Praise for David Weber's Safehold Series

"The personal ... ous characters are parti... nd Weber makes grand ... easily accessible to ca: ..."
— ... *Distressed*

"Another fascinating chapter in an SF epic with medieval trappings." —*Library Journal* on *By Heresies Distressed*

"Effortlessly exceeds the magnificence of its predecessor . . . I cannot emphasize how much I want to read the next chapter in the Safehold saga." —*Fantasy Book Critic* on *By Schism Rent Asunder*

"A brilliant new saga. Though his story encompasses meaty issues, such as the separation of church and state and the importance of a shared mythology, its focus remains on the people who embody the strengths and weaknesses of a flawed but ever hopeful humanity. Highly recommended." —*Library Journal* (starred review) on *By Schism Rent Asunder*

"Gripping . . . Shifting effortlessly between battles among warp-speed starships and among oar-powered galleys, Weber brings the political maneuvering, past and future technologies, and vigorous protagonists together for a cohesive, engrossing whole." —*Publishers Weekly* (starred review) on *Off Armageddon Reef*

"Vast, complex, intricate, subtle, and unlaydownable. This looks like the start of the biggest thing in science fiction since Isaac Asimov's Foundation series." —Dave Duncan on *Off Armageddon Reef*

"Fantastic in every sense of the word—the kind of book that makes you sit back and think about this reality that we call life. Who can ask for more than that?" —R. A. Salvatore on *Off Armageddon Reef*

TOR BOOKS BY DAVID WEBER

Off Armageddon Reef
By Schism Rent Asunder
By Heresies Distressed
A Mighty Fortress (forthcoming)

BY HERESIES DISTRESSED

·✦·

DAVID WEBER

TOR®

A TOM DOHERTY ASSOCIATES BOOK
NEW YORK

BY HERESIES DISTRESSED

Edited by Patrick Nielsen Hayden

Maps by Elissa Mitchell and Jennifer Hanover

A Tor Book
Published by Tom Doherty Associates, LLC
175 Fifth Avenue
New York, NY 10010

www.tor-forge.com

Tor® is a registered trademark of Tom Doherty Associates, LLC.

ISBN 978-0-7653-5399-3

First Edition: July 2009
First Mass Market Edition: March 2010

Printed in the United States of America

0 9 8 7 6 5 4

For Bobbie Rice and Alice Weber, two of
my favorite ladies. You both do pretty
good work!

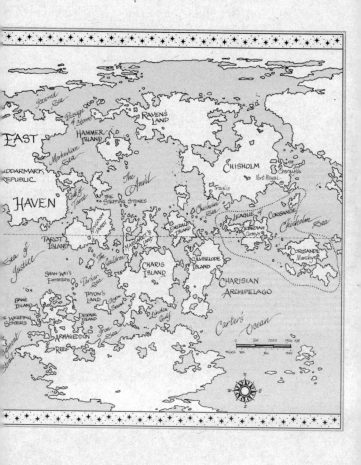

EAST

HAVEN

SIDDARMARK
REPUBLIC

Journal Sea

Passage of Storms

Markovian Sea

HAMMER ISLAND

RAVEN'S LAND

Gulf of Tarot

The Anvil

THE STEPPING STONES

CHISHOLM

Port Royal

Cherayth

Fralis

Chisholm Sea

LEAGUE

ZEBEDIAH Carmyn

CORISANDE

Chisholm Sea

EMERALD ISLAND

MARGARET'S LAND

CORISANDE Manchyr

TAROT ISLAND

Sea of Justice

The Cauldron

SILVERLODE ISLAND

SHAN-WEI'S FOOTSTEPS

Parker Sea

CHARIS ISLAND

CHARISIAN ARCHIPELAGO

TRYON'S LAND

Howell Sound

BANE ISLAND

WEEPING SISTERS

DESPAIR ISLAND

Linden Gulf

Iron Sea

Carter's Ocean

Lament Strait

ARMAGEDDON REEF

0   500   1000   1500 KM
MILES 0 500   1000

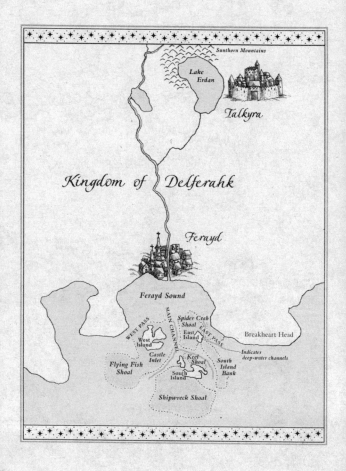

LANDS of the RAVEN LORDS

Chisholm Bight

WESTERN CROWN DEMESNE

WHITE CRAG

IRON HAT

WEST WATCH

LANNART

The Anvil

LAKE LAND

MOUNTAIN HEART

MAGUIRE

BLACK BOTTOM

LANTERN WALK

WINDSWEPT ISLAND

Rock Coast Keep

ROCK COAST

SWAYLE

BLACK HORSE

SAINT HOWAN

TRAYJIS

Zebe

EMERALD ISLAND

Northern Crown Demesne

Half-Moon Passage

HIGH HALLOW

HIGH MOUNT

THREE HILLS

BLUE SKY

EASTSHARE

Cherry Blossom Sound

GREEN MOUNTAIN

Teruyth

CHERAYTH

HARRIS ISLAND

Helena Sound

TURTLE ISLAND

THE SICKLE

SPRING ISLAND

HALLBROOK HALLOW

Cherayth

CHERAYTH

HELENA

CAPE HELENA

SHANG

MANDIGORA

WEST LAKE

LAKESHORE

BROKEN ROCK

GREENTREE

CREEK

DRAGON HILL

WINDSHORE

Port Royal

PORT ROYAL

TWO SWORDS

LOCK HAVEN

TREE

WEST ISLE

Sea

Sea of Chisholm

DIAH ISLAND

CHISHOLM

Corisande Island

E. OF CRAGG HILL

B. OF TAIRYS
E. OF GRAY SAND
E. OF THAIRNOS

B. OF KERSO
D. OF BARCAIR
E. OF ANVIL ROCK
E. OF DEEP HOLLOW

B. OF WIND HOOK
B. OF ROKALI
E. OF BLACK WATER
E. OF NORYST
B. OF GRANITE HILL

E. OF SHREVE

Rokali Inlet
E. OF WINDSHARE

Hard Shoal Bay
E. OF HARD SHOAL
E. OF ROCHAIR

Flower Island
E. OF TART

B. OF SHAI

West Margo Sound

D. OF MARGO

Margo Island

Margo Strait

Tear Island

CHISHOLM

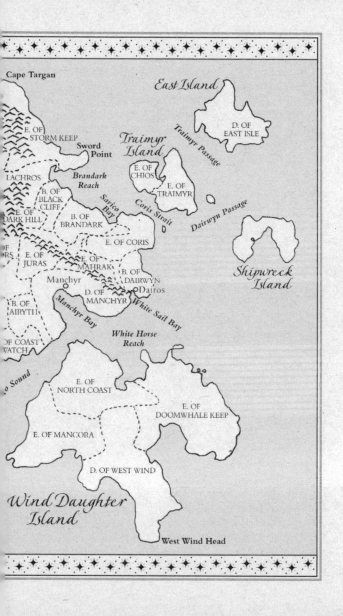

Cape Targan

East Island

D. OF
EAST ISLE

E. OF
STORM KEEP

Sword
Point

*Traimyr
Island*

Traimyr Passage

Brandark Reach

E. OF
CHIOS

LACHROS

B. OF
BLACK
CLIFF

E. OF
DARK HILL

*Sarico
Bay*

E. OF
TRAIMYR

Coris Strait

Dairwyn Passage

B. OF
BRANDARK

OF
RS

E. OF
JURAS

E. OF
MAHRAK

E. OF CORIS

B. OF
DAIRWYN

Manchyr

Dairos

*Shipwreck
Island*

B. OF
AIRYTI

D. OF
MANCHYR

White Sail Bay

OF COAST
WATCH

Manchyr Bay

o Sound

*White Horse
Reach*

E. OF
NORTH COAST

E. OF
DOOMWHALE KEEP

E. OF MANCORA

D. OF WEST WIND

*Wind Daughter
Island*

West Wind Head

OCTOBER,
YEAR OF GOD 892

·✦·

. I .

The Temple,
City of Zion,
The Temple Lands

The snow outside the Temple was deep for October, even for the city of Zion, and more fell steadily, thickly, only to be whipped into mad swirls by the bitter wind roaring in off Lake Pei. That wind piled thick slabs of broken lake ice on the bitterly cold shore, swept dancing snow demons through the streets, sculpted knife-edged snowdrifts against every obstruction, and chewed at any exposed skin with icy fangs. Throughout the city, its poorest inhabitants huddled close to any source of warmth they could find, but for far too many, there was precious little of that to be had, and parents shivered, watching the weather—and their children—with worry-puckered eyes as they thought about the endless five-days stretching out between them and the half-forgotten dream of springtime's warmth.

There was no cold inside the Temple, of course. Despite the soaring ceiling of its enormous dome, there weren't even any chilly breezes. The structure reared by the archangels themselves in the misty dawn of Creation maintained its perfect interior temperature with total disdain for what the merely mortal weather of the world might be inflicting upon its exterior.

The luxurious personal suites assigned to the members of the Council of Vicars were all magnificent beyond any mortal dream, but some were even more magnificent than others. The suite assigned to Grand Inquisitor Zhaspahr Clyntahn was a case in point. It was a corner apartment on the Temple's fifth floor. Two entire sides of its main sitting room and dining room were windows—the miraculous, unbreakable, almost totally invisible windows of the archangels' handiwork. Windows which were completely transparent from within, yet flashed back exterior sunlight like mirrored walls of finely burnished silver, and which were utterly impervious to the heat—or cold—which passed through and radiated from windows of mortal glass. Paintings and statuary, all chosen with a connoisseur's exquisite discernment, added their own luxurious beauty to the suite's interior, with its thick carpets, indirect, sourceless lighting, and perfect temperature.

It was far from the first time Archbishop Wyllym Rayno had visited the Grand Inquisitor's personal chambers. Rayno was the Archbishop of Chiang-wu in the Harchong Empire. He was also the Adjutant of the Order of Schueler, which made him Clyntahn's executive officer within the Office of Inquisition. As a result, Rayno was privy to far more of Clyntahn's innermost thought than anyone else, including his colleagues among the Group of Four, yet there were places inside Clyntahn where even Rayno had never been. Places the archbishop had never wanted to be.

"Come in, Wyllym—come in!" Clyntahn said expansively as the Temple Guardsman always stationed outside his chamber opened the door for Rayno.

"Thank you, Your Grace," Rayno murmured, stepping past the guardsman.

Clyntahn extended his ring of office, and Rayno bent to kiss it, then straightened and tucked his hands into the voluminous sleeves of his cassock. The remnants of a truly enormous meal lay strewn in ruins across the large dining table, and Rayno carefully avoided noticing that there had been two place settings. Most vicars practiced at least some discretion when it came to entertaining their mistresses within the Temple's sacred precincts. Everyone knew it happened anyway, yet there were standards to be maintained, appearances to be satisfied. But Zhaspahr Clyntahn wasn't "most vicars." He was the Grand Inquisitor, the keeper of Mother Church's conscience, and there were times when even Rayno, who had served him for decades, wondered exactly what passed through his mind. How the same man could be so zealous when it came to rooting out the sins of others even while he indulged his own.

Fair's fair, Wyllym, the archbishop told himself. *He may be a zealot, and he's definitely self-indulgent, but at least he's not hypocritical among his peers. And he does draw a remarkably sharp line between sins which are merely venal and those which constitute mortal offenses in the eyes of Schueler and God. He can be as irritatingly sanctimonious as anyone you've ever seen, but you've never heard him condemning any of his fellow vicars for weaknesses of the flesh. Spiritual weaknesses, yes; he can be utterly ruthless where they're concerned, but he's remarkably . . . understanding where those perquisites of high office are concerned.*

He wondered who tonight's visitor might be. All of Clyntahn's appetites were huge, and he craved novelty. Indeed, few women could hold his attention for long, and once his interest in them waned, he tended to turn to another with sometimes startling abruptness, although he was never ungenerous when he transferred his interest to another.

Rayno, as the Inquisition's adjutant, was well aware that there were those within the Temple's hierarchy who disapproved—in some cases, strenuously, if quietly—of Clyntahn's addiction to the pleasures of the flesh. No one was likely to say so openly, of course, and Rayno had very quietly quashed a few reports of condemnatory comments before they ever reached the Grand Inquisitor's ears. Still, it was only natural for there to be a certain . . . unhappiness. Some of it could probably be put down to pure envy, although he was willing to concede that there was genuine disapproval of such sensuality behind much of it. Indeed, there had been times when Rayno had found himself feeling much the same sort of disapproval. But the archbishop had concluded long ago, even before Clyntahn was elevated to his present office, that all men had flaws, and that the greater the man, the deeper his flaws were likely to run. If Clyntahn restricted his particular faults to the pursuit of fleshly pleasure, surely that was far better than what Rayno had observed in the occasional Inquisitor who found himself using the cover of his high office to indulge his own taste for unnecessary cruelty.

"Thank you for coming so promptly, Wyllym," Clyntahn continued as he ushered the archbishop to one of the Temple's incredibly comfortable chairs. He smiled as he settled Rayno and personally poured him a glass of wine. The Grand Inquisitor's normal table manners generally took second place—or even third—to the gusto he brought to food and wine, yet he could be an incredibly gracious and charming host when he chose to be. Nor was that charm false. It simply never occurred to him to extend it to anyone outside the circle of intimates he relied upon and fully trusted. Or, at least, trusted as much as he ever trusted anyone else.

"I realize your message didn't seem to indicate any immediate urgency, Your Grace. I had business in the Temple to attend to anyway, however, so it seemed best to respond to your summons promptly."

"I only wish I had a dozen archbishops and bishops who were as reliable as you are," Clyntahn told him. "Langhorne! I'd settle for six!"

Rayno smiled and inclined his head in a small bow, acknowledging the compliment. Then he sat back, nursing his wineglass in both hands while he gazed attentively at his superior.

Clyntahn was looking out the floor-to-ceiling windows at the swirling snow and wind. His expression was almost rapt as he contemplated the icy torrent of white for the better part of three minutes. Then, finally, he turned back to Rayno and leaned back in his own chair.

"Well!" he said, with the air of someone getting down to business at last. "I'm sure you've read all the reports about the seizures of Charisian merchant ships month before last."

He arched one eyebrow slightly, and Rayno nodded.

"Good! I was certain you would have. And since you have, you're undoubtedly aware that there were certain . . . difficulties."

"Yes, Your Grace," Rayno acknowledged as Clyntahn paused.

Of course the archbishop was aware that there'd been "difficulties." Everyone in Zion was aware of that much! What had been supposed to be an orderly seizure of unarmed, or at least only lightly armed, merchant ships as the first step in closing all mainland ports against the all-pervasive Charisian merchant marine had turned into something else entirely. Not everywhere, perhaps, but what the Grand Inquisitor was pleased to call "difficulties" was something the Charisians were going to call a "massacre" when word of August's events in the Kingdom of Delferahk's port city of Ferayd reached them.

Actually, Rayno corrected himself, *what they're undoubtedly already calling it, given the fact that at least some of their ships got away and most certainly sailed straight to Tellesberg.* The archbishop shuddered at the thought of what the schismatic Charisian propagandists were going to do with that many civilian casualties. *One thing's for sure,* he thought grimly, *they aren't going to* minimize *what happened.*

And that, Rayno realized, was what was truly on Clyntahn's mind. The Grand Inquisitor was speaking less of the fatalities involved than he was of the need to put the proper context on the part the Inquisition had played in the seizures. Few of those seizures had gone as badly awry as the ones in Delferahk—or not, at least, in the same way. Personally, Rayno found the implications of what had happened at Siddar City even more disturbing, in many ways. According to the Inquisition's agents there, everything had been proceeding far more smoothly than in Ferayd . . . right up to the moment, at least, when, for some unknown reason, every Charisian merchant ship had simultaneously decided to . . . expedite its departure. It was undoubtedly a mere coincidence that they'd decided to do that before Lord Protector Greyghor had gotten around to formally issuing the orders to implement the Church's instructions to seize them.

Of course it was.

There was no proof of who'd warned the Charisians, yet whoever it was, it had to have been someone deep in the Lord Protector's confidence. The only real question in Rayno's mind was whether the informant had acted solely on his own, or if Lord Protector Greyghor himself had made the decision to betray the Church's trust. Given the fact that his staff had somehow been unable to locate their inexplicably missing head of state and deliver Clyntahn's instructions to him for at least twelve hours, Rayno rather suspected that he wouldn't have cared for the answer to his own question if someone had provided it.

Whoever the traitor might have been, he hadn't acted entirely alone, no matter whose idea it had been. Siddar City wasn't the only Siddarmarkian port where every Charisian merchant ship had mysteriously departed mere hours before they were supposed to be sequestered by the Republic's authorities. The possibilities that suggested were far more unpalatable than a few score of dead Charisian sailors in Ferayd.

Not that we can expect everyone else on the Council—or even within the Order!—to see things that way, Rayno thought grumpily. The name of Samyl Wylsynn came forcefully to mind, and the adjutant reminded himself barely in time not to grimace. Not that Clyntahn would have disagreed with his subordinate's unloving thoughts where Vicar Samyl was concerned. If he decided Rayno's expression indicated the archbishop's disapproval of the decision to close the mainland ports to Charis, however, it could have unfortunate consequences.

"Well," Clyntahn said again, grasping the thread of the conversation once more, "as you and I have already discussed, it's essential that Mother Church put the true version of events into the hands of the faithful before any Charisian lies can take root there. I believe that may be especially important in this instance."

"Of course, Your Grace. How may I be of assistance?"

"It's taken longer than I could have wished," the Grand Inquisitor told him frankly, "but Trynair and Duchairn have just about agreed upon the text of a proclamation setting forth what happened, especially in Ferayd, and granting martyr's status to those murdered by the Charisians. It's still weaker than I would prefer. It stops short of declaring Holy War, for example. I suppose it does set the groundwork for the eventual declaration, but certain parties are still waffling. I think Duchairn actually entertains the belief—or the hope, at least—that this can all be patched up somehow. Deep inside, though, even he has to know he's wrong. It's gone too far. The Inquisition and Mother Church simply cannot allow this sort of direct challenge of God's will and His plan for the souls of men to pass unpunished. And the chastisement must be severe, Wyllym. Severe enough to prevent anyone else from even contemplating ever following in their footsteps."

Rayno simply nodded. There was very little new in what Clyntahn had just said—aside from the confirmation that the proclamation the adjutant had expected for five-days was approaching readiness. On the other hand, as much as Clyntahn enjoyed explaining things, it was unlikely he'd recapped all that history without a specific purpose in mind.

"I have to confess that the thing which is preying most strongly upon my own mind just now, Wyllym, isn't those damnable Charisians' open defiance. Oh, obviously that's going to have to be dealt with, but at least Cayleb and Staynair were rash enough to come out into the open. They've declared their allegiance to the pernicious doctrines Shan-wei is using to split Mother Church, marked themselves for the Church's justice and God's vengeance. In the fullness of time, they'll receive that justice and vengeance in full measure, too.

"But what happened in Siddarmark . . . *that's* another story entirely, Wyllym. Someone very highly placed in the Republic's government must have alerted the Charisians. And while I'm fully aware of all the diplomatic niceties which prevent Zahmsyn from coming right out and taxing Greyghor with responsibility, there's not much question in my mind as to who bears the responsibility. Even if he didn't give the specific order himself—and I wouldn't bet a mug of flat beer on *that* possibility!—it had to be someone very close to him, and there are no indications he's even remotely close to identifying the culprit, much less punishing him. That sort of insidious rot, the kind that hides behind a façade of loyalty and reverence, is deadly dangerous. Left to itself, hiding in the shadows, the infection will only grow more and more corrupt until we find ourselves with a second, or a third, or even a *fourth* 'Church of Charis' on our hands."

"I understand, Your Grace," Rayno murmured when the Grand Inquisitor paused once more. And the adjutant *was* beginning to understand, too. Had the "culprit" in question been found anywhere except in the inner circles of the Siddarmarkian government, Clyntahn wouldn't simply have been concerned about any future "rot." He would have been demanding the head of whoever had done it. Unfortunately, pressing Siddarmark too hard at this particular time was . . . contraindicated. The last thing the Church wanted was to engineer a marriage between Siddarmark's pikemen and Cayleb of Charis' navy.

"Unfortunately," Clyntahn continued, as if he'd been reading Rayno's mind (which wasn't something the adjutant was completely prepared to rule out as a possibility), "if Greyghor can't—or won't—identify the responsible party, there's very little we can do about it from the outside. For now, at least."

"I take it from what you've just said that you've been working on a means to change that, Your Grace?"

Rayno's tone was merely politely inquisitive, and Clyntahn snorted a grunting laugh as the adjutant arched his eyebrows delicately.

"Actually, I have," he acknowledged, "and the fact that Siddarmark is so stubbornly attached to its 'republican' traditions is part of my thinking."

"Indeed, Your Grace?" This time Rayno cocked his head to the side and crossed his legs as he awaited the Grand Inquisitor's explanation.

"One of the things that makes Greyghor so damnably stiff-necked and defiant behind that mask of piety and obedience of his is his belief that the voting citizens of Siddarmark support his policies. And, to give Shan-wei her due, he's pretty much been right about that. That's one of the considerations which has prevented us from turning up the pressure on him the way we really ought to have done long ago. But I rather doubt that public opinion in Siddarmark is quite as firmly united in approval of this schism of Charis' as Greyghor may think it is.

And if, in fact, his precious voters *disapprove* of Charis and of the things he's willing to do behind the scenes in support of the schismatics, then I suspect he'll change his tune."

"That sounds eminently sensible to me, Your Grace," Rayno said, nodding his head. "Exactly how do we . . . re-shape that public opinion in our favor, though?"

"Over the next few days," Clyntahn said, his tone a bit oblique, his eyes once again straying to the white maelstrom of the October blizzard, "several of the Charisians seized when their vessels were impounded will be arriving here in Zion. Actually, they'll be arriving here at the Temple itself."

"Indeed, Your Grace?"

"Indeed," Clyntahn confirmed. "They'll be delivered directly to the Order—to *you*, Wyllym." The Grand Inquisitor's eyes snapped back from the windows, boring suddenly into Rayno's. "I haven't gone out of my way to mention their impending arrival to the Chancellor or to the Treasurer General. I see no need to disturb them with what are, after all, the Inquisition's internal matters. Do you?"

"Clearly not at this time, Your Grace," Rayno replied, and Clyntahn smiled again, thinly.

"That was my thinking, as well, Wyllym. What we need to do is to . . . interview these Charisians. Shan-wei is the Mother of Lies, of course. No doubt she'll do her damnable best to protect these heretics lest they betray her by revealing her plans and perversions to the true children of God. But the Office of Inquisition knows how to strip away Shan-wei's mask and reveal the truth behind it. That will be *your* task, Wyllym. I want you to take personal charge of their questioning. It's essential that they confess what actually happened, admit their deliberate provocation of the civil authorities who were simply attempting to peaceably carry out their instructions from Mother Church and their own secular authorities. The world must see clearly where the true blood guilt lies, just as it must learn of the perverse practices and blasphemies which this so-called 'Church of Charis' has embraced and seeks to enforce upon all the children of God in the name of its own dark mistress. Not only does the redemption of these sinners' own souls hang upon their full

confession and repentance, but once the truth is revealed, it will
have a powerful effect upon 'public opinion' everywhere . . .
even in Siddarmark."

His eyes continued to bore into Rayno's, and the adjutant
drew a deep, steadying breath. The Grand Inquisitor was right
about the necessity of confession and repentance if a soul
which had strayed from the path of the archangels was ever to
find true redemption. And the Inquisition was accustomed to
its stern, often heartbreaking responsibilities. It understood
that the true love of the sinner's soul sometimes required that
sinner's body be dealt with harshly. It was sadly true that it
was often difficult to break into that fortress of self-pride, arrogance, and defiance and lead the lost soul hiding within it
back into the cleansing light of God's love once again. But
however difficult the task might be, it was one the Inquisition
had learned to discharge long-ago.

"How quickly do you need this accomplished, Your Grace?"
he asked after a moment.

"As soon as possible, but not instantly," Clyntahn replied with
a shrug. "Until my . . . colleagues are prepared to act openly, I
doubt that a confession from Shan-wei herself would carry
much weight with anyone who's already prepared to believe the
schismatics' lies. And, to be perfectly frank, I expect that
Duchairn, at least, is going to express all sorts of pious reservations and protests at the thought of the Inquisition's doing what's
necessary in this case. So, for now, this needs to be done very
quietly. Keep it within the Order and be sure that, even there, you
rely only on brothers whose faith and fidelity we *know* are trustworthy. I need to be able to produce this testimony when the
time comes, but in the meantime, we don't need any well-
intentioned weaklings who don't understand that, in this case,
too much kindness would be the worst cruelty of all, getting in
the way and hampering our efforts."

"I agree with you, of course, Your Grace," Rayno said.
"However, I do have a . . . tactical reservation, let's say."

"What sort of reservation, Wyllym?" Clyntahn's eyes had
narrowed slightly, but Rayno appeared not to notice as he continued in the same calm, merely thoughtful tone of voice.

"Everything you've just said about controlling the time at which this testimony is made public strikes me as completely valid. But you and I are accustomed to dealing with the pragmatic, often unpleasant duties and responsibilities inherent in attempting to reclaim the fallen for Langhorne and God. If—when—we obtain the apostates' confessions, some people are going to wonder why we didn't make those confessions public *immediately*. Some of that questioning will be completely sincere and legitimate, from people outside the Office of Inquisition who simply don't understand that sometimes saving the sinner is only the first step in combating a greater evil. But there will also be those, Your Grace, who seize upon any delay as an opportunity to discredit anything we may say. They'll argue that the penitents were coerced, that their confessions aren't reliable."

"No doubt you're right," Clyntahn agreed. "In fact, the same thought had occurred to me. But almost as soon as I thought about it, I realized I was worrying unduly."

"You were, Your Grace?"

"Yes." Clyntahn nodded. "I have no doubt that once you've managed to bring these people to the point of confession and repentance we'll discover that many of the 'Church of Charis' perversions and abominations are even worse—horrifically worse, in some cases—than anything we could reasonably suspect from here. Undoubtedly, as the painstakingly thorough guardian of the truth I've always known you to be, you'll insist on confirming as many as possible of those outrageous claims before making them public. It would never do to suggest such shocking possibilities if, in fact, it later turned out that the heretics had lied to you. So, obviously, until we have that confirmation, we couldn't possibly justify presenting our findings to the Council of Vicars . . . or to the citizens of Siddarmark who mistakenly believe that Cayleb, Staynair, and the others must have at least some valid justifications on their side."

"I understand, Your Grace," Rayno said, and he did.

"Good, Wyllym. Excellent! I knew I could trust your diligence and discretion in this matter."

"You can, Your Grace. Definitely. I suppose the only

remaining question I have is whether or not you want progress reports."

"Nothing written at this point, I think," Clyntahn said after thinking for a moment. "Written memos have an unfortunate habit of being taken out of context, especially by people who choose to take them that way in order to suit their own purposes. Keep me informed, but verbally. When the time is right, I want to produce as many as possible of the heretics who have confessed. And, of course, I'll want detailed, signed and witnessed written copies of their confessions, as well."

"I understand, Your Grace." Rayno rose and bent to kiss Clyntahn's ring of office once more. "With all due respect, Your Grace, I think perhaps I should return to my office. I need to do some personnel selection and make certain the brothers I choose fully understand your fears and concerns."

"I think that sounds like an excellent idea, Wyllym," Clyntahn said, escorting the archbishop back towards his chamber's door. "An excellent idea, indeed. And when you make your selections, remember that Shan-wei is cunning. If there should be a chink in the armor of one of your Inquisitors, never doubt she'll find it and exploit it. This responsibility is too serious, the potential consequences are too great, to let that happen. Be sure that they're fully protected in the armor of the Light and girded with the strength of will and purpose and faith to do that which must be done, however grievous the doing of it may seem. Our responsibility is to God, Wyllym. The approval or disapproval of mere mortal, fallible men cannot be allowed to sway us from the obligation to meet that dreadful responsibility, whatever it may demand of us. As Schueler taught and Langhorne himself confirmed, 'Extremism in the pursuit of godliness can never be a sin.'"

"Yes, Your Grace," Wyllym Rayno said quietly. "I'll see to it that I—that *all* of us—remember that in the days to come."

NOVEMBER,
YEAR OF GOD 892

✦

. I .

City of Ferayd,
Ferayd Sound
Kingdom of Delferahk

At least the Charisians were extending full military courtesies to their defeated enemies.

The thought ran through the back of Sir Vyk Lakyr's mind as he scaled the steep battens on the ship's high side, then stepped through the entry port onto HMS *Destroyer*'s deck. The bosun's pipes which had twittered painfully (and apparently endlessly) as he climbed fell blessedly silent, and the grave-faced young lieutenant waiting to greet him touched his right fist to his left shoulder in formal salute.

"The Admiral extends his respects and asks you to join him in his day cabin, My Lord," the lieutenant said.

My, how polite, Lakyr thought, acutely conscious of the lack of weight where his sword should have hung by his side. Of course, he hadn't seen that sword in the last two days. Not since he'd surrendered it to Admiral Rock Point's senior Marine officer.

"Thank you, Lieutenant," he said aloud, and the lieutenant inclined his head in a slight bow, then turned to lead the way below.

Lakyr tried not to gawk as they descended from the Charisian ship's upper deck—the "spar deck," they called it—to its gun deck. HMS *Destroyer* was huge, easily the largest ship he had ever been aboard, although at least one or two of its consorts anchored off what had once been the waterfront of the city of Ferayd looked larger than it was. What was even more impressive than its sheer size, however, was the number—and weight—of its guns. The short, stubby "carronades" on the spar deck had been bad enough; the monsters crouching on the gun deck were even worse. There had to be at least thirty of them, and he'd already seen the devastation their thirty-eight-pound round shot had wreaked upon the port's defenses.

Such as they were, and what there was of them, Lakyr thought.

Sunlight streamed in through the open gun ports, illuminating what was almost certainly normally a gloomy cavern. Or perhaps not all *that* gloomy, he reflected, as he and the lieutenant passed through a brilliantly lit, rectangular pool of light, streaming down through the long, narrow grating of the spar deck main hatch. The smell of burned gunpowder hovered faintly about him, despite the meticulously clean deck, scrubbed bulkheads, and canvas windscoops rigged to ventilate the ship. The smell was barely there, hovering at the backs of his nostrils, like something suspected more than actually experienced.

Or perhaps it was the scent of a more mundane smoke, he reflected. After all, there was a large enough cloud of that hovering black and dense above the city he'd been charged to protect. Even though the breeze was blowing towards shore, not away from it, the smell of burning wood had accompanied him aboard *Destroyer.* Clinging to the folds of his own clothing, no doubt.

They reached a closed door in a light bulkhead which was obviously designed to be taken down when the ship cleared for action. A uniformed Marine stood guard outside it with a bayoneted musket, and the lieutenant reached past him to rap sharply on the door with his knuckles.

"Yes?" a deep voice responded.

"Sir Vyk Lakyr is here, My Lord," the lieutenant said.

"Then please ask him to come in, Styvyn," the deep voice replied.

"Of course, My Lord," the lieutenant replied, then opened the door and stepped courteously aside.

"My Lord," he murmured, and waved gracefully at the doorway.

"Thank you, Lieutenant," Lakyr replied, and stepped past him.

Lakyr had expected to find his "host" waiting directly on the other side of that door, but his expectation was disappointed. The lieutenant followed him through the door, managing somehow—Lakyr was never certain afterward just how the young man accomplished it—to steer the visitor while still following a respectful half-pace behind him.

Thus steered, Lakyr found himself leading the way across the cabin towards a second door. His eyes were busy, absorbing the furnishings about him: a woman's portrait, smiling at any visitor as he entered; armchairs, a short sofa, a waxed and gleaming dining table with half a dozen chairs; a handsome ivory-faced clock ticking away; a polished wine rack made out of some dark, exotic tropical wood; a glass-fronted cabinet filled with crystal decanters and tulip-shaped glasses. They created a comfortable, welcoming space which only made the intrusion of the massive, carefully secured thirty-eight-pounder crouching with its muzzle touching a closed gun port an even greater contrast.

The lieutenant followed him through the second door, and Lakyr paused just inside it as he caught sight of the ship's great stern windows. He'd seen them from the boat rowing across the harbor, so he'd already known—intellectually, at least—that they stretched the full width of *Destroyer*'s stern. That wasn't quite the same thing as seeing them from the inside, however, he discovered. Glass doors at the center of that vast expanse of windows gave access to a sternwalk which, like the windows themselves, ran the full width of the warship's stern. Indeed, although he couldn't see it from where he stood, the sternwalk wrapped around *Destroyer*'s quarter galleys, as well.

The cabin into which he had just stepped was awash with light, bouncing up and through those windows as it reflected from the harbor's wind-flurried surface, and the man waiting for him was a black silhouette against that brightness.

"Sir Vyk Lakyr, My Lord," the lieutenant murmured.

"Thank you, Styvyn," the dark silhouette said, and stepped forward. There was something awkward about his gait. Lakyr couldn't quite put his finger on what it was, until the other man stepped clear of the windows' brightness and he saw the wooden peg which had replaced Admiral Rock Point's lower right leg.

"Sir Vyk," Rock Point said.

"My Lord." Lakyr bowed slightly, and what might have been the ghost of a smile flickered across Rock Point's mouth. Frankly, Lakyr doubted that was what it had been. Not given the vigor with which Rock Point had executed the orders he'd been given by Emperor Cayleb where Lakyr's city was concerned.

"I invited you aboard for a brief conversation before we return to Charis," Rock Point told him.

"Return, My Lord?" Lakyr asked politely.

"Come now, Sir Vyk." Rock Point shook his head, and this time his smile was more evident. "We never had any intention of *staying,* you know. Nor," his smile disappeared, "is there anything worth staying here to keep, is there?"

"Not any longer, My Lord." Lakyr couldn't quite keep the grimness—and the anger—out of his tone, and Rock Point cocked his head to one side.

"I'm not surprised you find the consequences of our little visit less than palatable, Sir Vyk. On the other hand, given what happened here in August, I'd say my Emperor showed considerable restraint, wouldn't you?"

A hot, angry retort hovered on Lakyr's tongue, but he swallowed it unspoken. After all, he could hardly disagree.

Rock Point turned and looked back out the stern windows at the pall of smoke swelling above Ferayd. More than a third of the city's buildings had helped to feed that looming mushroom shape, but Rock Point had allowed Lakyr's surrendered troops to demolish a semicircular fire break around the portion of Ferayd he'd been ordered to destroy. Emperor Cayleb's instructions had specified that not a building was to be left standing within a two-mile radius of the Ferayd waterfront, and Rock Point had carried out his orders with precision.

And also, Lakyr admitted unwillingly, with compassion. He'd permitted civilians whose homes had lain within the decreed radius of destruction to take away their most prized possessions—assuming they were sufficiently portable—before the torch had been applied. And the Charisian admiral had permitted no excesses on the part of his troops. Which, given what had happened to the Charisian merchant crews who'd been slaughtered here in Ferayd when Vicar Zhaspahr had ordered their ships seized, was far better than anything for which Lakyr had dared to hope.

Of course, he thought, regarding Rock Point steadily, *there's still that interesting little question about exactly what Rock Point's orders concerning the commander of the garrison who did the slaughtering might be.*

"I'm sure most of your citizens will be happy to see the last of us," Rock Point continued. "I'd like to think that with the passage of time, they'll realize we at least tried to kill as few of them as possible. However, there was no way we could allow what happened here to pass unanswered."

"I suppose not, My Lord," Lakyr admitted, and braced himself. The admiral's last sentence suggested he was about to discover precisely what Charis had in mind for the officer whose troops had committed the atrocity which had brought Rock Point to Ferayd.

"The real reason I invited you aboard *Destroyer,* Sir Vyk," Rock Point said, almost as if he had read the Delferahkan's mind, "was to deliver my Emperor's message to your king. This," he gestured with one hand at the smoke-choked vista invisible through the stern windows, "—is a part of that message, of course, but it's scarcely all of it."

He paused, waiting, and Lakyr's nostrils flared.

"And the rest of it is, My Lord?" he asked finally, obedient to the admiral's expectant silence.

"And the rest of it is, Sir Vyk, that we know who actually ordered the seizure of our ships. We know whose agents . . .

oversaw that seizure. Neither my Emperor, nor Charis, is prepared to hold Delferahk blameless over the murder of so many Charisian subjects, hence this." He waved at the rising smoke once more. "Should more of our subjects be murdered elsewhere, be assured Emperor Cayleb will respond equally forcefully there, as well. Nor will there be any peace between any who attack Charis, or Charisians, at the orders and behest of corrupt men like Clyntahn and the rest of the Group of Four. But our true quarrel lies with the men in Zion who choose to pervert and poison God's own Church. And that, Sir Vyk, is the real reason I asked you aboard. To tell you that although my Emperor must hold you, as any military commander, ultimately responsible for the actions of the men under your command, he understands that what happened here in Ferayd was neither of your seeking, nor what you intended. Which is why you will be returned ashore after our business this morning is concluded to deliver a written message from Emperor Cayleb to King Zhames."

"Indeed, My Lord?" Lakyr couldn't quite keep the surprise—and the relief—out of his voice, and Rock Point snorted in amusement.

"No doubt I would have anticipated a rather more . . . unpleasant outcome of this interview if I'd been in your shoes," he said. But then his expression hardened. "I'm afraid, however, that the unpleasantness isn't quite over yet. Come with me, Sir Vyk."

Lakyr's nerves had tightened once again at Rock Point's ominous warning. He wanted to ask the Charisian admiral what he'd meant, but he strongly suspected that he would find out altogether too quickly, anyway, and so he followed Rock Point out of the cabin without speaking.

The admiral ascended the steep ladders to the upper deck with surprising nimbleness, despite his wooden leg. No doubt he'd had plenty of practice, Lakyr thought, following him up. But then the commander of Ferayd's defeated garrison found himself standing once again upon the spar deck, and any thought about Rock Point's agility disappeared abruptly.

While the two of them had been below, in Rock Point's

cabin, *Destroyer*'s crew had been rigging halters from the ship's yardarms. There were six of them, one dangling from either end of the lowest yard on each of the ship's three masts.

As Lakyr watched in stunned disbelief, deep-throated drums began to rumble like distant thunder echoing across mountain peaks. Bare feet pattered and boots clattered and thudded as seamen and Marines poured onto their ships' upper decks in answer to that rolling summons, and then six men in priests' cassocks badged with the purple sword and flame of the Order of Schueler were dragged across the deck towards the waiting nooses.

"My Lord—!" Lakyr began, but Rock Point waved his right hand. The gesture was sharp, abrupt, the first truly angry thing Lakyr had seen out of the Charisian, and it decapitated his nascent protest as cleanly as any sword.

"No, Sir Vyk," Rock Point said harshly. "*This* is the rest of my Emperor's message—not just to King Zhames, but to those bastards in Zion. We know who provoked this massacre, and we know who ordered it *knowing* his minions would do precisely what they in fact did. And those who murder Charisian subjects will answer to Charisian justice . . . whoever they may be."

Lakyr swallowed hard, feeling the sweat suddenly beading his hairline.

I never even dreamed of this, he thought. *It never even crossed my mind! Those men are* priests—*consecrated priests, servants of Mother Church! They can't just*—

But the Charisians not only could, they were actually doing it. And despite his horror at the impiety of what was happening, a part of Sir Vyk Lakyr discovered that he couldn't blame them for it.

He saw Father Styvyn Graivyr, Bishop Ernyst Jynkyns' intendant, the Office of Inquisition's senior priest in Ferayd, among the prisoners. Graivyr looked stunned, white-faced . . . horrified. His hands were bound behind him, as were those of the other five inquisitors with him, and his shoulders twisted as his wrists fought against their bonds. He seemed almost unaware of his struggle against the cords as his eyes clung to the waiting noose, and he moved like a man trapped in the bowels of a nightmare.

He *never dreamed it might come to this, either,* Lakyr realized, and yet another emotion flickered through him. He was still too stunned himself to think clearly, but if he hadn't been, he might have been shocked to realize that at least part of what he was feeling was . . . satisfaction.

Graivyr wasn't the only inquisitor who seemed unable to believe, even now, that this could possibly be happening to them. One of them resisted far more frantically than Graivyr, flinging himself against the iron grip of the stone-faced Marines dragging him towards the waiting rope, babbling protests. And as Lakyr stared at the unbelievable events unfolding before him, he heard the rumble of other drums coming from other ships.

He wrenched his eyes away from *Destroyer*'s deck, and his face tightened as he saw more ropes hanging from other ships' yardarms. He didn't try to count them. His shocked mind probably wouldn't have been up to the task, anyway.

"We interviewed all of the survivors before my Emperor gave us our orders, Sir Vyk," Rock Point said, his harsh voice yanking Lakyr's attention back to him. "Before we ever sailed for Ferayd, we knew whose voices were shouting 'Holy Langhorne and no quarter!' when your men came aboard our people's ships. But we didn't rely solely on that testimony when we tried the guilty. It never even crossed Graivyr's mind that anyone else, anyone outside the Office of Inquisition itself, would ever read his secret files. Unfortunately for him, he was wrong. These men were convicted not on the basis of any Charisian's testimony, but on the basis of their own written statements and reports. Statements and reports in which they proudly reported, *bragged* about, the zeal with which they went about exhorting your troops to 'Kill the heretics!' "

The Charisian's eyes were colder than northern ice, and Lakyr could physically feel the rage within him . . . and the iron will which kept that rage leashed and controlled.

"Copies of those statements and reports will be provided to King Zhames—and to the Council of Vicars in Zion," Rock Point continued coldly. "The originals will be returning to

Tellesberg with me, so that we can be certain they won't mysteriously disappear, but King Zhames will receive Graivyr's own file copies. What *he* does with them, whether to publish them abroad, destroy them, or hand them back over to Clyntahn, is his business, his decision. But whatever he may do, *we* will do nothing in darkness, unseen by the eyes of men. We will, most assuredly, publish the evidence, and unlike the men and women—and children—they had murdered, Sir Vyk, every one of *these* men was offered the benefit of clergy after he was sentenced. And unlike the children who were slaughtered here on their own ships with their parents, there isn't one of them who doesn't understand exactly why he's about to hang."

Lakyr swallowed hard, and Rock Point twitched his head in Graivyr's direction.

"For centuries the Inquisition has meted out the Church's punishment. Perhaps there was once a time when that punishment was true justice. But that time has passed, Sir Vyk. God doesn't need savagery to show His people what He desires of them, and these men—and others like them—have hidden behind Him for far too long. Used Him to shield them from the consequences of their own monstrous actions. Used their office and their authority in the service not of God, or even of God's Church, but of vile and corrupt *men* like Vicar Zhaspahr. Now it is time they, and everyone like them, discover that the vestments they have perverted will no longer be permitted to protect murderers and torturers from justice. These men never dreamed *they* might face death for their crimes. They are about to discover differently . . . and perhaps at least some of their fellow inquisitors will be wise enough to learn from their example."

Lakyr stared at him, then cleared his throat.

"My Lord," he said hoarsely, "think before you do this!"

"Oh, I assure you, I *have* thought, long and hard," Rock Point said, his voice as inflexible as his title. "And so have my Emperor and my Empress."

"But if you do this, the Church—"

"Sir Vyk, 'the Church' sat by and watched when the Group

of Four planned the slaughter of my entire kingdom. 'The Church' has allowed herself to be ruled by men like Zhaspahr Clyntahn. *'The Church'* has become the true servant of darkness in this world, and deep inside somewhere, all of her priesthood must know that. Well, so do *we*. Unlike 'the Church,' we will execute only the guilty, and unlike the Inquisition, we refuse to torture in God's name, to extort confessions out of the innocent. But the guilty we *will* execute, starting here. Starting now."

Lakyr started to say something else, then closed his mouth.

He's not going to change his mind, the Delferahkan thought. *Not any more than I would, if I had my King's orders. And,* he admitted unwillingly, *it's not as if Mother Church hadn't already declared herself Charis' enemy. And he's not wrong about these men's guilt, either.*

A spasm of something very like terror went through Lakyr on the heels of that last thought, but he couldn't unthink it. It echoed somewhere deep down inside him, reverberating with his own anger, his own disgust, when Graivyr and his fellow Schuelerites turned what ought to have been—*could* have been—the bloodless seizure of the Charisian merchantmen here in Ferayd into bloody massacre.

Perhaps, a tiny little voice said in the shadowed stillness of his heart, *it really* is *time someone held those who do murder in the Church's name accountable.*

That was the most terrifying thought of all, for it was pregnant with the dreadful implication of other thoughts, other decisions, looming before not just Sir Vyk Lakyr, but every living man and woman. As he watched the nooses being fitted around the necks of the struggling men on HMS *Destroyer's* upper deck, he knew he was witnessing the seed from which all those other thoughts and decisions would spring. These executions were a declaration that men would be held accountable as *men* for their actions, that those who exhorted murder, who tortured and burned in "God's name," would no longer be permitted to hide behind their priestly status. And that was the true iron gage the Charisian Empire had chosen to fling at the Church of God Awaiting's feet.

The last noose went around the last condemned man's neck and drew tight. Two of the priests on *Destroyer*'s deck were frantically trying to fling themselves from side to side, as if they thought they could somehow break free of their rough-edged hempen halters, and it took a pair of Marines each to keep them on their feet as the drums gave one last, thunderous roar, and fell silent at last.

Lakyr heard one of the condemned inquisitors still babbling, pleading, but most of the others stood silent, as if they were no longer able to speak, or as if they had finally realized that nothing they could have said could possibly alter what was about to happen.

Baron Rock Point faced them from *Destroyer*'s after deck, and his face was hard, his eyes bleak.

"You stand condemned by your own words, your own written reports and statements, of having incited the murder of men—and of women and children. God knows, even if we do not, what other atrocities you may have committed, how much other blood may have stained your hands, in the service of that man-shaped corruption who wears the robe of the Grand Inquisitor. But you have convicted yourselves of the murders you did here, and that is more than sufficient."

"*Blasphemer!*" Graivyr shouted, his voice half-strangled with mingled fury and fear. "You and all your foul 'empire' will burn in Hell forever for shedding the blood of God's own priests!"

"*Someone* may burn in Hell for shedding innocent blood," Rock Point said coldly. "For myself, I will face God's judgment unafraid that the blood on *my* hands will condemn me in His eyes. Can you say the same, '*priest*'?"

"Yes!" Graivyr's voice gusted with passion, yet there was something else in it, something buried in its timbre, Lakyr thought. A note of fear that quailed before something more than the terror of impending death. At least one thin sliver of . . . uncertainty as he found himself on the threshold of mortality. What *would* he and the other inquisitors discover when they found themselves face-to-face at last with the Inquisition's victims?

"Then I wish you pleasure of your confidence," Rock Point told Graivyr in an iron-hard voice, and nodded sharply to the parties of seamen who'd tailed onto the ends of the ropes.

"Carry out the sentence," he said.

. II .

Merlin Athrawes' Cabin, HMS Empress of Charis, Chisholm Sea

Sergeant Seahamper was a natural shot, Merlin Athrawes decided as he watched Empress Sharleyan's personal armsman at pistol practice.

And so, he reflected wryly, *is Sharleyan herself! Not very ladylike of her, I suppose.* He chuckled silently. *On the other hand, the lady does seem to have a style all her own, doesn't she?*

Had anyone happened to glance into Merlin's small, cramped cabin aboard HMS *Empress of Charis,* he would undoubtedly have assumed Merlin was asleep. After all, it was already two hours after sunset aboard the fleet flagship, even though there were still several hours of light left back home in Tellesberg. That might be a bit early, but Captain Athrawes had the morning watch at Emperor Cayleb's back, so it made sense for him to get to bed as early as possible, and at the moment, he was stretched out in the box-like cot suspended from the overhead, swaying gently with the ship's motion, eyes closed, breathing deep and regular. Except, of course, that, whatever it looked like, he wasn't actually *breathing* at all. The individual known as Merlin Athrawes hadn't done that in the last nine hundred years or so. Dead women didn't, after all, and PICAs had no need to do anything so limiting.

There was no real need for him to be feigning sleep—or

breathing, for that matter—he supposed, either. No one was likely to barge in on Emperor Cayleb's personal armsman during his off-duty time, and even if anyone had, Merlin's reflexes were as inhumanly fast as his hearing was inhumanly acute. Someone whose "nervous impulses" moved a hundred times more rapidly than any organic human's would have had plenty of time to get his eyes closed and his "breathing" started up again. But Merlin had no intention of getting sloppy about the minor details. There were sufficient peculiar tales already circulating about *Seijin* Merlin and his powers as it was.

Of course, even the most peculiar tale fell far short of the reality, and he planned to keep it that way for as long as possible. Which meant *forever,* if he could only pull it off. That was the entire reason he had decided at the outset to assume the persona of a *seijin,* one of the warrior-monks who came and went through the pages of legend here on the planet Safehold. *Seijin* were reputed to have so many different marvelous capabilities that almost anything Merlin did could be explained away with the proper hand-waving.

Assuming the hand-wavers in question can keep a straight face while they do it, at any rate, he reminded himself.

So far, the tiny handful of people who knew the truth about Merlin had managed to do just that . . . helped, no doubt, by the fact that the truth would have been even more bizarre. Explaining that he was a *seijin* was ever so much simpler than explaining to a planet systematically indoctrinated with an antitechnology mindset that he was the Personality Integrated Cybernetic Avatar of a young woman named Nimue Alban who'd been born on a planet named Earth . . . and been dead for the better part of a thousand years. All too often, Merlin found it sufficiently difficult to wrap his own mind about that particular concept.

His artificial body, with its fiber optic "nerves" and fusion-powered "muscles," was now the home of Nimue's memories, hopes, dreams . . . and responsibilities. Since those "responsibilities" included breaking the Church of God Awaiting's antitechnology stranglehold on Safehold, rebuilding the technological society which had been renounced a thousand years ago in the name of survival, and preparing the last planet of human beings in the entire universe for the inevitable moment in which it reencountered the species which had come within an eyelash of exterminating humanity the first time they'd met, it was, perhaps, fortunate that a PICA was the next best thing to indestructible and potentially immortal.

It was also fortunate that no more than twenty-five people in the entire world knew the full truth of who—and what—Merlin was, or about his true mission here on Safehold, he reflected, then frowned mentally. All of those twenty-five people happened to be male, and as he watched Empress Sharleyan's personal detachment of the Imperial Charisian Guard punching bullets steadily through their targets on the palace firing range, he found himself once more in full agreement with Cayleb that there should have been at least one *woman* who knew the truth. Unfortunately, deciding who was to be admitted to the full truth about humanity's presence here on Safehold—and about Merlin—was not solely up to them. If it had been, Sharleyan would have been added to the ranks of those who knew both of those secrets long before Cayleb had sailed from Charis with the invasion fleet bound for the League of Corisande.

You can't have everything, Merlin, he reminded himself once again. *And sooner or later, Maikel is going to manage to bring the rest of the Brethren of Saint Zherneau around. Of course, just who's going to do the explaining to her with Cayleb—and you—the better part of nine or ten thousand miles away is an interesting question, isn't it?*

Personally, Merlin was of the opinion that Archbishop Maikel Staynair, the ecclesiastic head of the schismatic Church of Charis, couldn't possibly convince his more recalcitrant brethren soon enough. "Captain Athrawes" sympathized completely with the others' caution, but leaving Sharleyan in ignorance was shortsighted, to say the very least. In fact, the word "stupid" suggested itself to him rather forcefully whenever he contemplated the Brethren's hesitation. Sharleyan was far too intelligent and capable to be left out of the loop. Even without full information, she'd already demonstrated just how dangerously effective she could be against Charis' enemies. With it, she would become even more deadly.

Which doesn't even consider the minor fact that she's Cayleb's wife, does it? Merlin grimaced behind the composed façade of his "sleeping" face. *No wonder Cayleb's mad enough to chew iron and spit nails! It'd be bad enough if he didn't love her, but he does. And even on the most hard-boiled, pragmatic level, he's still right. She has a* right *to know. In fact, given the risks she's chosen to run, the enemies she's chosen to make in the name of justice and the truth, there's no one on this entire planet—including Cayleb himself—who has a* better *right! And if I were she, I'd be pissed off as hell when I finally found out what my husband's advisers had been keeping from me.*

Unfortunately, he thought, returning his attention to the images of the practicing guardsmen relayed through one of his carefully stealthed reconnaissance platforms, that was one bridge they'd have no choice but to cross when they reached it. All he could do now was hope for the best . . . and take a certain comfort from the obvious efficiency of her guard detachment. They wouldn't have the chance to explain *anything* to her if some of the lunatics who'd already attempted to assassinate Archbishop Maikel in his own cathedral managed to kill her, first. And given the fact that even with all of the advantages of Merlin's reconnaissance capabilities he still hadn't been able to determine whether or not those assassins had acted on their own, or how big any supporting organization might have been, Captain Athrawes was *delighted* by the evidence of Sergeant Seahamper's competence. He would have preferred being close enough to protect Sharleyan himself, but not even he could be in two places at once, and Cayleb needed looking after, as well. And at least if he couldn't be there in person, Seahamper made a satisfying substitute.

While Merlin watched, the sergeant finished reloading his double-barreled flintlock pistol, cocked and primed both locks, raised it in the two-handed shooting stance Merlin had introduced, and added two more petals to the ragged flower of bullet holes he'd blown through the target silhouette's head.

He was firing from a range of twenty-five yards, and the maximum spread of the group he'd produced was no more than six inches. For someone who'd never even fired a pistol until less than four months ago, that was a remarkable performance, especially with a flintlock he had to stop and reload after every pair of shots. Merlin could have produced a much tighter group, of course, but *Nimue* wouldn't have been able to when she'd still been alive. Of course, as Merlin, he had certain advantages which Seahamper—or any other mortal human being—lacked.

The sergeant was almost as good a shot with a rifle, although it was readily apparent that he was actually more comfortable with the pistol. And while Sharleyan's other guardsmen might not be quite up to Seahamper's standard, all of them had become excellent marksmen. As had the empress herself.

Merlin never doubted that quite a few Safeholdian males would have considered Sharleyan's interest in firearms distinctly unbecoming in a properly reared young woman of gentle birth. After all, they were noisy, smoky, dirty, smelly, and dangerous. Like all black powder weapons, they produced an enormous amount of fouling, not to mention blackening the hands—and faces—of everyone in the vicinity. And, besides, doing things like shooting holes in targets—or even in other people—was what the empress had *guardsmen* for.

Unhappily for those chauvinistic sticklers, Sharleyan Tayt Ahrmahk *liked* guns. The recoil from the guardsmen's rifles was undeniably on the brutal side, and the standard pistols were a bit too big and too heavy for her slender hands to manage comfortably. But Seahamper and Captain Wyllys Gairaht, the official commander of her guard detachment, had both known her since she was an imperious child-queen. They knew exactly what sort of force of nature she was. When she'd expressed a desire for weapons better sized for her not-quite-petite frame, they'd quickly commissioned just that. Besides, Merlin suspected that they found the notion that their charge could shoot considerably better than the vast majority of her guardsmen rather comforting.

He certainly did.

Now he spent a few more minutes watching through his distant remotes as Sharleyan methodically demolished her own silhouette.

She's going to need a bath before this evening's council meeting, he reflected with an inner chuckle, watching her smear the powder grime on her forehead as she wiped away sweat. *And when she sits down with the councilors, not a one of them would believe what she looks like right now!*

He smiled as he watched her guardsmen watching her accuracy with obvious, possessive pride, then, regretfully, turned his attention elsewhere. He was still a little surprised by how homesick he was for Tellesberg, but the city had been his home for almost three years. That was actually much longer than Nimue Alban had lived in any one spot from the day she'd graduated from the Naval Academy on Old Earth until the day of her death. Besides, home was where the people someone cared about lived.

Unfortunately, Merlin had already discovered that no one— not even a PICA who could (at least theoretically) go indefinitely without sleeping—could possibly keep track of everything *he* had to keep track of. He needed to know what was going on in Tellesberg, and on a personal level, he needed an occasional "fix" of watching over the people he and Cayleb had left behind when they sailed. Yet he couldn't afford to let himself spend *too* much time doing that, however tempting it might have been.

"Do you have that summary from Chisholm, Owl?" he asked over his built-in communicator without ever moving his lips.

"Yes, Lieutenant Commander," the AI hidden away in "Nimue's Cave," the distant cavern where Nimue's PICA had lain concealed for so many centuries, replied.

"Then I suppose I'd better take a look at it, too, shouldn't I?" Merlin sighed.

"Yes, Lieutenant Commander," Owl replied obediently.

"Well, go ahead and begin the transmission."

"Yes, Lieutenant Commander."

House of Qwentyn,
City of Siddar,
Republic of Siddarmark

It seems we're all present, gentlemen. Please, be seated."

The half-dozen men in the private dining room looked up as one when their host stepped through the expensive, paneled door and smiled at them. Answering smiles were notable for their absence.

If the immaculately groomed, silver-haired man was perturbed by the taut expressions of his guests, he allowed no sign of it to cross his own face. He simply stepped forward, with the assurance that went with both his age and his stature within the Siddarmarkian business community.

His name was Tymahn Qwentyn, and he was probably the wealthiest private citizen in the entire Republic of Siddarmark. At seventy-three years of age (sixty-six in the years of Old Earth, although no one in Siddarmark was even aware that a place called "Old Earth" had ever existed) he remained vigorous and actively engaged. It was said, not without reason, that there was not a business transaction in all of Siddarmark which didn't have a Qwentyn involved in it somewhere, and Tymahn was the acknowledged patriarch of the world-spanning family business. He was one of the Lord Protector's intimates and a financial adviser to dukes, princes, kings, and vicars. He knew everyone, everywhere, and he had built a lifetime reputation as a man whose word could be trusted and whose enmity was to be feared.

When Tymahn Qwentyn issued a dinner invitation, it *was* accepted. Even if some of the individuals on the guest list were more than a little anxious about just what he might have in mind. This evening's invitees strongly suspected the reason they'd been called together, and there was a general air of nervousness as they waited to find out if their suspicions were accurate.

"Thank you all for coming," Qwentyn said, exactly as if there'd been any probability that they might not have. "I'm sure that in these times of uncertainty, all of us can appreciate the necessity for men of goodwill to extend the hand of friendship to one another," he continued. "Especially when the well-being of so many other people depends upon the decisions those men of goodwill make."

The tension ratcheted slightly higher, and he smiled as if he both sensed their increased anxiety and was amused by it.

"I'm quite confident that all of us know one another," he said, seating himself at the head of the table. "That being the case, I see no particular need for introductions."

One or two heads nodded in agreement. Most of them did, in fact, know one another, but there were definitely times when official anonymity was greatly to be desired.

"I'll come directly to the point, gentlemen," Qwentyn continued. "I invited you here not simply in my private capacity as a senior stockholder in the House of Qwentyn, but also as a concerned citizen of the Republic. I have concerns of my own, obviously, but I have also been the recipient of certain statements of anxiety from other citizens, both within and without the government. Obviously, those anxieties have been expressed as one private individual speaking to another private individual, so please do not make the mistake of assuming that this meeting bears any particular official . . . stamp of approval, as it were."

No one bothered to nod this time. Despite any qualifications he might voice for the record, Tymahn Qwentyn did not mention contacts with anyone "within and without the government" unless he was, in fact, speaking for that government. Or, at least, for those with very powerful interests within it. And given his close personal relationship with the Lord Protector, the chance that he would even consider acting against Greyghor Stohnar's expressed desires was effectively nonexistent.

The only question in the minds of his guests was not whether or not he was being used as a sub rosa conduit by the

Lord Protector, but rather exactly what it was that Stohnar wanted to tell them.

"Recent events both here in the Republic and elsewhere," Qwentyn continued after a moment, "have resulted in extraordinary dislocations of business and finance. I'm certain all of you have experienced some of the dislocations to which I refer. And, as myself, I feel certain, you're deeply distressed by the open schism between the Kingdom of Charis—excuse me, the *Empire* of Charis—and the Knights of the Temple Lands. In a time rife with so much uncertainty, it becomes inevitable that markets will be depressed, that trade will be dislocated and businesses will falter, and that some of those businesses will fail, with disastrous consequences not simply for their owners and shareholders, but also for those who depend upon them as a means to earn their own livelihood.

"While I feel confident none of us would dispute the Knights of the Temple Lands' right to formulate their own foreign policy as they see best, or contest the will of the Grand Inquisitor when he acts to protect all of us from potential heresy and spiritual contamination, we may, perhaps, be aware of certain consequences of those decisions which have not occurred to those charged with making them. In particular, the decision to ban all Charisian-flag merchant vessels from the ports of the Republic—and, for that matter, of every other mainland port— is already producing business failures. At the moment, that's largely due to the panic effect, but the consequences—the ultimate consequences—will be only too real. To be blunt, the collapse of more than a few trading houses would appear to be imminent, and if and when those houses fail, their collapse will be like stones dropped into pools of water. Ripples of additional failure will sweep outward from them, crossing and crisscrossing with potentially disastrous effects which will know no limitations of flag or border."

He paused, and four of his guests very carefully did not look at the remaining two. Silence lingered for several minutes, and then one of the men no one else was looking at cleared his throat.

"No doubt your analysis is as accurate and pertinent as always, Master Qwentyn," he said with a pronounced Charisian accent. "And I trust you'll forgive me if I might seem to be getting ahead of events, or perhaps even appear to be putting words into your mouth. But may we assume that one of the reasons for your invitation this evening is to discuss ways in which those unfortunate repercussions could be . . . ameliorated?"

"In a manner of speaking, certainly," Qwentyn replied. Then he leaned back in his chair, folding his hands before him on the tabletop, and smiled almost whimsically. "Obviously, the spiritual well-being of the Church's flock must be the first responsibility and concern of the Grand Inquisitor. No one could possibly dispute that fact. Nonetheless, there have been occasions in the history of the . . . Knights of the Temple Lands when their policies have required the interpolation of those outside the Temple Lands if their true objectives were to be accomplished. Several people I've spoken to over the last few five-days are of the opinion that it's at least possible this may be another of those occasions."

"In what way, Master Qwentyn?" one of his other guests asked in guarded tones.

"It seems evident that the Grand Inquisitor's objective is to minimize contact between potentially apostate Charisians and the citizens of the Republic," Qwentyn said calmly. "One can hardly draw any other conclusion from his directives, not to mention his explicit instructions to the Lord Protector and to the other heads of state of the major mainland realms. The possibility that the consequences of his directives may very well exceed his intentions clearly exists, however. It's been suggested to me that perhaps it would not be inappropriate for those of us deeply involved in international trade and investment to consider ways in which certain of those unanticipated consequences might be minimized.

"For example, the Grand Inquisitor has specifically directed that our ports are to be closed against any and all Charisian-flag vessels. None of us, I'm certain, would ever even consider setting our own will in opposition to the commands of the

Grand Inquisitor. However, his directives refer specifically to the realm where a ship is *registered;* there was nothing in them which pertained to where a ship might have been *built,* or even where its cargo might have originated." He smiled benevolently at his listeners. "My own House has recently signed a long-term lease-purchase agreement by which we have taken possession of several dozen Charisian-built merchant ships. Since the agreement is a lease-*purchase,* it's obviously in our best interests to secure our ownership interest in the vessels, especially in these troubled times. Accordingly, their registries have been transferred from those of the kingdom in which they were built to the Republic, where their current owners are located."

Eyes narrowed around the table as his guests digested that. It was true that the Grand Inquisitor's orders had specified the seizure of Charisian-*owned* vessels. If ships were no longer registered in Charis, and if their owners were no longer Charisian subjects, then the letter of Vicar Zhaspahr's commands would no longer apply. Still. . . .

"Have you discussed these 'lease-purchases' with the Chancellor's office?" the Charisian-accented guest asked slowly.

"There's been no need to involve the Chancellor in such routine transactions," Qwentyn said tranquilly. "Obviously, his office is aware of them, however, since it's responded most favorably and promptly to our requests to expedite the registration of the transfers of title."

"I see."

The Charisian and the others seated around the table digested that, as well. Given the fact that the vessels themselves would be useless without crews to man them, and given the fact that the Siddarmarkian merchant marine was virtually nonexistent, a rather delicate question arose. After several seconds, one of the other guests cleared *his* throat.

"I can well appreciate how the transactions you've described would go far towards meeting the Grand Inquisitor's desires while simultaneously providing the necessary bottoms to keep essential commerce moving. My own shareholders might well be interested in participating in similar transactions, but, alas, we do not possess a stock of trained sailors from which to provide crews."

"As a matter of fact, that presented certain difficulties to *us,* as well," Qwentyn said, nodding gravely. "We determined that the simplest decision was to hire the additional sailors we required. In fact, the sellers were kind enough to provide us with the trained seamen we needed. The simplest solution, actually, was simply to hire the passage crews who delivered the vessels to us. Obviously, they were already familiar with the ships in question, and the majority of them had no objection to sailing under Siddarmarkian colors. One ship is very like another, after all."

Eyebrows rose. It was abundantly clear that the legal maneuver Qwentyn was describing was no more than a paper transaction. And if that was clear to them, they felt confident it would be clear to others. The possibility that Zhaspahr Clyntahn would be . . . unhappy when he learned of it appeared significant, but it was obvious Qwentyn was, in fact, acting as the Lord Protector's messenger in this instance. And while it was undoubtedly true that the Grand Inquisitor's wrath and the disapproval of the "Knights of the Temple Lands" was not something to be lightly contemplated, it was also true that the Lord Protector was far closer to them. With winter closing in, it was even conceivable that some five-days would pass before anyone in Zion learned of this particular maneuver. And if—or when—Vicar Zhaspahr learned of it, the Church's long-standing policy of not pushing Siddarmark too hard would undoubtedly come into play. The most probable negative outcome would be a forced repudiation of the "lease-purchases," and it was highly probable that the Republic's diplomats (and law masters) would be able to spin even that out for months. Months during which the official owners of the vessels in question would be making money hand-over-fist in markets where the general reduction in shipping would enforce scarcity and drive prices steadily upward.

And if the Lord Protector's administration was prepared to pursue *this* arrangement, who knew what *other* arrangements it might be prepared to sanction, as well?

Several eyes slid sideways, towards one of the guests, in particular. He was neither Charisian nor Siddarmarkian, and his tunic sleeve carried an embroidered crown surmounted by crossed keys. The crown in question was orange, not white, which meant he was a senior bailiff for a member of the Council of Vicars, and not some lowly archbishop or bishop. His presence had been unexpected, and more than one of the other guests waited to hear him denounce what Qwentyn had just said.

Instead, he simply frowned thoughtfully. If he felt the intensity of the regards directed at him, he gave no sign of it, but after a few moments, he nodded.

"As you say, Master Qwentyn, the consequences of the exclusion of Charisian-owned shipping have already been profound. And, like most of the people in this room, I'm responsible for serving the best interests of my patrons. Clearly, the upward surge in prices is making that significantly more difficult. I feel quite confident that my employers would wish me to explore every possible avenue by which those rising prices might be controlled. I think this lease-purchase arrangement of yours has a great deal to recommend itself as a means whereby the Grand Inquisitor's directives and intentions can be given effect without bringing about a total collapse of our maritime commerce or imposing disastrously high prices. In fact, it would seem to me that the purchasing approach you've chosen to follow is only one of several possible options. For example, had you considered—"

The atmosphere around the table shifted noticeably as the bailiff leaned forward, his eyes intent. *Business is business.* They could almost physically hear him saying that, although they all knew he would never, under any circumstances, admit that he had.

The arrangements they were discussing probably wouldn't last, yet they might very well hold up for quite some time. And if the Lord Protector remained as willing to pursue . . . innovative solutions as he clearly was at this moment, some fresh arrangement would undoubtedly be waiting in the wings when the Church finally got around to quashing this one.

Which suggested all sorts of interesting future possibilities. . . .

. IV .

Priory of Saint Hamlyn,
City of Sarayn,
Earldom of Rivermouth,
Kingdom of Charis

Excuse me, My L—Sir," the rather plainly dressed young man said.

The almost equally plainly dressed older man looked up with a chiding expression, but he permitted the self-correction to pass unremarked.

This time.

"Yes, Ahlvyn?" he said instead.

"There's a messenger from Tellesberg," Ahlvyn Shumay told him.

"Really?" The older man, who tried very hard to remind himself that he was no longer Bishop Mylz Halcom— officially, at least—sat back in his chair and quirked an eyebrow.

"Yes, Sir. From . . . our friend in Tellesberg."

Halcom's raised eyebrow smoothed magically. As a matter of fact, he'd discovered quite a few "friends" in Tellesberg— more, really, than he'd hoped for, after his hasty departure from his own see in Hanth Town. At this particular moment, however, there was only one of them for whose messages Shumay would have interrupted him. And if his aide sometimes had trouble breaking the habit of addressing Halcom as a bishop, he'd demonstrated a much greater ability to remember never to mention names unless he absolutely had to.

"I see." Halcom gazed thoughtfully at Shumay for a handful of seconds, then shrugged very slightly. "Is there anything I need to do about it immediately, Ahlvyn?"

"As a matter of fact, no, Sir," Shumay replied. "I just thought you'd like to know that he seems to have experienced no undue difficulty in making the arrangements you asked him to see to."

"Thank you, Ahlvyn. That's very good news."

"Of course, Sir," Shumay murmured, and withdrew.

Halcom gazed after him for a moment, then turned back to the brown-bearded man in the white lamp-badged brown habit of an upper-priest in the Order of Bédard. That robe was girdled by the white rope belt which marked him as the head of a monastic community, a fact which had a great deal to do with Halcom's presence in this remarkably spartan office.

"Please excuse the interruption, Father Ahzwald," he said. "I'm afraid I may have overly impressed Ahlvyn with the need to deliver messages promptly."

"Please, My Lord." Father Ahzwald shook his head. "Don't concern yourself. Father Ahlvyn has been with you in the dragon's mouth. If he thinks you need to know something, then I'm quite content to leave that decision in his hands."

"Thank you," Halcom said, managing not to frown as the other man used his ecclesiastic title.

Actually, he supposed, it didn't really matter that much in this case. Father Ahzwald Banahr was the head of the Priory of Saint Hamlyn, and the priory was located in the city of Sarayn, well over two hundred and fifty miles from Tellesberg. It was unlikely that Baron Wave Thunder, King—no, *Emperor*—Cayleb's spymaster, had infiltrated any of his agents into a relatively small priory that far from the capital. And particularly not into a priory of the same order which "Archbishop Maikel Staynair" called his own.

Still, good security was a matter of developing the proper habits, and as Banahr had just pointed out, Halcom had survived more than a few five-days in the dragon's mouth in Tellesberg, itself. And, once his business here in the Earldom of Rivermouth was completed, that was precisely where he'd be returning.

"Well," he said, "to return to our earlier discussion, Father. I fully realize how eager you are to strike a blow in the name of God and His Church, but I'm very much afraid that, as I said, your value to His cause is much greater where you already are."

"My Lord, with all due respect, neither I nor the brothers I've called to your attention are afraid of anything apostate heretics might do to us. And the fact that we're members of the same order from which the author of this abomination sprang gives us a special responsibility to do something about it. I really think—"

"Father," Halcom interrupted, his tone as patient as he could make it, "we have the swordarms we need. We have a plentiful supply, actually, of good and godly men prepared to do God's will in opposing what you've so rightly described as an 'abomination.' What we need more than anything else is a support network. A community of the faithful—of those the schismatics have so disdainfully labeled 'Temple Loyalists'—prepared to gather supplies, stockpile weapons, offer shelter, serve as message conduits, pass funds as necessary. To be totally, brutally blunt, we need that sort of network much more than we need additional fighters."

Father Ahzwald couldn't hide the disappointment in his expression, assuming he'd actually *tried* to hide it.

Well, that's just too bad, Halcom thought, *because everything I just told him is the absolute, literal truth. Although I do hope we can instill at least a rudimentary sense of security into Father Ahzwald! I'm confident Wave Thunder isn't wasting time looking in his direction yet, but that can always change, especially once we start staging our operations through the monastic community.*

"I understand what you're saying, My Lord," Banahr said after a moment. "And I suppose, if I'm honest, that I can't really argue with your logic. Still, I can't help feeling that a 'fellow Bédardist' might well be able to get close enough to Staynair to settle the business."

"It wasn't a case of failing to get close enough, Father," Halcom responded, and his voice was much grimmer than it had been a few moments before. "Believe me, our brothers got close enough to do the job easily enough. Or they *would* have been close enough, if not for '*Seijin* Merlin.'"

The bishop showed his teeth in an expression no one could ever possibly have confused with a smile.

"We owe the good *seijin* quite a debt," he continued, recalling the reports of Emperor Cayleb's personal armsman standing balanced on the rail of the royal box in Tellesberg Cathedral, smoking pistols in hand, as he shot down the three volunteers who'd actually gotten close enough to physically lay hands on the apostate "archbishop." "Without him, Staynair would be dead this very moment. The time will come when we settle with *him,* too, Father."

"We've heard rumors about him, even here," Banahr said, his expression troubled. "Some of the things he's supposed to have done sound . . . preposterous. Impossible."

"Oh, I don't doubt that for a moment," Halcom replied. "He's extraordinarily handy with a sword—and, obviously, with these 'pistols' Cayleb and his cronies have invented—and he has an incredibly irritating knack for being in exactly the wrong place at exactly the wrong time."

"Is it possible he has . . . assistance in managing that, My Lord?" Banahr asked in a very careful tone.

"Is he receiving demonic assistance, do you mean, Father?" Halcom asked in reply, and chuckled. "I suppose anything is possible, but I'm inclined to think the superstitious give him rather too much credit. Most of the 'impossible' things he's supposed to have done are much more probably the products of overactive imaginations than of reality! Strangling krakens with his bare hands? Single-handedly slaughtering two hundred, or three hundred—or was it *five* hundred?—Corisandian sailors and Marines aboard *Royal Charis*?" The bishop shook his head. "Athrawes is definitely a *seijin,* Father, and it would appear that the ridiculous legends about the martial capabilities of *seijins* in general have a solid core of truth, after all. But sooner or later, he's going to arrive too late, or someone is going to manage to get a sword—or an arbalest bolt, or an arrow, or a bullet—through his guard, and that's going to be the end of *Seijin* Merlin."

"I'm sure you're right, My Lord, but still. . . ."

Banahr let his voice trail off, and Halcom snorted.

"At the moment, Father, it clearly suits the purposes of Staynair, Cayleb, and their cronies to . . . *emphasize,* shall we say, Athrawes' abilities and accomplishments. After all, he's Cayleb's personal armsman. Encouraging people to think he's some sort of infallible superman is likely to discourage direct attempts on the Emperor's life. And having someone capable of 'miraculously' intervening to save Cayleb, or Staynair, is another way for them to pretend God truly favors their apostasy. After all, would He have sent a protector like '*Seijin* Merlin' to look after Cayleb, to save Staynair from certain death, if He *didn't* favor them? So it's scarcely in their interests to downplay his accomplishments, is it?"

"I suppose not," Banahr said a bit doubtfully, and Halcom suppressed a sigh. The prior's fixation on Captain Merlin Athrawes' apparently more-than-human capabilities actually only underscored what Halcom had just said. Many of those who supported Cayleb in his insane, arrogant challenge to the authority of God Himself saw in Athrawes the imprimatur of God's approval, instead. It was tempting to take advantage of the concern Banahr and others like him felt and label Athrawes a servant of demons—or even a demon, himself. In many ways, it might be an effective tool, especially among the more poorly educated and more credulous. But it had been over seven hundred years since anyone had last seen a true demon. Labeling Athrawes as one now would probably lose them as much support among the better educated and informed, and if they were going to successfully combat the schism, they couldn't afford to lose that support. Besides, the opportunity it would provide for the schismatic propagandists to mock the Temple Loyalists' "ridiculous claims" was something which had to be avoided.

Mind you, there are times I'm more than half-tempted to sign on to the same belief, Halcom admitted. *For example, I have no intention of telling Banahr about the way Merlin "just happened" to turn up in the nick of time to save that bastard Mahklyn from the bonfire we'd arranged for him. But if he really were a demon, he'd have gotten there in time to save the* rest *of their precious Royal College, as well.* The bishop smiled mentally, thinking about the literally decades of records which had gone up in the flames. *They're never going to be able to put all of* that *back together again, and a* true *demon would have recognized that and gotten there a half hour or so sooner. And a true demon would have simply arranged to have our brothers arrested—or killed—before they ever got close enough to strike at Staynair, too. Killing them the way he actually did was certainly spectacular, but letting us get that close first only proved how deep—and committed—the opposition to their precious "Church of Charis" really is.*

"Trust me, Father," he said aloud, "God isn't going to permit any demonic intervention. Not openly, at any rate. Staynair is right in at least one respect, damn him to Hell. God did create Man with free will. It's the exercise of that free will by men who have willingly embraced evil that we confront, but God isn't going to permit demons to openly intervene on the side of blasphemy and heresy. If that were what this 'Merlin' truly is, we'd see angelic intervention to deal with him. *The Book of Chihiro* makes that abundantly clear."

"Yes." Banahr brightened visibly. "Yes, My Lord, that's true. I shouldn't have forgotten that. I suppose,"—he grinned almost sheepishly—"that I've been so shocked by what's happening that I'm starting to jump at shadows."

"You're scarcely alone in *that,* Father," Halcom said dryly. "On the other hand, in some ways, that only underscores what I was saying earlier about our need for a secure communication network. And, frankly, for what I suppose you might call 'safe houses' where those who are openly striking at the forces of the apostate can feel secure between attacks. Someplace where they can gather and recoup their faith and their spiritual wholeness before going back out to face the schismatics once more."

"Yes." Banahr nodded, slowly at first, but with gathering enthusiasm. "Yes, My Lord, I can see that. And, however much I might hunger to strike one of those blows myself, it's clearly my duty to serve in the most effective way possible. Not to mention the fact that, so far as I know, you're the only *legitimate* bishop remaining in the entire Kingdom. As such, anyone truly loyal to Mother Church must obviously place himself under your direction."

"I believe there are more members of the clergy of this accursed 'Church of Charis' who would agree with you in their heart of hearts on that point than Cayleb and Staynair dream," Halcom said in a hard voice. "And the fact that they keep their faith secret, securely hidden, is a good thing, for now, at least."

Banahr nodded, and Halcom's nostrils flared. Then he gave himself a small shake.

"Now, Father," he said more briskly. "I don't want to get into too many particulars at the moment, but I can tell you that we have at least one or two quite wealthy supporters here in Charis. Some of them are prepared to place that wealth at the Temple Loyalists' service. Obviously, we can't permit any one of them to contribute too heavily."

Banahr looked a bit confused, and Halcom shook his head.

"Think about it, Father," he said patiently. "It's unlikely that someone like Wave Thunder isn't making a list of people—especially wealthy or powerful people—he might suspect of Temple Loyalist sympathies. If a sizable percentage of one of those wealthy suspects' wealth should suddenly disappear, it would ring all sorts of alarm bells in Wave Thunder's mind. So it's essential that any contributions to our cause be both carefully hidden and not so large as to obviously impact upon the wealth of the contributors."

Banahr was nodding again, and Halcom sat back in his chair and raised both hands, palms uppermost.

"Fortunately, I've managed to make contact with a few people—some of them in Tellesberg, some of them not—who are prepared to channel 'charitable contributions' through various monasteries and convents and into our hands. That, to be honest, would be the greatest service Saint Hamlyn's could provide to our cause at this time."

No one on Safehold had yet reinvented the term "money-laundering," but Halcom had the essentials of the practice down pat.

"Of course!" Banahr said promptly.

"Think about it carefully, Father," Halcom cautioned. "The possibility that, sooner or later, Wave Thunder or one of his spies is going to come up with something that could be traced back to you definitely exists. And for all of Cayleb's sanctimonious disavowal of 'repressive measures,' he's also made it clear that anyone who lends himself to supporting armed resistance to the Crown or to Staynair's corrupt régime within the Church will face the sternest penalties."

"I'm not in love with the concept of martyrdom, My Lord," Banahr replied somberly. "I'm not *afraid* of it, either, though. If it's God's will that I should die doing His work, then I will have been blessed above all other men."

"That's true, Father," Halcom said quietly, his eyes warm. "That's very true. In fact, it's that truth which makes it possible for me to go back into the 'dragon's mouth,' as you put it. And sooner or later, Cayleb and Staynair—and, yes, even *Seijin* Merlin—are going to discover that no one can ultimately defeat men who remember that. And when they discover that, they're also going to find themselves giving account to God and Langhorne, and *that,* Father Ahzwald, is something they're *not* going to enjoy."

FEBRUARY,
YEAR OF GOD 893

✦

. I .

Cherayth,
Kingdom of Chisholm,
Empire of Charis

Welcome to Cherayth, Your Majesty."

The man who'd been waiting at the foot of the gangway bowed deeply as Cayleb Ahrmahk, Emperor of Charis, stepped off it onto the stone quay and set foot for the very first time upon the soil of the Kingdom of Chisholm. Cayleb had never met the tall, silver-haired Chisholmian with the deep, strong voice, but he'd been looking forward to making the older man's acquaintance. Not, unfortunately, without a certain amount of trepidation. Fortunately, the Chisholmian's greeting seemed sincere, although it was hard to be certain, since just hearing him was more than a bit difficult, under the circumstances. The harbor behind Cayleb was crowded with Charisian warships and Charisian transports packed to the gills with Charisian Marines. Even the enormous waters of Cherry Bay seemed congested and crowded well beyond their maximum capacity, and the defensive waterfront batteries were wreathed in smoke. But the fleet behind Cayleb was no invasion force come to pillage Cherayth, and the gunsmoke drifting away on the biting breeze of a northern winter (whose teeth made Cayleb's southern blood devoutly grateful for his heavy cloak) was from the twenty-four-gun salute which had just roared its way into silence. And if the guns had fallen silent, the shouting voices of the bundled-up Chisholmians packed black and dense into every vantage point they could find had not.

There was enthusiasm in most of those shouts. Not all—
Cayleb hadn't expected that—but most. Yet however welcome that might be, they still made it hard to hear.

"Thank you, My Lord," Cayleb replied, raising his own
voice against the background tumult, then stepped forward
and extended his right hand. Mahrak Sahndyrs, Baron Green
Mountain and the first councilor of the Kingdom of Charis,
seemed surprised at the gesture. He hesitated for a fraction of
a second, then straightened from his bow and clasped forearms with the man who had become *his* emperor.

The cheering redoubled, and Cayleb smiled, ever so faintly.
He supposed there were rulers who would have felt it was imperative to stand upon their imperial dignity when meeting
someone in Green Mountain's position for the first time. The
baron had been the mentor, protector, and, effectively, second
father of Queen Sharleyan of Chisholm ever since Sharleyan
had ascended to the throne as a mere child, and in many ways,
he was every bit as popular with her subjects—her *common-
born* subjects, at least—as she was. Many princes or kings
who'd abruptly found themselves in Cayleb's position would
have felt legitimate concern about the ultimate loyalty of a
man who'd been all of those things and enjoyed so much support and trust. The mere fact that Sharleyan had become
Cayleb's wife and the Empress of Charis, Cayleb's coruler,
might not have been enough to keep some other Green Mountain from seeking control of Chisholm for himself—especially
since Sharleyan had remained behind in Charis, rather than
returning with Cayleb—and too much familiarity with a man
of such ambitions might all too easily prove fatal.

Yet Cayleb felt no concern about that at all. Mostly because *Sharleyan* didn't, and Cayleb trusted her judgment
(and her hardheaded realism) implicitly. Almost as important, however, Captain Merlin Athrawes shared Sharleyan's
judgment, and Captain Athrawes possessed certain . . . advantages which were not available to other men when it came to
evaluating the actions and beliefs of others. If Merlin Athrawes
told Cayleb a man was trustworthy, the emperor was quite

prepared to take him at his word. A word which had been amply confirmed by Merlin's reports on how firmly and ably Green Mountain and Queen Mother Alahnah had looked after Sharleyan's affairs in Chisholm during her absence.

Of course, Green Mountain had no way to know anything of the sort, and just as Cayleb had never met Green Mountain, Green Mountain had never met *him*. Now Cayleb held the baron's arm in his clasp for a few moments longer. He looked levelly across at him, letting Green Mountain look into his own eyes, and Sharleyan's first councilor accepted that invitation as he had accepted the emperor's proffered hand. He looked deep, and Cayleb met that searching gaze without flinching, his own eyes steady, until something inside Green Mountain's expression—something no one could actually have seen, or described—seemed to ease somehow.

"Your Majesty, I—"

"A moment, My Lord," Cayleb interrupted, his voice pitched just a bit lower, to form a sort of private alcove at the heart of the thunderous cheers still rising about them. Green Mountain's eyebrows arched, and the emperor smiled at him. "There are many things I'd like to say to you at this moment," Cayleb continued. "Unfortunately, I'm well aware that there are any number of *official* things we need to be discussing, instead, not to mention all of the public folderol we're both going to have to put up with. I assure you, I have my public face ready to put on for all of that. But first, the Empress, my wife, charged me most sternly, as my very first duty in Chisholm, to give you and her Queen Mother all of her love."

"I—" Green Mountain stopped and cleared his throat. "I thank you for that, Your Majesty," he said after a moment, his own voice just a bit husky. His hand tightened on the emperor's forearm for a second. Then his nostrils flared as he inhaled deeply.

"And now that you've delivered her message, Your Majesty, we really do have those formalities to deal with, I'm afraid." His head twitched ever so slightly, indicating the gorgeously clad ranks of aristocrats—some of whose expressions seemed just a bit less welcoming than his own—standing behind him at a respectful distance on the jam-packed quay.

"Will you come and meet your Chisholmian subjects?"

▼ ▼ ▼

Welcome heat poured from the vast fireplace to Queen Mother Alahnah Tayt's left as she sat at the foot of the table, gazing up its length across the glittering silver and polished glass and china at the dark-haired young man sitting at the table's head. For the past several months, that chair—the one at the table's head—had been Alahnah's, and it felt odd to see someone else sitting in it.

Especially this *someone else,* she thought. *It wouldn't bother me a bit to see* Sharley *sitting there again!*

She watched Emperor Cayleb turn his head, laughing at something Baron Green Mountain had said, and she discovered that her eyes were examining his profile intensely. It was as if by staring at him she could somehow have a glimpse of her daughter once again. Then, without warning, Cayleb stopped laughing at Green Mountain's comment and looked straight at her, and she found her eyes gazing directly into his.

They were dark in the lamplight, those eyes. Dark and deep and surprisingly warm. Almost . . . gentle.

Odd. "Gentle" was the one adjective it would never have occurred to her to apply to the victor of Rock Point, of Crag Hook and Darcos Sound. And yet it was the only one which really fitted. The young man sitting in her daughter's chair met her gaze directly, not challengingly, but with understanding. With compassion.

A peculiar little tingle danced somewhere deep inside her at the thought. It was as if in that moment she had finally allowed herself to realize—or, at least, to *admit*—something she'd refused to face directly from the moment Cayleb's proposal of matrimony arrived in Cherayth. Fear. Fear that the man who'd won those smashing victories, who'd threatened to sink every one of the Earl of Thirsk's ships, without quarter or mercy, unless his surrender terms were accepted, must be as hard as his reputation. As cold as the sword at his side. Fear that her daughter had gone to wed a man as merciless, in his own way, as the kraken which was the emblem of his house. It wasn't that she'd feared Cayleb might be *evil,* the monster of depravity depicted in the Group of Four's propaganda. But a man need not be evil to be cold. To recognize all of the ways in which political calculation must trump mere human emotions when the prize was the life or death of entire kingdoms, and to act accordingly.

But she wasn't seeing that man. Oh, she had no doubt that a man with that chin, those eyes which had seen too much blood and death already for a man of twice his years, *could* be just as hard and cold as any steel blade. Whatever else he might be, Cayleb Ahrmahk was no weakling, no captive to indecision or to vacillation. Yet who she was seeing in this moment was the young man—the *husband*—Sharleyan's letters had described. Not the emperor. Not the invincible admiral, or merciless dictator of terms, or leader of schism against God's Church, but her daughter's husband.

Oh my God, a quiet voice said softly, almost prayerfully, in the back of her mind. *Sharley* wasn't *just trying to reassure me. She was telling me the truth. She truly loves him . . . and maybe even more important,* he *truly loves* her.

Alahnah Tayt had watched her daughter sacrifice too much already on the altar of responsibility, give too much to the weight of the crown she had been forced to assume when other girls were still playing with dolls, surrender too many of the joys which should have been hers. Sharleyan had never complained, never wasted effort on self-pity or admitted she missed those things, yet Alahnah had missed them for her. In the lonely watches of the night, she had prayed for her daughter's happiness, begged God to give her some small scrap of *personal* love and joy as partial compensation for all of the cold, demanding prestige, power, and wealth of her queenship. *Surely* God could not have condemned her to a bitter, cold marriage after all He had already demanded of her! Yet that was exactly what Alahnah had feared . . . and if Sharleyan had never admitted it, her mother had known it was what *she* feared, as well.

Now, for just an instant, the queen mother's lips trembled, and then—to her astonished embarrassment—she burst into totally unanticipated tears. Green Mountain rose quickly, stepping urgently around to her, going to one knee beside her chair and taking her right hand in both of his, and she heard his soft, urgent questions. Heard him asking her why she wept. But she couldn't answer him. She could only stare down the length of the table at the young man who had so unexpectedly, without saying a single word, told her that her daughter had found the one thing in the world her mother had most feared she would never know.

▼   ▼   ▼

Cayleb Ahrmahk watched Queen Mother Alahnah weep, listened to Green Mountain speaking softly and urgently to her. He'd been as surprised as Sharleyan's first councilor by the queen mother's tears, but only for a moment. Only until he'd recognized the way her eyes clung to him, even through her tears, and recognized that the one thing in which she did not weep was sorrow.

He patted his mouth with his napkin, laid the snowy linen aside, and pushed back his own chair. At his express request, he, Alahnah, and Green Mountain were dining privately. Even the servants had withdrawn, waiting to be summoned by the ringing of Queen Mother Alahnah's bell if they were needed. Even Merlin Athrawes stood outside the private dining chamber's door, guarding the privacy of all its occupants, and now Cayleb went to one knee at the other side of Alahnah's chair. He took her free hand in his own, raised it to his lips and kissed its back gently, then looked up at her—or, rather, across, for he was as tall kneeling as she was sitting.

"Your Grace," he murmured, "I feared the same thing myself, in many ways."

" 'Feared,' Your Majesty?" Alahnah repeated, and he nodded, then reached up with his left hand. A gentle thumb brushed tears from her cheek, and he smiled softly, almost sadly.

"You feared your daughter had been caught in a trap," he told her. "You were afraid of a loveless marriage of state, a thing of cold calculation and ambition. From what Sharleyan's told me, I believe you recognized the reasons for that calculation, understood the necessity behind the ambition, but still, you feared them. As did I. I had reports of your daughter, descriptions. I knew her history. But I didn't know *her*, and I was afraid—so afraid—that if she accepted my proposal, I would be condemning both of us to a necessary but loveless union. That like so many other princes and princesses, kings and queens, we would be forced to sacrifice our own hopes of happiness on the altar of duty to our crowns.

"Sharleyan changed that for me. She changed it by being someone I could love, and someone who could love me. By being as brave, as warm and loving, as she was intelligent. As compassionate as she was pragmatic. As gentle as she could be ruthless at need. I would have proposed this marriage no matter what her character might have been, and I would have wed her with all honor, even if there'd been no love at all between us, just as she would have wed me. But God was good to us. We had no need to make that choice, because we truly do love one another. I wish, more than I could ever possibly say, that she were here to tell you that herself. She can't be. God, in His mercy, may have spared us from a cold, unfeeling marriage, yet our other duties, our other responsibilities, remain. And it would be impossible for Sharleyan, as I know I need not tell you, to leave those responsibilities unmet, those duties undone. You—and Baron Green Mountain—taught her that, just as my father taught me, and neither of us will be unworthy of our teachers."

"I know," Alahnah half-whispered. "I *know*, Your Majesty, truly. And I see now that Sharley's letters told me nothing but the simple truth when I feared she was trying desperately to offer me false comfort. Forgive me, Your Majesty, but I half-suspected—feared, at least—that the true reason she hadn't accompanied you home to Cherayth was that it *was* a loveless marriage and you feared I might realize that when I finally saw the two of you together."

"Your Grace, I told you Sharleyan would never lie to you about something like that," Green Mountain said softly, and she gave him a watery smile.

"Dear Mahrak!" She pulled her hand out of his to touch him lightly on one cheek. "Of course you did. I know that. Just as I fully realize that you would lie Shan-wei out of Hell if that was what it took to protect Sharleyan or me."

"Your Grace, I never—" he began, only to have her interrupt him with a soft gurgle of laughter.

"Of course you would have! And don't make it worse by trying to convince me otherwise."

He looked at her with an oddly hopeless expression, and she laughed again, then turned her attention back to Cayleb.

"Get up, Your Majesty! It's not fitting that you should be on your knees to me."

Her voice, Cayleb noticed, was much stronger than it had been, with a scolding note he had not previously heard from her. It was one he recognized, though. The last time he'd heard it—from someone besides Sharleyan herself, at least—it had been from his own mother, and he felt something warm within his heart.

"Yes, Your Grace. Immediately, Your Grace. To hear is to obey, Your Grace," he said meekly, brown eyes twinkling with devilish delight, and she laughed again.

"That's quite enough of that, too, Your Majesty," she told him. "You aren't going to turn *me* up sweet with a few words and an easy smile! That may have worked with my young and impressionable daughter, Sir, but it won't work with me!"

"Your Grace, I am shocked—*shocked,* I say—that you could possibly impute such base motives to me!"

"Of course you are," she said dryly, then pointed firmly with her free hand at the chair he had abandoned. He held her left hand a moment longer, still smiling at her, then rose and walked obediently around to seat himself once more in the indicated chair.

"With all due respect, Your Majesty," she continued, "I hope you'll forgive me if I inform you that you are a charming, utterly unprincipled young rascal. No doubt you've found that smile of yours has always gotten you out of trouble before. I suspect you'll find it rather less effective in my own case, however!"

"Well, there went all my hopes and plans to use my irresistible charm to . . . steer you into doing things my way."

"Somehow," Green Mountain said, his tone even drier than the queen mother's, "I rather doubt that you've resorted to anything as uncertain as 'irresistible charm' in quite some time, Your Majesty."

"Indeed not," Alahnah agreed, her eyes narrowing as she considered the exotically dressed young man sitting at the far end of the table. "Mind you, it's already obvious to me that you *can* be quite charming, when it suits you, Your Majesty. And to be frank, if I were twenty years or so younger, I would undoubtedly find that charm almost as 'irresistible' as Sharleyan obviously has. In my own case, however, you have something much more valuable and convincing."

"I do?" Cayleb arched one eyebrow, his head cocked politely, and she snorted.

"Of course you do," she said in a much more serious tone. "You have the truth. And you have the partnership you and Sharleyan have obviously forged. I already knew that much from her letters."

"And does the rest of Chisholm share that belief with you, Your Grace?" Cayleb asked softly.

"Not all of it, Your Majesty," Green Mountain answered for the queen mother. "Not all of it. But for most of your people, most of Queen Sharleyan's subjects, there's more than enough trust—in her and her judgment—to offset the fears of those who don't agree. For now, at least."

"That was the impression we'd both drawn from your letters to her, My Lord," Cayleb said, carefully never mentioning the reports he'd had from one Merlin Athrawes, as well. "I hope this visit will help to convince at least some of those stubborn holdouts that their fears are groundless."

"If you mean our own Temple Loyalists are going to find it a bit difficult to continue describing you as Shan-wei come back to Safehold, complete with horns, cloven hooves, and hairy tail, you're probably right," Green Mountain replied dryly. "On the other hand, I'm sure you don't need me to point out that where power and politics are concerned, most men really don't need Mother Church to inspire them with 'distrust.' Especially if they scent the possibility of siphoning some of that power into their own hands."

"The fact that you left Sharley at home in Tellesberg, trusted her at your back, with all of the levers of power in your own kingdom, is going to go a long way towards reassuring those whose concerns were genuine, Your Majesty," Alahnah said. "And, frankly, the fact that Mahrak and I accept your authority, not to mention taking both you and Sharley at your word when you claim to be true partners and coequals, is going to be just as reassuring. Unfortunately, mere reassurance isn't going to inspire the ambitious to suddenly abandon their own designs. Nor," her eyes darkened, "is it going to magically convince those Temple Loyalists Mahrak just mentioned to acquiesce in your 'blasphemous' defiance of Mother Church."

"Perhaps not," Cayleb agreed calmly, sitting back in his chair—the comfortably upholstered, ornately carved chair in which Sharleyan had sat so many nights—before the softly roaring fire. The priceless emeralds set into the golden chain about his neck danced with hearts of green fire as he fingered it, and he smiled. "Perhaps not. On the other hand, when all of the Charisian sailors and Marines I've brought with me come ashore and begin telling Sharleyan's people how she already has every single one of *my* subjects eating out of her hand, I suspect those Temple Loyalists of yours may find it just a bit more difficult to foment distrust. And I'd imagine that all the marks they're going to be spending in your taverns and taprooms—not to mention your brothels, if you'll pardon me for bringing that up—will make them rather more welcome visitors. Which, of course," his smile grew thinner, baring his teeth, and this time Queen Mother Alahnah felt a profound satisfaction as she saw in it all of the cold steel and ruthlessness she'd been so afraid of seeing such a short time before, "completely leaves aside the fact that if any of your Temple

Loyalists—or ambitious nobles—should have been cherishing any notions about challenging Sharleyan's decision to link Chisholm's fate with that of Charis, it's just remotely possible that finding forty or fifty thousand Charisian Marines in the vicinity will cause them to . . . rethink their options, shall we say?"

"Oh, I believe it's entirely possible you're correct about that, Your Majesty," Green Mountain said with a satisfaction which matched Alahnah's own. "And in the meantime," he continued with a smile, "might I tempt you to sample just a little more of this truly excellent chicken?"

. II .

Royal Dockyard,
City of Cherayth,
Kingdom of Chisholm

Thank you, Commander Ahzmynd," Captain Andrai Gyrard said as the Chisholmian officer behind the desk signed off on the requisition order for replacement spars. Properly speaking, Gyrard ought to have left this interview to his purser. A full captain, the commanding officer of one of the Imperial Charisian Navy's most powerful galleons, had far better things to do with his time than to spend it hobnobbing with dockyard officers just because he wanted a few spare spars before heading off to conduct an invasion. And if that was true of most galleon skippers, it was especially true of the man who commanded Emperor Cayleb's flagship. Handling routine chores like this one so that their captains didn't have to was precisely the reason the Navy had pursers in the first place.

"You're welcome, Captain Gyrard," the Chisholmian said, setting his pen back into its desktop holder as he looked up from the document with a smile. "At least this is one requisition

I can be certain is going to end up where it's supposed to end up, rather than on the black market somewhere!"

Gyrard chuckled, although, truth to tell, he wasn't certain whether or not Commander Ahzmynd truly had been making a joke. Prior to Chisholm's involuntary participation in the Group of Four's attack on Charis, the Royal Chisholmian Navy had been fighting a losing battle against corruption and peculation. Certain of its officers, secure behind the protection of highly placed aristocratic patrons, had been far more interested in finding ways to line their own pockets than with safeguarding their navy's combat readiness. All sorts of vital supplies had "mysteriously disappeared," and all too often, officers who'd tried to do something about it had paid a stiff price in highly placed aristocratic *enemies*.

So it was entirely possible that this particular Chisholmian was referring to the sweeping reforms which had been rammed through his own navy by the Earl of Sharpfield, its senior officer, as part of the navy's mobilization before his departure for Emerald and the Battle of Darcos Sound. Any truly competent officer must have welcomed those reforms, after all.

There was another possibility, however, and that second possibility helped to explain why Gyrard had come to deal with this matter in person. Much of Safehold accepted the stereotype of the Kingdom of Charis as "a kingdom of moneylenders and shopkeepers," populated by greedy, scheming Charisians who were always on the lookout for ways to squeeze a mark out of any opportunity which came their way. There was an enormous amount of unspoken envy in that stereotype, of course, but that made it no less real. And there were more than a few Safeholdians who would have added "unscrupulous, dishonest, and shifty" to all the other adjectives. After all, if they hadn't been unscrupulous, dishonest, and shifty, then they wouldn't have been so much wealthier than those far more worthy souls who cherished the stereotype in the first place!

Since the invasion fleet had arrived in Cherry Bay, its Charisian officers had encountered quite a few people who obviously shared that stereotypical view of them.

"Seriously, Sir," Ahzmynd said, "it's been a privilege to be able to supply your requirements. And," his eyes hardened ever so slightly, "I, for one, was delighted to have the opportunity to do it. Especially here."

Those no-longer-smiling eyes met Gyrard's, and Cayleb's flag captain felt himself relax internally. Not everyone in what had been the Royal Chisholmian Navy before its merger into the new Imperial Charisian Navy would have shared Kynai Ahzmynd's opinion on this particular subject. The invasion fleet's decision to bypass Kraken Bay, where the city of Port Royal had been built almost a century ago expressly to serve as the Navy's primary base, to anchor in Cherry Bay, so much farther to the north, might not have been the most subtle possible way to deliver a message, but it had certainly been effective. The incredible mass of galleons anchored off Chisholm's capital city—and especially the fifty thousand Imperial Charisian Marines embarked aboard the transports—was something not even the most ambitious Chisholmian aristocrat could overlook. As pointed suggestions went, this one was more pointed than most. And those who had found the greatest personal advantage under the old system had understood exactly who been intended to absorb that point.

"I'm glad you feel that way, Commander," Gyrard said now. "And I've been impressed by the professionalism you and most of the other dockyard officers have displayed."

"It's been a relief to be *able* to display it," Ahzmynd said, with rather more frankness than Gyrard had expected, even now. "I won't pretend that anyone in the Navy was happy about what you Charisians did to us at Darcos Sound." His mouth tightened briefly, and his eyes darkened, but then he shook himself, and his mouth relaxed. "On the other hand, it wasn't exactly like you'd been left a lot of choice, was it? Most of us understood that, too. The ones of us who could *think,* at least. And," he bared his teeth in a tight smile, "since Earl Sharpset got home, those of us who found that difficult to understand seem to have been finding ourselves with quite a lot of, um, *free time* on our hands."

The Chisholmian's dust-dry tone was so biting Gyrard

snorted in amusement. Sharpset had returned to Chisholm with the surrendered galleys Emperor Cayleb—although he'd been *King* Cayleb at the time, of course—had "spontaneously" returned to Chisholm even before he had proposed marriage to Chisholm's queen. Since the earl's return, and especially since Queen Sharleyan had accepted Cayleb's proposal, Sharpset had attacked the twin problems of his own navy's lingering corruption and the challenge of preparing for the merger of the Chisholmian and Charisian fleets with vigor. In the process, quite a few Chisholmian officers had found themselves abruptly turfed out of their comfortable, profitable assignments. At the same time, those of them who appeared to be prepared to resist the merger had also found themselves summarily relieved of duty.

"Fair's fair, Commander," the flag captain replied after a moment. "Most Charisians understand how little choice Chisholm had about obeying the Group of Four's commands. We know it wasn't *your* idea to attack us, and most of us deeply regret how many of your people were killed or wounded in someone else's war. At the same time, I won't pretend there aren't also Charisians who aren't exactly prepared to simply forgive and forget. And, by the oddest happenstance, those officers who share that attitude seem to be finding themselves with quite a bit of unanticipated 'free time' of their own."

"I thought that was probably the case, Sir." Ahzmynd's swivel chair creaked gently as he leaned back slightly. "In fact, I didn't see how it could be any other way, to be honest."

"No, it couldn't be," Gyrard agreed. "People are people. Some of them aren't going to be able to put the past behind them no matter what. It doesn't even mean they aren't trying to, sometimes. It's just the way it is. So it's not really hard to understand why some officers would be . . . uncomfortable with all the changes coming at them, even completely disregarding all of the religious implications."

He watched Ahzmynd's eyes as he spoke, but the Chisholmian only nodded.

"You're right about that one, Sir." He shrugged. "I don't think anyone in Chisholm, except maybe Her Majesty and

Baron Green Mountain, ever expected things to come to a head with the Group of Four this way. It really hasn't helped smooth the way for our Navy to combine with yours, either."

He paused and frowned for a moment, then shook his head.

"Actually, that's not quite true," he said. "It's created problems with a lot of people, of course—I think we've probably got more 'Temple Loyalists' here in Chisholm than you have in Charis, for a lot of reasons—but for other people, it's actually helped." He looked back into Gyrard's eyes once more. "Charisians aren't the only ones who could see what was happening in Zion, you know."

"Yes, I do know." Gyrard nodded.

"Well, Sir, I won't say that anyone here in Chisholm is doing handsprings of delight at the prospect of open warfare with Mother Church, but you might be surprised by how many of us already agreed with you 'schismatic' Charisians, at least in principle. And once Her Majesty decided to marry the Emperor, well—"

He broke off with another, much more eloquent shrug, and Gyrard nodded once more. Sharleyan's nobles might have been—or, at least, *wanted* to be—more fractious then Cayleb's, but the flag captain had come to the conclusion that she'd been even more beloved by Chisholm's commoners than King Haarahld had been by their Charisian counterparts before his death. That was saying quite a lot, and that deep reservoir of trust and devotion had carried her people with her. It also helped to explain why Cayleb's demonstration that she truly was his coruler, not simply his consort, had legitimized his own authority in their eyes as probably nothing else could possibly have accomplished.

"Tell me, Commander Ahzmynd," Gyrard said, asking the question he'd had no intention of explicitly voicing when he came ashore for this meeting, "how do you think your fellow Chisholmians feel about Charisians now?"

"Now, Sir?" Ahzmynd chuckled. "They still think every single one of you is out to turn a fast mark, and, to be honest, I think many of us are more than a little uneasy about all these changes—all these new weapons and ways of doing things—you seem intent on introducing. Certainly when you first arrived, most people here in Cherayth were bracing themselves just a bit. They expected an onslaught of moneychangers, loan krakens, and political hangers-on out to make a profit out of Chisholm. I think that despite everything, there were people who believed the Emperor's marriage proposal was really only a ploy designed to let Charis get its hands on everything worth having here in Chisholm.

"That much, at least, is changing. Or that's the way it seems to me, at any rate. I could be wrong, of course." He twitched his shoulders in another brief shrug. "From where I sit, though, I think that what the Emperor's had to say so far, coupled with the fact that he's made absolutely no political changes here in Cherayth, hasn't brought in any of his own political favorites from home and handed them plum assignments, *and* the fact that he and Baron Green Mountain and the Queen Mother are obviously on such excellent terms, really has turned most of that suspicion around. The fact that your sailors and Marines have been spending so freely hasn't hurt anything, either. I haven't heard any of the dockside tavernkeepers complaining, at any rate! Mind you, I can think of quite a few lords and ladies who probably don't like the new arrangement a bit, but that's more than offset—I think, at least—by how much the common folk have been reassured. They've always regarded the Queen—the Empress, I mean—as one of their own, someone they can trust to look out for them. Now most of them seem willing to at least tentatively accept that the Emperor feels the same way she does. And I think we've at least reached a point where all but the most dyed-in-the-wool Temple Loyalists are willing to wait to hear his address to Parliament before they really decide what they think of him. If he says what I rather suspect he's going to say, that trust in Her Majesty is going to attach itself to him—provisionally, at least—and they'll decide they can trust *him,* too."

"I certainly hope you're right, Commander," Gyrard said quietly. "And it's true, you know. His Majesty *does* feel the same way Her Majesty does, although, to be honest, the battle lines between the common folk and the nobility are less sharply drawn in Charis."

"Really?" Ahzmynd cocked his head to one side, lips pursed. "I'd heard that that was the case, Sir," he continued after a moment. "From my perspective, it's a bit difficult to really accept, though. It's so different from the way things have been here in Chisholm for as long as anyone can remember."

"Well, Commander," Andrai Gyrard said, sitting back in his own chair with a smile as tight as anything Ahzmynd had produced, "we'll just have to see what we can do about changing that, won't we? The Emperor has a saying: 'If it isn't broken, don't fix it.' I'd say that's probably one of the main reasons he and Her Majesty haven't set out to make any political changes here in Cherayth. Baron Green Mountain and Queen Mother Alahnah are doing just fine. But if anyone thinks *His* Majesty is going to be any more tolerant than *Her* Majesty where great nobles with . . . delusions of grandeur, shall we say, are concerned, they're sadly mistaken."

"Really?" Ahzmynd repeated, then smiled back at his Charisian visitor. "Somehow, Sir, I can't quite seem to find it in my heart to regret that. Odd, isn't it?"

. III .

Parliament Hall, City of Cherayth, Kingdom of Chisholm

It's a good thing Sharleyan warned me, Cayleb thought wryly as he and his mounted bodyguard arrived outside Parliament Hall.

Chisholm's Parliament had a much more magnificent home than its Charisian equivalent. Unfortunately, that owed rather more to the Chisholmian nobility's delusions of grandeur (and appetite for power) than it did to any reverence for popular participation in the Kingdom's government.

The sprawling building's windows flashed back the cold northern sunlight, and its white marble gleamed like chilled alabaster under a sky of palest blue, burnished with a few high puffs of cloud. The Kingdom's banner snapped and popped from two of the flagstaffs above it, flanking the tallest, central staff, which bore the banner of the new Charisian Empire: the traditional black field and golden kraken of Charis, quartered with the blue and white checkerboard of Chisholm. An icon of the Archangel Langhorne in his role as Lawgiver crowned the roof above the Hall's portico, scepter raised in stern benediction and admonition; gold leaf glittered; and deep, detailed bas-relief sculptures decorated the Hall's enormous bronze doors. Doors whose sculptures, by the strangest turn of fate, seemed oddly dominated by heroically posed nobles on their prancing chargers, with precious few peasants, merchants, sailors, mechanics, or manufactory owners anywhere to be seen.

The more I see, the more impressed I am that she managed to survive, *much less retain her throne,* Cayleb thought much more soberly as he took in the monument to the aristocracy's traditional domination of political power here in Chisholm.

He'd always known the political equation in Chisholm was fundamentally different from the one in Charis. He hadn't realized before becoming privy to the Brethren of Saint Zherneau's hidden influence just why Charis was so different from so many other kingdoms and principalities, but he'd always realized that commonly born Charisians had far more say than commoners in other lands when it came to the way in which they were ruled.

Chisholm had been one of those "other lands," at least until Sharleyan's father had taken the throne. The Chisholmian aristocracy had secured a firm grip on the levers of power when a not-quite-rebellious alliance of his most powerful nobles forced Sharleyan's great-grandfather, Irwain II, to "graciously grant" the Charter of Terayth. According to Merlin, the terms imposed upon the Crown at Terayth had been similar to those of something called the "Magna Carta" back on Old Earth, except that they'd been substantially more restrictive of the Crown's prerogatives.

The situation probably still wouldn't have been irretrievable except for the unhappy (from the Crown's perspective, at least) fact that her grandfather, Irwain III, had been a well-meaning but weak monarch. Sharleyan had once told Cayleb that her grandfather would have made a truly excellent minor baron back in the hills somewhere, but he'd been a disaster as a reigning king. Instead of regaining the ground his father had lost, Irwain III had sought compromise rather than conflict. He'd dreaded the thought of what open warfare would have cost his subjects and refused to inflict it upon them in defense of royal prerogatives . . . and so he'd seen the nobility make even more inroads into the king's authority. By the time he died, the great nobles had reduced him to little more than a figurehead.

Unfortunately (from the great magnates' perspective, at least), however, they hadn't *quite* completed the process at the time of his death . . . and Sharleyan's father, King Sailys, had been made of sterner stuff. The fact that he'd grown to young manhood watching his own father's humiliation as he kept steadily losing ground had probably had something to do with it, but he'd also been aware that factionalism among "his" nobles threatened to split Chisholm into warring fragments. That civil war would soon inflict all the bloodshed and horrors his father had bartered away the Crown's authority trying desperately to avoid . . . unless he made it his business to prevent it. He did, and he'd found the two men whose support he needed to accomplish his seemingly hopeless task. Mahrak Sahndyrs had been Sailys' chief adviser and confidant, but the king had been ably assisted by his future brother-in-law, the Duke of Halbrook Hollow, as well.

Irwain III had been stripped of everything the nobility recognized as a source of power, but he'd retained his status as the head of state . . . and the Crown had retained the power to summon—and dissolve—Parliament. When the old king died, and Crown Prince Sailys assumed the throne, the law of the Kingdom required that Parliament be summoned to confirm the new monarch and to swear fealty to him.

Everyone had known it was a mere formality, of course, but they'd been wrong. What none of Irwain III's aristocratic masters realized was that Sailys and his friend Mahrak Sahndyrs had spent the last ten years of King Irwain's life planning for the day that summons would be issued. Along with a few very carefully chosen and recruited members of the House of Lords, they had steered the new Parliament in directions no one else had anticipated, and they'd done it so quietly, so skillfully, that their intended victims had never even seen it coming.

That first Parliament of King Sailys was referred to now as the "Parliament of Love" in most of Chisholm's histories. Ostensibly, that was because everyone had been so carried away with their enthusiasm for their charismatic new king that they'd gladly acquiesced in the "modest changes" he'd requested. Foremost among those "modest changes," although Sailys and Green Mountain had been careful to bury it as deep in the underbrush as they could, had been the formation of the core of a small standing army. That particular proposal was justified on the basis of the growing threat from Corisande, and—according to those same official histories—Parliament had gladly supported such a farsighted request. In fact, the Lords had seen the minuscule authorized strength of the new "Royal Army" as little more than giving their youthful monarch a shiny new toy with which he could amuse himself rather than interfering in the serious business of running the Kingdom.

Some toys were more dangerous than others, however, and before the great nobles had awakened to their danger, the king and his handful of trusted advisers had created a *genuine* royal army, one which was both rather larger than the nobility had anticipated and answerable directly and solely to the Crown. *And* one which was independent of the feudal levies upon which previous monarchs had been forced to rely.

They should *call it the Parliament of Idiots,* Cayleb thought bitingly. *Not that I mind the fact that they were idiots, but how in God's name could they have let him get* away *with it?*

Actually, he had a pretty shrewd notion of exactly how it could happen. Chisholm's military traditions had been so backward by the standards of the great kingdoms of the mainland that it had still relied on feudal levies on the rare occasions when an army was required. That was the way it had always been, and Sailys' nobles had been so accustomed to thinking in terms of those same feudal levies—which *they* controlled, not the Crown—that it had never occurred to them that a professional standing army could actually pose a threat.

Unfortunately for them, they'd been wrong. The Royal Chisholmian Army might not have been particularly large by the standards of mainland realms, but it had been large enough. And its troops had all been volunteers, raised from the ranks of commoners. That had made them a dragon of a different color compared to the conscripted peasants who had filled out the ranks of the traditional levies. Among other things, they'd had a cohesiveness, an awareness of themselves as servants of the Crown and as voluntary members of something far greater than the usual noble's drafted levies ever attained. More than that, they'd had a very good idea of who was most likely to get ground into dust in the course of any fighting between their betters' competing factions, as well, which probably helped to explain why they'd been so impervious to aristocratic blandishments or threats once the nobility finally woke up to what was happening.

With Sailys shrewdly playing the nobility's factions off against one another to prevent them from combining against him while Green Mountain adroitly managed the Kingdom's financial affairs and Halbrook Hollow commanded the Army, the king had broken the three most powerful of those factions, one by one, within six years of taking the throne. The other factions, made wise by the misfortune of their fellows, had finally combined against him and attempted to cut off funding for the Army through their control of Parliament, rather than face it in battle. But while they'd been looking at Halbrook Hollow's campaigns in the field, they'd missed Green Mountain's rather quieter yet ultimately more deadly efforts inside

Parliament Hall. Until, that was, the traditionally browbeaten Chamber of Commons had suddenly defied its rightful lords and masters and ranged itself at the Crown's side under Green Mountain's leadership. Even worse, the alliance Sailys and Green Mountain had quietly concluded with a sizable chunk of the lesser nobility (who had resented the great nobles' self-aggrandizing monopoly of power just as much as the Crown had) made common cause with the Chamber of Commons. Instead of depriving the Army of funding, Parliament had actually voted to increase its size!

Ten years after assuming the Crown, King Sailys had made himself the master of his own house. In the process, he'd established the precedent of the Crown's alliance with the Commons which had been maintained during Sharleyan's reign. The Chisholmian aristocracy was far from resigned to the permanent curtailment of its power, but it had at least learned the rudiments of discretion. The fact that Chisholm had become progressively more powerful and prosperous under Sailys had probably helped it swallow the painful medicine he, Green Mountain, and Halbrook Hollow had forced down its collective throat. Unfortunately, that power and prosperity had also posed a threat to Prince Hektor of Corisande's plans, which explained Hektor's subsidization of the "pirates" who had ultimately succeeded in killing Sailys.

The more disgruntled of Sailys' nobles had publicly mourned their king's death even while they laid quiet plans for dealing with their new child-queen as their own great-great-grandfathers had dealt with Queen Ysbell. But if Sailys had been killed, Green Mountain and Halbrook Hollow were still very much alive, and Sailys' daughter proved even more capable—and, when necessary, ruthless—than he had been himself . . . as the Duke of Three Hills and his allies had soon discovered.

There was no doubt that the aristocracy retained a larger share of political authority in Chisholm than its Charisian counterparts did in Tellesberg, but that authority had been drastically reduced. And it was only a shadow of that which the nobility continued to enjoy in most other Safeholdian realms. Yet the trappings of its four-generations-ago dominance remained in Parliament Hall's decoration and procedures, and Cayleb made it a point to keep reminding himself that the Chisholmian tradition of royal authority was younger—and probably weaker—than the Charisian tradition.

On the other hand, we're establishing all sorts of new traditions, aren't we? Cayleb thought. *And—so far, at least— Alahnah and Green Mountain have the situation in hand. Probably*—his lips twitched in an involuntary smile—*at least partly because these people really don't want to see Sharleyan coming home to deal with any . . . unruliness herself!*

As always, the thought of his wife's proven capabilities was deeply comforting . . . and sent a tremor of loneliness through him. It was still a marvel to him that someone should have become so deeply, almost painfully, vital to him in so short a time. And not just on a pragmatic level. In fact, if he was going to be honest with himself, not even *mostly* on a pragmatic level, any longer.

He glanced over his shoulder to where Merlin rode at his back in the uniform of the new *Imperial* Charisian Guard. The blackened armor remained, as did the black tunic, but the golden kraken on Merlin's breastplate now swam across a kite-shaped shield in the blue-and-white of the House of Tayt. Sharleyan's personal guard detachment wore the same uniform, except that hers bore Chisholm's doomwhale in place of the kraken.

"Impressive, isn't it?" the emperor said quietly, twitching his head at the building looming before them, and Merlin snorted.

"So is the Temple," he pointed out, equally quietly. "The wrappings are less important than the contents."

"Is that one of those wise *seijin* proverbs?" Cayleb asked with a grin.

"No, but it probably should be." Merlin cocked his head, studying the Hall's imposing façade. "I wish Her Majesty were here to play tour guide," he added.

"So do I," Cayleb admitted, then stopped speaking as they reached their destination and halted in the space a cordon of halberd-armed Royal Army infantrymen had kept clear before Parliament Hall.

The emperor swung down from his saddle, accompanied by the sharp-eyed, handpicked Imperial Guard troopers of Merlin's detachment. Those guardsmen were even more alert than usual, Cayleb noticed. None of them were oblivious to just how convenient certain parties would find it if something fatal were to overtake one Cayleb Ahrmahk.

Despite the cold temperature, which struck Cayleb and the majority of his Charisian-born bodyguards as outright frigid, a substantial crowd had assembled outside Parliament Hall. The overwhelming majority of the spectators standing there amid steamy clouds of exhaled breath were commoners, probably because most of the nobles in the capital were already sitting snugly in their seats inside the Hall, Cayleb thought just a bit enviously as the cheers began to rise. The crowd's enthusiasm meant he had to proceed slowly, graciously, acknowledging their greetings rather than scurrying towards the Hall's waiting warmth.

His guardsmen almost certainly shared his desire to get inside and out of the wind as quickly as possible, but they allowed no sign of that eagerness to distract them from their duties. They formed a loose ring around him, wide enough to keep anyone who might break through the Army cordon from getting to him with a knife. Ranged weapons were more problematical, of course, but Cayleb took a certain satisfaction from the knowledge that Merlin and Owl, the *seijin*'s computer henchman, had provided him with garments made out of the same sort of "antiballistic smart fabric" (whatever *that* was) from which they'd made Archbishop Maikel's vestments. Even if some unfriendly soul with an arbalest or a rifle were crouched behind one of the windows overlooking Parliament Hall, nothing he could do was likely to leave Cayleb with anything more than a painful bruise or two.

Well, that and the need for some fairly inventive explanations, I suppose.

His lips quirked at the thought, and then he heaved a surreptitious sigh of relief as he managed to get inside the building's comforting warmth at last.

It was much quieter inside Parliament Hall than it had been outside, although he wasn't certain it was all that much of an improvement. However happy the members of the Commons seated on the western side of the Hall's grand meeting chamber might be to see him, the Lords seated on its eastern side appeared to find it remarkably easy to restrain any unseemly enthusiasm *they* might be experiencing.

I suppose it's hard to blame them for that, Cayleb thought as the Speaker came towards him to offer formal greeting. *They must have been unhappy enough with only Sharleyan to worry about. Now there's* me, *as well . . . and any of them who have been awake enough to smell the chocolate have to be aware of how Charis' Parliament operates. Whatever else they may be expecting out of me, it's not going to be anything that will* improve *their position here in Chisholm.*

"Somehow," he heard Merlin murmur very, very softly into his ear, "I don't feel all warm and loved."

"*You* don't?" Cayleb snorted back, then adjusted his face into an expression of proper formality as the Speaker bowed to him in greeting.

"Welcome! Welcome, Your Majesty!"

"Thank you, My Lord Speaker," Cayleb replied graciously.

"Both Houses await your pleasure with eagerness," the Speaker continued more diplomatically, Cayleb was certain, than accurately, at least where the Lords were concerned.

"Then let us not keep them waiting," Cayleb said.

▼   ▼   ▼

He looks *like an emperor,* Mahrak Sahndyrs thought from his place among his fellow nobles as the Speaker ushered Cayleb to the lectern which had been draped in the new imperial flag to await him. Personally, Sahndyrs would have preferred to be seated on the western side of the Hall, among the commoners who were his staunchest allies. Unfortunately, he was a peer of the realm, and tradition demand that he be seated among his fellow aristocrats.

Besides, it gives them all the opportunity to remind themselves—and me, of course—that while I may be First Councilor, I'm also still a mere baron.

Sharleyan had offered several times to do something about that, but Green Mountain had always declined. He could put up with the pretensions of snobbish earls and dukes all day long, if he must, and his decision to remain a "mere baron" was important to his commoner allies. They understood that the queen's senior minister had to be a nobleman, but they found a "mere baron" far more acceptable than they would have found an earl or a duke. Now he watched the young man in the embroidered thigh-length tunic and loose-fitting breeches which still looked undeniably exotic to most Chisholmians standing where Sharleyan had stood so often, the emerald-set chain of a Charisian king flashing about his neck, and leaned back comfortably in his own chair. He'd half-expected Cayleb to come in full imperial regalia, and he still wasn't sure the younger man's decision not to hadn't been a mistake, but the baron had to admit that he'd never seen a more kingly young man in his life.

Clothes don't make the man, nor a crown a king, he reminded himself. *Not really, whatever certain other people may think. That has to come from within, from a man's own strength, confidence, and willpower, and this young man has those qualities in plenty.*

Somehow, he expected to enjoy the next half hour or so rather more than one of those earls or dukes he wasn't one of.

▾ ▾ ▾

"My Lords and Ladies," Cayleb said after the Speaker's fulsome, flowery introduction had finally ended, "I greet you in the name of Charis, and I bring you a message from your Queen and Empress."

He paused for a moment, letting his eyes sweep over the assembled members of Parliament's houses. Even those who undoubtedly least wanted to hear what he was about to say were listening attentively, and he smiled as he pitched his voice to carry to every one of those ears.

"Your Empress—my wife—bade me tell you that she wishes she could be here to speak to you in person. Unfortunately, the great challenges and tasks which our new Empire faces do not always let us do what we would like to do. Queen Sharleyan— *Empress* Sharleyan—remained behind in Tellesberg because she, and only she, has the power and authority to make binding decisions in both our names. While I take the field against our common enemies in Corisande, *she* has assumed the heavy burden of governing both our realms, and I need not tell *you* that those realms could not be in better hands."

He paused again, waiting while what he'd already said sank home. There was nothing new in it, not really. Yet this was the first time he had formally enunciated to Chisholm's Parliament *his* acceptance of Sharleyan's full equality as his coruler.

"At this time, as we face the Group of Four and the mainland realms under its sway across the Anvil and the Gulf of Tarot, Her Majesty finds herself confronting not simply political and financial decisions, but the military decisions required to defend our people against our enemies, as well. Even now, our forces will have completed their operations against Delferahk in punishment for the Ferayd Massacre, and it will be her responsibility to decide what other actions may be necessary. It is not a task anyone else could conceivably have undertaken, and it is one which I implicitly trust her to discharge successfully, but we must not delude ourselves that she will find it an easy one.

"My Lords and Ladies, the dangers which we face, the decisions we must undertake, the prices we must pay are unique." His eyes swept slowly across the seated peers and the members of the House of Commons. "No one else in the history of Safehold has faced the enemy we face. No other realm, no other people, have found themselves at war with the Church which was meant to be mother to us all. We, the combined people of the Kingdoms of Charis and Chisholm, know our enemy. In

Charis we were forced to defend ourselves against a totally unjustified—and unjusti*fiable*—onslaught ordered by the corrupt men in Zion who have perverted everything Mother Church was ever meant to be. Thousands of my father's subjects—and my father, himself—gave their lives stopping that attack, defending their homes and families and the belief that men and women are meant to worship *God,* not bow their heads at the feet of four corrupt, venal, arrogant, blasphemous men whose actions profane the vestments they wear and the very air they breathe."

He paused again, for just a moment, then continued in a softer voice, clear and yet pitched low enough his audience was forced to listen very carefully to hear him.

"Oh, yes, My Lords and Ladies. Thousands of Charisians died. But so did thousands of Chisholmians. Chisholmians whose only 'crime' was that the Group of Four had *ordered* Queen Sharleyan to join her own kingdom's worst enemy in an attack upon a friend who had never harmed Chisholm in any way. She had no choice. They spoke with the authority of God—or so they claimed—and all the coercive authority of the Inquisition and Mother Church. And so she was forced to bend to their will, and how many of *your* fathers, sons, husbands, and brothers died with *my* father because she had no choice?"

Dead silence reigned in Parliament Hall, and he let it linger. Then, slowly, he drew himself up to his full height.

"My Lords and Ladies, never doubt the courage your Queen showed when she accepted my proposal of marriage. It was not a decision she reached lightly, but it was the *right* decision. It was the decision of a queen who will not see her people's lives sacrificed, thrown away as if they were no more important than deciding which shoes to wear today, at the whim of four corrupt and evil men. The decision of a queen who knew that if the Group of Four's ambition was not checked, if their corruption of Mother Church was not cleansed, the Kingdom of Charis would have been but the first of many victims, and the keeper of men's souls would have become the means of their destruction.

"I know there are those here in Chisholm, as in Charis, who fear the course upon which we have found ourselves forced to sail. Do not think your Queen and I don't understand those fears. That we don't share them. To set our own mortal wills, our own mortal hands, against the might and majesty of Mother Church? To set our understanding of God's will against those who wear the orange? To set our defiance against those who grip eight in ten of all Safeholdians in the iron fist of their power? Of course we have tasted fear of our own. Of course we came to this moment in trembling, and only because those vile men in Zion left us no choice . . . and because the other men in Zion did not stop them. Only because we will live and die as men and women who worship God joyously, not as the cringing slaves of a corrupt clique who have set their own power, their own greed, in the place of God's will. Make no mistake; we will *never* bow the knee to Zhaspahr Clyntahn and his cronies!"

Spines straightened throughout Parliament Hall, and Cayleb nodded to them slowly.

"That was the reason your Queen agreed to become my wife. The reason she agreed to merge our realms into a single greater whole. The reason she, too, has drawn the sword of resistance. This is not Charis' war. It isn't Chisholm's war, or Cayleb's war, or Sharleyan's war. It is *everyone's* war. It is the war of every child of God, of every man and woman who believes in justice. *That* is the war your Queen had the high courage to join when she might have tried to close her eyes to the truth and avoid that dreadful decision."

Even some of the peers seemed to sit taller in their seats, eyes brighter, but it was in the eyes of the Commons that Cayleb saw the true fire.

"There is not a single soul in Tellesberg, or anywhere in the Kingdom of Charis, who does not recognize the decision Queen Sharleyan made," he told those burning eyes quietly. "No one who fails to understand the danger she chose to face with her eyes wide and her head high. And that, My Lords and Ladies, is why the Kingdom of Charis has taken her to its heart. They, as you, have come to know her, and in knowing her, they have come to trust her. To love her. Perhaps the subjects of another realm might question whether or not they have. Might be unwilling—or unable—to believe anyone could win the heart of a strange and new kingdom so quickly. But you already know her, have watched the girl who was forced to take her father's throne untimely grow under the challenges she has faced. Seen her grow from the sorrowing child into a queen who is Queen indeed, in the full power and majesty of her reign. You *know* what the people of Charis saw in her—what *I* see in her, every time I look at her—and because you know her, you know how she could have won her new subjects in Tellesberg so quickly."

There was sober agreement and satisfaction in faces throughout Parliament Hall, and nods, and—here and there—smiles of memory and pride, as well. Cayleb saw them, and smiled back at them.

"We have not yet been granted the time to complete the arrangements, the reorganization, which was a part of the marriage agreement between Queen Sharleyan and myself—between Charis and Chisholm. The press of events, the threat of our enemies, has forced us to move more quickly even than we had expected. But those arrangements are too important, too fundamental, to be put aside, and so I charge you, My Lords and Ladies, to select from your number those who will represent you in our new, imperial parliament. You must choose them within the next month, and you must send them to Tellesberg, where they will sit with the men and women chosen by the Parliament of Charis, under Empress Sharleyan's personal direction, and forge that new *Imperial* Parliament. I entrust this vital task to your hands, to the hands of Queen Mother Alahnah and Baron Green Mountain. I do not fear that you will fail me, or Her Majesty, in this essential duty."

He saw astonishment in the faces of many members of his audience, and disbelief in not a few of them, as they realized what he was saying. When they grasped the fact that he would allow *Sharleyan* to create the new institutions of imperial government without even looking over her shoulder the entire time. That he truly trusted her *that* much.

"For at least the immediate future, My Lords and Ladies," he told them with a crooked smile, "my own time bids fair to be more occupied with tasks of the sword than with tasks of the council chamber. I wish it were not so, but what I *wish* cannot change what *is*. Yet never doubt that whatever Empress Sharleyan does, whatever decision she makes, it will also be *my* decision, and if I cannot join her in the council chamber, I can—and will—support her outside it."

His voice hardened, turned grim, almost harsh, with the final sentence, and his brown eyes were dark. He turned those eyes on the assembled peers of Chisholm, and no man or woman in Parliament Hall misunderstood his meaning . . . or his warning. Here and there one or two of Sharleyan's nobles sought to meet his eye with defiance. They did not succeed.

"A mighty challenge and a daunting task lie before us, My Lords and Ladies," he said quietly into the intense silence, "and I do not believe God sends great challenges to the unworthy, or that He chooses weaklings for the burdens He lays upon men and women. He expects us to meet those challenges, to straighten our backs under those burdens, and so we shall. We face the sternest test that any have ever faced since the days of the archangels themselves, and we shall be worthy of the challenge He has sent us, of the trust He has shown in us. Here we stand. We can do no other, and we will not retreat or yield. We *will* prevail, however long the journey, however great the cost, so help us God."

City of Cherayth,
Cherry Bay,
Kingdom of Chisholm

Cayleb Ahrmahk stood once again at the foot of his flagship's gangway. The weather was different today—even colder, but with a heavy overcast and a raw, wet humidity. Baron Green Mountain had assured him there would be snow by nightfall, and a part of him wished rather wistfully that the snowfall would go ahead and begin. It wasn't something anyone saw very often in Tellesberg, after all.

Unfortunately, he really couldn't stay to watch snowflakes. In fact, he'd spent a five-day and a half longer here in Cherayth than his schedule had originally allowed for already. The harbor was less crowded now, since Bryahn Lock Island had taken the majority of the invasion fleet—and the Chisholmian galleys which had been added to its escorts—on ahead. *Empress of Charis* and the rest of her squadron should be able to overtake the lumbering main body without any difficulty. It felt decidedly odd to look out across Cherry Bay's waters and not see Charisian transports lying to their anchors, though, and he couldn't help feeling impatient. The extra delay on his part might not have made any difference at all in the timing of the invasion of Corisande—in fact, he knew it hadn't—but it didn't *feel* that way.

Not that he could begrudge the extra days here in Sharleyan's capital. He'd spent most of them conferring with Mahrak Sahndyrs, Queen Mother Alahnah, and their closest allies from Sharleyan's royal council, and he'd sensed the gradual relaxation of muscles and spines . . . especially after his address to Parliament. Even those closest to Sharleyan had nursed inevitable reservations about their new "emperor." Cayleb could hardly blame them for that. In fact, he was gratified—and more than a little surprised, if he was going to be honest about it—by how quickly they'd managed to get beyond it. Taking the time to accomplish that would have been worthwhile entirely on its own merits, but that wasn't all he'd managed to accomplish with Green Mountain and Alahnah's assistance.

Of course, not everyone's *been so delighted with my visit, have they?* he mused with a certain gleefulness.

Despite their outwardly expressed enthusiasm following his appearance in Parliament Hall, his speech had more or less confirmed the Chisholmian nobility's worst suspicions. But if they'd been dismayed to discover just how completely their new emperor shared their queen's view of the proper balance between royal (or imperial) authority and that of the aristocracy, they'd been careful not to show it too openly. The *Commons,* on the other hand, had been downright exuberant—one might almost have said jubilant—at the same confirmation. And much of the uncertainty and even fear many Chisholmians had nourished about Cayleb's own religious views had been ameliorated, if not totally dismissed, by the masses he had attended in Cherayth Cathedral at the queen mother's side. The hard-core Temple Loyalists weren't going to care *what* he did, but his obvious piety had greatly reassured those who'd been concerned by the tales of heresy, apostasy, and Shan-wei worship put about by the Group of Four and their adherents.

How little they know, he thought, rather more harshly, as he looked up at the dark gray clouds riding above the steel-colored winter waters of Cherry Bay. *How little they know.*

A part of him had found it increasingly difficult to go through the motions of the Church's liturgy ever since he'd read Saint Zherneau's journal. In fact, he often thought, the Church propagandists were far closer to the truth than they ever suspected when they accused him of Shan-wei worship. If there'd been any of the so-called "archangels" worthy of reverence, it had been she and the members of the original colony command crew who had stood with her in their defiance of "the Archangel Langhorne's" megalomania. Which was why Langhorne had murdered all of them, of course. Knowing the entire Church of God Awaiting was one huge perversion, a monstrous lie, deliberately calculated to bind an entire planet into an antitechnology mindset and based upon the murder of any who opposed it from the very beginning, made it difficult to pay even lip service to its doctrines.

But Maikel was right about that, too, the emperor reflected. *Men can tell all the lies they want about God, but it doesn't change the truth. And the worship of those lied to by the Church is no less real, no less sincere, simply because they don't know the truth.*

And the brethren were right about "the impatience of youth" where I'm concerned in at least one respect, he admitted grimly. *I really* do *want to yank away the mask, tell everyone on Safehold the truth. It sickens me not to.*

Perhaps it did, he reflected now, gazing out across the crowded harbor. Yet however sickened he might be, he also knew Maikel Staynair was also right that they dared not reveal the truth about "the Archangel Langhorne's" divinity. Not yet. The truth *must* be told, on that point the Archbishop of Tellesberg and the Brethren of Saint Zherneau were as grimly determined as Cayleb himself. But it *could* not be told yet. The tyrannical power of the Church of God Awaiting must be broken before the lie upon which that power was based could be denounced. Every single human being on the planet of Safehold had been reared in the Church, taught since childhood to believe the lie, and they did. To attempt to denounce that lie would only give the Group of Four and Council of Vicars a priceless—and almost certainly fatal—weapon.

The Church of Charis' position in Chisholm was a bit more precarious than its position in Charis itself. That wasn't too surprising, given the fact that Chisholm had no equivalent of the Brethren of Saint Zherneau. There'd been no one to do the work of preparing the ground, the way Staynair and his predecessors among the brethren had done in Charis. Still, Pawal Braynair, who had become the Archbishop of Cherayth when Sharleyan made her decision to defy the Group of

Four, had not impressed Cayleb as much as Maikel Staynair. Of course, Staynair was a hard act for anyone to follow, and the fact that Cayleb had known him literally for his entire life only made that even more true.

Braynair seemed a bit more timid, a bit less willing to confront opposition head-on, and less flexible. Cayleb never doubted the man's sincerity, but Archbishop Pawal lacked that intensely, almost radiantly *caring* aura which enveloped anyone who came within ten paces of Maikel Staynair.

Well, of course he lacks it! Cayleb scolded himself. *Just how many Maikel Staynairs do you think there* are *in a generation, Cayleb? Spend your time thanking God for the one you've got, not complaining about the others you* didn't *get! And don't hold the fact that Braynair isn't up to Maikel's weight against him, either.*

At least there was no doubt in his mind—or in Merlin's, for that matter—that Braynair's espousal of the Church of Charis' doctrines and denunciations of the Group of Four's perversions of the Church were genuine and heartfelt. He might not be another Staynair, but he appeared to have his own dogged, unflinching internal strength. If he never struck the sparks of spontaneous love which Staynair evoked so effortlessly from his own flock, he would be there to the very end, shoulders hunched against the blast, facing any storm that came his way. And that, Cayleb told himself, was all that any emperor had a right to ask of any man.

There was no telling how someone like Braynair would have responded to Saint Zherneau's journal, assuming he were ever given the opportunity to read it. Which only underscored the strength of Staynair's argument against bringing the truth to Safehold too quickly. No. They had to let the lie stand at least a little longer, until the Church of Charis, at least, had been given time to think untrammeled by the Inquisition's heavy hand.

But the day will come, Langhorne, Cayleb promised the ghost of Eric Langhorne in whatever corner of Hell it had been banished to. *The day* will *come. Never doubt it. Merlin and I will see to that.*

He glanced sideways to where Captain Athrawes stood waiting patiently, those "unearthly blue *seijin* eyes" sweeping alertly for any sign of threat, even as his invisible overhead sensors did the same thing, and felt a familiar rush of wonder and confidence. The mind, the thoughts and the soul, behind those sapphire eyes were even older than the lie. Nimue Alban had already deliberately sacrificed her life to defeat it; Cayleb Ahrmahk had no doubt that the *seijin* she had become in death would succeed, however long it took, whatever the cost.

Merlin glanced at him, one eyebrow slightly arched, as if he'd felt the pressure of Cayleb's eyes. And perhaps he had. *Cayleb* certainly wasn't prepared to set limitations upon the esoteric senses of a PICA! Although, now that the emperor thought about it, it was more likely Merlin had simply seen him looking through one of those invisible "sensors" of his.

The thought touched his mouth with a fleeting smile, and Merlin smiled back, then returned his attention to the task of keeping Cayleb alive.

And I should stop wasting time trying to delay the inevitable and get on with my own *job*, Cayleb told himself firmly. *It's just that . . . I don't want to.*

He admitted the truth to himself, then turned to the main reason he didn't want to.

Queen Mother Alahnah had accompanied Baron Green Mountain to the docks to bid her son-in-law farewell. Now, as he looked into her eyes—northern eyes, as gray and clear as the Chisholm Sea itself—he saw the same awareness.

"I don't want to leave," he told her softly, his voice all but lost in the sound of wind and water and the murmuring sound of the watching crowd.

"I know, Your Majesty . . . Cayleb." She smiled at him, those gray eyes misty, and her lips trembled ever so slightly as she smiled at him. "I don't want you to, either. But if we could order the world in the way we would have it, none of this would have happened, and you and I would never have met, would we?"

"The *Writ* says the world works as God would have it,"

Cayleb replied. *And that much, at least, is true,* he reflected. "I think we would have met, anyway."

"Perhaps so," Alahnah said. "Perhaps so."

She reached out to touch his cheek gently, and he saw her eyes looking deep into his own, searching for an echo, a reflection, of her daughter. And he saw her expression lighten as she found it . . . even as he found its twin in *her* eyes.

"Take care of her, My Lord," he said, moving his eyes to Green Mountain's watching countenance.

"Of course, Your Majesty." Green Mountain bowed slightly, then straightened with a crooked, whimsical smile of his own. "You might say I've had some experience in that direction."

"You have, haven't you?" Cayleb returned his smile, then drew a deep breath. "And now, I really do have to go. If we miss the tide, we probably won't make our scheduled rendezvous with the main fleet. And if we don't do that, Captain Gyrard and Admiral Lock Island will never forgive me!"

"Well, we can't have that, can we?" Alahnah said. Cayleb looked back at her, and she shook her head at him. And then, with absolutely no warning, she threw her arms around him and hugged him tightly.

Like her daughter, she was a slender, small-framed woman, while Cayleb was a muscular, deep-chested man. That chest still had some filling out to do, but those arms couldn't quite reach all the way around him even now. Yet if they were slender, those arms, almost frail, still he felt the strength of Chisholm itself in them. His eyes widened in surprise. Then his own arms went about her, and he felt her head resting on his shoulder.

A thunderous roar of approval went up from the watching crowd, and Cayleb wondered if a single member of the aristocracy would ever believe the embrace was unplanned, unchoreographed. He doubted they would, and he couldn't have cared less.

"My daughter chose well," she told him softly, raising her head and meeting his eyes once more. Tears glistened, and he

eased his embrace enough to use the index finger of his right
hand to wipe them away. She smiled again and shook her head.
"I never had a son before," she said.

"Things change," he told her.

"Yes. Yes, they do." Her nostrils flared as she inhaled
deeply, and then she released him and stood back once again.
"But we really can't have your captain and your admiral upset
with you, can we? Not with a *Charisian* emperor!"

"No, I don't suppose we can."

He touched her face one more time, nodded to Green Mountain, then turned and marched up the gangway to his flagship
through the raw northern cold and the roar of the spectators'
approval.

. V .

Vicar Zhaspahr Clyntahn's Office,
The Temple,
City of Zion

Vicar Zhaspahr Clyntahn, Grand Inquisitor of the Church of
God Awaiting and Father General of the Order of Schueler,
looked up from the paperwork on his desk, eyebrows knitting
in anger, as the door to his sumptuous office in the Temple
was opened abruptly. The upper-priest who had opened it so
unceremoniously bobbed in a rushed bow, and Clyntahn's
eyes flashed dangerously. Father Dahnyld Fahrmyr had been
one of his confidential secretaries for almost eight years. He
knew better than to burst in upon his patron without so much
as knocking first.

"What—?!" Clyntahn began thunderously, but the upper-
priest actually had the temerity (or desperation) to interrupt
him.

"I most humbly beg your pardon for intruding so abruptly,

Your Grace," Fahrmyr said, speaking so rapidly the words came out almost in a babble. "I would never have done so if it hadn't been—that is—I mean . . ."

"Oh, spit it out, Dahnyld!" Clyntahn snapped, and the upper-priest swallowed hard.

"Your Grace, Vicar Zahmsyn is here!"

Clyntahn's corrugated eyebrows flew up in surprise.

"Here?" he repeated, his tone as close to incredulous as it ever came. "In the office?"

"Yes, Your Grace!" Father Dahnyld nodded almost spastically, but there was relief in his voice, as well. As if he were astounded he'd gotten his message out without being incinerated on the spot by the thunderbolts of Clyntahn's well-known temper.

The Inquisitor General sat back in his chair, mastering his expression of astonishment while his brain raced.

No wonder Fahrmyr seemed so stunned. The Chancellor of the Church of God Awaiting didn't just casually "drop in" on the Grand Inquisitor without scheduling his appointment well in advance. In fact, *no one* "dropped in" on the Grand Inquisitor without an appointment.

Clyntahn spent a handful of seconds trying to think of any reason for Zahmsyn Trynair to have just suddenly appeared in his office anteroom, but no explanation suggested itself to him. Not, at any rate, any suggestion that he cared to contemplate.

"I assume, since you haven't told me why he's here, that he hasn't told you, either," he said in a tone which suggested that that had *better* be the reason Fahrmyr hadn't already told him, and the upper-priest shook his head sharply.

"No, Your Grace." Fahrmyr's own intense uneasiness at such a radical breach of procedure showed in his eyes, but his voice was coming back under control. "He just . . . walked in the door and 'requested a moment of your time.'"

"He did, did he?" Clyntahn snorted like an irritated boar, then shrugged. "Well, in that case, I suppose you'd better show the Chancellor in, hadn't you?"

"Yes, Your Grace. At once!"

Fahrmyr disappeared like a puff of smoke. He was back a

moment later, followed by Zahmsyn Trynair. The Chancellor's expression had been trained by decades of experience—first as a priest, then as a diplomat, and finally as the true ruler of the Council of Vicars—to say whatever he told it to say. This time, though, there was a glitter in his eyes, a tightness to his mouth. Those who didn't know him well might have missed seeing that, but Clyntahn *did* know him, and he felt his own stomach muscles tightening.

"Good morning, Zahmsyn," he said.

"Good morning." Trynair's response came out half-snapped, and Clyntahn looked over the Chancellor's shoulder at Fahrmyr.

"That will be all, Father," he said, and Fahrmyr vanished with even more alacrity. Whatever curiosity he might feel—and Clyntahn suspected he felt quite a lot of it—the upper-priest didn't want to be anywhere in the vicinity. Obviously, he, too, had read the storm flags flying in Trynair's expression.

Of course, only a blind man could have missed *seeing them,* the Grand Inquisitor thought dryly.

"To what do I owe the pleasure?" he asked, since there seemed little point in indulging in polite nothings.

"To *this*, Zhaspahr." Trynair reached into the breast of his orange cassock and extracted a sheaf of paper.

"And 'this' would be exactly what?" Clyntahn's voice was more brusque as his hackles rose in response to the other man's obvious anger. Anger which appeared to be directed at Clyntahn himself. The Grand Inquisitor wasn't accustomed to confronting anyone with the courage—or the stupidity—to show open anger with him, and he found that he didn't much care for the experience.

"It's a semaphore message, Zhaspahr. A message from King Zhames in Talkyra. Or, rather, from Bishop Executor Frayd *for* King Zhames. And himself, of course."

Clyntahn had never heard that particular note out of Zahmsyn Trynair. The Chancellor's voice sounded like hammered metal, and the emotion in his eyes burned hotter than ever.

"Obviously something about it has upset you," Clyntahn said, trying to make his own voice come out more naturally.

He wasn't accustomed to trying to defuse someone else's anger, but it looked as if Trynair was whipping himself into an even greater rage with every word he said. "And presumably, since you've come storming into my office without even warning anyone you were coming, whatever it is that's upset you concerns me, or the Office of Inquisition."

"Oh, yes," Trynair agreed. "Yes, indeed, Zhaspahr! I think that would be a very *good* way to put it."

"Then tell me what it is and let's get on with it," Clyntahn said flatly.

"All right, Zhaspahr, I *will* tell you." Trynair dropped the folded sheets of paper onto Clyntahn's desk. "King Zhames and Bishop Executor Frayd have sent word that the Charisians have burned half or two-thirds of Ferayd to the ground. You remember Ferayd, don't do, Zhaspahr? The place where all of those Charisians 'foolishly resisted' the *Delferahkan troops* who attempted to sequester their vessels on your orders?"

Clyntahn's facial muscles tightened ever so slightly, but he declined to rise to Trynair's verbal bait—if that was what it was—and simply nodded.

"Well, Cayleb and Sharleyan appear to have decided how they intend to respond to such incidents in the future. They sent twenty or thirty of their galleons into Ferayd Sound, they pounded the defensive batteries into rubble—then blew them up, after they surrendered—and burned every structure within two miles of the Ferayd waterfront."

Anger fumed up in Clyntahn's own eyes as Trynair listed the catalog of Charisian reprisals. He started to open his mouth, but Trynair cut him off with a quick, sharp wave of his hand.

"I'm not quite done yet, Zhaspahr." This time the Chancellor's voice was icy, not fiery hot, and his eyes bored into Clyntahn's. "Despite the fact that they burned down most of the city, the Charisians were extremely careful to inflict as few Delferahkan casualties as possible. They even allowed the civilian population of Ferayd to remove their portable valuables from homes inside the area they intended to burn. Not exactly the response one would have anticipated out of heretics and blasphemers after Delferahkan troops massacred their fellow heretics and blasphemers, wouldn't you say?"

Clyntahn's jaw muscles clenched, but he said nothing, and Trynair's nostrils flared.

"I thought it showed remarkable restraint on their part, actually," the Chancellor continued. "Of course, the reason for it was that they fully intended to punish those actually responsible for the deaths. Which is why, Zhaspahr, Admiral Rock Point of the Imperial Charisian Navy had sixteen—*sixteen,* Zhaspahr—consecrated priests of Mother Church hanged."

Clyntahn's eyes flew wide. Despite Trynair's obvious anger, despite his realization that the contents of the semaphore message must be shocking, he'd never anticipated that! For several seconds, he could only sit, staring at Trynair. Then he shook himself and started to shove up out of his chair, his jowly face going dark with fury.

"Those *bastards*! Those goddamned, murderous—!"

"I'm not *finished* yet, Zhaspahr!" Trynair's voice cracked like a musket shot, and the white-hot fury in his eyes stunned Clyntahn. No one looked at the Grand Inquisitor that way— *no one*!

"What?" he made himself bite out the single word, and Trynair's lips twisted.

"Every one of those priests," he said, and his voice was deadly now, each word precisely uttered, cut off as if with a knife, "was a member of the Order of Schueler. In fact, by an odd turn of chance, they were all servants of the Office of Inquisition." He watched Clyntahn's expression turning even darker, and there was something almost like . . . satisfaction mixed with the anger in his eyes. "And the reason they were hanged, Zhaspahr—the *reason* that a Charisian admiral *executed* sixteen consecrated priests of Mother Church as if they were common felons—is that the massacre of Charisians in Ferayd may have been carried out by Delferahkan *troops,* but it wasn't at Delferahkan *orders.* It was carried out, as I feel sure *you* knew very well, under the de facto command of Father Styvyn Graivyr, Bishop Ernyst's intendant, and fifteen other members of the Order of Schueler."

Clyntahn had opened his mouth once more. Now he paused, and Trynair glared at him.

"You *lied* to us, Zhaspahr. Lied to all of us."

There was no question in Clyntahn's mind who the "us" Trynair referred to might be. After all, *all* of the members of the Group of Four had . . . creatively reconstructed certain events for the *rest* of the vicarate.

"And what makes you immediately jump to *that* conclusion?" he demanded, instead of denying the charge outright. "Are you that prepared to take the word of schismatic *heretics*? It never occurred to you that *they* might have every motive in the world to lie about what happened and blame it on Mother Church in order to justify their own murderous actions?"

"Of course the possibility occurred to me. Unfortunately, they sent King Zhames certain . . . documentary evidence. I'm sure there were already copies of most of it in your files, Zhaspahr."

"What do you mean?" A thin note of caution had crept into Clyntahn's voice, and Trynair's lips tightened.

"You know perfectly well what I mean! They captured Graivyr's *files,* Zhaspahr! The originals of the reports he and his fellow Inquisitors sent to *you,* detailing the role they played. In fact, I was quite astonished at how openly and honestly Graivyr admitted in his correspondence with you that the first shot was fired by one of the Delferahkans, not by the Charisians. Or the fact that as soon as the first shot was fired, his handpicked Schuelerites immediately took command of the detachments to which they were assigned and ordered—*ordered,* Zhaspahr— the massacre of Charisian women and children! My God, man! The idiot *boasted* about it, and you knew he had, and you never warned us!"

"He didn't 'boast' about it!" Clyntahn snapped back.

"Oh, yes, he did!" Trynair retorted. "I've read the reports now, Zhaspahr. He was *proud* of what he did!"

"Of course he was!" Clyntahn's eyes flared with contempt. "They were heretics, Zahmsyn. *Heretics,* you understand? They were God's own enemies, and they deserved exactly what they got!"

"Some of them were only *eight years old*, Zhaspahr!" For the first time in Clyntahn's memory, someone leaned across a desk and shouted at him. "How in Shan-wei's name are you going to convince anyone with a working brain that an eight-year-old child was a *heretic*? Don't be insane!"

"They were the *children* of heretics," Clyntahn grated. "Their parents were responsible for putting them in that position, not me! If you want to blame someone for their blood, blame Cayleb and Staynair!"

"The Charisians are going to publish these reports, Zhaspahr. Do you understand what that means? They are going to *publish* the documents, the very words in which Graivyr and his . . . his *accomplices* wrote down, for the record, *in their own words*, exactly what the Charisians accused them of doing!" Trynair glared at his colleague. "I can't think of a more effective piece of propaganda we could have handed them if we'd *tried*!"

"And I say *let* them publish!" Clyntahn snapped back. "I've already got confessions out of those bastards, too, some of them!"

"Oh?" Trynair's eyes were suddenly much colder. "Would those be the confessions Rayno tortured out of the Charisian prisoners you had secretly transferred to Zion without mentioning it to the rest of us?"

Clyntahn twitched, and the Chancellor shook his head, his expression disgusted.

"I know you're the Grand Inquisitor, Zhaspahr. I know you have agents everywhere, more than I could possibly have. But don't make the mistake of thinking that I'm stupid, or that I don't have agents of my own. Of course I knew about your orders to Rayno!"

"Then if you disagreed with what I was doing, you should have said so at the time!" Even Clyntahn seemed to realize his retort sounded remarkably lame, and Trynair snorted.

"*I'm* not the Grand Inquisitor," he pointed out. "As far as I was concerned, if you could get confessions out of some of them, it might at least have ameliorated the disaster I was already afraid Ferayd could be turning into. Of course, not even

I had any reason to suspect the full magnitude of the catastrophe you and Graivyr were busy cooking up for us, did I?"

Clyntahn sat back down, tipped back his chair, and glowered sullenly.

"As you say, you aren't the Grand Inquisitor; *I* am. And the bottom line, Zahmsyn, is that I'll do whatever God requires of me *as* his Grand Inquisitor. If that means a few innocents are going to get caught up in bloodshed that was provoked by their own parents, then that's going to happen. And before you tell me anything more about Graivyr or the other Inquisitors in Ferayd, let *me* point out to *you* that without the blasphemy, without the schism, being pushed by the goddamned Charisians, *none* of this would be happening! Forgive me if I seem just a bit more concerned with the future of God's Church and the protection of the souls of God's people than with the well-being of a few dozen Charisian heretics or their miserable brats!"

For just a moment, Trynair looked as if he were literally about to explode. The Chancellor's entire body seemed to quiver, and a neutral bystander might have been excused for thinking he saw lightning flickering from the ends of his hair. But then, visibly, he fought for calm.

It's just like you to blame every bit of this on the Charisians, Zhaspahr, he thought icily. *It was you and your "final solution to the Charisian problem" which started all of this! I should never have let you push us all into accepting your proposals!*

Yet even as he thought that, a small voice somewhere deep inside was reminding him that he *had* let Clyntahn push—or, at least, draw—the rest of the Group of Four into doing things his way. And he'd let Clyntahn do that because it hadn't seemed important enough to him *not* to let him do it. Which meant, however much he might try to worm out of admitting it, that the disaster which had resulted was as much *his* fault as Clyntahn's.

Of course, unlike Zhaspahr, I've at least been trying to make things better *since then!*

Still, he couldn't honestly pretend that at least some of the blood wasn't on his own hands. And however furious he might be with Clyntahn just now, the fact remained that it could be dangerous—even fatal—to push the Grand Inquisitor and the Order of Schueler too far. Ostensibly, and possibly even actually, Trynair's power and authority as Chancellor was greater than Clyntahn's. Even the Office of Inquisition was legally bound to accept the direction of the Grand Vicar, after all, and Grand Vicar Erek would direct the Inquisition to do whatever *Trynair* decided needed to be done. But if it came to an open showdown between him and Clyntahn, it was far from certain that the Order of Schueler would bother to remember to whom it owed formal obedience.

"Listen to me, Zhaspahr," he said finally, his voice calmer than it had been since the conversation began. "This entire episode in Ferayd has the potential to do us enormous damage. It's got to be handled very carefully from this point out."

"Like hell it does!" Clyntahn's native belligerence was rousing as surprise began to ease a bit. "They've murdered *priests,* Zahmsyn. They can call it whatever they want, but the fact is that they've *killed* men consecrated to the service of God! Yes, it's a pity children were killed in the original confrontation. And, yes, servants of the Office of Inquisition were involved. But we're in the midst of a fight for the very survival of Mother Church. This is no time to handle things 'very carefully'! It's a time to counterattack. They don't have any proof of the authenticity of the documents they're claiming to have. Call them on it. Denounce their claims as lies and convict them of murdering *priests*! Then go ahead and call for Jihad—proclaim Holy War and burn out the canker of rebellion and apostasy and heresy in Charis once and for all!"

"No." Trynair said the single word softly, but there was nothing at all soft about his flint-hard eyes.

"Damn it, what are you *waiting* for?!" Clyntahn demanded. "For the fucking Charisians to invade the Temple Lands?!"

"If it weren't for what just happened in Ferayd, I'd be a lot more willing to proclaim Holy War," Trynair said bitingly. "Unfortunately, we have a little problem just now."

"What problem?" Clyntahn half-sneered.

"The problem that while they may not have 'proof' of the

authenticity of the documents in their possession, they do have the documents themselves, don't they? Trust me, when they publish those documents abroad there are going to be enough people—especially sitting on various thrones scattered around the planet—who recognize the truth when they hear it. My office is the one in charge of Mother Church's diplomacy, Zhaspahr. Believe me, I *know* what's going to go through the minds of all those throne-sitters, and we aren't going to like it very much. Because, Zhaspahr, they'll also recognize what happened to Ferayd after King Zhames did exactly what *we* instructed him to do for what it was. They're going to see these hangings as completely justified, whatever we may say, or whatever *they* may say openly."

"So?"

"So how many Greyghor Stohnars do you want to create, Zhaspahr?"

Trynair's question was sharp, and Clyntahn paused abruptly. Greyghor Stohnar, Lord Protector of the Republic of Siddarmark, and his predecessors had been the worst nightmare of the Group of Four and *their* immediate predecessors for years. There was no doubt in Zhaspahr Clyntahn's mind that Stohnar would gleefully have overthrown the Church of God Awaiting in his own lands if he'd imagined for a moment that he could make the attempt and survive. For his part, Trynair had never shared Clyntahn's suspicion that Stohnar was actively seeking a pretext to break with Mother Church. *His* fear had been simply that someday some difference of opinion between Siddarmark and the Church would spill over into open confrontation whether either side wanted it to or not. But in its own way, that difference between his own and Clyntahn's view of Stohnar only lent his question even more point.

"What do you mean?" Clyntahn demanded after a moment, and Trynair smiled sardonically.

Fool yourself if you want to, Zhaspahr, he thought, *but don't expect me to do the same thing. You know* exactly *what I mean.*

Of course, he couldn't actually say that out loud.

"What I mean," he said instead, "is that we've already seen

Nahrmahn turn his coat and Sharleyan actually marry Cayleb. From all the reports I've seen, it seems likely Duke Zebediah is going to do exactly the same thing Nahrmahn did—and that even *Hektor* would, if he thought for a moment Cayleb would settle for anything short of his head. Now every other prince and king on the face of the world is going to look at what happened in Ferayd and realize that in Cayleb's place, they would have done exactly the same thing."

"The hell they would have!"

"I said they would *realize* that in Cayleb's place they would have done the same thing," Trynair said. "Although, to be fair, perhaps I should have said that they would have done exactly the same thing *if they'd had the courage to*. But the main point is this. Given the way Charis is going to present what happened, we don't have a leg to stand on. No," he raised his voice and jabbed the air with an index finger when Clyntahn tried to interrupt, "we don't. Especially not after we've already been telling the entire world what *you* told the rest of us—that the *Charisians* started it. Well, they have the proof before them now that the Charisians *didn't* start it, Zhaspahr. They're going to be thinking about that if the Church suddenly declares Holy War and summons them to battle. You saw what happened when Chisholm was forced to fight a war it didn't believe in. Do you want to see the same thing happen with, say, the Desnarian Empire? Do you *want* to hand Stohnar the pretext he can use, stand upon as 'a matter of principle,' to refuse to answer that summons? And before you tell me you don't trust Stohnar not to do that anyway, let me point out to you that whatever the rest of the world may think, our resources aren't actually unlimited. There's a limit to the number of fronts we can afford to fight on simultaneously, Zhaspahr."

"But it's going to come to Holy War inevitably in the end, whatever we do," Clyntahn pointed out. "It has to. Unless you actually believe there's some way Cayleb might think he could patch things up with Mother Church after murdering her own priests?"

" 'In the end' is not the same thing as right this minute," Trynair replied, his voice as frosty as the winter snows outside the Temple. "Of course it's going to come to Holy War sooner or later. The only one of us who doesn't already understand that is Rhobair, and even he has to suspect that no other outcome is possible. And I agree with you that what Rock Point's done only makes it more inevitable, ultimately. But we not only have to be aware of what other secular rulers may be thinking, Zhaspahr. We have to be aware of what other members of the *vicarate* are thinking."

Clyntahn started to fire something back, then paused, his eyes narrowing in thought as he recognized what Trynair had actually said. What the Church could survive and what the *Group of Four* could survive weren't necessarily the same thing, after all.

"There might be fewer of those other vicars to worry about than you know, Zahmsyn," he said after several moments, his eyes flickering with a slyness Trynair found more than a little disturbing. "Trust me. The number of our . . . critics could find itself rather drastically reduced."

It was Trynair's turn to look thoughtful, eyebrows furrowed. It was obvious he was running through a mental checklist of the Group of Four's present and potential opponents, but then he shook his head.

"We can't afford to get too far ahead of ourselves, Zhaspahr," he said much more calmly. "This . . . situation in Ferayd is going to cause enough problems as it is. If we simultaneously convince the other vicars that we're planning on purging our opponents, then those opponents are far more likely to be able to whip up some sort of opposition block on the Council. In fact, they'd probably use what happened in Ferayd as the public basis for their opposition to us."

"We can't afford to be too hesitant, either," Clyntahn countered. "If those opponents you're talking about decide we're weak, or that we're vacillating, it's only going to embolden them."

"Perhaps so." Trynair's nod acknowledged Clyntahn's warning, but his expression never wavered. "The problem is that we can't uncouple Ferayd from someone like the Wylsynns—not now that Charis is planning on exploding it all in our faces. We may be able to weather Ferayd, and we may be able to weather the Wylsynns, but the odds of our weathering both of them at once are far worse."

"So what would you do?" Clyntahn challenged.

"You won't like it." There was a warning note in Trynair's voice, and Clyntahn snorted.

"And you think I've liked anything else you've had to say this afternoon?"

"Probably not," Trynair replied. "But, as I see it, we have no choice but to take the Charisians' charges against Graivyr and the others seriously."

"What?!" Clyntahn's jowls darkened furiously.

"Zhaspahr, whether we want to admit it or not, the truth is that what happened in Ferayd is exactly what the Charisians *say* happened. How we got there, whether or not Graivyr and the others were justified, is really beside the point in most ways. It certainly doesn't alter the physical facts of who attacked whom and who was at the head of the Delferahkan troops when it happened. The Charisians are going to say their subjects were set upon by what amounted to lynch mobs led by priests of the Office of Inquisition. They're going to point out that many of the dead were women, and that many more were children, and that children that young can scarcely have chosen to be heretics. For that matter, Zhaspahr, you know as well as I do that at least some of those Charisians probably were no more heretics than you or I are! There are devout Charisians who are horrified by this entire schism, you know. It's entirely likely that some of those killed in Ferayd would fall into that category, and don't think for a minute people like Wylsynn aren't going to point that out if we don't."

"If *we* don't?" Clyntahn's eyes glittered with sudden suspicion.

"I know you won't like it—I told you you wouldn't—but it's the only answer I see," Trynair said stubbornly. "And it's the only answer Rhobair is going to settle for, which isn't a minor consideration in its own right. Unless, of course, you'd like to contemplate what would happen if Rhobair decided to join hands with the Wylsynns?"

Clearly, Clyntahn didn't want to do anything of the sort, and Trynair smiled thinly.

"I didn't think you would."

"And we avoid this precisely how?" Clyntahn demanded, his face still dark and his eyes more suspicious than ever.

"We hold our own inquiry, and we conclude that the Charisians were right," Trynair said flatly.

"Never!"

Trynair didn't even flinch. It wasn't as if Clyntahn's instant, explosive response were something he hadn't anticipated all along.

"We don't have any choice, Zhaspahr. Either we hold the inquiry, and at the end of it we condemn Graivyr's actions, or else Wylsynn and the other waverers on the Council—not to mention secular rulers like Stohnar—realize we're whitewashing them. We can't afford that, Zhaspahr. Especially not in light of the evidence Cayleb and his Charisians are prepared to present. Besides, it's not as if Graivyr was still alive, is it? He's dead. Nothing we say or do is going to affect him in any way, and even if we end up condemning his actions, *we* won't be obliged to punish him; Cayleb's already taken care of that little chore for us. Besides, think of all the points we'll get. Faced with proof of wrongdoing by those pledged to Mother Church, even if that proof came from heretics and apostates, we will have acted."

Clyntahn frowned, but at least he wasn't shouting anymore, and Trynair pressed his advantage.

"Let's be clear on one thing here, Zhaspahr. I realize there were special circumstances in Ferayd's case, but you realize as well as I do that priests actually guilty of the 'crimes' Charis has accused them of are subject under Church law to exactly the punishment they received. In fact, according to *The Book of Schueler,* they were liable to far *worse* punishment. I know, I know!" He waved his hands as Clyntahn's started to fire back. "It should have been done through a proper Church tribunal, and the extenuating circumstances ought to have been taken into consideration. But the fact remains that, aside from the way in which Church law was profaned when a *secular* authority judged and executed ordained priests, what happened to Graivyr and the others is completely in accordance with charges framed the way Cayleb's framed *these* charges. We couldn't deny that even if we wanted to, and, frankly, we *don't* want to. Not at this moment."

From the look in Clyntahn's eyes, he, for one, obviously didn't agree with that last statement. Not deep inside, at any rate. But he clamped his jaw on any protests, and Trynair continued.

"We're not going to be ready to take the war to Charis until our new fleet is built and manned," he pointed out. "If we were to declare Holy War tomorrow, it wouldn't bring the day we could actually begin operations even an hour nearer. But what we *can* do with that time is use it to improve our own position before the day we can declare Jihad. Convene a special commission to investigate what happened in Ferayd, Zhaspahr. Look at *all* of the evidence, including anything from Charis. And if your special commission should conclude that Graivyr did what Charis accuses him of doing—and what you and I both know he actually did—say so. Publicly acknowledge what happened, express contrition on behalf of the Office of Inquisition, possibly even impose a public penance upon yourself—even upon me and the other two—for *permitting* it to happen. In the end, we'll emerge with even more moral authority because we dared to admit wrongdoing within the Church at a time like this."

"I don't like it." Clyntahn appeared to be oblivious to the fact that he was repeating something Trynair had already said several times. "I don't like it a bit. This is a time for strength, not for weakness!"

"It's a time for guile as well as for open confrontation," Trynair countered.

"It will delay the final confrontation."

"Not necessarily. Or, at least, not for long. Remember, we still need to build a navy before we can do anything effective against Charis, anyway."

Clyntahn fumed silently for several seconds, then drew a deep breath.

"You really think this is necessary?"

"It may not be absolutely necessary," Trynair acknowledged, "but it's the best way I can think of to defuse Charis' attack. For that matter, you know I've always thought it would be a mistake to declare Holy War any farther in advance of the ability to take that war to Charis than we can help. I know you and Allayn haven't agreed with me entirely on that point. And I know Rhobair finds the entire notion of Holy War frightening. This is the best way I can think of to control when and where that declaration gets made. It leaves the initiative in our hands, and it allows us to stake out a claim to the moral high ground. After all, we'll have shown the world we're willing to consider *genuine* charges that servants of Mother Church—as *individuals*, Zhaspahr, not as Mother Church herself—are capable of criminal acts. And when we condemn Graivyr and the others, it will be one of those 'more in sorrow than in anger' affairs. In the end, we'll actually be able to turn some of this at least partly to our own advantage."

"If you can call *that* an 'advantage,'" Clyntahn muttered. He sat silently for a well over a minute, gazing sightlessly at his own blotter, then shrugged.

"Very well, Zahmsyn," he said. "We'll try it your way. As you say," he showed his teeth in a white smile that contained very little humor, "we'll have proved our willingness to go the extra mile, to be sure of our ground before we make charges or allegations."

"Exactly," Trynair agreed, making no particular effort to hide his relief at Clyntahn's agreement. "Trust me, if we can establish that, get it fixed in everyone's mind, we'll have an enormous advantage in the battle between our propagandists and theirs."

"Well, in that case," Clyntahn said, "I suppose it's time I had Father Dahnyld start pulling copies of Graivyr's reports. I'll need them for the investigation, won't I?"

HMS Empress of Charis,
Hannah Bay,
Grand Duchy of Zebediah

Cayleb Ahrmahk stood on the quarterdeck of HMS *Empress of Charis* once again as the column of galleons wended its way past Grass Island. Shoal Island lay almost thirty miles to the north, and the broad waters of Grass Reach stretched before them. It was almost ninety miles yet to the harbor of the city of Carmyn, and he tried very hard not to feel closed in by the surrounding land.

It wasn't especially easy, even though his intellect stubbornly insisted that it ought to be.

His flagship and the squadron which she had rejoined were just over twenty-six hundred miles south-southwest of Cherry Bay. That meant the local climate was much closer to the one to which Cayleb was accustomed. If anything, it was *too* hot, despite the fact that it was technically winter, since they were still—barely—north of the equator at the moment, but that wasn't the reason he felt uneasy.

Hannah Bay measured almost two hundred and forty miles from east to west. That was a lot of water, especially when the Imperial Charisian Navy was effectively the *only* navy in these waters. Still, it was four hundred and seventy miles from Carmyn to the mouth of the Talisman Gulf. Four hundred and seventy miles between the capital of Zebediah and the open waters of Carter's Ocean.

Four hundred and seventy miles moving deeper and deeper into the embrace of the enormous island of Zebediah.

He didn't like being that far from the open sea. For him, as for almost any Charisian, the sea meant safety. It meant room to maneuver, to dodge, and it meant an element of which

Charis was the mistress . . . and a place where the lesser seamen of other lands intruded at their peril.

Stop being an old woman, Cayleb! he scolded himself. *"Open sea," indeed. Just what do you call thousands of square miles of seawater if it's not "open"? And it's not exactly as if anyone could sneak up on you, even if anyone had anything to do the sneaking with!*

He glanced for a moment at Merlin Athrawes, standing protectively at his right shoulder even here. At that particular moment, Cayleb knew, Merlin was watching through those SNARCs of his. The emperor was confident that he still had only the most imperfect grasp of exactly what a "SNARC" was, but he didn't have to know *exactly* what it was as long as Merlin knew. All Cayleb had to know was that Merlin's invisible, wyvern's-eye view encompassed not simply all of Hannah Bay, but the Gulf of Talisman—and all the other waters stretching about Zebediah like all-enveloping arms—as well. If there'd been a single warship out there in a position to threaten his fleet's stately progress, Merlin would have known it.

Actually, Cayleb reflected, *the real danger probably lies in coming to rely too heavily on Merlin's "special abilities." They may not always be available. For that matter, they* certainly *won't be available to anyone besides me, because he's my bodyguard. So maybe it's just as well if I go on feeling nervous, even knowing Merlin is keeping an eye on things, as long as I don't let that nervousness distract me from what has to be done. After all, I also need to bear in mind the fact that he won't be available to other commanders when I assign them their missions. Wonderful. I just found something* else *to worry about!*

His lips twitched as he considered his own perversity. It was remarkable how much that helped his mood, and he half-turned to face the shortish, rotund prince standing beside him.

"Any last-minute advice, Your Highness?"

"Not really, Your Majesty." Prince Nahrmahn shrugged.

"You simply need to continue to think about the Grand Duke much the way I'm certain you grew up thinking about *me*. Never forget that he's a naturally treacherous, oily sort of fellow, with a fondness for assassins and all the personal charm and warmth of a sand maggot, and you can't go too far wrong. I won't say he's actively allergic to the truth, mind you. Although, on mature consideration, I do feel relatively confident that any completely truthful statement which accidentally found its way into his mouth would cause him acute indigestion, at the very least."

"An . . . interesting characterization," Cayleb observed with something that sounded suspiciously like a chuckle.

"But an accurate one, I think." Nahrmahn looked up at the taller and younger emperor, and his expression had become very serious. "At this particular moment, Your Majesty, Grand Duke Zebediah is trapped between the kraken and the doomwhale, and he knows it."

"But which is which?"

"On balance? I'd say the Empire is definitely the doomwhale, but Hektor of Corisande makes a very respectable kraken. And then there's the fact that Zebediah knows as well as we do that the true struggle ultimately lies not between you and Hektor, but between you and the Temple. He's fully aware that at this time you have the power to crush him like an eggshell if he isn't accommodating to you, but he's equally aware that Hektor isn't simply going to forgive and forget if he turns his coat to support Charis. It may not be very likely Hektor is going to survive, but Zebediah won't be prepared to rule that possibility out completely. And whether Hektor survives or not, the Group of Four will most definitely still be waiting when the smoke clears here in the League."

"Which means he's going to be extraordinarily accommodating . . . as long as I keep my dagger firmly at his throat," Cayleb said.

"Precisely, Your Majesty." Nahrmahn inclined his head slightly. "You know, I always found your house's stubborn tendency to survive and its general all-around competence extremely irritating. It's remarkable how my attitude in that respect has changed over the last few months."

"Flattery, Your Highness?" Cayleb's eyebrows arched, and his brown eyes gleamed with amusement.

"Oh, of course!" Nahrmahn smiled. "After all, I *am* one of your courtiers now, am I not?" He swept the emperor a deep bow, surprisingly graceful for one of his physique, and Cayleb smiled back at him. But then the Emeraldian prince sobered once again.

"Jesting aside, Your Majesty, I must admit that I'm both surprised and impressed by the maturity of the judgment you've consistently demonstrated. To be blunt, you're extraordinarily young for any ruler, far less for the ruler of an empire the size of the one you and the Empress are busily hammering together. That's enough to make a man nervous, at least until he gets to know the two of you."

"Indeed?" Cayleb cocked his head, and Nahrmahn nodded.

"You've demonstrated a remarkable palette of abilities, actually," he said in an almost detached, analytical tone. "Military capability, skilled diplomacy, a steadiness which is quite remarkable in someone as young as you still are, integrity—which, I'm discovering, can be an extraordinarily dangerous weapon when it comes to diplomacy; probably because we encounter it far too infrequently to build up defenses against it—and intelligent ruthlessness coupled with what I can only call a pragmatic compassion." He shook his head. "That collection of abilities would be rare in a man twice your age. Your father was obviously an even better teacher than I'd ever realized."

"I believe he was," Cayleb agreed softly.

"And then there's the Empress," Nahrmahn continued with a quirky smile. "In her own way, I suspect she's actually even more dangerous than you are. She's certainly one of the two smartest women I've ever met in my life, and the fact that she managed not simply to survive but to actually strengthen the power of the Chisholmian Crown despite the best efforts of a pack of noblmen four or five times her age only underscores her own capabilities. Frankly, the two of you together are positively frightening, if you'll excuse my frankness."

"I'll not only excuse it, I'll take it as a compliment."

"Probably you should. And," Nahrmahn pursed his lips thoughtfully, "there's another aspect to it, too. One that hadn't occurred to me until I'd had the opportunity to meet both of you and acquire a firsthand impression of you."

"And what aspect would that be?" Cayleb asked when the Emeraldian paused.

"For a time, at least, I'm inclined to think your adversaries may well be going to underestimate you simply because you *are* young. They're going to assume that however intelligent you may be, you'll still be prey to the impetuousness of your youth. In fact, I must admit that was my own first thought when I heard the details of the ultimatum you delivered to Earl Thirsk after Crag Reach. The way they were reported to me, you were quite . . . bloodthirsty about the consequences he'd face if he rejected your surrender terms. They struck me as the sort of, um, extravagant intentions one might have expected out of youthful inexperience, let's say."

"Good." Cayleb chuckled. "They were supposed to."

"Indeed, Your Majesty?"

"Oh, don't mistake me, Nahrmahn. If he'd rejected my terms, I *would* have renewed the action . . . and there would have been no more offer of quarter until every last one of his ships had burned or gone to the bottom. Never think I wouldn't have done it."

Nahrmahn Baytz looked into the no longer gleaming brown eyes which had gone hard as frozen agates and recognized the truth when he heard it.

"And I'll also admit that I wanted to make the consequences of attacking *my* kingdom crystal clear, not simply to the Earl, but to the entire world. The next ruler the Group of Four bribes or coerces into attacking Charis will never be able to pretend he didn't know ahead of time exactly how Charis was going to respond. And in case anyone missed that after my conversation with Thirsk, I rather suspect they'll take my point after our message to King Zhames."

"But I also figured it wouldn't hurt for people like Clyntahn and Trynair to think they heard a young man's arrogance talking. My father once told me it was a wonderful and always-to-be-treasured thing to be loved by your friends, but that it was essential to be *feared* by your enemies. And after fear, the next most essential thing where your enemies are concerned is that they *under*estimate you. Better never to be attacked at all, but if you are going to be attacked, the more overconfident your enemy is, the better."

Nahrmahn gazed for several seconds at the young man who had become his emperor, and then he bent his head in a gesture of respect.

"I'm feeling better and better every day about the fact that I ended up losing to you and your father, Your Majesty."

"Really? Because I'm such a splendid and lovable fellow?"

"No, not really," Nahrmahn said dryly, and Cayleb snorted in amusement. Then the Emeraldian continued. "The reason I'm deciding I don't feel so bad after all is that at least I didn't lose to someone who simply stumbled into the ability to kick my well-padded arse up between my conniving ears."

▼ ▼ ▼

The scorching sun was hot high overhead as *Empress of Charis* hove to outside the breakwater of the city of Carmyn.

Zebediah's capital didn't look especially impressive to someone who'd grown up in Tellesberg, Cayleb decided, but he had to admit that the anchorage itself was superb. Protected by the full extent of the Gulf of Talisman and Hannah Bay—not to mention the sheltering land masses of Grass Island and Shoal Island—it offered excellent security from the elements, which was a not insignificant reflection in these latitudes, especially during hurricane season. And the approaches to the port were just as good, with deep water and very few hazards to navigation until one got quite close to the city.

Of course, the fact that it was also barely fifty miles north of the equator produced a climate in which even a Charisian felt as if he were being roasted on a spit whenever he stepped out into the direct noon sunlight.

The harbor waterfront was reasonably well guarded by shore batteries, but Grand Duke Zebediah had sadly neglected the fortification of the islands dotting the approaches to his capital. There were several places where batteries would have seriously inconvenienced, at the very least, an attacking fleet, but no guns had been emplaced.

Which might not owe a thing to Zebediah's neglect, now that I think about it, he reflected. *After all, Hektor knows the Grand Duke even better than Nahrmahn does. He probably made damned sure his navy wouldn't have to fight its way past those batteries if any little unpleasantness arose. And that might not be a bad thing for me to be remembering, either, I suppose.*

The other ten galleons Cayleb had brought with him lay protectively about *Empress of Charis,* with their guns run out and manned. That might not be considered the most diplomatic stance possible, but Cayleb didn't really care about that. His own flagship's guns *weren't* manned, and that was about all the concession to international proprieties he intended to make.

He watched the ornate barge pulling out of the harbor towards *Empress of Charis,* then glanced at Merlin, who was examining the same barge through a spyglass. The emperor suppressed a temptation to smile as he privately bet himself that Merlin's eye was actually closed. After all, a mere spyglass would only get in the way of someone with Merlin's "natural" eyesight. It did give him an excuse to ask the *"seijin"* questions. However.

"I take it the rowboat with all the gold paint is our friend the Grand Duke?"

"I believe that's correct, Your Majesty," Merlin replied gravely, never lowering the spyglass. "At any rate, there's a fellow sitting in the stern sheets who's *got* to be about ready to suffer heatstroke, given all the gold and embroidery he's wearing."

"That would be Zebediah," Nahrmahn agreed from Merlin's other elbow. "He's always been insistent about maintaining the 'proper appearance.' "

The Emeraldian wore tastefully embroidered and tailored garments, but, like Cayleb, they were as utilitarian as they were elegant, and their cotton silk and steel thistle silk were as light and cool as was physically possible. Despite the extra weight Nahrmahn was carrying about with him, he looked far more comfortable than the approaching grand duke could possibly feel.

"In that case, perhaps we should keep him here on deck while we talk?" Cayleb suggested with an evil smile. "If he's about to melt down into a puddle of fat, he'll scarcely be at his naturally treacherous best."

"Tempting, Your Majesty," Nahrmahn agreed with a smile of his own. "But not very practical, I fear. I'm sure he's already memorized everything he intends to say, and I'd be extraordinarily surprised if anything as silly as rational thought or debate was likely to change any of it. That being the case, I think the advantages for *your* thinking of getting into the shade outweigh the remote possibility that he might suffer the *seijin*'s heatstroke."

"It's not *my* heatstroke, Your Highness," Merlin remarked mildly, lowering the spyglass at last and turning to look at Nahrmahn. "I was merely offering an analytical statement, not expressing any sort of personal desire."

"Oh, of course not," Nahrmahn agreed.

"Stop it, both of you," Cayleb half-scolded.

It was remarkable how well Merlin and Nahrmahn got along, he reflected. In fact, it was obvious they actually liked one another, which wasn't something Cayleb would have been willing to place any wagers on. And, he admitted, he found the fact that Merlin did like Nahrmahn remarkably reassuring.

"Stop what, Your Majesty?" Merlin inquired innocently. "All I said was—"

"I heard exactly what you said," Cayleb said severely. "And let me remind you, that it's most unbecoming of a Charisian Imperial Guardsman to think it would be a good idea for a visiting nobleman to suffer a fatal heatstroke. Until *after* he's signed the surrender terms, at least."

"Surrender terms, Your Majesty?" Nahrmahn's eyebrows rose. "Somehow I don't recall that particular phrase having been used in any of the correspondence you've exchanged with Grand Duke Zebediah. Or, at least, in any of it which you've shared with your advisers."

"That's because it wasn't used," Cayleb said with another of those thin smiles. "Believe me, though, Your Highness. Before the Grand Duke gets back into his rowboat this afternoon, there's not going to be much doubt in his mind about what he's just signed. He can *call* them whatever he wants, but I don't think he's going to be left in any uncertainty over what they really are . . . or what's likely to happen to him if he should chance to violate them."

"That doesn't sound extraordinarily 'diplomatic' to me, Your Majesty," Merlin observed. The emperor looked at him, and the *seijin* shrugged. "Not that I have any problem with the desired outcome," he added. "Personally, I think reasoned dialogue and fair-minded negotiation are overrated at times. I mean, yes, they have their place, and they *can* work. But sometimes a good, hard punch in the mouth is more effective than any number of diplomatic notes. Well, more enjoyable, anyway. And from all I've heard, this sounds to me like it might be one of those times."

"Good."

▼ ▼ ▼

Prince Nahrmahn, Cayleb decided as he exchanged bows with Tohmas Symmyns, the Grand Duke of Zebediah, on *Empress of Charis'* quarterdeck, had a pronounced gift for accurate thumbnail descriptions. If Zebediah could have been rendered down, his natural oil content could have lit every lamp in Tellesberg Palace for at least a year.

Which would probably be the best use to which he could possibly be put.

The grand duke was a man of average height and average

build, with a prominent nose, thinning dark hair, and eyes which appeared to be only about a quarter of an inch deep. They met other people's gazes with laudable steadiness, but there was an opacity, an armor, just under the surface, that reminded Cayleb of certain species of poisonous hedge lizards.

"It was most kind of you to come all this way to meet me, Your Grace," Cayleb said, straightening from his own bow.

"You're an emperor, Your Majesty," Zebediah said, showing large, even, white teeth in a gracious smile. "Emperors, like kings, are entitled to their little quirks and foibles. And, to be completely honest," he allowed his smile to fade into an expression of sobriety, "under the circumstances, I would have been astonished if your advisers had even considered allowing you to anchor your flagship within range of the harbor batteries of someone with whom your realm is still officially at war."

"True enough." Cayleb produced an expression which was almost a pout, and glanced sideways at the expressionless bodyguard towering at his shoulder in the livery of the House of Ahrmahk. Then the emperor returned his attention to the grand duke. "There are times when those 'advisers' of mine can be just a little . . . overprotective. It's been even worse since Father's death. There are times I think I'm *never* going to be allowed to do anything spontaneous again."

"I'm afraid great rank and great responsibility bring with them their own limitations, Your Majesty," Zebediah said sympathetically.

"I know." Cayleb sighed, then drew a deep breath and straightened his shoulders.

"Forgive my manners, Your Grace," he said. "Here I stand, keeping you talking on deck, rather than getting you into the shade and offering you some refreshment. Will you join me in my cabin?"

"I would be honored to," Zebediah assured him.

▼ ▼ ▼

"Well, I thought that went rather well," Cayleb remarked, some hours later as he stood on *Empress of Charis'* quarterdeck once more, watching Zebediah's ornate barge pull back towards the city.

"You did, did you?" a deep voice asked, and Cayleb smiled up at Merlin. The two of them stood by the rail, with one of the quarterdeck carronades between them, and out of easy earshot of anyone else, as long as they kept their voices down.

"Of course I did," the emperor replied, returning his attention to the departing barge. "Didn't you?"

"I think Grand Duke Zebediah thinks you're still a drooling teenager, at least when your 'advisers' aren't around," Merlin said.

"So do I," Cayleb said with obvious satisfaction, and Merlin snorted.

"All well and good to be 'underestimated,' Cayleb. As long as someone like Zebediah doesn't end up underestimating you so badly he does something stupid, that is. Something that gets a lot of people killed."

"I agree." Cayleb looked back at Merlin, his expression serious. "I think, though, in this case, that Nahrmahn was probably right. Zebediah knows he doesn't have any choice but to give us the basing rights I demanded from him. And of course he showed more than a flicker of interest in the notion of his remaining as the first-ranking noble of Zebediah when we formally add the island to the Empire. And he fully intends to be my loyal and supportive ally and vassal right up until the first opportunity he sees to leave a dagger planted between my shoulder blades."

"Which is precisely why it may not be a good thing for him to underestimate you too badly."

"You're missing my point, Merlin. It's not a question of *if* he'll see an opportunity to betray me; it's only a question of *when.* And, that being the case, I'd really prefer for him to feel overconfident, rather than underconfident. I don't want him to be so afraid of me that he actually ends up taking effective precautions. For that matter, I'd just as soon have him make his try before we're directly engaged against the Church's own forces. Better to have him hatch some sort of treason when we're not distracted by a more serious threat, don't you think?"

"You may well have a point," Merlin said slowly. "I'm not sure I agree with your logic, but I have to admit that it *is* logical. It seems a bit . . . convoluted, though."

"There are times, Merlin, when I find it easier than usual to believe you really did grow up in that 'Terran Federation' of yours."

"I beg your pardon?" Merlin's left eyebrow arched, and Cayleb chuckled harshly.

"In a more kindly and straightforward world—like the one you grew up in, at least where its politics were concerned—I'd just go ahead and quietly remove Zebediah. I'd 'fire him' as Grand Duke, and find someone else for the job. Preferably one of my Charisians who I know is loyal to me and deserves a proper reward for his services. Unfortunately, I can't do that. Or, rather, I *could,* but only at the expense of making the next noble who might be tempted to reach an accommodation with me wonder if I plan on stripping him of *his* titles as a present for one of my favorites as soon as it's convenient, as well.

"I didn't greet Nahrmahn with open arms just because of his diplomatic contacts, or his undeniable value as an adviser, Merlin. And while it's fortunate that he's actually a rather likable old bugger—when he's not trying to assassinate me, of course—I planned on treating him as *if* I'd liked him even if he'd turned out to be an unmitigated pain in the arse. But I didn't greet him so warmly or betroth Zhan to Mahrya on the basis of those things. I did it because it sent a message to other princes, other dukes and earls. And that message was that I was prepared to be reasonable and pragmatic, not to insist upon vengeance. And that so long as a man honors his promises to me, *I'll* honor my promises to *him* . . . including the promise that he'll be allowed to keep his titles, and to pass them on to his heirs in the fullness of time. Unless, of course, he does something which gives me legitimate grounds to attaint him for treason. If he does that—if he obviously breaks his oaths, obviously supports my enemies—then I'll be totally justified in stripping him of his titles and crushing him like a bug. But I need him to give me that obvious justification if I don't want others to regard me as capricious and untrustworthy."

Merlin stroked his waxed mustachios, his expression thoughtful, then nodded slowly.

"You're right, that aspect of it *hadn't* occurred to me," he admitted.

"That's what I meant about believing you grew up somewhere else. It's second nature to a dynast like me or Nahrmahn to think in those terms. Or, at least, it's second nature to think that way if we're reasonably *intelligent* dynasts. Which brings me back to my original point about the advantages of having Zebediah underestimate how smart I really am."

"You know, Cayleb, it's rather unsporting of you to challenge an unarmed man to a duel."

"Oh? Is that what I've just done?"

"No, it isn't. It's just the closest analogy I can come up with . . . at least until I think of something even nastier."

MARCH,
YEAR OF GOD 893

·✦·

Tellesberg Palace,
City of Tellesberg,
Kingdom of Charis

I never imagined Admiral Rock Point was going to find this sort of evidence," Sharleyan Ahrmahk said as she finished scanning the last page of the admiral's report and laid it on the conference table in front of her.

"Neither did Clyntahn . . . or Graivyr, Your Majesty," Baron Wave Thunder agreed. Cayleb's old spymaster, who remained responsible for both espionage and security in the Kingdom of Charis—which was rapidly coming to be known as "Old Charis" in order to distinguish it from the new empire to which it had given its name—nodded at the sheet of paper the empress had just set aside. "Trust me, it never even occurred to them that this sort of documentary evidence might fall into anyone else's hands, and especially not *ours*!"

There was considerably more satisfaction in Wave Thunder's tone, and he smiled nastily.

"Not only that," he continued, "but their reports about the Massacre are only the tip of the iceberg, Your Majesty. We got *all* of the Church's files from Ferayd, and they were so confident that they didn't take even the most rudimentary of precautions. We have complete copies of half a dozen of their most secure ciphers now. Obviously, they're going to change them as quickly as they can, but it's going to take time. And even after they change them, there's no telling what older documents we might come into possession of. And that doesn't even begin to consider all of the other documents and files the Admiral's shipped home."

He shook his head, his expression almost reverent.

"We're going to need months just to sort through it all and catalogue it. I can already tell you, though, that there's an incredible amount of . . . potentially embarrassing information in here."

"I realize that, My Lord," Sharleyan said. "At the moment, however, I'm afraid my own attention is rather more sharply focused on those reports about the Massacre. And on the consequences for the report writers."

"Admiral Rock Point carried out his instructions from you and His Majesty to the letter, Your Majesty," Rayjhis Yowance pointed out. The Earl of Gray Harbor was the first councilor of Old Charis, and was clearly on the way to becoming first councilor of the Empire of Charis, as well. Some people might have expected all of that to mean Cayleb had left him home in order to be certain Sharleyan didn't get carried away by an overly inflated notion of just how much authority she truly possessed. No one seated in this council chamber was likely to make that mistake, however, and Gray Harbor's voice was both respectful and perhaps just the tiniest bit apprehensive.

"Don't worry, My Lord." Sharleyan smiled at him, and that smile was cool. "I agree that the Admiral did precisely what he was instructed to do. And I approve his actions completely. I can see why Cayleb and the rest of Charis have so much faith in his judgment. I simply never anticipated that he would have such clear-cut evidence upon which to proceed. Or, for that matter, that so many of Clyntahn's inquisitors would stand self-convicted."

"With all due respect, Your Majesty, I think that if anyone had anticipated that they would, those instructions might have been somewhat more limited," another voice said, and she turned her head to look at the speaker.

Paityr Sellyrs, Baron White Church, sounded worried, almost querulous. In fact, Sharleyan thought sourly behind her calm expression, he sounded downright whiny. White Church was the Keeper of the Seal for Old Charis, and he had quite a few useful political allies here in Tellesberg, which she suspected helped to explain how he'd come to hold his present office. If she had anything to say about it, however (and she did), he would not be the *Empire's* Keeper of the Seal.

"I disagree, My Lord," she said now, calmly but with absolutely no hesitation. "If there had been a hundred guilty men—or a thousand—and not sixteen, the sentence would have been no less just, and its execution would have been no less appropriate. I'm surprised, My Lord. I am *not* dismayed."

"Your Majesty," White Church said, "I'm not suggesting you should be dismayed. Nor am I suggesting that these men, priests or not, didn't amply merit the punishment visited upon them. I'm only saying that to effectively cast the heads of no less than sixteen consecrated priests at the Group of Four's feet may not have been the most productive thing we could have done."

Gray Harbor started to say something, then paused as the empress smiled affably at White Church. Given that smile, and what he'd seen so far of this young woman, he rather doubted that his intervention was either necessary or desirable.

Sharleyan considered White Church, her head cocked slightly to one side, for two or three heartbeats. It wasn't so much what he'd said as the way he'd said it. She'd heard that same patient tone of voice before, although not recently; the survivors among her councilors had learned better from the unfortunate fates of those who had adopted it. She watched him, recognizing the patronizing edge of his own smile, and wondered if he had the least idea she could see it. Probably not, she decided. He wasn't actually stupid enough to deliberately provoke her, after all. That, unfortunately, wasn't quite the same thing as saying he *was* smart, however.

He's Cayleb's *Keeper of the Seal, Sharley,* she reminded herself. *You don't know all the reasons Cayleb might have chosen him. And even if you did, you aren't the one who appointed him to the Council. So do you* really *want to do this?*

Yet even as she asked herself that question, she knew the answer. It was the same answer Mahrak Sahndyrs had taught a frightened girl-child so many years before. She could rule, or she could simply reign. She'd made *that* choice when she was barely twelve, and Cayleb Ahrmahk hadn't married her because she was weak.

"Allow me to explain to you, My Lord," she said, speaking coolly and precisely, "why your concern is groundless."

White Church seemed to stiffen in his chair as her tone registered, but she continued as if she hadn't noticed.

"As you may recall, we've already informed the Group of Four, and the Council of Vicars, for that matter, that we reject their authority. That we know them for who and what they are, and that we intend to hold them accountable for their crimes against not simply the people of Safehold, but against Mother Church, and even God Himself. Are you suggesting that, having so informed them, the proper course of action when men of proven guilt—men whose written reports, whose own testimony, shows the pride and satisfaction they took in ordering the murder of *children*—fall into our hands is that we shouldn't execute justice upon them?"

"Your Majesty, I only—"

"Please answer my question, My Lord." Sharleyan's voice was noticeably frostier. "Is this a time to demonstrate weakness? To suggest not simply to the Group of Four, but to all of Safehold, that we do not truly have the strength of our own beliefs? The confidence of our own principles?"

White Church's expression was acutely unhappy, and his eyes flitted around the council table, as if seeking someone to save him from the empress' ire. What he saw were a great many eyes which obviously agreed with *her,* and his Adam's apple bobbed as he swallowed.

"No, Your Majesty. Of course not!" he said.

"I'm glad we find ourselves in agreement on such a fundamental principle, My Lord," she told him, holding him impaled upon her hard, brown gaze. "I love the shedding of blood no more than the next man or woman," she continued. "Moreover, the Emperor and I have made it as clear as humanly possible that the Empire of Charis will *not* simply murder people because they disagree with us, or because they are opposed to the Church of Charis and our conflict with the Group of Four. But the corollary of that must be equally clear." She released him from her gaze at last in order to let her eyes sweep around the rest of the table. "We *will* punish the guilty when their guilt be proven, and the vestments they have perverted and betrayed will not protect them. Unlike them, we will not shed innocent blood, but we will hold them accountable for all of the blood *they* have shed. Is there some reason anyone seated around this table has failed to grasp that essential point of our policy?"

No one spoke. In fact, Gray Harbor thought, the odds were good that very few of them were even breathing at the moment, and he was almost certain White Church wasn't. The empress had never even raised her voice, but the Keeper of the Seal looked remarkably like a man who wished he could melt and ooze down under the council table.

Idiot, the first councilor thought without much pity.

In some ways, it wasn't all that difficult to sympathize with White Church. Part of his worries was easy enough to understand in terms of simple human self-interest. White Church was a wealthy man, but most of his personal and family wealth was tied up in trade, and in the sizable merchant fleet they collectively owned. No doubt he was delighted that Rock Point had managed to recover all but two of the ships originally seized in Delferahk, yet a part of him seemed unable to grasp that the confrontation between Charis and the Temple had moved into a realm which made even the trade vital to the Empire's existence a secondary issue. Perhaps that wasn't so surprising, since *any* Charisian understood, on an almost instinctual level, just how vital that commerce was. Unfortunately, deep down inside somewhere, White Church obviously wasn't able to recognize the need to prioritize on a realistic basis. Or, at least, to set aside his own, personal interests in the interests of Charis as a whole. Anything likely to interrupt the Empire's trade, to close ports to those ships of his, threatened his family's future, and he'd been a persistent voice of caution from the beginning.

But there were other reasons for his position as well, and

most of them were considerably less self-interested. That didn't mean Gray Harbor agreed with them, but at least he understood the reasoning behind them.

The responsibilities of the man's office included the official drafting and receipt of the Kingdom's diplomatic correspondence. He was accustomed to thinking not in terms of great and sweeping struggles, but in terms of communications between a relatively small number of people whose decisions governed the fates of realms. He hadn't yet made the transition to understanding that the forces unleashed here in Charis went far beyond the councils of kings and princes, or even priests and vicars. Those decision-makers remained vitally important, but the tides against which they must contend had fundamentally changed.

Unfortunately, if White Church hadn't already grasped that, it was unlikely he ever would. And whether he had the wit to do *that* or not, he was obviously tone-deaf where the realities of the new Charisian political equation were concerned.

He probably thinks Sharleyan belongs in the royal bedchamber, pregnant and punching out heirs to the throne, Gray Harbor thought bitingly. *As if Cayleb would have married a mere brood mare! Or as if* she *were likely to put up with that kind of kraken shit!*

"I'm relieved and gratified to discover we're all in agreement upon that point, My Lords," the empress observed now, her smile marginally warmer. "I trust we won't find it necessary to . . . revisit it in the future."

White Church seemed to cringe ever so slightly, although she wasn't even looking in his direction as she spoke. Then she sat back in her chair at the head of the table.

"Clearly, Rayjhis," she said to Gray Harbor, deliberately using his first name, "we have to consider the fact that the execution of so many priestly murderers *is* going to have an impact both in Zion and elsewhere. I would appreciate it if you and Baron Wave Thunder—and you, Your Eminence—" she added, glancing at Maikel Staynair, "would give some thought to that very point. I'd like your analysis of how the more immediately important rulers are likely to react."

"Of course, Your Majesty," Gray Harbor murmured. "Do you have any particular concerns you'd like us to consider?"

"Obviously, in many ways, I'm most interested in how the Group of Four is likely to respond. I realize, however, that any advice you could give me on that particular topic would be little more than speculation. By all means, go ahead and speculate—I have great respect for your judgment, and I'd like to hear anything you have to say about it. I'm more immediately concerned, however, with people like Lord Protector Greyghor, and perhaps King Gorjah."

"Gorjah, Your Majesty?" Surprise startled the three-word question out of Gray Harbor, and Sharleyan actually chuckled.

"I do fully realize, My Lord, that King Gorjah isn't particularly . . . well thought of here in Tellesberg, shall we say?"

Several of the other people seated around that table chuckled this time. The Kingdom of Tarot had been a Charisian ally for decades, and King Gorjah of Tarot had been obligated by treaty to come to Charis' assistance against attack. Instead, he'd joined the "alliance" the Group of Four had hammered together for Charis' destruction. And, unlike Sharleyan and Chisholm, there was precious little evidence that Gorjah had hesitated for a moment.

"All the same," Sharleyan continued, her voice and expression both rather more serious and intent, "Prince Nahrmahn wasn't very well thought of, either, and with a much longer history of enmity, at that. Eventually, we're going to have to deal with Tarot, one way or another. It's simply too close to Charis itself *not* to be dealt with, and it, too, is an island."

Her eyes swept the council chamber once more.

"We lack the resources, the manpower, to establish a foothold on the mainland. Oh," she waved one slender hand, "I don't doubt we could seize a single port—like Ferayd, let's say—and even hold it for an extended period of time. Given our control of the sea, we could support such a garrison indefinitely, and if the time came that supporting it seemed too costly, we would be well placed to withdraw. But we have neither the time, the manpower, nor the wealth to waste on such adventures.

"By the same token, however, we *do* control the sea, and if we lose that control, we're all doomed, anyway. I think, therefore, that we should be making our plans on the basis that we will *not* lose control. Would you not agree with that, My Lords?"

Despite years of experience at the very highest levels of politics, Gray Harbor found himself forced to raise a hand to hide the smile he could not restrain as Empress Sharleyan's councilors looked back at her and nodded like marionettes.

"Excellent, My Lords!" The empress' white teeth flashed in a broad smile of her own. "If we're in agreement upon that point, however, it would seem to me to follow that we should be seeking every opportunity to make *use* of our seapower. Admittedly, we must be careful not to overreach, yet anywhere there is a strip of seawater, that water belongs not to the Group of Four, but to Charis."

Spines straightened subtly around the table, and Gray Harbor's temptation to smile faded into sober appreciation of the empress' skill, her grasp of her listeners' psychology.

"We've already added Emerald—and Chisholm—" she allowed herself a more rueful smile, "to the Empire. By this time, I feel confident, His Majesty has done the same with Zebediah, as he will soon do with Corisande."

Her smile disappeared completely with the final word, and her nostrils flared slightly as she shook her head.

"With the exception of Corisande, all of those other additions were accomplished reasonably peacefully, with little or no additional loss of life. And all of those lands will remain secure so long as Charisians remain masters of Safehold's seas. As would Tarot. Inevitably, Tarot *will* be added to the Empire. In many ways, we have no choice in that regard, and I strongly suspect that King Gorjah understands that. Moreover, given the existence of the Tarot Channel and the Gulf of Tarot, we would be well placed to retain Tarot without greater effort than we would already be forced to expend to ensure the security of Charis itself. And at the same time, while I would never wish to appear too coldly calculating, let us not overlook the fact that Tarot's proximity to the mainland would almost certainly make *its* conquest inviting to the Group of Four as a staging point for any future invasion of Charis. In short, it would provide a bait, a prize dangled before them to draw them out into the waters of the Channel and the Gulf where we could trim back their naval strength without risking the invasion of Charis itself, should they somehow manage to sneak past us."

Gray Harbor felt his own eyes narrowing in appreciation of the empress' analysis. Chisholm had become a significant seapower only during the reign of King Sailys, yet Sharleyan clearly appreciated the way in which the command of the sea, properly applied, could hold even the most massive land power in check. She *understood,* he thought—understood the mobility advantages, the defensive possibilities, the way in which seapower made the most economic use of available manpower practical.

"Under the circumstances," the empress continued, "I believe it behooves us to think in terms of encouraging Gorjah to accept the peaceful amalgamation of his kingdom into the Empire. I would hope that the fact that Cayleb saw fit to marry one of his adversaries, and to unite our house by marriage with that of yet *another* of his adversaries, as well, would already suggest to Gorjah that a resolution which leaves him not simply with his head, but even his crown as our vassal, is within the realm of possibilities. If we can contrive to offer him further motivation to consider such an outcome, I believe we certainly ought to be doing just that. Would you not agree, My Lord Gray Harbor?"

"Most assuredly I would, Your Majesty." Gray Harbor half-rose from his chair to bow to her across the council table. "It simply hadn't occurred to me to consider it in quite the terms you've just used. Nor, to be frank, would it have occurred to me to consider whether or not what happened in Ferayd would be likely to affect his thinking."

"Nor to me, I confess, Your Majesty," Archbishop Maikel said, his expression wry. "Yet, now that you've mentioned it, I must admit your point could be very well taken. On the one hand, what Domynyk did to Ferayd must weigh in the thinking of anyone who finds himself opposed to Charis, especially if he has cities in reach of the sea. No one will want the same thing to happen to one of *his* seaports, after all.

"At the same time, however, there's the moral dimension to consider, and despite his ready acquiescence in the Group of Four's plans, King Gorjah has never struck me as being willfully morally blind. The evidence of the Inquisition's direct and intentional complicity in the Ferayd Massacre, and our much more measured response to it, won't be lost upon him. Coupled with your own marriage to His Majesty and the generous terms granted to Emerald, it is, in fact, very likely he would believe, on the one hand, that any terms you and His Majesty chose to offer him would be honored, and, on the other hand, that Ferayd proves you are not, in fact, the slavering monsters the Group of Four has sought to portray in its propaganda. And, for that matter, I have no doubt Gorjah will be personally revolted by Graivyr and his fellows' gloating pride in their part in mass murder. I don't say he'll be inspired to spontaneously offer his allegiance to Charis, but I do think it's entirely possible his mind will be inclined towards accepting Charis' sovereignty when the time comes."

"I hope you're correct about that, Your Eminence," Sharleyan told him. "And my point is simply that if you are, the time to begin preparing the ground is now."

"As you say, Your Majesty," Gray Harbor replied.

"Excellent. Now," she continued more briskly, "given Admiral Rock Point's return, we find ourselves with considerably greater naval strength in home waters. It seems to me that it would be an unthrifty use of that strength to let it sit idle. I realize it's winter, and that Charisians seem to lack a Chisholmian's taste for winter weather," she smiled, and this time one or two of the councilors laughed out loud, "yet it occurs to me that we might find employment for some of our cruisers completing the hunt for Delferakhan shipping wherever it may be found. In addition, however, I see no reason not to use some of them to make life as unpleasant as possible for the Group of Four in the Markovian Sea and the northern Gulf of Tarot, as well. I see no need to cast our net for *Siddarmarkian* merchantmen, or—especially—for those Charisian ships which seem to be flying Siddarmarkian flags these days. Nonetheless, all of our intelligence reports indicate that the Group of Four's naval building programs are continuing to accelerate. I think it would be an excellent idea to disrupt the flow of strategic materials."

She turned her head to look at Ahlvyno Pawalsyn, the Baron of Ironhill. Ironhill was the Keeper of the Purse, effectively the treasurer of Charis.

"I see from the report you handed us yesterday, My Lord, that even though Clyntahn's distrust for Siddarmark is excluding the Republic from their building programs, they seem to be buying a great many of the naval stores they need from Siddarmarkian sources?"

"That's correct, Your Majesty," Ironhill said. "And even more from Fallos."

"Well, in that case, I believe we should do something about that. I don't imagine any of those naval stores are moving in those Charisian ships flying Siddarmarkian flags?"

"Ah, no, Your Majesty," Wave Thunder replied with a crooked grin. "I think the 'owners' of those particular ships feel it might be . . . impolitic. For that matter, it would appear Clyntahn's distrust of Siddarmark extends to keeping Siddarmarkians as a group as far removed as possible from their shipbuilding projects. At any rate, Maigwair is using almost exclusively non-Siddarmarkian bottoms to move his more critical naval stores. In fact, his quartermasters are avoiding Siddarmark-owned ships even when that policy occasions significant delays in delivery times."

"How very thoughtful of him," Sharleyan murmured with a lurking smile. Then she straightened in her chair and glanced at Gray Harbor again.

"My Lord," she said, "I realize we already have privateers operating in those waters. Nonetheless, I want you to instruct Admiral Rock Point to deploy as many of his cruisers as he deems prudent to those same waters with orders to take, burn, and destroy any shipping employed by Vicar Allayn and his associates on their naval projects."

"As you wish, Your Majesty." Gray Harbor's inclined head indicated as much approval of his instructions as obedience to them, and she smiled fleetingly at him.

"And if we're going to employ our Navy most profitably, My Lord Ironhill," she said, turning back to the Keeper of the Purse, "we're going to have to come up with ways to pay for it. I've reviewed your latest revenue proposals, and I believe most of your points are well taken. However, I'd like you to consider in somewhat greater depth the possible impact on our own carrying trade of the new export duties you've sketched out. My concern is that although the rate doesn't seem excessive, it will nonetheless drive up the prices our manufactories are forced to charge to foreign customers. At the moment, given the Group of Four's efforts to close all mainland ports against us I'm loath to adopt any measure of our own which might chill our markets. And, to be honest, I think I'd prefer to avoid setting a precedent of *export* duties any sooner than we have to. Had you, perhaps, considered increasing *import* duties rather more, instead? I suspect we would be better placed to absorb even a substantial increase in the prices of luxuries, and more moderate increases in the cost of raw materials and foodstuffs, than we would be to absorb a drop in foreign demand for our own goods."

Ironhill's eyebrows arched in mingled surprise at her perceptiveness and respect for the point she'd raised, and Gray Harbor leaned back in his own chair with a faint smile. Ahlvyno Pawalsyn was one of his closer friends, and he respected the baron's mind. At the moment, however, the Keeper of the Purse's surprise frustrated the first councilor almost as much as it amused him.

Come on, Ahlvyno, he thought sardonically. *You're smarter than that. God knows, you're ten times as smart as* White Church, *at any rate! I know she's young, I know she's foreign-born, and I know she's female. But you—and the rest of the Council—better start figuring out that it's entirely possible she's even smarter than Cayleb, and at least as forceful. Because, trust me, anyone who doesn't figure that out is really, really not going to enjoy what she does to him.*

The earl propped his elbows on the arms of his comfortable chair, crossed his legs, and watched the young woman seated at the head of the table effortlessly controlling and directing almost twenty men, the youngest of whom was probably at least twice her own age.

Those idiots in Zion haven't got the least idea of what they turned loose against themselves when they pissed her off, he thought gratefully and perhaps—just perhaps—a tiny bit complacently. *They may think they've seen bad, already. They're wrong about that, though. They haven't even* begun *to see bad yet . . . but it's coming.*

▼ ▼ ▼

"Did I push too hard, do you think, Your Eminence?" Sharleyan Ahrmahk asked much later that evening as Archbishop Maikel joined her for supper.

"At the Council meeting, Your Majesty?" Staynair chuckled and shook his head with a small smile. "I wouldn't worry about that. I'm sure you stepped on a few male toes here and there, but I don't think you trod on any that didn't *need* stepping on. And even those who may still be inclined to discount your ideas because of your youth and sex seem to end up accepting their logic."

"I wouldn't worry about it as much back home in Cherayth," she confessed, leaning forward to reach for her wineglass and then settling back in her chair once more. "Once upon a time I *would* have, of course, but I've had years to . . . polish my relationship with my Chisholmian Councilors."

" 'Polish'?" Staynair repeated with a deeper chuckle. "Beat into submission is what you really mean, isn't it?"

"Oh, Langhorne, no!" Sharleyan rounded her eyes and shook her head. " 'Beat into submission' would be *such* an unladylike thing to do!"

"I think there's a very unladylike element to your personality, Your Majesty," Staynair replied. "And thank God for it!"

"So you don't think I'm driving too hard to assert my own

authority?" she asked more seriously. He crooked an eyebrow at her, and she shrugged. "I'm not concerned about my own ability to control the situation, Your Eminence. I suppose what I'm really concerned about is whether or not I appear to be attempting to undercut Cayleb's authority. Or, even worse, whether or not it turns out that, without meaning to, I actually *am* undercutting his authority."

"Emperor Cayleb's authority isn't so fragile as all that, Your Majesty," Staynair said dryly. "I think it will survive any unintentional chips or scratches you might inflict upon it—especially since it's obvious to me that you have no intention of 'usurping' his authority. And, frankly, I believe the possibility that you might encroach upon his prerogatives—which, now that I think about it, would be difficult for you to do, since they happen to also be *your* prerogatives—is far less dangerous to us than it would be for you to begin vacillating, or hesitating, for *fear* of encroaching. Charis—the Empire, not simply 'Old Charis'—needs a strong, firm hand on the tiller, especially now. And at this moment, that hand is—must be—yours."

"I know," she confessed, then sipped a little wine, as if buying time to sort through her own thoughts. "I know," she continued, "and if I'm going to be honest, I suppose I should admit that there's a part of me that doesn't come truly alive except when I'm dealing with decisions that *matter.* I've often wondered if that's the sin of pride speaking."

"And have you discussed your concerns with Father Carlsyn?" Staynair asked in a slightly more neutral tone. Carlsyn Raiyz had been Sharleyan's personal confessor ever since she ascended to the Chisholmian throne, but Staynair, for obvious reasons, had never even met the man before he arrived in Tellesberg at Sharleyan's side.

"I have." She smiled crookedly. "Unfortunately, he's *my* confessor; I'm not *his.* He's reassured me several times, and imposed a penance or two on the rare occasions—well, possibly not all *that* rare—when he felt I'd clearly stepped on someone harder than I had to. Confidence, he says, is a good thing in a ruler. Capriciousness isn't."

"Sound doctrine," Staynair said with a smile of his own. "Good philosophy, too. And, if I may, Your Majesty, could I also ask you if you've discussed the schism with him?"

"Not the way we've discussed other concerns," Sharleyan admitted, her eyes darkening. "He hasn't pressed me on it, which probably says a great deal, right there. But the truth is, I'm almost afraid to ask him how he feels about it. If he's prepared to accept my decisions without openly condemning them, that's better than some others have already done."

Her voice was far more somber, and Staynair's expression softened sympathetically.

"Your uncle, Your Majesty?" he asked gently.

Sharleyan's head snapped up. She looked at him intently across the dinner table for several seconds, and then her firm mouth seemed to quiver for a moment.

"Yes," she admitted softly, and the archbishop nodded.

Very few people in Charis had been particularly well acquainted with the internal political dynamic of Chisholm prior to Sharleyan's marriage to Cayleb. Staynair certainly hadn't been, but he'd made it a priority to learn all he could about that dynamic since. And one thing which had become abundantly clear to him was that the Duke of Halbrook Hollow had been far more than simply one of Sharleyan's senior nobles. Indeed, he'd been more than "just" an uncle. As the commander of the Royal Army, he'd been her sword, even as Green Mountain had been her shield. And now . . .

"Your Majesty," Staynair said after a moment, "it's easier to command fleets and armies than to command the human heart. Your uncle has already discovered that, and if it should happen that it's a lesson *you* haven't already learned, then I fear it's one you have no choice but to master now. I believe your uncle loves you. I don't pretend to know him well, especially since he's kept me—as all of the 'Church of Charis'— at arm's-length or beyond, but I believe he does love you. Yet you've asked him to accept something he can't. When I look at him, I see a man grieving over his niece's decisions, and one of the reasons he grieves is *because* he loves her."

"I suppose that's reassuring," Sharleyan said. Then she

shook her head. "No, I don't 'suppose' it is; it *is*. But it doesn't change the fact that the . . . estrangement between us over the Church is becoming increasingly evident. Or the fact that there are those here in Tellesberg Palace who think it's dangerous to have someone with such obvious Temple Loyalist sympathies so close to the throne."

"They may be correct about that, Your Majesty." Staynair's expression was serene. "In the end, what your relationship with him is—or becomes—is a matter for your decision, however, not for anyone else's. And it's not as if he were attempting to dissemble, to conceal those sympathies. It would appear to me that he is who he is, and what more can one fairly ask of anyone?"

"I'm a queen, Your Eminence—an empress. Can I afford to be 'fair' to someone as close to me as he is?"

"Perhaps it does constitute a danger to do so," Staynair replied. "Perhaps you might even argue that it's your responsibility as a queen and an empress to put him out of the way, somewhere he can do no harm. And perhaps if you fail to do so, you may face serious consequences in the fullness of time. All of that *may* be true, Your Majesty. But what I know *is* true is that you, too, must be who you are. Too much danger, too many threats from others, already confront you. I believe that the one thing you dare not do is to permit yourself to undermine who you are, who you've always been, with doubts from within. If you love him as deeply as you obviously do, you must listen to that love as much as to the pragmatic caution of the ruler you are. It would be better for Charis for you to risk what harm he might do than for you to maim your own spirit, your own confidence and all the good *you* have still to do, by hardening your heart and denying that love."

"But I've already taken steps to protect myself against him," she confessed. "That's the entire reason I didn't leave him behind in Chisholm with Mahrak. I couldn't leave him in command of the Army when he so obviously disagreed with what I was coming to Charis to do."

"I assumed that was the case." Staynair shrugged. "And there, I suspect, you see the clearest proof of just how unlikely you are to allow your love for him to blind you to your duties."

The empress nodded slowly, and Staynair sipped from his own wineglass, watching her and wishing more strongly than ever that he, Cayleb, and Merlin had succeeded in convincing the rest of the Brethren of Saint Zherneau to allow Cayleb to tell her the truth. If she'd known, as Staynair did, how Captain Athrawes could keep an eye on even the most skilled of conspirators, it might have set her mind at ease.

And easing her mind wherever and whenever we can is the least we can do for her, he thought sympathetically behind the serenity of his eyes. *She deserves that. And even if she didn't, simple commonsense would demand that we do it anyway. We* need *her—need her functioning at her best,* using *all that intelligence and willpower, not wasting it by belaboring herself over issues she can never hope to resolve, anyway.*

"Your uncle, in many ways, is a mirror of Safehold itself, Your Majesty," he said out loud. "The struggle in his heart and mind is the same struggle going on in the hearts and minds and souls of every man and woman in this world. Each of us must, in the end, make our own decisions, our own choices, and the pain that will bring to altogether too many of us will be terrible. Yet we *must* choose. The worst sin of all, the one unforgivable sin, is to *refuse* to choose. And whatever we may think or believe ourselves, we cannot deny that choice to others simply because we believe they will choose differently from ourselves.

"You understand your uncle's inability to agree with you. Now you must accept his right to *dis*agree with you. Don't judge him for that disagreement. Take steps to protect yourself against its possible consequences, yes, but remember that he remains the uncle you loved as a child, and the army commander who served you so well for so long. If *he* decides, if *he* chooses, to allow the breach between you to damage or destroy his love for you, or even impel him to join your enemies, that, too, is his decision. Yet never forget that it truly is possible to deeply love someone with whom you fundamentally disagree, Your Majesty. I'm a Bédardist, and that's one of the essential principles of my order's teaching. And another principle is that it's very *difficult* to love someone with whom you fundamentally disagree. Difficult, and hard on both of you. Don't make it any harder than you must, any sooner than you must."

Sharleyan looked at him for a moment, then inhaled deeply, and nodded.

"You're right, Your Eminence," she said softly. "It is hard. But I'll try not to make it any harder than I have to."

. II .

Privateer Brig *Loyal Son*, Desnarian Merchant Galleon *Wind Hoof*, Markovian Sea

Steel-gray water heaved under a slate-gray sky like a vast bowl of ice-burnished wind. That same wind hummed and whined through the rigging as the brig *Loyal Son* made her way across the vast wasteland of the Markovian Sea. Symyn Fytzhyw, *Loyal Son*'s owner and captain, stood on the brig's tiny quarterdeck, his legs spread wide against the ship's motion, and shivered, despite his thick, warm coat.

Fytzhyw was just under thirty Safeholdian years old, and he had no children of his own. His older brother, on the other hand, had five already, including not one, but two sets of twins. The eldest was only seven, and none of them had ever been outside the city of Tellesberg . . . or its climate. They'd found Uncle Symyn's thick winter coat hilarious when they'd "helped him pack," but Fytzhyw didn't find its thickness the least bit humorous at this particular moment. In fact, he wished fervently that it was even thicker and heavier.

Spring was a month off yet, and winter in the Markovian

could be as cold and bitter as anything south of the Icewind Sea itself, as the current weather seemed bent upon proving. At least, he thought gratefully, there was no longer anything falling out of the sky. Yesterday's rain had turned into freezing sleet, and the standing rigging was coated in ice, like tree branches in a winter-struck forest. The temperature hadn't climbed enough to melt it yet (assuming it ever intended to climb that high again), but chunks of it rattled and banged on deck from time to time. The carronades gleamed under their own thin coating of glassy ice, and more ice came slithering to the deck in crystal shards from the running rigging whenever the sails were trimmed.

I wonder why this seemed like a good idea before we left port? Fytzhyw asked himself rhetorically as he looked up at the northern sky.

Actually, he knew the answer perfectly well. The waters south of the Markovian had been thoroughly fished out by other privateers. The Gulf of Tarot, the Tarot Channel, the Tranjyr Passage, and the Sea of Justice had been thoroughly swept, and if there were still twenty merchantmen in the world flying the Tarotisian flag, Fytzhyw would have been astonished. The waters off Delferahk, still farther south, had been even more thoroughly hunted out over the past several months as Charisian ships swarmed over the Delferahkan coast and went through the Kingdom's coastal waters like feeding doomwhales in the wake of the Ferayd Massacre, and the Empire of Charis wasn't at war (yet) with the Desnarian Empire. Effectively, that left only the Harthian Sea and the Gulf of Harchong, far to the west, and that was really too far for a vessel the size of *Loyal Son*.

Besides, Symyn Fytzhyw hadn't become a privateer just for the money. Not that he had any objection to piling up a satisfying heap of marks, of course, but what he really wanted to do was to hurt those bastards in Zion any way he could.

And that was the real reason he was where he was this frigid, blustery, thoroughly miserable day. He couldn't match the size of many another privateer vessel, and he couldn't match the wealth of many another shipowner, but he still had his father's network of contacts, including several in the independent Duchy of Fallos.

The island of Fallos measured almost nine hundred miles from its extreme northern tip to its extreme southern tip, but its total population was less than that of the city of Tellesberg, alone. By and large, no one paid much attention to Fallos, but the duchy did have one extraordinarily valuable natural resource: trees. Lots and *lots* of trees. Trees which produced some of the finest shipbuilding timbers in the world. Most Fallosians—those who weren't farmers or fishermen—were woodsmen, and they showed a respectable profit selling timber to various mainland realms. Charis wasn't usually one of Fallos' markets, given that the forests which still covered much of Charis and almost all of the huge island of Silverlode had even more (and arguably better) timber to offer far closer to home. But far more of the mainland had been logged off, and second-growth forest couldn't match the magnificent timbers for masts and spars which came out of Fallos' virgin forests. Turpentine was another major Fallosian product, and so was pitch.

Under normal circumstances, Fallos made a reasonably comfortable living off of its forestry products, but the duchy was scarcely in danger of becoming wealthy. Circumstances, however, had been anything but "normal" since the Battle of Darcos Sound. The Group of Four's decision to build its enormous new navy had produced a demand for timbers and every sort of naval store such as the world had never before seen. Suddenly, Fallosians were making money at a rate even a Charisian could envy . . . and the waters between Fallos and the mainland swarmed with freighters.

Given the growth demands of the Charisian Navy and the brawling Charisian privateer fleet, a merchantman loaded with already-cut ship timbers could bring a reasonable return, even in timber-rich Charis. It wouldn't be a particularly handsome profit, which was the reason most privateers tended to hunt elsewhere, but it would certainly cover Fytzhyw's operating expenses, and taking those same timbers away from the Church held a certain appeal all its own. That wasn't the real reason he and his grumbling ship's company were out here just now, however. He was perfectly willing to snap up any timber-hauler which crossed his path (in fact, he'd already taken two of them), but that was a task better suited to regular Navy cruisers, who didn't have to present profit and loss statements to shareholders or business partners. All they had to worry about was hurting the enemy's actual capabilities; a privateer had to worry about paying the bills, as well. Which was why what Fytzhyw was really looking for was the ship his Fallosian informant assured him was even then on her way to the duchy . . . and carrying several thousand marks of cold, hard cash destined to pay for all of those felled trees.

The only problem was that his target should have been along at least two days ago. There were many possible explanations for its tardiness, including the storm which had worked its way across the Markovian the previous five-day and left *Loyal Son* in her glittering icy cocoon in its wake. Despite that, Fytzhyw was beginning to feel considerably less cheerful than he had when he set out.

Face it, he told himself brutally, *the real reason you're beginning to feel less cheerful is that the most likely "explanation" for the reason you haven't seen it is that it sailed right past you in the dark. Or it chose a passage further north or further south. Or—*

"Sail ho!" The wind-thrashed shout came down from the mainmast lookout. "Sail on the larboard bow!"

Fytzhyw twitched, then strode rapidly to the larboard bulwark, peering down to leeward. For several minutes he saw nothing at all from his much lower vantage point, but then something pricked the horizon. He pounded gently on the bulwark rail with gloved hands, waiting impatiently. It seemed to take forever, and the masthead which had broken the hard line of the horizon was far clearer and sharper from deck level before the lookout peering through his spyglass finally announced—

"Deck, there! She's flying a Church pennant!"

"Yes!" Symyn Fytzhyw hissed jubilantly. Then he wheeled

from the bulwark and sucked in a burning lungful of frigid air.

"Hands to quarters!" he bellowed. *"Hands to quarters!"*

▼ ▼ ▼

Alyk Lizardherd, captain of the galleon *Wind Hoof,* swore inventively as his lookout finally got around to reporting the ship headed purposefully to meet him.

"Very well, Master Hairaym," he said in a disgusted tone when he'd finally exhausted his supply of profanity. "Thanks to that blind idiot at the masthead, it's too late to try to run for it. Go ahead and clear away the guns."

Such as they are, and what there are of them, he did not add out loud.

"Yes, Sir." Gorjah Hairaym, *Wind Hoof*'s first lieutenant, was a good twelve years older than his skipper, who was no spring hedge lizard, himself. In the cold, gray light of the wind-whipped afternoon, the older man's unshaven face looked wrinkled and old as he acknowledged the order. From the look in his eyes, he knew as well as Lizardherd just how pointless the instruction was if that other vessel was what both of them were confident it was. However—

"And I suppose you'd better tell Lieutenant Aivyrs, too," Fytzhyw said heavily.

"Yes, Sir," Hairaym acknowledged, then turned away and began bawling orders to man the galleon's pop gun broadside of catamounts. They were heavier than the wolves most merchant galleons carried in swivel mounts on their bulwarks, yet the shot they threw still weighed little more than three pounds. They might have been enough to discourage most converted merchantmen which turned into privateers (or turned outright pirate), but they were scarcely likely to dissuade a *Charisian* privateer.

And that's what that bastard is, just as sure as Hell's a mantrap, Lizardherd thought grimly. *It's sure as hell* not *another merchant ship, that's for certain! Not heading* towards *us with all the craziness going on in the world just now. Besides, that idiot at the masthead may not have noticed her coming for a day or two, but he's sure she's Charisian-rigged.*

To be fair to his lookout—which, at that particular moment, was remarkably low on Lizardherd's list of priorities—he knew the man was cold, two-thirds frozen, and no doubt exhausted as he awaited the end of his stint in the crow's-nest. He was, however, an experienced seaman, which meant his identification of the oncoming vessel as Charisian was almost certainly accurate. Relatively few ships outside Charis had yet adopted the new sail plans Charis had introduced, after all. *Wind Hoof* had been *scheduled* to be rerigged on the new plan almost three months ago. She would have been, too, if Lizardherd's contact in Resmair hadn't quietly passed the word that the Church's shipping factors were being chary about awarding charters to ship masters who seemed too eager to adopt the heretics' innovations.

I should've told him to piss up a rope, Lizardherd thought now, grumpily. *Sure, it's a fat charter.* Actually, he knew, there was enough graft going on that his charter fee—which he was already charging at better than half again his normal rate—was probably no more than two-thirds (if that much) of what the Church factors were reporting to Zion when they sent in their accounts. *But no charter's fat enough to get* killed *over!*

He looked up at the set of his own canvas—his *inefficient* canvas, compared to the hunter sweeping down upon him on the wind—and grimaced. As he'd already told Hairaym, there was absolutely no point trying to outrun the other ship. And there was no point hauling down his Church pennant at this point, either, since the oncoming brig had to have already seen it. Not to mention the fact that Lieutenant Lewk Aivyrs, the Temple Guard officer whose detachment had been sent along to keep an eye on the money chests, would probably have a little to say about any such outbreak of prudence.

I guess I'm just going to have to hope that fellow over there doesn't want to start a war with Desnair on top of everything else, he thought morosely. *And fat fucking chance of that!*

▼ ▼ ▼

"She's Desnairian-flagged, Sir," Fytzhyw's first officer pointed out as the range fell to a thousand yards.

"Yes, Tobys, she is," Fytzhyw agreed.

"I just thought I'd point it out," Tobys Chermyn said mildly. "We're not at war with Desnair, at the moment, you know."

"I am aware of the fact," Fytzhyw acknowledged, turning to raise one eyebrow at his shorter lieutenant.

"Well, I was just thinking, it's sort of nice to have *someone* we're not at war with. Yet, at least." Chermyn grinned at him. "Do you think we're about to change that?"

"I don't know. And, to be totally honest about it, I don't really care, either," Fytzhyw told him, swinging back to look at the high-sided, wallowing Desnairian galleon. "First, Desnair hasn't got a navy. Second, Desnair is already busy *building* a navy for those sanctimonious pricks in Zion, so we might as well already be at war with them. And, third, Tobys, if they don't want to get themselves taken, then they shouldn't be flying that fucking pennant."

Chermyn nodded without speaking. The practice of flying a Church pennant whenever a vessel was in the service of the Church went back almost to the Creation itself. Traditionally, there were very good reasons for that, including the fact that only the heartiest—or most insane—pirate was going to trifle with a Church galleon. Those traditional reasons had been . . . somewhat undermined of late, however. It seemed to be taking a while for the rest of the world to figure out that flying that pennant these days had much in common with waving a red flag at a great dragon, at least where Charis was concerned, but Chermyn supposed old habits were hard to break.

And to be fair, not even every Charisian's as pissed off by the sight of it as the Old Man, he reflected.

In point of fact, Chermyn was at least a few years older than Fytzhyw, but it never crossed his mind to use another label for *Loyal Son*'s master. Symyn Fytzhyw struck most people as older than his years. Partly that was his size, no doubt—he stood a head taller than most other Charisians—but more of it stemmed from his indisputable *solidness*. And not just the solidness of his undeniably brawny muscle and bone, either. For all his youth, Fytzhyw was a purposeful, disciplined man, which helped to explain how someone his age not only captained but owned his own galleon.

But he was also a man of iron convictions. No one could accuse him of being narrow-minded, or of refusing to look before he leapt, yet once his convictions were engaged, there was no shaking him. Chermyn knew Fytzhyw had entertained his doubts initially about the wisdom of the schism between the Church of Charis and the Temple Loyalists. Those doubts had weakened with King Haarahld's death, and they'd vanished completely as he'd seen Archbishop Maikel and Emperor Cayleb turning their words into reality. The attempt to assassinate the archbishop in his own cathedral, what had happened to Archbishop Erayk, the lies coming out of Zion, and the Ferayd Massacre had replaced those initial doubts with fiery commitment.

And the Old Man doesn't do anything by halves, Chermyn told himself. *Which suits me right down to the ground, when you come to it.* He bared his teeth at the Desnarian galleon. *I wonder if that fellow over there's smart enough to realize just how quickly he'd better get that pennant down?*

▼   ▼   ▼

"Shit."

Alyk Lizardherd said the single word with quiet intensity as the Charisian brig—and they were close enough now to see the national banner which confirmed that she *was* Charisian—sliced through the water in surging bursts of white foam. He had to admire the other captain's ship handling, but that was just a bit difficult to remember when he saw the seven opened gun ports grinning in his direction. He'd never—yet—had the opportunity to examine one of the new Charisian guns, but he knew what he was seeing as the squat, short-barreled weapons were trundled forward. His catamounts threw three-pound shot; if those were what he was certain they were, they'd be throwing at least *eighteen*-pound shot. *Wind Hoof* was considerably larger than the Charisian brig, but not enough bigger to be able to survive that sort of imbalance in firepower!

"Sir?" Hairaym said tautly, and Lizardherd looked at him.

"I don't think they look particularly concerned about firing on a Desnairian ship, do you, Gorjah?"

"No, Sir, I don't," Hairaym said after a moment, yet even as he spoke, his eyes shifted forward to where Lieutenant Aivyrs and his ten Temple Guardsmen stood waiting on the main deck.

"Yes, that *is* a problem," Lizardherd agreed very softly. Hairaym's eyes darted back to him, and the captain smiled thinly. "If we don't strike our colors and heave to, those guns over there are going to turn us all into kraken bait, and pretty damned quickly. Or, for that matter, I'm sure they've got enough manpower over there to take us by boarding, assuming they somehow know enough about the cargo we're carrying to worry about sinking us with a careless cannon shot. But Lieutenant Aivyrs is going to insist that we *not* strike our colors and heave to, and I'm sure his men will follow his lead if—and when—he cuts down the first man to lay a finger on a flag halyard. Not to mention the fact that if we were so careless as to lose the Church's money by surrendering to a heretical Charisian 'pirate,' his report would undoubtedly have . . . unfortunate consequences."

"Yes, Sir," Hairaym acknowledged in an even quieter voice.

"Trapped between the dragon and the deep blue sea," Lizardherd murmured. No one could possibly have heard him through the noise of a sailing ship at sea, but Hairaym had been with him for a long time. He knew what his skipper was thinking, and he looked acutely unhappy.

Well, he can look as unhappy as he likes, Lizardherd thought waspishly. *He's going to look pretty frigging unhappy when we go to the bottom of the Markovian, too!*

"Tell the Bosun I need to speak to him," he said out loud, holding Hairaym's eyes with his own. "I believe he's up forward handing out the muskets."

For just a moment, Hairaym appeared not even to breathe. Then he inhaled deeply, squared his shoulders, and nodded.

"Yes, Sir. I'll see to it."

▼   ▼   ▼

Well, I don't see any signs of sanity breaking out over there yet, Fytzhyw thought. *Unless of course it's just that they're all stone blind and don't even realize we're here!*

He grimaced and raised his speaking trumpet.

"Master Chermyn!"

"Aye, Sir?" Tobys Chermyn shouted back from the foredeck.

"Clear away the pivot gun! It seems we need to attract these people's attention!"

"Aye, aye, Sir!"

▼   ▼   ▼

Lizardherd stood by the aftercastle rail, gazing steadily—one might almost have said fixedly—at the Charisian brig. He'd discussed his plans for defending the ship with the bosun, who'd been with him considerably longer even than Hairaym, and the bosun had moved all twelve of *Wind Hoof*'s matchlock-armed seamen into the waist of the ship, more conveniently located to Lieutenant Aivyrs.

The brig had a single longer gun forward. It looked as if it were mounted on some sort of turntable. Although Lizardherd had never heard of anything like it, he could see the advantages of such a mounting, and he concentrated on it rather than risk glancing towards the Guardsmen. Any time now. . . .

▼   ▼   ▼

"Fire!"

Loyal Son's pivot-mounted fourteen-pounder crashed, spitting its round shot across the gray-green waves. It landed well clear of the Desnairian galleon, exactly as warning shots were supposed to do, but its message was crystal clear, and Fytzhyw watched the other ship intently. If that ship's master had an ounce of sense, that Church pennant would be coming down any instant. Unfortunately, Fytzhyw had already spotted at least a handful of Temple Guardsmen on the galleon's deck. *They* weren't going to take kindly to the notion of surrender. On the other hand, their presence suggested that this was, indeed, the ship for which he'd been waiting. And whether they were likely to surrender or not, he still had the responsibility to at least give them the opportunity. Personally, he'd just as soon have handed each of those Guardsmen a round shot and kicked him over the side, but rules were rules. And, he conceded almost unwillingly, following the rules was one way a man could keep himself from waking up and discovering he'd become someone he didn't very much like. On the other hand—

He stiffened suddenly. *Loyal Son* was upwind of the Desnairian, but the popping sound of what was unmistakably musket fire reached him anyway, and his eyes narrowed. Exactly what did that idiot over there think he was going to do with muskets—especially *matchlock* muskets—at this sort of range? It was the *stupidest* thing he could have—

Symyn Fytzhyw's thoughts broke off again as the Church pennant came fluttering down from the other ship's masthead.

▼ ▼ ▼

"Heave to," Alyk Lizardherd commanded, and turned away once more as Hairaym passed the order.

One problem solved, he thought with a sort of lunatic detachment. *Of course, it does leave me with a few others.*

He glanced—briefly—at the eleven bodies sprawled across *Wind Hoof*'s deck. He regretted that. Lieutenant Aivyrs had seemed a nice enough young man, if a trifle overly earnest, but he hadn't been picked for his present assignment because of any weakness of faith. Even though he must have realized as clearly as Lizardherd did that nothing they might do could possibly affect the ultimate outcome of the Charisians' attack, he would have insisted on fighting. And when he did that, a lot of Lizardherd's crewmen—all of whom had been with him one hell of a lot longer than Aivyrs had—would have gotten themselves killed uselessly. So might one Alyk Lizardherd, although, to his own surprise, that possibility had played a relatively minor role in his final decision.

Somehow, I don't think the Inquisition is going to accept the theory that the Charisian marksmen concentrated on shooting down just the Guardsmen, he reflected sardonically. *Especially not when all of the bullets seem to have miraculously struck them from* behind. *And when you add that to all the money we've got onboard, they're bound to consider the possibility that it was an inside job. Maybe even that we never met up with any* Charisian *thieves at all.*

It irritated him that, in fact, it *wasn't* an inside job. If he was going to be suspected of making off with the Church's money, then he would have preferred at least to actually be guilty!

Well, he'd just have to see. Fortunately, he himself had no immediate family waiting for his return, and most of his seamen were unmarried. So was Hairaym, for that matter. He could always ask if the Charisians would be interested in acquiring one slightly used Desnairian galleon. They might even be willing to part with enough of *Wind Hoof*'s cargo to allow the crew of the galleon in question to begin new lives under new names somewhere far, far away from the Desnairian Empire.

Or we might be able to get them to agree to let us take to the boats long enough for them to put a couple of broadsides—hopefully nonfatal *broadsides—into the ship. Then anyone who wanted to go home could sail her back, while those of us more interested in seeing the world shipped along with the Charisians. That should provide enough other "buried at sea"* fatalities to keep anyone from commenting on the fluke of Charisian accuracy that hit only Guardsmen.

He shrugged. There was only one way to find out what sort of arrangement might be possible, and he raised his leather speaking trumpet.

"Ahoy, there!" he bellowed across the tumbled waste of water. "We're ready to receive a boat!"

. III .

Royal Palace,
City of Manchyr,
League of Corisande

Lamps burned late in the small council chamber as Prince Hektor walked through the door, followed by two of his body-guards. As usual, Hektor was impeccably attired, yet something about his appearance suggested he'd dressed rather more rapidly than usual this time. Or perhaps it was merely that the men awaiting him already knew he had.

He walked across to the head of the conference table with a quick, determined stride, and settled into the chair waiting for him there. Then he looked around the table with hard, grim eyes.

The Earl of Anvil Rock, Admiral Tartarian, the Earl of Coris, and Father Mahrak Hahlmyn, one of Bishop Executor Thomys' senior aides, were already seated there, waiting for him. The prince's eyes might have hardened briefly as they brushed across Hahlmyn, but if they did, he banished the hardness quickly and nodded respectfully to the upper-priest.

"I'm sorry to have summoned you on such short notice, Father," he said.

"Don't be concerned about it, Your Highness," Hahlmyn replied, his expression and tone both grave. "Shan-wei's machinations wait on no man, and the *Writ* tells us news of them has a habit of coming at inconvenient moments. I only regret that the Bishop Executor and Father Aidryn are both away from the city tonight. I have, of course, informed them of your message by carrier wyvern. And the Bishop Executor has asked me by return wyvern to tell you he and Father Aidryn will set out on their return at dawn. In the meantime, I am instructed to offer whatever assistance Mother Church can provide at this time."

"Thank you, Father." Hektor gave him a brief smile, then inhaled deeply. "The first thing I believe Mother Church could do for us this evening would be for you to ask the intervention of God and the Archangels on our behalf."

"Of course, Your Highness." Hahlmyn made the sign of Langhorne's Scepter, then bowed his head. "O God, we beseech You in the name of Your Holy Archangels to grant us Your strength and the true knowledge of Your will in this hour of trial. As the Holy Langhorne taught us, You and You alone are the true refuge of the righteous. Defend us from the malice and poison of Shan-wei, and strengthen us as we put upon us the armor of Your champions against those who would defile and defy Your Holy Church in the Evil One's dark name. There is no day so dark Your light cannot fill it, no enemy so powerful Your strength cannot subdue it. Lead us, guide us, and make us your sword against the powers of Hell. In Langhorne's holy name, amen."

"Thank you, Father," Hektor said again, his voice a bit softer, as he raised his head once more. His eyes circled the table again, then settled on Earl Coris.

"I take it you've already seen Taryl's dispatch, Phylyp?"

"I have, My Prince." Coris' expression was grim.

"And your thoughts on the matter?"

"My Prince, Admiral Tartarian's judgment would be far more reliable than mine in a matter such as this, I'm sure."

"That's probably true. However, I'd like to hear your thoughts before we hear from him. I have the greatest possible respect for the Admiral's judgment, and for Rysel's, but they're both professional military men. I think it's at least possible something will occur to you which might not occur to them precisely *because* they're professional military men. If that should happen to be the case, I'd like to hear it before something they say sends all our minds in another direction."

"Of course, My Prince." Coris pursed his lips for a moment, obviously marshaling his thoughts, then leaned forward slightly.

"The first thing that occurs to me, My Prince, is that the sighting report put the Charisians off Cape Targan, not Tear Island. From the report, it sounds as if they were making for either Tralmyr Passage or Coris Strait." The earl grimaced at the thought of how close to his own earldom the Charisian Navy was about to pass. "That's scarcely the most direct route from Charis, but it would make sense if Cayleb came by way of Port Royal to make rendezvous with Sharpset and what's left of the Chisholmian Navy, I suppose. Somehow, though, I don't think the answer is quite that simple . . . or palatable."

"Why not?" From Hektor's tone, he already knew where his spymaster was headed.

"Because Sir Farahk Hyllair is Grand Duke Zebediah's brother-in-law, My Prince," Coris said in a flat voice, and Hektor grimaced. Sir Farahk Hyllair was the Baron of Dairwyn, and there were times the prince regretted the marital connection he'd urged Dairwyn to form with Grand Duke Zebediah. At the time, like a great many things, it had seemed like a good idea to anchor Zebediah to one of his more trusted barons. And one whose relatively lightly populated barony needed all of the royal patronage it could get.

"The fact that Cayleb has chosen to circle all the way around into the Chisholm Sea to come at us from the north, instead of the south, could mean several things, of course," Coris continued. "The most likely, though, I'm afraid, is that he stopped off at Carmyn en route."

"Do you really think Dairwyn would betray you, Your Highness?" Anvil Rock asked quietly.

"Frankly? I don't know." Hektor shrugged. "Ordinarily, I'd say no. For several reasons. But these aren't exactly ordinary conditions, are they? Much as I hate to admit it, almost everyone has to be looking over his shoulder at the moment, wondering what's going to happen to *him* if we lose to Cayleb. And as Phylyp has just pointed out, Dairwyn is Zebediah's brother-in-law."

"We've had no indications that Sir Farahk might even be contemplating anything of the sort," Coris said. "What I'm afraid of is that Zebediah's turned *his* coat. If he has, it would be just like him to send letters along with Cayleb urging his brother-in-law to do the same thing."

"With all due respect, Your Highness," Tartarian said, entering the conversation for the first time, "I know Baron Dairwyn. I don't believe he'll be that easily swayed into betraying his loyalty to you."

"I think you're probably right," Hektor replied thoughtfully. "On the other hand, if Zebediah did send a letter like the one Phylyp is suggesting, then Cayleb may have decided it would be worth trying to get Dairwyn to come over to his side. Dairos is a good, relatively deepwater port right there on White Sail Bay. It's a bit on the cramped size for a really large fleet, but it's big enough to provide a decent anchorage at a pinch if his fleet's still tied down when the storm season really picks up in the next month or two . . . and it's only about two hundred miles overland from Manchyr. Admittedly, the Dark Hills are between Dairwyn and Manchyr, but that works both ways. If they'd be an obstacle for his army moving west against Manchyr, they'd also give his own base of operations some protection if we manage to concentrate our own forces against him. But the key point is that he's going to need a port *somewhere* at this time of year. If there's even a chance that Dairwyn might give him Dairos intact and without a fight, it's probably worth his while to at least give it a try."

"And if Dairwyn doesn't go over to him, Dairos isn't anywhere nearly as heavily defended as the ports along the Margo Sound coastline," Tartarian agreed unhappily.

"We had to prioritize our forces and the new artillery somehow, Taryl." Hektor waved one hand. "You and Rysel were right when you pointed out—as I just did—that the Dark Hills cover Manchyr from the east. So it made sense to concentrate on fortifying the southwestern ports, instead."

"Which could also be another indication Cayleb has been in contact with Zebediah," Coris pointed out. "Zebediah's had plenty of time to discover where we were concentrating our forces. I expect it's exactly the kind of information he would have been gathering up to offer Cayleb as proof of his value."

"It could indicate that," Hektor acknowledged. "By the same token, it's hard to hide new coastal batteries, Phylyp. Any one of the merchant ships passing through the Sound could have reported the information to Cayleb."

"And even if that isn't what happened, it probably wouldn't have required a military genius to figure out the way we'd approach the problem," Anvil Rock added.

"Exactly." Hektor nodded. Then he grimaced. "All right, I think all of that was worth thinking about, but now we have to concentrate on what we're going to do if they *are* headed for Dairwyn."

"I wish we had a better estimate of their total strength, My Prince," Tartarian said. "The good news is that, thanks to the semaphore, we know they're coming at least a five-day before something as slow as an invasion fleet can reach Dairos. The bad news is that we really don't know how much fighting strength they're bringing with them when they come. I know what Phylyp's reports have been telling us about the size of their fleet, the hundreds of galleons they've been assembling to send after us with every man in the Kingdom embarked as elite Marines. But as I've been saying all along, I don't trust our sources at this point."

"With good reason, I'm afraid," Coris muttered, and Hektor's mouth tightened slightly.

It was always difficult managing spies at distances as great as the one between Manchyr and Tellesberg, yet the fiendish effectiveness Charisian security had developed over the past couple of years was still something of a sore point. He'd been forced to accept that it wasn't really Coris' fault, since Nahrmahn and all of Cayleb's other enemies appeared to have been experiencing precisely the same sort of difficulties. Despite which, the fact that they were forced to rely upon secondary sources, the kinds of intelligence Coris' agents could pick up by questioning merchant captains or frequenting taverns in other realms' seaports to listen to sailors' gossip, left him feeling off-balance and half-blind.

"I'm prepared to admit that the Charisians—especially now that Chisholm has thrown in with them—can put together an impressive fleet and find the transports they need to lift a fairly substantial army as far as Corisande," Tartarian continued. "I'll believe he has two hundred war galleons and a hundred thousand men when I actually see them, though. Assuming we're actually facing a merely mortal foe, I don't see how he could have as many as *one* hundred war galleons, and I'd be astounded if he'd been able to find the troop lift for more than fifty to sixty thousand men. Not to mention the fact that he's had to raise and train his army virtually from scratch. That's going to limit the total manpower he can actually deploy here in Corisande just as effectively as his troop lift will."

"I agree," Anvil Rock said, nodding vigorously. "Another thing to consider is that after a voyage as long as the one between here and Charis—or even between here and Chisholm—his cavalry mounts and draft animals are going to need at least a five-day or two on land before they're going to be ready for any sort of serious campaigning."

"Against which he'll have the advantage of offshore mobility," Tartarian pointed out. "We still don't have the naval strength to face him, which means he can use his transports as aggressively as he likes. And, frankly, he'll be able to move his troops faster and farther than Rysel and Koryn can possibly march *our* troops overland.

"Having said that, though, he's not going to want to try anything too tricky right away," the admiral continued. "He's going to make sure he has a solid foothold here in Corisande before he does anything else. So, wherever he ends up going ashore—and, like you and Phylyp, My Prince, I think Dairos is his most probable immediate objective—he's going to spend at least some time establishing a solid defensive perimeter. The point Rysel just made about the condition of his cavalry mounts and draft dragons is also valid, and I suggest we do what we can to make it worse by ordering every horse, mule, and dragon in the Dairos area swept up and moved west, out of easy reach from the coast, before his first Marine hits the shore. Let's keep him from impressing any of *our* animals to make up any deficits. That should slow him down some. In fact, I believe we can probably count on at least another two or three five-days, even after he reaches Dairos, before he starts sending any spearheads off to find a way across the Dark Hills."

"His best route would be by way of Talbor Pass," Anvil Rock put in. "Well, his shortest and most direct route, at any rate. And I agree with Taryl. We've got time to get Koryn into position to cover Talbor before he can get there. For that matter, assuming Taryl's estimate of his troop strength is accurate, we can get Koryn there with almost twice the fighting strength. If we start soon enough, we could actually hit Cayleb while he's still east of the Dark Hills. We might even be able to get Koryn into position soon enough to pin him down in Dairos."

"At which point he burns down Dairos, re-embarks his troops, and sails off to attack us somewhere else, leaving Koryn and the bulk of our army in his wake," Hektor said sourly.

"All we can do is the best we can do, My Prince," Tartarian said reasonably. "If we can concentrate our troops quickly enough to attack before he's firmly established in Dairos, there's at least the possibility of driving him into the sea. We may not be able to fight him effectively *at* sea just now, but if this new army of his suffers a major reverse and heavy casualties, we'll probably get at least another six months to a year in which to build up our own strength. But if we're going to have any chance of doing that, we've got to take some chances, uncover ourselves in other places, in order to concentrate the troops we need where we have at least the chance of accomplishing something significant."

Anvil Rock nodded again, his expression sober, and Hektor's nostrils flared. They'd been over much of this same ground before, and he knew Tartarian and Anvil Rock were right. Now that the moment was actually upon him, however, he discovered that his intellectual agreement with their arguments was far less comforting than it had been when that moment had lain somewhere in a threatening yet still indeterminate future.

"All right," he said, and looked at Hahlmyn. "Father, if you would, I'd like to use the Church's semaphore to begin passing orders to Dairos, Baron Dairwyn, and Sir Koryn. Cayleb can move troops and men faster than we can, but at least we can pass *messages* faster than *he* can. With the Bishop Executor's permission, I think it's time we put that advantage to work for us."

. IU .

Dairos,
White Sail Bay,
Barony of Dairwyn,
League of Corisande

Fresh thunder rumbled and crashed, and a fresh wall of dirty-white smoke billowed up, shot through with flashes of flame, as the line of Charisian galleons sailed majestically past the floating batteries once more.

The rapid, disciplined bellowing of their guns was having its effect. Three of the anchored batteries had already been silenced, reduced to shattered ruin despite their heavy bulwarks. Wooden vessels were extraordinarily difficult to sink using solid shot, mainly because the holes those shot punched were relatively small and most tended to be above the waterline. It could still be done, however, and one of the big, stoutly constructed rafts was listing steeply, beginning to settle as water poured into it. Another was heavily aflame, and the third had

simply been shot through and through. The other four were still
in action, although their fire was beginning to falter, and bodies
floated in the water around them, where they'd been pushed
out of the gun ports to clear space for the surviving gun crews
to serve their weapons.

From this distance, with the city of Dairos and the sparkling
waters of White Sail Bay as a backdrop, it could almost have
been a magnificent spectacle, a tournament arranged to entertain
and enthrall. But only if the spectators hadn't experienced the
same things themselves, and Cayleb Ahrmahk *had* experienced
those things. He knew what happened to the fragile bodies of
men when round shot came crashing through heavy timber bulwarks in a cloud of lethal splinters. When the man standing beside you was turned into so much bloody gruel by a twenty- or
thirty-pound round shot. When the screams of the wounded cut
even through the deafening thunder of your own guns. When the
deck which had been sanded for traction before action was
splashed and patterned and painted in human blood.

He knew what he was truly seeing, and he stood tight-
mouthed as he watched the contest with his hands tightly
folded behind him. He was unarmored, without even a sword
at his side, and that was part of the reason his mouth was set in
such a harsh line.

Unfortunately for what he truly wanted to be doing at this
moment, his official advisers—and Merlin—had had a point.
The contest against the city of Dairos' defenses could have
only one outcome. Gallant as the men behind the guns of
those beleaguered rafts might be proving themselves, they
couldn't possibly stand off the firepower of Cayleb's fleet for
very much longer. For that matter, trying to employ the full
galleon strength under Cayleb's immediate command against
them would have been foolish. The ships would only have
gotten in one another's way, and the possibility of crippling
collisions between friendly units would have been very real
under such crowded, smoke-choked conditions.

And, as Merlin had remorselessly pointed out, if it wasn't
practical to use all of his galleons, anyway, then there was no

possible excuse for using *Empress of Charis*. It wasn't as if Cayleb had anything to prove about his personal courage in order to motivate the men under his command. And "sharing the risk" when there was no pressing military necessity for him to do so—and when he and Sharleyan had yet to beget an heir—would have been not simply unnecessary but criminally reckless. One unlucky round shot could have catastrophic consequences, not simply for Cayleb, but for all the people he was obligated and pledged to defend.

The obligation argument, in Cayleb's opinion, had been a particularly low blow, even for Merlin. Nonetheless, he'd been forced to concede the point, and so he'd been standing at *Empress of Charis'* quarterdeck rail, watching from safely outside artillery range, for the last three hours as other ships took the brunt of combat.

It hadn't been entirely one-sided. As Cayleb and his senior commanders had estimated (in no small part on the basis of *Seijin* Merlin's "visions"), Hektor of Corisande had, indeed, gotten the new-style artillery into production. He still had nowhere near as many of the new guns as he undoubtedly would have wished, but he obviously *did* have his equivalent of Edwyrd Howsmyn. In addition to all of the brand-new guns which had been emerging from his foundries, some infernally clever Corisandian busybody had figured out how to weld trunnions onto existing cannon, just as Howsmyn had done. He'd apparently been busily doing just that for months, too, which helped to explain why two of Cayleb's galleons had been forced out of the battle line to make repairs and why the ships engaging those floating batteries had already suffered upward of two hundred casualties of their own.

"Why can't those idiots recognize the inevitable and strike their colors before any more people get killed . . . on *either* side?" he half-growled and half-snarled.

"Probably because they know their duty when they see it, Your Majesty," Merlin said quietly. Cayleb's jaw muscles tightened, and his brown eyes flashed angrily at the infinitely respectful note of reproval in his chief bodyguard's tone. But then the emperor's nostrils flared as he inhaled a deep breath, and he nodded.

"You're right," he acknowledged. It wasn't exactly an apology, but, then, it hadn't exactly been a rebuke, either. He turned his head to give Merlin a crooked smile. "I just hate seeing so many men killed and wounded when it's not going to change anything in the end."

"In the ultimate sense, you're probably right about that," Merlin agreed. "On the other hand, they might get lucky. A shot in exactly the wrong place, a spark in a magazine, a smashed lantern somewhere below decks . . . as Earl Gray Harbor is fond of pointing out, the first rule of battle is that what *can* go wrong, *will* go wrong. And, as your father once pointed out to *him,* that's true for both sides."

"I know. But the fact that you're right doesn't make me like it any better."

"Good." The emperor's eyebrows arched at Merlin's reply, and the sapphire-eyed guardsman smiled a bit sadly at him. "An awful lot of people are going to get killed before this is all over, Cayleb. I know it's going to be harder on you, but I hope you'll forgive me if I say that the longer it takes for you to begin taking that for granted, the better man—and emperor— you'll be."

On Cayleb's other side, Prince Nahrmahn's eyes narrowed thoughtfully as he watched the emperor nod in grave agreement with the *seijin*'s observation. It wasn't that Nahrmahn disagreed with Merlin's observation. If the truth be told, Nahrmahn himself was perfectly capable of utter ruthlessness when necessity required, but he wasn't naturally bloodthirsty. In fact, his ruthlessness was almost a reaction against the sort of bloodthirstiness some rulers—Hektor of Corisande came to mind—often displayed. He'd always had a tendency to focus his ruthlessness on narrowly defined targets, key individuals whose surgical elimination would most advance his plans, and wholesale mayhem offended him. It was messy. Worse, it was sloppy, because it usually indicated he'd failed to properly identify the critical individual or individuals whose removal was truly necessary. Which, among other things, meant he'd probably killed more people in the end than he'd had to.

It was also the reason why, even though he would infinitely prefer an emperor who was a bit more ruthless than he had to be to an emperor who wasn't *sufficiently* ruthless, he had no quarrel with the *seijin*'s statement. There were other reasons, as well, though, and some of them had been rather unexpected. To his surprise, Nahrmahn had actually come to like Cayleb. He was a thoroughly decent young man, which was rare enough *outside* the ranks of heads of state, and Nahrmahn would prefer to keep him that way as long as possible, particularly since Cayleb was also going to be the brother-in-law of Nahrmhan's daughter. But setting that personal consideration completely aside, the last thing Safehold needed was for the young man who had been regretfully prepared to sink the Earl of Thirsk's entire fleet if his surrender terms had been rejected to turn into a young man who wouldn't have regretted it at all.

Yet however much Nahrmahn might approve of Merlin's statement, it wasn't the sort of thing one's bodyguards normally said to one. Especially not when one was an emperor. Nahrmahn had been prepared for a close relationship between Cayleb and the *seijin*. That kind of bond between an aristocrat and his most loyal and trusted servants was only to be expected, and Merlin had saved not only Cayleb's life, but also those of Archbishop Maikel and the Earl of Gray Harbor, not to mention the *seijin*'s superhuman, already legendary effort to save King Harahld's life at Darcos Sound. What wasn't to be expected was for that servant to be almost a . . . mentor to an emperor. "Mentor" wasn't exactly the right word, as Nahrmahn was well aware, but it came close. Cayleb *listened* to Merlin, and he treasured the *seijin*'s views and opinions on an enormous range of decisions. Of course, unlike altogether too many rulers, Cayleb had the incredibly valuable (and unfortunately rare) ability to *listen* to his advisers. No one would ever mistake him for an indecisive man, but his very decisiveness gave him the confidence to seek the opinions of others whose judgment he trusted before he reached a decision. Still, there was something different about the way he listened to *Merlin's* opinions.

Don't do it, Nahrmahn, the prince told himself. *That curiosity of yours is going to get you straight back into trouble yet, if you're not careful. If Cayleb wanted you to know why he respects* Seijin *Merlin's advice as much as he does, no doubt he'd already have told you. And, no, you* don't *need to be wondering how much the* seijin *has to do with all of those remarkable intelligence sources Wave Thunder was very carefully not telling you about.*

He snorted in quiet amusement at the direction of his own thoughts. Then his head snapped up as a thunderous explosion rolled across the smoke-layered waters of White Sail Bay. One of the floating batteries still in action against the Charisian galleons had just disappeared in an enormous fireball, and flaming fragments traced lines of smoke across the sky as they arced outward.

"A spark in a magazine, I believe you said, Merlin," Cayleb said harshly.

"Probably," Merlin agreed sadly. "On the other hand, they still haven't figured out how to produce corned powder. Even with bagged charges, the way their gunpowder tends to separate and throw out dust clouds is dangerous enough under any circumstances. Given what it has to be like aboard those batteries by this time . . ."

He shook his head, and Cayleb nodded in agreement. Then he looked over his shoulder at *Empress of Charis'* captain.

"Make a signal, Andrai. Instruct Admiral Nylz to temporarily disengage. That's better than half their batteries gone, and even the ones still in action have to be in bad shape. Let's give them a chance to think about the advantages of surrender before we kill any more of them."

"Of course, Your Majesty," Captain Gyrard said, and bowed to his monarch. Gyrard had been promoted to his present post after being wounded in action while serving as first lieutenant aboard Cayleb's last flagship. He, too, had only too good an idea of what it must be like aboard those shattered batteries, and his expression made it obvious he agreed wholeheartedly with Cayleb's decision as he nodded to his signal officer, who'd been standing by, waiting for instructions.

"You heard His Majesty. Make the signal to disengage."

"Aye, aye, Sir." The lieutenant touched his shoulder in salute, then began issuing orders of his own.

As the signal flags started to climb the halyards, Cayleb turned back to the still-rising column of smoke where the battery had exploded, and grimaced.

"I could wish we'd been wrong about Hektor's ingenuity," he said. "If he's managed to cobble up something like this to defend Dairos, what has he come up with for one of his *major* ports?"

"Probably more than we'd care to tangle with unless we absolutely have to," Merlin replied.

"At least his logistics problems have to be more complex than ours, if only because of his ammunition problems, Your Majesty," Captain Gyrard pointed out, and Cayleb grunted in agreement.

The Royal Charisian Navy had standardized the armament of its galleons long before it had become the *Imperial* Charisian Navy. Ships like *Empress of Charis* carried the newest artillery, which was actually a bit lighter than the guns Cayleb had taken to Armageddon Reef and Darcos Sound. Ehdwyrd Howsmyn and Baron Seamount had seen no choice before the previous year's campaign but to use the existing kraken for their standard artillery piece. It had already been the closest thing to a standard heavy gun the Navy had boasted, so there'd been enough of them to give the fleet a useful initial stock, once Howsmyn had figured out how to add trunnions.

But although it had been the only practical choice, it hadn't been the one Seamount had really wanted, for several reasons. The biggest one was that the "standard" kraken, unlike the larger and longer "great kraken," or "royal kraken," had been intended as a comparatively short-ranged, smashing weapon. Even with the new powder, its relatively short barrel length had reduced the velocity and range of its shot, with a corresponding drop in accuracy at longer ranges. In addition, when Howsmyn had reamed out the bores to standardize them and reduce windage, he'd had to go to a heavier weight of shot than Seamount had wanted. The baron had experimented with several different shot weights, trying to find the best balance between hitting power and the speed with which human muscles could load the weapons. Especially the *sustained* speed with which they could be loaded. Those experiments had suggested that reducing shot weight even slightly would help substantially, so he and Howsmyn had designed somewhat different models and adopted them once they began producing only newly cast weapons.

The new-model weapons had longer gun tubes, but they also had reduced bores, so they weighed no more than the older guns. The change hadn't made much difference where the upper-deck carronades were concerned, but it had given the much longer and heavier main-deck guns greater muzzle velocity and striking power, despite the reduction in each shot's weight by almost eight pounds.

The change had its downsides, of course. The most prominent one was that it had introduced at least some ammunition complications, since the older galleons still mounted their original converted krakens, whose ammunition was not interchangeable with that of the guns mounted aboard the newer vessels.

Compared to most navies, however, the Charisian Navy's ammunition arrangements were simplicity itself. Howsmyn and Seamount had settled on a total of four "standard" long guns: the "new-model kraken" with its roughly thirty-pound shot, an eighteen-pounder, a fourteen-pounder (intended specifically for chase armaments, with an especially tight windage to enhance accuracy), and a ten-pounder (for the same role aboard lighter ships). Their carronade "stablemates" were a fifty-seven-pounder, a thirty-pounder, and an eighteen-pounder. That was an enormous improvement over the "old-model" artillery, which had included no fewer than fifteen "standard" long gun calibers. (Not to mention the fact that guns of nominally the same bore size frequently hadn't been able to use the same round shot because different foundries' "inches" had been a different length from one another before King Harahld's draconian enforcement of the new official standards of measurement.)

They'd sought to further simplify things by decreeing that each individual ship must mount the same caliber of carronades and long guns, at least for broadside armament. They were willing to be a bit more flexible where the chase armament was concerned, but the fact that all of the broadside weapons fired identical projectiles made both the gunners' and the purser's lives ever so much easier. For the moment, at least. Personally, Merlin suspected it wasn't going to be long before the neat "official establishment" began to leak. As more specialized galleon designs evolved and the differentiated frigate/cruiser and ship-of-the-line/battleship emerged, topweight considerations and designed combat roles were going to begin dictating a reversion to mixed armaments.

The Corisandians' rush to improvise as many as possible of the "new-model" guns had left them in a far less enviable position, however, with no time to waste working out any sort of standardized table of naval ordnance. Their *new* guns appeared to come in no more than one or two calibers, but the conversions with the welded-on trunnions had pressed as many existing guns as possible into service. One of the floating batteries engaged against them in Dairos' defense had obviously mounted at least three, and possibly four, different calibers, which must have created nightmares for the man responsible for getting the right size and weight of shot to each gun.

Which, unfortunately, Cayleb reflected, *doesn't keep those guns from being damnably effective when the gunners* do *get the right shot size.*

"Your Majesty, we've just received a signal from General Chermyn." Gyrard's polite voice interrupted Cayleb's thoughts, and the emperor turned to the flag captain.

"And what did the General have to say?" he asked.

"Brigadier Clareyk has reported by heliograph, Your Majesty. He has his entire brigade ashore, and the second wave of Brigadier Haimyn's troops are landing now. Brigadier Clareyk estimates both brigades will be in their assigned positions within the next thirty to forty minutes. An hour at the outside, he says."

"Good!" Cayleb's tight expression lightened slightly.

One of the new Charisian innovations had been the introduction of the heliograph, using reflected sunlight to transmit messages in what another world in another time would have called "Morse code." Another had been the construction of specifically designed landing craft. They came in two sizes, with the larger capable of landing field artillery or up to a hundred men at a time, while the smaller (and faster) version could land only forty. Although both designs were capable—theoretically, at least—of making extended independent passages under sail, the shallow draft and flat bottoms designed to make over-the-beach landings possible also made them less than ideal blue-water vessels at the best of times. Sir Dustyn Olyvyr had improved things at least a bit by providing them with retractable leeboards, but the smaller ones (almost half the total) had made the voyage from Charis as deck cargo, and the captains responsible for getting them to Corisande had not been delighted by their assignment.

At the moment, Cayleb's sympathy for their unhappiness was limited, to say the least. The deck cargo landing craft had been swayed out the day before to join their bigger, rather more weather-worn sisters who'd made the passage the hard way, and while Dairos' defenders' attention was glued to the galleons systematically reducing the harbor's seaward defenses to wreckage, Clareyk and Haimyn had busied themselves putting their two Marine brigades ashore just out of sight of the town's fortifications. They had only four batteries of field guns, and no siege artillery at all, to support them, but four thousand rifle-armed Marines wouldn't need a lot of artillery support.

"Someone ask Father Clyfyrd to join us. I think it's time to send another note ashore." The emperor showed his teeth in a tight smile. "I realize Baron Dairwyn wasn't especially impressed by his brother-in-law's letters. Frankly, I wouldn't have been impressed by anything from Grand Duke Zebediah, either. But the beating his batteries have taken ought to be enough to incline him to see reason even without having Clareyk and Haimyn ashore behind him."

"It seems likely, at any rate, Your Majesty," Captain Gyrard agreed.

"It better," Cayleb said in a harder, somehow darker voice. "If we have to storm his town, it's going to get ugly. I realize our men are better disciplined than most, but even Siddarmarkian pikemen's discipline can slip if they take heavy casualties. Especially if they take them storming a position everyone on both sides knows couldn't hold out against them in the end. Besides, even if our people behave themselves perfectly, there are civilians—lots of them, including women and children—in Dairos."

"Were you thinking of making that point to the Baron in your note, Your Majesty?" Merlin asked, and Cayleb barked a laugh at his bodyguard's painstakingly neutral tone.

"As a matter of fact, yes. But tactfully, Merlin—*tactfully*. I wasn't thinking of handling this the same way I handled Earl Thirsk, if that's the point you were delicately raising. Observe."

Father Clyfyrd had arrived, portable writing desk in hand, while Cayleb was speaking. The emperor watched his secretary setting up the desk and pulling out a pad of notepaper. The brisk breeze blowing across the deck caught at the edges of the pad's sheets, ruffling them exuberantly, and Cayleb quirked an eyebrow at Laimhyn as the priest grabbed the pad, set it on the desk, and jabbed a pair of pushpins through the bottom corners of the top sheet to tame its gyrations.

"Would it be easier on you if we went below, Clyfyrd?" the emperor asked then with grave courtesy . . . and careful timing.

"No, thank you, Your Majesty." Laimhyn's deadpan expression would have done credit to any trained stage actor, and he shook his head courteously. "By the strangest turn of fate I appear to have just this *instant* finished tacking down the notepaper. A peculiar coincidence of timing, I'm certain."

"Goodness," Cayleb said demurely. "That *is* astonishing, isn't it?"

A sniff, barely audible over the sound of wind humming through *Empress of Charis'* rigging, might have escaped from Laimhyn. Then again, it *might* have been only the onlookers' imagination.

"Truly," Cayleb said, his expression much more serious, "are you ready, Clyfyrd?"

"Of course, Your Majesty," Laimhyn replied, his tone equally serious, and dipped his pen in the desk's inkwell.

"Make sure it's properly addressed," Cayleb told him. "Use some of that correspondence of Zebediah's to be sure we get the details straight. And I'll rely on you to choose a properly polite salutation."

"Yes, Your Majesty."

"Very well."

The emperor cleared his throat, then began.

"My Lord, your men have fought with a gallantry and determination which deserves only praise and honor, but their position is now hopeless. Your defensive batteries are destroyed or too badly damaged to effectively defend themselves any longer, and my infantry is now ashore in strength and will shortly be prepared to assault your landward defenses. Men who have shown such bravery in action deserve better than to be killed when their position has become obviously untenable, and Dairos is a city, not a fortress citadel. I am confident that neither of us desires to find civilians—especially women and children—caught in battle in the middle of their own town, amid their own homes, churches, and shops. In order to avoid additional and ultimately profitless loss of life, both military and civilian, I once again urge you to surrender your position. I will guarantee civil order, the safety of your civilian population, and the preservation of private property in so far as the exigencies of war allow, and men who have fought as valiantly and steadfastly as your men have this day deserve, and will receive, honorable and correct treatment under the laws of warfare."

He paused, as if considering adding something else, then shrugged.

"Read that back, please, Clyfyrd."

"Of course, Your Majesty." The priest read the entire brief message aloud, and Cayleb nodded.

"I think that should just about do it. Make a clean copy for my signature. And let's be certain it's properly sealed, as well as addressed. I don't want the Baron thinking we dashed it off hastily, now do I?"

"No, Your Majesty."

Laimhyn bowed to the emperor, and this time he did retire to the shelter of Cayleb's day cabin to produce the formal note on Cayleb's personal stationery, complete with the properly correct and ornate calligraphy.

"There," Cayleb told Merlin. "You see? No crude threats. Just one reasonable man sending a note to another reasonable man."

"Much smoother than your conversation with Thirsk, Your Majesty," Merlin agreed respectfully. "I especially liked the bit at the end when you *didn't* say 'or else.' "

"Yes, I thought that was well done myself," Cayleb said with a smile.

. V .

The Laughing Bride Tavern,
City of Tellesberg,
Kingdom of Charis

The man who stepped through the Laughing Bride's front door was plainly dressed. The hot, humid March night was blacker than the inside of a boot, but thunder rumbled out over Howell Bay, and occasional flashes of lightning lit the banks of heavy cloud rolling steadily in across the city of Tellesberg. Even though no rain had fallen yet, the fact that the visitor wore a poncho was certainly understandable, despite the temperature, under the circumstances.

"Can I help you?" the tavern's owner asked as he stepped across to personally greet the newcomer. It was late, and with the threatening weather, the Laughing Bride was scarcely packed.

"I'm looking for someone," the man in the poncho said. "I was told to ask for Master Dahryus."

"Ah." Something might have flickered deep inside the publican's eyes. If so, it disappeared as quickly as it had come, like one of the cloud-buried lightning flashes out over the Bay, and he nodded. "He's taken the private taproom for the evening. Through that arch," he pointed, "and down the hallway. Last door on the right."

"Thank you." The man in the poncho nodded and headed down the indicated hallway. He paused outside the door of the taproom for just a moment, almost as if he were drawing a deep breath. Then he knocked once, crisply.

The door opened quickly, and he found himself facing a youngish man dressed like a moderately successful merchant or shop owner.

"Yes?" the younger man said courteously.

"I have a message for Master Dahryus," the man in the hallway said once more.

If there might have been a flicker of something in the tavern-owner's eyes, the brief tightening of the younger man's expression was unmistakable. But he stepped back courteously enough, inviting the other man into the small taproom, then closed the door behind him. There were just under a dozen other men present, and all of them turned their heads, looking at the newcomer with expressions which varied from calmness to obvious uneasiness. In some cases, possibly even fear.

"Ah, *there* you are!" another voice greeted the new arrival as yet another man—this one considerably older and rather better dressed than the fellow who had opened the door for him—looked up from a quietly intense conversation with one of the others seated around the small tables.

"I apologize for my tardiness . . . Master Dahryus," the

newcomer said. "It was a bit difficult to get away without raising any questions."

"That wasn't a criticism," the man called "Master Dahryus" said reassuringly. "I'm just happy and relieved to see you after all."

The man in the poncho bowed slightly, and Master Dahryus' waving hand invited him over to take a seat.

"Seriously," Dahryus continued as the late arrival obeyed his unspoken invitation, "I was beginning to feel a bit anxious. Baron Wave Thunder's agents have proven even more effective than I'd anticipated."

"I've noticed the same thing, My Lord."

"I believe we might stay with simple 'Master Dahryus,' even here," Dahryus said.

"Of course." The man in the poncho colored very slightly, and Dahryus chuckled and reached across the table to pat him on the shoulder.

"Don't worry about it so much, my son. Old habits die hard, and this isn't exactly something any of us expected to be facing, now is it?"

"No, it isn't," the other man said feelingly, and this time two or three of the others snorted or chuckled in harsh agreement.

"Unfortunately, we are facing it," Dahryus continued, "and given that we've all just agreed that Wave Thunder's agents appear to be everywhere, we'd all best get into the habits of successful conspirators. Which is why, even though I realize one or two of you already know one another, I think we'll avoid using any names tonight. Agreed?"

Everyone nodded, and he smiled thinly.

"Very well, my friends. In that case, it's time we were getting down to business. We have much to discuss—much which will come as a surprise to many of you, I suspect. And, as I promised when first we came together, the time to strike draws rapidly closer. Indeed, if tonight's meeting goes as planned, that time is almost upon us."

The others looked back at him in silence, their expressions

a blend of excitement, anticipation, determination, and fear, and his smile grew broader and warmer.

"Yes, we do indeed have much to discuss and to plan. But first, will you join me in a moment of prayer?"

▼   ▼   ▼

"—confident you can see why the arrangements near the convent are critical to our success," Master Dahryus said some hours later. "And given the location of your manor, you're definitely the one of us best placed to see to those details. So, if you're willing to shoulder the responsibility—and the risk—we'll leave their arrangement in your hands. The most important thing to remember is that none of the rest of us can play our part until those arrangements are solidly in place. If any problem should arise, or if you should discover that you require additional funds or any other assistance, you must let us know promptly so we can adjust our schedule. Father Tairyn will know how to contact me at any time, should there be need. It may take some days for any message from him to reach me, but be assured that it will."

"Of course, Master Dahryus," the man to whom he'd been speaking said, and pushed back his chair. He stood, bowed to Dahryus and the two others who were still present, then left the taproom.

Even as he stepped through the doorway, the abrupt, torrential rush of a thunderstorm came pounding down on the Laughing Bride's roof. Thunder crashed suddenly almost directly overhead, shaking the tavern about its bones, and Dahryus shook his head as the door closed behind the departing man.

"I fear Langhorne is providing an appropriate backdrop for this evening's meeting," he said.

"In more ways than one," the man who'd arrived late agreed dourly. "I'm not looking forward to the walk clear back to the Palace through *this*."

He twitched his head in the direction of the taproom's shuttered windows, and the man who'd assumed the name of Dahryus chuckled.

"At least it should mean you're unlikely to meet anyone who might wonder where you've been, Father," he pointed out, relaxing his own security rules in recognition that all of those remaining already knew one another's identities. "In fact, that might be the very reason God provided this little shower."

"If He did, I'm sure He knows best, My Lord," the priest said. "On the other hand, not every task God sends us is equally enjoyable."

"No," Dahryus said, his tone and expression both darkening. "No, it isn't."

"My Lord—I mean, Master Dahryus—" one of the others began, his voice quiet in the rushing-water sound of the thunderstorm.

"I think we can be a little less circumspect at this point, Mytrahn," Bishop Mylz Halcom said.

"Yes, My Lord. Thank you." The other man smiled briefly, but his obvious unhappiness didn't ease appreciably. "I was just going to ask . . . is *this* task really necessary?"

"Unfortunately, I believe the answer is yes," Halcom said. "It's not the sort of thing I ever thought God would call me to do, and I don't expect it to be easy for any of us. Yet the truth is, my sons, that when Shan-wei works her evil in the world of mortals, sometimes men who stand for the Light find themselves called to hard tasks."

The man who'd asked the question nodded, but his expression remained troubled, and Halcom gave him a gentle, sad smile.

"When Sharleyan voluntarily joined with Cayleb in his attack upon Mother Church, she made herself an enemy of God, Mytrahn," he said. "I've never actually met her, of course. Everything I've ever heard of her would seem to indicate she's always been a good ruler, with a deep interest in justice and the well-being of her people. But whatever she may have been in the past, she no longer is. It may well be she truly believes what she and Cayleb are doing is God's will. If so, however, both of them are wrong. And, in many ways, a good and sincere person mistakenly serving Shan-wei's ends, with absolutely no evil *intention*, is the most deadly threat of all. Those who openly and obviously serve corruption are easily denounced, easily discredited. Those who fall into sin through good but misguided intentions and mistaken understanding often sound reasonable and convincing. They have no evil *motives,* however evil the ultimate outcome of their actions may be, and people such as that are far more seductive than the open and deliberate enemies of God.

"That's always true, but it takes on an even greater significance in Sharleyan's case, I'm afraid. Just look at how her popularity here in Charis is already working to bolster Cayleb and the other schismatic leadership, even in the face of excommunication and interdict."

Heads nodded around the table, and more than one face tightened. The writs of excommunication for Cayleb Ahrmahk and Maikel Staynair, along with the proclamation of the interdiction of the entire Kingdom of Charis, had arrived less than two five-days earlier. The shock, however, had been less profound than one might have anticipated, given the severity of the penalties involved, and there was very little sign of any significant reaction against the authority of the Crown or of the Archbishop of the Church of Charis. Partly, no doubt, that was because Staynair and Cayleb had foreseen the probability of such an action from the very beginning and had carefully warned their supporters that it might be coming. Another major factor was that the Church itself in Charis had blithely ignored the proclamations. Despite the interdict, churches were open and sacraments were administered. When the priesthood scorned the legitimate decrees and proclamations of Mother Church, how could the laity be blamed for following suit? Especially when the very grounds for the schismatics' rejection of Mother Church's authority further undercut the legitimacy of those writs through their scorching condemnation of the corruption of the vicarate which had issued them?

But there was another factor, as well, Halcom felt certain. Sharleyan had *not* been excommunicated, obviously because no one in Zion had anticipated the possibility of her marriage to Cayleb when the writs were originally issued two months earlier. The fact that she hadn't been, coupled with the way in which she had taken the heart of Charis by storm, made her a sort of legitimating source of the authority and fealty the Church had formally stripped away from Cayleb.

"At the moment," he continued, "Sharleyan's very reputation as a good and just ruler, the fact that she's so *likable*, has put a smiling face on Shan-wei's corruption. That's bad enough. But she genuinely believes in what she's doing. She hasn't been misled or deceived by Cayleb, and her commitment, in my judgment, is every bit as powerful as his own. She isn't going to allow herself to be used as a weapon against something in which she truly believes. That's why I believe our friend in the Palace is mistaken."

"I'm afraid you're right about that," the priest who'd shed the poncho said heavily. "I believe he's sincere, although I'm also inclined to think his motivations aren't quite as selfless as he says. In fact, I think they aren't quite as selfless as he truly *believes* they are. And, of course, there are all of those other, more personal, factors involved in his thinking. But however sincere he may be, he simply doesn't want to face hard, unpleasant facts."

"Which ones?" the man who'd questioned Dahryus asked, and the priest raised his hand, counting off points on his fingers as he made them.

"First, I don't think he truly wants to admit she's become an enemy of God. He desperately wants to believe she's only temporarily mistaken. That, given time, she'll return to her senses. And, second, he doesn't want to admit how deeply and sincerely attached to her the majority of her subjects actually are. I think he underestimates the importance of her support among the common-born folk on this issue, probably because he's not one of them himself. That's more than a little ironic, in light of past events, but I suppose it's also possible that he's fooling himself on this point because he doesn't want to face the logical implications.

"But whatever he may be thinking, or why ever he may be thinking it, the truth is that she's genuinely loved. In fact, his entire plan revolves around using that love for our own ends, and superficially, it's a very attractive concept. When she not only held the throne after her father's death but also proved to be one of the strongest rulers in Chisholm's history, she won their hearts as well as their loyalty. Despite how deeply they respect her, the common folk also feel actively possessive about her, almost as if she were a favorite, beautiful sister or daughter, not just their monarch. Our friend is well aware of that, but what he's persistently overlooking is that a huge percentage of Chisholmians will follow her straight into apostasy and heresy simply because of how much they love her. Every dispatch from Green Mountain and the Queen Mother only underscores that fact. He simply doesn't want to admit it, just as he's underestimating, in my opinion, the degree to which the Chisholmian commons are going to be automatically suspicious of anything which holds even the slightest possible taint of some sort of aristocratic cabal. Every other scheme he's come up with for actually discrediting her has foundered on that same rock, but he honestly believes this one will work because it's supposed to discredit the *reasons* for her decisions, rather than the decisions themselves, and do it in a way she can't directly counter. Unfortunately, I don't think it will have the effect he's predicting . . . and without Green Mountain's active support—which even he realizes would be impossible to secure—I'm even more doubtful about his ability to manage the commons well enough to keep the situation under control in the long run."

"So am I," Halcom said, nodding slowly and regretfully. "And if he's wrong, if he can't discredit her policies *and* deprive her of the power to counterattack his actions, then we have no choice but to consider more . . . direct action."

"I understand," the man who'd asked the initial question said. "I still wish there were some way to avoid it, though."

"So do we all," Halcom replied. "So do we all."

He sat silent for several seconds, then returned his attention to the priest.

"I take it you have his answer to our latest counterproposal?"

"I do. He believes what you've suggested should be practical, given conditions in both Charis and Chisholm. He's agreed to help push events in the necessary direction."

"And is he making any plans of his own to consolidate things in the aftermath?" Halcom's eyes sharpened as he asked the question, and the other man shrugged.

"He says there's no point in trying to do so at this time. Or, rather, that it would be unduly risky to attempt to involve anyone *else* in his planning at this stage. As he says, his present base of support isn't especially strong, and he's not completely positive who among his apparent supporters might prove less than enthusiastic if they knew the full plan. So he intends to wait until the moment comes, then 'play it by ear.' I think he entertains at least some hope of recruiting additional supporters when the Chisholmian delegation to this new Imperial Parliament arrives in Tellesberg. Even if he fails in that, or decides it's too risky to attempt after all, the fact that he's the only one in the Palace who will know ahead of time that anything is coming should allow him to capitalize upon it. That's what he says, at any rate, and I'm strongly inclined to agree he's telling us the truth about his plans and intentions."

"Which tends to lend additional credence to your own comment about his motivations, doesn't it?" Halcom said a bit sadly.

"I suppose it does. On the other hand, don't forget that his objections, his stipulations, are completely sincere. That's my evaluation of them, at least. There are clear limits beyond which he's not prepared to go."

The note of warning in the priest's voice was clear, and Halcom nodded.

"I realize that. And if I believed his analysis of the consequences of his own proposal was accurate, I'd be fully prepared to respect those limits. Unfortunately, he's wrong. What he wants to do is far too likely to come crashing down around his ears, and if it does, it will come crashing down on us and upon *our* task, as well. In fact, I believe that ultimately his idea is likely to make things worse by actually strengthening Sharleyan's hand in the fullness of time. Never forget, my sons, that this new Empress of ours is a formidable, intelligent, and determined woman. One who not only has enormous popular support in Chisholm, but who's been steadily winning the hearts and loyalty of all of Charis, as well. That's what makes her such a dangerous weapon in Cayleb's hand, and striking her *from* his hand is going to be far more difficult than our friend believes."

"I . . . regret that," the priest said softly. "As you said a moment ago, she isn't and never has been an *evil* woman, despite the horrible sin she's fallen into."

"Evil seduces," Halcom replied almost equally softly. "It cannot conquer by force of arms unless godly men allow it to do so, and if its mask were not so fair and so seductive, then Hell would be empty of all save Shan-wei herself. But Hell is not empty, my son, and however good Sharleyan's intentions may originally have been, however good she may still sincerely believe they *are,* she is fully in the service of Shan-wei now. And so, however likable she may be, no matter how physically or even spiritually attractive she may be, she is the enemy of God. And there can be no quarter, no compromise, with His enemies."

The others nodded in solemn silence, and he redirected his attention to the priest once again.

"Very well. When you have the opportunity to speak to him once again, tell him it will take at least a short while to make the arrangements from our side. If he seems to be feeling impatient, point out to him that the difficulties involved in finding a secure and, if necessary, defensible location for our base after the actual strike are far from trivial. Tell him we'll complete our preparations as quickly as possible and inform him when everything is in place. And it might be as well to suggest to him that he begin thinking of ways to bring Saint Agtha's to the Empress' attention."

"With all due respect, do we want to have him do that before our preparations are complete?" the priest asked.

"I think it will be better to lay the groundwork as far in advance as possible," Halcom replied. "Given how complicated and busy her life must be at the moment, however many of Cayleb's advisers may still be available to assist her, it's unlikely she'd be able to free the time in her schedule to visit the convent before we could be prepared. Even if our friend is clumsier than I would expect about mentioning Saint Agtha to her, she isn't going to be able to go haring off on a moment's notice."

The priest nodded, and Halcom inhaled deeply, pushed back his chair, and stood.

"In that case, my sons," he said, raising his hand and signing the scepter, "go now, with God's blessing and in Langhorne's keeping. Remember the devotion and love due to God and the Archangels, and let the strength that love brings you strengthen and guide your hands, hearts, and minds as we give ourselves to the service of God and Mother Church against all enemies of the Light."

. UI .

The Temple,
City of Zion,
The Temple Lands

Well, this ought to be an interesting dog and dragon show," a voice muttered quietly, and Vicar Samyl Wylsynn looked up as his brother settled into the chair beside him.

"Not, perhaps, the most tactful—or safe—thing to say," Samyl replied even more quietly.

"Maybe not, but that doesn't make it inaccurate," Hauwerd Wylsynn half-growled.

"No," Samyl agreed.

"Well, then." Hauwerd shrugged, and Samyl grimaced.

Actually, there was a sufficiently wide moat of empty chairs around the two Wylsynn brothers that the likelihood of anyone overhearing a private conversation between them was virtually nonexistent. On the other hand, Samyl hadn't survived this long by running unnecessary risks. Still, he understood his younger brother's profoundly mixed feelings as they waited, along with perhaps forty or fifty other vicars and senior archbishops, for the tribunal to convene.

How many years have we been collecting evidence of corruption—especially in the Office of Inquisition? Samyl asked himself. *We must have enough of it to fill a dozen trunks by now!* Large *trunks. Yet with all those years, all that effort, we have yet to secure a serious indictment of anyone. And now* this.

There had been times when Samyl had been sorely tempted to abandon his quixotic quest. The chances of success, even if he somehow, someday, found himself stepping into the office Clyntahn and his successors had corrupted so thoroughly, were slim. He knew that. He'd always known it. And even if he somehow achieved that goal, it would be only to find himself battling literally generations of entrenched opposition and self-interest. Yet he was who he was, and the unending (and generally thankless) task of reforming the Church and purging it of its many abuses had become a Wylsynn legacy.

And a damned risky "legacy" it is, too! he thought moodily.

He'd actually preferred charges against at least a dozen of his fellow Schuelerites over the years, whenever he could produce the necessary evidence without exposing the Circle's broader, covert, and far riskier activities. At least twice he'd had absolutely conclusive evidence that the Inquisitors in question had been using their office (and all the grisly threats associated with it) to extort money out of completely innocent men and women. And once he'd had *almost* absolutely conclusive evidence of murder. Yet the most severe punishment he'd ever managed to secure had been no more than a one-year suspension from the Order of Schueler . . . and that had been for one of the *extortionists*, not the murderer.

It sickened him that his own order, the order charged with preserving the sanctity of the Church's own soul, was even more corrupt than the other orders it was supposed to guide and police, yet there was no point in pretending that wasn't true. And the worst of it was that many of those corrupt inquisitors didn't even realize they *were* corrupt. They were part of a system far larger than themselves, performing their duties exactly the way they'd been taught to perform them by Zhaspahr Clyntahn and his immediate predecessors. The thought that they genuinely believed they were serving God's will was frightening, yet he'd long ago come to the conclusion that—for many of them—it was also true.

I sometimes wonder if even Clyntahn truly realizes how corrupt he is. In fact, I doubt he does. He doesn't see it as corruption at all, which is probably the most damnable thing about him. I think he genuinely sees no discrepancy between what he *wants and the will of God. They're exactly the same thing, which is why he's justified in doing anything—anything at all—to achieve his own ends. Anything that maintains and strengthens the Church's authority (and his) is good and godly; anything that* threatens *the Church's authority (and his) is the work of Shan-wei herself. And no one else, except for the Circle, cares a damned thing about it as long as it keeps working for* them, *keeps squeezing out money and power and privilege for* them.

The truth was, although Samyl hadn't told anyone, even among his brothers of the Circle, that he actually *agreed* with Maikel Staynair and the Church of Charis. The Church of God Awaiting *was* hopelessly corrupt, trapped in the grip of men like Clyntahn and the rest of the Group of Four. Even if he could somehow topple Clyntahn and Trynair, there was no point deceiving himself into the belief that there weren't at least a score of other vicars prepared to step into the Group of Four's place and maintain "business as usual." It was simply the way things were.

But there truly are good and godly men among the vicarate, as well, he told himself stubbornly. *You* know *there are. That's the only reason you haven't given up and fled to someplace like Charis yourself.*

Perhaps so, but it was getting harder to cling to that belief. And the air of desperation, the sense of men willing to reach for any avenue of escape, which had permeated the Church at her highest level since the Charisians had bidden the Group of Four defiance was frightening. What had been merely dangerous before had become something far worse, and after the ghastly fate handed out to Erayk Dynnys, Samyl Wylsynn was under no illusion about that. Frightened men would turn savagely upon anyone who appeared to threaten their own safety, their own positions, and Zhaspahr Clyntahn was more than prepared to use that fear to support his own ends.

Perhaps it's time, he thought. *If the key wasn't given for a moment like this one then why* was *it given? Surely an internal threat to the Church is just as deadly as an* external *one?*

Yet it wasn't the same thing, and he knew that as well as Hauwerd did. Perhaps the time was coming, but until it did—

Samyl Wylsynn's ruminations broke off abruptly as the members of the tribunal filed into the large chamber and seated themselves behind the enormous conference table. There were eight of them, but only one who really mattered, and Wylsynn's face tightened as Wyllym Rayno, the Archbishop of Chiang-wu and Adjutant of the Order of Schueler, leaned forward and rapped lightly on the small bell hanging in its stand before him.

The sweet, silvery notes floated through the chamber, and the quiet buzz of side conversations ended abruptly.

"This tribunal is now in session," Rayno announced. "Let us pray."

Heads bowed throughout the chamber, and Rayno raised his voice.

"O God, Creator of all men, maker of all things, designer and architect of all that has been, is now, or ever shall be, we come before You in awe and trembling. We beseech You to guide us in this, our solemn task to maintain the sanctity, the purity, and the truth of Your word and Your Church as handed down to us by the Archangel Langhorne on the very day of Creation itself. We thank and bless You for giving us that sacred instruction and guiding us in its preservation and teaching, and it is with a heavy heart we bring You the result of the deliberations and decisions to which Your Office of Inquisition has been called by recent events. Be with us, we beseech

You, as we contend with the forces of Darkness in Your most holy name. In Langhorne's name we pray, amen."

A chorus of answering "amens" rumbled back, but Samyl Wylsynn's was not among them. Nor was his brother's.

Rayno raised his head, waited for his listeners to settle themselves comfortably once again, then cleared his throat.

"I'm confident that everyone in this chamber is fully conversant with the events which led to the assembly of this tribunal," he said. "Since that is the case, there seems little point in summarizing them yet again."

One or two heads nodded among the audience, and Rayno looked over his shoulder at one of the aides assembled against the tapestry-covered wall behind the tribunal's members. The aide, a remarkably young-looking upper-priest of the Order of Schueler, promptly handed him a thick folder, and Rayno placed it on the conference table before him. He opened it and leafed through the first few sheets of paper for several seconds. Then he looked back up at the waiting clerics.

"This tribunal was impaneled to consider the circumstances surrounding the deaths of sixteen consecrated priests of the Order of Schueler," he said. "There is no question about the causes of those deaths, or who was responsible for them, but certain charges leveled at the priests in question were so serious, so disturbing, that the Grand Inquisitor, with the Grand Vicar's strong agreement, felt a formal inquiry and investigation was mandatory.

"This tribunal has now concluded that inquiry and investigation to the satisfaction of its members and is prepared to announce its findings."

It was scarcely a surprise, but even so a stir went through the audience, like a stiff breeze rustling its way through a field of ripened wheat.

"According to the allegations published by the so-called 'Church of Charis,'" Rayno continued, "the sixteen priests who died in Ferayd were guilty of instigating the murder of women and children in that same city last August when King Zhames, in obedience to Mother Church's instructions, ordered the seizure of the Charisian shipping then in Ferayd. In support of those allegations, the so-called 'Church of Charis' has published what purports to be reports written by those very priests in which they openly admitted their complicity in those 'murders.'

"This tribunal has considered those reports, including the documentary evidence sent to us by King Zhames of Delferahk. That evidence consisted primarily of what the Charisians claimed were the official file copies of those reports, captured during their vicious attack upon the people of Ferayd.

"Needless to say, the initial response of any reasonable man must be to reject allegations and charges from those who have blasphemously announced their own defiance of God's own Church. When those allegations and charges come also from the hands of men who have themselves so recently caused the deaths of so many innocent civilians—including women and children—and burned an entire city to the ground, the reasons to doubt the . . . reliability of their testimony redouble. This tribunal is confident that no one will be surprised to learn that the initial reaction of the Grand Inquisitor and the Chancellor of the Council of Vicars was to pay those charges no heed."

Rayno paused, and his jaw tightened visibly in obvious unhappiness and pain. Samyl Wylsynn's jaw tightened, as well, if for rather different reasons, as he recognized the theater of his order's adjutant.

"Even though that was the Grand Inquisitor's initial reaction," Rayno continued after a moment, "he was not unmindful of his responsibility as the head of the Office of Inquisition. Even the most unlikely allegations must be tested when they touch upon the integrity of Mother Church and, especially, on the Inquisitors charged with protecting that integrity. And so, despite his own profound skepticism, he ordered this tribunal to convene and to consider the possibility that there might be some basis to the 'Church of Charis' preposterous allegations.

"We have now concluded our inquiry, and we must regretfully, with the most profound remorse and dismay, announce that it is our belief that the priests who died in Ferayd were, indeed, guilty of the actions charged against them by the so-called 'Church of Charis.' "

Both of the Wylsynns had already known what Rayno intended to announce. To judge by the sudden wave of whispers which hissed its way across the chamber, at least some of those in the audience hadn't.

Rayno paused once more, his expression one of bitter regret, until the chamber was once again silent.

"Brothers in God," he said then, "it is, alas, true that even God's priests can err. Even the best of men is not the equal of the Archangels, and the *Writ* bears ample witness that even the Archangels themselves could fall into error. In this instance, there seems very little doubt that the Inquisitors of Ferayd did just that. They did, indeed, assume the leadership of the parties of Delferahkan troops detailed to sequester the Charisian merchant ships in Ferayd. And when fighting broke out, they did, indeed, order those troops to kill the Charisians who resisted the attempt to sequester their vessels, and as a direct result of those orders, what had been intended as a peaceful seizure became, indeed, a massacre of innocents, as well.

"This tribunal believes the reports forwarded to us by King Zhames were, indeed, written by the priests who died in Ferayd. We cannot, of course, know if these file copies are complete, or whether or not there might be some extenuating or exculpatory evidence which was also contained in the Inquisition's files and which was not transmitted to King Zhames by the Charisians. Despite that, the tribunal does not believe that any amount of extenuating or exculpatory evidence could excuse the actions of the Inquisitors of Ferayd.

"No servant of Mother Church can take any pleasure in rendering such a verdict, yet this tribunal has no choice. It is the tribunal's solemn duty to proclaim the truth, however painful, however much we might wish to avoid that duty, or that the truth were otherwise than it in fact is. The tribunal believes that Father Styvyn Graivyr and his fellow Inquisitors committed these . . . excesses—no, these *crimes*—not out of any personal animosity or any hope of personal gain. The tribunal believes that their wrongful acts sprang from their own deep and sincere concern over the seriousness and danger of the schism being forced upon Mother Church by the heretical leadership of the so-called 'Church of Charis.' In their zeal to obey their instructions from the Grand Inquisitor, they allowed themselves to succumb to the dark side of their own fallible, mortal natures. Men whom Shan-wei cannot corrupt into sin in their own interests may sometimes be drawn into sin even in the name of their most holy beliefs, and that, this tribunal believes, is what happened in this instance."

He paused once more, then visibly squared his shoulders and drew a deep breath.

"It is also this tribunal's conclusion that at least some of the responsibility for these actions resides not in the priests who actually committed them, but in the instructions those priests were given. The way in which those directives were phrased, the stern injunction to secure the Charisian galleons in Ferayd at all costs which those instructions contained, lent itself to the misinterpretation which Father Styvyn and his fellows placed upon them. There is no question that Father Styvyn and the other Inquisitors in Ferayd grossly exceeded the intent and the letter of those instructions, yet this tribunal has no choice but to observe that the Grand Inquisitor's own directive to Father Styvyn played a not insignificant part in Father Styvyn's later wrongful actions. Accordingly, we must assign at least a portion of the guilt for what the so-called 'Church of Charis' has termed the 'Ferayd Massacre' to the Grand Inquisitor himself."

If there'd been a whisper of consternation at the announcement of the *priests'* guilt, it was as nothing to the reaction provoked by Rayno's last sentence. There were gasps, hisses of surprise, even one or two half-voiced imprecations.

Rayno let them die most of the way away, then cleared his throat once again. The sound wasn't especially loud, but it produced instant silence, and he continued.

"The tribunal's conclusions concerning the actions of Father Styvyn and his fellow Inquisitors, and concerning the extent to which the Grand Inquisitor's instructions may have contributed to them, will be formally communicated both to the Grand Inquisitor's office and, at his own specific instruction, directly to the Chancellor and the Grand Vicar, as well.

"In addition to determining the facts about those actions, however, this tribunal was also charged with investigating the deaths of the Inquisitors in question. The Charisian admiral who destroyed Ferayd has confirmed, by his own words, that he personally ordered the executions, and, moreover, that he did so upon the express instructions of the excommunicate Cayleb and Sharleyan of Charis. The tribunal does not intend at this time to issue any formal conclusions about the devastation and civilian death and suffering visited upon the innocent citizens of Ferayd by that same admiral. Those matters lie beyond the scope of this tribunal's charter, and it is the tribunal's understanding that King Zhames is conducting his own inquiry, and will share its conclusions with Mother Church when it is completed.

"Nonetheless, this tribunal *is* charged with investigating and reporting upon the actual circumstances of the Ferayd Inquisitors' deaths. And it is the inescapable conclusion of the tribunal that, notwithstanding the guilt of the Inquisitors in question, their 'executions' constitute, in fact, acts of cold-blooded and most impious murder. The *Holy Writ* itself, in both *The Book of Langhorne* and *The Book of Schueler*, establishes for all time that Mother Church, and specifically the Office of Inquisition, is responsible for judging the actions of God's priests, for determining guilt or innocence when those priests stand accused of crimes, and for the execution of judgment upon them if they are found guilty. That solemn responsibility and duty resides solely in Mother Church and the Office of Inquisition. Any man who sheds the blood of a consecrated priest upon his own authority, or that of any mortal entity, stands guilty before Schueler, Langhorne, and God Himself, of murder. Not simply of murder, but of blasphemy. It is an act of defiance not of mortal, fallible humanity, but of God and His Holy Archangels. There can be no doubt, no question, of the blood guilt the so-called 'Church of Charis' must bear in the eyes of Mother Church, of all godly men, and of God Himself.'"

His voice was harsh as hammered iron, and he swept his cold, hard eyes across the chamber.

"It may be that Shan-wei tempted Father Styvyn and his fellows into sin by appealing to and twisting their determination to do God's will as they understood it upon the basis of their instructions from the Grand Inquisitor. No doubt their immortal souls will pay a heavy price because of their grievous failure, and no priest of Mother Church can condone their actions. Not when those actions led not simply to the deaths of self-professed heretics, but to the deaths of children who had no choice, no voice, in their parents' actions. The blood of such innocent victims must stain even the most devout of souls.

"But even though all of that be true, the men who slew those priests were guilty of an even darker and more heinous crime. They hanged Father Styvyn and his fellows—hanged consecrated priests of God—in the white-hot fury of revenge. In the passion of their own blasphemous bloodlust, they overstepped the bounds God Himself has set upon mortal men. There can be no pardon for actions such as that, and the day must surely come when they will answer both to Mother Church and the Inquisition and to God for their unforgivable sins."

. VII .

A Cotton Silk Plantation,
Barony of Dairwyn,
League of Corisande

So, they're finally on the move," Sir Koryn Gahrvai murmured.

He stood on the shady veranda of the cotton silk planter's house his staff had commandeered for his headquarters. The house—obviously that of a wealthy man—was finely furnished, if on the small side for the headquarters of an entire army. On the other hand, a back corner of his mind reflected, his "army" was on the small side for anything one of the great mainland realms like Harchong or Siddarmark would have used that particular noun to describe.

And at least Cayleb's army seems to be even smaller than mine is. *That's something, at any rate.*

"How reliable are these reports, Alyk?" he asked in a louder voice, looking up at the handsome, splendidly dressed man standing beside him.

Gahrvai had known Sir Alyk Ahrthyr, the Earl of Windshare, since boyhood. They'd been good friends for many years, and there was no one Gahrvai would rather have at his side in a fight. Unfortunately, for all of his pugnacity and undeniable courage, Windshare wasn't the most brilliant man Gahrvai had ever met. He took his responsibilities seriously, he had a seemingly boundless store of physical energy, and he was the most superb horseman Gahrvai had ever seen. Give him an enemy across an open field, a saber in his hand, and a troop of cavalry at his back and he was invincible. He was a little shakier where the reconnaissance and screening aspects of the cavalryman's profession were concerned, however, and his natural preference when faced by an enemy position was to attack first and figure out what the odds had been for his after-battle report. On the other hand, he'd taken enough hard knocks to be aware of his own weaknesses.

"I think they're very reliable," he said now. "My lead regiment's had them under observation since they left Dairos. We haven't been able to keep scouting parties operating along their flanks since they headed into the woods, but we're still falling slowly back in contact with their advance guard. From the route they've taken so far, they're definitely headed for Talbor Pass. And you were right, they don't seem to have much cavalry of their own." Windshare sniffed. "If it came down to a straight fight between my troopers and theirs, we'd be done before lunch."

"But it isn't going to do that, is it, Alyk?" Gahrvai asked, and Windshare shook his head gloomily.

"Probably not. Although," the earl brightened noticeably,

"if you and Charlz manage to break their formations, my lads and I will be delighted to finish them off for you."

Gahrvai smiled, but the smile faded into a frown as he considered one, in particular, of the dispatches Windshare's cavalry screen had sent back to him.

"What do *you* make of this, Charlz?" he asked the man lounging back in a commandeered chair on the other side of the improvised map table. Gahrvai tapped the offending dispatch with an index finger, and the other man shrugged.

"Pretty much what you do, I expect," Sir Charlz Doyal said.

He was several years older than Gahrvai or Windshare, and he owed his present position to the fact that he was one of Prince Hektor's favorites. On the other hand, he'd become one of the prince's favorites because of his penchant for accomplishing difficult tasks. The tall, rangy, dark-haired Doyal was more noted for indolence than physical hardihood, but he had all of the intellectual sharpness Windshare often seemed to lack. His role as Gahrvai's senior artillery officer suited him well, and between the two of them, he and Windshare normally formed a remarkably effective sounding board for Gahrvai's strategy sessions.

He was also, however, unfortunately fond of the occasional cryptic comment, and Gahrvai made a rude gesture in his direction.

"Perhaps you'd care to be a bit more specific?" he suggested.

"It's exactly what your father discussed with us," Doyal said with a shrug. "We went for the short-barreled guns; from what Alyk's scouts are telling us, the Charisians went for longer tubes. It doesn't sound like their field guns are built to exactly the same pattern as naval guns; the barrel length is too short for that, assuming the scouts' estimates are accurate. But they're longer than ours are, and that means they're going to outrange us, that's for sure. Whether that range advantage is going to make up for how much lighter their shot are going to be is more than I could tell you at this point, though. There's simply no way to know before we start actually shooting at one another, unfortunately."

"You're right; that is what I was thinking," Gahrvai admitted.

"Koryn, I know I always prefer going straight ahead and damn the consequences," Windshare said. "And I know that more than once I've managed to land myself up to my arse in slash lizards by doing just that. But I've got to say, they're coming to us on our terms. I think we've got to hit them, and hit them hard."

Gahrvai nodded. Windshare's awareness of his own weaknesses, as well as his strengths, was one of the better things about him. And he was right—his tendency to charge straight ahead *had* led him to the very brink of disaster more than once. Not just on fields of battle, either, and Gahrvai's lips tried to twitch into a smile despite the seriousness of the current moment as he recalled some of the dashing earl's other misadventures. Windshare's rakish good looks, added to his . . . impetuosity and taste for the ladies, had led to at least one duel (fortunately without any fatalities on either side) and generally kept him in constant hot water for as long as anyone could remember. Indeed, there'd been occasions in their shared youth when he'd very nearly taken Gahrvai into amorous disaster with him, as well.

But this time Alyk had a point, Gahrvai thought. The whole reason for advancing this far from the Dark Hills was to attack the Charisian invaders as quickly and as vigorously as he could and, if possible, drive them straight back into the sea.

Of course, another reason for attacking them is to find out just how badly we've underestimated whatever new capabilities they've developed for their Marines, as well as their navy, he reflected.

He looked back down at the map. He'd advanced with no more than a third of his total force, and he wondered again if he'd been wise to do so. The problem was that the roads through the Dark Hill Mountains weren't very good. That was especially true of the smaller, flanking roads, and while the royal highway itself wasn't *too* bad, there was a distinct limit to the number of troops which could be moved rapidly along it without using those flanking roads. Worse, that cramped cluster of roads was his only really reliable supply line, as well, now that Dairos was firmly in Charisian hands. He could probably have gotten a larger percentage of his forces forward, but only at the expense of making it extraordinarily difficult to keep them fed and supplied with ammunition and weapons once he had them deployed.

Not to mention just how ugly things could get if that many men suddenly found themselves trying to retreat simultaneously. He gave a mental shudder as he imagined the scenes of chaos, congestion, and panic which were all too likely to ensue under those circumstances. *But does worrying about what would happen if I have to retreat mean I'm going into battle already half-defeated in my own mind? Is thinking about it prudence or cowardice?*

It was amazing all the ways a man could find to doubt and second-guess himself. And whatever the limitations of the roadways in his own rear might be, the road over which the Charisians were currently advancing was even worse, in many ways. So if *they* were the ones who had to retreat . . .

"I think you're right, Alyk," he heard himself saying. "And if they're kind enough to keep coming to meet us, especially without an adequate cavalry screen of their own, then I think we should plan on greeting them right about here."

He tapped a symbol on the map, then bent closer to peer at the name.

"Haryl's Crossing," he read aloud.

"Ah?" Doyal climbed out of his chair and leaned forward, studying the map.

The town Gahrvai had selected wasn't very large. Its total population, including the outlying farm families, probably didn't exceed four thousand, and many of them had found urgent reasons to be elsewhere once armies began heading in their direction. It sat directly on the Talbor River, which flowed out of the mountain gap of the same name, where the royal highway crossed the stream on a stone bridge. The artillerist considered the terrain east of the river thoughtfully for several seconds, then nodded.

"It looks reasonable to me," he agreed. "This might be a bit of a problem if things don't go smoothly, though."

He indicated the single stone bridge.

"There's what looks like a fairly big wooden bridge down here, to the south, at Haryl's Priory," Gahrvai countered, waving his finger at another map symbol, this one representing a substantial monastery. It lay south of Haryl's Crossing and on the western side of the river, where the foothills of the Dark Hill Mountains began to rise. "There are fords north of the priory, as well, according to the map, at any rate."

"Let me see it," Windshare requested. He bent over the map, lips pursed, then looked back up at Gahrvai.

"I've got a report somewhere about this wooden bridge," he said. "It's not in very good shape, if I'm remembering correctly. We could probably get infantry across it, but only a lunatic would try to take cavalry or artillery across. On the other hand, I think my scouts also indicated that the river is pretty shallow along here, where the map shows your fords. I know we could get cavalry across even without the bridge, although I wouldn't want to make any promises about infantry without double-checking. And we definitely don't want to take any of Charlz' artillery across this thing."

"Do any of Sir Farahk's militiamen know the area well enough to provide us with more information?" Doyal asked.

"I can check," Windshare replied. "I wouldn't be a bit surprised if they do, though. They've been remarkably helpful so far."

The earl sounded almost bemused, as if he still found it peculiar that the Baron of Dairwyn's men had been so useful. Gahrvai wondered if part of that was because of how . . . unsoldier-like the baron's militia were. They were obviously civilians who intended to go back to being civilians as soon as they possibly could, and they didn't care who knew it. At least equally obviously, some of them, like the inhabitants of Haryl's Crossing, would have preferred to be somewhere else. *Anywhere* else, if it came to that. But they appeared to feel a degree of loyalty to their baron which was rarely seen, and their assistance not simply as guides, but as go-betweens for the army and the local farmers, as well, had been invaluable. No farmer ever really wanted to see an army—*any* army— marching through his district, and unhappy locals could create all sorts of problems if they put their minds to it. So far, at least, the ability of Dairwyn's men to put a friendly face on Gahrvai's army had kept that sort of thing from happening. Whether it would remain effective once the two sides came to grips and combat started turning fertile fields into wastelands was an entirely different question, of course.

And one to which the answer is almost certainly "no," Gahrvai thought sourly.

"I'm sure they'll have some useful additional information," he said aloud. "Please do check with them."

Windshare nodded, and Gahrvai returned his attention to the map.

"I take your point about the bridge, Charlz," he said reflectively, folding his arms while he contemplated the terrain once more. "And fighting with a river in your rear is usually considered a bad idea, even when you don't have to worry about getting artillery across a single bridge. Still, if we take up a position on *this* side of the river, then whoever's in command over there is going to stop on his side and send back for reinforcements. Which means we'd have to fight our way across the river to get at him."

"It also means he'd have to fight *his* way across to get at *us,*" Doyal pointed out. "And the longer he stays put out here, the longer your father and Prince Hektor have to get more troop strength transferred to us."

"Unless Cayleb decides to just sit here with a part of his army and demonstrate how determined he is to attack us while he's actually loading all the rest of his troops back aboard his transports to strike directly at Manchyr," Gahrvai replied. "And as for getting more troops to us, how are we going to feed and supply them all through Talbor Pass? That's over twenty-five miles of narrow road and bottlenecks, especially as you get towards the eastern end. We could feed our entire army through the *western* half, but I doubt we could support more than thirty thousand men on this side of the mountains. Not if they're going to have to sit in one place for very long, at any rate. We'd run out of forage pretty quickly, and somehow I don't think even Baron Dairwyn would be able to keep the local farmers friendly once we've eaten all their cattle, trampled all their crops, and emptied all their granaries."

"And seduced all their daughters," Windshare added with a grin. "Besides, we're supposed to do it my way—you know, charge straight in and smash everybody up instead of trying to get fancy."

"And hitting them on their side of the river will at least give us a chance of catching their advance guard and cutting it up in isolation," Gahrvai agreed with a nod. "If Alyk's scouts are right, they can't have more than a couple of thousand men—five thousand, at the outside. We've brought over *twenty* thousand with us."

"And how many of them are still *west* of the river at the moment?" Doyal countered.

"If everyone's where they're supposed to be—and you know as well as I do how likely it is that none of our movement orders managed to go astray for a change—we've got roughly fourteen thousand, including seven batteries of your field guns, either east of the river already or close enough to be there by nightfall. That ought to be enough to take care of five thousand Charisians, especially since they seem to have only three or four batteries with them."

"Unless they speed up a lot, most of their column won't be here until late tomorrow morning. Maybe not even until early afternoon," Doyal pointed out. "We could get almost everybody across by then, if we worked at it."

"No." Gahrvai shook his head. "There's no point wearing the men out—not to mention probably getting a lot of them lost—marching around after dark. Besides, fourteen thousand men and thirty-five guns ought to be enough to get the job done. Piling in still more men would only cramp our mobility. And if four- or five-to-one odds *aren't* enough to get the job done, I don't want to complicate things if we have to retreat."

Doyal and Windshare both looked at him as if they weren't

quite certain they'd heard him correctly, and he snorted sourly.

"Let's do this my way," he suggested. "We'll see what happens. If they bring up more strength of their own, then I'll think seriously about putting still more of our men across the river before we attack. But if they're as short on cavalry as they seem to be, then their scouting has to be spotty, at best. They probably don't have a clue how many men we've already managed to concentrate in front of them. If we can keep it that way, keep them confident enough that they don't stop their advance guard where it is until they can reinforce it, I think we can hit them tomorrow morning. With any luck at all, we'll roll right over them and smash them up quick and dirty.

"To be perfectly honest, that's what I expect to happen. But let's not forget that everybody 'expected' Duke Black Water to smash up Haarahld's navy, too. I don't see any way they could be hiding some sort of 'secret weapon' from Alyk's cavalry, but I'm not going to rush to any potentially unfortunate assumptions, either. This will let us test the water without getting in too deep. If we're right, we crush their advance guard, and Alyk's cavalry gets to spend the afternoon riding down and sabering fugitives. If it turns out that they do have some horrible surprise waiting for us, we lose at worst a fifth part of our total force."

Windshare looked moderately rebellious, but he nodded without further argument. Doyal cocked his head, contemplating the map once more, then shrugged.

"I think you're probably worrying more about surprises than you need to," he said. "On the other hand, given your reminder about what happened to Black Water, I can live with a little over-caution. Better that than the reverse, at least! And to be honest, I'd prefer to blood my gunners under the most benign conditions we can arrange. I think they're ready, but none of them have ever been under fire as a unit before."

"I think they'll do just fine, Charlz," Gahrvai said. "Believe me, my 'over-caution' doesn't have a thing to do with any concern over the quality of our troops. Especially of your gunners."

"I never thought it did," Doyal assured him. "That doesn't mean it isn't something else to bear in mind, though."

"I'd like to spend some time this afternoon actually looking at as much of the terrain as possible," Gahrvai continued, turning back to Windshare. "I'll need a cavalry escort. You wouldn't happen to know a good officer to put in command of it, would you, Alyk?"

"As a matter of fact, I would," Windshare told him with a grin, then glanced at Doyal. "Would you care to come along with us, Charlz?"

Windshare's tone was more than half-teasing, given Doyal's well-known aversion to any unnecessary physical activity. To his surprise, the older man promptly nodded.

"As a matter of fact, I'd like to check my impressions from the map against the actual terrain. There are a couple of places that look pretty close to ideal for artillery deployment. I'd prefer to make sure they really are good positions before I order my people into them, though."

"Excellent!" Gahrvai said approvingly. "Charlz, show Alyk the spots you particularly want to see. I've got to go draft a couple of dispatches for Father and the Prince before we go wandering off. Alyk, once you and Charlz have discussed where we need to go and what we need to see, make sure we really do have an adequate escort. I'm not feeling especially vain this afternoon, but it occurs to me that if the army loses its senior field commander, his cavalry commander, and the closest thing we have to a genuine expert on field artillery, it wouldn't be the very best possible beginning to our campaign, would it?"

"If we let *that* happen," Doyal said with a smile, "the only good thing I could see about it would be that all three of us would be safely dead, which would at least spare us from your father's analysis of all the truly stupid things we must have done to bring it about."

"And what exactly in my record to date convinces you that I'm not fully capable of doing truly stupid things if I put my mind to it?" Gahrvai inquired.

Emperor Cayleb's Headquarters,
City of Dairos,
Barony of Dairwyn,
League of Corisande

I wish we were up against the Temple Guard," Cayleb Ahrmahk grumbled as he stood looking down at a map of Corisande.

"Dare I ask *why* you'd prefer that?" Merlin inquired.

"Because Allayn Maigwair is an idiot, and Koryn Gahrvai isn't," Cayleb replied succinctly, in something very like a growl.

"No, he isn't," Merlin agreed, stepping closer to the map table.

He and Cayleb were alone, for the moment, in the library of the Baron of Dairwyn's townhouse. It was a palatial temporary home for Cayleb's headquarters, although their reluctant host had managed to take at least some of his most valuable knickknacks with him. Cayleb didn't really begrudge Sir Farahk his personal treasures, however. After all, the emperor had the baron's entire city, in exchange.

Baron Dairwyn had been unable to deny any of the points Cayleb had made in his final note to him. And, to give him his due, his concern over what might happen to the citizens of his barony's capital if it had come down to fighting in the streets had played a major role in his decision to surrender Dairos to Cayleb. He, himself, however, hadn't been included in the package. He'd delegated authority to the city's mayor to treat with Cayleb, while he and his personal armsmen had hastily mounted and galloped off towards the Dark Hill Mountains, evading Clareyk and Haimyn's Marines en route.

Most of Cayleb's men, and at least some of his officers, had taunted Dairwyn in absentia for his "cowardice." Cayleb didn't agree. Dairos might have fallen, but the baron was responsible for defending the *rest* of his barony. Besides, he'd clearly recognized how valuable his firsthand report would be to Prince Hektor. Or, at least, to Sir Koryn Gahrvai. At this particular moment, the baron had joined Gahrvai, and his armsmen and the subjects of his barony who'd been pressed into service as militia were busy serving as Gahrvai's local guides. Which, Cayleb admitted, was probably the most useful thing they could possibly have been doing for the other side.

Over the last six days, the majority of Cayleb's Marines had been landed. Dairos couldn't possibly have absorbed fifty thousand men, even if the citizenry had been happy to see them. Aside from a strictly limited garrison, whose primary responsibility was keeping the peace, the Charisian troops had poured through the city like water through a net and settled into vast, neat encampments outside the city limits. So far, they'd behaved themselves extraordinarily well, too. Part of that was undoubtedly due to the fact that they hadn't yet had to do any real fighting, which meant they had no casualties to "avenge" upon the local citizenry. Another part of it was the eagle eye the chaplains were keeping on them, and their officers' stern injunctions about the importance of not providing the Group of Four's propaganda mills with the free gift of any atrocity fodder.

And, of course, there were the bloodthirsty field regulations Emperor Cayleb, Admiral Lock Island, and General Chermyn had composed. Every man in the invasion army had heard those regulations read out in formation at least once per fiveday. And none of them doubted for a moment that Cayleb and his commanders would enforce every stringent penalty upon any violators.

The invasion's supplies, unlike its troops, were still coming ashore in a steady stream. Dairos had many things to recommend it, including some fairly spectacular beaches, if anyone had had time to consider going for a dip, but no one would ever confuse its waterfront with Tellesberg's. Wharf space was limited, its warehouses were far smaller and sparser, and aside from one or two main thoroughfares, the city's streets were much narrower and more constricted. All of that conspired to turn Dairos into a logistical bottleneck.

Cayleb and his planners had realized that was going to happen, and they'd allowed for it in their original timetable. His engineers were busy building new wharves and extending existing ones, and some public buildings and houses were being demolished to widen roads and improve traffic conditions. The astonishment of the homeowners when Cayleb insisted on actually *paying* them for their houses had been palpable, but that hadn't stopped them from accepting the compensation with alacrity. Or from complaining loudly to their neighbors about how coin-pinching the payments had been.

In the meantime, the invasion force's horses and draft dragons required enough time to regain their land legs before moving into the field, anyway, so Cayleb and his advisers had always planned on spending at least the first couple of five-days consolidating their hold on Dairos while their animals recovered and their supplies came ashore. They hadn't quite made sufficient allowance for the limited warehouse space in the city itself, and more of their supplies than anyone liked were being stacked up under canvas, instead of a solid roof, which wasn't exactly a pleasant thought with the storm season coming on. But at least they'd been able to send almost half their troopships back to Port Royal under escort by a third of the Chisholmian galleys. That had relieved much of the port's congestion, and the shore patrol Chermyn had organized and rigorously trained as military police had kept things moving smoothly and relatively peacefully as their forces ashore built up.

On the other side of the coin, Gahrvai had already concentrated the majority of his eighty thousand–man force in the vicinity of Talbor Pass before coming farther east with his own advance guard. Another twenty-five thousand men were on their way to join him, and should be arriving within the next five-day or so. When they did, he would outnumber Cayleb's entire invasion army by better than two-to-one, and Hektor had at least another thirty thousand men within a hundred miles or so of Gahrvai's main position. Those numbers didn't make for pleasant contemplation.

"I don't like how carefully Gahrvai is thinking these things through," Cayleb said more seriously, clasping his hands behind him and rocking gently up and down on the balls of his feet. "I'd be ever so much happier if someone like Windshare were in command over there!"

"It *would* be nice," Merlin agreed almost wistfully.

In fact, he had an even better feel for Sir Koryn Gahrvai's irritating competence than the emperor did, since it was Merlin's SNARCs which had been keeping an eye on Hektor's field commander for the past several months. He'd been focusing even more closely on that for the last five-days, although his ability to monitor all of the sensors he had deployed here in Corisande (and elsewhere), even with Owl's assistance, was being stretched to (and beyond) its limits. The fact that his hacked PICA's software had disabled his high-speed data interface was becoming an increasingly significant handicap. He couldn't really complain too much, given the fact that if Dr. Elias Proctor *hadn't* hacked the software, it would have automatically shut Merlin down and dumped his entire memory after ten days of autonomous operation, but that didn't prevent it from causing significant problems. He had to review the data at little more than "human speed," and even the fact that he could go so long without "sleep" couldn't put enough hours into even one of Safehold's lengthy days to examine all of the reports and recordings he ought to be examining.

"You're sure he's going to come across that river and hit Clareyk and Haimyn?" Cayleb asked.

"As sure as I can be, before he actually does it. He's already started moving the bulk of his planned striking force across it, after all."

"Damn." Cayleb said the word remarkably mildly, given his expression, and his eyes flashed. "Why the hell couldn't he have just sat on the defensive and concentrated on digging in?"

"Because he *is* competent."

"What I'd like to do is pull Clareyk and Haimyn back," Cayleb said. "I know they've spent months training for

exactly this, but they've got barely four thousand men between them, and odds of three- or four-to-one don't strike me
as the best ratio for their first serious battle."

"And how would you justify pulling them back?" Merlin
asked. Cayleb turned his head to shoot him a sharp glance,
and the man who'd once been Nimue Alban shrugged. "It's
one thing when you're there yourself, Cayleb. When you can
use your 'seaman's instinct' to explain why you're 'playing a
hunch' with the fleet. But all of Chermyn's reconnaissance reports continue to indicate that there are only a few thousand of
Hektor's troops on this side of the Dark Hills. You and I know
those reports are wrong—or, at least, not complete. But we
can't tell anyone that without their wondering just how it is
that we do know. And Clareyk and Haimyn are doing precisely what all of your plans and discussions called for them
to do until we encounter Hektor's troops in strength."

"I could still order them to stand fast until we get more
troops up with them," Cayleb argued.

"Yes, you could. But look at the terrain where they are
right now. It's all second-growth forest, wire vine, brambles,
and woodlots. Our people's main advantage is going to be the
ranges at which they can engage, and that kind of ground cuts
visibility to as little as ten or fifteen yards—even less than
that, in places."

Merlin considered mentioning an Old Earth general
named Grant and a place called The Wilderness, but decided
against introducing the distraction.

"At that range, a smoothbore's just as effective as a rifle,"
he continued, "and a third of the musketeers on the other side
have been equipped with flintlocks of their own. Those musketeers are going to be able to fire almost as rapidly as ours
can, and given the absolute numbers on each side, those pro-
portions mean Gahrvai's got as many flintlock muskets as we
do, with twice that many matchlocks to support them. If we
want to maximize our advantages, give our people the best
chance for victory, then we need more open terrain. Which, as
it happens, is exactly what Gahrvai is looking for, as well.
Without knowing all our musketeers are actually *riflemen*,

he's deliberately seeking a battlefield which will give him clear enough lines of fire for him to use his advantage in artillery most effectively."

"Which will just happen to do the same thing for our rifles," Cayleb agreed. "I know that. It's just the numbers on each side, Merlin. If I could at least warn them, tell them what's coming, how many men Gahrvai has on the other side of the hill . . ."

"Cayleb," Merlin said quietly, his sapphire eyes soft with sympathy, "once upon a time, back on Old Earth, there was a statesman named Winston Churchill. He was the leader of a nation very much like yours, in a lot of ways, actually. An island nation, which had relied upon its own navy and naval tradition to protect its freedom for hundreds of years. But when Churchill became prime minister, that nation—Great Britain—was fighting for its life against something that was just as evil as, and even more vicious than, the Church of God Awaiting is today here on Safehold."

The emperor had stopped rocking up and down. He stood very still now, listening intently as the voice of the PICA named Merlin gave life once more to a past so dusty no living man on Safehold had ever even heard of it.

"Great Britain was at least as alone as Charis ever was, but, like you, the British had certain advantages. One was that they were intercepting their enemy's communications. Those messages were being transmitted in a very advanced and complicated code, one which their enemies—the Nazis—believed was unbreakable. But the British *had* broken the code. As a result, they knew a great deal about what the Nazis were going to do before it ever happened. And one of the things they discovered was that one of their cities, the city of Coventry, was going to be heavily attacked by bombers."

" 'Bombers'?" Cayleb repeated, tasting the peculiar word on his tongue.

"Machines that flew through the air at a couple of hundred miles an hour loaded with bombs, like very big, very powerful versions of the 'shells' Seamount is experimenting with. They were dropped from high up in the air, and they weren't

202 / DAVID WEBER

very accurate at the time I'm talking about. The Nazis couldn't hope to hit specific targets or military installations, but they were going to send over hundreds of bombers. What they planned was a deliberate attack on a civilian target—it was called 'terror bombing'—and all of the prewar projections had indicated that an attack like the one they were planning would kill thousands and thousands of people, most of them civilians."

It was very quiet in Baron Dairwyn's library.

"The bombers were going to be attacking at night, under cover of darkness, to prevent the defending aircraft from spotting them and shooting them down short of their target. Navigating would be a problem, but they'd come up with a way to solve it for this particular attack. So there wasn't anything the British could do to stop it. It was *going* to happen.

"Under those circumstances, the question became whether or not the citizens of Coventry should be warned. Should Churchill order the evacuation of the city? Or should he simply see to it that the city authorities knew at least a few hours before the attack that it was coming so they could get their people—those *civilians,* including women and children—into the strongest, best protected bomb shelters they had?"

"What did he do?" Cayleb asked when Merlin paused.

"He didn't tell them at all," Merlin said softly. Cayleb's eyes widened, and Merlin shook his head. "He couldn't tell them. If he'd warned them, if he'd tried to evacuate the city or to bolster its defenses before the attack, people would have wondered how he'd known. Questions would have been asked, and there were some very bright people working for the Nazis, as well as for the British. Rather as we're discovering is the case with Gahrvai, working for Hektor. If the Nazis had realized Churchill must have known in advance, they might have begun to wonder about the security of their codes. Were they as impossible to intercept and break as they'd thought they were?

"It was always possible, perhaps even probable, that they'd decide the British had figured it out some other way, through some sort of spy, perhaps. But they might not have. They might have wondered. And all they would have needed to do to nullify the intelligence advantage which had become one of Britain's most vital weapons would have been to change their cipher system 'just in case.' Churchill decided he couldn't take that chance, and so he said nothing to Coventry, and the bombers flew over it, and they did enormous damage. Not as bad as the prewar pundits had predicted, but terrible enough."

"And you're saying that if I warn Clareyk about what's coming, people may begin to wonder how I knew?"

"I'm saying that if you warn your field commanders too often, people *will* begin to wonder." Merlin shook his head. "There's not a lot any of your enemies could do to prevent my SNARCs from spying on them even if they knew all about them. In that respect, your situation is very different from Churchill's. But if the fact that I have 'visions' which guide your decisions gets out, you know what the Group of Four is going to say. You don't need—you can't *afford*—to give them a pretext for charging you with trafficking with demons. It's entirely possible charges of that sort are going to be levied against you before this is all over, anyway. But if they charge that *I'm* a demon, it will create all manner of problems. Not least because we can't possibly prove I'm not. For that matter, according to the doctrine of the Church of God Awaiting, I *am* one."

Cayleb looked at him in silence for several seconds, then drew a deep breath.

"All right," he said. "You're right. For that matter, I already knew everything you've just said. Not the part about 'Churchill' or 'bombers,' but the rest of it. It's just so *hard,* Merlin. I know men are going to be killed no matter what I do or how well I do it. However much I may not like that, I haven't had any choice but to accept it. But if I can keep *any* of them from being killed or maimed, I *need* to do it."

"In the long term, that's exactly what you *are* doing, Cayleb. It's just that you're going to have to be very careful, very selective, about when and *how* you do it. And what you can do with it in a strategic sense, when it comes to planning and projecting operations, or what you can do by feeding 'classified intelligence sources' to someone like Nahrmahn and letting him make the recommendations *I* can't make openly, is one thing.

Using that same information for something like this is something else entirely."

Cayleb nodded unhappily. Then he looked back down at the table, eyes distant while he obviously imagined the men represented by the tokens on the map. He stayed that way for several seconds, then straightened his shoulders and looked back up at Merlin.

"What about this?" he asked. "Suppose I send a message forward to Clareyk, who's already worked with you and me both and probably knows a lot more about your 'visions' than he's ever let on? I won't tell him what Gahrvai and his commanders are discussing, or what they had for dinner. I'll just tell him I have a 'feeling' our reconnaissance reports have been less than complete. That shouldn't be particularly surprising, when we've got so little cavalry and everyone knows the horses we do have are still trying to regain their land legs. I won't pull him back, since there's no concrete evidence to support my 'feeling.' Instead, I'll simply instruct him to be particularly alert in the next couple of days and to operate on the assumption that the enemy may be much closer to him, and in considerably more strength, than our scouts' reports so far have indicated."

Merlin considered it for a moment, then nodded.

"I think that's unlikely to create any problems," he said. "Especially not if you don't include any specific numbers. 'In considerably more strength' is a good, cautionary phrase which shouldn't suggest any definite knowledge we shouldn't have. And I don't suppose it will hurt a bit for the troops to decide that that 'seaman's instinct' of yours translates into land battles, as well."

"I'd still prefer to pull them back," Cayleb said, looking back at the map. "Even if Clareyk and Haimyn take any warnings from me fully to heart, it won't change the numbers against them. And even if you see Gahrvai doing something else—throwing out a cavalry force to cut their line of retreat, for example—there won't be anything we can do about it. We probably couldn't get word to them quickly enough for it to do any good even if we didn't have to worry about people's wondering how we'd 'guessed' what was coming."

"That's going to become something we have to live with more and more often, I'm afraid," Merlin said. "And to be perfectly honest, the times when we *can* use my 'visions' are only going to make the times when we *can't* use them hurt even more. But like everything else, there are limits to this, as well. We're simply going to have to accept them."

"I know." Cayleb smiled crookedly. "I suppose it's just human nature to always want more. You're already the greatest unfair advantage any commander's ever had. I suppose it's churlish of me to want an even bigger unfair advantage, but there it is. I guess I'm just naturally greedy."

"There was a saying back on Old Earth," Merlin told him. "I don't approve of it for many things in life, but I think it's applicable to military operations."

"What sort of saying?"

"'If you're not cheating, you aren't trying hard enough,'" Merlin said. Cayleb's mouth twitched and the somberness in his eyes was lightened by a flicker of amusement, and Merlin shook his head. "Your father understood that the object in a war wasn't to see who could 'fight fairest.' Mind you, he was one of the most honorable men I ever knew, but he recognized that a commander's greatest responsibility is to his own troops. To keep as many of them alive as possible, and to do his very best to ensure that those who die anyway die for a *purpose*. That their deaths aren't wasted. And that means not asking them to take stupid chances in the name of 'honor.' It means figuring out the best way you can shoot their enemies in the back. It means taking every advantage you can find, buy, steal, or invent and using it to keep your people alive and, as another person from Churchill's war put it, make the other poor dumb son-of-a-bitch die for *his* country."

"That isn't a very chivalrous concept of war," Cayleb observed.

"I'm not a very chivalrous sort, in that respect, at least,"

Merlin replied. "And neither is any king—or emperor—worthy of his people's loyalty."

"Then I suppose it's a good thing I'm a naturally sneaky sort of fellow. I mean, I'd hate to disappoint you or make you go looking for someone else who's sufficiently underhanded, devious, cunning, and unscrupulous to suit your nefarious purposes."

"Oh, I wouldn't worry about that," Merlin said with a broad smile. "Given your little explanation about what you have in store for Grand Duke Zebediah, I really don't think I *could* find anyone who was more underhanded, devious, cunning, and unscrupulous than you are."

"Gosh, thanks." Cayleb grinned, then gave himself a shake. "And now that we've got that settled, let's get a signalman in here to get my 'I've got a bad feeling' message off to Clareyk."

. IX .

Near Haryl's Crossing,
Barony of Dairwyn,
League of Corisande

Brigadier Kynt Clareyk contemplated the dispatch in his hand, then looked down at the map spread out before him. Despite the Archangel Hastings' world-spanning atlas, the map in front of Clareyk was far less detailed than he could have preferred. Mostly that was simply a matter of the scale at which he was operating, but the fact that the Archangel's original maps were eight hundred years out of date, and that mere mortals had been responsible for updating them in the meantime, didn't help. In fact, it didn't help a bit.

His own limited handful of cavalry, his scout-sniper teams, and his attached engineering section had added a good bit of cartographic detail, but, unfortunately, mostly it was detail about places they'd already been.

"What do you make of it, Kynt?" Mahrys Haimyn asked quietly.

"'Make of it'?" Clareyk repeated, glancing up at his fellow brigadier. Haimyn looked at him for a moment, then smiled slightly.

"Don't give me that innocent look," he said. "You and I both know you spent the better part of a year working directly with His Majesty and *Seijin* Merlin. Did you really think I wouldn't figure out that His Majesty's little note says more to you than just the words he actually wrote down?"

"I don't have any idea what you're talking about." Clareyk's innocent tone wasn't very convincing. Then again, he hadn't intended for it to be.

"Of course not. Now, to repeat my earlier question. What do you make of it?"

"I think," Clareyk said, speaking slowly, his expression far more serious than it had been, "that we're about to walk into a shit storm."

"That's funny. That's what I thought it might mean, too."

"Yes. Well, somehow I doubt the Emperor would have sent us a personal message like this one if he wasn't pretty sure his 'hunch' was accurate."

"You mean *Seijin* Merlin's hunch, don't you?" Haimyn asked quietly.

The look Clareyk gave him this time was far sharper, and the other brigadier snorted.

"Forget I asked that." Haimyn shook his head. "It's not really any of my business, I suppose. But, just between the two of us, you might want to mention to the Emperor that I'm not the only one who's noticed how many new things started happening right about the time the *seijin* turned up in Charis."

"Oh?"

"*I'm* not complaining!" Haimyn assured him. "In fact, I think it was a damned good thing he did turn up. I just thought you might want to let His Majesty know."

"Contrary to what you may believe, Mahrys," Clareyk said

mildly, "I really don't spend all of my free time hobnobbing with the Emperor. Or with *Seijin* Merlin, for that matter."

"Of course not," Haimyn agreed politely. Then he twitched his head at the dispatch still in Clareyk's hand. "And in the meantime?"

"In the meantime, we figure out what we plan on doing if we should happen to run into any unfriendly souls."

"That suits me right down to the ground. And, to be honest, I'd really like to find better ground than this." Haimyn waved his hand at the tangled trees and dense underbrush which surrounded them. "I know this is good defensive terrain, but from a rifleman's perspective, it sucks."

Clareyk chuckled sourly at the junior brigadier's succinct description. Which, he conceded, summed up his own opinion quite handily.

At the moment, they stood in a clearing which was little more than a wide spot in what passed for the royal "highway" between Dairos and Manchyr. To be fair, it was probably entirely adequate for the traffic which normally passed along it, but that traffic didn't include armies. Fatigue parties were busy widening the roadway by cutting back the encroaching tree cover and undergrowth and filling in the worst ravines and gullies, but they were far behind Clareyk's and Haimyn's brigades. Fortunately, the two brigadiers had barely four thousand men between them, so the less than marvelous state of the road was nowhere near as big a problem for them as it might have been for General Chermyn's main body. *Un*fortunately, they had barely four thousand men between them, so if they ran into sizable numbers of Corisandians, they might just find themselves short on firepower.

And if we wind up having to retreat under fire, the fact that we only have one main road is not *going to be a good thing*, he reflected.

"All right," he said finally. "According to this," he tapped the map, "there's a large village or a small town another few hours' march up the road. It looks like there's a good-sized monastery or priory of some sort southwest of the town, too.

I'd think that if people actually live out here, they must have cleared farmland, wouldn't you?"

"Probably." Haimyn looked down at the map himself. "I wish we had better information on the contours," he continued, running his finger across the map sheet. "It *looks* like the ground's probably higher on the far side of this river." He grimaced. "I suppose that makes sense, since we're marching towards the mountains. If I were in command on the other side, and if I were looking for a defensive position, that would appeal to me."

"Agreed. But if you were in command on the other side and if you figured you had a sizable numerical advantage, would you be looking for a *defensive* position at all?"

"Assuming all I had were smoothbores against rifles, damn straight I would," Haimyn said.

"But according to all of our intelligence estimates," Clareyk's eyes rose to meet Haimyn's for a moment, and he twitched the dispatch he still held very slightly, "this Gahrvai doesn't know anything about our rifles."

"True." Haimyn rubbed his chin. "If it should happen those estimates are actually accurate, then you're probably right. Gahrvai *ought* to be thinking about jumping on us and smashing us up."

"Exactly. And in addition to that, I'm sure he'd prefer to keep us from getting a foothold on the far side of the river, especially if you're right—and I think you probably are—about the rising ground over there."

"You think he'll come across the river? Fight with it in his rear?"

"I do." Clareyk nodded sharply. "We don't know enough about bridges, or whether there might be practical fords, to really be able to estimate how serious an obstacle it may be. And I'll almost guarantee you he has a lot better information on where *we* are, and in what strength, than we have about him. It's for damned sure he's got a lot more cavalry swanning around out there to *tell* him about us, at any rate, and I'm going to assume he's smart enough to know what to do with it."

"Suits me," Haimyn agreed.

"Well, in that case, he's probably got a pretty fair notion of how many men we've got. If I were him, I'd be thinking in terms of putting enough of my men on *this* side of the river to eat a force our size for breakfast. I don't think I'd put any more of my total manpower over here than I figured I'd need for the job, though. That way, if it turned out I was wrong and I had to retreat, I wouldn't be stacked ten deep trying to get across the bridges. And I'd have the bulk of my troops available on the far side of the river to hold the high ground and cover the advanced force if it *did* have to retreat."

"Makes sense," Haimyn said after considering it briefly.

"Well, assuming this little exercise in mind-reading has any merit, I think it's also safe to assume he wouldn't want to give us the gift of any better defensible terrain than he has to when he attacks us. If I were him, and if I was feeling really clever, I'd figure on fighting somewhere in here." Clareyk's finger traced a rough oval around the town and the monastery. "He'll want open ground so he can close with us as quickly as possible, especially if he's thinking about plowing us into the ground with pikes or cavalry. And he'll want us as far forward out of these miserable woods as he can get us, so that when we break, we'll be jammed up against the trees trying to funnel down the road."

Haimyn nodded again, and Clareyk smiled thinly.

"The one good thing about this miserable patch of trees and briars is that if there's only one road through it, at least it's not easy to get lost."

"Meaning?"

"Meaning we can continue marching after dark without losing entire companies down side roads. There *aren't* any side 'roads.' The most there are is paths and foot trails no one is going to confuse with the main right-of-way."

"We've got another two or three hours of daylight, too," Haimyn observed.

"Yes, we do." Clareyk looked over his shoulder at a grizzled-looking man in the uniform of a sergeant major. "Mahk?"

"Yes, Sir?" Brigade Sergeant Major Mahkynty Dragonmaster replied.

"Find me a runner. Then figure out exactly where Colonel Zhanstyn is so we know where to send him."

Zhoel Zhanstyn was the commander of the ⅓rd Battalion—First Battalion of the Third Brigade. He was also a cool and levelheaded man, which qualities had made him Clareyk's choice to lead the advance.

"Aye, Sir!" Dragonmaster's broad shoulders straightened as he came to an abbreviated position of attention. Then he turned away from the two brigadiers with a purposeful air.

"I'm going to send Zhanstyn on ahead," Clareyk continued, turning back to Haimyn. "If he pushes, he should be able to get to more open ground near the town before sunset, and if we're reading Gahrvai's intentions the right way, he's going to be patient. He won't jump Zhanstyn the instant the First clears the woods, because he'll want more of us in his trap. He might have some pickets out to skirmish with us, convince us to stop for the night, or at least advance more slowly, but he might not even do that. More likely, he'll settle for posting a few scouts well in advance of his own positions just to warn him if we keep coming. Then he'll wait for us to stick our heads firmly into the noose before he yanks it tight."

"Very devious of him," Haimyn said dryly.

"I'd rather assume he's more devious than he is than make the mistake of assuming he's *less* devious than he turns out to be."

"Oh, I'm not complaining," Haimyn assured him.

"Good. What I want Zhanstyn to do is to move as quickly as he can to the edge of the more open ground we think is up there. But then I want him to advance just a little way more and start settling in for the night. Once it's *dark*, though, he'll put his men back into motion and—"

▼ ▼ ▼

"So they're taking it a little easy, are they?" Koryn Gahrvai murmured to himself.

The sun had set an hour and a half before, and insects buzzed and zinged around the lanterns illuminating his veranda command post. His thigh muscles ached just a bit from the time he, Windshare, and Doyal had spent in the saddle, but the personal reconnaissance had been worth it. He had the terrain around Haryl's Priory and the town of Haryl's Crossing firmly in his mind now. He'd found himself wondering exactly who the "Haryl" who'd strewn his name around this locale so generously had been, but that idle curiosity had taken fourth or fifth place on his "Things to Wonder About" list.

Now he sat in a comfortable, cushioned wicker chair gnawing on a fried chicken breast and trying not to get greasy fingerprints on his map while he worked his way through the latest dispatches from Windshare's mounted pickets.

Alyk's done himself proud, Gahrvai reflected. *He may not be the very brightest star in the heavens, but Langhorne knows he works* hard *with the wit God gave him.*

He reached the final message, read it as carefully as he had the first, then handed his plate to one of his staffers and frowned thoughtfully.

I'd be happier if they'd moved further forward, he admitted to himself. *If the cavalry reports are accurate, that's no more than a third, maybe even a quarter, of their total strength. And given the crappy nature of the terrain they've been advancing through, we could be underestimating their strength significantly.*

His frown deepened as he acknowledged that possibility. On the other hand, if the Charisians were present in greater numbers, then they were going to be even more jammed up than he'd hoped for on the section of highway through the tangled wilderness in front of his chosen battlefield.

Should I move further forward?

He closed his eyes, considering the ground he'd ridden over. It was tempting, in many ways. In fact, if his objective had been simply to *stop* the Charisians, that was exactly what he would have done. But he didn't want to stop them; he wanted to *smash* them, and for that he needed them out in the open where he could get at them.

Besides, like I told Charlz earlier, if I try moving units around in the dark, they're only going to get lost. Or, worse, someone's going to blunder into the enemy and tell them we're here. Of course, unless they're imbeciles, they must realize we're out here somewhere. *That doesn't make it a good idea to confirm* our positions *for them, though.*

He pondered his mental map for several more seconds, then opened his eyes once more and beckoned to his clerk.

"Yes, Sir?"

"Message for Earl Windshare."

"Yes, Sir."

The clerk readied his notepad, and Gahrvai tipped back in his chair.

"My Lord Earl," he began. "From your scouts' latest reports, the enemy seems to be planning to hold his present position until morning, before resuming his advance. I anticipate that he will continue towards Haryl's Crossing tomorrow, with the intention of securing the bridge there. He may also intend to direct a smaller column on the Priory in order to secure the wooden bridge, assuming he knows—or learns—of its existence.

"In either case, I believe we may assume he will continue advancing along the highway at or shortly after dawn. From his present position, he will be required to advance approximately six miles before he encounters our forward positions. If our estimate of his total troop strength is accurate, that advance should take long enough for his entire strength to clear the undergrowth behind him and emerge into the more open ground between the woods and the town.

"If that should prove to be the case, it is my intention to cut off and destroy his entire force. To that end, you are directed to prepare a force of cavalry adequate to advance into his rear and cut the highway behind him after he clears the woods. However, I do not desire for you to engage his infantry unless he attempts to force his way past you in order to escape my own forces.

"Given the importance of keeping him in ignorance of our own positions, intentions, and strength, I do not wish you to move until after daylight. You are to keep the highway under observation, if at all possible, and to advance into his rear only after he has fully emerged from the woods, unless otherwise directed by myself. To this end, I wish for such force as you deem adequate to the purposes of this instruction to be prepared for movement one hour before dawn, but to remain in position until the conditions stipulated in the above paragraphs have been met."

He paused, considering whether or not to add anything else, then shrugged mentally.

"Read that back," he directed, and listened carefully as the clerk complied. Then he nodded. "Very good. Write up a fair copy for my signature. I want it delivered within the hour, if at all possible. And I want a receipt from the Earl's staff to confirm its delivery."

▼   ▼   ▼

"We seen a few cavalry kind of driftin' around out there, Sir," the sergeant told Colonel Zhoel Zhanstyn. He spoke softly, as if he were afraid the enemy might overhear him, which made his Lochair dialect even more difficult for Zhanstyn's Tellesberg-born ears. The precaution was probably unnecessary, too, but that wasn't something Zhanstyn was going to criticize, under the circumstances.

"Do you think they know you saw them?" he asked.

"Hard t' say, Sir, t' be honest," the sergeant admitted. "We kept t' cover much as we could, just like you said. And I didn't pick no city boys, begging your pardon. We weren't making much noise, and a man on a horse's easier t' see nor a man on foot, but it could be they saw us. And if they were smart and put somebody out on foot in front of them so's we'd see the mounted ones and not notice t' others, I couldn't swear we'd've spotted 'em at it, and that's a fact, Colonel."

"Understood, Sergeant." Zhanstyn nodded. However rustic the noncom might have sounded, there was nothing at all wrong with his brain, and Zhanstyn made a mental note to commend him in his own report. The explosively expanding Charisian Marines desperately needed competent officers, and the sergeant might just make one of them. On the other hand, they needed experienced, capable, and *smart* sergeants just as badly, as any officer worth his salt was well aware. And the "scout-sniper" units Brigadier Clareyk had organized needed them worse than most.

"You did well, Sergeant Wystahn," he said now. "Very well. Thank you."

"Yes, Sir. Thank you, Sir."

Zhanstyn couldn't see Wystahn very clearly in the darkness, but he could hear the sergeant's smile of pleasure at the well-deserved words of praise. The colonel did a little smiling of his own, then frowned as he considered Wystahn's report.

It fitted well with all of the other reports he'd so far received. The Corisandians had cavalry pickets scattered across an arc that extended about three thousand to thirty-five hundred yards from where the highway cleared the woods with the concave side towards Zhanstyn's battalion. That gave him some room for maneuver, but not enough to carry out his orders.

He pondered it for several more minutes, then shrugged. He could have sent a messenger back to the Brigadier with a dispatch summarizing the situation and asking for fresh instructions. But the Marine tradition had always been that once a superior officer's intentions were understood, it was up to a junior officer to show a certain degree of initiative in accomplishing those intentions. He knew what Brigadier Clareyk wanted to happen; it was just a matter of seeing to it that it did.

And there's a way, he mused, his thoughtful frown turning into a cold, thin smile. *I'm afraid Sergeant Wystahn isn't going to get much rest this evening.*

▼   ▼   ▼

"What was that?"

"What was *what*?" the corporal in charge of the three-man cavalry picket demanded irritably.

"I heard something," the private who'd spoken up said.

"Like what?"

The corporal, the private noted, wasn't getting any less irritable.

"I don't know what," the trooper said a bit defensively. "A sound. A branch breaking, maybe."

The corporal rolled his eyes. Given the stiff breeze sighing through the tall wheat around them, the chance that the other man could actually have heard something was remote, to say the least. He started to rip a strip off of the unfortunate private's backside, then stopped himself. The man might be an idiot, but better an idiot who reported an imaginary sound he *thought* he'd heard than the sort of idiot who wouldn't report something he really *did* hear for fear of being reamed out.

"Look," he began as patiently as he could, "it's dark, we're all tired, we know the bastards are out there," he waved one arm in an arc to the south, "and we're all listening as hard as we can. But there's enough wind stirring this crap around to make a man think he's hearing just about anything. So—"

The patient corporal never completed his final sentence. The hand which snaked around him from behind, cupped his chin, and yanked his head back for the knife in the *other* hand saw to that.

The picket leader's blood fountained from his slashed throat, spraying over the nearer of the other two troopers. That unfortunate soul jumped back, mouth opening to shout something, but his instinctive recoil from the dying corporal took him directly into the arms of a second Charisian Marine, and a second combat knife went home with a gurgle.

The alert trooper who'd thought he'd heard something was a quick-witted fellow. He didn't waste time trying to get to his horse; he simply turned and bolted into the darkness. That took him directly away from the two Marines who'd been detailed to cover the horses. Unhappily for him, it took him directly into the path of Sergeant Edvarhd Wystahn. Still, he made out better than his fellows, although he might be forgiven for not realizing that immediately as Wystahn's rifle butt slammed into the pit of his belly. The cavalryman folded up with an agonized, wheezing gasp, and the sergeant struck him again—this time a scientific blow across the back of his neck that didn't quite pulverize any vertebrae.

"Good work," Wystahn told the other members of his squad softly as they filtered out of the darkness around him and the single, unconscious survivor of the cavalry picket.

Unlike the majority of the men of Brigadier Clareyk's Third Brigade, Wystahn and his men wore single-piece garments of mottled green and brown, rather than the traditional light blue breeches and dark blue tunics of the Royal Charisian Marines. Their rifles were also shorter than the standard weapon, with browned barrels, and the brims of their traditional, broad-brimmed black hats were sharply rolled on the right side.

Their distinctive garb marked them as scout-snipers. None of them were aware that the inspiration for their organization had come from a chance remark *Seijin* Merlin had dropped in conversation with Brigadier Clareyk when he'd been only a major. What they *were* aware of was that they'd been selected and trained specifically as a small, elite force to be attached to standard Marine formations. They were intended for missions exactly like the one they'd just carried out, and their function once combat was joined was to serve as covering skirmishers in the early stages and to specifically target any officer they could identify on the other side. Quite a few of them had enjoyed previous careers as hunters or, in some cases, poachers, and they'd developed a distinctive swagger which was guaranteed to . . . irk any other Marine whose path they happened to cross in a tavern or bordello. Many of them, as a consequence, had come to know the shore patrol quite well.

This was the first time they'd actually been used in the field, of course. Sergeant Wystahn was well aware that he, his men, and the entire scout-sniper concept were on trial. Although it might not have occurred to him to describe it in precisely those terms, he was determined that they were going to prove themselves, and so far, he had nothing to chew anyone out for.

So far.

"Zhak, go back and tell the Lieutenant where we are. Tell him the last picket on the list's gone. The rest of us'll wait here."

"Aye, Sarge."

The indicated Marine nodded, then went loping off into the darkness.

"The rest of you take position," Wystahn continued, and the others filtered out to form a loose perimeter around the former picket's position.

Wystahn watched them critically, then grunted in satisfaction and squatted to check on the surviving Corisandian's condition.

. X .

Haryl's Crossing,
Barony of Dairwyn,
League of Corisande

Sir Koryn Gahrvai made himself look patient as he waited for the early dawn light to creep back into the world. He could smell rain, but it didn't feel very imminent, and its approach suggested that the day might at least be a little cooler than yesterday had been. That would be nice, although if things went as he'd planned, today would be hot enough to satisfy anyone.

There, he thought, watching the first hint of salmon and gold creep across the eastern horizon. *It won't be much longer now.*

He'd left his headquarters at the planter's house and ridden forward to keep a personal eye on things, but he hadn't gone beyond the town itself. Tempting though it was, he knew he had no business with his most forward formations. Nothing they might gain from his presence in terms of improved morale or steadiness would be worth the possibility that he might be taken out of action . . . or the much greater *probability* that he would find himself bogged down in some purely local situation when he ought to be supervising the overall battle.

After considering carefully, he'd chosen the steeple of Haryl's Crossing's biggest church as his forward command post. It would give him the best view over the greatest area, it offered good height for the semaphore mast his engineers had rigged overnight, and it was a prominent enough landmark (especially now that it had the mast stuck on top of it) that couriers trying to locate him with messages from his subordinate commanders shouldn't find their task difficult. Now he yawned, cradling a cup of hot chocolate in both hands, while the sky gradually brightened and details began to emerge from the darkness.

He was glad he'd made his decision to get the troops into position yesterday. Either Windshare's scouts had misreported the Charisian column's position earlier in the day, or else the Charisians had picked up the pace considerably yesterday afternoon. He was inclined to believe it was probably a combination of the two. Estimating the enemy's position accurately in such heavily overgrown terrain would have been difficult at the best of times, and he would have liked to ascribe the Charisians' unanticipatedly early arrival solely to a perfectly natural mistake on the cavalry's part. But he didn't think it was that simple, and he wondered if the Charisians might somehow have caught wind of his own presence at Haryl's Crossing. He didn't see how they could have gotten any of their own scouts close enough for that without even being detected, but it was always possible one of the locals had provided information to the other side, whether involuntarily or in return for payment.

He sipped chocolate, savoring the rich flavor, and fresh energy seemed to trickle through his veins. It shouldn't be much longer now. . . .

There. Those were the standards of his farthest forward battalions. He still didn't have as many muskets, flintlock or matchlock, as he would have preferred. Worse, according to his own cavalry scouts' reports, every single one of the Charisians they'd seen so far appeared to be armed with a flintlock musket, whereas a third of his own men were still armed with pikes. Fortunately, he had a lot more men than the

Charisians did, and while he might be weaker, proportionately, in firepower, the difference in total manpower meant he actually had more of them, absolutely. And whatever the relative numbers of firearms might be, those pikes were going to be a nasty handful if the infantry formations ever managed to close.

The light was still too poor for him to use his spyglass, but he squinted his eyes, peering eastward to where the shadows of the tangled woodland continued to conceal the single Charisian battalion which had encamped just this side of them. They ought to be about—

Gahrvai's eyes widened in sudden astonishment. Surely it was only a trick of the light!

He set his chocolate cup aside, and stepped closer to the open side of the belfry. He was conscious of the cool breeze, the awakening twitter of birds and gentle whistling of wyverns, and the dew-slick, man-sized bell, hanging just behind him like some watching presence. And he was also conscious of the handful of staff officers and aides in the belfry with him. That was the reason he forced his expression to remain calm, kept his hands still as they rested on the waist-high safety railing. The light continued to improve, and his eyes tried to water with the intensity of his gaze.

"Sir!" one of his aides blurted suddenly. "I thought—"

"I see it, Lieutenant," Gahrvai said, and he was pleased—and more than a little surprised—by how calmly he managed to speak.

The evening before, a single battalion of Charisian infantry had been bivouacked in a restricted arc whose broad side had been centered on the highway where it emerged from the tangled wilderness. Now, somehow, that battalion had advanced at least a full mile without any of his cavalry pickets having spotted a thing. Worse, the battalion had been substantially reinforced. His scouts had estimated the Charisian column at a maximum of five or six thousand men. Assuming that the higher number was accurate, it looked as if at least two-thirds of the enemy's total strength had somehow managed to magically appear in front of his own men.

His jaw clenched as he attempted to estimate frontages and strengths. In close formation, each infantryman covered a frontage of approximately one yard. In open formation, that frontage doubled. So a four hundred–man battalion in close formation, with three companies up in a double line and the fourth in reserve, covered a front of around a hundred and fifty yards. In a three-deep line, their frontage shrank to only a hundred yards. The scouting reports suggested that the Charisian battalions were larger than his own, probably about five hundred men, instead of four hundred. Assuming each of them retained one company as a reserve, that meant each of their battalions should cover about two hundred yards in close formation, dropping to only a hundred and thirty if they went to a triple line. Which seemed. . . .

The light was significantly stronger than it had been, and he raised his spyglass, then frowned. Details were still hard to make out at this distance, even with the glass, but one thing was obvious; they weren't in close formation at all. Instead, they were in a peculiar, almost staggered open formation.

What the hell *are they up to?* he fretted. *If it ever comes to a general melee, we'll go through them like shit through a wyvern even without a single pike! So why . . . ?*

Then he realized. That formation wasn't intended for hand-to-hand combat at all. His own flintlock muskets could fire much more rapidly than the old-style matchlocks. He'd already assumed the Charisians had to be able to fire *at least* as rapidly as his own flintlocks, and that formation was obviously optimized to allow the greatest number of muskets to fire at any given moment. It wasn't a melee formation at all; it was one which had been specifically designed around the rate of fire of the new weapons.

Which ours haven't been, he thought grimly. *That's going to be . . . painful.*

The fact that the Charisians had managed to get so many more muskets forward and out of the constricted woodland behind them was also worrisome, although now that the surprise was beginning to ebb, that particular discovery bothered him less. The object had been to draw the enemy forward, after all. The fact that the Charisians had obliged him should scarcely have been a matter for concern.

Except that they did it on their own terms, not mine. And except for the fact that Alyk had cavalry pickets out there expressly to warn us if they tried something like this. Not only that, but those bastards' front is on this *side of where some of those pickets were posted. So they didn't just keep Alyk's troopers from spotting them; somehow, they took out every single picket without anyone's firing a single shot or a single man getting away to warn us. Now that's . . . bothersome.*

"How did they manage that, Sir?" the same aide muttered behind him, and Gahrvai shrugged.

"I don't have the foggiest idea, Lieutenant," he admitted. "And just between you and me, the fact that they did manage it without our catching even a sniff of what they were up to bothers me. On the other hand, all they've really accomplished is to shove their heads deeper into the noose for us. Not only that, but they're a good thousand or fifteen hundred yards this side of the woods. If Earl Windshare's cavalry can get into that gap, cut them off from retreat . . ."

The lieutenant was nodding now, his eyes intent, and Gahrvai discovered that the youngster's response actually made *him* feel a bit better, too. If the lieutenant thought what he was saying made sense, it probably did. Even better, other people might be thinking the same thoughts instead of worrying about how the hell the Charisians had managed to magically move that many men that far forward without anyone happening to notice.

That thought was still percolating through the back of his mind when he heard the faint, distant call of bugles.

They weren't *his* bugles, and as he watched, the Charisian formation shivered, then stirred into motion.

▼   ▼   ▼

"Now that's an unpleasant sight, isn't it?" Brigadier Kynt Clareyk murmured to himself.

He and his staff had attached themselves to Colonel

Zhanstyn's headquarters group. Each of the two Charisian brigades had three of its battalions up in line, with the fourth battalion in reserve, and Zhanstyn's 1/3rd Battalion formed the center of Third Brigade's line on the Charisian left.

At the moment, Clareyk had paused on a slight knoll, peering through his own spyglass over the heads of his advancing riflemen at the Corisandian formation waiting for them.

The Corisandian lines were far denser than his own—deeper, bristling with pikeheads. That tighter frontage and greater depth were going to provide them with much greater shock value if it came to a melee, but that possible advantage had been obtained by decreasing each Corisandian battalion's maximum firepower. Or, rather, by decreasing it in comparison with the *Charisian* battalions. It looked as if Clareyk might be about to find out whether or not his theories about firepower trumping shock power were going to turn out to have been accurate after all.

Something fitting about that, he mused as he swung his spyglass steadily, sweeping across the front of the enemy's position. *It's only fair that the fellow who thought he was so clever when he worked it all out should get to test his own concepts under fire, as it were. Odd. Somehow I don't really find myself looking forward to the opportunity.*

"I make it about eight or nine thousand men, Sir," a voice said quietly at his elbow, and he turned his head, quirking one eyebrow at Major Bryahn Lahftyn, his senior staff officer. "In their main formation, I mean," Lahftyn added.

"Ah, yes. In their *main* formation," Clareyk said dryly.

"Well, yes, Sir." Lahftyn looked rather uncomfortable for a moment, then saw the glint of humor in his brigadier's eye.

"Somehow," Clareyk said, "the odds didn't seem so bad until just now." He grinned crookedly. "I've just discovered that seeing all of those fellows standing over there sort of takes the concept of 'outnumbered' out of the merely intellectual category."

"It does do that, Sir," Lahftyn agreed. "And look over there, in the center of their line."

Clareyk gazed in the indicated direction, and his mouth tightened ever so slightly.

The terrain between the tangled wilderness through which they'd marched and the river, some six or seven miles farther west, consisted primarily of cotton silk fields, cropland, and pastures, with belts of orchards closer to the town nestled around the stone bridge. There were scattered sections of woodlot out there, as well, although none of them seemed as choked with wire vine as the wilderness they'd slogged through to get here. At least some of the pastures were separated by carefully trained hedges of wire vine, and there were several stone walls, as well. Fortunately, the walls were obviously intended as property markers rather than significant obstacles, and very few of them rose much higher than midthigh.

Overall, it was as close to ideal terrain as he was likely to find. It did slope steadily uphill towards the feet of the Dark Hill Mountains. In fact, the foothills on the far side of the river were actually closer to low bluffs, he thought, and he had no doubt they were solidly manned by the additional troops the Corisandian commander had declined to cram into his relatively limited battlefield. The river was too broad for smoothbore muskets atop those bluffs to dominate the lower, flatter eastern bank, although it would be quite a different matter for field artillery, even the carronade-style artillery the Corisandians had developed. Aside from that, though, the ground in front of him was close to perfectly fitted to his own tactical needs, while the denser, deeper Corisandian formations were going to find the relatively minor terrain obstacles much more hampering than his own men would.

Unfortunately, the reason it was ideal for his riflemen was because the Corisandians had been seeking exactly the same sort of clear fire zones for their *artillery*, and they'd placed no fewer than thirty or forty field pieces at the center of their own front. That was what Lahftyn had spotted, and Clareyk's mouth tightened a bit more as he contemplated what those guns would do to his own battalions if they got the chance.

We'll just have to see that they don't *get the chance, won't we, Kynt?*

"Signal Major Bryndyn," he said. "I want our field guns and Lieutenant Hahthym deployed in the center. Tell him he's not to come within five hundred yards of their pieces with his own guns."

"Yes, Sir."

Lahftyn scribbled busily in his notebook, then read back the brief message. Clareyk listened, then nodded in satisfaction, and the youthful major went jogging across to the heliograph which shared the top of their knoll. The signalman manning the device read over the major's note, trained his sight on the mounted officers clustered around the twelve-pounder field guns and their draft dragons, and reached for the lever on the heliograph's side. A moment later, the shutters began to clatter as he flashed the instructions in coded flickers of mirrored sunlight.

Lahftyn waited until Major Bryndyn's acknowledgment had been received. As it happened, there wasn't yet enough light on Bryndyn's position for him to use his own heliograph, but his signal party displayed the single green flag which indicated a message had been received and understood. It wasn't as good as having the text of the message repeated back to be sure it wasn't garbled, but if Bryndyn had been in any doubt about what he was supposed to do, his signalers would have displayed the red flag which requested that the message be repeated.

"Message acknowledged, Sir," Lahftyn announced as he rejoined Clareyk.

"Thank you, Bryahn. I saw the flag myself."

Lahftyn nodded, and then he and his brigadier stood side-by-side, watching as four thousand Charisians marched steadily towards well over *ten* thousand Corisandians.

▼   ▼   ▼

"Sir, they're marching straight *towards* us!"

The young lieutenant—he couldn't be much over nineteen, Gahrvai thought—sounded aggrieved, almost indignant. And he also sounded puzzled. Which, Gahrvai decided, could have been said of the lieutenant's commander, as well.

They couldn't have known how many men we had waiting for them, he told himself firmly. *Not when they advanced to their present positions last night, at least. On the other hand, unless they're blind, they can sure as hell tell we've got more than they do* now! *So why are* they *coming to* us?

Koryn Gahrvai would have given a great deal if he could have been positive the answer was Charisian arrogance or stupidity. Unfortunately, he doubted it was either of those.

Still, if they didn't expect to see this many of us, that could explain why they're as far forward as they are. And it could just be that having put themselves in a position where their only avenue of retreat is down a single, narrow roadway, they figure their best chance is to hit us and hope we break rather than see their unit organization go straight to hell trying to wiggle away through that miserable rat hole of a road.

His chain of thought broke off as more bugles sounded. This time, they were his, and he watched his own infantry begin rolling forward as planned.

He scratched the tip of his nose reflectively, forcing his expression to remain calm, while a sudden craven temptation to call his troops back ran through him.

Don't be an idiot, he told himself sternly. *You're about to panic yourself into deciding to retreat before a single shot's even been fired! You're supposed to be attacking them, not waiting for them to attack you! Besides, if you can't take them with odds this heavily in your favor, what's the point of even trying?*

▼ ▼ ▼

Brigadier Clareyk nodded in something very like satisfaction as the Chisholmians began to move forward. That massive artillery battery of theirs stayed put, not surprisingly. They'd put their guns in an almost perfect position, along the crest of a long, sharply rising slope. The artillerists had a wide open field of fire, well placed to fire over the heads of their own advancing infantry. Of course, there were downsides to that, as well. For example, firing canister or grapeshot *over* your own troops wasn't a very good idea. The patterns spread rapidly—

vertically, as well as laterally—which meant you tended to kill quite a few of your own men if you tried something like that, and the infantry, for some peculiar reason, didn't much care for that.

Which probably explains why no one is advancing directly in front of their guns, Clareyk told himself dryly. *I wonder if they've had decent artillery long enough to figure out about grazing fire?*

His and Baron Seamount's own experiments had quickly demonstrated that field artillery firing solid projectiles was most effective when the ground was hard enough to produce ricochets and the gunners had learned how to judge the strike of their shot in order to bounce it through an enemy formation. Grapeshot and canister could benefit from the same effect, although they couldn't hope to match the effective range of round shot.

In this instance, the ground was almost certainly too soft for good grazing fire, he reflected. Still, he would have liked to know whether or not the Chisholmians had reached the same conclusions. Sooner or later, they *were* going to wind up fighting each other when the ground was hard enough, and it would be nice to not have it come as a surprise if the Corisandians were prepared to bounce their shots into his men.

Let's see, he thought. *I see lots of infantry out there in front of me. What I* don't *see is their cavalry. I wonder. . . .*

He gazed speculatively north, once again wishing that he had a decent mounted element of his own. If this Gahrvai was as good as he was supposed to be—and the fact that he'd produced this much fighting power in what had to seem like an ideal position on the basis of everything he knew about the Marines' weaponry certainly indicated that he was—then that cavalry had to be somewhere. And the most likely place for it to be was waiting where it ought to be able to cut off Clareyk's retreat back into that blasted wilderness.

"We need another message, Bryahn," he said.

▼ ▼ ▼

"All right, I don't like this," Sir Charlz Doyal muttered.

The Charisian artillery, despite the fact that it had only a dozen pieces, was angling across the developing battlefield straight towards his own thirty-five guns. That indicated either terminal stupidity (which, given what Charis had recently done to the navies of its various opponents, didn't seem particularly likely) or else that the gunners on the other side knew something he didn't. Which seemed entirely *too* likely.

Maybe they're just counting on their greater range, he thought. *We don't know how much greater it is, but if they stay more than five or six hundred yards out, we won't be able to reach them effectively even with round shot. Not on ground this soft. And I'll bet you* they've *got a range closer to a thousand or even fourteen hundred yards. This is going to be unpleasant.*

Still, ultimately the only function of the artillery on either side was to support the infantry. And the infantry battalions on both sides were continuing to march straight towards each other. Eventually, that was going to bring the Charisians into Doyal's range, whatever their own artillery might be up to. And if he and Sir Koryn's infantry could kill enough of *their* infantry, then their guns wouldn't be enough to stem the tide of disaster.

▼ ▼ ▼

"Steady. Steady, lads," Sergeant Wystahn murmured, even though all but two of the men of his platoon were well outside earshot. If he'd thought about it at all, he would have admitted it was really more of a supplication to whichever of the archangels might be listening than an admonition to his Marines.

The rest of the Third Brigade was advancing steadily behind him through what struck him as a profoundly unnatural quiet. The pipes began to skirl, but even that seemed distant and far away. He could still hear distant birdcalls and the hum and zing of insects buzzing about in the tall, almost ripe wheat in which he and his men lay concealed.

He raised his head cautiously, lifting just the crown of his hat above the wheat. At the moment, that hat looked far less martial than it did on the parade ground, which didn't bother Edvarhd Wystahn one little bit. The overwhelming majority of the scout-snipers were farm boys like Wystahn himself. Most of them had hunted—some, like the senior corporal of Wystahn's own platoon, had probably supported themselves as poachers, in fact—and they understood how concealment worked. The handful of city boys who made it through the rigorous scout-sniper training program had to learn that, and most of them thought it was funny as hell the first time they were ordered to attach random greenery to their hats. That amusement tended to disappear quickly, though, as soon as they discovered how simply breaking up the outline of a human head could make it disappear into background vegetation. Which just went to show that even city boys could learn if their sergeants were prepared to kick them in the arse hard enough.

He brushed that thought aside while he raised his eyes just high enough to see across the gently waving sea of wheat, then grunted in satisfaction. The Corisandian infantry formations were moving forward, as well, and he tried to tell himself he was glad to see it. He didn't quite manage to convince himself of that, though. Satisfied that the enemy was performing as hoped, yes; glad to see several thousand armed men moving straight towards him, no.

Oh, hold your water, Edvarhd! he told himself sternly. *And while you're doing that, check your priming.*

▼ ▼ ▼

Captain Ahntahn Illian was young enough that excitement and anticipation almost overwhelmed his anxiety.

Almost.

His youthful self-image didn't like admitting that that qualifier applied, but given the sweatiness of his grip on his sword hilt and the queasiness stirring around in his belly, he couldn't very well deny it. Not that he intended to let any of his men see it. His battalion commander and his senior sergeant, at least, knew this was going to be his very first battle, and he rather hoped they'd kept that information to themselves. He'd been very careful not to tell anyone else that it *wasn't,* but he also hadn't gone out of his way to admit he'd never yet smelled powder smoke in actual combat, and he'd just as soon not have any of the members of his company figure it out at this particular moment. Somehow, he doubted the discovery would have contributed to their confidence in his leadership.

He looked up as the sound of the Charisian bagpipes rose against the morning quiet. It still seemed distant, faint, like a backdrop behind the closer-to-hand swishing sound of thousands of boots behind him, moving through the waist-high, dew-slick wheat. Behind the muted clatter, jingle, and scrape of weapons, the distant shouts of command from his fellow officers and leather-lunged sergeants, and his own breathing. Morning sunlight was warm on his face, although rain clouds were gathering in the west behind him. It wasn't going to be as hot as yesterday, and he found himself suddenly hoping desperately that he'd be around to see the rain when it finally began to fall.

He rested the flat of his drawn sword across his shoulder, as he'd seen his more experienced fellows doing, and concentrated on striding confidently. His breeches were already soaked from the morning's dew, and his lips quirked in sudden amusement.

At least this way no one's going to be able to tell it if I piss myself when the shooting starts!

They were starting to get closer to the enemy, and he glanced back over his shoulder to check the major's position. He wasn't worried about dressing his own company's ranks; his sergeants knew their business far better than he did, and they would have resented the very suggestion that they needed his oversight to do their jobs properly. At the moment, *his* job, like that of every other company commander in the leading battalions, was to look confident as he walked straight towards the enemy with unquestioning assurance that his perfectly formed up company was following on his heels.

It's a lot harder to do this when there are real people with real guns waiting for me, he reflected. *And they do have a* lot *of muskets. In fact, I don't see a single pike over there.*

His eyes narrowed as he realized he truly didn't see a single pike. Corisande's new flintlock muskets had a much higher rate of fire than old-fashioned matchlocks, and he had no doubt the Charisians' weapons could fire at least as rapidly. Even so, it was unlikely musket fire alone would keep a determined enemy from closing, and if *that* happened, they were going to miss those pikes—badly. But the Charisians had to know that at least as well as he did, so why . . .?

He forced himself to set that question aside, although the back of his mind suggested that he'd just seen one of the reasons there were no pikemen on the other side of the field.

He glanced back at the major again, waiting for the signal. The distance between the opposing front lines had closed to little more than five hundred yards. According to their orders, they were supposed to advance to seventy-five or eighty yards before firing. If their firepower proved as effective as everyone expected—or hoped, at least—they would stay at that range and pound away until the Charisians broke. If it turned out that, for some reason, their fire *wasn't* as effective as expected, the pikemen would charge with the musketeers following in support. Since the Charisians were advancing towards them, as well, it was up to the major to indicate exactly where and when he wanted his battalion halted, which was why Illian was watching him. And, undoubtedly, why the major was watching the colonel, who had to decide where the entire regiment would halt.

▼ ▼ ▼

Sergeant Wystahn's eyes narrowed as the Corisandians continued to wade through the tall wheat towards him. It was odd. He'd felt more than a little nervous when Colonel

Zhanstyn had given him his orders and informed him that it was up to *him*—Sergeant Edvarhd Wystahn—to decide when to fire the very first shot of the battle. Now that the moment was almost upon him, that particular nervousness had vanished. He couldn't say he missed it, but he did wish it could have taken all of his other nervousnesses with it.

He had to admit the Corisandians were maintaining almost perfect formation as they advanced. That wasn't easy, especially when the troops had to trample their way through wheat this high, and it didn't do much for the wheat fields in question, either. The local farmers were going to be pissed off, he thought. The field behind the oncoming enemy had been trampled as flat as a pavement by thousands upon thousands of feet. One of the horse-drawn reapers couldn't have cut the unharvested wheat any shorter. Rabbits, hedge lizards, grass lizards, quail, and white-ringed field wyverns rustled and swarmed through the still-standing wheat, fleeing before those oncoming, trampling feet, and Wystahn felt a certain sympathy for them. He'd like to be fleeing, too, if he was going to be honest about it, and he wondered what would happen when the wildlife running away from the Corisandians ran into the wildlife running away from the Charisians?

A large grass lizard, at least a foot and a half long, ran directly into Wystahn's chest as the sergeant knelt in the wheat. The impact was enough to make the Marine grunt as the lizard bounced off him, and the already terrified creature gave a high-pitched squeak of panic. It landed with all six feet already churning and disappeared somewhere beyond him.

Well, that *hurt,* the sergeant reflected. *Not to mention almost making my heart stop. And I'm glad I took a leak before I settled in.*

The thought made him snort, and he glanced back at the oncoming enemy. The lead Corisandians were almost up to the farmer's scarecrow he'd moved last night to serve as a range marker.

At an overall length of sixty-four inches, the scout-snipers' weapons were a half-foot shorter than the standard rifled musket of the line formations, although their barrels were only about two inches shorter, thanks to what someone from Old Earth would have called the rifle's "bull pup" design. The shorter barrel's rifling also had a tighter twist, and the weapon was equipped with a peep sight graduated out to five hundred yards. In theory, a man should be able to shoot accurately out to a thousand yards, but what with bullet drop, the difficulty in judging the range in the first place, and the sheer difficulty of picking out a target at such extended distances, it wasn't really a practical option for the majority of people. A single platoon of elite marksmen in each scout-sniper company was equipped with rifles that were actually sixteen inches *longer* than the standard infantry weapon, with flip-up aperture sights graduated all the way out to twelve hundred yards. In the proper hands, that rifle could register a headshot at five hundred yards and reliably hit man-sized targets at twice that range, assuming of course that the target cooperated by holding still. At the moment, however, those marksmen were all concentrated elsewhere, probably where the Corisandian artillery had been emplaced.

Wherever they were, they, too, were waiting for *him*. Now, as he watched one of the junior officers leading the Corisandian battle line walk past the scarecrow, he slowly and carefully cocked his rifle. The front rank of musketeers reached the scarecrow and shouldered it aside, and Edvarhd Wystahn raised his weapon, captured his sight picture, and squeezed the trigger.

▼ ▼ ▼

Captain Illian heard the first shot.

His head snapped up in astonishment. The closest Charisian was still at least three hundred yards away!

That thought flashed through his brain, but then he saw the powder smoke in the wheat field. It was to his left, and far closer than the main Charisian formations.

But it's still a hundred and fifty yards away from—

Ahntahn Illian stopped thinking abruptly as another Charisian scout-sniper squeezed *his* trigger and a fifty-caliber bullet punched straight through his breastplate.

▼ ▼ ▼

Sir Phylyp Myllyr stiffened as the "pop-pop-pop" of musket fire rippled across the front of his advancing regiment.

Like Captain Illian, he couldn't quite believe his own ears for the first heartbeat or so. The enemy was much too far away for either side to be shooting at the other! But then he, too, saw the smoke blossoming out among the tall wheat. There were dozens—scores—of the sudden, white puffs, and his jaw muscles ridged as he realized what they were shooting at.

▼ ▼ ▼

Wystahn felt a wave of mingled satisfaction and something like guilt as he watched his target collapse like a broken toy. Other scout-snipers were firing, taking their cue from him, and all along the Corisandian front, officers and standard bearers were going down.

The company commanders who'd been acting as living guidons for their men were the primary targets, and the deadly accurate rifle fire went through them like a reaper. As far as Wystahn could tell, every single one of them was hit at least once, and behind them, unit standards toppled as other riflemen targeted their bearers.

The entire enemy formation wavered in shock, but Wystahn was no longer looking. He was too close to the Corisandians to waste time admiring his own marksmanship, or even that of his men. Even with paper cartridges instead of a powder horn, reloading a single-shot rifle took time. Especially if a man was trying to do that while hiding in three-foot wheat. Which was why none of the scout-snipers were even trying to do anything so foolish. Instead, they were busily scuttling towards the rear—much like the grass lizard, a corner of Wystahn's brain reflected—while doing their dead level best to stay completely concealed.

▼ ▼ ▼

Myllyr swore viciously as he realized the Charisians had
just picked off at least half of his regiment's company commanders.

He'd known every one of those officers personally, and
most of them had been young enough to be his sons. Despite
that, the rage he felt at seeing them deliberately shot down
would have astonished him if he'd had time to really think
about it. Officers had always been high-priority targets, after
all. The only difference this time was that the Charisians had
done it in a carefully coordinated, preplanned ambush. The
range was so great, and the accuracy of the executions—and
that was what they had really been: cold-blooded, carefully
planned executions—was so high, that the men who'd carried
them out must have been armed with rifles. And that meant
the Charisians were fielding specially trained and equipped
marksmen for the express purpose of ambushes just like
this one.

They couldn't have a great many of them, given rifles' slow
rate of fire. No weapon whose tightly fitting ball had to be
hammered down the barrel to force it into the rifling could
possibly be fired as rapidly as a smoothbore. That was the reason no field commander could sacrifice that much firepower
from his regular line units, no matter how accurate rifles
might be. Unfortunately, that didn't mean the tactic couldn't
be hellishly effective, and his jaw clenched as his immediate
flash of fury receded just a bit and he recognized what the loss
of so many officers was going to mean for unit cohesion and
morale. The steadiness of an infantry company, its ability to
stand the pounding of combat without crumbling, was hugely
dependent on its officers. On their knowledge of their human
material, their awareness of who would be towers of strength
and who would have to be watched carefully when the pressure came on. And, perhaps even more, on the confidence of
the men in their leadership. They knew their own officers.

They listened for their voices in combat, read their own fate and the course of the battle in the tone in which orders were given.

Now what should have been a source of strength had been transformed into a source of weakness, and the men those dead and wounded officers had commanded would recognize as well as Myllyr that what had happened had been a deliberate, well-planned, brilliantly executed tactic . . . designed to do exactly what it had.

▼   ▼   ▼

Colonel Zhanstyn's mouth stretched in a tight, teeth-baring grin as the scout-snipers decimated the other side's junior officers. Had he known the thoughts passing through Phylyp Myllyr's mind at that moment, he couldn't have disagreed with a single one of them. It *had* been a deliberate assassination, and while Zhanstyn was no more eager to kill people than the next man, he would have done it again in an instant.

The Corisandians' meticulously dressed lines were no longer as neat as they had been. Here and there—especially where some company commander had been miraculously missed—individual subunits had continued advancing at the same steady pace. Other units had stumbled to a halt as their commanding officers went down. Others had continued to move forward, but more slowly, almost hesitantly, as the men in the ranks waited for one of the company's platoon commanders to take over the unit. Unfortunately, quite a few of those platoon commanders had also become casualties.

The portions of the line which had continued advancing halted abruptly when they realized so many of their compatriots had fallen behind. They stood where they were, waiting for the disorganized units to get themselves fully back under control, which happened, among other things, to give the scout-snipers the time they needed to make good their withdrawal to their own lines.

The camouflage-clad marksmen came filtering through the line companies' ranks, sliding adroitly through the openings without impeding their comrades' steady advance. Here and there, someone took a hand from his own rifle to slap the returning snipers on the back, and Zhanstyn himself nodded in greeting when Sergeant Major Sahlmyn led Sergeant Wystahn up to the command group.

"Good work, Sergeant. I'm glad to see you made it back in one piece." The colonel gave Wystahn's shoulder a congratulatory squeeze. "And I believe you timed that just about perfectly, too."

"I hope so, Sir." The scout-sniper sergeant shook his head, his expression grim. "Begging your pardon, but I'd just as soon not be doing that again anytime soon. Shooting rabbits and mountain lizards is one thing. This, though . . ."

"We can hope, Sergeant." Zhanstyn squeezed his shoulder again. "We can hope."

Their eyes met for a moment, and then Zhanstyn looked back at the steadily narrowing gap between the two forces and shook his head.

"Now that you've done your job so well, Sergeant, I suppose it's up to the rest of us to do ours."

▼ ▼ ▼

Gahrvai was too far behind his advancing regiments to see what had happened. He'd seen the sudden white puffballs springing up out of the wheat fields like loathsome toadstools, and he'd realized instinctively that his troops had just encountered a screen of dispersed skirmishers. What he didn't realize was that there'd been over four hundred of them, and that they'd just inflicted shattering damage on the command structure of altogether too many of his leading battalions.

He was a little slower than Myllyr to realize the skirmishers in question must have been rifle-armed, as well. Mostly because his position so far to the rear made it hard to judge the range at which the shots had been fired . . . and even more so because he had no idea how devastatingly accurate they'd been.

His mouth tightened as his entire formation halted, even if

only briefly, to dress its ranks and try to reorganize around the loss of so many of its key cadre. Without any way of realizing how many officers and noncoms had just been eliminated, he didn't understand the pause. Surely a scattering of musket balls shouldn't have caused a battle line over *two miles* wide to stop in its tracks!

It was a brief pause, but even small things could accumulate into an avalanche on a field of battle. He felt himself leaning forward, willing the solid lines and blocks of infantry to resume their movement. Priceless seconds dragged away into even more irreplaceable minutes, and still the lines stood in place. It looked as if his left wing was waiting for his right, and he gritted his teeth.

Sir Zher Sumyrs, the Baron of Barcor, was in command of his left. He was also the oldest of Gahrvai's senior officers. He'd been a soldier for the better part of thirty years, but he'd seen precious little serious action in those three decades. His campaigning had been mostly against brigands, aside from a couple of forays against rebellious Zebediahans, not against trained soldiers, and he had a pronounced tendency to go by The Book. Worse, he was still attached to the *old* Book. He'd had more trouble than most getting his mind wrapped around the new concepts Gahrvai and his father had been introducing, yet his firmly entrenched position in the army command structure (and in the political structure of Corisande) had prevented Gahrvai from easing him out to pasture.

At the moment, Gahrvai would cheerfully have shot him on the spot, and hang the political consequences. All of his own prebattle orders had stressed the necessity of getting to grips with the Charisians as rapidly as possible. Coordination was good, and confusion was to be avoided at all costs, but speed of execution was most important of all, and Barcor's right was firmly covered by Doyal's massive artillery battery. He didn't need to maintain perfect alignment with the Earl of Mancora, on Gahrvai's right. And someone with all the experience Barcor was fond of mentioning damned well ought to be aware of the potential consequences of allowing a line of battle to lose momentum. Hektor Bahnyr, Earl Mancora, was half Barcor's age, with a military career *less* than half as long, but Mancora would never have made the mistake Barcor was busy making.

But it's still only a pause, *Koryn,* he reminded himself. *And each wing has five thousand men in it. That's got to be more than the Charisians' total strength, so even if Barcor screws up, Mancora should still be able to do the job.*

He told himself that with as much assurance as he could. Then his head snapped to the right as artillery began to thunder.

▼ ▼ ▼

Langhorne! I hadn't counted on their stopping that *far out!*

Sir Charlz Doyal winced in dismay as the Charisian artillerists abruptly stopped and began unlimbering their pieces.

He was reasonably comfortably ensconced in the branches of a nearoak tree, and he'd been watching their approach through his spyglass. He'd also been experiencing a deep sense of envy as he watched. Their gun carriages were significantly different from his own—proportionately more lightly constructed, and with larger wheels. Nor had it occurred to anyone in Corisande to incorporate what looked like a private ammunition wagon into each individual gun's equipment. Each gun appeared to be paired with a much larger ammunition wagon, as well, but the bigger vehicles had been stopped well back, out of harm's way, while the guns continued to advance.

The draft dragons weren't actually harnessed to the guns themselves, at all. Instead, they were harnessed to the smaller, two-wheeled ammunition cart, and the gun was hooked in turn to the cart. Both vehicles together were little larger and more cumbersome than a single one of Doyal's own guns, and it reduced the number of draft animals the Charisians required to actually move the gun in and out of action by almost fifty percent. Not to mention the fact that everywhere the gun went, its own ammunition cart obviously went with it.

If only Alyk and his blasted cavalrymen had realized what

they were seeing, this wouldn't have come as such a damned surprise!

Doyal had been scribbling notes to himself in pencil from the moment he first saw the Charisian equipment with his own eyes. Between notes, he'd concentrated on reminding himself that neither Windshare nor his troopers had any experience with true field artillery. Of course they hadn't realized what they were seeing—why should they have?

And it wouldn't have made that much difference, anyway. There wouldn't have been anything you could have done about it in the last fifty-two hours, even if they'd described every last detail to you!

That thought chased itself through the back corridors of his brain as the Charisians brought their pieces to battery. They went about the task with a polished efficiency, and the peculiar cart-and-carriage arrangement clearly speeded the evolution. Despite the fact that their guns' six-foot barrels were almost twice as long as those of his own weapons, they had the guns fully deployed in little more than two-thirds of the time his own crews would have required.

His jaw tightened as he contemplated the range at which they were doing that deploying. Without his glass, he would have been hard put to pick out individual limbs, but belts and packs were still visible, and the division between the Charisians' upper and lower bodies remained relatively clear. That put the range at more than five hundred yards but less than seven. In fact, it looked to be at least six hundred, although he might be being at least a little pessimistic. He hoped he was, at any rate, because six hundred yards was right on the very limit of his stubby twenty-six-pounders' effective range. In fact, it was outside that range. His gunners might just be able to reach them at maximum elevation, especially given his height advantage, but he wouldn't have cared to bet any substantial sums on the probability. And even if they could *reach* the Charisians, "inaccurate" would be a grossly inadequate description of their ability to actually *hit* them.

The question, of course, was whether or not that would be true for the Charisians, as well.

▼ ▼ ▼

Well out in the wheat field, invisible to Doyal among the three-foot stalks, were the thirty men of Lieutenant Alyn Hathym's specialized sniper platoon. The marksmen of that platoon were the elite shots of an elite outfit, and they knew it. Most platoons consisted of only twenty men, but the sniper platoon was divided into fifteen two-man teams. Every man was a trained and deadly marksman, but normally only one of them was assigned the shooter's role while his partner used a spyglass to identify and pick out targets.

Which was precisely what they had been doing for the last quarter of an hour or so.

▼ ▼ ▼

Doyal never heard the shots. Nor was he looking in the right place to spot the rifle smoke. The snipers were actually *beyond* and to either side of the deploying Charisian artillery, which—by definition—meant they were far out of any range at which small arms fire could possibly threaten Doyal's guns.

His gunners knew that as well as he did, and many of them had climbed up out of their gun pits, craning their necks to get a better view of what was going on to either side of them. Which meant they were totally exposed when fifteen rifles with fifty-eight-inch barrels, loaded with what an inhabitant of Old Earth would have called spitzer-pointed bullets, specially formed in compression dies, fired practically as one.

Doyal's eyes flared in astonishment as eleven of his men went down virtually simultaneously. Two of them had obviously been hit at least twice, and his brain seemed to freeze for just an instant as it registered the fact that both of them had been officers, with the distinctive sashes and hats which indicated their rank. In fact, all but two of the casualties were officers, which meant that somehow musketeers he couldn't even see were picking individual targets with deadly precision.

It took an instant or two for the unwounded gunners to realize death had just come striding through them. Then, as if a single hand had reached up and grabbed them by the ankles, they disappeared back into the protection of their gun pits, leaving eight dead men and three wounded ones grotesquely sprawled behind them.

▼ ▼ ▼

"*Commence firing!*" Major Dahryn Bryndyn shouted on the heels of Lieutenant Hathym's snipers' volley. The one real drawback to the snipers' specialized weapons was that they were long and clumsy. That made it unlikely they would have time to reload before their targets took cover, so it was up to *his* men now, and a solid wall of smoke erupted as the twelve field guns of his two batteries bellowed.

At five hundred and fifty yards, they were a good hundred yards outside what would have been effective canister range for his twelve-pounders. At five degrees of elevation, they could throw a solid shot almost seventeen hundred yards, but maximum canister range was no more than a quarter of that.

Grapeshot, now, though . . . that was another matter entirely. Instead of the thirty one-inch-diameter balls of a canister round, a stand of grape consisted of only nine miniature round shot. But each of those shot was *two* inches in diameter and weighed almost eight times as much as a ball of canister. And *they* could carry five hundred and fifty yards quite handily from one of Baron Seamount's twelve-pounders.

▼ ▼ ▼

Doyal was still trying to come to grips with the preposterous accuracy and range of the Charisian musketry when the enemy gun line vanished behind its own muzzle smoke and the first patterns of grapeshot came screaming into his position.

Some of his subordinates had thought he was taking caution to the point of timidity when he'd insisted they dig proper gun pits. They'd known they had the Charisian guns outnumbered by a factor of almost three-to-one, after all. But despite some grumbling, they'd carried out his orders, digging each gun into its own individual pit so that its muzzle just cleared the shallow wall of spoil thrown up on the side towards the enemy by the excavators' spades.

The Charisian snipers' brutally unexpected harvest had driven his uninjured personnel back into those pits in the instant before the twelve-pounders fired, which meant Doyal's "timidity" had just saved quite a few of those subordinates' lives.

For now, at least.

The sound as the grapeshot came slashing in was like wind rushing through leaves. A sort of sibilant, many-voiced hissing that ended in the heavy thuds, like a vast fist, punching the ground, of the shot plowing into their targets.

Some of those targets were *not* the low earth berms protecting the gun pits, and fresh screams started.

In actual fact, the Charisian gunners' accuracy was considerably less than pinpoint. Unlike a specialized sniper rifle, grapeshot was an inherently inaccurate projectile, and even for the longer-barreled Charisian guns, five hundred and fifty yards was a stretch. But grapeshot also had the advantage of buckshot; someone firing it didn't really need pinpoint accuracy to achieve lethal results.

Most of the individual shot buried themselves harmlessly in the dirt. Of those which didn't, only two actually hit human beings. One man's head simply disappeared; the other jerked to his feet, screaming as he stared at the shattered, spurting ruin of his left arm. But horses and draft dragons were much larger targets than human beings, and Doyal realized instantly that he hadn't had them moved far enough to the rear when he deployed his own guns.

At least half a dozen horses went down in the first salvo, most of them shrieking like tortured women at the sudden unexpected agony they had absolutely no way to understand. The sound twisted a man's nerves like pincers, yet the dragons were worse. The high-pitched, agonized howl of a wounded dragon was indescribable. The whistling, ululating screams seemed to fill the universe, and injured beasts lunged frantically against their pickets.

Doyal shoved his notepad into his pocket and came slithering down the tree in a shower of bark splinters. He hit the ground already running, charging into the battery's central gun pit.

"Draw the charges! *Draw the charges!*" he bellowed. "Load with round shot! Load with round shot, damn your eyes!"

Some of his surviving division officers and gun captains had already anticipated his instructions. He'd ordered *his* guns loaded with grapeshot because musketeers would have to come into his effective range if they were going to be any threat to his battery. Despite his own insistence on digging the guns in properly, he hadn't really expected the Charisians to embark upon an artillery duel, unsupported by infantry, when they had barely a third as many guns as he did. Grapeshot and canister were the most effective anti-infantry ammunition any artillery piece had, and he'd never imagined that any infantry in the world could engage effectively from outside *grapeshot* range. Now, even as he cursed and goaded his men into reloading, he made a mental note for the artillerists' manual he was still drafting. Rule Number One: *Never* load your weapons until you know—positively *know*— what type of ammunition is going to be required.

Oh, shit! he thought suddenly. *What the* hell *am I doing wasting time* drawing *charges? Why didn't I just order them to* fire *the damn grapeshot to clear the guns?!*

Because, he realized, he was experiencing his own version of panic as he registered just how badly the Charisians outranged his own guns. That wasn't going to help anyone, and so he made himself pause and suck in a deep, steadying breath, even as the second and third salvos of grapeshot came hissing, whistling, and thudding into his position.

Slow down, Charlz! At least you've got the right idea, but slow down. Good ideas are fine, but you've got to think long enough to make the right decisions, as well!

Still more sniper bullets were hidden inside the artillery storm, and they continued to reap their own grim harvest from any man who exposed himself incautiously. Doyal couldn't pick the snipers' victims out of the general chaos, but he was harshly aware that he was losing men in steady twos and threes, despite the protection of their gun pits. One of the unseen bullets clipped the tip off the feathered officer's cockade on his own hat, and he started to duck down behind his gun pit's sheltering berm. He stopped himself barely in time, not because he was feeling especially heroic, but because of his awareness of his men's wavering morale. So instead of withdrawing into cover like a sane man, he played the lunatic role his command responsibilities required of him. He took off his hat to examine the cropped cockade, then looked at the men around him and waved it over his head.

"All right, boys!" he shouted. "They've gone and ruined my hat, and that's really pissed me off! I don't know if we can mark the bastards from here or not—but I damned well intend to find out! How about you?"

More than thirty of his gunners were down by now, at least half of them dead, but the others responded with echoes of his own fierce grin, and gun captains' hands rose as their crews finished extracting the charges of grape and reloading with round shot.

"*Fire!*"

▼ ▼ ▼

Dahryn Bryndyn watched the sudden eruption of smoke from the Corisandian guns. Its sheer volume was intimidating, and he held his breath as the twenty-six-pound round shot sliced through the air towards him.

Unfortunately for Charlz Doyal's gunners, they simply didn't have the range to reach Bryndyn's guns. The round shot thudded into the earth well short of the Charisian officer's batteries, and he'd been right about how soft the ground was. The Corisandian shot were the next best thing to six inches in diameter, but the rich, damp, well-watered topsoil was almost four feet deep, and it simply swallowed them down. Some of them plowed channels across the wheat fields before they finally stopped, and clods of dirt spattered outward, yet not a man or a draft animal was even wounded, and Bryndyn smiled grimly.

"All right! Let's put it to the bastards!" he shouted.

▼   ▼   ▼

Doyal jumped up onto the edge of the gun pit, exposing himself recklessly as he tried to see through the smoke of his own fire. Some small, very fast-moving object went by his right ear with a sizzling sound, and he realized that his new position went beyond anything that could be justified on the basis of encouraging his men. But he stayed where he was long enough for the breeze to roll away the battery's smoke, and his jaw tightened painfully.

So far as he could tell, not a single one of his shot had reached the enemy. He could see rips and gouges in the deep, even green of the wheat fields which must have been left by his fire, but none of them even came close to the Charisians.

He jumped back down into the gun pit, his heart like lead. His men were doing a better job of staying under cover while they served their weapons now—the slow learners were probably all already dead or wounded—but they *had* to expose themselves to work the guns. And because they did, they continued to go down, in a bloody, brutal erosion of his strength, and they couldn't even *reach* the men killing them.

It's time to withdraw, he thought, astonished that he could have accepted defeat so rapidly, yet unable to think of any other alternative. *I've got to get these guns out of here while I still have the animals to move them and the men to man them. Koryn will just have to under—*

His thoughts broke off abruptly in a stupendous, far louder explosion of musketry.

▼   ▼   ▼

Gahrvai's steeple perch let him see the entire panorama of his chosen battleground, but only until the clouds of smoke streaking the heavens started obscuring parts of it. *Critical* parts, he realized as the opposing batteries wrapped themselves in gunsmoke his spyglass couldn't penetrate.

Unaware of the deadly sniper fire sizzling in on Doyal's position, or of the fact that his own guns couldn't even reach the Charisian artillery's exposed position, he had no idea of how one-sided that confrontation was turning out to be. Instead, he felt a cautious stir of optimism that the enemy wasn't having it all his own way. And that sense of optimism grew stronger as Barcor and Mancora finally resumed their interrupted advance.

▼ ▼ ▼

The Charisians had never halted *their* advance, however. Or, rather, they'd simply continued closing until the range had fallen to about two hundred yards. Then they'd stopped, meticulously dressing their own formation, letting the Marines catch their breath, while the Corisandians recovered from the disorganization the scout-snipers had imposed. When the enemy resumed his advance, they were ready.

▼ ▼ ▼

Gahrvai's budding optimism vanished into icy horror when the entire Charisian line of battle vanished behind a sudden, fresh eruption of smoke. He might have been too far to the rear to realize the range at which the scout-snipers had fired, but he was close enough to tell the Charisian line battalions had opened fire at at least twice his own troops' maximum effective range.

From the elevated advantage of the steeple, he saw the front line of his own battalions ripple, like trees in a high wind, as the deadly volley ripped through their tight formation, and all too many of them toppled before that wind's dreadful strength. They were packed so closely together that any Marine who missed his own target could be virtually certain of hitting someone else's, and the big, soft-lead bullets struck like mangling hammers that shattered limbs and bodies in grotesque sprays of blood. Gahrvai couldn't hear the screams of the wounded, but he could almost taste his men's panic as they realized just how badly outranged they were.

My God, they're going to massacre *us!*

The thought ripped through his mind as a second, equally massive volley of rifle fire crashed out from the Charisians. It wasn't quite as deadly as the first one, but that was only because the previous volley's smoke prevented the Marines from seeing their targets as clearly. And it was deadly enough. Still more Corisandians went down, and Gahrvai's front began to waver.

▼ ▼ ▼

Hektor Bahnyr, the Earl of Mancora, watched in disbelief as the rifle fire smashed into his lead regiments' battalions. Reorganizing around the loss of so many junior officers had been bad enough. Now this!

He clenched his jaw, his mind working furiously as he sought some answer to the looming catastrophe he already saw rumbling down upon his wing of Gahrvai's army. It was deliberate, he realized. The pinpoint removal of so many company commanders, so many standard bearers, had been intended to make a point, as well as to ravage his command structure. The Charisians had been telling him—telling all of his *men*—that their marksmen could pick—and hit—individual targets at preposterous ranges. Now they were making the even more devastating point that even their line units could fire at those same insane ranges.

And however they were doing it, it wasn't with any sort of rifle Mancora or any other Corisandian had ever heard of. It *couldn't* be a rifle—not with the deadly speed with which volley followed upon volley. The bastards were actually firing *faster* than any of his own flintlock-equipped musketeers could have! Yet at the same time, those *had* to be rifles, because no unrifled musket could possibly have so much range!

He felt his own nerve wavering as the implications hammered home. All of the priests' fiery rhetoric, their condemnation of the "apostate Charisian heretics," came back to him in that moment. To be honest, he'd never really believed the wild tales about Charisian heresy, about the way they'd opened the doors to Shan-wei and her dark temptations. But now, as that impossible weight of fire mowed down his men, he wondered.

No! There was nothing demonic, no violation of the Proscriptions, in the new Charisian artillery. He didn't know how they'd managed what they were doing to him now, but he told himself that it had to be something else like the new artillery mountings. Some cunning new trick, yes, but something any mortal man could have devised.

Which did nothing at all to rescue his command.

He glared at the rising wall of smoke above the Charisian firing line, then drew a deep breath.

"Sound the charge—*now*!" he barked.

▼ ▼ ▼

Brigadier Clareyk heard the Corisandian bugles. They were faint and distant through the wailing of his own bagpipes and the crash and thunder of artillery and massive rifle volleys, but he recognized them, and he nodded in ungrudging understanding.

Whoever that is in command over there, he's quick, the brigadier thought. *Not quick enough . . . probably. But quick.*

The two sides were a little more than two hundred yards apart. Advancing at the double, infantry would require at least two minutes to cross that gap, and it was most unlikely the Corisandians could hold together for two minutes under his brigade's rapid, massed fire. Each rifleman was firing approximately once every fifteen seconds, and he had fifteen hundred of them in his two-deep firing line. In the two minutes it would take the enemy to reach them, those fifteen hundred men would fire twelve thousand rounds at no more than *five* thousand targets.

The opposing commander couldn't know that, though. If he'd had time—time to think about it, time to analyze the weight of fire ripping through his men, to truly grasp the rapidity of that fire as well as its accuracy and range—he almost certainly wouldn't have tried it. But he *didn't* know, hadn't had that time. Which meant, under the circumstances, that he'd put his finger on the only slim chance he had—or ought to have had—for victory. A stand up firefight between his musketeers and Clareyk's riflemen could have only one ending, but if he could charge, get to grips with his greater total number of men, he might still carry the field.

Only that isn't going to happen, Clareyk thought grimly.

▼   ▼   ▼

Gahrvai grasped Mancora's thinking as rapidly as Brigadier Clareyk had. Unlike Mancora, however, he wasn't trapped in the very forefront of the disaster sweeping over his army like some inrushing tidal wave. He didn't have to make the decision in the midst of bloodshed, carnage, screaming wounded, blinding waves of gunsmoke, and the smell of shed blood and riven and torn bodies. He never blamed Mancora for a moment, knew he would probably have made the same choice in the earl's position.

And he knew it was the wrong one.

Barcor, on the other hand, showed no sign of launching any charges. For what Gahrvai was privately certain were all the wrong reasons, Barcor was doing the right thing, while Mancora—for all the *right* reasons—was about to make a disastrous mistake.

"Signal Baron Barcor!" he snapped over his shoulder, never taking his eyes from the field before him. "Instruct him to begin falling back immediately!"

"Yes, Sir!" one of his aides blurted, and Gahrvai heard boots thundering across the planking as the young man dashed for the signal station.

Of course, with all this smoke, the odds are no better than even that Barcor will even see *the semaphore,* Gahrvai thought bitterly. *On the other hand, he's . . . cautious enough he may turn tail and run on his own any minute now.*

It was already far too late to stop Mancora, but it was possible he might still salvage at least the majority of Barcor's men if he could only withdraw them from the perfect killing ground he'd provided for the Charisian rifles. The realization that he was the one who'd chosen exactly the right terrain for the Charisians' new tactics filled him like poison, and the fact that he actually wanted one of his subordinate commanders to be gutless enough to run away from the enemy was bitter as gall. Yet it was also true, and his face set like congealing stone as Mancora's infantry advanced into the dreadful maelstrom of the Charisians' fire.

Why? The thought went through his brain. *Why are You doing* this, *God? We* aren't *the schismatics trying to tear Your Church apart—they* are! *So why are You letting a good man, a good commander, take his troops into a meat-grinder like this one while a cretin like Barcor won't even advance?*

There was no answer. He knew there wouldn't be one, and his eyes were hard as he realized he'd actually be forced to *commend* Barcor after this battle—assuming God and the Archangels weren't merciful enough to get the baron killed—rather than stripping him of his command as his timidity so justly deserved.

▼ ▼ ▼

Earl Mancora's infantry hurled themselves forward.

How the handful of survivors from the winnowed ruin of his forward ranks managed to advance instead of running away in terror or simply flinging themselves to the ground was more than the earl was prepared to say. But somehow, they did it, and his heart wept within him at the gallantry with which they responded to the bugles.

They moved forward, stumbling over the bodies of dead and wounded comrades. They waded into the smoke, forged ahead into the stormfront of rifle fire like men leaning into a hard wind, and the meaty thuds and slapping sounds of heavy caliber bullets ripping through human flesh were like hail.

The Charisians watched them come, and even the men killing them recognized the courage it took to keep advancing. Yet courage was not enough in the face of such a totally unanticipated tactical disadvantage. It wasn't Gahrvai's fault, wasn't Mancora's. It was *no one's* fault, and that changed nothing. Almost eight hundred half-inch bullets slammed into them every fifteen seconds, and they were only flesh, only blood.

The advancing Corisandian battalions were like a child's sand castle in a rising tide. They melted away, shredded, broken, shedding dead and wounded with every stride. They marched straight into a fiery wasteland like the vestibule of Hell itself, roofed with smoke and fury, filled with the stink of blood, the thunder of the Charisian rifles, and the shriek of their own wounded, and it was more than mortal men could stand.

The men of the leading battalions didn't break. Not really. There weren't enough of them left to "break." Instead, they simply died.

The battalions behind them were marginally more fortunate. They realized that all the courage in the universe couldn't carry them across that beaten zone of fire. It simply couldn't be done, and they *did* break.

▼ ▼ ▼

"*Yes!*" Clareyk shouted as the Corisandian formation disintegrated.

Pikemen dropped their cumbersome weapons, musketeers discarded their muskets, men threw away anything which might slow them as they turned and ran. A harsh, baying cheer of triumph went up from the Marine riflemen, and yet, in its own way, that wolf-like howl was almost a salute to the courage of the Corisandians who had marched into that furnace.

"Sound the advance!" Clareyk commanded.

"Aye, Sir!" Colonel Zhanstyn acknowledged, and Third Brigade swung into motion once more.

▼ ▼ ▼

Charlz Doyal swore savagely as Mancora's wing came apart. He understood exactly what had happened, not that understanding changed anything. He'd still just lost the infantry covering the right flank of his beleaguered grand battery, and it wouldn't be very long before the Charisian left swung in on his own exposed right. The range at which they'd dismantled Mancora's infantry told him what would happen when their massed volleys joined the blasts of grapeshot and pinpoint sniper fire already tearing into his men. But if *he* pulled back, if he tried to get his guns out, then Barcor's right would be uncovered, as well. And if the Charisian left could advance fast enough, they might actually reach the highway bridge *before* Barcor. If they managed that, trapped Barcor between themselves and their advancing fellows . . .

Doyal's jaw clenched so tightly his teeth ached as he watched Barcor's wing falling back with alacrity. He had no more doubt than Gahrvai about *why* Barcor was doing what he was, yet whatever the man's reasoning, it was the right thing. He was still going to lose heavily to the Charisians' fire, but his retreat was the only thing that might get half of Gahrvai's advance guard out of this disaster reasonably intact. And if that meant sacrificing Doyal's thirty-five guns and six hundred men to save five thousand, it would still be a bargain at the price.

Besides, he thought with a sort of ghoulish humor, *I've already lost so many dragons and horses I couldn't get more than half of the battery out of here, anyway.*

His heart ached at what he was about to demand of the men he'd trained and led, yet he drew a deep breath and turned to the commander of his right flank battery. The major who had commanded that battery half an hour ago was dead. The captain who'd been his executive officer up until ten minutes ago was wounded. Command of the entire battery had devolved onto the shoulders of a lieutenant who couldn't have been more than twenty years old. The young man's face was white and set under its coating grime of powder smoke, but he met Doyal's eyes steadily.

"Swing your battery to cover our flank, Lieutenant," Doyal said, and forced himself to smile. "It looks like we're going to get a bit lonely."

APRIL,
YEAR OF GOD 893

✦

. I .

The Temple
and Madame Ahnzhelyk's,
City of Zion,
The Temple Lands

The side conversations in the Grand Council Chamber were
more hushed than usual this year.

The chamber itself had been meticulously prepared for the
afternoon's ceremony. Ancient tradition said the Archangel
Langhorne himself had sat in council with his fellows in this
very chamber, and its magnificent wall mosaics and the enormous, beautifully detailed map of the world—four times a
man's height—inlaid into one wall certainly supported the
tradition. Portraits of past Grand Vicars hung down another
wall, and the floor, paved in imperishable, mystically sealed
lapis lazuli like the floor of the Temple sanctuary itself, was
covered with priceless carpets from Harchong, Desnair, and
Sodar. An entire army of servants had spent the past five-day
dusting, mopping, polishing, honing the chamber's normal
magnificence to the very pinnacle of splendor.

The glittering crowd of vicars seated in the chamber's lux-
uriously comfortable chairs made a fitting match for the enormous room in which they had gathered. Jewels glinted and
flashed, bullion embroidery gleamed, and priests' caps glittered with gems. The air in the chamber circulated smoothly,
soundlessly, warmed to exactly the proper temperature by the
Temple's mystic wonders, despite the snow falling outside the

Temple Annex in which this treasure box of a meeting room was housed. Perfect, softly glowing illumination poured down from the chamber's lofty ceiling, lighting every detail of priceless artwork and sumptuous clothing. A long buffet table of delicacies stretched across the short end of the chamber (although "short" was a purely relative term in such an enormous room), and servants circulated with bottles of wine, ensuring that the vicars' glasses did not suffer a sudden drought.

Despite the comfort, despite the splendor which underscored the majesty and power of God's Church, a curiously fragile tension hovered in the chamber's atmosphere. Voices were lowered, in some cases almost to the level of whispers, and some of the wineglasses required more frequent replenishment than usual.

Zahmsyn Trynair sat in his own chair, the one reserved for the Chancellor of the Council of Vicars, located just to the right of the Grand Vicar's empty, elevated throne. Zhaspahr Clyntahn's chair flanked the throne from the other side. Each had chatted easily with the members of his staff, making the occasional small joke, showing his calm assurance, but after exchanging a single, smiling nod of greeting, the two of them had made a point of *not* speaking to one another since they'd taken their seats.

Rumors of their recent . . . disagreement had filtered throughout the Temple's hierarchy. No one knew precisely what it had been about, although a great many people suspected that it had owed something to the explosive news from Ferayd. The totally unprecedented findings of the Ferayd Tribunal certainly suggested that it had, at any rate. Even the most jaded Temple insiders had been astonished by the tribunal's conclusions, and the penance Clyntahn had been assigned by the Chancellor, speaking for the Grand Vicar, had been equally unheard of.

Clyntahn had accepted his penance with every outward sign of humility, humbling himself before the high altar, leading memorial masses for the innocents who had been slain along with the obvious heretics in Ferayd. He had even performed his five-day of service, laboring in the Temple kitchens to feed his far humbler brethren, serving plates with his own two, well-manicured hands.

However humble he might have chosen to appear, no one believed for a moment that he had *enjoyed* the experience, and there were persistent rumors that he held Trynair personally responsible for his humiliation. Needless to say, neither Trynair nor Clyntahn had confirmed any such thing. Indeed, they'd both taken considerable pains to establish that whatever their confrontation had been about, it had constituted—at worst—a *temporary* rift between them. Of course, some of the Temple insiders would suspect that their obvious rapprochement was all a mask, a disguise to prevent their many enemies on the Council of Vicars from scenting blood. Showing just the right degree of friendliness and cooperation to warn any potential enemies that an attempt to exploit any division among the ranks of the Group of Four would be . . . unwise was a delicate task, and never more than today. Too much or too effusive a display of friendship would transmit the wrong message just as surely as too cold and formal an attitude. Especially today. It would never have done for either of them to have seemed as if he might be suffering some sort of last-minute attack of nerves, after all.

Theater, Trynair thought. *It's all theater. I wonder if there's a single man in this Chamber who couldn't have earned his living on the stage if he hadn't been born to be elevated to the orange?*

There were other differences between this year's Address from the Throne and those of years past. Normally, there would have been a standing crowd of junior archbishops and senior bishops behind the seated vicars. In theory, the members of that crowd would have been selected randomly, in reflection of the universal equality of the priesthood's members. In fact, of course, invitations to the Address from the Throne were carefully considered tokens of power for the vicars and of prestige and influence among the recipients. This year, however, there was not a single bishop, nor any member of the laity, present. Even some of the more junior archbishops had been excluded, and the senior archbishops were virtually silent in the presence of their superiors.

Maybe it's not all theater, after all, Trynair thought more somberly. *Not this year, at any rate.*

A single, musical chime echoed suddenly, and the hushed conversations stilled abruptly. That, too, was unusual. Normally, at least some of those side conversations would have continued even through the Address itself. After all, every vicar would have already received his copy of the text. Some of them might not have bothered to read it yet, but it would have been waiting for them in their offices when they got around to it. Besides, everyone would already have known what was in it, even if he hadn't received a copy.

Today was very different, however. No one had yet seen the text of this year's Address—no one outside of the Grand Vicar, Trynair, the other three members of the Group of Four, and the Chancellor's most trusted aides, at least. And the rumors concerning its probable content had swirled throughout the ranks of the vicarate like a spring riptide as one report after another underscored the challenge the Kingdom of Charis had thrown into the Church's very teeth.

Word of the marriage between Cayleb of Charis and Sharleyan of Chisholm had reached the Temple only three five-days before, hard on the heels of word of what had happened at Ferayd, and the news had shaken the vicarate to its core. The fact that news of the marriage and the creation of this new "Empire of Charis" had taken so long to reach Zion, even allowing for the winter weather, was only one more sign of the threat to the Church's power. The chains of Temple couriers who would normally have carried that word across the Cauldron to the semaphore stations, winter gales or no winter gales, had been broken for the first time in the history of Safehold. And the messages from the bishops and senior priests whose correspondence would have announced and analyzed the event had never been written, for the men who now held those offices were loyal not to Zion and the Temple, but to Cayleb and Sharleyan.

That would have been sobering enough. The realization

that Chisholm had voluntarily joined Charis in its defiance of Mother Church had gone beyond sobering to frightening, and the execution of sixteen consecrated priests had hit even harder, in many ways. Even those who had held quietly to the belief that the Group of Four's heavy-handed misman-agement had driven the Charisian crisis had found them-selves confronting the emergence of a brand-new empire which, in the fullness of time, must inevitably take its place among the great kingdoms and realms of Safehold. An em-pire solidified not by simple conquest, or mere dynastic mar-riage, but upon the common foundation of its defiance of Church authority—a defiance it had underscored with brutal finality in Ferayd. And one which had already added the Princedom of Emerald to its territories and would certainly move upon the League of Corisande within five-days or months, if it had not already.

Two years ago no member of the Council of Vicars could even have imagined a world in which such a political and re-ligious grotesquerie could have existed. Now, all of them found themselves face-to-face with the hideous specter of a schism which not only had not been crushed but was actively growing, spreading steadily from the initial source of corrup-tion in Tellesberg.

In a world so much of whose certainty had crumbled, the Grand Vicar's annual address loomed with enormous impor-tance, and all eyes and heads turned quickly towards the Grand Vicar's throne as that single chiming bell announced his arrival.

As the Church's oldest traditions required, Grand Vicar Erek XVII, the secular and temporal head of the Church of God Awaiting, God and the Archangel Langhorne's steward on Safehold, entered the Grand Council Chamber alone and unat-tended. In this room, on this day, he was officially only one more vicar, come to report to his brother vicars on the state of God's Church throughout Safehold. If the nature of his entry proclaimed his equality, however, the glittering crown upon his head, the magnificent robes of state (which, with their weight of pearls, gems, and fine embroidery weighed more than most suits of armor), proclaimed a very different message. *They* underscored the absolute power which lay in the hand of the master of the church which was mistress of all the world.

Erek certainly looked the part of a proper grand vicar, Trynair thought sardonically. He was a tall man, with broad shoulders, hair which had silvered with the passing years (and the judicious assistance of the Grand Vicar's valet and hairdresser), piercing eyes, a powerful, arched nose, and a high and noble brow. Fortunately for Trynair's purposes, the man inside that impressively regal appearance understood the realities of Temple politics at least well enough to take direction properly.

Now the Grand Vicar proceeded to his throne through the hushed silence. He seated himself upon it, looking out across the rows of vicars and archbishops, and his expression was calm. Despite the fact that every member of his audience knew his expression was a part of the carefully scripted theater they were all here to observe, many of them actually found themselves relaxing, at least slightly, as they beheld it. Trynair observed their reaction with satisfaction. Erek's ability to project that air of reasoned, calm assurance was, after all, one of the primary reasons Trynair had selected him for elevation to the Grand Vicarate.

"Dear brothers in God," the Grand Vicar said after a moment, "we welcome you, and we thank you for the godly brotherhood in which we have all gathered that we might report to you the state of God's Church and work among the millions upon millions of souls committed to our pastoral care by the all-powerful hands of God and His servant Langhorne."

His voice was another reason Trynair had selected him. It was a deep, magnificent, velvety bass that reached out to its listeners with the assurance that here was a man who knew what he was about, was as confident internally as his expression proclaimed externally. That impression was further reinforced by his ability to memorize lengthy speeches, like the Address, and deliver them sincerely, passionately, and without so much as glancing at notes or a script. If Erek had possessed the force of intellect to match his other qualifications for the grand vicarate, he would have been a man to be feared . . . and Zahmsyn Trynair would have sought a different puppet.

"Much has transpired in the past year," the Grand Vicar continued gravely, delivering the lines Trynair had composed for him with measured, earnest sobriety. "Much of that has been good, redounding to the glory of God and the salvation of His Faithful. Yet, as all of us are aware, we have also found ourselves confronted, as no previous Grand Vicar or Vicarate since the days of Langhorne himself, by Shan-wei's open challenge in this world. The Dark Mother of Evil has thrust her finger once again into the perfection of God's work, once more seeking to mar and subvert all which is good into the service of evil."

One or two of the vicars appeared to stiffen, and Trynair concealed a mordant smile behind his own carefully schooled expression. Obviously at least some of the vicarate's members had continued to hope this could all just be made to go away. Precisely what might have inspired them to cling to such a futile hope was more than the chancellor would have ventured to say. No doubt some of them—the name of Samyl Wylsynn came to mind—had clung to the belief that some sort of compromise might still have been patched up between the Church of Charis and the legitimate Church of God Awaiting. Well, it was time to knock that notion on the head once and for all, assuming the Ferayd Tribunal hadn't already done for it.

"All of us," Erek continued, "are only too well aware of the events which have transpired in Charis, and now in Chisholm. We have heard the pretexts upon which the schismatics have based their apostasy, their defiance of Mother Church's legitimate, God-given authority over the souls and spiritual well-being of all of God's children. We've heard their lies, recognized their distortions. And more recently, we have seen evidence of their willingness to resort even to the bloody-handed murder of God's own priests. To take into their own secular, unsanctified hands the consecrated judgment of God's priesthood which the *Holy Writ* has reserved solely for the Office of Inquisition and Council of Vicars, acting with all due deliberation and under the guidance of God Himself and the Archangels."

He paused, surveying his audience solemnly, then continued in that same level voice.

"All of those crimes, those perversions, are sufficiently dreadful to fill any godly soul with horror and repugnance. Yet I must tell you, my brothers, that the Office of Inquisition has amassed fresh evidence, new knowledge, which makes it plain that this schism, this defiance, is part of a long and carefully nurtured conspiracy. That the baseless accusations the schismatics have leveled against Mother Church are the opening wedge not for a mere defiance of Mother Church's authority, but for a heretical rejection of the most basic and fundamental doctrines handed down to us from the Archangels themselves."

Throughout the vast Grand Council Chamber faces tightened and eyes narrowed. Zhaspahr Clyntahn had seen to it that carefully crafted, fragmentary rumors about the confessions of the Charisians in the Inquisition's custody had reached the proper ears. But they'd been *only* fragments, deliberately fashioned to prepare the ground for the Grand Vicar's address without giving away that address' content.

"Much of what we have recently learned confirms things we have believed to be true. That belief was foremost in our mind when we took the grave step of excommunicating the schismatic leadership and placing the entire realm of Charis under the heavy burden of the interdict. Yet we have not made them public, nor shared them even with our brothers among God's vicarate, because we found them so disturbing, so difficult to credit, that we demanded evidence. We will not share with you even now all that we have learned. To be honest, we continue to believe additional evidence must be provided before such serious charges may be publicly levied against any child of God. In the fullness of time, when that evidence is in hand and the time to deal with God's enemies has fully arrived, we will share with you—and with the entire body of God's Church—the full nature of the enemies who have arisen to dispute God's mastery of His own world.

"And do not be deceived, brothers. Whatever they may

claim in Tellesberg and Cherayth, their ambition is nothing less than to overthrow, forever, Mother Church's legitimate authority as God's and the Archangels' chosen shepherd. The violence which wracked the peaceful city of Ferayd in August has been far surpassed by the brutal attack, devastation, and sack which the so-called Charisian Navy carried out so savagely little more than a month ago. And the murder—for such it was—of sixteen of our consecrated brethren, sixteen servants of Mother Church and the Office of Inquisition, was but the tip of an iceberg of murder and rapine in that unhappy city. Two-thirds of that city—*two-thirds,* brothers—lies in broken and burned ruins, littered with the bodies of its defenders and all too many of their wives, daughters, and children."

He shook his head gravely.

"Who can look upon such actions, such savagery and destruction, without recognizing the hand of Shan-wei herself? And who but the servant of Shan-wei would use tales of the 'guilt' of the Inquisitors of Ferayd in an attempt to buttress all of their *other* lies and false, blasphemous accusations against Mother Church? Shan-wei is crafty, my brothers, and her snares are cunning. See how they fasten upon the failures of a handful of God's priests and proclaim that *all* of God's priests are corrupt and fallen! How they strive to convince the foolish, the credulous, that God's Church—the hand of God Himself in this world—is responsible for atrocities, for groundless persecutions, for corruption.

"It was with heavy heart that we reviewed the findings of the Ferayd Tribunal, and we will not deceive you; we were gravely tempted to order those findings sealed. To turn away from confronting such painful things, for we already knew how the schismatics had fastened upon those sad and tragic events as a weapon against God. Yet however tempted we might have been, we recognized that temptation itself as the work of Shan-wei. We realized that we dared not fail in any least aspect of our duties before God—and most assuredly not in a duty as grave and heart-wrenching as this—lest we display weakness before God's foes. And so we accepted the tribunal's finding, and thus we demonstrated who the true guardians of the Church are. We demonstrated that we would take even the allegations of schismatics seriously when there was evidence of wrongdoing on the priesthood's part, and that we would not permit impious rebellion against Mother Church's authority to prevent us from doing our duty as Langhorne's steward on Safehold.

"Yet all of this is nothing more than the beginning. Nothing more than the attempt to set in place the lies and deceptions the schismatics will use, in the fullness of time, to justify their all-out assault on Mother Church, on the authority of the Archangels, and upon God's own plan for the safekeeping of men's souls. Believe me, my brothers, what has happened in Delferahk is but a shadow, the merest foretaste, of what they intend for Zion and the Temple Lands in the fullness of time."

The normally inaudible motion of the chamber's circulating air could actually be heard when the Grand Vicar paused. The men seated in their orange cassocks to listen to him might have been carved from stone, and he shook his head once more, slowly, regretfully.

"Brothers, there is a reason we have chosen to deliver our yearly Address only to the most senior of Mother Church's servants. We charge you to remember in your own utterances, your own discussion of what we say here today, that the enemies of God have ears in all places. The time is not yet meet for us to further alarm the members of our flock. Yet it *is* time we shared with you, our brothers and the guardians of Mother Church, our belief that full-scale Holy War lies before us."

Some of the seated vicars flinched visibly, and Trynair hoped the members of his staff who'd been briefed to watch for that exact reaction had gotten all of their names.

"As we say, the time is not yet. Just as there are preparations to be made, plans to be cast, weapons to be built and forged, there is also the heavy responsibility laid upon us as God's true servants to establish once and for all, beyond any question or contradiction, the true depth and depravity of our enemies' plans and intentions before resorting to such stern and awful measures. No matter how just the war, how imperative the action, the innocent will suffer as well as the guilty, as, indeed, events in Ferayd have already demonstrated so tragically. No true son or daughter of God could contemplate all the horrific consequences of such a conflict without fear and trembling. Without the necessity of *knowing* that no other option, no other course of action, lay open to them. And we do not utterly foreclose the possibility of some less drastic resolution. It is our hope, our earnest prayer, that the subjects of the rulers who have made themselves the enemies of God will recognize their responsibility to rise in righteous fury and cast off the servants of Shan-wei who have led them into this apostasy and sin. It is for this reason that we issued our writs of excommunication and our proclamation of the interdict upon Charis and have subsequently extended it to Chisholm and Emerald. Yet however earnestly we may pray for that eventuality, we cannot rely upon it. It is our responsibility, as God's steward, to make timely preparation for the more drastic measures which we greatly fear have become inevitable.

"In the fullness of time, God will assuredly grant victory to those who strive in His most holy name. We have no doubt of that, and we know that your faith, as our own, is the unshakable rock upon which God's Church rests. That faith will not be disappointed, nor will God permit it to be dismayed. Yet dark days lie before us, my brothers. Let none of you be misled into believing otherwise. We have been called to the sternest test mere mortals have ever faced. We stand in the place of the Archangels themselves, face-to-face with the menace of Shan-wei, and we cannot command the *rakurai,* as Langhorne did. We cannot reach out our hand and smite the corruption of Charis and Chisholm with the cleansing fire of God's purifying wrath. But what we *must* do, we *can* do. We face not Shan-wei herself, as Langhorne faced her in the fullness of her own perverted divine power. We face only her servants, only those who have given their souls into her dark service, trusting her to bear them up. Yet those mistaken, lost, and accursed souls would have done well to recall that Shan-wei is the Mother of Lies and the Mistress of Betrayal. We, who trust in the fidelity and the authority of God's chosen Archangels, have a surety and a fortress which Shan-wei can never provide. And because this is so, because we do battle in the armor of God Himself, our victory is sure, for it will be *His* victory, and God does not suffer Himself to be defeated."

The Grand Vicar paused, surveying the faces of the assembled vicars, and the Grand Council Chamber was hushed and still.

"The time has not yet come to openly draw Langhorne's sword," he said then, "but that day draws near. And when it arrives, my brothers, when Langhorne's sword is unsheathed in the pure service of God, it will not be returned to its scabbard while even one of His foes breathes."

▼ ▼ ▼

Despite her sitting room's warm fire, Ahnzhelyk Phonda shivered inside as she reread the letter on her desk.

Unlike many of the letters which passed through her hands, this one was unencrypted, although there were code words and codenames scattered throughout it which would have made no sense to most readers. It was printed in neat block characters, rather than handwritten, but she recognized Samyl Wylsynn's characteristic phrasing. She supposed there'd been no point in putting it into cipher when it had been accompanied by the complete text of the Grand Vicar's annual Address from the Throne. There were only so many people it could have come from, after all.

She laid the single sheet back on her blotter and looked out the frosty windowpane at the snow-choked streets of the city.

She couldn't see it from where she sat, but she knew about the curl of smoke emerging from the roof of the shed her gardener normally used for summer storage. As was her custom, she'd made the shed available to some of Zion's poor for the winter. It was pitiful enough housing for Zion's climate, but at least she'd made sure the shed's walls were wind- and weathertight, and she'd quietly arranged to keep the coal bin alongside the shed door filled. She didn't know how many temporary tenants she'd acquired this winter, but she did know that when the city's snow finally cleared, at least some bodies would be found. They always were, and the greatest number were always huddled near the Temple's vents, where the waste heat breathed out into the freezing cold.

Her lovely mouth tightened at the thought and anger stirred deep in her expressive eyes as she thought about Grand Vicar Erek's Address and all of the condemnation showered upon the "apostate heretics" of Charis and Chisholm by the men who lived in the sumptuous comfort of the Temple. Men immune to hunger and cold, who never gave a single thought to the pitiful poor trying desperately to keep themselves and their families alive by crouching around the vents of their own magnificent dwelling place. She knew exactly what it was that had actually triggered her decision to join the reformists like Samyl Wylsynn, and it hadn't really been any one event, any one realization.

Her own life, the studied rejection and denial of her own father and the power of office which had allowed him to do it, had left her ripe for rebellion—she knew that much, admitted it freely—but there were so *many* ways she might have rebelled. Of course, she might also have simply disappeared, faded away into invisibility as one more cast-off, bastard daughter seeking refuge in a nun's vocation. Even her adoptive parents had undoubtedly wished that she'd been able to accept that fate, although her beloved older sister had always known better.

Yet the exact form that rebellion had taken had grown gradually, nurtured in the quiet stillness of her own mind and soul as she witnessed the incredible luxury of the great Church dynasties in a city supposedly dedicated solely to the service of God. In a city where starvation and exposure collected their grim tolls every winter in sight of the Temple itself. That was what had opened her eyes to the truth of the Church's internal corruption, moved her awareness to the casual callousness of the Church as a whole, not simply of her own vile excuse for a father. However he might have abused the powers and perquisites of his own birth and office, he'd been able to do it only because the other men who ruled and perverted the Church with him had allowed him to. Because so many of them had done precisely the same sorts of things, and the consequences for so many others had been so much more terrible than the ones for her. That was what had impelled her outrage . . . and it was her love of what the Church was supposed to be which had fueled her rebellion against what it *was*.

And now this.

She looked at the transcript of the Address from the Throne once more, and like the man who'd written the accompanying letter, she saw only one thing. The men—and women, she thought, the ice in her eyes warming as she thought of Adorai Dynnys and Sharleyan of Chisholm—who had dared to raise their hands openly against the corruption she'd fought in secret for so long were to be crushed. She knew as well as any member of the Council of Vicars who had actually written that Address, and she recognized the official enunciation of the Group of Four's policy.

I don't understand why I can still feel so . . . surprised by it, she thought. *It's been obvious it had to come to this. I suppose it's just that deep down inside, I wanted so badly to believe that it might not, after all.*

Her mind turned to Adorai. She'd had only a single carefully and circuitously delivered letter from Erayk Dynnys' widow since she'd reached Charis safely. Her description of Archbishop Maikel and King—no, Emperor—Cayleb and Empress Sharleyan had warmed Ahnzhelyk's heart. The safety Adorai and her sons had found, the protection she'd been given, and her description of the "heretics" of Charis told Ahnzhelyk Phonda who was truly on God's side in the titanic, looming contest whose storm clouds were spreading steadily through Safehold's skies.

She sat thinking for a moment longer, then inhaled sharply, squared her slender shoulders, and gathered up the sheets of paper on her desk once more. She jogged them neatly together, then slid them into the hidden compartment cunningly built into the desk, and her mind was busy as she considered the unsigned letter's instructions. She wondered what Wylsynn and the other vicars and senior clerics of his circle of reform were going to decide about the so-called "Church of Charis." Judging from his direction to see to it that the transcript of the Grand Vicar's Address reached Charis, they, too, had few illusions about who truly served God and who followed corruption. But had they gone far enough to realize consciously what their hearts had obviously recognized already?

She didn't know. Just as she didn't know whether or not this new Empire of Charis would prove strong enough to resist the tempest gathering to sweep across it. But she did know where *she* stood, and she nodded slowly as she reflected upon that point.

She stood, walking to the window, looking out onto the bleak winter beauty of the snow, and her brain was busy, sorting through all of the other information she'd acquired about the Council of Vicars and the Group of Four's intentions. She'd passed all of it along to Wylsynn and his circle, but she'd kept copies of all of it, as well. She didn't know how much of it might be useful to Charis, but she didn't have to make that decision. Adorai could decide after Ahnzhelyk got all of it into her hands.

Is it really that easy? Her eyes followed a pedestrian as he slogged along, head bent against the wind, huddled deep inside his cloak. *That easy to go from agent of reform to schismatic spy?*

She had no answer . . . but she felt confident God would understand.

. II .

White Horse Reach,
and
Royal Palace,
City of Manchyr,
League of Corisande

The schooners' white sails sliced across the blue waters of White Horse Reach like the dorsal fins of krakens as they closed upon their prey.

They flew the new flag of the Imperial Charisian Navy, but the single light galley fleeing desperately before them flew the green and gold banner of the Church. The three schooners had reacted to the sight of that flag much as actual krakens would have responded to blood in the water, and the leading pursuer had already cleared away her forward chaser. A puff of gray-white smoke erupted from her foredeck and a thin plume of spray kicked up just ahead of the galley.

The fleeing vessel ignored the demand to stop, and the schooner fired again. This time, it was no warning shot. The fourteen-pound round shot slammed into the galley's stern, and splinters flew. One of the schooner's consorts began to fire, as well, and more splashes erupted around the fugitive's fragile hull. After another fifteen minutes—and at least three more direct hits—the galley finally surrendered to the inevitable. Her sail came down, and so did the proud golden scepter of the Church of God Awaiting.

It was a scene which had become unusual in the waters off the island of Corisande only because there was so little prey left for the Charisian Navy to pursue. In the last month, no Corisandian-flagged ship had been safe. Navy cruisers like the schooners—and a few privateers—with brooms lashed to their mastheads had swept the seas clear of Hektor of

Corisande's ships. The few merchant ships still flying the Corisandian flag huddled defensively in harbors—preferably neutral ones, when they could find them, where the Charisian Navy might not send in cutting-out expeditions after them—while the ships of the Corisandian Navy waited to defend their anchorages against the inevitable onslaught.

Even as the schooners came alongside their prize, someone standing on their decks could have seen half a dozen plumes of smoke rising from the Corisandian shore where naval landing parties, covered by Marines, were busily burning naval stores, sawmills, warehouses, highway bridges, and anything remotely of military value all along the coast of the Duchy of Manchyr. In a few places, the landing parties had found themselves facing garrisons or batteries. When that happened, they simply withdrew, confident they would soon find easier prey, or else they circled around any unsupported batteries to take them from their unprotected landward side. With the Corisandian Navy blockaded in port, even light units could operate with impunity, and no army detachment could march fast enough and far enough to keep pace with a warship, or to intercept a landing party before it reembarked once more. There was no way Prince Hektor's troops could prevent, or even seriously inconvenience, the Charisian onslaught, and his coast bled from a hundred tiny wounds every day.

▼ ▼ ▼

"—put a stop to this . . . this *piracy*!"

The speaker glared at Admiral Tartarian, and the earl reminded himself not to glare back. Not that he had any constitutional objection to letting some of the air out of this pompous windbag. Exactly what he and the other property owners being . . . inconvenienced by their Charisian visitors thought Tartarian could do about their problems eluded him. On the other hand, as the commander of the Corisandian Navy, he supposed it was inevitable that he would be the recipient of their ire.

What I ought to do is tell them to take it up with Cayleb, he thought bitingly. *Unfortunately, that's not a very practical response.*

"I realize the situation is bad," he said instead, addressing the entire delegation crowded into his office. "Unhappily, all I can tell you at this time is that it's likely to get still worse before it gets any better."

"But—!" the complainer began, waving both hands in the air.

"I'm sure all of you are well aware of the danger the entire League faces," Tartarian continued, overriding the other man ruthlessly. "At this time, all of our available warships are tied down defending major ports. I'm afraid it's simply impossible to free any of them up to protect our shipping." *Assuming even for an instant that they could somehow fight their way out of harbor against the Charisian Navy,* he added to himself. "As I've already told you, Earl Anvil Rock has agreed to assign every available man to coast defense. What *can* be done *is* being done, and I assure you all that we will continue to search for additional measures we can implement. But in all honesty, our resources are so heavily committed to resisting the invasion that I very much doubt we'll be able to make much difference against these shipping and coastal raids. I'm sorry, but that's simply the way it is, and I'm not going to sit here and lie to you by making promises I can't keep."

The loudmouth with the waving hands had opened his mouth again while Tartarian was talking. Now he closed it with a snap and looked around him at his fellow "delegates." Most of them looked as angry and unhappy as he did, but several of them were also shaking their heads at him, and Tartarian felt a trickle of relief. What he'd just told them obviously wasn't what they wanted to hear, but there was no way any reasonable man could have disputed a single thing he'd said.

Fortunately, there were enough reasonable men in the delegation to get them back out of Tartarian's office without his actually having to order the loudmouth taken out and shot.

Not, the earl reflected, standing as his "visitors" filed back out the door, *that it wouldn't have been much more satisfying to just go ahead and have him shot. Surely the Prince wouldn't begrudge me* one *little execution after all of the crap I've diverted from the Palace!*

The thought restored some needed balance to his day, and he snorted in harsh amusement. Maybe he owed that big-mouthed idiot some thanks after all. It wasn't likely that he was going to find anything else to amuse him today.

He glanced at the clock ticking away on his wall and grimaced. If he left now, he'd just be in time for this afternoon's meeting of Prince Hektor's senior advisers.

Which, he thought, *is probably going to be even less amusing than* this *meeting was.*

▼ ▼ ▼

"My Prince, I don't want to sound like I sympathize overmuch with the pain-in-the-arse bleaters who have been besieging Taryl's office, but they do have a point," Sir Lyndahr Raimynd said almost apologetically.

Prince Hektor gave him a moderately ugly glance, but the treasurer didn't flinch. First, because what he'd said was true, and second, because he knew Hektor's ire wasn't actually directed at *him.*

"I'm not saying I plan on shedding any tears over their personal losses, My Prince," he said. "I'm only trying to point out two things. First, we're suffering not simply property and financial losses, but also the loss of capabilities we may need badly later. And, second, the perception that the Charisians can operate with impunity along the coast of the capital duchy itself is beginning to have a serious impact on your subjects' morale. I can see definite signs of that among the members of the merchant and manufactory associations, and I'm sure it's affecting all of our people to at least some extent."

"I can't disagree with anything Lyndahr's just said, My Prince," Tartarian said, before Hektor could speak. "The problem is that I don't see anything we *can* do about it. Cayleb's scouts have located every warship we have. He has his damned schooners patrolling off of every port where they've found one of my galleons, and every one of those schooners has a squadron or so of *Charisian* galleons waiting, just out of sight from shore, to be summoned if any of my captains tries to put to sea."

"Could we possibly transfer some additional strength from the Dark Hills?" Raimynd asked anxiously, looking back and forth between Hektor and Earl Anvil Rock.

"I don't see how—" Anvil Rock began, but Hektor cut him off.

"No," he said firmly, almost harshly. Then he shook his head, like a horse irritated by a fly, and smiled a little crookedly at Raimynd. "I'm not trying to bite your head off, Lyndahr. To be honest, I'd *like* to bite someone's head off, if only to relieve my frustration. But I don't intend to start with the man who manages my finances and who's only trying to tell me the truth."

Raimynd returned his prince's smile and bobbed his head in acknowledgment of the semi-apology, and Hektor continued.

"At the moment, Koryn's position at Talbor Pass is the only thing keeping Cayleb's entire army out of Manchyr. I rather suspect that what he could do with forty or fifty thousand Marines, especially since all of them seem to have those Shan-wei-damned rifles, would dwarf what we're seeing now. Not to mention costing me the capital, which would also have a somewhat negative effect on morale."

"I understand that, My Prince," Raimynd said. "At the same time, though, I'm worried about the possibility Taryl raised at the very beginning. What if Cayleb decides to use his transports to swing his entire army around behind Sir Koryn without ever attacking his position at Talbor?"

"He might still do that," Anvil Rock said.

The earl looked older than he had a month or two before. The shocking totality of his son's defeat at Haryl's Crossing—and the news that Sir Charlz Doyal had been seriously wounded and captured by the Charisians—had shaken him badly. As he and Hektor had pored over Gahrvai's reports, they'd realized that what had happened was certainly not his fault. Or, for that matter, anyone else's. The fact that he'd gotten even four thousand of his infantry, and virtually all of his cavalry, out of the Charisian trap was remarkable, under the circumstances . . . and also explained what had happened to Doyal and virtually all of his artillerists. But what had happened at Haryl's Crossing was a grim warning that any future battle in anything remotely like open terrain would be an expensive proposition.

And it hadn't done the confidence and morale of his troops one bit of good, either.

"He might still do it," Anvil Rock repeated. "In fact, I half expect him to. At the moment, according to our own scouts, he's short of the troop lift he'd need to reembark his entire army. It sounds as if he had too much shipping for Dairos and sent the rest of his transports back to Chisholm or Zebediah to ride out the storm season. That's probably what's stopping him for now. He doesn't want to send *half* of his army out to the end of a limb Koryn might manage to saw off behind him. And he's also still very short of cavalry. It doesn't look like he has more than four or five thousand horse, total, which means that once he gets inland, *we* have the mobility advantage."

"Do you think he'll move to his right? Use one of the more northern passes, instead?" Tartarian asked, and Anvil Rock shook his head.

"I doubt it, for a couple of reasons. First, as I just said, he's very short on cavalry. If he starts pulling troops away from Talbor and sending them north, Koryn has Windshare's cavalry scouts hovering off Cayleb's flanks, watching for exactly something like that. If he heads inland with an infantry army, Windshare will definitely be able to get a force into position to block any of the other passes before he reaches them. Cavalry alone isn't going to stop Charisian Marines with rifles, of course. But Windshare's troopers will at least slow them down, and Koryn's infantry can march just as quickly as Charisians can. Not only that, but there are defensive positions in most of those passes which are almost as good as the ground at Talbor. Not quite, but almost. So he's not going to gain any significant tactical advantage by moving north, and doing that would also take him further away from his own base of operations and from the coast, where he can best utilize his seapower advantage effectively."

"Which he isn't going to want to do," Tartarian said, nodding in understanding and agreement.

"Exactly." Anvil Rock grimaced. "I'm not proposing any sort of boundless optimism here, but I'm beginning to think Cayleb may plan on staying put in Dairwyn until he decides he can risk the weather and bring his transports back to Dairos. At that point, of course, I'm afraid he *is* going to look for ways to break his army loose in Koryn's rear by hitting us here, closer to the capital."

"He won't take on Manchyr's batteries," Hektor said confidently. "And by the time he could get here, the earthworks you and your men are throwing up to cover the landward side of the city are going to be almost as tough."

"Agreed." Anvil Rock nodded, but his expression remained unhappy. "I'm not really concerned about the capital's immediate security, My Prince. He can have all of the rifles he wants, but as long as our men keep their heads down behind a good, solid earthwork, he won't be able to get at them without coming into musket range. And as nasty as his field artillery is, it doesn't have the range or the weight to stand up to the heavy guns we're mounting in the fortifications. He'd need siege artillery for that, and we've seen no sign of such heavy guns yet. Of course, he can always land dozens of heavy guns from his fleet, but he's going to want to have a secure anchorage somewhere close to Manchyr before he does that. He's certainly not going to want to drag naval guns and carriages any further overland than he absolutely has to!

"But if he manages to pen up a substantial portion of our troop strength as a garrison here in the capital, that frees his own forces to maneuver against other cities, or inflict damage on our manufactories and farms that would make anything we've seen out of his landing parties so far seem like no more than a minor annoyance. If he puts the capital under siege, our situation is going to be about as grim as it gets."

"If he manages that, then I may have to go ahead and sue for terms." Hektor looked like a man sucking on sour persimmon figs.

"My Prince—" Earl Coris began, his own expression concerned, but Hektor shook his head.

"Don't say it, Phylyp. And don't think you're worrying about anything *I* haven't worried about. Still, that fat little bugger Nahrmahn seems to have made out remarkably well, doesn't he?"

Hektor's expression turned more sour than ever. Anything less like a cat-lizard than the rotund Prince of Emerald would be difficult to imagine, but the little bastard had most definitely landed on his feet. Hektor didn't know which irritated him more. The fact that Nahrmahn had so promptly and effortlessly deserted to the other side—and done so damnably *well* out of it!—or the fact that he himself had obviously been underestimating the Emeraldian for years.

"With all due respect, My Prince—" Coris said.

"Oh, I know how much Cayleb hates me. To be honest, I can't say I blame him; in his shoes I'd probably feel the same. No, let's be fair. If I were in his shoes, I *would* hate my guts. After all, I've been trying to break Charis for years now, and it was my Navy which managed to kill his father at Darcos Sound. On the other hand, Haarald died in open battle, and *I'm* not the one who tried to have Cayleb himself assassinated and conspired with his cousin to usurp his father's throne. Oh, and let's not forget that a successful usurpation would have required his father's murder, as well. And probably his younger brother's, too."

"No," Coris acknowledged in the voice of a man edging delicately into dangerous waters. "Still, My Prince, don't forget that Cayleb is a married man now. And however he might feel about you, I don't believe there's much question about how *Sharleyan* feels."

"Believe me, that's not a point I'm likely to forget." Hektor showed his teeth in what definitely was *not* a smile. "If it weren't for that unfortunate little fact, I might already have tried opening negotiations with him. Still, if he has the choice between making at least minimal concessions to me or seeing several thousand more people killed—and this time, quite a few of them would be *his* men, not just ours—he may decide to turn reasonable. Whatever else he may be, and leaving aside our own propaganda on that point, he's not *really* a bloodthirsty monster, you know. An extraordinarily dangerous—and pissed-off—young man, I'll grant you, but not a monster."

Coris looked dubious, but he allowed the point to drop, and Hektor turned his attention back to Anvil Rock and Tartarian.

"I don't know if I'm completely convinced by your logic, Rysel. It sounds reasonable, mind you, and I don't have any better analysis to offer. I just don't want us to get too wedded to the belief that he's going to simply sit there until he's recalled more of his transports. For now, though, I see no option but to continue as we are while pressing the fortification of the capital as hard as we can.

"In the meantime, though, there is one precaution I want to take."

He paused, and his advisers looked at one another as the silence stretched out. Finally, Coris cleared his throat.

"Yes, My Prince?"

"I want Irys and Daivyn safely out of Corisande."

Hektor said the words as if they cost him physical pain, and Coris' eyebrows rose in astonishment.

"I know Irys will fight me on this one," Hektor continued. "And I know there are risks involved, and not just the ususal ones of a normal voyage long enough to get them somewhere more or less safe. Outside my protection, the two of them become potential hostages. But if they're outside Cayleb's reach, as well, they also represent a potential trump card tucked away in my tunic pocket. He can't simply arbitrarily reject an invitation to negotiate in favor of taking my head when he knows that Daivyn will still be alive to be used against him even if both Hektor and I are killed. And, to be honest, I'm not *quite* as confident as I'd like to be that he won't decide it's time to be rid of the House of Daykyn once and for all. Or of its *male* members, at any rate," he added just a bit more harshly, and his face turned briefly hard as marble.

"But where would you send them, My Prince? And how would you get them past Cayleb's navy?"

"I'll get them past Cayleb by selling half my soul and my left testicle to the Siddarmarkian ambassador," Hektor said dryly. "He's almost Charisian in his taste for nice, tall stacks of marks. I think he'll agree to grant them sanctuary if I come up with the right inducement, and any ship flying his personal standard is the same as his own embassy. Siddarmark is too important to Charis for Cayleb to violate its flag, I think, even if he knows Irys and Daivyn are aboard."

"My Prince," Tartarian said very seriously, "I advise against relying on that." Hektor raised an eyebrow, and Tartarian shrugged. "First, Siddarmark is friendly enough with Cayleb that I'm not completely convinced we can trust Stohnar's ambassador in something this important. Secondly, I wouldn't be a bit surprised, given that friendship, if Cayleb isn't already receiving regular spy reports from someone on his staff. And if Cayleb *does* learn Irys and Daivyn are onboard that ship, he certainly will intercept it. No doubt he'll be properly horrified by the way one of his captains has exceeded his orders and violated Siddarmarkian neutrality. I'm sure he'll promptly release the vessel, and probably apologize profusely and pay a handsome indemnity, to boot. But if he does, I can assure you that your son and daughter will *not* be aboard that ship when she docks in Siddarmark."

"You may be right," Hektor said after a long, silent pause. "But I still want them in safety. And not just for political reasons, Taryl."

"My Prince, all of us know that," Tartarian said gently. "But if that's what you desire, please let us try to find a way which is less likely to deliver them directly into your enemies' hands."

"Such as?"

"Not even Cayleb's navy can be everywhere at every moment, My Prince. I doubt very much that I could possibly get

any of our war galleons to sea without having them inter-
cepted. I think it would be possible to get a single small, fast
vessel out of one of the secondary ports which isn't as heavily picketed, however. Especially if we pick our time and
weather carefully. And once a small, unimportant-looking
vessel flying, say, Siddarmarkian or Harchongese colors is
well away, it's unlikely any Charisian cruiser or privateer is
going to bother her, even if they manage to sight her in the
first place."

Hektor looked suddenly more thoughtful.

"You really think that's possible?" He looked at Tartarian
with the eyes of an anxious father, as well as a prince, and his
naval commander nodded.

"My Prince, I know how much you love all your children,"
he said, very carefully not saying the word "daughter," then
raised one hand, palm uppermost. "I can't say there's no risk
involved in my suggestion. I won't say that. But I will tell
you, as one father speaking to another, that if they were my
own children, this is still what I would recommend. Of course
there's risk involved. I simply believe it's the lowest risk
available to us."

"Let me think about it," Hektor said. "You've raised some
very telling points, and I'll be honest. The thought of exposing them to this sort of risk, even aboard one of our own
ships, frightens me."

"If you do send them out of the princedom, My Prince,
where would you send them to?" Coris asked.

"I don't have a very long list to choose from," Hektor said
dryly. "For what it's worth, I think they'll probably be safest
with Zhames of Delferahk at the moment."

The others frowned, clearly considering what he'd just
said. Delferahk was scarcely the most powerful of the mainland realms, but Queen Consort Hailyn was Hektor's fourth
cousin. That would give Irys and Daivyn at least some blood
claim upon King Zhames' protection. And the fact that
Delferahk wasn't a player in the traditional power struggles
of the mainland's larger kingdoms should minimize the
temptation to use Hektor's children as pawns. In addition, re-

ports of what had happened to Ferayd had reached Manchyr. It seemed unlikely Zhames was going to feel like doing any favors for Cayleb anytime soon, so he was most unlikely to simply turn Irys and Daivyn over to Charis.

Which left—

"My Prince," Coris said quietly, "do you think the Temple will allow them to remain in Delferahk?"

"I don't know," Hektor confessed, his face tightening. "If Clyntahn decides any surrender I arrange shows I'm disloyal to the Temple—or, at least, to his precious Group of Four—there's no telling how he'll react. And if we're wrong, if Cayleb does decide he needs my head, and if anything happens to Hektor, Irys and Daivyn will suddenly become even more valuable than they are now. It's not a good solution; it's only the best one I can come up with."

Coris nodded, but his expression was still troubled, and Hektor smiled faintly.

"I have come up with one way to give them at least a little additional protection, Phylyp."

"You have, My Prince?" Coris' tone was suddenly the slightest bit wary, and Hektor's smile grew broader.

"Indeed I have. In addition to getting Irys and Daivyn out, Taryl is going to get *you* out. I'll provide you with a writ of authority as Irys' guardian until she comes of age, and of regency in Daivyn's name, in case, well—"

He shrugged, and Coris frowned.

"My Prince, I'm honored by your trust, but—"

"Don't say it. I know a lot of people are going to assume the worst about how you 'came by' those writs. After all, you *are* my spymaster, aren't you? However, it will be witnessed by the entire Council, and I think you'll be able to make its legitimacy stand up. More to the point, I'm going to *need* someone like you looking out for them. Someone who's accustomed to outthinking other players. I know you don't want to go, and I fully realize that if Cayleb is feeling vengeful here in Corisande, your chances of retaining your earldom won't be very good. But of everyone I can think of here in Manchyr, you're the one best suited to advise Irys and keep her out of the Church's clutches for as long as you can."

Coris looked as if he was tempted to argue. But then, instead, he closed his mouth and nodded.

"Of course I will, My Prince," he said quietly.

Hektor met his eyes for a moment, then nodded briskly.

"Very well," he said crisply. "In that case, I think we're done here for the day."

. III .

Helen Island,
Kingdom of Charis

Empress Sharleyan angled her parasol carefully as she crossed the mountain valley's grassy field at Earl Gray Harbor's side. The first councilor had wanted to provide her with a carriage, but after one look at the narrow, twisting track—calling it a "road" would have constituted physical assault on a perfectly respectable noun—Captain Gairaht and Sergeant Seahamper had flatly rejected *that* possibility. Fortunately, Sharleyan had always been an excellent horsewoman, although she suspected her style of horsemanship had come as something of a shock to her new Charisian subjects. Well, that was too bad, and she hoped their sensibilities hadn't been bruised, but she wasn't about to begin learning to ride sidesaddle at this late date.

At least she'd had time to have the palace seamstresses run up a new riding habit for her, with the divided skirt made of cotton silk rather than the heavier—and sweatier—fabric she would have been wearing in Chisholm at this time of year. She'd found that her northern complexion was profoundly grateful for the Charisian innovation of the parasol, but she'd also decided which five months of the year she wanted to spend in Charis and which in Chisholm. Snow was all very well in its place, and no doubt she would eventually miss February in Cherayth. Probably by the time she was, oh, sixty or so, at the very latest.

She smiled slightly at the thought, but the smile faded as she considered the loose ring of bodyguards surrounding her alertly even here.

Gairaht and Seahamper kept an eagle eye on everything around her. She considered suggesting that they might relax just a little bit, but she knew better. She'd had far too many years to grow accustomed to that sort of omnipresent protectiveness. Besides, it would have hurt their feelings, and at least they'd managed to get over a dozen of Cayleb's Charisian guardsmen integrated into their own detail, and still more would be joining it over the next few months. She suspected Gairaht had been tempted to protest, at least initially, but if he had, he'd been far too smart to succumb to the temptation. Sharleyan wasn't about to surround herself with a "bunch of foreigners" as if she didn't trust the Charisians to protect her. And she was rather amused by "her" Charisians' reaction to their new assignment. If anything, they were even more fanatical about protecting their new empress than her original Chisholmians were about protecting their old queen.

And the fact that the Church has finally gotten around to placing the entire Kingdom under the interdict—and I'm sure they'll extend it to the rest of the Empire (and me) as soon as they find out the Empire exists—only makes things worse.

She managed not to grimace as she realized that she'd probably *already* been excommunicated. Surely the Temple had learned about her marriage by now, in which case the Group of Four's response ought to be arriving fairly shortly.

The more fanatical Temple Loyalists probably wouldn't have worried about it either way, but now even the more hesitant among them can console themselves with the knowledge that the Church has formally absolved them of any lingering loyalty to Cayleb and the Archbishop. God only knows where that's likely to lead! No wonder Wyllys and Edwyrd—and all the rest of them—are so nervous. And I don't like to think about the way Chisholm is likely to react when word reaches

Cherayth. Uncle Byrtrym may be more alarmist than he has to be, but that doesn't mean he's completely wrong, either.

She did grimace—mentally at least—at that thought, but then she made herself put it aside. There wasn't anything she could do about it, anyway, except to trust her bodyguards here in Charis, and Mahrak Sahndyrs and her mother in Chisholm. And so she'd deliberately reached for the distraction of what had brought them here.

"I'm really looking forward to this, My Lord," she told Gray Harbor quietly as one of Seamount's aides tapped him on the shoulder and he turned to see her approaching. They were still a good two hundred yards away, though, and Gray Harbor looked at her as they continued to stroll towards the naval officer and his assistants.

"To be honest, Your Majesty, I'm not at all sure that I am," the earl admitted. She arched a surprised eyebrow, and he grimaced. "I was a sea officer for too many years, Your Majesty, and Cayleb, Seamount, and Howsmyn have already managed quite enough innovations to give an old sea dog like me nightmares. Solid shot is hard enough on a wooden hull without adding *this* to it. And if Seamount and Howsmyn can figure out how to make this work, then so can someone else. So eventually, we're going to find other people's navies firing the same sort of thing at *us,* and I don't expect we'll enjoy *that* very much. For example, I don't like to think what could have happened to the Ferayd attack if *their* batteries had been equipped with some of these 'shell'-firing guns Seamount is talking about."

"I see your point," she said thoughtfully, although the mention of Ferayd reminded her of other worries.

No one in Charis knew—yet—how the Group of Four was going to respond to the inquisitors' executions. Not that anyone had any intention of sitting around, paralyzed by indecision, while they waited to find out. Copies of the documents Admiral Rock Point had captured had been handed to the printers, and the presses had turned out thousands of additional copies for distribution throughout the Empire . . . and every mainland seaport. She had no intention of rethinking that decision, yet she had to admit that she felt more than a little wary whenever she contemplated the Group of Four's possible responses.

She'd written her husband a long letter which had been *mostly* about political matters and decisions, and enclosed a copy of Rock Point's official report, as well as printed copies of the captured documents, along with it. She knew he was going to be as grimly satisfied with the outcome as she'd been, and she'd already suggested that perhaps some additional knighthoods might be in order. But as she reviewed that same report mentally once more, she realized that Gray Harbor had every right to be concerned about what explosive shells might have done to the admiral's galleons.

Or might do to some other *admiral's ships in the future,* she thought rather more grimly.

"I see your point," she repeated out loud. "On the other hand, Cayleb said something to me on the same head." It was Gray Harbor's turn to raise an eyebrow, and she shrugged. "He said that once the slash lizard is out of its egg, your only option is to ride it or get eaten. So in this case, our only real choices are whether *we'll* introduce the changes or find out the hard way that someone *else* has already done it."

"He's said much the same thing to me, and so has . . . Seamount." For just a moment, Sharleyan had the oddest sensation that he'd been about to mention another name and changed it to the commodore's at the last moment. "And I suppose they're both right about that," he continued before she could pursue that thought. "Even if they aren't, we can't afford to overlook any advantages when the odds against us are so long. So I tell my bad dreams to leave me alone and try to concentrate on what a nasty surprise it's going to be for someone else, at least the first time we use it."

"I hope some of the Baron's other 'surprises' are serving Cayleb as well in Corisande." Sharleyan's voice was suddenly lower, darker, and Gray Harbor glanced across at her. "I know I probably shouldn't, but I worry about him," she admitted softly.

"Good," he said, equally softly, and smiled at her expression.

"Your Majesty, I think the way you and Cayleb obviously feel about one another may be one of the best things that's ever happened to Charis. You go right on worrying about him. Don't take counsel of your fears and let them rule you, but don't pretend—especially to yourself—that you *aren't* worried."

"I'll try to bear that in mind, My Lord." She reached out and gave his arm an affectionate squeeze. "I just wish it didn't take so long for letters to travel between here and Corisande!"

"So do I. But so far, if you'll pardon my saying so, you've done an excellent job ruling in Cayleb's absence."

"How far wrong can I go with your advice, and Archbishop Maikel's, to keep me straight?" she replied with a smile.

"Your Majesty," Gray Harbor's answering smile actually looked rather more like a grin, "forgive me, but you are a remarkably stubborn young woman. That's a *good* thing in a ruler, in many ways, you understand, so don't think I'm complaining. But I strongly suspect that if Maikel and I both advised against a course of action you thought was the proper one, you'd listen very carefully and courteously and then be exquisitely polite when you informed us that we were all going to do it *your* way."

She started to shake her head, then paused. After a moment, she gave a gurgle of laughter, instead.

"I'm glad you had an opportunity to get to know Mahrak Sahndyrs before you had to leave for home with me. I have the oddest feeling, though, that the better you get to know me, the more you're going to sympathize with Mahrak. And vice versa, I'm quite sure. He's told me more than once that I could outstubborn a slash lizard with a toothache."

Gray Harbor chuckled.

"Why do I suspect that when you were younger, Your Majesty, you knew how to pitch a truly royal temper tantrum?"

"What do you mean, 'when I was younger,' My Lord?" she murmured provocatively, and his chuckle turned into a laugh.

"I await the moment with trembling and dread," he assured her.

She started to say something else, then stopped as they

reached Seamount. She gave Gray Harbor one more smile, then turned to greet the commodore.

"Your Majesty," Seamount said, bowing deeply.

"Baron," she replied, and he straightened once more. "I've quite been looking forward to your demonstration ever since I received your last report," she continued.

"Well, Your Majesty, I only hope it performs as promised. It has so far, but I've discovered that the first law of demonstrations for royalty is the same one Earl Gray Harbor is fond of quoting about battles."

"Indeed?" Sharleyan glanced at the first councilor, and Gray Harbor shrugged.

"What can go wrong, *will* go wrong, Your Majesty," he told her. "Although Ahlfryd is probably doing himself an injustice. Most of his demonstrations perform as promised. On the other hand, I must confess, when one of his little displays does go awry, it tends to do so rather . . . spectacularly. Ah, you may have noticed, for example, that he has you at least a hundred yards away from his new infernal device. I'm sure it will prove an unnecessary precaution, of course."

"Oh, of *course,* My Lord." Sharleyan chuckled and returned her attention to Seamount. "Well, now that you've both conspired to lower my expectations, I trust you're prepared to dazzle me with your success, instead."

"I certainly hope so, Your Majesty," Seamount said more seriously. "And while Earl Gray Harbor is correct when he suggests that I would really prefer not having you physically closer to the weapon than you have to be during the test firings, I would be honored to allow you to examine it *before* the test."

" 'Test,' My Lord?" Sharleyan repeated. "I thought you'd just referred to it as a 'demonstration.' "

"Up until the moment we actually deploy a weapon, Your Majesty, all demonstrations are also tests," Seamount replied promptly, and she snorted.

"A splendid recovery, My Lord!" she congratulated him. "And now, I truly would like to see this new wonder of yours."

"Of course, Your Majesty. If you would accompany me, please?"

290 / DAVID WEBER

Seamount led the way across to the weapon in question, and Sharleyan's eyes narrowed as she inspected it. It looked rather like a cross between a standard field gun and a carronade, she thought. The barrel was shorter and stubbier than one of the twelve-pounders she'd seen demonstrated, but it was longer in proportion to its diameter than a carronade. There was also something a bit peculiar about the way it was mounted on its carriage. It took her a moment to figure out what it was, but then she had it. This weapon had been designed to be elevated to at least twice the elevation of a normal field gun. Not only that, but instead of the wooden wedge all of the other Charisian cannon she'd seen used as a spacer under the breach to hold the gun at its desired elevation, this weapon's cascabel was pierced by a wrist-thick screw with a crank handle on its upper end. Obviously, the gun's elevation was supposed to be adjusted by running the screw up and down, and there was a metal pointer and a scale graduated in degrees to measure precisely what that elevation was.

"This is an ingenious idea," she commented to Seamount, tapping the crank handle. "Do you intend to go back and apply it to our naval cannon, as well, My Lord?"

"Probably not, Your Majesty." Seamount seemed pleased by the fact that she'd obviously grasped how the new arrangement worked. "First, it adds to the expense and the foundry time required to produce each weapon. More to the point, perhaps, shipboard guns don't require the same fine degree of control. Or perhaps what I should say is that the practical limitations of shipboard gunnery mean this degree of control wouldn't be extraordinarily useful. Ranges are short, both the firing ship and its target are usually moving—in more than one direction at the same time, given the normal action of wind and wave—and ruggedness of design and the ability to make quick, *rough* adjustments in elevation are much more important features than being able to know the *exact* elevation of the weapon."

"Is the exact elevation truly that critical, My Lord?"

"It will be, Your Majesty," he said very seriously. "Dr. Mahklyn is working on the mathematics for me now, but eventually, using this basic design concept—I imagine it will require a great deal of refinement first, you understand—we should actually be able to fire accurately on targets we can't even see from the gun pit."

"Indeed?" Sharleyan's eyebrows rose. "Your report didn't mention that possibility, My Lord."

"Mostly because it's still theoretical, Your Majesty. However, as I'm certain you've observed, this gun can be elevated to a much higher angle than our standard field guns. In fact, to distinguish it from our normal field guns, I've dubbed this a 'high-angle cannon.' I imagine, sailors being sailors and Marines being Marines, that will undoubtedly be shortened to 'angle-cannon' or even just 'angle.' " He sighed. "They *do* have a way of rather brutally simplifying precise terminology."

"I see." Sharleyan's lips twitched, but her voice was commendably steady as she continued. "I assume, however, that there's a specific reason for this 'high-angle cannon's' greater elevation?"

"Indeed, Your Majesty. What I've done is to attempt to recapture some of the catapult's ability to fire on an arced trajectory so as to drop the fired round onto its target at a relatively high angle. That should both increase range for a given projectile velocity and allow us to use 'indirect fire' to engage targets on the other side of walls or hills, the way a skilled catapult crew could."

Sharleyan's eyes widened as the implications of Seamount's explanation sank home.

"That, My Lord," she said after a moment, "would be an enormous advantage."

"At least until our enemies figure out how to duplicate it, Your Majesty," Gray Harbor pointed out, and she flashed him a smile at the reminder of their earlier conversation.

"That, unfortunately, is unavoidable, Your Majesty," Seamount said rather more heavily. "There's no way we could—"

"Baron Seamount," Sharleyan interrupted, "there's no need for you to apologize for—or explain—the inevitability of Earl Gray Harbor's observation. I assure you, the Emperor and I are both perfectly aware of that. And, as he pointed out to me, if our enemies adopt our innovations, then ultimately, they'll be forced to become increasingly *like* us, which means the Group of Four's grip on things will start fraying rather badly. And if they *don't* adopt our innovations, then they systematically undercut their own chances of ever actually defeating us militarily."

Seamount nodded respectfully, and Sharleyan turned her attention to the ammunition cart parked beside his "high-angle cannon." The bagged charges of gunpowder were familiar enough, but the gun's projectiles were unlike anything she'd ever seen before. One of them had been laid out for her examination, and she studied it thoughtfully. Instead of a spherical round shot, it was an elongated cylinder with rounded ends, as if someone had stretched a standard round shot to perhaps five or six times its normal length without increasing its diameter. And its smooth skin was interrupted by a series of studs, arranged in three rows, which projected outward from it and encircled the projectile in an angled spiral pattern.

"These, I take it," she said, touching one of the studs gingerly with a fingertip, "are what engage in the rifling grooves your report described?"

"Precisely, Your Majesty."

Seamount looked even more pleased than before at the evidence Sharleyan had studied his report with the attention it deserved, and she smiled at him.

"And this," he continued, picking up a wooden plug, "is our fuse. At the moment, at any rate. There are some problems I'm still working on."

Sharleyan nodded. Seamount, she thought, would *always* be working on "some problem." He was the sort of man who was constitutionally incapable of accepting that anything had attained perfection.

"You mentioned that there was a problem with the 'shell's' impact," she said.

"Exactly. This," he waved the wooden plug in his hand, "works . . . adequately for timed detonation. We're still working on refining the composition of the powder we use to improve the consistency with which it burns, but the basic principles are relatively simple. The plug is drilled out and filled with a powder train. The walls of the central cavity are thin enough that they can be easily pierced with an awl. By piercing it at the proper point along the fuse's length before inserting it into the shell, the flash from the powder charge when the shell is fired is admitted to the powder filling, which then burns down to the powder filling of the *shell,* causing it to detonate.

"The problem is that this type of fuse is actually going to work better on a spherical shell, such as might be fired from a smoothbore gun, like our current twelve-pounders. In fact, Master Howsmyn is already beginning to produce shells for our field artillery, as well as larger ones for the Navy's thirty-pounders, in case they're needed for siege work. We ought to be ready to ship the first of them to Corisande within another month, at the outside."

"And why is—? Oh, I see! These," Sharleyan tapped the elongated shell again "—are always going to land point-first, aren't they?"

"Yes, they are," Seamount agreed, nodding vigorously. "We've already discovered that putting the fuse on the side of the shell *towards* the propellant charge doesn't work very well. That means we have to put it on the front—or, on one of these, on the nose—and, fired out of a rifled gun, the shell will always land nose-first, which will quite often tend to destroy or crush the fuse before it can explode. With a spherical shell, on the other hand, there's no way to tell which part of the shell will land first. That means the chances are actually quite good that it *won't* land fuse-first, in which case a fuse which hasn't burned all the way down yet would still have an excellent chance of detonating the shell after all."

"I see." Sharleyan frowned. "Surely there has to be a solution for the problem, though, My Lord. It seems to me that what we really need is a fuse which will detonate the shell only *after* it strikes its target. It would obviously simplify things enormously if it didn't matter whether or not the powder burned completely consistently in the fuse, or whether the range had been estimated absolutely correctly. For that matter, there must be any number of instances in which it would be much more desirable for the shell to *penetrate* its target before it exploded."

The empress, Gray Harbor realized, had just turned Seamount into her adoring slave. Her nimble mind's quick grasp obviously delighted the pudgy artillerist, and he beamed at her as if they were co-conspirators.

"That's *exactly* right, Your Majesty!" he agreed, nodding vigorously. "In fact, that's the very thing I'm working on now."

"And how are you approaching the problem?"

Sharleyan's expression was intent, and Gray Harbor realized something else. If she'd just captivated Seamount, it was because she was genuinely fascinated by what the baron had accomplished. She *was* Seamount's co-conspirator, and the first councilor had a sudden picture of her in the commodore's workshop, sleeves rolled up, hands grimy, dirt smudged across her nose, and as happy as a little girl in a candy shop.

"Actually, I'm thinking that what we need is some sort of incendiary composition," Seamount told her. "Something that doesn't need a spark for ignition. Something that ignites from *friction,* for example. Gunpowder can do that. It's one of the dangers we look for in magazines where it's stored. But gunpowder won't work for this. We need something else. I'm trying several different compositions at the moment, and Dr. Mahklyn and the Royal College are also working on the problem. In the end, I think, the solution is going to be to make a fuse which is a closed vessel, with its walls coated in the composition we've managed to devise, and something like a heavy ball coated in more of the composition that flies forward when the shell lands and—"

"And strikes the walls of the vessel, setting off whatever compound you finally come up with, and detonates the shell on impact!" Sharleyan finished for him with a huge smile.

"Yes!" Seamount beamed back at her. For several seconds,

they simply stood there, grinning at each other. Then the baron gave himself a shake.

"Your Majesty, I trust you'll forgive me for saying that you're even quicker at grasping possibilities than the Emperor. And that's saying a great deal, indeed."

"Thank you, My Lord. That's a compliment I'll treasure," Sharleyan told him. Then she inhaled deeply.

"And now, Baron Seamount, I believe you were about to demonstrate to me how to fire an explosive shell to the other side of a wall?"

. IV .

The Laughing Bride, City of Tellesberg, Kingdom of Charis

Excuse me, My Lord, but this just arrived."

"Ahlvyn, Ahlvyn!" The man seated at the table looked up, waved an admonishing finger at the younger man standing in the doorway, and shook his head. "How many times must I remind you that I'm a simple merchant?" Archbishop Mylz Halcom asked chidingly.

"Excuse me, My Lo— Sir." The younger man colored slightly at the familiar reprimand. "I'm afraid I'm more of a creature of habit than I'd thought I was."

"We all are, and in some ways, that's a good thing. But it's also something that anyone—even a priest—needs to be aware of and guard against. Especially now."

"Of course, Sir." The younger man bent his head in a brief bow of acknowledgment, then held out a sealed envelope. "As I was saying, this just arrived."

"I see."

The man seated at the table took the envelope and turned it slowly in his hands. It was addressed to "Edvarhd Dahryus, at the Laughing Bride," and he rather thought he recognized the handwriting.

"Thank you, Ahlvyn," he said.

The younger man gave him another brief bow and withdrew from the room. "Dahryus" watched him go, then reached to the narrow bookshelf beside his worktable and withdrew a copy of *The Life of Saint Evyrahard* which had been printed right here in Tellesberg. He laid the book on the table, unsealed the envelope, and extracted the several thin sheets of fine, expensive, gilt-edged paper it contained. They were covered in columns of numbers—the new numbers, which had originated here in Charis—and he smiled thinly. The cipher in which the letter had been written was based on a technique the Church had worked out centuries before, but it amused him, in a grim sort of way, that the Charisians' own new numbers had made it so much simpler and more effective now that he found himself forced to employ it against them.

He laid out another pad of paper, inked his pen, and opened the book. The numbers were arranged in groups of four, and he started turning pages. The cipher was both simple and impossible to break without the key, albeit at the price of a certain cumbersomeness. The first number in each group referred to a specific page in Saint Evyrahard's biography. The second number referred to a paragraph on that page, the third referred to a sentence in that paragraph, and the fourth referred to a specific word in that sentence. Without knowing which book the cipher was based upon, no one could possibly break the code.

Which is undoubtedly a good thing at the moment, he reflected as he began laboriously counting. *I think, though, that it might not be a bad idea to suggest that our friend use less expensive paper in the future. Wave Thunder might not be able to break the cipher, but I'll bet his agents could probably locate everyone who sells this particular paper . . . and find out who they sold it to.*

He worked his way slowly but steadily through the entire letter, transcribing the indicated words without really trying to read them. He knew his own impatience, and he was well aware of his ability to allow himself to succumb to distraction when faced with tasks like this one. As a young monk, he'd always found the traditional discipline of the scriptorium boring beyond words, not to mention pointless, given the existence of printing presses and moveable type. In fact, he'd been disciplined more than once for finding ways to amuse himself when he ought to have been attending to his copyist's duties. But although his present task's demand for exact accuracy and laborious precision was just as great, its purpose was deadly important, and so he forced himself to complete the entire task before he turned back to the very beginning and began methodically reading.

It took him several minutes to complete the transcribed text, and his eyes narrowed as he worked his way through it. Then he sat back, gazing up at the ceiling while he contemplated what he'd read. He stayed that way for the better part of half an hour, then straightened abruptly.

"Ahlvyn!"

"Yes, sir?"

Ahlvyn Shumay reappeared in the doorway as if by magic, and despite the tension the letter from the palace had generated, Halcom smiled slightly. The youthful priest would never admit it, of course, but Halcom knew he'd been hovering outside the door, consumed by curiosity. Then the bishop thought about what that letter had actually said, and the temptation to smile disappeared.

"We need a letter. Two letters, actually. One to our friend in the Palace, and one for our friend in the mountains."

"Yes, Sir." Shumay sat down on the opposite side of the table, took the pen Halcom had laid aside, and prepared to take notes. "Whenever you're ready, sir."

"According to our friend here in Tellesberg," Halcom began, tapping the letter he'd decoded, "the Duke has mentioned Saint Agtha's to the Empress, and as expected, she's expressed an interest in visiting the convent. Unfortunately, the Royal Guard—excuse me," he smiled thinly, "I mean the 'Imperial Guard,' of course—is being rather more solicitous of her security than we'd hoped. Our friend doesn't yet know just how strongly they intend to reinforce her normal body-guards for any excursions outside the Palace, but he says they definitely will be reinforced. So, to our two letters.

"First, to our friend in the Palace. Inform him that we cannot risk exposing our presence and our capabilities unless we're as certain as humanly possible of success. If we make an attempt of this nature, and we fail, it's unlikely enough of us will survive to make another attempt. And even if that weren't the case, an unsuccessful attempt will certainly cause them to increase their bodyguards and all of their other security precautions. Because of that, I will not authorize the operation, even if Sharleyan does carry out her plans to visit Saint Agtha's, unless we have accurate information on the strength of her bodyguard at least several days before she departs the Palace. I don't wish him to run any extraordinary risks in acquiring that information. Stress to him that he'll be more valuable where he is in the future, even if this operation is never attempted, than he would be unmasked and executed. Not to mention the fact that if he *is* unmasked and executed, it will mean this particular operation will be a failure, anyway. Nonetheless, he needs to be aware that we simply can't act without that knowledge."

"Yes, Sir," Shumay said, pen flying as he jotted down the bishop's points.

"Now for our friend in the mountains." Halcom frowned, then inhaled deeply. "I'm very much afraid we're going to have to risk widening our contacts," he said. "We're simply going to need more men than we already have, and that means actively recruiting the people who can provide them. Tell him I'm assuming on the basis of present information that we'll have to increase the size of our force by at least another third, and possibly as much as half. I realize we've discussed the possibility that something like this might arise, and that he's done some preliminary planning already, but tell him to be extremely cautious about who he admits to his plans and how deeply he allows them to become involved—and informed—before the actual strike itself."

"With all due respect, Sir," Shumay said, "but would it be wise to involve anyone who isn't aware, at least in a general sense, of what will be asked of them?"

"A valid point," Halcom conceded. "You're concerned that if they aren't aware of what we intend to do before the actual operation, some of them may balk when they do find out?"

"That's my major tactical concern, Sir," Shumay agreed. "There's also the moral issue, of course."

"There is indeed." Halcom smiled affectionately at his aide. "And you're quite right that we can't forget our priestly calling and responsibilities simply because we find ourselves called to a sort of service we never contemplated when we first took our vows. Still, I'm afraid our greater responsibility to defend Mother Church against her enemies outweighs many of our purely pastoral concerns. At this moment, and especially for this particular operation, we must think first and foremost in pragmatic terms about the tactics and precautions necessary to success.

"Every individual we recruit increases the number of people who may inadvertently betray us, our plans, and God, even if that individual is completely and totally trustworthy. Should someone *not* be trustworthy, not be fully committed to what we ask of him in God's name, then the danger of betrayal increases many times over. And should we recruit someone who might—as you're quite right to be concerned over—balk at the last minute, then that person would be much more likely to inform one of Wave Thunder's agents if he learned early on exactly what our objectives are. Finally, should someone feel inclined to balk at the very last moment, after our force has already assembled to launch the strike, it will, to put it bluntly, be too late. The mere fact that he's already joined us under arms in what the Emperor and Empress, despite their excommunication and the interdict, will quite properly construe as an act of 'treason' against them will mean he stands condemned before the Emperor's Bench of a capital crime whatever happens. Not only that, but if he attempts to withdraw, or even to actively resist our plans, we'll have the additional men available to prevent him from doing so."

He paused, regarding his aide's troubled expression across the table, and smiled sadly.

"In some ways, I suppose, I'm guilty of allowing expediency to overrule conscience. And I'm definitely taking precautions which will make it effectively impossible for everyone involved in God's work to have made a fully informed decision about taking up that task. But I'm a bishop of Mother Church, Ahlvyn, just as both of us are priests. We have a responsibility not simply to the individuals who may be involved in this particular effort against the schismatics, but also to all of the other souls which may be lost forever to Shan-wei if our effort is unsuccessful. However much we may regret it, we must make our decisions on the basis of that larger responsibility."

The bishop's expression darkened, and he shook his head.

"I know I'm asking much of the loyal sons of Mother Church, Ahlvyn. And it grieves me to do so without being completely honest with them beforehand. Yet, in my defense, I've asked as much or more of you. And of myself. We both have vows of obedience and loyalty to God and Mother Church, of course, and more is asked of any priest than of the souls in his care, but I never expected when I took those vows that those responsibilities would require me to set my hand to something like this. I know Sharleyan has made herself God's enemy. I know who she truly serves. And I genuinely believe that what we intend to do is the most effective blow we could possibly strike against the unholy alliance gathering to assail Mother Church. All of that's true. Yet when I face God and the Archangels in my evening prayers every night, I find myself begging for their forgiveness."

"Do you, Sir?" Shumay asked softly. Halcom quirked one eyebrow, and the younger cleric shrugged. "I find myself in the same situation," he explained.

"Of course you do," Halcom said sadly. "You're a priest. Priests are charged to care for their flocks, not to plan acts of violence and rebellion against secular authority. It's how we think, as well as who we are. And that's why we both find ourselves asking forgiveness for doing the very thing we know Langhorne now calls us to. I sometimes think that the darkest thing of all about Shan-wei is her ability to contrive situations in which good and godly men find themselves forced to choose between evils in the service of God. Is it more evil for us, as individuals, to act as we are, or would it be more evil for us to *refuse* to act and allow this monstrous challenge to God's plan for all mankind to go unchecked?"

The plainly furnished little room was silent for several seconds, and then Halcom shook himself.

"I know how you've already answered that question, Ahlvyn. If you continue to have doubts, continue to question some of the actions to which we are called, that's completely human of you. Indeed, I think it would worry me more if you *had* no doubts. Even when the shedding of blood is necessary, it should never be easy, never be a trivial decision, arrived at without questioning, without being as positive as one can be that it *is* necessary. That should be true of any man, and particularly of any priest. But I believe you know as well as I do that in this case it is necessary, and that we must do whatever we may to ensure that we succeed in doing God's work."

He gazed into Shumay's eyes, and the younger man nodded.

"You're right, Sir, of course." He tapped the sheet of notes in front of him. "If you'll give me a few moments, I'll draft the letters for your approval before we encrypt them."

MAY,
YEAR OF GOD 893

·✦·

. I .

Talbor Pass,
Dark Hill Mountains,
League of Corisande

Sir Koryn Gahrvai kept low as he made his cautious way to the forward redoubt.

Coming this far forward in daylight was risky, although that wasn't a consideration which would have occupied his mind as little as two months before. Now, however, he and the men of his army had learned the hard way that to expose oneself anywhere within a thousand yards of a Charisian marksman was likely to prove fatal. Even now, he could hear the occasional distant, distinctively whip-like crack of their damnable long-range rifles, and he wondered if whoever was firing actually had a target.

Probably. But not necessarily. He grimaced. *They managed to put the fear of their riflemen into us at Haryl's Crossing; just reminding us by firing an occasional shot, even at random, is one way to make sure we don't forget.*

Not that anyone who'd survived Haryl's Crossing was ever likely to forget. Of course, he reflected sourly, there weren't that many who *had* survived and were still with his army. Most of those who'd actually faced the Charisian Marines' rifle fire—and survived—were prisoners.

Despite that, his men's loyalty remained unshaken. And so, more than a little to his own surprise, did their confidence in their leadership. In him.

I owe a lot of that to Charlz, he thought bleakly. *We may have fucked up, but without Charlz and his gunners, we wouldn't have gotten* anyone *out. The men know that, just as they know he—and I—never even considered running for it ourselves until we'd gotten out every single man we could.*

Gahrvai only wished Doyal hadn't left it quite so late. A handful of artillerists who'd managed to escape death or capture had told him how Charlz had moved continually from gun pit to gun pit, exposing himself recklessly to the deadly Charisian rifle fire, as he rallied his men. He'd been everywhere, encouraging, threatening, pointing guns himself, even wielding the rammer with his own hands on one of the last guns still in action while two-thirds of its crew lay dead or wounded around it. Without his example, the men in that battery would have broken and run far earlier . . . and the trust Gahrvai's troops were still willing to extend to their commanders would probably be a much flimsier thing.

Gahrvai knew that, but he missed Doyal more with every passing day. He'd counted upon the older man's sharp mind and imagination even more than he'd realized before he lost them, and he was painfully aware of their absence now. Besides, Charlz was a friend.

At least you know he's still alive, Koryn, he told himself. *And he's likely to stay that way, according to Cayleb's letter. That's something. In fact, it's quite a lot. And you've still got Alyk, too. That's nothing to sneeze at, either, given what almost happened to* him*!*

Windshare had recognized the unfolding disaster and attempted to do something about it by getting his cavalry into the Charisians' rear, in the gap they'd obligingly left between their own formations and the woodland through which they'd advanced. Unfortunately, the Charisians had detailed an entire battalion of their infernal riflemen expressly to prevent him from doing just that. They'd hidden it in an arm of second-growth trees which had extended out into the farmland surrounding Haryl's Crossing, with enough trees and undergrowth to make their position effectively cavalry proof, and their deadly rifle fire had more than decimated Windshare's lead squadrons when they attempted to ride past them to the infantry's assistance. Fortunately, horses were bigger targets than men, and Windshare's human casualties hadn't been as severe as the earl had first feared. They'd been bad enough, though, and the loss of so many horses had been decisive. Windshare himself had had his horse shot out from under him, and he'd dislocated his shoulder when his mount went down. But one of his staff officers had gotten him remounted and safely out of the cauldron, and, to Gahrvai's intense relief (and not a little surprise), the earl had called off his advance rather than taking even worse casualties trying to bull his way through.

I really ought to stop feeling surprised when Alyk does something right, he scolded himself. *He isn't* stupid, *whatever else, and he's probably the best cavalry brigade commander in Corisande. It's just—*

The sudden *"wheeet"* of one of the Charisians' infernal bullets, passing unpleasantly close to his head, reminded him forcibly that he was almost to the front line and that it was unwise to allow his mind to wander.

And, he thought with wry bitterness, quickly ducking back down behind the sheltering parapet, *it's also the reason I ordered all of my officers to take the damned cockades off their hats!*

He scrambled the last fifty or sixty yards along the communications trench to the redoubt he'd come to visit. The major commanding it saluted sharply as Gahrvai entered the work, and Sir Koryn returned the courtesy with equal sharpness. He suspected that some of his subordinates thought it was silly of him to insist on maintaining proper military etiquette at a time like this, but Gahrvai was convinced the familiar requirements helped keep the men focused, not to mention maintaining their sense of identity as *soldiers*, rather than a frightened rabble huddling in their fortifications.

And I'm not going to let them turn into *a rabble, either,* he promised himself—and them—grimly.

"Good afternoon, Major," he said now.

"Good morning, Sir."

"How have things been today?"

"More of the same, Sir." The major shrugged. "I think some of their light infantry was sneaking around out there early this morning, before dawn. We haven't seen any sign of them since sunrise, though."

"And their marksmen?"

"A pain in the arse, Sir," the major said frankly. Then he grinned crookedly. "As usual," he added.

"How bad are your losses?"

"Actually, Sir, I think they're a little off their game today. I've got two wounded, only one of them seriously. That's about it."

"Good!" Gahrvai slapped the younger man on the shoulder, wondering if it sounded as bizarre to the major as it did to his own ears to call two wounded in return for no enemy casualties "Good."

On the other hand, that's exactly what it is, so there's no point pretending otherwise. Besides, I wouldn't be fooling anyone if I did.

Gahrvai climbed up onto the redoubt's firing step and very cautiously lifted his head above the parapet. No Charisian bullets screamed around his ears immediately, but he made a mental note not to assume things would stay that way as he rapidly scanned the approaches to his present position.

Talbor Pass was the shortest, most direct route through the Dark Hill Mountains, although at just under twenty-seven miles "short" was a purely relative term. It was also a thoroughly unpleasant place to fight a battle. "Shortest" and "most direct" didn't say a thing about "straightest," and no general in his right mind would launch an offensive battle in a place like this. Which was precisely why Sir Koryn Gahrvai's army was here.

The western half or so of the pass was fairly broad and really did have extensive stretches of good going, but as one moved farther east, it became increasingly narrow, twisting, and steep-sided . . . among other things. The handful of places that weren't bare rock, or a thin coating of dirt *over* bare rock which might support a threadbare patch of alpine grasses, were covered in tangled thickets of wire vine and dagger thorn. Whatever the wire vine didn't manage to entangle, the dagger thorn's six-inch, knife-edged thorns ought to cut to ribbons quite handily. Best of all, from Gahrvai's perspective, places where firing lines were more than a hundred and fifty yards long were virtually impossible to find. In many places, the longest field of fire available was less than *fifty* yards, which suited his smoothbores as well as it did the Charisians' rifles. And it also meant the shorter-ranged Corisandian batteries could count on holding their own against the Charisian guns.

He couldn't keep the Charisians from sending their marksmen scurrying up the steep slopes to find suitable positions, but it had quickly become evident that the number of Charisians capable of those truly astounding long-range shots was limited. They managed to inflict a steady, painful stream of casualties, a handful here and a handful there, but there weren't enough of them to be a serious threat to his ability to hold his ground. Especially not with the redoubts and connecting earthworks he'd ordered built. Most of them had been thrown up before what was left of his retreating advance guard had reached the pass, and they'd been steadily improved by working parties each night thereafter. By now, Gahrvai was completely confident of his ability to hold any frontal assault . . . assuming someone as smart as Cayleb would suffer a sufficiently severe case of temporary insanity to launch any such assault.

Part of Gahrvai was deeply tempted to pull back behind Talbor. He could have left perhaps a quarter of his total infantry strength to hold the fortifications, and it probably would have eased his supply problems. He'd fallen back to the west of the worst bottleneck before he'd ever dug in, so getting supplies forward to his advanced positions in sufficient quantity wasn't *quite* impossible. The bulk of his army lay spread out along the wider portions of the pass behind him—close enough to move forward quickly if the opportunity to do so presented itself; far enough to the rear to make supplying it relatively easy. That didn't make those problems magically go away, by any stretch of imagination, however, and moving forty or fifty thousand men out of the pass would have helped a lot.

I ought to do just that, he told himself for perhaps the thousandth time. *But if I do, then I lose the ability to threaten Cayleb's rear if he suddenly decides to go somewhere else. Besides, there's that little surprise we're working on for him.*

He grimaced as he gazed eastward, then ducked as a puff of smoke blossomed high on the side of the pass and a bullet thudded into the parapet close enough to throw dirt into his face.

"See what I mean about being off their game, Sir?" Gahrvai turned his head and saw the major crouched beside him, grinning. "Most days, that bugger would have nailed you."

Despite himself, Gahrvai found himself smiling back. He supposed some generals might have reprimanded the youngster for his familiarity, but Gahrvai treasured it. The major's *"what-the-hell-we're-all-in-this-together"* grin was the clearest indication possible that despite its awareness of how its enemies' weapons outclassed its own, his army was still far from defeated.

"Well, Major, I suppose I've seen what I came to see, anyway. No point giving him an opportunity to improve his score, is there?"

"I'd really prefer for you to get shot on someone else's watch, Sir. If you insist on being shot, that is."

"I'll try to bear that in mind," Gahrvai chuckled, and patted the young man on the shoulder. Then he looked back the way he'd come, squared his shoulders, and drew a deep breath.

"Well, back to headquarters," he said, and set off on the cautious trek towards the rear.

There hadn't really been any need for him to make the trip forward this morning in the first place. He'd already known exactly what he was going to see, it wasn't as if his personal reconnaissance was going to change anything, and it could certainly be argued that exposing the army's commanding officer to an incapacitating wound (or death) without some damned compelling reason wasn't a particularly bright move.

But he'd made it a point to spend at least part of every day in one of the forward positions, primarily because he felt he *did* have a compelling reason. He was no more fond of the sound of bullets whizzing past him than anyone else, and his personal opinion was that an officer who deliberately exposed himself to fire when there was no need for him to do so wasn't proving his bravery, just his stupidity. Unfortunately, there were times when a commanding officer had no choice. Nothing could destroy morale faster than a sense that an army's officers were keeping themselves safely out of harm's way while leaving their subordinates exposed to the enemy. That was the very reason he'd found the major's reaction to his own near-miss so welcome.

And I suppose, if I'm going to be honest, I did have a need to see the front line with my own two eyes. Just to be sure the damned thing was where I left it last night.

He snorted at the thought, then glanced up at the sky. One of the storm season's tropical storms was moving in on Corisande from the east, across the Great Western Ocean. To Gahrvai's experienced eye, it was obvious that plenty of rain and high winds were about to sweep in across Dairwyn and the Earldom of Coris yet again. It would be the second storm since he'd dug in here, which meant he had a pretty fair idea of what was going to happen when it hit. It was going to be thoroughly unpleasant here in the pass when the water began flooding his earthworks and trenches, but it wasn't going to be any picnic for the Charisians, either. And it should at least keep the damned marksmen off the slopes for a day or two.

And the longer Cayleb will let us sit here, the better. It may be hard work keeping the men fed, but it's the best damned defensive position this side of Manchyr. And Cayleb is about to get a surprise of his own if Father's last semaphore message is accurate.

The Charisians' rifles had come as a nasty—one might as well be honest and say "terrifying"—surprise to Gahrvai and his army. They'd come as an equally unpleasant surprise, if at secondhand, to Earl Anvil Rock. No one had been able to imagine how the Charisians had managed to equip every single one of their Marines with a rifle which actually fired *faster* than most smoothbore muskets.

Not until one of Gahrvai's surgeons recovered a half-dozen bullets from the bodies of his wounded men.

The bullets had been badly deformed from their mangling passage through human flesh and bone, but they'd been sufficiently intact for Gahrvai to realize what he was looking at. It was another of those damnably simple "innovations" Charisians seemed so fond of. He'd been sure there were aspects of it which had required experimentation on the Charisians' part, but the underlying principle was absurdly easy to grasp. Instead of hammering an oversized bullet down the bore, which was the way everyone *else* forced it to take the rifling, the Charisians had simply designed a hollow-based, conical bullet. When the powder detonated, the force of the explosion spread the base of the bullet, forcing it into the rifling and sealing the bore behind it, and the bullet's stretched shape meant it was heavier than a spherical ball of the same diameter. It was probably also a better shape for driving through the air, although Gahrvai wasn't certain about that. *And* the fact that, before the base expanded on its way to its target it was actually a looser fit in the barrel than a regular musket's round ball made it faster to load one of the new rifles than it was to load even one of his own men's smoothbore muskets.

The critical point was that once the surgeon had realized what he was looking at and drawn it to Gahrvai's attention, Earl Anvil Rock and his artisans had assigned the highest possible priority to figuring out exactly how the Charisians had made the design work . . . and how to duplicate it. According to his father's last message, they seemed to have done just that. There was no way they would have time to manufacture anything like the numbers of rifled muskets the Charisians had, but his father was scraping up every single sporting rifle he could find and turning out new bullet molds for them. Gahrvai would be surprised if there were more than a couple of hundred rifles in the entire Duchy of Manchyr. They were expensive toys, which only wealthy hunters could afford, and the fact that they came in such a wide diversity of calibers meant each of them would require its own specifically designed bullet mold. But even fifty of them in the hands of trained marksmen of his own would be a nasty surprise for the Charisians who were steadily pecking away at his men.

And if Cayleb will just give me another month, say—just to the end of the storm season, for example—then Father will be able to start putting worthwhile numbers of rifled muskets into production. We still won't have anything like the same total numbers, but we'll have enough to . . . convince Cayleb to approach us more cautiously than he did at Haryl's Crossing. And if it should happen that the next time we fight an open field battle I've got a few hundred, or a couple of thousand, rifled muskets of my own and he doesn't know *it . . .*

Sir Koryn Gahrvai knew he was indulging in wishful thinking. Still, it could work out that way. And for now, at least, he had a cork firmly in the bottle of Talbor Pass, and he had no intention of pulling it back out again.

▼ ▼ ▼

"—still say we ought to go ahead and hammer him, Your Majesty." It was hard to imagine a *respectful* growl of disgust, but Hauwyl Chermyn managed to pull it off. Cayleb's senior Marine stood on the far side of the map table, glowering down at the broken-backed snake of Talbor Pass, and from his expression, he would have liked to personally throttle Sir Koryn Gahrvai with his own large, sinewy hands.

"That's only because you're constitutionally opposed to doing nothing, Hauwyl," the emperor said mildly. The general looked up at him and had the grace to blush, and Cayleb chuckled. That chuckle was not a sound of unalloyed amusement.

"Trust me," he said. "I'm not incredibly in love with the idea of sitting on our hands, either. But in your saner moments, you know as well as I do that hammering straight into the positions Gahrvai's managed to build for his troops is going to produce nothing but a bloodbath, rifles or no rifles. And not, unfortunately, a *Corisandian* bloodbath."

Chermyn looked very much as if he would have liked to disagree, but he couldn't, and so he nodded unhappily, instead.

"You're right, of course, Your Majesty. I just hate the thought of *sitting* here. We've got virtually the entire Marine Corps camped out here, and we haven't done a thing since Haryl's Crossing. We're giving them *time*, Your Majesty, and we're wasting time of our own."

"Granted." Cayleb didn't even glance at the tall, sapphire-eyed guardsman standing behind him. "The problem is that we don't have enough mobility on land to slip around Gahrvai. If we had more troops than he does, we could try stretching out our right flank, forcing him to garrison other passes until he thinned out Talbor enough for us to punch through it. Unfortunately, *he* has more men than *we* do. And he also has a lot more—and a lot better—cavalry than we do. Charisians are seamen, not horsemen. You might want to get Admiral Lock Island's view on the proper degree of familiarity between sailors' arses and saddles. Believe me, he doesn't think they should spend any more time in contact with one another than they can possibly avoid. And that, unfortunately in this instance, pretty well sums up the Navy's attitude in general."

"All of that's true, Your Majesty, but—"

"We knew it was going to be like this," Cayleb pointed out. "Oh, I don't believe any of us thought it would be quite *this* bad, but we recognized from the beginning that we were going to face a problem rather like this one. So, while I fully understand why you're feeling so impatient, I think we'll stick to our original strategy."

If he'd been speaking to anyone else, Chermyn would have puffed his mustache at Cayleb. Since he happened to be speaking not simply to his superior officer, but to his emperor and commander-in-chief, he didn't. And in all fairness to the Marine, Cayleb knew Chermyn understood exactly what he was saying. After all, the general had helped build their original strategy in the first place.

"You're right, of course, Your Majesty," Chermyn said after a moment. "It just goes against the grain to sit here, doing nothing."

"As it happens, General, 'nothing' is exactly what we *aren't* doing," Cayleb said with a nasty smile. Chermyn's eyes narrowed, and the emperor chuckled again. This time it was a much more pleased sound.

"The longer he's prepared to sit there, the better I like it, Hauwyl," Cayleb told him. "I'm still pushing the thought around in my brain, but believe me, if we can convince him to give me another month or so to work with, he'll really, really wish he hadn't."

"I'll take your word for that, Your Majesty," Chermyn said with simple sincerity, then bowed and withdrew from the room. The door closed behind him, and Cayleb turned to Merlin.

"That," he remarked, "is an impatient man."

"Not so much impatient as tenacious, I think," Merlin replied. "He reminds me of a lot of Marines Nimue knew. Their instinct was always to attack, to push the pace and keep the other side off-balance whenever possible. When the Gbaba pushed us completely back onto the defensive, they *hated* it . . . and not just because it meant we were losing."

"I can see that." Cayleb nodded. "For that matter, I tend to be that way myself. The notion of giving the other side time to get set has never really appealed to me. Or, at least, not usually."

He and Merlin smiled nastily at one another, then looked back down at the map of Corisande on the table before them.

The real problem, Cayleb reflected, was that no one involved in crafting the overall Charisian strategy had considered making their landing in Dairwyn until very late in the planning process. The possibility that Grand Duke Zebediah might be able to convince his brother-in-law to come over to the Charisian side hadn't occurred to any of them until they learned of Prince Nahrmahn's correspondence with the grand duke. Their earlier plans had called for landing in either the Barony of Brandark or the Earldom of Coris, if they'd landed east of the Dark Hills, or else much farther to the west, in the Earldom of Rochair, if they'd landed on the Margo Sound coast. In either case, the idea had been that they would establish a firm foothold, then use their amphibious capability to offset the Corisandians' greater mobility on land by leapfrogging along the coast in a series of amphibious "hooks."

Unfortunately, the combination of the speed with which Dairos had fallen and the promptness with which Gahrvai had marched out to meet them had taken Cayleb's planners by surprise. When they hadn't been planning on landing in Dairwyn to begin with, they'd expected it to take much longer for the main bodies of the opposing armies to make contact with one another. And because that had been true, they hadn't dared to count upon fighting a decisive battle quite that quickly. And, to be fair, judged purely by the casualties inflicted as a percentage of Gahrvai's total strength, it would have been hard to call Haryl's Crossing "decisive." Judged by those casualties as a percentage of the strength he'd actually had on the field—and, especially, as a demonstration of the relative capabilities of the two armies—that was precisely what it had been, however, and Gahrvai had been far quicker to draw the appropriate conclusions than Cayleb could have wished he'd been.

The Corisandian field commander's decision to withdraw as quickly as possible into Talbor Pass had precluded the possibility of another, larger scale Haryl's Crossing. He knew what Charisian rifles and artillery could do now, and even though Merlin's remotes confirmed that his father was working on providing him with an improvised force of riflemen of his own, he wasn't about to offer battle on Cayleb's terms unless he absolutely had to. And so, Cayleb had found himself in undisputed possession of the entire Barony of Dairwyn, the southern portion of the Earldom of Coris, and a goodly chunk of the eastern part of the Earldom of Mahrak, far earlier than anyone had expected him to. And with the Corisandian Army far closer to intact than anyone had wanted it to be.

The fact that the storm season promised to be just as active as Merlin had warned Cayleb it would be on the basis of his "meteorological satellites" (whatever *they* were) didn't help things a bit, either.

Thunder grumbled quietly from the east, as if to remind Cayleb of that very fact, and he grimaced. The storm season was bad enough in Charis, but Charis very seldom saw the powerful hurricanes which could sweep across Corisande. The sheltering bulk of Silverlode Island, which did get its share of hurricane-like storms, did much to explain that, although according to Merlin the pattern of ocean currents had at least as much to do with it. At any rate, the storms which came roaring in off the Great Western Ocean to hit Corisande were even more violent than the ones Charisians were accustomed to dealing with closer to home.

As he listened to that distant rumble of thunder, Cayleb was glad, for several reasons, that he'd sent so much of his shipping back to shelter in Zebediah and Chisholm. One reason, of course, was that it reduced congestion in Dairos and got his vital transports as safely out of the way of foul weather—and far enough north to be outside the normal hurricane zone entirely, in Chisholm's case—as he could. And if Zebediah was still right in the middle of the threat zone, the presence of a substantial number of Charisian transports and their galley and galleon escorts in Hannah Bay was a pointed reminder to Grand Duke Zebediah that any . . . adventures which might tempt him would be a bad idea.

Useful though that was, however, the ships sheltering in *Chisholm* were almost certainly even more valuable. The continued presence of so many Charisian ships and Charisian sailors (who just happened to have Charisian *marks* burning holes in their purses) continued helping to buttress the Chisholmians' view of themselves as part of the new, larger Charisian Empire. Even more of the Chisholmians who'd nursed reservations about the entire idea were finding themselves feeling much more comfortable with it as the deep and genuine respect with which the Charisians had already come to regard Empress Sharleyan sank fully home. And as they listened to the Charisians' tales of the fortunes to be reaped by anyone who could go a-privateering.

All of that was true, but however useful those other accomplishments might be, what Cayleb truly wished was that he had that shipping right here, closer to hand, instead. Without it, he simply didn't have the troop lift for the amphibious tactics which had been the linchpin of their strategy from the beginning. He was sorely tempted to try using the shipping he'd retained in Dairos to carry out the same sorts of operations, despite the season, if only on a reduced scale. Gahrvai's decision to settle down in Talbor Pass with his entire army, however, had dissuaded him. The Corisandian commander's position offered him a prize that was far too tempting to pass up. But claiming that prize would require a much larger landing than he currently had the troop lift to support, while a series of smaller landings was likely to provoke Gahrvai into changing his present dispositions, at the very least.

"Is he really going to go on sitting there?" Cayleb asked now, and Merlin shrugged.

"That's what it looks like," he said, and Cayleb's eyes narrowed slightly. There was something about Merlin's voice . . .

"Merlin," the emperor asked slowly, "are you *tired*?"

Merlin's eyebrows rose, and Cayleb shrugged.

"I'm sorry, but it's just occurred to me that I don't believe I've ever actually seen you tired. Once you and Maikel told me the truth, I realized why that was, of course. But now . . . I don't know, there's just something . . ."

"I'm not really *tired*, Cayleb." Merlin grimaced slightly. "PICAs aren't subject to physical fatigue. On the other hand, until *I* came along, no one had ever operated a PICA in autonomous mode for more than ten days at a time, so no one had any actual experience on the long-term effects on the personality living inside one. From my own experience, I don't really need *sleep* the way a flesh-and-blood human would, but it turns out I do need . . . downtime. A few hours, at least, every few days, when I can just shut down. It's my equivalent of going to sleep, I suppose, and I really need it if I'm going to stay mentally fresh and alert."

"And you aren't getting it, are you?" Cayleb asked shrewdly.

"There's too much that needs doing," Merlin replied

obliquely. "I've got SNARCs and remote sensors out all over the place, Cayleb, and Owl and I are the only ones who can monitor them."

"Can you possibly monitor *all* of them, whatever you do?"

"No, that's part of the problem. I spend too much of my time trying to figure out which ones I absolutely *need* to monitor, which reduces the time I have to do the monitoring *in*. And it's virtually certain that I'm *not* monitoring at least one of the ones I ought to be watching. Then there's—"

"Stop," Cayleb said, and Merlin's mouth closed.

"That's better. Now, listen to me for a moment, Merlin Athrawes. Your ability to tell me what's going on all over the world is an enormous advantage. Frankly, it's even more important than the new artillery. In fact, I think it's the single most important factor in giving us a chance to survive. I know that. Maikel and Dr. Mahklyn and Father Zhon all know it. But as you yourself have pointed out, you aren't really an Archangel. You can't be everywhere and do everything. You can't even *watch* everything that happens across an entire world. Maybe you don't need sleep the same way I do, but I can't believe you're so different from the rest of us that you don't need to rest at least occasionally. Frankly, I think you're just as likely to miss something because you aren't . . . how did you put it? Because you aren't 'mentally fresh and alert' as you are because it didn't occur to you that something needed to be watched in the first place. People—including *you*, Captain Athrawes—make sure *I* get my sleep because I'm an emperor, and because I need to be rested and clearheaded when the time comes to make decisions. Well, you need to be rested and clearheaded for the same reasons. And also, in your case, because of how much I rely on you when it comes time for *me* to make decisions. If resting is what you need to do to stay that way, then I want you to do just that. Besides, you're my friend. I don't want you driving yourself too hard simply because you can."

Merlin looked at him for several seconds, then sighed.

"I don't know if I can do that, Cayleb," he admitted.

"Try," Cayleb advised him. "Try hard. Because if you

don't, I'm going to order you back to Dairos." Merlin stiff-ened, and Cayleb shook his head. "I'm not going to argue about it with you, Merlin. Either you're going to get—What? Two hours a night?—of the 'downtime' you were just talking about, or else I'm going to send you back to Dairos, so you can get the downtime during the day instead of watching my back. It's not open to discussion."

For a moment, brown eyes locked with blue, and then Mer-lin sighed again.

"It was bad enough when you were just a crown prince," he complained. "Now this 'Emperor' stuff has obviously gone to your head."

"Was that a 'yes' I heard?"

"All right, Cayleb." Merlin shook his head, his expression wry. "I'll be good."

. II .

Vicar Zahmsyn's Suite,
and
Vicar Zhaspahr's Suite,
The Temple,
City of Zion

"—response to the Address is still coming in, especially from the more distant bishoprics," Zahmsyn Trynair said over his wineglass. "Frankly, I'm not entirely satisfied with what I'm hearing, though."

"No?" Zhaspahr Clyntahn smothered a fresh roll in butter and took a huge bite. "Why not?" he asked a bit indistinctly as he chewed.

"I'm not convinced all of them fully understand the seriousness of the situation, even after what happened in Fer-ayd," Trynair replied. "Of course, they only have the expur-gated version of the Address, without the specific references to Holy War, and it's probably taking time for the reports of the hangings to circulate, given this winter's weather. I sup-pose that could explain the fact that they don't seem to me to show the proper degree of urgency in all cases."

Clyntahn's face tightened ever so briefly at mention of the Ferayd executions. Although he'd endured his own public penance with every outward appearance of humility and ac-ceptance, there was no point pretending that the humiliation of "admitting his own fault" hadn't filled him with white-hot fury. Or that he didn't still blame Trynair as the person re-sponsible for that humiliation. The fact that his intellect was capable of understanding exactly why the Chancellor had in-sisted upon it—and even the fact that he'd been perfectly cor-rect to do so—didn't do much about his sullen resentment. There was a new, undeniable strain in their relationship as a result, but by the same token, both of them were even more aware than ever of just how much they needed one another. And, for all his anger, Clyntahn knew it had never been per-sonal. Or not *very* personal, at any rate. When it came to the survival of Mother Church (and the Group of Four), business was business, as far as the Grand Inquisitor was concerned.

Even if it did still piss him off.

Now he washed down the mouthful of roll with a hefty swallow of wine and shrugged.

"If they don't understand now, they will, soon enough," he said a bit more clearly, and reached for his fork once more.

Despite how little he and Trynair might like one another, particularly these days, both of them knew they were the two true poles of power within the Group of Four. As such, they'd taken to dining privately together at least twice a five-day, in addition to the larger suppers when Rhobair Duchairn and Allayn Maigwair were invariably present, ever since the Charisians had decided to create so much havoc. As was cus-tomary when serious Church business was to be discussed, the two vicars had dismissed their servants, and the Grand Inquisitor refilled his own glass before he looked back across the table at Trynair.

"I've already made my displeasure clear to that idiot Jynkyns down in Delferahk." He scowled. "If he'd kept proper control of the situation, we never would have had all that unpleasantness in Ferayd."

Trynair managed to nod without grimacing, despite the way what had happened in Ferayd remained a sore point between them. What bothered him even more about it, though, if he was going to be honest with himself, was that Clyntahn seemed in a fair way towards convincing himself that his own version of events there was the accurate one, despite the official findings of the Ferayd Tribunal and his own public confession and penance. It was bad enough trying to manage the repercussions of that entire disaster without having the Grand Inquisitor actively deluding himself about it!

I wonder if he's always actually been able to do that? Trynair thought. *Is it possible that what I've always put down to cynicism and pragmatism has actually been complete—if delusional—sincerity? An ability to make his version of reality the "truth," whenever the actual truth would be . . . inconvenient? Or is this something that's only come out in him—or gotten stronger, at least—since the Charisians didn't oblige him by all dying on schedule after all?*

The Chancellor had no idea how to answer his own questions, but at least he knew now there were currents inside Clyntahn which even he hadn't recognized before. Potentially dangerous currents, and not simply dangerous to the Group of Four's opponents.

Yet even if that was true, or perhaps *especially* if it was true, it simply became more important than ever to keep Clyntahn both focused and under control.

As if I didn't have enough to worry about already! I don't really know which is worse—Zhaspahr's dragon-in-a-glassworks approach to anything remotely Charisian, Rhobair's refound piety, or Allayn's stupidity! I really am *starting to feel like Master Traynyr!*

His raised wineglass hid his smile as his lips quirked involuntarily. He was well aware of the whispered Temple cloakroom puns linking his own surname with that of the traditional stage manager of puppet theater. No one was going to repeat any such jokes where he could hear them, of course, but they'd never really upset him particularly. After all, that was how he'd seen himself, in many ways.

But the play used to be so much easier to direct, he reminded himself, and his smile faded.

"I'm not as convinced as you appear to be that Bishop Ernyst could have prevented what happened originally, Zhaspahr," he said mildly as he lowered his glass after a moment. "And, frankly, I don't see how he could possibly be held responsible for the outcome of the Charisians' attack on the port."

"No? Well, *I* damned well can," Clyntahn growled. "If he'd insisted from the outset that the Inquisition have complete control of the ship seizures, without letting those ham-fisted, so-called 'soldiers' screw things up first, then none of the damned Charisians would have gotten out. Probably, as many of them wouldn't have been killed, either, but even if they had been, Cayleb and his bunch of deviants wouldn't have gotten the wildly exaggerated reports of what happened that put such a wild hair up their arses about Ferayd!"

Despite his resolve not to renew his quarrel with Clyntahn, and despite all of the excellent reasons he had for that resolve, Trynair's lips tightened. It was one thing to avoid conflict within the ranks of the Group of Four; it was another to let one of the two most powerful of its members engage in such dangerous self-delusion. Especially when the *Charisians'* version of what had happened in Ferayd was getting such broad circulation.

The letters and printed broadsides they'd left behind when they withdrew from Ferayd had included the proclamation from "Emperor Cayleb and Empress Sharleyan" which had made their reasons for attacking the city and burning the better part of it to the ground crystal clear. And as that bastard Rock Point had promised, the contents of Graivyr's files had also been broadcast. It was hard to be certain exactly where they'd first been distributed, but printed copies of every single self-condemnatory word of the executed Inquisitors' reports had mysteriously appeared from *somewhere*. And despite Clyntahn's best efforts, at least some of them were being circulated throughout the mainland realms, especially in Siddarmark and Delferahk itself. The Charisians' grasp of the value of propaganda, Trynair was discovering, was at least as good as the Church's, and it seemed impossible to stop their printed broadsides and pamphlets from getting out.

All of which only makes it an even better thing I insisted that we had to address the situation ourselves, however Zhaspahr feels about it, the Chancellor thought grimly. *I suppose he's right when he argues that the tribunal's findings help to buttress the Charisians' claims about what happened, but it looks like an awful lot of people find our own "openness" and "honesty" deeply reassuring. And it gives them an out. They can accept that at least some of the Charisians' claims are true, but they can go ahead and reject the points where their accusations don't coincide with our own admissions. Like the question of just how much of the city was burned, and just how many civilians were killed.*

As far as Tryair knew, *no* Delferahkan civilians had been killed in the Charisian attack, but there was no way for Charis to prove that. No handy, captured reports which were bound to get out, anyway, and leave all sorts of embarrassing mud on the Church's face.

None of which meant that the Charisians hadn't demonstrated a fiendish ability to distribute their propaganda—like their version of Ferayd—whenever and wherever they chose.

Clyntahn seemed particularly irate about that. No doubt because he'd believed the Inquisition's ability to intercept such inflammatory documents was adequate to the Church's needs. What he was discovering, unfortunately, was that much of the Inquisition's previous success had been due to the fact that no realm or kingdom had ever before dared to openly proclaim its opposition to the Church. These were no smudgy, poor-quality sheets run off on a hidden press in some malcontent lunatic's cellar. These were every bit as professionally produced as anything the Inquisition or Office of Instruction had ever distributed, and literally thousands of them were mysteriously appearing in every port city.

And unlike our efforts, they have the unfair advantage of actually telling the truth, don't they, Zhaspahr? the Chancellor reflected grimly.

Trynair considered asking the same question aloud, but only briefly. First, because it didn't really matter a great deal either way, after the fact, and second, because nothing he could say would change Clyntahn's view, and he knew it. Just as he knew that attempting to challenge the Grand Inquisitor's version could actually be . . . hazardous.

"At any rate," Clyntahn went on after a moment, "I've sent out instructions to every intendant and to every senior inquisitor. We'll still use the silk glove approach with the laity—for a while, at least—but it's time for them to begin making clear to the clergy that the possibility of some sort of patched-up compromise is long past . . . if it ever existed in the first place! Trust me, they'll soon understand that no defeatism or lack of enthusiasm will be tolerated."

"I could wish, Zhaspahr," Trynair said after a brief pause, "that you'd at least informed me of your intentions before you sent out those instructions. I am Chancellor, you know. The archbishops and bishops should have received a letter of instruction from me at least simultaneously."

"The actions of the Order of Schueler, Mother Church's intendants, and the Office of Inquisition are *my* responsibility, Zahmsyn," Clyntahn said coldly. "You may send whatever instructions you like to the archbishops and bishops, but it's the Inquisition's task to see to it that all of Mother Church's priests know precisely what is expected of them—and what will be *demanded* of them—where matters of spiritual and doctrinal purity are concerned."

Trynair's nostrils flared, but he sat on his own instant surge of anger. What Clyntahn had just said—in his own, thankfully inimitable fashion—was true. Trynair never doubted that the way Clyntahn had handled it, like his current half-glare, owed a great deal to the fashion in which the Chancellor had . . . discussed Ferayd with him, but that didn't make what he'd just said inaccurate. Nor did it change the importance of handling him carefully. Still, there was a point here which had to be made.

"I never said it wasn't the Inquisition's responsibility to ensure the reliability and purity of doctrine, Zhaspahr," he said in a calm but firm voice. "I merely indicated that there are long-standing traditions and procedures by which such messages and instructions are supposed to be distributed. You know that as well as I do . . . and so do the bishops. If we begin sending out directives which obviously haven't been coordinated with one another, it's only going to engender a sense of confusion and make them wonder if we're truly in control of the situation. I don't think either of us wants that to happen, do we?"

He met Clyntahn's eye levelly, forcing himself not to flinch, despite any inner qualms. It wasn't easy, and he felt rather like an animal trainer facing down a dangerous beast in a cage. But, after a moment, Clyntahn nodded, almost as if against his will.

"Point taken," he said shortly. "I'll try to at least keep you informed—in advance—of any additional directives I feel must be distributed in the Inquisition's name."

"Thank you." Trynair poured fresh wine into his own glass with a hand which, he was pleased to note, didn't tremble at all.

He passed the glass under his nose, savoring the bouquet while he gazed out the windows. Spring had come late, hard, and cold to Zion, but at least there was no more blowing snow. Not that he was convinced icy rain and mud were that much of an improvement, even when all he had to do was view it from the comfort of his own suite. That suite was every bit as luxurious as Clyntahn's own, although he'd preferred one with a smaller expanse of windows, and not just because he didn't like looking at snow or rain. He knew the Temple's mystic glass permitted the human eye to see through its windows in only one direction, yet something deep inside him always felt somehow exposed when they dined in Clyntahn's chambers.

Perhaps that's because I know Zhaspahr makes a habit of mounting his mistresses in front of those windows, he thought sardonically. *I wonder what it says about the way his mind works that he wants to be able to look out across the entire city of Zion at a moment like that?*

"I suppose that's just about everything for this evening, then," he said aloud after a moment.

"Just about," Clyntahn agreed. "I did just receive a dispatch from Father Aidryn in Manchyr, however."

"You did?" Trynair looked up sharply.

"Yes, but it arrived by courier less than an hour before we were scheduled to dine, and it came in in cipher. There wasn't time to get it deciphered before I had to leave. I'll see to it that you get a clean copy tomorrow morning."

"Thank you." Trynair leaned back in his chair, wondering whether or not his "clean copy" would also be a *complete* copy.

"I'm not happy about what we've heard so far about Cayleb's campaign," he admitted after a moment. "And I have to confess I was most unpleasantly surprised when we found out he'd managed to launch both his invasion of Corisande and his expedition against Ferayd virtually simultaneously."

"There I have to agree with you," Clyntahn said, and his voice was quite different from the tone in which he'd discussed Ferayd. In fact, his entire body language was different. He sat straighter in his chair, his eyes narrowed, and he set his wineglass down in front of him, folded his arms on the edge of the table, and leaned slightly towards the Chancellor.

"Actually, one of the things that most disturbs *me* about Cayleb's ability to operate with such impunity is that I've come to the conclusion that Allayn's new fleet is going to be about as useful as tits on a boar dragon."

"What?" Both of Trynair's eyebrows arched. "This is the first time you've mentioned *that*!"

"It's taken a while for some of the evidence to come together for me," Clyntahn admitted. "I'm not a naval man, or a soldier. And, to be blunt, I've had my own responsibilities and I've been forced to assume Allayn was adequately discharging *his* responsibilities. Unfortunately, I'm rapidly coming to realize he hasn't been."

"That's a very serious allegation, Zhaspahr."

"Oh, *fuck* 'allegations,' Zahmsyn." Clyntahn unfolded his arms long enough to wave one hand dismissively. "I'm not accusing him of playing some sort of games, or of *shirking* his responsibilities. The problem is that his imagination is about the size of a dried pea. A *small* dried pea. And it's at least partly—maybe even mostly—our fault for not riding herd on him more carefully. You and I both know he's the weak link in our group, after all."

Trynair was privately surprised by Clyntahn's frankness. At the same time, he couldn't disagree with anything the Inquisitor had so far said.

"He may be the weak link, but we can't really afford to dispense with him, especially now," the Chancellor pointed out, and Clyntahn shrugged his broad, beefy shoulders.

"Not unless we're prepared to strip him of his office and pick Mother Church a new Captain General," he agreed. "And, like you, I don't believe we can afford to risk any appearance of internal dissension. But that's really a bit beside my point where the new fleet is concerned."

"Then what is your point?"

"We're building the wrong ships," Clyntahn said flatly. "I've been reading over reports from my intendants and inquisitors. Obviously, many of them have been deeply concerned about the nature and extent of the Charisians' innovations and their violations of the Proscriptions of Jwo-jeng. As part of that concern, they've been reporting on every instance of those innovations' use which has come to their attention. And it's disturbingly clear to me, now that I've had time to think about it, that these new galleons of theirs are far more effective than any galley."

"Even the new, bigger galleys?"

"Than *any* galley," Clyntahn repeated in that same flat voice. "It's a simple enough proposition, Zahmsyn. A ship which doesn't rely on rowers can be bigger, heavier, and tougher. We can make our galleys bigger and more seaworthy—which we *are* doing—but at the price of making them slower and requiring more rowers under oars. That's what the Charisians had already done before they started turning to galleons. But a *galleon* can eventually be made bigger and heavier than anything that's going to be able to move under oar power. And a ship which doesn't have oars all down the side can mount a lot more guns in that same space, as well. So when you combine bigger, heavier ships—which means ships which can carry heavier *weights*—with a hull design which lets them cram more guns into a broadside, you get a ship which can do what Cayleb's ships have been doing to us for the last year and a half. I'm sure the new ships Allayn is building will be more effective than older style galleys. Unfortunately, I'm coming to suspect that 'more effective' in this case simply means one of Cayleb's galleons will need *three* broadsides to sink them, instead of only one."

"Sweet Langhorne," Trynair murmured as he reflected on how much Rhobair Duchairn had already disbursed on the Temple's massive new naval programs. It was, as the Treasurer General had pointed out a few five-days earlier, the largest single outlay of funds in the history of Mother Church, and the entire enormous first wave of galleys they'd ordered was nearing completion. In fact, scores of them had already been launched, in Dohlar and the southern ports of Harchong. But if Clyntahn's biting analysis was accurate, then those ships represented a colossal waste of timber, money, and time. Especially time.

"How long ago did you reach this conclusion?" he asked after a moment, and Clyntahn shrugged again.

"I actually started suspecting it a few five-days ago," he admitted. "Given how much we've already committed to the building program, and the extent to which Allayn's prestige is tied up in it, I decided to take the time to think about it and be certain of my conclusions before I shared them with anyone."

"I can understand that, I suppose."

Trynair stared out the window again, his eyes distant, and Clyntahn chuckled sourly.

"I wasn't any too happy about it when it first occurred to me, either," he said. "As a matter of fact, I still don't find it particularly amusing. The Address warned the entire vicarate we were planning to declare Holy War, and now it turns out we still don't have a navy we can use to launch a Jihad after all! On the other hand, it's a lot better to figure it out now than after we send a galley fleet—*another* galley fleet—out to be turned into driftwood by Cayleb and his galleons."

"That's true enough," Trynair agreed slowly.

"Well, after I'd realized that, I also realized the present program hasn't been a complete waste of time. If nothing else, we've assembled the shipbuilding teams, established the yards, and generally streamlined the construction process. Rhobair's not going to be happy about it," Clyntahn smiled nastily, "and I expect to hear him pissing and moaning about the additional expense. With reason, I suppose, however irritating he can sound. But at least we've got the men and the tools in place if we're going to have to start building galleons, instead."

"But dare we embrace all of these Charisian innovations?"

"We'll dare to do anything we *have* to do to crush these schismatics. As Grand Inquisitor, I can grant special dispensations to anyone, if I need to."

"That wasn't really my point," Trynair said, shaking his head. "What I meant is that we've stressed the Charisian willingness to violate the Proscriptions. If we're going to accuse them of having done that, and then we turn around and do exactly the same things they're doing . . ."

He let his voice trail off, and Clyntahn grunted in understanding. But the Inquisitor seemed far less concerned over the possibility than Trynair was.

"We can duplicate their new galleons, and almost certainly this new artillery of theirs, as well, without breaching the Proscriptions. And the artillery and the new ship designs are only a fragment of all of the 'innovations' they've been introducing. The mere fact that we're very cautiously adopting a tiny part of what they've done isn't going to magically make all of their other, far more serious violations disappear. Besides, the entire nature of the contest is shifting. It's about Mother Church's legitimate primacy, now, and all the doctrinal implications which hang on that dispute. If we emphasize that firmly and steadily, I don't think we'll have any problems over introducing a few new guns and a few new ships of our own."

"I hope you're right," Trynair said. "But whether you're right about that or not, if we're going to have to build yet *another* completely new navy, it's going to throw a major kink into our plans."

"I believe I can safely say that that's a substantial understatement," Clyntahn said dryly.

"And unless we do want to get rid of Allayn and try to find another Captain General we think we can trust, we're going to have to be careful about how we go about changing our building plans," Trynair continued, his expression thoughtful as his brain got past the shock of Clyntahn's announcement and began grappling with its implications. "If we don't handle this properly, it's going to create a crisis in confidence among the rest of the vicarate where Allayn is concerned."

"Frankly, that might not be the worst thing that could happen," Clyntahn pointed out. "Except, as you say, that finding another Captain General we can trust, especially if we find ourselves being forced to drop Allayn under pressure from other vicars, isn't going to be simple. I'm pissed off with him about this, but I suppose it's only fair to point out in his defense that all of us had the same information, and I'm only just now figuring this out myself. Given the fact that Allayn is possibly a third as smart as you or I—I'm being generous here, you'll note—it's probably unfair of me to be *too* pissed off with him."

"I think it might be best to have Allayn reach the same conclusions you have on the basis of reports from Ferayd," Trynair said after a moment. "If we stress that no one else had realized all of this and point out that the Ferayd attack is the first one on which we've really received adequate reports, then perhaps we can convince everyone Allayn recognized the inherent weaknesses of galleys forced to fight galleons as soon as he had an opportunity to review a sufficiently detailed account."

"I suppose that could work," Clyntahn agreed a bit sourly. "Although I have to admit that I'm getting a bit tired of 'admitting' things just to head off the damage when someone *else* starts screaming about them. Still, I think we're in a better position to control the spin on this one . . . assuming, of course, that no one else finds out about the reports Admiral

Thirsk and Admiral White Ford sent Allayn after Rock Point and Crag Reach."

Trynair grimaced and wished Clyntahn could have refrained from that last observation. Still, those reports had scarcely been broadly circulated. It wouldn't be that hard to discreetly "disappear" them.

"This is going to make things even worse where Corisande is concerned," he said after a moment. "I've been assuming that if Hektor could only hold out until the spring ice melts up here, we could send a fleet to his support. One capable of at least fighting its way through with additional troops."

"I think we can assume that *that's* not going to happen," Clyntahn agreed.

"Well, that probably pretty much guarantees that Corisande's going to be lost to us, along with Chisholm and Emerald. Which, in turn, means this 'Charisian Empire' of Cayleb's may actually come into existence."

"For a while," Clyntahn said grimly. "For a while."

"Maybe only for a while, but if Corisande goes down, especially after Chisholm and Emerald have voluntarily joined Charis, and after Cayleb has burned Ferayd to the ground and hanged sixteen Inquisitors with apparently total impunity, *and* after we've announced we have to start building yet another new navy from the ground up, it's not going to do very much for morale. And if Hektor does the same thing Nahrmahn did, it's going to be even worse."

"It won't be good, no," Clyntahn said much more calmly than Trynair would have expected. "On the other hand, if it's going to happen, it's going to happen. Panicking about it ahead of time won't accomplish anything. Besides, you might be surprised." He smiled unpleasantly. "I've been working on a little insurance plan. One I think will turn Hektor into an asset even if Corisande voluntarily surrenders to Charis."

"Insurance plan? What *sort* of insurance plan?"

"Ah!" Clyntahn wagged an index finger chidingly. "I told you I'm still working on it. It's not what I'd call really finished yet, and even if it were, everyone likes his little surprises. I think you'll be impressed, but I'm not quite ready to share it yet."

Trynair frowned at him, but Clyntahn only chuckled and reached for the wine bottle again.

▼ ▼ ▼

It was considerably later that evening when Clyntahn strolled into his own suite in a pleasant glow.

Of the entire Group of Four, only Trynair's wine cellar really matched Clyntahn's own, and the Grand Inquisitor always enjoyed drinking someone else's wines and whiskeys more than he cared for sharing his own. Besides, Trynair's attempts to inveigle him into sharing his plans for cushioning the impact of Hektor's eventual defeat had amused him enormously, especially after the way in which he'd been forced to humiliate himself over Ferayd. And so he was in an expansive mood as he returned home.

"Good evening, Your Grace," his valet said, bowing to him.

"Evening," Clyntahn responded.

"I'm sorry, Your Grace, but you have a visitor," the valet continued.

"A visitor? At this hour?" Clyntahn frowned, and the valet grimaced.

"I did point out the lateness of the hour, Your Grace, and inquire as to whether or not he could come back at a more convenient time. He informed me, however, that it was important he speak to you. He seemed quite insistent, in fact."

"And who might this visitor be?"

"It's Archbishop Nyklas, Your Grace."

Clyntahn's eyes narrowed. Nyklas Stantyn was the Archbishop of Hankey in the Desnairian Empire, but he was scarcely one of Clyntahn's intimates. In fact, the Grand Inquisitor had never thought too highly of the man's basic intelligence. Besides, Stantyn had been one of those who had favored Samyl Wylsynn in the contest between Wylsynn and Clyntahn for the Grand Inquisitor's office. Only vicars had been allowed to vote, of course, but the campaigning had been vigorous, and Stantyn had done quite a bit of Wylsynn's legwork. That was one reason he was still a mere archbishop instead of having been elevated to the vicarate, despite his well-connected birth and seniority.

"Did he say what's so important?"

"I'm afraid not, Your Grace. His Eminence informed me that it was a matter for your ears alone."

"Indeed?" Clyntahn frowned for a moment, then shrugged. "I assume he's waiting in the library?"

"Yes, Your Grace."

"Very well. If what he has to say is so important, I suppose I'd best hear him out. And if it's for my ears only, I suppose you'd best leave us to it. If I need you, I'll ring."

"Of course, Your Grace."

The valet vanished with well-trained alacrity, and Clyntahn continued through to the library. Stantyn sat in a chair, gazing out into the snowy night, and Clyntahn's face smoothed into a mask of non-expression as he saw the archbishop's tense shoulders and noted the other man's nervously drumming fingers.

Stantyn twitched around from the window, then stood abruptly as he saw Clyntahn.

"Your Eminence," Clyntahn said, stepping fully into the library and extending his ring. "What brings you here at such an hour?"

"I beg your pardon for disturbing you so late in the evening, Your Grace," Stantyn said as he straightened from kissing the proffered ring. "I realize this is highly irregular, but I felt a great need to speak to you. Privately."

The Desnairian's voice might have sounded calm to another's ears, but Clyntahn's were the ears of the Grand Inquisitor. People often tried to sound calm when they spoke to him—especially when what they actually felt was something very different. And this, he decided, was one such time.

"My door is always open to any child of God who feels the need to speak to me, Your Eminence. And if that's true for all children of God, how much more true must it be for my own brothers within the episcopate? Please, tell me how I can serve you."

"Actually, Your Grace . . ." Stantyn's voice trailed off, and he looked like a man who abruptly wondered what he could possibly be doing. But Clyntahn was accustomed to that, as well.

"Come now, Your Eminence," he said chidingly. "We both know you wouldn't be here at this late hour unless you'd felt it was essential that we speak. And I fear the office I hold has made me somewhat . . . sensitive to hesitance when I see it. It's too late for you to pretend you didn't feel compelled to come here."

Stantyn looked at him, and his face seemed to crumple. Something happened inside him—something Clyntahn had seen more times than he could count.

"You're right, Your Grace," the archbishop half-whispered. "I did feel compelled. I . . . I'm afraid. Too much is happening. The Grand Vicar's Address, what's happened in Ferayd, the Charisians' defiance . . . It's all changing the ground under our very feet, and what seemed so *clear* before isn't clear anymore."

"Like what . . . Nyklas?" Clyntahn asked gently, and Stantyn inhaled deeply.

"For the last several years, Your Grace, I've . . . been involved with certain others here in the Temple. At first, and for a long time, I was certain I was doing the right thing. The others are all men I've known and respected for many, many years, and what they said seemed to make so much sense to me. But now, with this schism changing everything, I'm not sure anymore. I'm afraid that what seemed to make sense is something else entirely."

He stared appealingly into Clyntahn's eyes, and it took all of the Grand Inquisitor's decades of experience to keep his own eyes gently sympathetic instead of narrowing them in sudden, intent speculation. He knew the steps to this dance entirely too well. What Stantyn wanted was the Inquisition's promise of immunity before he continued with whatever had driven him here. And the fact that an archbishop of his seniority thought he *needed* immunity suggested that whatever had brought him here was at least potentially of enormous importance.

"Sit back down, Nyklas," Clyntahn said soothingly. "I

know moments like this are always difficult. And I know it can be frightening to admit the possibility that one *may* have fallen into error. But Mother Church is God's loving servant. Even those who have fallen into error may always be received back into her welcoming arms if they realize their error and turn to her in a true spirit of contrition."

"Thank you, Your Grace." Stantyn's voice was barely audible, and for a moment Clyntahn thought the man was actually going to break into tears. "Thank you."

"Now," Clyntahn continued, settling into a chair of his own as Stantyn sat back down, "why don't you begin from the beginning?"

"It was several years ago," Stantyn began. "Shortly after your own elevation to Grand Inquisitor, I was approached by Archbishop Zhasyn. I didn't know him as well as I knew many others within the episcopate, but I respected and admired him. When he invited me to discuss our shared duties as archbishops of Mother Church, I was both surprised and, I suppose, flattered. In the course of those discussions, however, he began to gently lead the conversation into the direction of Church politics, rather than the discussion of pastoral tasks with which we'd begun."

The Desnairian paused, his hands clasped tightly in his lap, then met Clyntahn's compassionate eyes once more.

"Eventually, Your Grace, I learned Archbishop Zhasyn was a member of a larger group, a circle, here within the Temple. And that circle was concerned about what it saw as Church corruption. Its members were . . . unwilling to bring their concerns before the Office of Inquisition, and so they were amassing their own evidence. Exactly what they intended to do with that evidence was not immediately made clear to me, but Archbishop Zhasyn did make it plain that they wished to recruit me as another reformer, and he asked me to begin to take note of any evidences of corruption I might see. At that time—"

Clyntahn's expression never even flickered, and he leaned back, listening.

JUNE,
YEAR OF GOD 893

✦

. I .

Elvarth,
Earldom of Storm Keep,
League of Corisande

Are we there yet?" Prince Daivyn asked plaintively.

Compared to his older brother, Phylyp Ahzgood reflected, the query was *only* plaintive. Crown Prince Hektor would have asked the question in something uncomfortably more like a whine, and there would have been no doubt that it was a complaint.

"Not quite yet, Daivyn," Princess Irys said soothingly. She leaned over and tucked the boy's cloak more snugly about him. "Go back to sleep. I'm pretty sure we'll be there by the time you wake up."

Daivyn looked at her, his eyes puckered with worry in the dim light of the single turned-down lantern hanging from the carriage's roof. Then he nodded, obviously as reassured by her manner as by her words, and settled back down on the comfortably padded seat. It was more than big enough as a bed for a boy of his age, and he closed his eyes obediently.

Irys sat looking down at him for several minutes, her eyes tender, but then she drew a deep breath, leaned back in her own seat, and looked across at the Earl of Coris.

"I hate this," she said very quietly, speaking softly to avoid disturbing the boy who was obviously already drifting back off despite the rapidly moving carriage's swaying, frequently jouncing motion and the sounds of their cavalry escort's hooves.

"I know you do, Your Highness," the earl replied just as quietly. "I don't blame you. *I* feel like I'm running away, as well."

"You shouldn't." She shook her head. "I know perfectly well that the only reason you're here is because Father ordered you to be."

"Your Highness, it's my honor, as well as my duty—" he began, but another shake of her head cut him off.

"Can we just go ahead and consider all of the obligatory comments already said and accepted?" she asked, and smiled wearily at his expression. "I'm sorry, Phylyp. I didn't mean to suggest for a moment that what you were saying was anything but sincere. I've known you too long to think anything else. But I'm so tired of saying what we all have to say, playing the parts we all have to play."

"I can understand that," he said after a moment. "Still, you are a princess of Corisande, and I am, by your father's appointment, your legal guardian and your younger brother's first councilor, if it should come to that. I'm afraid those are parts we can't stop playing, Your Highness."

"Given how long we've known one another, and the fact that I'm sure you were there on at least one occasion when my diaper was being changed, do you think you could call me 'Irys' rather than 'Your Highness,' at least when we're alone, Phylyp?"

He started to reply quickly, then paused.

"I'm not sure that's a good idea," he said finally. "Under the circumstances, it's particularly important that your dignity and Daivyn's are as effectively protected as possible. If I address you too familiarly, it's going to undercut your authority in your person as your father's daughter. And, from a more selfish perspective, I wouldn't want anyone to think I'm presuming on the position your father assigned me to for personal advantage."

"I don't disagree with any of that. That's why I said 'at least when we're alone.' But it's going to be difficult enough in Delferahk, whatever happens. I'd like to have at least one person I know I can trust who's willing to call me by my name at least sometimes. And if my 'legal guardian' can't do that, then who can?"

"Very well . . . Irys." His own smile was bittersweet. "And you're right; I was present when your diapers were changed."

"Good!"

A gleam of genuine amusement flitted across her expression. It didn't last long, but he thought he saw a few less shadows in her eyes when it had passed. It was difficult to tell under the present lighting conditions, of course.

"I wish he hadn't done it," she said.

"Sent you away with Daivyn?"

"Sent me away at all," she corrected, and if there were fewer shadows in her eyes, the lantern light touched the diamond gleam of tears on the ends of her long lashes. "I know he didn't have any choice—not if he was going to send Daivyn at all. But I ought to be with *him*, Phylyp!"

"Don't think for a moment that this was an easy decision for him," Coris said gently. "In fact, I haven't seen any others that were harder."

"I know. I know!" She shook her head. "And I promise I don't want to sound like a petulant, spoiled princess, either."

He started to reply to that, then stopped and simply shook his head with a small smile.

Irys sat silent for several more minutes, reaching down to smooth her brother's hair across his forehead. Finally, she looked back up at Coris.

"I suppose, since there's not any point crying about the basic decision, I ought to spend my moaning time on the travel arrangements, instead," she said with a determinedly lighter air.

"They do leave a bit to be desired, don't they?" Coris acknowledged wryly as the carriage went over a particularly solid bump. "Call it another inconvenience to blame on Cayleb and his Charisians."

"Oh, believe me, I've got quite a list of 'inconveniences' to . . . discuss with *Emperor* Cayleb some fine day." Her tone was whimsical; the anger in her eyes was not.

"Under the circumstances, I think Admiral Tartarian was entirely correct, though," Coris continued, and she nodded.

At the moment, their carriage, even at its rapid speed, was still some hours from the minor city—little more than a glorified fishing port, if the truth be known—of Elvarth. The journey overland from Manchyr had been an exhausting and lengthy ordeal, especially for Daivyn (who still didn't really understand all that was happening), since Elvarth lay in the Earldom of Storm Keep, at the northern tip of the island of Corisande. But the town had three significant advantages. First, it was so small and insignificant that it hadn't occurred even to Cayleb of Charis that it needed to be blockaded. Second, it was about as far away from Manchyr as it was possible to get. And, third, there'd happened to be a small galleon already anchored there, taking refuge from the Imperial Charisian Navy.

"I'm sure the Admiral was right," Irys agreed. "And I'm glad he was able to give us Captain Harys."

Coris nodded again. In many ways, he supposed, command of the galleon *Wing* was something of a step downward for Zhoel Harys. The onetime commander of the galley *Lance* had been promoted to command one of Tartarian's first armed galleons, the *Cutlass. Wing*, unlike *Cutlass*, carried only a handful of falcons and wolves, and she was no more than half *Cutlass*' size. Of course, there'd been the distinct probability that *Cutlass* was going to find herself pounded into a bloody wreck by the Imperial Charisian Navy sometime soon, but Harys' appointment to command her had represented an enormous professional step upward.

Despite that, he'd responded with every appearance of genuine pride when he'd learned that his prince had chosen him to transport his daughter and younger son to safety, and Coris never doubted that the captain would do everything humanly possible to carry out his mission successfully.

Tartarian's plan for doing just that ran back through Coris' mind once more. The notion of sailing east, rather than west, had a great deal to recommend it, in Coris' opinion. The Charisian Navy was overwhelmingly concentrated in the waters around Corisande and Zebediah, and its attention was focused on the area between the League of Corisande and

Charis proper. A single small vessel sailing east, rather than westward into that area of interest, was far more likely to get through unintercepted.

There were still risks, of course. The Trellheim pirates came to mind, and so did the swarms of Charisian privateers operating in Dohlaran waters. On the other hand, *Wing* wouldn't be flying Corisandian or Dohlaran colors. Harys had quite a selection of national colors laid in, along with a splendidly falsified set of Harchongese papers, and *Wing* had been chosen almost as much for the cargo she'd carried when the Charisian threat drove her to ground at Elvarth as for her out of the way location. So far, at least, all information available to Coris indicated that the new Charisian Empire was leaving Harchong's limited merchant marine strictly alone. If the reports about Harchong's involvement in building the Group of Four's new navy were accurate, that immunity from Charisian attack was unlikely to last long. For now, though, it appeared to be holding, and they should be able to make Shwei Bay without interception. From there, it would undoubtedly be safer to travel overland to Delferahk.

Especially traveling incognito, Coris thought a bit grimly. *You're far too valuable a prize, Irys. Far better for you to be simply my niece, Lady Marglai, traveling with me to Delferahk.*

That, too, had been suggested by Tartarian. It made at least some sense for Hektor to have sent his most trusted councilor off to Dohlar and Delferahk in search of aid. And if any of Corisande's enemies decided to interpret his mission as an effort on his own part to get out of Corisande before the final shipwreck, that was perfectly all right with Coris, as well. The additional cover story that his sister-in-law had asked him to take her daughter and son to safety in Delferahk also made sense. Marglai Ahzgood was a few years older than Irys, and Kahlvyn Ahzgood was a few years younger than Daivyn, but the match was close enough, and the Ahzgoods had relatives in Delferahk who might be expected to provide their distant cousins with a safe haven in these troubled times.

344 / DAVID WEBER

There were still far too many opportunities for something to go wrong, even if one completely disregarded the possibility of natural disaster overtaking a galleon at sea. Still, under the circumstances, it was probably the best plan available.

"Do you really think this will all work?" Irys asked quietly, as if she'd been reading his mind.

"Honestly?" He looked at her, then shrugged ever so slightly. "I do think it will work. I won't pretend there aren't a lot of things which could still go wrong, but I think it's the best plan, with the best chance of success, anyone could have come up with under the circumstances."

"Then that's just going to have to be good enough, isn't it?" she said simply, then adjusted her own cloak about her, leaned back in her seat, and closed her eyes.

▼   ▼   ▼

Merlin Athrawes frowned in unhappy agreement with the Earl of Coris' assessment. Although Merlin had been late in picking up on Hektor's decision to get his daughter and younger son safely out of Corisande, he'd realized almost a full five-day ago what was happening. Unfortunately, Hektor's instructions to his daughter's coachman and accompanying cavalry escort had included the order to move as rapidly as possible. By the time Merlin had become aware of what was happening, there'd been insufficient time to get word to the handful of light cruisers covering the waters between Sword Point and East Island before Irys and Daivyn could reach Elvarth.

He'd considered using his recon skimmer to intercept them himself, but only very briefly. The skimmer could have gotten there in time, but what was he supposed to do after he arrived? He could hardly destroy the galleon tied up to the town's wharf without raising at least a few eyebrows. And he wasn't prepared to simply sink the ship with all hands—including a teenaged girl and her younger brother—once the galleon got to sea, either. Nor could he and Cayleb send word to the privateers operating in Dohlaran waters—not in time for it to do any good, at any rate—without raising all sorts of unpleasant questions about just how they'd come by the information that Princess Irys and Prince Daivyn were taking a cruise.

He'd told Cayleb about it, of course, and the emperor had shared his own unhappy conclusions. If they were lucky, one of their patrolling schooners would happen across *Wing*, snap her up, and discover an incredibly valuable prize. If they were unlucky (which, frankly, given Captain Zhoel Harys' general level of competence, was much more likely), then Irys and Daivyn were going to arrive unintercepted at King Zhames' court.

Neither he nor Cayleb liked the notion of allowing them to slip through their fingers, but it was unlikely that their successful escape to Delferahk was going to have much effect on events here in Corisande. Not, at least, in the short term. In the long term, it was likely to prove . . . inconvenient, of course. In fact, it was almost certainly going to prove far worse than that. Which was why Captain Athrawes was spending his time hoping that one of their schooners would get lucky.

. II .

Duchy of Manchyr,
League of Corisande

The surf boat could have been a slightly more solid piece of the moonless night as it came nosing in from the southeast. It had been carefully painted matte black, and the sailors manning the oars rowed steadily but carefully. The last thing anyone needed was for the boat to broach to in the surf and soak its passengers' gunpowder. Among other things.

Sergeant Edvarhd Wystahn sat on the forward thwart with his rifle standing upright between his knees while he peered at the featureless, black blur of the coast. Aside from a pale froth where the gentle surf piled up on the beach of tawny sand, he could make out no details. He thought he could just see the loom of the hills beyond the beach, standing up against the starry sky, but he was fairly sure that was his imagination.

I've spent too long studying the damned maps, he thought wryly. *For the last five-day, I've even been* dreaming *about them!*

Actually, that wasn't such a bad thing. One of the primary tenets of the scout-snipers was that it made far more sense to wear themselves out ahead of time planning and training for an operation than it did to take casualties a little forethought might have avoided.

"Easy!" the petty officer in charge of the surf boat hissed. "Toss oars. Styv, Zhak—over the side!"

The boat swooped over the last swells, held bows-on to the beach by the sea anchor streamed over her stern, and the indicated seamen swung themselves over the gunwales and into the chest-deep water. They half-floated towards the shore, leaning their weight against the boat to guide it. Their feet found purchase as the water grew quickly shallower, and then the bow slid onto the sand with a quiet *"scrunch."* The sound was just audible through the noise of wind and wave, and the petty officer nodded to Wystahn.

"This is where you get out, Sergeant," he called softly, and Wystahn saw the faint flash of white teeth in a broad grin. "Good hunting."

Wystahn nodded back, then turned to the other members of his double-squad.

"All right, lads," he told them. "Let's be going."

He stepped over the side and waded through the wash of water, with the waves surging knee-high as they slid up the shelving beach on the last of their dying strength. Sand swirled away from under his boot soles, carried back out to sea by the receding water, and the flow plucked playfully at his calves. The solid ground seemed to curtsy underfoot as he stepped clear of the surf at last, but he ignored that—and the seawater squelching in his boots—while he looked around, then up at the stars, trying to get his bearings.

"It looks like the swabbies put us in the right spot . . . for a change," he said, and several of his men chuckled softly. "It's blacker nor the inside of a dirty boot," he continued, "but I'm thinking that's our hill yonder."

He pointed, then gave the stars one more look, taking his bearings, and nodded to Ailas Mahntyn, the senior of his two corporals.

"Off you go, Ailas. Try not t' fall over your own flat feet!"

Mahntyn snorted and started off through the darkness. Wystahn and the rest of the scout-snipers allowed the corporal to open a suitable lead, then followed him up the beach and into the high, stiff grass that rustled and whispered back to the murmuring sea in the steady wind.

▼ ▼ ▼

"I hope this brilliant idea of mine is going to live up to its billing," Emperor Cayleb remarked as he stood on *Empress of Charis'* sternwalk and gazed up at the same stars Sergeant Wystahn had just consulted. No hills were visible from where Cayleb stood, but he could see starlight glimmering on the sails of at least a half-dozen galleons, and he shook his head. "I don't think Bryahn is particularly happy about closing the land in the middle of the night this way," he added.

"Nonsense," Merlin said from where he stood "guarding" Cayleb even here. "Why should any admiral be concerned about sailing directly towards a beach he can't even see with twelve warships and sixty transport galleons loaded with fifteen or twenty thousand Marines?"

"Oh, thank you." Cayleb turned to lean his back against the sternwalk railing and looked at him. "You do know how to bolster someone's confidence, don't you?"

"One tries," Merlin told him, stroking one of his waxed mustachios. Cayleb chuckled, and Merlin smiled, but his smile faded quickly as he remembered another night on another ship's sternwalk and his final conversation with King Haarahld.

Oh, give it a rest! he told himself. *And stop looking for bad omens, too. Cayleb's hardly going ashore in the first wave!*

"How are they doing?" Cayleb asked in a considerably more serious tone, and Merlin shrugged.

"So far, so good." He considered the schematic Owl was transmitting to him from the SNARCs watching over the small groups of Charisian Marines filtering inland. "Most of them landed within a thousand yards or so of the right spot," he continued. "We've got one group that managed to get itself put ashore over a mile south of where it's supposed to be, but it's one of the dummies. At the moment, it looks like the rest of them are pretty much on schedule."

"Good."

Cayleb turned and stood gazing out into the night once again for several moments. Then he inhaled sharply and shook himself.

"Good," he repeated. "Now, as Domynyk recommended to me before Rock Point, I think it's time I got some sleep."

"I think that's an excellent idea," Merlin agreed.

"Well, there's not anything else useful I can do until dawn," Cayleb pointed out. He sounded much calmer about it all than Merlin knew he actually was, but he also waved one finger in Merlin's direction. "As for you, *Seijin* Merlin, under the circumstances, I'll grant you a dispensation on your 'downtime.' But only for tonight, mind you!"

Merlin snorted and bowed ironically to him.

"Yes, Your Imperial Majesty. Whatever you say, Your Imperial Majesty," he said unctuously.

▼　▼　▼

Wystahn sighed in relief as Ailas Mahntyn rose silently out of the steep hillside's grass. The sergeant's raised hand stopped the men following along behind him in their tracks, and Mahntyn pointed farther up the slope.

"Right where they said she'd be, Sarge," the corporal murmured through the steady sigh of the wind. "Four of 'em. Got them a signal mast and some flags. Looks like a signal fire, too. Two of 'em 're asleep. Got one man sittin' up on a big old rock—reckon he's got th' duty. Last one's making some tea or somethin'. Lookout's 'bout fifty yards that way." He pointed upslope and to the right. "Cooking fire an' th' signal gear's that way." He pointed to the left. "Got their tents and other gear on th' back side of th' slope."

"Good work," Wystahn replied quietly.

Ailas Mahntyn had even less formal education than Wystahn did, but he'd grown up in the Lizard Range Mountains, and his ability to move silently—not to mention his ability to see in apparently total darkness—was phenomenal. He had a woodsman's eye for terrain and a hunter's ability to put himself inside the mind of his quarry, and his own brain was dagger-sharp, despite any lack of schooling. Wystahn was working with him on his letters, since literacy was one of the requirements for a scout-sniper sergeant. Privately, although he'd been careful not to mention it to Mahntyn, he wouldn't be a bit surprised if the corporal ended up an officer, assuming he ever got a firm grip on reading and writing. Which wasn't a certain thing, unfortunately. Mahntyn was trying harder than he would have cared to admit to anyone, but letters were more elusive than any prong lizard as far as he was concerned.

The sergeant brushed that thought aside, then turned and beckoned for the rest of the double-squad to close up on him and Mahntyn.

"Say it again for them," he told the corporal, and listened himself, just as carefully the second time as he had the first. When the corporal had finished, Wystahn started handing out assignments.

"—and you've got th' lookout," he finished two minutes later, tapping Mahntyn on the chest.

"Aye," the corporal replied laconically, and nodded to the other three men of his section.

They were just as taciturn as he was, and almost as quiet. Wystahn might have heard a single boot scrape quietly over a rock . . . but he might not have, too. In either case, he had no worry about what was about to happen to the lookout. He'd given that task to Mahntyn partly because the corporal was the best man for the job in a general sense, but also because Mahntyn had already spotted the Corisandian. He knew exactly where the lookout was, and Wystahn was sure he'd already worked out the best way to approach him. The man making tea, or whatever he was doing, would be illuminated by his cook fire, and his night vision would be nonexistent, if he'd been sitting there looking into the fire while he worked. The other two were asleep in their tents, which meant none of the three of them were likely to notice anyone creeping up on them. The lookout, on the other hand, was sitting there in the dark with his eyes fully adjusted, and the nature of his duty meant he was at least supposed to be alert. Soldiers being soldiers, and given the fact that not even one of the archangels could have seen anything more than a few hundred yards offshore under the available light conditions, he probably wasn't as alert as he ought to have been, but Edvarhd Wystahn wasn't going to assume that. And if the Corisandian was paying attention to his duties, sneaking up on *him* was going to be a significantly more difficult task.

"All right," the noncom said to the men he hadn't sent off with Mahntyn, "let's go wake these lads up."

▼ ▼ ▼

Emperor Cayleb stepped onto *Empress of Charis'* quarterdeck and gazed up at the sky. Wispy cloud was moving slowly in from the east, but it was obviously high and thin, not the storm clouds which had been entirely too common for the previous couple of months. The stars continued to shine overhead, but those thin banners of cloud were a lighter gray, as if the sun were beginning to peer over the edge of the world, and the night had that feeling dawn sends ahead of itself. Captain Gyrard and his officers gave the emperor a respectful distance as he strode to the taffrail and looked astern.

HMS *Dauntless* followed in the flagship's wake, and it was definitely easier to see her than it had been earlier.

Captain Athrawes had been talking quietly to Captain Gyrard until the emperor arrived. Now the *seijin* nodded to Gyrard and walked across the deck to stand behind Cayleb with his hands clasped behind his own back in an attitude of respectful waiting.

The emperor completed his survey of sky, sea, and wind, then turned to his personal armsman.

"Well?" he asked softly.

"Well," Merlin agreed, equally softly, with a very slight bow.

No one with ears less acute than Merlin's could possibly have heard the exchange through the inevitable background noises of a sailing ship underway at sea. No one else needed to hear, however, and somehow, without actually changing a bit, Cayleb's expression seemed to lighten.

Merlin's expression didn't, but, then, he'd already known the answer to Cayleb's question. The boat parties of scout-snipers had been carefully briefed on exactly where they were supposed to go once they were ashore. As far as General Chermyn and his officers were concerned, they'd been dispatched to *suspected* lookout posts—the places where Emperor Cayleb had decided *he* would have placed sentinels to watch his seaward flank if he were Sir Koryn Gahrvai and feeling particularly paranoid.

Some of the Marines had felt the emperor's precautions were excessive. Others had privately questioned whether their emperor, for all his prowess as an *admiral,* had enough of a landsman's eye for terrain to pick out actual observation points from a map. Any of those doubting souls, however, had been wise enough to keep their opinions to themselves. And Cayleb had covered himself just a bit by spending two days aboard one of the fleet's schooners, perched in her foretop—much to her skipper's considerable anxiety—personally surveying the coastline through a glass. The schooner had obviously been on "routine patrol," without the crowned personal standard which officially indicated the emperor's presence on board, and Cayleb had dutifully jotted down an entire pad full of notes. No one else had to know that the content of those notes had actually been dictated to him by the *seijin* sitting beside him (ostensibly to make certain the emperor did nothing foolish, like tripping over his own feet and making a large, messy spot on the schooner's deck).

As it happened, Koryn Gahrvai was, indeed, "paranoid" enough to have arranged observation posts. He was only too well aware of the risk he'd taken by adopting his forward deployment in Talbor Pass, and he knew what could happen if a sufficiently large force could be landed in his rear. He had no intention of allowing Cayleb to do anything of the sort, however, and he'd established an entire series of interlocking lookout posts that stretched almost fifty miles westward along the Manchyr coast from the tip of the Dark Hill Mountains. Each of those posts was equipped with signal flags, and semaphore masts had been located at central points. He'd sought out the highest elevations he could find, in order to give his lookouts the greatest visual command of the waters of White Horse Reach, and given the relatively low speed of even Charisian galleons, those lookouts would give him a minimum of six hours' notice before any hostile landing could commence.

They were, of course, dependent upon daylight. If the Charisians were sufficiently confident to risk grounding by approaching the coast under cover of darkness and began landing at the very crack of dawn, they could deprive Gahrvai's sentinels of that half-dozen hours of approach time. But the lookouts would still be able to flash a warning to him long before any Charisian Marines could reach the southern terminus of Talbor Pass, especially without cavalry. Getting his own infantry out of the pass before the Charisians could seal it behind him would become a chancier proposition under those conditions, but he had posted Earl Windshare's cavalry to watch his back.

Overall, he had every reason to feel confident that any Charisians in his vicinity would be to the *east* of him, and he planned to keep them there. If they managed to flank him out of Talbor anyway, he intended to fall back as rapidly as possible on Manchyr and the extensive fieldworks whose construction around the capital his father had overseen. In the long run, any waiting game was in Corisande's favor, especially now that Anvil Rock knew about the Charisian rifles and had begun duplicating them. The one thing Corisande could not afford was the destruction or neutralization of Gahrvai's field force, and Gahrvai was supremely unconcerned by the very real possibility that anyone might question his courage for retreating from one heavily fortified position into another one in the face of an army little more than half the size of his own.

Unfortunately for Sir Koryn, he had no idea of the reconnaissance capabilities Merlin Athrawes made available to Cayleb Ahrmahk. Merlin had sat in on his staff and officers' meetings, had watched and analyzed each of his commanders, studying their strengths and weaknesses. He—and Cayleb, based on his reports—knew exactly why Gahrvai had made the command arrangements he had, and, overall, Cayleb would probably have made the same ones, given the same conditions. But the emperor also knew from Merlin's reports that there was a potentially fatal flaw in Gahrvai's command structure, and that was the reason he'd had Merlin pinpoint every one of the Corisandians' observation posts. Merlin had also plotted their lines of communication and located the positions of the semaphores which formed those lines' central nodes. And equipped with that information, Cayleb had planned the nocturnal landings which had put Sergeant Wystahn and his fellows ashore.

He'd been very careful to select some "suspected lookout posts" where, in fact, no one had ever been posted. And he'd been equally careful *not* to select several which did exist but which reported through one of the central nodes rather than having a direct signal link to Gahrvai's army. It would never have done for him to have unerringly dispatched attacks against *every* observation post, any more than it would have done for him not to have come up dry at least once or twice.

Hopefully, no one would notice that the *only* ones he'd missed "just happened" to be unable to tell anyone what they'd seen by signal. Runners were something he couldn't do anything about, but it would take a minimum of several hours for anyone from the surviving positions to get word to Gahrvai—and that assumed the runners in question figured out what was happening and headed directly for Talbor Pass instead of first running over to check on why the relay post to which they'd reported hadn't acknowledged their signals.

It wasn't a perfect solution to the problem. It was simply a solution which not even the wisest and most cunning of enemy commanders could possibly have seen coming.

Gahrvai's good enough to deserve better than this, Cayleb thought. *It feels like cheating. But, as Merlin says, if I'm not cheating, I'm not trying hard enough.*

The emperor turned his head to sweep his eyes across the eastern horizon one more time. The sky was definitely beginning to brighten, and additional galleons were becoming visible beyond *Dauntless.* There'd be enough light for his needs by the time the assault boats reached the beaches, he decided, and walked across the broad quarterdeck to Captain Gyrard. The sound of his heels on the dew-slick planking was the only sound which was not born of wind or sea, and the flag captain came to respectful attention as Cayleb stopped in front of him.

"Very well, Captain Gyrard," the emperor said formally. "Show the signal."

"Aye, aye, Your Majesty." Gerard touched his shoulder in salute and nodded to Lieutenant Lahsahl.

A moment later, the lit signal lanterns went soaring up to *Empress of Charis'* mizzen peak.

▾   ▾   ▾

"Now isn't that a pretty sight?" Edvarhd Wystahn murmured.

He stood on the rock where the Corisandian lookout had been perched the night before, and he had to admit that the fellow had had a breathtaking view out across the sparkling waters of White Horse Reach. At the moment, Wystahn had come into possession of that view, however, and he suspected that its former owner would have been much unhappier than he was at what he saw so far below him.

The transport galleons lay anchored or hove-to while their own boats pulled strongly towards the shore. The flat-bottomed assault boats had already landed the men they'd brought with them all the way from Dairos, and delighted they must have been to hit the sand, Wystahn thought with a grin. Those assault boats had amply proven their worth, but they were Shanwei's own bitch in any sort of seaway, and it was as certain as anything could possibly be that at least one or two of the embarked Marines aboard any one of them would fall victim to seasickness.

And once the first poor unhappy sod pukes, everyone starts to. I'll bet every one of 'em was grass-green and heaving by the time they got ashore!

If so, they'd shown no sign of it as the first wave of infantry formed up into columns and headed inland. The boats had landed Brigadier Clareyk's Third Brigade and Brigadier Haimyn's Fifth Brigade first, followed by Brigadier Zhosh Makaivyr's First Brigade. Now those six thousand men were spreading out to screen the inland side of the landing zone while their assault boats headed out to the waiting galleys to help fetch the other nine thousand men prepared to come ashore behind them.

Personally, Wystahn figured the odds were less than even that they were going to manage to fully pull off the emperor's plans. There was too much chance that they'd missed an observation post, or that some random cavalryman would stumble across them, or that some inland signal post would spot them before they could get fully around into the Corisandians' rear. But that was fine with Edvarhd Wystahn. If it worked, it worked, and the war would probably be well on its way to being over. And even if it didn't work, it would force the Corisandians to pull out of that damnable position in the pass without Wystahn and his fellow Marines being forced to assault those formidable earthworks head-on. Which meant

Ahnainah Wystahn, of the Earldom of Lochair, was much less likely to find herself a widow.

▼ ▼ ▼

"What?!"

Koryn Gahrvai stared at his aide. The lieutenant looked back mutely, his eyes huge, then held out a sheet of paper.

"Here's the signal, Sir," he said.

Gahrvai managed—somehow—to not quite snatch the paper out of the young man's hand. He stepped closer to the open fly of the command tent to get better light, and his eyes flashed over the lines of smudgy pencil. Then he read it again. And a third time.

It didn't get any better.

He raised his head, gazing sightlessly out of the tent at the everyday business of the encampment around him for what seemed a short eternity. Then he turned back to the senior officers' conference which had just been so abruptly interrupted.

"Somehow, Cayleb's gotten round behind us," he said harshly.

Heads jerked up in disbelief, and the officers standing around the map table looked back at him with expressions which were almost as stunned as *he* felt.

Baron Barcor's expression went a bit further than that, however. *His* face froze for a heartbeat, and then Gahrvai could actually see the blood flowing out of it as it turned the color of cold, congealed gravy. Which was scarcely reassuring, given the fact that Barcor had been promoted to command the entire army's rear guard after his performance at Haryl's Crossing. Gahrvai had picked him for the position because it was prestigious enough to serve as an ostensible reward for the man while actually making him, in effect, a mere administrator for the forward positions' reserves. Gahrvai had never intended to commit any of "Barcor's" men to action under the baron's own command; instead, he'd planned to slice off battalions and regiments as required and "temporarily" assign them to the command of men like Earl Mancora.

Mancora, who'd been slightly wounded at Haryl's Crossing but had somehow made it back to the rear with a pitiful handful of his wing, looked equally astounded, but lacked the "stunned draft dragon" expression in Barcor's eyes. Unfortunately, Mancora had been assigned to command the farthest *forward* of the positions in Talbor Pass.

Which means I've got exactly the wrong men in exactly the wrong places . . . again, Gahrvai thought bitterly. *Mancora would have his men on the road within the hour. Langhorne only knows how long it's going to take Barcor to get his arse in motion!*

"How bad is it, Sir?" Mancora asked quietly.

"I'm not sure," Gahrvai admitted. "According to this, though," he waved the dispatch, "they somehow got ashore in the sector closest to the pass without a single one of our observation posts warning us."

"But that's *impossible!*" Barcor blurted, then added a hasty "Sir."

"That's exactly what I would have thought," Gahrvai agreed grimly. "Unfortunately, we'd both be wrong, My Lord. They must have landed right at dawn. How they managed to eliminate our lookouts before they got a single message out is more than I could say, but from this, they're already within fifteen or twenty miles of the western end of the pass."

Barcor's stunned look was beginning to turn into something entirely too much like panic to suit Gahrvai.

"Do we have any strength estimate, Sir?"

The question came from Colonel Ahkyllys Pahlzar, the man who'd been Charlz Doyal's second-in-command. Pahlzar had assumed command of Gahrvai's artillery following Doyal's capture by the Charisians, and he really should have been officially promoted when he did. It was a temporary oversight Gahrvai intended to rectify as soon as possible, and at the moment Pahlzar's calm voice was a welcome contrast to Barcor.

"No, Colonel. I think, though, that we can assume he's

present in strength. We've already determined that he's not the sort of commander to throw out a weak and unsupported force to be chopped up."

Barcor winced visibly at Gahrvai's reminder of what had happened at Haryl's Crossing. Some of the other officers present seemed equally unhappy, but others—like Mancora and Pahlzar—only nodded.

"All right." Gahrvai shook himself, then stepped briskly across to the map table and looked down at the dispositions indicated on it. He would have given anything to be magically able to transform his command arrangements. Unfortunately, miracles were beyond him, and so he looked up at Barcor and forced himself to radiate confidence in his subordinate.

"I want you to return to your command as quickly as possible, Sir Zher. We can't afford to let them pin us in the pass. There's a good position here." He tapped the map at a point about four miles west of the pass proper, where the royal highway passed between a pair of hills. A small farming town named (accurately, if not precisely originally) Green Valley sat in the saddle between them, straddling the highway. "If you can get there quickly enough, your men can dig in in and around the town and make *them* come to *you*. If they refuse to attack you, or try to maneuver around you, it'll buy us time to reinforce you and get more of our men out of the pass. If they don't do either, we'll be able to continue moving out of the pass and around the northeastern edge of your men, as long as you hold your position."

Barcor stared at him, then nodded almost convulsively. Gahrvai hovered on the point of relieving him and handing command of the rear guard to someone else, like Mancora. But there wasn't time for that, either. If he wasted precious hours getting someone else into Barcor's place—and getting word of the change of command to all of Barcor's subordinates—Cayleb's steadily advancing Marines would be knocking on his army's backdoor before the first man marched out of his encampment.

Of course, that's altogether too likely to happen anyway, if

I leave Barcor in command. But I'm just going to have to take my chances on that.

"In the meantime," he continued out loud, "I'll signal immediate orders to Earl Windshare to harass and delay the enemy. It doesn't sound as if they have *any* cavalry of their own with them. With any luck, he'll be able to slow them down enough to let you get into position."

"Yes, Sir." Barcor's response sounded strangled, and he cleared his throat harshly. "With your permission, Sir," he said in a more normal-sounding voice, "I'd best be getting back to my men."

"Of course, My Lord." Once again, Gahrvai projected all the confidence he could as he clasped forearms with Barcor firmly and thanked God that the baron couldn't possibly know what he was really thinking. "The rest of the army will be right behind you."

"Thank you, Sir."

Barcor released Gahrvai's forearm and headed out of the tent looking almost like a resolute commander who knew what he was about. Gahrvai allowed himself a moment to hope there was more truth than usual in that impression, then turned back to the rest of his officers.

"My Lords," he said, "please be thinking about what we have to do while I draft Earl Windshare's instructions. Earl Mancora."

"Yes, Sir?"

"It's remotely possible that this is only a diversion, intended to panic us into falling back from our current position. To safeguard against that possibility, I want you and your men to stay right where you are. At the same time, however, I want you to begin planning now for a rapid withdrawal if it turns out Cayleb really is behind us in strength. Be sure you and Colonel Pahlzar coordinate the withdrawal of his artillery carefully."

"Of course, Sir."

"As for the rest of us," Gahrvai surveyed the other officers around the table, "I want every unit behind Earl Mancora's ready to move west within the next two hours." One or two expressions blanked, and he smiled thinly. "Gentlemen, we're like beads on a string here in this pass. None of us can move until the man immediately to our west is already in motion. Don't think Cayleb hasn't considered that, either. So, yes. Two hours I said, and two hours I meant. Is that clearly understood?"

Heads nodded, and his smile turned a bit warmer.

"I would recommend that each of you send one of your aides back to your command immediately with instructions to begin preparing to move. I'll try to have all of you personally back to your men as quickly as possible. Now, if you'll excuse me?"

▼ ▼ ▼

Cayleb and his mounted bodyguard cantered briskly up the flank of the marching column of Marines. They were accompanied by a hundred-man cavalry company, one of the very few the Marines had. It wouldn't be enough to beat off any sort of serious attack, but the entire compact force was fast and agile. Besides, the column was always available for them to fall back on, and if an entire brigade of Marines couldn't stave off an attempt to kill or capture the emperor, then this entire operation was already effectively doomed.

That was Cayleb's view of the situation, at any rate, and he was sticking to it. Merlin had done his dead level best to argue the youthful emperor into changing his mind, but Cayleb was adamant. And, Merlin had to agree, there was quite a bit of logic on the emperor's side, whether he liked it or not. For good or ill, Cayleb was the only interface through which Merlin was able to directly affect the deployment of the Charisian field force. Merlin certainly couldn't turn up in Brigadier Clareyk's command area and start telling him where to move his troops to meet threats his own scouts hadn't detected. Cayleb could give whatever orders he wanted, and the troops were rapidly coming to the conclusion that his ability to read a tactical situation on land was just as good as it was at sea. Given that set of circumstances, Merlin had been forced to admit that having Cayleb at the point of the Charisian spear made at least some sense.

Besides, Cayleb was the emperor—a point he wasn't particularly loath to make whenever it suited his purposes.

It's a good thing he really is smart as a whip, Merlin reflected as he rode just behind and to the emperor's right. *Stubborn as he is, we'd be in an incredible mess if he decided to get up on his "emperor's horse" this way and he wasn't a bright fellow. I suppose we're fortunate he has the habit of command, too, all things considered. It's a hell of a lot better than indecisiveness, God knows! But I hope Sharleyan and I can keep him from getting* too *confident. It's going to be really hard for someone with his authority to avoid the trap of always* insisting on going his own way, especially as he gets older.

The head of the column came into sight, and Cayleb and his escort slowed down as they spotted Brigadier Clareyk's mounted command group under the brigade's dovetailed standard with its embroidered kraken and huge "3" in scarlet and gold. The brigadier had obviously been informed that they were on their way, and he and his staff trotted to meet the emperor.

"Your Majesty," Clareyk said, bowing from the saddle.

"Brigadier," Cayleb acknowledged. "I hope you won't feel I'm trying to joggle your elbow," the emperor continued, "but I've discovered that there are only so many times I can sit around safely aboard ship while I send my Marines off to get into trouble without me."

He'd raised his voice slightly, and Merlin saw several of the nearby Marines grinning as they marched past. The emperor's remarks would spread throughout the brigade within the hour, he felt quite sure. By nightfall, they'd probably have spread through the entire expeditionary force west of the Dark Hills.

"Of course, Your Majesty," Clareyk agreed with a smile, although Merlin was quite certain that at this particular moment the brigadier wished Cayleb were just about anywhere on Safehold *except* with Third Brigade. But then Clareyk glanced rather oddly in Merlin's direction, and the man who had been Nimue Alban suddenly wondered just how much Clareyk really had guessed about him.

"Have your scouts reported any sign of Gahrvai's cavalry?" Cayleb asked more seriously, and Clareyk grimaced.

"My *mounted* scouts are unfortunately thin on the ground, Your Majesty, and I haven't wanted to let foot patrols get too far out on the column's flanks, under the circumstances. So far, we've had a handful of run-ins with the other side's cavalry, but only in ones and twos."

"Their scouts running into our scouts," Cayleb agreed with a frown of his own. "Has there been any fighting?"

"I've had a couple of reports." Clareyk nodded. "So far, it's worked out in our favor in each case. On the other hand, I expect I'd only hear back about the ones where it *did* work out in our favor," he added with a wintry smile.

It was Cayleb's turn to nod, and he scratched thoughtfully at the wiry whiskers of the short, neatly trimmed beard he'd grown since leaving Charis. He gazed off to the northeast, obviously thinking hard, then looked back at Clareyk.

"I think we can expect Earl Windshare to come calling," he said. "In fact, I'm a bit surprised he hasn't already arrived. I know we discussed the possibility in our planning sessions, Brigadier, but I've got a feeling he's going to arrive in greater strength than we'd anticipated."

"I see, Your Majesty," Clareyk said calmly, then let his eyes flick sideways to Captain Athrawes before he looked gravely back at his emperor. "Do you have any suggestions to make?"

"Actually," Cayleb said, his own eyes narrowing slightly, "I do. It's occurred to me that the fact that Windshare hasn't arrived yet probably indicates we did take them by surprise. It may also indicate," he looked directly into Clareyk's eyes, "that their infantry has been slower about getting into motion than they'd hoped. In fact, I suppose it's even possible Gahrvai's infantry hasn't actually started moving at all yet."

"If our spies' reports that Baron Barcor's been placed in command of his rear guard are accurate, I'd say that was certainly at least a possibility, Your Majesty," Clareyk agreed.

"Well, if that should be the case, then I'd expect someone like Windshare would be particularly determined to slow us down, especially if he has more of his men with him than we'd anticipated he would. As a matter of fact, I believe he'd probably be looking for an opportunity to do just that by launching a decisive attack on our leading column. *Your* column, Brigadier."

"Yes, Your Majesty."

"If he should be tempted to do that, then the opportunity would arise for *us* to decisively defeat *him*, instead. How confident would you feel about your ability to deal with, say, three or four thousand cavalry?"

Clareyk's eyes narrowed as Cayleb threw out the number. He cocked his head to one side, obviously considering the figures, then turned in the saddle to survey the terrain through which he was currently advancing.

"Assuming, of course, that your numbers are close to correct, Your Majesty," he said, flicking another of those lightning glances in Merlin's direction, "and given the openness of most of the ground between here and Green Valley, I think we could handle that many cavalry without too much difficulty. We're more spread out than I might wish, but they aren't going to be able to sneak into charge range without our seeing them in plenty of time to form square."

"I realize that," Cayleb said a bit more slowly. "But if you form square, and if Windshare is smart enough—and patient enough—to simply sit there, he wins. All he really has to do is delay us long enough for Gahrvai to get his infantry out of Talbor. If he settles for holding you under threat, keeping you formed up in one place in square, instead of continuing to advance, he'll buy Gahrvai the time he needs."

"And you'd like me to tempt him into *not* being smart and patient enough, Your Majesty?"

"Exactly." Cayleb nodded. "Every report I've seen on Windshare says he's aggressive. Someone even described him as 'thinking with his spurs.' I think that's probably unfair—if he's not the sharpest man ever born, he's not exactly stupid, either—but his instinct is definitely to hit hard and fast. Given the threat we pose to the rest of Gahrvai's troops, and the fact that he probably doesn't have the most lively faith in the world in Barcor's quickness off the mark, he's going to be even more tempted to do that if he thinks he sees an opportunity. So I'd like to convince him that he does."

"Risky, if you'll permit me to say so, Your Majesty," Clareyk observed.

"Agreed. But if you can pull it off, the return could be decisive."

"I can see that. At the same time, Your Majesty, I trust you'll forgive me for saying that if I'm about to try something risky, I'd really prefer for you to be somewhere else while I do it."

"Everyone seems to keep saying that to me," Cayleb replied with a tight grin. "And, usually, I can talk myself into going along with them. But this time, I think not, Brigadier. I'm asking you and your men to run a greater risk than we'd discussed earlier. I'm not going to do that while I sit somewhere in the rear."

"Your Majesty, my entire brigade is worth far less to Charis than you are," Clareyk said bluntly. "With all due respect, I must respectfully decline to unnecessarily endanger your person in a situation like the one we're discussing."

"Brigadier—" Cayleb began sharply, then made himself bite off his sentence. His jaw clamped for a moment, and then he inhaled sharply.

"You really intend to be stubborn about this, don't you?"

"Your Majesty, I'm sorry, but I do." Clareyk faced his monarch squarely. "It's your prerogative to relieve me of my command, if you so choose. But the Empire literally cannot spare you at this time. You know that as well as I do. If you want me to bait a trap for Earl Windshare, I'll do that. But I won't risk your life on the possibility that Windshare might get lucky."

Cayleb half-glared at Clareyk, but the brigadier didn't flinch. Then his eyes flickered sideways to Merlin for a third time.

"Very well, Brigadier," the emperor said after a long, simmering moment. "You win. And you're wrong about my prerogative to relieve you." He showed his teeth. "I'd get away with it about as long as it took for the Empress to find out what you'd done to piss me off."

"I'll admit that that thought *did* occur to me, Your Majesty."

"I'm sure it did. However, if I allow you to chase me back to the rear, I'd at least like to leave . . . call it a personal representative behind. Someone who can report to me in person as soon as whatever happens happens."

"May I assume you have someone in mind for that duty, Your Majesty?"

"I thought I'd leave Captain Athrawes." Cayleb held Clareyk's eyes levelly with his own. "I've always found Merlin's reports extremely accurate, and I trust his judgment."

"As do I, Your Majesty." Clareyk smiled ever so slightly. "If you feel you can spare the *seijin*'s services, I'd be honored to have him remain with the Brigade."

▼ ▼ ▼

Sir Alyk Ahrthyr stood slapping his riding gloves impatiently against his thigh as the courier galloped up to him. He was out of direct contact with the semaphore masts Gahrvai had ordered constructed all across his rear areas. He could communicate only by old-fashioned dispatch riders, and that left him feeling even more edgy and irritated than he'd been when he received Gahrvai's original, stunning message. Not that he needed much in the way of additional irritation.

"*Well?*" he growled as the courier drew up beside him.

"I'm sorry, My Lord," the dust-covered young lieutenant replied. "The Baron hasn't marched yet."

"Then what in the name of Shan-wei is the idiot *waiting* for?!" Windshare snarled. Diplomacy had never been his strong suit, and unlike Gahrvai, he saw no reason to waste what little diplomacy he had on someone like Barcor.

I may not be the smartest man in the world, he thought savagely, *but there's at least* one *who's a lot stupider than I am, by God!*

"My Lord, I—" the courier began, but Windshare waved him into silence.

"Of course you don't have an answer, Lieutenant. That was what General Gahrvai would have called a 'rhetorical question.'" The cavalry commander surprised himself with a sharp bark of laughter. "Not exactly what people expect out of me, I admit."

The lieutenant, rather wisely, simply nodded this time. Still, it was amazing how much better the exchange made Windshare feel . . . for the moment, at least.

He turned and stumped back over to the hilltop nearoak under whose broad-branched shade he had established his temporary command post. Dry seed cones crunched under his boots, and he found himself wishing the crunching sounds could have been coming from Baron Barcor. His staff looked up at him, and he grimaced disgustedly.

"The fat-arsed idiot hasn't even started marching yet," he growled. Very few of his staff saw any more reason than he did to conceal their opinions of Barcor, and one or two of them actually spat on the ground.

"My Lord, if he doesn't start moving soon, then this army is well and truly fucked," Sir Naithyn Galvahn said harshly.

Major Galvahn was Windshare's senior aide, effectively his chief of staff, although the Corisandian Army didn't use that particular term. Like virtually all of Windshare's other officers, Galvahn was exceedingly wellborn. That was inevitable, given the fact that the cavalry tended to attract the nobly born like a particularly powerful lodestone. There was nothing wrong with Galvahn's brain, however, and Windshare knew he tended to lean on the major.

"I know, Naithyn. I know," he said, and looked out from the small hill, glaring at the dust clouds rising above the local turnpike which connected with the royal highway less than three miles from where he stood at this very moment.

Galvahn was right about what was going to happen if the Charisians managed to seal the western end of Talbor Pass while Gahrvai's army was still trapped inside. Unfortunately, everyone seemed to understand that except the one man responsible for getting the army's rear guard the hell out into the open to prevent it from happening!

Windshare didn't want to admit just how desperate he was beginning to feel. Cayleb's move to flank Talbor by landing a force west of it had scarcely been unexpected, but his ability to somehow eliminate the observation posts specifically placed to detect any such landing definitely was. He'd used the advantage of surprise he'd gained ruthlessly, and at this point, Windshare hadn't even been able to form a clear, hard notion of how many men were ashore. It wasn't for lack of trying, but against an army whose every soldier was equipped with a rifle, his cavalry patrols hadn't been able to get as close to the Charisian columns as he would have liked.

It wasn't his troopers' fault. His men had no shortage of courage or horsemanship, but the ability of cavalry armed with lances, sabers, and horse bows or arbalests to stand up to massed rifle fire was . . . limited, at best. The only real advantages the horsemen retained were mobility and speed, and neither of those was great enough to offset their newfound *disadvantages*. The worst of it was that cavalry required open terrain if it was going to operate efficiently, but open terrain only allowed riflemen to begin killing them sooner, at longer ranges. And most of the terrain between Cayleb's landing point and Green Valley consisted of rolling, open grasslands, rising steadily towards the east as they merged with the Dark Hills' western foothills.

In light of his scouts' inability to maintain close contact with the enemy, his notion of the Charisians' strength was problematical, at best. The most anyone could say on the basis of the reports he'd received so far was that Cayleb had landed somewhere between ten thousand and eighteen thousand men. Windshare personally inclined towards the lower figure, but he was frustratingly aware that he had nothing concrete upon which to base his feeling. And even if Cayleb had "only" ten thousand men with him, Windshare had less than four thousand of his cavalry actually present. Another eight thousand of them were scattered along the line of the Dark Hills, watching the passes farther north from Talbor, but there was no way to recall any of those detachments in time to do any good. So here he sat, with not quite four thousand men and orders to harass a numerically superior force equipped with much longer-ranged weapons in order to delay its advance until Baron Barcor got his thumb out of his arse.

Which, at this rate, isn't going to happen before Langhorne returns to gather up the world, he thought disgustedly.

"All right, Naithyn," he said finally, turning back from the oncoming dust clouds. "We're going to have to do something, and you're right, we're going to have to do it quickly. I want everyone we've got moved to those cotton silk plantations west of Green Valley. Their columns are going to have to tighten up where the highway passes through that belt of woodland. I know it's not very deep, but it should at least cramp them, and the ground on this side of the woods is the best place we're going to find for cavalry."

"Sir, those woods aren't that thick or overgrown. Certainly not anything like the approaches to Haryl's Crossing. Loose-order infantry can probably get through them without a lot of difficulty, and if they send riflemen forward into the trees, they'll be able to use them for cover and—"

"Don't worry, I'm not planning on deploying a nice juicy target for them inside rifle range. I'm not going to object if they do waste time sending their marksmen into those woods, mind you. What I'm thinking, though, is that there's that nice rising slope this side of the woods. If we take position just over its crest and they know we're there, they won't be able to shoot at us, but they'll have to respect the possibility of a charge. If nothing else, it should encourage them to halt in place until they can bring up additional infantry. And given the fact that they don't seem to have any cavalry of their own on this side of the mountains, they may not realize we're there in strength at all. If they advance up that slope, away from the protection of the woods, and get close enough to us . . ."

He let his voice trail off, and Galvahn started nodding. Slowly, at first, and then with increasing enthusiasm. Much as the major respected Windshare as a fighter, he wouldn't have trusted the earl as a strategist. He was the ideal regimental or divisional commander, in many ways, but he probably would have been a disaster as an *army* commander. One of his virtues, however, was an excellent eye for terrain, and he was right. The plantations' fields, covered in roughly knee-high cotton silk plants, offered a stretch of fairly level ground almost four miles wide. It was a fan-shaped stretch, widest at its western end and narrowing as it climbed towards the east. And, as Windshare had just pointed out, the land along its eastern edge broke down into a shallow trough before it started climbing again. The resultant depression was big enough—probably—to allow Windshare to conceal the bulk of his cavalry from the approaching Charisians until they were right on top of him. Nothing could magically erase the advantage the Charisians' rifles bestowed upon them, but Windshare's chosen spot was the closest thing to ideal ground they were likely to find.

Aside, of course, from the fact that it was barely a mile and a half west of Green Valley. If they couldn't convince the Charisians to halt there, it was virtually certain Cayleb's Marines would take Green Valley without a fight. And if *they* held Green Valley, the chances of any infantry force breaking out of Talbor Pass would be slim.

"Yes, My Lord," he said now. "I'll see to it at once."

▼ ▼ ▼

"Excuse me, Brigadier."

Brigadier Kynt Clareyk looked up from his conversation with Colonel Arttu Raizyngyr, the commanding officer of the 2/3rd Marines.

"Yes, Captain Athrawes?"

"I wonder if I might have a word?" Merlin asked diffidently.

Clareyk looked at him thoughtfully for a moment, then nodded.

"I need to catch up with Colonel Zhanstyn's battalion, anyway, *Seijin* Merlin," he said. "Why don't you ride along with me?"

"Thank you, Sir," Merlin replied, and waited until Clareyk had mounted his horse once again.

Cayleb's surrender to Clareyk's insistence that he had no place at the point of the spear had surprised Merlin more than a little. And, truth to tell, it had left him in two minds. On the one hand, he was delighted to get Cayleb back where he belonged. On the other hand, Cayleb's decision to leave *him* behind had made him feel undeniably uneasy. The rest of Cayleb's bodyguards, not to mention the cavalry company surrounding him, ought to be capable of dealing with anything the emperor might run into, but Merlin had already lost Cayleb's father. Whether that had been his fault or not, he still felt bitter regret every time he thought about King Haarahld's death, and he had no intention of feeling that way over *Cayleb's* death.

Then there's that other *minor consideration,* he thought dryly as Clareyk concluded his brief conversation with Raizyngyr and headed for his horse. *I could wish I'd had a little more time to think about how I'd handle this situation. I'm not even sure whether all those glances in my direction meant what I thought they did or not.* He snorted suddenly in amusement. *Now, if I were still Nimue, I could think of another reason for him to've been doing that. And, truth to tell, he's cute enough I don't think I'd have minded it at all. . . .*

He managed not to smile as he watched the brigadier swing gracefully into the saddle. Unlike too many Marine officers, Clareyk obviously felt right at home on a horse's back as he fell easily into place beside Merlin's mount.

And he's got really nice buns, too, Merlin thought.

"Now, *Seijin* Merlin," Clareyk said, thankfully unaware of the *seijin*'s appreciative thoughts, as the two of them started forward, followed at a respectful distance by Major Lahftyn and the other members of Clareyk's command group. "I believe you had something to say to me which you'd prefer no one else heard?"

Well, that answers that *question, doesn't it,* "Seijin Merlin"*?* Merlin thought sardonically.

"I beg your pardon, Brigadier?" he said politely aloud.

"I realize I'm not really supposed to know this, *Seijin*," Clareyk said with a crooked smile, "but I didn't spend that long working with you, the Emperor, and Baron Seamount without realizing you're considerably more than just one of the Emperor's bodyguards. Or even 'just' a *seijin* who happens to know all sorts of interesting things, and have even more interesting ideas. I still remember how neatly you maneuvered *me* into suggesting the creation of the scout-snipers, for instance. And who it was who suggested the name for them. And I suppose I should go ahead and admit I've heard a few whispers of rumors about 'visions' of yours. In fact, I've found myself wondering on occasion just how much of the Emperor's uncanny ability to predict what the enemy is likely to do stems from those visions you may or may not be having."

Merlin managed not to wince, but only because he'd already suspected at least some of what was coming. He hadn't anticipated the *full* of it, however, and he found himself wondering if Clareyk was still holding back even more suspicions.

Well, you knew he was a smart man when you and Cayleb picked him to develop the new infantry tactics. It would appear he's even sharper than you'd realized, though, and sharp blades tend to nick fingers if you handle them carelessly. So I think it's about time you started handling this one the right way:

"Brigadier," he said, "obviously I can't go into all of that without the Emperor's permission. On the other hand, there's not much point pretending you aren't generally correct. I *do* have visions, of a sort, at least. And they have been quite useful to the Emperor—and to his father—on several occasions. Which, for obvious reasons, explains why all of us have been to some pains to prevent the rumors you referred to from getting any sort of broad circulation."

"I can see why that would be, yes," Clareyk agreed.

"Since you've figured out at least some of it, I suppose I should go ahead and tell you that while I can 'see' many things, I can see neither the future nor the past—only the present. Obviously, even that much can sometimes provide a major advantage, but it means, for example, that I couldn't simply buff up my crystal ball—and, no, I don't *actually* use one—and tell Cayleb ahead of time what Gahrvai and Windshare would do when they found out we'd landed behind them."

Clareyk pursed his lips thoughtfully, then nodded, and Merlin continued.

"Although I can't see the future, I can tell you Earl Windshare is assembling the better part of four thousand troopers about another two miles down the road from here. It's actually quite a good position from his perspective, and I believe he's counting on the terrain to keep you from realizing how close he is until you blunder into him."

"Which presents a possible opportunity to carry out His Majesty's intentions," Clareyk said thoughtfully.

"Yes, it does. But the place he's found gives him a much better chance of actually pressing home a charge than I think Cayleb wanted you to give him."

"Maybe so. But if his position is that good, then if we can't entice him into charging, we'll be forced to stop, at least until Brigadier Haimyn can come up to support us. So it's either find a way to convince him to fight or else let him pin us down, possibly long enough for Gahrvai to get out of the trap."

Merlin nodded, and Clareyk frowned pensively.

"Tell me more about this terrain Windshare's chosen, *Seijin*," he said.

▼ ▼ ▼

The Earl of Windshare frowned, listening carefully as rifle shots popped distantly on the other side of the crest line. They were coming steadily closer, and he hoped his forward pickets weren't taking too many casualties.

Damned rifles, he thought resentfully.

He remembered his own incredulity at Haryl's Crossing when the rifles hidden in the woods had opened up on him. At first, he'd literally been unable to believe it was happening. No one could *possibly* shoot that far or that rapidly—the very idea had been unthinkable!

Unfortunately, the Charisians *could*. Windshare couldn't quite agree with Gahrvai's opinion that the new rifles were going to overturn all accepted battlefield tactics, just as their galleons had already overturned all accepted naval tactics, but even he had to admit the consequences were going to be profound. He wasn't prepared to assume they'd just made cavalry obsolete as a decisive arm, but he was honest enough to admit that at least part of that reluctance might be pure, bullheaded stubbornness on his part.

A war in which cavalry was reduced solely to a scouting force, capable of occasional hit-and-run raids but helpless against any unshaken infantry position? Nonsense. Ridiculous! Unthinkable! Yet vehemently as Windshare had rejected the notion, he couldn't free himself of a gnawing suspicion that Gahrvai had a point.

Even at an extended gallop, a typical cavalryman could cover less than five hundred yards in a minute. Against slow-firing smoothbore matchlocks, with a maximum effective range of no more than a hundred yards, that meant musketeers would have time for only a single shot each before the horsemen were on top of them. But these damned Charisian rifles fired four or five times as rapidly as matchlocks, and to four or five times the effective range. Which was the reason the skirmishers deployed to screen the oncoming infantry columns were able to keep Windshare's scouts at a distance. By the same token, the skirmishers had to stay close enough to their columns to fall back on them if they were threatened by a cavalry charge, but the ability of an *infantry* force to move virtually at will, even in the presence of superior numbers of cavalry, seemed like a perversion to an old-school trooper like Windshare.

Well, Koryn may have a point, Windshare granted unwillingly. *I still think he's overreacting to what happened at Haryl's Crossing, but I'm willing to admit I could be wrong about that. Even if I am, though, those bastards don't have a single pikeman. If they'll just come close enough . . .*

"My Lord."

Windshare shook himself up out of his introspection as Galvahn trotted up beside him.

"Yes, Naithyn?"

"They have two battalions on this side of the woodline. Another is just beginning to emerge, but they've allowed the marching interval between it and the other two to widen to over three hundred yards."

"They have?" Windshare's eyes brightened, and Galvahn smiled.

"Yes, My Lord. And their lead battalion is heading straight towards us. Our pickets are falling back in front of it as you instructed. That's the firing you can hear." He twitched his head in the direction of the whip-crack rifle shots. "They've kept the range open, too, just like they were supposed to, and we haven't lost very many men. We've got over a dozen horses down, but I think we've only had two or three *men* hit."

"Good!" Windshare slapped his gauntlets against his thigh. "Good, Naithyn!"

The earl climbed back into his own saddle and looked around at his staff.

"Gentlemen, I believe it's time we discouraged these people," he said.

▼ ▼ ▼

Merlin Athrawes found himself hoping Brigadier Clareyk wasn't being overconfident.

His two lead battalions—Colonel Zhanstyn's First Battalion and Colonel Raizyngyr's Second Battalion, which together made up the Third Brigade's First Regiment—marched straight along the royal highway towards Green Valley in time with the battalion pipers and with rifles slung. Although their battle casualties had been ludicrously low, sickness and injury had reduced both battalions from a nominal strength of five hundred men each to a combined total of just over eight hundred. Which, for any animal-powered army Nimue Alban had ever studied, was an incredibly low sick rate. Traditionally, back on Old Earth, especially in preindustrial armies, attrition from illness had vastly exceeded combat losses. It hadn't been until the period of World War I that deaths from enemy action had actually outnumbered deaths from disease, but "the Archangel Pasquale's" teachings had produced a level of hygiene and preventive health measures which created a very different situation here on Safehold.

None of which changed the fact that Zhanstyn and Raizyngyr were outnumbered by roughly five-to-one by the cavalry waiting just on the far side of the hill.

Merlin glanced at Clareyk as the brigadier rode along, seemingly without a care in the world. He'd stayed with Zhanstyn's command group, and if he was particularly concerned about Windshare, his expression showed absolutely no sign of it.

▼　▼　▼

The Earl of Windshare sat in his saddle watching his retreating cavalry pickets withdraw up the hillside towards him exactly as Major Galvahn had described. The long, gradual slope behind them was dotted with the bodies of dead and wounded horses who'd obviously been brought down by the skirmishers moving fifty or sixty yards in advance of the main infantry column, but he saw only a very few human bodies out among them.

His spyglass showed him the Charisians, marching with their rifles slung. To his considerable surprise, they were marching with fixed bayonets, as well, which was more than simply odd. Bayonets were musketeers' last-ditch defense, and a clumsy substitute for proper pikes, at best. Worse, men with the circular hilts of bayonets shoved down the muzzles of their muskets could neither fire nor reload, so what in the world could the Charisians be thinking of?

Deep inside, a little voice suggested to him that someone like Gahrvai might have been able to come up with an answer short of assuming that his opponents had succumbed to lunacy. It should, perhaps, have occurred to him that none of his earlier reports had mentioned anything about bayonets. On the other hand, that wasn't the sort of detail cavalry scouts normally included in their reports, and at the moment, Windshare had other things on his mind. Like the fact that, bayonets or no, they were coming hard, concentrating on covering ground as quickly as they could without exhausting themselves, and the way they'd allowed themselves to become more spread out indicated that they weren't spending a lot of energy worrying.

No reason they should be, he thought grimly. *We've been shadowing them—and they've been killing and wounding my men—for hours now, and I doubt their maps are as good as ours. As far as they're concerned, this is just more of the same, and they probably don't even know what the ground looks like between here and Green Valley. No reason for them to think I could have over four thousand cavalry hidden away.*

He smiled hungrily, watching the enemy approach.

It was going to be ticklish getting his men up and over the crest line. Not only was there the slope to consider, but the terrain would be constricted until they crossed the crest, where the fan-shaped prospective battlefield began to open out once more. No trooper liked to start a charge headed uphill, for a lot of reasons, and in this instance, they were going to be packed like apples in a basket, forced to adopt a deeper formation than he would have preferred, until they cleared the top of the slope. On the other hand, there were those bayonets. Even if the Charisians' muskets were loaded, they'd still have to remove the bayonets before they could fire, and his troopers would have the downslope on the far side to help them build and maintain speed once they got started. The trick was going to be timing. He needed to start the charge soon enough to give his men time to come over the hill and gain speed, but at the same time, he wanted to give the Charisians as little time as possible to react.

Still, he thought, studying those slung muskets, *surprise is bound to keep them from reacting instantly.*

▼ ▼ ▼

Merlin had deliberately looked away from Clareyk. In fact, he'd turned in the saddle to look back down the length of the column behind them to where the first battery of twelve-pounders had just come through the belt of trees in road column. It probably wasn't strictly necessary, but he wanted to make it clear to any potential observer that he wasn't even thinking about the brigadier at this particular moment.

Of course, he wasn't really looking at the *column,* either, as he waited, watching and listening through his SNARC.

▼ ▼ ▼

"Now!" Windshare snapped, and Major Galvahn stood in the stirrups, waving the red signal flag vigorously.

▼ ▼ ▼

Merlin might not have been watching Clareyk, but the brigadier had been very attentively—if unobtrusively—watching *him.* Which was why the Marine saw the bodyguard reach up and remove his helmet in order to wipe sweat from his brow.

"*Now,* I think, Bryahn," he said crisply.

Major Lahftyn looked at him for just a moment, then glanced up the slope before them. Obviously, he couldn't imagine what had prompted Clareyk to give the order at that precise moment, but it was an order he'd been expecting. He hesitated for no more than a heartbeat, then nodded to the bugler at his side.

"Sound 'Form square,' Corporal," he said.

▼ ▼ ▼

Windshare's massed horsemen started up the slope. First, at a walk, but moving rapidly to a trot, with the smoothness of years of experience and the demanding training Windshare had put them through ever since assuming command of Gahrvai's cavalry.

The lead squadrons reached the crest in an eight-deep line, moving at a hard trot, covering just over two hundred yards per minute, and the front two ranks accelerated rapidly. By the time they'd covered another forty yards, they were moving at a full, extended gallop, hooves showering clods of moist earth, lances and sabers glittering in the sunlight, while the next two ranks thundered along thirty yards behind them. About them and behind them came the music of bugles, the drumming thunder of sixteen thousand hooves, and a deep, baying cheer as they turned on their enemies at last.

Windshare himself came over the crest with the third doubleline, sixty yards behind the first. He rode in the exact center of the line, his standard snapping and popping in the wind of his passage, and his eyes glittered with fierce satisfaction.

But then those eyes widened in astonishment.

▾   ▾   ▾

The men of Clareyk's first two battalions had been waiting for the bugle call, and they responded instantly. Both battalions unraveled, moving with the speed and precision only endless, brutally demanding drill could have instilled. They spread out, First Battalion moving to its right while Second Battalion moved to its left, forming not a column, not a line, but a single hollow formation. It wasn't literally a "square"; the ground was too uneven for that, and it was more of a rectangle than a square, anyway. But that compact, steady, unshaken, *unsurprised* formation bristled with bayonets, facing outward in every direction, and, in direct contravention of every standard safety regulation, the rifles upon which those bayonets were mounted had been carefully loaded and primed before they were ever slung.

▾   ▾   ▾

Windshare couldn't believe it.

He'd never seen infantry move that quickly, that precisely, even on the drill field. Surely there was no way they could have responded that instantly! It wasn't possible!

Yet the Charisians had done it, and it was too late for him to change his own mind. Half his total force—including Windshare himself—was already at a full gallop, pounding downhill towards the enemy at over seven yards a second in a series of lines which were each a hundred and twenty-five men across. His lead elements had little more than a hundred and fifty yards to go, and the front rank of the second half of his force was already moving up and over the crest line behind him, ready to exploit his charge's success.

And the bastards still *have their damned bayonets fixed, too!* he realized, and grinned savagely. *They may* think *that'll keep my lads from closing with them, but they're about to find out just how wrong they are!*

▼ ▼ ▼

Brigadier Clareyk sat his horse in the middle of First Battalion's square, watching the enemy come. His expression was as calm as ever as he glanced over at Merlin.

"I suppose this is where we find out just how clever I really am," he remarked.

The front of his square, where it faced uphill, was three ranks deep, instead of two. The front rank knelt on one knee, rifle butts braced, bayonets thrusting up and out at a sharp angle . . . right about at chest height on a horse. The second and third ranks waited, rifles cocked. The temptation to fire as soon as possible was almost overwhelming as they watched two thousand cavalry thundering towards them, but they didn't. They waited.

Colonel Zhanstyn waited with them. His battalion formed the long side of the square closest to the enemy, and he'd dismounted to stand beside the battalion standard, sword in hand, his eyes on the enemy.

There wouldn't be time to reload before the first wave was

upon them, whatever happened, and he had no intention of wasting the shock value of a massed volley by firing too soon. It wasn't just a matter of range or accuracy; it was also a matter of *timing,* of hitting those cavalrymen not simply with the physical impact of his Marines' bullets, but with their *morale* effect, as well—and doing it at precisely the right moment.

▼　▼　▼

The Corisandian cavalry thundered downhill, opened up into proper double-lines. Now the leading troopers tightened in the saddle, bracing for impact as they hurtled straight at the Charisian formation. The hedge of unwavering bayonet points glittered wickedly in the early-afternoon sunlight, but at least they weren't *pikes.* In another few seconds—

The universe came apart in a sudden, thunderous roll of rifle fire.

▼　▼　▼

There were roughly eight hundred men in the Charisian square, with four platoons—roughly eighty men—in each of its short sides, covering either flank. Another hundred men formed its rear face, facing downhill, covering the backs of the two hundred and twenty men in its front face, and a forty-man reserve stood ready in the middle of the formation, prepared to reinforce any weak spot. Its long face was roughly a hundred yards from side to side, barely a third of the oncoming cavalry's frontage, and it looked impossibly frail in the face of such a threat.

If the Charisians in that square realized that, they gave no sign of it.

As Windshare's cavalry charge poured down the hillside like a river of horseflesh and steel, the hundred and fifty rifles in the square's second and third ranks flamed as one.

The impact of that deadly volley was staggering, and in more than one way. Every man in Windshare's charge had seen those bayonets, and because they'd never heard of "ring bayonets," which mounted *around* a rifle's muzzle instead of being shoved down into the weapon's bore, they'd *known* that the musketeers behind them couldn't possibly fire. The surprise when they went right ahead and fired anyway was total. Even if those bullets had inflicted no casualties at all, the sheer shock of experiencing yet another surprise at Charisian hands would have dealt the cavalry's confidence and determination a deadly blow.

And, unfortunately for Corisande, the Charisian bullets *did* inflict casualties, as well.

Horses were big targets; men were relatively small ones. No more than twenty or thirty of Windshare's troopers were actually hit by the Charisian fire. Those who *were* hit went down hard as the massive bullets smashed through breastplates and the fragile bodies beneath them, yet they represented only a handful of that onrushing wave's total numbers.

But the horses were another matter. Holes appeared abruptly in the center of the Corisandian line as screaming horses smashed to earth. Riders were flung out of their saddles, only to find themselves in the path of the second line of troopers behind them. Ordinarily, a horse will do almost anything to avoid colliding with a human, but there was no way *these* horses could. They were moving too fast, with too much momentum, with too many *other* horses right behind them, and they trampled the dismounted cavalrymen into bloody mud.

The bodies of the fallen horses were a more serious obstacle, and the face of the charging formation splintered as the horses still on their feet tried frantically to avoid the tangled wreckage of their dead and wounded fellows. Many of them failed, plowing into the barrier, shrieking as legs broke, riders went flying, and fresh, thrashing bodies were added to the heap.

Zhanstyn had timed his volley almost perfectly. There was time enough to break the cavalry's momentum, distance enough for the leading edge of the charge to spread out around the sudden obstacle and lose cohesion, but too little time for it to begin to recover. And, just as horses will instinctively seek

382 / DAVID WEBER

to avoid trampling a downed human, they have a pronounced aversion to charging straight into the solid barrier of a glittering wall of sharpened steel. With their momentum broken, their ranks staggered, their riders unnerved, they refused the challenge. Instead, they split around the square, flowing down its short sides, and fresh rifle volleys ripped out as their momentum carried them across the flank platoons' field of fire.

Then they were past the square . . . and its *rear* wall fired a deadly volley into their backs.

▼ ▼ ▼

There wasn't time for Windshare to even begin to analyze what had happened to his first wave before his *second* wave came thundering in, ten seconds later.

Those ten seconds hadn't been quite long enough for the firing ranks to reload, but the kneeling *front* rank hadn't fired against the first wave. Now, the second rank advanced its bayonets at the thrust, reaching well forward over the heads of the front rank, while that front rank raised its rifles and fired its own vicious volley at point-blank range.

It was only half as heavy as the volley which had broken the first charge, but it was enough to stagger the second, especially with the writhing drift of dead and wounded horses and bodies from the first double-line's wreckage to help disorder the Corisandian formation, and the surviving horses of the second wave were no more eager than their fellows had been to thrust themselves against those waiting bayonets. They fought their riders, and even as they did, the square's third rank finished reloading, leveled its rifles, and fired at a range of less than thirty feet.

The carnage was incredible, yet even in the midst of the blood, the smoke, and the screams, some of Windshare's troopers actually managed to close with the Marines. Lances crossed with bayoneted muskets, swords flashed, and blood splashed across the grassy hillside, and then the *third* wave plowed into the melee.

In most places, the square held. Unshaken infantry in tight formation and under firm tactical control stood an excellent chance against cavalry. It was *broken* infantry, or an unsteady formation, which formed cavalry's legitimate prey, and the Charisians refused to be broken. Yet the Corisandians were just as determined, and Charisians began to die, as well.

A hole opened in the square's front as Windshare's third line slammed home. One of the reserve platoons moved quickly to seal the gap, but half a dozen Corisandian horsemen burst through it before they could. Brigadier Clareyk's command group were the only mounted troops under his command, and he slapped home his heels, spurring to meet the breakthrough with his staff officers.

One rider had started moving an instant before the hole actually opened, however. He wore the black and gold kraken on the blue checkerboard shield of the Charisian Imperial Guard, and his katana flashed in his hand. He went into the oncoming Corisandians like a battering ram, and a head flew. Before that first head hit the ground, Merlin's blade had claimed a second.

He passed through them like the archangel of death, then drove his horse directly into the gap and flung himself from the saddle to wield his sword two-handed while Clareyk and his staffers dealt with the two Corisandians he hadn't killed on his way through. In the handful of seconds it took for the reserve platoon to reach him, he killed another nine men.

▼ ▼ ▼

The Earl of Windshare found himself unhorsed once more, and this time with no dislocated shoulder. The bayonet wound in his right thigh bled badly, and he sat up, squeezing the leg with both hands, trying to staunch the flow of blood. Horses stamped and reared and screamed all about him, steel beat on steel with the dull, hideous blacksmith sound of a battlefield's death mill in full production, but he could feel the battle's tempo. When the hole had opened, he'd hoped they might still at least break this square. Now he knew they wouldn't. The shock of the Charisians' preposterously rapid response—the fact that they'd been able to fire after all, and the *effectiveness* of their fire—had broken his men's resolve, and he could already hear additional rifles, and artillery, firing from farther down the slope, where two more Charisian battalions had deployed into a standard firing line to cover the square's flanks with their preposterously long-range fire. He could also make out the sound of his own bugles, still blowing the charge, sending more of his men forward into the maelstrom, and something inside him cringed at the thought. Even if his men kept trying, all they could accomplish would be to die in even greater numbers, and—

Some instinct warned him, and he looked up just as one of those shrieking horses reared high and then came toppling down straight at him. There was nothing he could do, but then a human-shaped hand closed on the back of his weapons harness, and his eyes went wide as it effortlessly yanked him out of the falling horse's path.

He found himself being supported with one hand by a tall, broad-shouldered Charisian in the black-and-gold of the House of Ahrmahk. He had no idea what an Imperial Guardsman was doing in the midst of this insane carnage, but however the man had gotten there, he'd just saved Windshare's life. And, as the earl watched, the sword in the Charisian's *other* hand cut off one man's arm and took another's head.

Don't be silly, a corner of his brain told him. *No one can do that one-handed! You're wounded. Blood loss can make a man imagine all kinds of things.*

Then, charging out of the confusion, a platoon of Charisian Marines appeared to seal the opening in the square's front, and Windshare felt himself being dragged back from the fighting.

"I apologize for the rough treatment, My Lord," the man hauling him to safety said, "but I think General Gahrvai would prefer you alive."

Tellesberg Palace,
City of Tellesberg,
Old Kingdom of Charis

Well, I'd say we have our work cut out for us, Your Majesty,"
Rayjhis Yowance said quietly as he stood beside Empress
Sharleyan and watched the ballroom fill.

The two of them were ensconced in a waiting room off
Tellesberg Palace's grand ballroom. They'd chosen this particular waiting room because the artfully arranged and wrought
ornamental grillwork in the wall between it and the far larger
ballroom allowed someone inside the waiting room to watch
the ballroom without being seen in return. And they'd chosen the grand ballroom for today's assembly because there
wasn't another room in the palace large enough for their requirements.

"I don't understand why you should take that position, My
Lord," Sharleyan said with a slightly lopsided smile. "Surely
all these loyal servants of the Charisian and Chisholmian
crowns couldn't possibly have assembled in anything less
than the wholehearted spirit of cooperation! *I* certainly don't
expect anything less out of them!"

She elevated her nose with a slight but clearly audible
sniff, and Earl Gray Harbor turned to smile up at her.

"Your Majesty," he said, "I trust you won't take this in the
wrong spirit, but I don't think you should consider changing
vocations. You'd make a very poor salesman if you can't
learn to lie better than that."

"For shame, My Lord!" she scolded.

"Oh, trust me, Your Majesty," he assured her with a gracious bow, "no one will ever be able to discern the way I really
think about these . . . people. Unlike you, I'd make an *excellent* salesman."

Sharleyan chuckled and shook her head at him, but when she turned back to the grill covering their peephole, she had to admit Gray Harbor had a point.

And the reason he does is mainly thanks to Chisholm, she acknowledged sourly.

She had no fears where the Charisian delegates to the new Imperial Parliament were concerned. Well, very few fears, at any rate. There were a handful of them she could have done without, but all of them had been selected by a joint committee of the Lords and Commons. In Charis, those two bodies had a tradition of actually working together cooperatively, and their members, by and large, considered themselves accountable to their colleagues, so it was unlikely any of them would ignore their official instructions. There'd been some tiffs, and one or two knock-down, drag-out fights, especially over which of the Kingdom's nobles should be seated in the new Imperial House of Lords. And there'd been a few disagreements (and quite a bit of political dragon-trading) over who would replace the representatives named to the new Imperial House of Commons in the Charisian House of Commons. For the most part, however, all of those disputes had been settled relatively amicably. No one was completely happy with the final list of selections, but no one was completely unhappy with it, either, and that was almost certainly the best anyone could reasonably have expected.

Chisholm, however, hadn't done things quite the same way.

The letter from Green Mountain and Sharleyan's mother had apologized profusely for that, but she knew she couldn't really blame them. For that matter, she couldn't blame Cayleb, either, though a part of her was just a bit frustrated because she couldn't. His decision to stay out of the selection process had undoubtedly been the correct one, even if it had left her with a sticky, potentially nasty mess.

The Chisholmian Commons had been quite willing to cooperate with their own Chamber of Lords, but the Lords had flatly refused to cooperate with the Commons. They, and they alone, would decide which of their members would be sent to Tellesberg to represent them in the new Parliament.

And that's exactly why they're going to be such a pain in my posterior, Sharleyan thought grimly. *They aren't here to represent Chisholm; they're here to represent* themselves.

Well, it wouldn't be the first time she'd crossed swords with the Chisholmian nobility, and this time she had some truly formidable allies.

▼　▼　▼

"—and so, My Lord Speaker, I most urgently request that this body give its immediate attention to this matter."

Sharleyan grimaced as she leaned back in the comfortable chair in the same waiting room she and Gray Harbor had occupied that morning. There were a great many other urgent tasks upon which she could have been spending her limited time, but she badly wanted to hear at least the first day's deliberations with her own ears. She trusted Gray Harbor and Archbishop Maikel—both of whom were formal members of the Imperial Parliament the delegates were attempting to organize—and for the most part, she would be completely satisfied with their reports as the organizational meetings proceeded. For now, though, she wanted to get a feel for the delegates' mood and where those deliberations of theirs were likely to go.

What I really *want,* she admitted to herself grumpily, *is to be in there, kicking their posteriors—or possibly shooting one or two of them out of hand—to get this job done right!*

In the end, she and Cayleb would almost certainly get pretty much what they wanted. She knew that, and if anyone in that ballroom-turned-meeting-chamber thought otherwise, they would soon discover differently. Unfortunately, she couldn't just dictate her own terms and decisions—not if she wanted this new Parliament's legitimacy to be fully accepted by its own members, much less the rest of the Empire. These people, however irritating some of them might be, were the representatives of the Empire's subjects. If they were truly going to represent Lords and Commoners, then they must be allowed to voice their own opinions, organize their own affairs, and reach their own decisions. If the Crown disagreed with those decisions, then it was clearly the Crown's job to do something about that, but not by brazenly setting aside or openly trampling upon them. And not without listening to them and attempting to work *with* them first, since it was highly likely that they had something worth saying, even if it *wasn't* what the Crown wanted to hear.

No matter how exhausting, frustrating, and just plain irritating it could be.

For that matter, Sharleyan reflected with a lopsided smile, *sitting out here instead of in there may actually be doing me some good. I can work off—or at least work* through—*the worst of my temper tantrums before* I *have to start dealing with them.*

That wasn't a minor consideration, and the man who had just finished speaking and resumed his seat was an excellent example of why it wasn't. Pait Stywryt, the Duke of Black Horse, had ambitions (which were less well concealed than he apparently thought) to succeed where the previous Duke of Three Hills had failed. Nor was he alone in that. He and the man seated next to him—Zhasyn Seafarer, the Duke of Rock Coast—were close allies in the Chisholmian House of Lords. Not too surprisingly, Sharleyan supposed, given the fact that their dukedoms neighbored one another in southwestern Chisholm and their families had been intermarrying for generations. Or that both of them were about as stubborn, pigheaded, and shortsighted as it was possible for a breathing human being to be. For that matter, she suspected most *corpses* were less pigheaded than they were! And yet, by the oddest turn of fate, both of them, and the almost equally revolting (from Sharleyan's perspective) Earl of Dragon Hill, had been chosen by their fellow peers to represent them in Tellesberg. Fortunately, Sir Ahdem Zhefry, the Earl of Cross Creek, had also slipped through the selection process somehow. Cross Creek was the Earl of White Crag's brother-in-law, and one of the senior members of the Chamber of Lords who was actually a stalwart ally of the Crown.

At the moment, Duke Black Horse was staking out the

grounds for what Sharleyan had anticipated from the beginning would be one of the Chamber of Lords' tactics. There were far fewer dukes and earls and far more barons in Charis than in Chisholm, and the marriage contracts which had created the Empire had specified that all preexisting patents of nobility would remain unchanged and, upon the formal merger of the two crowns, would become *imperial* titles. Now the Chisholmian peers were taking the position that seats in the new Imperial Parliament's House of Lords should be assigned strictly on the basis of precedence of title, without regard as to the kingdom from which the holders of those titles might come.

It was a brazen attempt to ensure that the Chisholmian aristocracy would dominate the new Parliament's upper house, and while Sharleyan had anticipated a move in this direction, she hadn't expected them to try pushing it this quickly. Admittedly, Black Horse had much in common with a dragon in a glassworks, but he'd learned at least a modicum of tactical timing in Chisholm. Surely he should have had the wit to realize it would only be prudent to at least test the waters here in Tellesberg before he plunged in headlong. And to remember that the heraldic symbol of Charis was a kraken.

Apparently not, she thought tartly. *Which doesn't exactly break my heart. If there are any Charisian nobles with delusions of power-grabbing, this should at least ensure that they don't think they can cut some sort of deal with* my *idiot aristocracy!*

In fact, she could already see quite a few fulminating Charisian peers. Obviously, the Chamber of Lords' tactic hadn't come as a complete surprise to them, either. Not that having anticipated it made the Charisians any less . . . irked when their anticipation was confirmed. And not that realizing Black Horse had jumped too quickly made what he was saying one bit less irritating to Sharleyan.

He and his allies had wrapped their proposal up in the camouflage of her own and Cayleb's insistence that there was no "senior" or "junior" partner in the merger of their two kingdoms. If Chisholm and Charis were truly going to merge into a single entity, Black Horse was arguing, then the national boundaries which had once separated them would no longer exist. All of their peers should be considered members of a single unified peerage, just as all of the commoners from both of the now legally deceased realms should be eligible for election to the new House of Commons. And if that was the case, then, obviously, the seats in the new House of Lords ought to be assigned strictly on the basis of precedence of title without regard to whether it was a Chisholmian or Charisian title. After all, were they not all to become the loyal servants of a single, united Crown?

Just like that lying cretin, she thought waspishly. *But does he actually think this noble patriot act is going to fool anyone? I'd like to "loyal" his "servant"! And I've got a dungeon cell somewhere which would fit him just fine. I'm sure I do, even if Cayleb did forget to tell me where it was. Maybe if I ask Rayjhis he can—*

"My Lord Speaker," another voice said, and Sharleyan's grimace eased just a bit as Samyl Zhaksyn, the Duke of Halleck, asked for recognition.

Halleck of was one of the relatively small handful of Charisians whose titles would take precedence over virtually any Chisholmian. Indeed, he, the Duke of Korinth, and the youthful Duke of Tirian were three of the four most senior noblemen of the entire Old Kingdom of Charis, and all three of them had been chosen as delegates, despite the fact that young Rayjhis Ahrmahk, the Duke of Tirian, was barely twelve years old. Obviously, the choices had been made expressly because the Charisians had expected something like this. Although, Sharleyan smiled rather nastily, the fact that young Rayjhis' regent was his grandfather, the Earl of Gray Harbor, had probably had a little something to do with it, as well.

"His Grace, the Duke of Halleck, is recognized," the Speaker announced, and Halleck nodded gravely in thanks.

"While I feel confident that I speak for most of my fellow Charisians—I beg pardon, for my fellow *Old* Charisians, for as His Grace of Black Horse has just pointed out, we are all

Charisians today—when I say that I wholeheartedly approve of our Chisholmian fellow subjects' willingness to accept that we are all now a single Empire, and no longer separate kingdoms, I fear Duke Black Horse may be getting just a bit ahead of himself. With all due respect, and while fully agreeing that the Empire has already come into existence, I invite His Grace's attention to the marriage agreement between His Majesty and Her Majesty. In particular, I note in section four that it is specifically stated that the crowns of Chisholm and Charis will not be formally united until both of them are inherited by Their Majesties' heir. As every patent of nobility in Old Charis is currently held in fealty to the King of Charis, and every patent of nobility in Chisholm is currently held in fealty to the Queen of Chisholm, we cannot, however much we might wish to, consider them to be part of a seamless whole at this time."

Black Horse scowled. Rock Coast didn't seem much happier, although Edwyrd Ahlbair, the Earl of Dragon Hill, was actually nodding gravely, his lips pursed in obvious thought. Then again, Dragon Hill had always been a smoother operator than either of the two dukes.

"Indeed," Halleck continued, "unless I misread section *three* of the marriage contract rather badly, the function of this assembly is to organize our new Imperial Parliament with what might most accurately be described as a House of Lords and a House of Commons, each of which has two chambers: one whose membership is drawn from Old Charis, and one whose membership is drawn from Chisholm. All of the members of that new Imperial Parliament will, of course, be equal colleagues of one another, regardless of the kingdom from which they may come, but my own strong feeling at this time is that the membership of those two chambers in each House ought to be determined by the parliament of the kingdom which they will be representing. I believe it would be presumptuous of us at this time to make any attempt to dictate to either of those sovereign bodies. Surely it would constitute an unjustified infringement upon their prerogatives and ancient legal rights and responsibilities."

Halleck seated himself, and there was a buzz of side conversations. The majority of them were approving, judging from their tone, and Sharleyan chuckled as she watched Black Horse's expression.

Did he really think Charisians were too stupid to have anticipated something quite that *obvious?* she wondered scornfully. *Of course, he—and Rock Coast and Dragon Hill—are all three stupid enough to go on hoping that they're going to be able to wiggle out from under the foot Mahrak, Mother, and I have firmly on the backs of their necks in Chisholm. So maybe they* were *dumb enough to think they could get away with something like this so quickly.*

She shook her head, and then her eyes narrowed as she saw Black Horse's head twitch in the direction of yet another Chisholmian nobleman. Sir Paitryk Mahknee, the Duke of Lakeland, was gazing attentively at the Speaker, apparently oblivious to Black Horse, but Sharleyan felt an abrupt prickle of suspicion. At thirty-six, Lakeland was no callow youth, yet he was very new to his title. His father had been killed in a fall from a horse when Lakeland was only eleven, which had made him his grandfather's heir. But that grandfather, who had died less than a year ago, had been well over eighty, and still vigorous, still fully in charge of his duchy and all its responsibilities, up to the very day of his death. The previous duke had also been closely allied with Black Horse and Rock Coast, longing for the "good old days" of Irwain III, which he had remembered only too well. Despite his mental vigor, however, he'd been understandably frail, no longer up to the demands of making long journeys to the capital, and Sir Paitryk had always been a dutiful grandson, carrying out his grandfather's instructions to the letter whenever he had deputized for the old man in Parliament Hall. The assumption had been that he agreed with those instructions, but Sharleyan was suddenly less certain of that.

I've always known he was smarter than his grandfather, she thought. *Is it possible that he's also a lot* sneakier? *And that perhaps—just perhaps—he* wasn't *in agreement with his grandfather's political ambitions all these years? If he wasn't, and if he was both smart and sneaky enough not to let his grandfather' allies* realize *that he wasn't . . .*

Perhaps she'd been wronging Black Horse just a bit. It had still been a particularly stupid opening move, but was it possible the stupidity hadn't been entirely self-grown? That someone else, someone like the Duke of Lakeland, might have suggested the ploy to him to deliberately maneuver him and his allies into a false step? One which would make it crystal clear to everyone, Charisian and Chisholmian alike, exactly where that line of battle was going to be drawn?

I really have to get to know Lakeland a little better, she told herself. *If he's truly that devious, I need to make certain he really is on the Crown's side, too. Cayleb and I certainly don't need him on the* other *side!*

. IU .

Empress Sharleyan's Dining Chamber,
Tellesberg Palace,
City of Tellesberg,
Old Kingdom of Charis

Well, I think that probably went rather better than you'd anticipated, Rayjhis," Sharleyan said cheerfully much later that evening as she dined with Gray Harbor and Archbishop Maikel.

"Actually, Your Majesty," Gray Harbor pointed out in a gently corrective tone, "I think it went rather better than *either* of us had anticipated."

"Nonsense." Sharleyan chuckled. "I never doubted for a moment."

"Remember what I said about career changes, Your Majesty." Sharleyan laughed out loud and shook her head. Then she emptied her wineglass, and the archbishop refilled it for her.

"Thank you, Your Eminence," she said.

"You're entirely welcome, Your Majesty. Although, as a priest, I must feel some slight concern for the state of your soul if you continue to prevaricate the way you just did."

"Oh, no, Your Eminence! You're quite wrong. I didn't 'prevaricate' at all. I *lied*."

"Oh, that's much better." Staynair's eye twinkled. "Or more direct, at least."

"I try, Your Eminence."

"Indeed you do, Your Majesty," Gray Harbor agreed. "And if I may be permitted to steer this conversation into slightly more serious territory, you have a point about how well things went today."

"I know." Sharleyan leaned back in her chair, her own expression more serious, and nodded. "Were either of you watching Black Horse after Duke Halleck cut his legs off?"

"What a charming turn of phrase, Your Majesty," Staynair observed. She made a face at him, and he smiled, then shook his head. "Actually, I must confess that I wasn't. May I ask why?"

"Because I'm not at all certain his stupidity was entirely his own idea," Sharleyan said. She explained her own thoughts about the Duke of Lakeland, and both the first councilor and the archbishop looked thoughtful when she'd finished.

"Obviously, Your Majesty, you know both Black Horse and Lakeland far better than Maikel or I do," Gray Harbor said. "I'd certainly like to think you're right about this, though. Frankly, I suspect that arm-wrestling your Chisholmian noblemen is going to get exhausting fairly quickly."

"It may," Staynair said. "Then again, it may not. Obviously, if Your Majesty is right about Lakeland, it means we've managed to acquire an ally behind enemy lines, as it were. On the other hand, Halleck's point that we can scarcely dictate to either kingdom's parliament without infringing its prerogatives was a particularly nasty thumb in the eye for Black Horse and his friends. It wouldn't happen, would it, that you and he might have discussed that before this morning's session?"

"I suppose it's remotely possible," Gray Harbor admitted.

"I thought I detected your touch." Staynair smiled. "At any rate, it's probably going to cause at least some of Black Horse's more conservative fellows to think hard about whether or not they want to undermine their own prerogatives back home. And I have to admit that I've been rather pleasantly surprised by the attitude of Archbishop Pawal's delegates."

"You have?" Sharleyan looked at him.

"Assuredly, Your Majesty." The archbishop inclined his head in a seated bow. "On several levels. First and foremost because I've detected no reservations on their part about the legitimacy of our quarrel with the Temple Loyalists. One or two of them obviously have major concerns about precisely where we may be headed in a theological and doctrinal sense, but they clearly support our basic position about the corruption of Mother Church. Archbishop Pawal's letters make it quite clear that he feels the same, and that he's readily prepared to accept the Church of Charis' existing hierarchy and the primacy of the Archbishop of Tellesberg, which is nothing to sneeze at. Emerald has already done the same thing, of course, but despite Princess Mahrya's betrothal to young Zhan, the fact remains that most of the world is going to see Emerald as essentially a conquered province. Clyntahn and Trynair will be able to argue fairly convincingly that Cayleb constrained the Emeraldian Church to accept the Church of Charis.

"That's not the case in Chisholm. Or, at least, not nearly as much the case. That makes Archbishop Pawal's willingness to openly and willingly accept the Chisholmian Church's position within the Church hierarchy both far more valuable and more courageous. He can't hide behind the threat of Charisian bayonets, can't pretend we 'made' him do it, yet he's openly embraced the schism and its implications. The attitude of his representatives convinces me his letter is completely sincere, as well. Mind you, he's already drawn my attention to several areas in Chisholm where both firmness and patience—and wariness—are going to be required, but overall, he's managed to put to rest most of my most pressing concerns.

"On another level, however, and the one which actually brought it to mind at the moment, I've also read his instructions to his representatives where the Imperial Parliament is concerned. Essentially, they've been instructed to take their lead from myself in political as well as temporal matters, and he's impressed upon them that it is his desire, as their archbishop, for them to assist the Crown in whatever ways may be possible."

"Oh, good." Sharleyan nodded in satisfaction. "Mahrak—Baron Green Mountain—and Mother both told me they expected something very like that from him. I'm glad to see they were right."

"They most certainly were, Your Majesty."

"And," Gray Harbor said, his satisfaction undisguised, "the delegates from the Chamber of Commons are already forming working partnerships with their counterparts here in Charis. Zhak Blackwyvern and Sir Samyl Waismym tell me that they've already been in conversation with a Wyllym Watsyn and Tobis Samylsyn, Your Majesty."

"I know both of them well." Sharleyan nodded again. "Watsyn, especially, has been one of Mahrak's closer allies in the Commons for years. I'm not a bit surprised he's taking the offensive here in Tellesberg, as it were."

"It's my impression that that's exactly what he's doing," Gray Harbor agreed. "Although Zhak tells me he's gotten the impression that Master Samylsyn may have more substantial reservations about our 'schismatic' policies than Master Watsyn does."

"Really?" Sharleyan frowned slightly, then gave her head a little toss. "That could well be. Tobis is an extraordinarily loyal man by nature. He isn't the very smartest man in the world, but he's uncommonly levelheaded, which is one reason he and Watsyn usually work in tandem. Watsyn can be downright brilliant, but he can also be a bit . . . erratic, from time to time. Tobis helps keep him centered. But Tobis also extends that loyalty of his to more than just the Crown. In fact, that's one of the things I've always liked most about him; he brings that same steadiness, that same sense of responsibility, to *all* of the important things in his life. And the Church is important to him."

"Is that likely to become a problem, Your Majesty?" Gray Harbor's eyes were much more serious than they had been. "From what Zhak had to say, both he and Sir Samyl believe Watsyn and Samylsyn may well be the two most important delegates from the Chamber of Commons."

"They almost certainly are the two most important delegates," Sharleyan agreed. "And I suspect that one reason Tobis was chosen was because the other members of the Chamber know he has at least some doubts about the schism. He'll abide by whatever instructions they sent with him—or, at least, if he decides he can't abide by them in good conscience, he'll resign and withdraw from the process rather than *violate* them—but I'm sure there are quite a few other Chamber members who have reservations of their own. They trust his integrity, and they also trust him to address those reservations."

"Should I seek to set to rest any concerns he might have, Your Majesty?" Staynair asked quietly.

"I think that would be a very good idea," Sharleyan said after a moment. "I don't think you're going to have to go looking for him, though, Your Eminence. Unless I'm very mistaken, *he's* going to come to *you*. As I say, he's very levelheaded, and I believe, now that I've thought about it, that he'll probably want to discuss those reservations of his directly with you at the earliest possible moment. And I think he'll do his best to listen to what you have to say with an open mind, when he does."

"I can ask no more than that of any man." Staynair smiled another of his serene smiles. "If he's truly willing to listen, I expect God will be able to make Himself heard, even if He has to use a fallible conduit like myself."

Sharleyan shook her head. In most men in Staynair's

position, that last sentence would have been an example of pure false modesty. In Maikel Staynair's case, it was entirely genuine.

"You may not be able to ask more than that of any man, Maikel," Gray Harbor's voice was considerably more sour than the archbishop's, "but I could wish that you got it a bit more often."

"And what brought that on, My Lord?" Sharleyan asked, quirking an eyebrow.

"That idiot Kairee, Your Majesty," Gray Harbor growled. "I wish I knew what the Commons were thinking when they added *him* to their list of delegates!"

Sharleyan grimaced. Traivyr Kairee was one of the handful of Charisian delegates about whom she cherished serious reservations. She, too, had wondered what could possibly have inspired the rest of the House of Commons to choose him to help speak for them, and she still hadn't been able to come up with an answer she liked.

"Most of it was simply wealth talking, Rayjhis," Staynair said, his tone considerably calmer than the first councilor's. "Do I really have to explain to you just how many other members of the House of Commons owe him money, favors, or both?"

"No," Gray Harbor groused.

"Well, I think that's probably the primary reason, right there." The archbishop shrugged slightly. "I wouldn't be a bit surprised if he called most of those favors in to get himself selected."

"I have to say I agree with Rayjhis," Sharleyan said, and the harshness in her voice surprised even her just a bit.

Sharleyan Tayt Ahrmahk had come to love Charis, and most of the things about it. Not *everything,* of course, but most things. Traivyr Kairee, on the other hand, represented almost everything she *disliked* about Charis. He was fabulously wealthy (due as much to his father's efforts as to his own), and every negative stereotype the rest of Safehold cherished about Charisians fitted him like a glove. He was greedy, scheming, and totally unconcerned about the well-

being of his workforce. He was one of the manufactory owners who'd campaigned most vigorously against the new child
labor laws, and she knew Ehdwyrd Howsmyn and Rhaiyan
Mychail both despised him and didn't particularly care who
knew it. From all she could see, he felt exactly the same way
about them, with the addition of intense resentment for the
fact that both of them were substantially more wealthy even
than he was.

Sharleyan would have been prepared to regard the man
distastefully on that basis, alone, but she had her own deeply
personal and individual reasons for loathing Kairee. Although he had substantially moderated his strident criticism
since, he'd made no secret of his original opposition to the
decision to defy the Group of Four's authority. Sharleyan was
less surprised about that than some had been. For all his os-
tentatious devotion to the Church—and whatever else she
thought of him, no one could dispute the fact that he'd always
given generously to the Church—it was readily apparent to
her that he'd never even made a gesture towards applying the
Writ's admonitions of brotherhood to his own hapless em-
ployees, nor was there any evidence of any particular right-
eousness in his own life. In fact, in her opinion, he'd been a
perfect fit for the Group of Four. His "gifts" to the Church,
like his highly public lip service to the Church's teachings,
had represented an attempt to bribe God, not any sort of genuine, heart-deep piety. Which meant the Church of Charis
represented a challenge to the swindle he'd spent his life per-
petrating upon God and the archangels.

Sharley, you just might *be being a little harder on him than
he deserves,* she reminded herself.

Maybe I am, herself replied. *Then again, maybe I'm not.*

Despite his efforts to downplay his original opposition to
Charis' rejection of the Group of Four, Kairee remained at
best only imperfectly resigned to the existence of the Church
of Charis. He'd embraced at least the form of the Church's
reformation in Charis, but Sharleyan was one of those who
doubted that his heart was truly in it. The war against the
Church was simply producing too many contracts, worth too

much money, for him to stand on principle and let all those lovely marks fall into someone else's cashbox.

That would have been more than enough to prejudice Sharleyan against him, but he hadn't stopped there. Her uncle, the Duke of Halbrook Hollow, was one of the twenty or so wealthiest men in the Kingdom of Chisholm, and Kairee had spent the last couple of months enticing him into investing in Kairee's various Charisian business enterprises. It wasn't that Sharleyan resented her uncle's involvement in Charisian ventures, but if he was going to invest with anyone, why couldn't it have been with someone like Howsmyn or Mychail? Someone who was at least remotely principled?

He's preying on Uncle Byrtrym's *principles,* she thought resentfully. *He knows how unhappy Uncle Byrtrym is with my decisions, and he's using his own reputation for dedication to the Church to convince Uncle Byrtrym to pour money into his pocket! By now, Uncle Byrtrym is convinced Kairee is actually his* friend—one of the very few *friends he has here in Charis—and the last thing* I *need is for the uncle whose loyalty to the Church of Charis is already questionable to be publicly spending time with someone with Kairee's reputation!*

She closed her eyes for a moment, scolding herself yet again. Her uncle could scarcely be blamed for associating with one of the handful of Charisians of rank or wealth who didn't eye him with open suspicion. And although she'd dropped a few hints to Halbrook Hollow, she couldn't bring herself to be any more explicit in her efforts to drive a wedge between him and Kairee. She ought to. She *knew* she ought to. But he had so few friends in Charis, and she was the one who had compelled him to come here. However much *she* might detest Kairee, he obviously saw the man in quite another light.

And it's always possible your view of Kairee is distorted specifically because *you resent Uncle Byrtrym's relationship with him,* she told herself.

"I would be considerably happier myself if Kairee were far, far away from not just the Imperial Parliament, but from the House of Commons, as well," Archbishop Maikel admitted.

"On the other hand, perhaps it's as well to have him where he is."

"And why might that be, Maikel?" Gray Harbor asked tartly. "Aside, of course, from the convenience of always knowing where he is when it's time for the headsman?"

"Because, Rayjhis," Staynair said, "he's not unique. He's far more irritating than many, more visible than most, and almost certainly more hypocritical than anyone else I can think of right offhand, but not unique. There are many others here in Charis, and in Chisholm, who undoubtedly feel the same way he does."

He didn't even glance in her direction, Sharleyan noted, remembering another conversation with him.

"It's important that those who do not agree with the Church of Charis not be deprived of their own right to a public voice," the archbishop said. "This is a struggle over principles, over the right and responsibility of individuals to make choices, and as Cayleb's said, we cannot win a war for freedom of conscience if we *deny* freedom of conscience to those who simply happen to disagree with us. If that means we must put up with a few Kairees, even in Parliament, then that's a price we must be willing to pay."

"In theory, I agree," Gray Harbor said. "And God knows I've spent enough time in politics to realize that genuinely trying to listen to opposing viewpoints is always messy. But Kairee—" He shook his head, his expression one of disgust. "Why couldn't the Temple Loyalists at least have chosen themselves a spokesman who had an ounce of genuine principle *somewhere* in his bones?"

"I suppose it's a case of settling for what they can find," Sharleyan said tartly. Then she shook herself.

"But that's enough about Master Kairee," she continued. "We have far more important things to worry about. Like exactly when the delegates should 'spontaneously' invite me to address them."

"Your Majesty," Gray Harbor said, "that sounds extraordinarily calculating and cynical, especially for someone of your own tender years."

"Not calculating and cynical, My Lord, just practical," she replied. "And my question stands. When should we arrange to have the invitation extended?"

"There's no need to move too quickly, Your Majesty," Staynair said. "My own advice would be to give all of them at least a few more days to stew in their own juices. Let us hammer our rough edges off a bit—and give us time to begin shaking down into recognizable factions—before you come in and use your own mallet on us."

"Wait until I've got recognizable targets, you mean?"

"Something like that, yes."

"You don't think it would be a better idea for me to get in a few blows while everything is still more or less in a state of flux?" Sharleyan's tone wasn't argumentative. She was simply an expert tactician discussing tactics with her fellow experts.

"Your Majesty, whatever you might do immediately isn't going to keep factions from forming," Staynair pointed out. "That's simple human nature. I'm of the opinion that it would be wiser to allow water to seek its own level, to let the factions form naturally, so that we can identify both friends and foes, before we draw our swords."

"My, what a martial metaphor," Gray Harbor murmured. Staynair quirked an eyebrow at him, and the first councilor laughed. "I'm not disagreeing with you, Maikel! In fact, I think you're right."

"I believe I do, too," Sharleyan said thoughtfully.

"Good," Gray Harbor said. "In that case, I'll have a word with Sharphill. He's already primed to start the ball rolling by—as you said, Your Majesty—'spontaneously' moving that the delegates entreat you to address them. All he needs is a nod."

"Fine." Sharleyan smiled. Sir Maikel Traivyr, the Earl of Sharphill, was Ehdwyrd Howsmyn's father-in-law. He also had sufficient seniority in the Charisian peerage to ensure a hearing even from a Chisholmian noble, and he was very carefully keeping his head down and giving as little indication as possible of his own thoughts at the moment. Sharleyan had liked Sir Maikel from the moment she met him, and she could readily understand why Howsmyn thought as highly as he did of his wife's father.

"Well," she said, picking up her wineglass once again, "I have to say, gentlemen, that I'm feeling considerably more cheerful than I was this morning. Whatever else happens, at least Cayleb and I seem to have allies in most of the necessary places."

" 'Allies,' Your Majesty?" Gray Harbor repeated innocently. "Don't you actually mean spies, provocateurs, and saboteurs?"

"*My Lord!*" Sharleyan said in shocked tones. "I cannot *believe* that a royal councilor of your many years of experience could possibly be guilty of dabbling in *candor* at a moment like this! What *were* you thinking?"

"Forgive me, Your Majesty," he said earnestly. "It was only a temporary lapse! I don't know what came over me, but I promise I'll do my best to refrain from such unseemly outbursts in the future!"

"I should certainly *hope* so," Empress Sharleyan of Charis said primly.

. V .

Galleon *Wing*,
Off East Island,
League of Corisande

Your Highness, I think you'd better go below," Captain Harys said quietly.

Princess Irys opened her mouth, prepared to protest, then closed it again, protest unspoken, and glanced at the Earl of Coris. It wasn't an unspoken appeal for him to override the captain. It came close, but it stopped short, and Coris felt a fresh surge of pride in her as, almost against his will, he found himself once again comparing her to the older of her two brothers.

"If you think best, Captain," she said to Harys after a moment. "Do you think I need to go below immediately, or can I watch for a few more minutes?"

"I'd really feel more comfortable—" Captain Harys began, turning to the princess, then paused in midsentence. It was her eyes, Coris thought with a half-hidden smile, despite the very real potential danger of the moment. They met the captain's steadily, levelly, and in the end, Coris decided, it was the fact that, look into those eyes as he might, Harys saw neither fear nor petulance, but did see a promise to accept his decree, whatever it might be.

"I'd really feel more comfortable if you went below now," the captain continued his interrupted thought. "On the other hand, I don't suppose it would hurt if you stayed a little longer, Your Highness. I would appreciate it, however, if you would take His Highness below in time to get him thoroughly settled in case we should have . . . visitors."

"Of course, Captain." Irys smiled at him. There was no doubt that she understood exactly what he'd been implying, but those eyes of her dead mother met his unflinchingly, and Zhoel Harys found himself smiling in approval.

"I'll tell you when it's time to go, Your Highness," he told her, then bowed ever so slightly, as if he thought watching spyglasses might detect a more profound gesture of respect, and turned away to shade his eyes with one hand and peer across the sun-struck water at the low-slung, kraken-like schooner slicing steadily nearer.

Irys stepped a bit closer to Coris, without ever taking her own eyes from the Charisian warship. The earl didn't think it was a conscious action on her part, although he was sorely tempted to put an encouraging arm around her straight, slender shoulders. Instead, he simply stood there, watching with her and hoping for the best.

He found himself wishing they'd been aboard Harys' *Cutlass* instead of *Wing*. The thought of being able to meet the

Charisian ship's firepower on an even footing was incredibly attractive at the moment. But there'd never been any hope of getting *Cutlass* or one of her sisters past the blockaders watching Manchyr, of course. And since it had been impossible to use a proper warship, Tartarian—and Harys—had undoubtedly been correct in their argument that putting additional Marines aboard *Wing,* or trying to fit extra guns into her somewhere, would have been a serious mistake. Their best hope had been to avoid Charisian cruisers entirely. Failing that, their *only* hope was to appear as innocent and unexceptional as possible. The last thing they could afford was to attempt to explain to one of the heavily gunned Charisian schooners why they had twenty or thirty Corisandian Marines on board a merchant galleon flying the colors of Harchong.

To that end, *Wing*'s seamen wore the motley assortment of garments one might have expected to find aboard a merchant ship whose owners were too tightfisted to provide a well-stocked slop chest. The men *wearing* those garments, however, had been carefully selected by Captain Harys and Earl Tartarian as much for their years of experience in the merchant service as for their demonstrated loyalty and intelligence during their naval service. They knew exactly how a merchant crew ought to be acting under these circumstances.

Now Coris kept his eyes on the Charisian and hoped that Harys and Tartarian had been right.

▼ ▼ ▼

Zhoel Harys stood on *Wing*'s aftercastle, watching the Charisian maneuver. The galleon's aftercastle was much lower than it would have been aboard a warship, and Harys concentrated on looking as calm as he could. It wouldn't have done to look *too* calm, of course; any merchant skipper facing a potential naval boarding party would feel plenty of natural apprehension, after all.

Which I *bloody well do,* he told himself. *The trick is to look nervous* enough *without looking* so *nervous they decide I have to be hiding something.*

In fact, he was discovering that his belly had been less tightly knotted at Darcos Sound, when he'd realized what the Charisian guns could actually do, than it was now.

The princess and her younger brother had gone below without protest, settling into their cramped cabin. *Wing* had never been intended to transport passengers in luxury, and—in keeping with all the rest of their disguise—Princess Irys and Prince Daivyn had been assigned quarters which were relatively comfortable, but downright spartan. They and the Earl of Coris were all covered with false identities in *Wing*'s log, but everyone would be much happier if the Charisians never paid any attention at all to the plainly dressed daughter and son of a merchant factor.

The Charisian was sliding easily downwind towards him, her guns run out, and he could see her captain standing on his own quarterdeck, gazing at *Wing* through a spyglass. He hoped the Charisian was taking note of the fact that not a single one of *Wing*'s seamen was anywhere near the galleon's pathetic broadside of falcons. Nor had any of the ship's wolves been mounted on their swivels.

We're absolutely no threat at all, he thought very hard in the other captain's direction. *Just another scruffy little merchant ship with a cargo for Shwei.*

The schooner came still closer, till it was less than fifty yards off *Wing*'s windward side as the galleon broad reached on the starboard tack. The Charisian cruiser loped along, easily matching *Wing*'s best speed under these wind conditions with only her own foresail and headsails set, and Harys felt an abrupt stab of envy. Excited as he'd been to receive command of *Cutlass,* he knew the galleon could never have matched the speed and agility of that schooner, and the Charisian's broadside of thirty-pounder carronades was almost as heavy as *Cutlass'* new broadside.

And I bet they're not assigning the damned schooners to just anybody, he thought grimly. *They'll want men who can think, as well as fight, in command.*

"Ahoy, *Wing*!" The Charisian captain's voice floated across the water between the two ships, amplified and directed by his leather speaking trumpet.

"And what can I do for you this fine morning?" Harys bawled back through his own speaking trumpet.

"Heave to, if you please!" the Charisian replied.

"On whose authority?" Harys tried hard to put the right note of bluster into the question.

"You know whose authority, Captain!" The Charisian's voice sounded more amused than anything else, Harys noticed, and he used his speaking trumpet to gesture in the direction of the kraken banner flying above his own ship.

"This is an imperial merchant ship!" Harys shot back.

"And we're not at war with the Empire," the Charisian told him. "But we *are* at war with people who might *pretend* to be Harchongese. Now heave to, Captain, before I start to think you might be one of them."

Harys waited a few moments longer, then allowed his shoulders to slump.

"All right," he growled back in a frustrated tone, and turned to his first officer. "Heave to," he said.

"Aye—yes, Sir."

Harys frowned, but the other officer *had* caught himself before he gave the formal naval acknowledgment of an order, and he'd managed not to salute, either. Which, given the fact that men tended to respond the way they'd been trained to under pressure and that he had to be feeling just as anxious as Harys did, was probably about the best Harys could have expected.

Wing hove to without the snap or efficiency one might have anticipated out of a warship. Her big courses were brailed up, her spritsail disappeared, and her fore topsail and main topsail were braced around, trying to drive her in opposite directions and holding her almost motionless under their opposed forces.

The schooner matched her maneuver much more smartly, and a launch was dropped over her side and manned. It rowed swiftly across the gap between the two vessels, and came alongside *Wing*.

"Permission to come aboard, Sir?" the youthful lieutenant in command of the boarding party asked, respectfully enough, as he climbed the galleon's side to the entry port.

Harys allowed himself to glower at the young man for a second or two, then grimaced.

"Since you've seen fit to invite yourself, I suppose you might as well," he growled.

"Thank you, Sir," the lieutenant said. He climbed the rest of the way through the entry port and waited while ten Charisian Marines followed him aboard.

"My Captain instructed me to apologize for the inconvenience, Captain," he said then. "He realizes that no one ever likes to be stopped and boarded by a foreign navy. If you'll show me your papers, we'll try to get this over with as quickly as possible."

"That'll suit me just fine," Harys replied. "Come with me."

"Thank you, Sir."

The lieutenant nodded to the sergeant commanding the squad of Marines. One of them attached himself to the lieutenant; the others stayed where they were, just inside the entry port. They made no overtly threatening gestures, although neither Harys nor any of his men doubted that the muskets grounded unthreateningly on the deck were loaded.

The lieutenant and his single accompanying Marine followed Harys into his cabin under the aftercastle. They paused just inside the door and waited patiently while Harys rummaged about in a desk drawer for *Wing*'s papers. He took a few minutes to find them, then hauled them out, along with the carefully prepared log, and passed them across to the lieutenant.

"Thank you, Sir," the Charisian said again. He stepped a little farther into the cabin, holding the ship's papers under the light coming through the cabin skylight, and examined them closely. He clearly knew what he was looking for, and Harys was abruptly grateful that the men who'd forged those papers had known what they were about, too.

The lieutenant set the papers aside after a moment, then flipped quickly through the log. He didn't try to read the entire thing, but it was obvious he was looking for any discrepancies . . . or any sign that newer entries had been made among the older ones.

Thank Langhorne we made it up from scratch, Harys thought from behind his calm expression. *Even if I did think I was going to die of writer's cramp before we finished the damned thing.*

Most of the entries were in his own hand, although he'd used several different pens and inks. Other entries, scattered throughout, were in the handwriting of his first and second officers, and Earl Coris' forgers had aged the pages nicely. A couple of entries had been so water-damaged as to be almost illegible, and most were the sort of curt, one- or two-line entries one might have expected from a merchant skipper, while a few had been expanded into larger descriptions of specific events.

"Could I ask what you're doing in these waters, Captain?" the lieutenant asked finally, looking up from the log and neatly gathering up *Wing*'s registration, customs, and ownership papers once more.

"Sailing to Shwei Bay . . . just like the log says," Harys replied a bit tartly.

"But why this way?" The lieutenant's tone was still polite, but his eyes had narrowed. "According to these, you sailed from Charis. Wouldn't it have been a considerably shorter voyage going west, not east?"

"I'm sure it would have," Harys acknowledged. "On the other hand, the waters off the southern coasts of Haven and Howard are swarming with privateers these days—or hadn't you've heard, Lieutenant?"

"I believe I have heard something about that, yes, Sir." The lieutenant's lips twitched, and Harys snorted.

"I'm sure you have. Any road, it seemed to me I'd be less likely to run into a privateer going east, since all of them seemed to be hunting westward from Charis. And it also seemed to me—no disrespect, Lieutenant—that every so often, a privateer's likely to get a mite . . . overenthusiastic, if you take my meaning. I'd just as soon avoid situations where something unfortunate might happen. The owners wouldn't like it if something did."

"I see." The lieutenant gazed at him for several seconds, eyes thoughtful. Then he shrugged. "I imagine that makes sense, as long as the length of your passage doesn't matter too much."

Harys snorted again.

"It's not going to bother a cargo of farming gear a lot if it takes a few extra days, or even a few extra five-days, to arrive, Lieutenant! It's not like I was hauling a cargo of perishables."

"Farming gear?"

"Reapers, cultivators, and harrows," Harys said tersely. "We loaded it in Tellesberg."

"May I examine it?"

"Why not?" Harys flipped both hands in a gesture which combined exasperation and acceptance. "Follow me."

He led the lieutenant back out on deck and beckoned to the naval lieutenant who'd been assigned the role of *Wing*'s purser.

"He wants to see the cargo," he said. "Show him."

"Yes, Sir," the purser acknowledged, and looked sourly at the Charisian. "Try not to leave too big a mess for me to clean up," he said.

"I'll try," the Charisian agreed sardonically.

Four of *Wing*'s seamen knocked out the wedges and lifted the battens from the main hatch cover, and four of the Charisian Marines clambered down into the hold. Where they found exactly what the manifest said they ought to have found.

The farm equipment had come from one of Ehdwyrd Howsmyn's manufactories, although it *hadn't* been bought in Tellesberg. In fact, it had been purchased in Chisholm and had been bound for the Duchy of West Wind when the first tide of Charisian privateers had swept across the waters around Zebediah and Corisande and *Wing* had taken refuge at Elvarth. It was still in its original crates, however, and those crates bore the customs marks of Tellesberg. They didn't bear *Chisholmian* customs marks, however, since they'd somehow evaded Chisholm's customs inspection. Queen Sharleyan had formally prohibited trade between Chisholm and Corisande even before she sailed to Tellesberg. Unfortunately, at least some of her subjects—especially those who'd already accepted orders from Corisandian customers—had decided she surely couldn't have meant her prohibition to apply to *them* . . . and had taken steps to see to it that it didn't.

That had been the final, decisive factor in Earl Tartarian's choice of *Wing* for her present mission. After all, few things could possibly have looked less threatening, or less suspicious, to a Charisian boarding party than goods manufactured in Charis, itself.

The Marines clambered around in the hold for several minutes, then climbed back on deck.

"Matches the manifest, Sir," the senior Marine told his lieutenant, and the lieutenant turned back to Harys.

"Well," he said, handing *Wing*'s papers back over, "I suppose that's that, Captain. Thank you for your cooperation, and, once again, please accept my Captain's apologies for inconveniencing you."

"No harm done, I suppose," Harys allowed just a bit grudgingly. Then he shook his head and grimaced. "Truth to tell, Lieutenant, I don't blame you or your Captain. Mind you, I think all of you Charisians have lost your minds, but under the circumstances, I'd probably've done the same thing in your boots."

"I'm glad you understand, Sir." The lieutenant bowed slightly, then twitched his head at his Marines. The sergeant came briefly to attention and then started chivying his men back down into the launch.

"I hope you and your ship enjoy a safe voyage to Shwei Bay, Captain," the lieutenant said, then followed his Marines.

Harys stood at the bulwark, watching as the launch's oars dipped, then pulled strongly back towards the schooner. A part of him felt almost sorry for the lieutenant, but the truth was that the young man had done his job well. He'd looked in exactly the right places, and he'd found exactly the right documents and cargo, and who in his right mind would have suspected such an elaborate ruse designed solely to get three passengers to Shwei Bay? The very idea was preposterous.

Of course, I suppose the question of just how preposterous it is depends on who the passengers are, doesn't it?

Zhoel Harys smiled wolfishly at the thought and discovered that, for the first time, he was perfectly content to be commanding *Wing* instead of *Cutlass*.

. VI .

Archbishop's Palace,
Tellesberg,
Empire of Charis

Your Eminence," Father Bryahn said, "Madame Dynnys is here."

"Of course, Bryahn!"

Archbishop Maikel rose and walked around his desk, smiling broadly, as Ushyr bowed Adorai Dynnys through his office door. He extended his hand, and Erayk Dynnys' widow returned his smile warmly as she took it. He'd come to know her far better in the months since her arrival in Tellesberg, and he wasn't surprised when she rose on tiptoe and kissed him lightly on the cheek.

"Thank you for agreeing to see me, Your Eminence," she said as he tucked her hand into his elbow and escorted her across to one of the office's chairs. "I realize it isn't easy to fit someone into your schedule on such short notice. Especially not with all the details of the new Parliament still being settled."

She had not, Staynair noticed, added *all the details of the merger with that other batch of heretics in Chisholm* to her list of his duties. That was tactful of her.

"Fitting you into my schedule is never a problem," he told her. "Well, sometimes it can be a bit difficult, I suppose, but it's never an *unwelcome* difficulty."

"Thank you," she said, and he considered her carefully if unobtrusively.

The lines worry and grief had carved in her face were less prominent than they had been. They would never fade entirely, just as he suspected that the occasional flashes of sorrow in her eyes would never entirely go away. Yet she'd settled into her new life in Tellesberg better than he would have been prepared to predict. It was possible that Cayleb and Sharleyan's decision to house her in the palace and make her an official member of their own household had something to do with that, but Staynair thought it had more to do with the fact that, for the first time in her life, she could openly oppose the corrupt system which had ensnared her husband. She'd become one of the most vocal and effective supporters of the Church of Charis' rejection of the present Church's leaders' corruption. That made her anathema to the Charisian Temple Loyalists, of course, but the Church of Charis' supporters, already disposed to welcome her after they learned the details of Archbishop Erayk's hideous death, had taken her to their hearts in her own right, and Sharleyan had assigned her two personal armsmen as a precaution.

"To what do I owe the pleasure of this particular visit?" he asked now.

"Actually, Your Eminence, I need your advice. I—"

She broke off as Ahrdyn poked his sleek, round, earless head up out of his basket. Adorai Dynnys was one of the cat-lizard's favorite people. She could always be relied upon to allow him to extort endless petting from her, and he hopped up and ambled across the office floor to leap up into her chair with a hum of welcome.

Well, Staynair thought, *I suppose it* could *be welcome. Personally, I think it's triumph.*

The cat-lizard settled down across her lap, and she stroked his short, luxuriant coat with a smile.

"You *do* realize, don't you, that the sole value human beings have for cat-lizards is the fact that they have hands?" Staynair asked.

"Nonsense, Your Eminence. They also have pitchers of milk."

"Well, yes. I suppose there *is* that, as well," Staynair allowed with a smile. Then, as Adorai sat back, still stroking the cat-lizard, he cocked his head. "I believe that, before we were interrupted, you were about to explain why you might desire my advice?"

"Yes." Her fingers never stopped moving, but her expression faded into one of intense seriousness. "Actually, 'need your advice' probably wasn't the best way to put it, but I do need your spiritual counsel, I think."

"Of course," he murmured, his eyes darkening with concern as he absorbed her expression and the tone of her voice.

"I have a letter for you, Your Eminence—one I've been instructed to share with you and with the Emperor. It's from a very dear friend of mine, and my friend has made an offer which could be of great value to Charis. But if that offer is accepted, it could also be very dangerous for . . . my friend. So, I've come to you to bring you the letter and also to ask your advice. You're not only a member of the Imperial Council, but a priest. My friend has already risked a great deal in a great many ways. I'm . . . hesitant to let still more risk be added to that, yet I'm not sure I have the right to make this decision for someone else. So before I pass that offer on to Empress Sharleyan, I want to tell *you* a little bit about this letter, the reason it was written, and what it implies."

"And ask my opinion on whether or not you should allow your friend to run the additional risk to which you've just referred?" he asked gently.

"Yes." She looked into his eyes. "Politically, I know what your answer ought to be, Your Eminence. But I've also come to know you as one of God's priests. I ask you to consider this matter *as* a priest."

"Always," he told her simply, and she inhaled in what might have been relief.

She sat for a few more seconds, petting Ahrdyn, then shook herself.

"Your Eminence, when I first arrived here in Tellesberg, you and the Emperor and Empress all expressed your relief and surprise that I'd managed it. Well, I wouldn't have without the help of a dear friend. Let me tell you about her.

"Nynian's father was Grand Vicar Zhoel, who, as you may be aware, was my uncle. Unfortunately, her mother died two years after she was born, and my uncle—who I'm sure must have had *some* worthwhile qualities beyond his truly outstanding gifts for hypocrisy and selfishness and an undeniable skill at manipulating Temple politics, although I never personally saw them, you understand—was unwilling to acknowledge his bastard daughter."

Adorai's lips tightened in remembered anger, and her eyes were hard.

"Fortunately, Uncle Zhoel hadn't become Grand Vicar yet. He was only a vicar at the time, as was my father. Father and Mother were sufficiently angry at him not to allow a mere vicar's resentment to keep them from taking her in, and until she was twelve years old, she was raised in my parents' home. They called her Nynian, because she was such a beautiful baby, and she grew up to be as beautiful as the original Nynian. For all intents and purposes, she was my sister, not simply my cousin, although not even Father and Mother were prepared to openly acknowledge her blood relationship to us. There were 'appearances' to be maintained, after all.

"Then her father was elected to the Grand Vicarate, and everything changed. He insisted my parents send Nynian away, and this time, they felt they had no choice but to agree. So they sent her off to convent school to be educated. I think they hoped she might discover a vocation, which would keep her safely out of my uncle's sight, and I suppose, in a way, she did."

This time, Adorai's lips twitched in what was obviously amusement.

"I'm sure a Bédardist like yourself would have a field day

deciding exactly why she chose the particular vocation she did. And I don't doubt that the circumstances of her own birth played a part. But I genuinely don't think she did it simply because she could be certain it would keep her father spinning in his grave for centuries. At any rate, what she did was to change her name and—"

▼   ▼   ▼

"—and that's how 'Ahnzhelyk' came to be able to help me and the boys escape to Charis," Adorai finished, some time later. "She has all manner of contacts, and one of them managed to smuggle us aboard ship without any of the Schuelerites looking for us realizing who we were."

"She sounds like a rather amazing woman," Staynair said. "I wish I could have the opportunity of meeting her someday."

"Do you really mean that, Your Eminence?" Adorai asked, her eyes searching his face, and he nodded.

"If you're asking me if I would condemn her for her choice of—vocation, I believe you called it—the answer is no," he replied serenely. "I won't say it's exactly the one I would have wished for for my own daughter, but, then again, *my* daughter never had to fend for herself simply because she would have been an embarrassment to my high and holy position. And from all you've told me about her, she obviously managed to become a strong person and a loyal and loving friend—and sister—despite her father's manifold shortcomings."

"Yes," Adorai said softly. "Yes, she did. Although I must confess that both of us felt more than a little odd over her relationship with Erayk."

"I scarcely see how you could have felt any other way, Adorai." Staynair shook his head. "The lives we live are not always the ones we might have chosen, but with two such extraordinary women in his life, I begin to see that there must always have been rather more to Erayk Dynnys than I realized at the time. Enough more that perhaps we should not all have been so surprised at the final decision *of* his life."

"I don't really know about that, Your Eminence. I'd like to believe you were right, and perhaps I do. But, at the moment, the point is that Ahnzhelyk—Nynian—has sent me this."

She set Ahrdyn aside and reached into the handbag she'd brought with her. Ahrdyn obviously felt intensely annoyed by her misguided interruption of the proper relationship between human fingers and cat-lizard fur. He gave her one disgusted look, then hopped down to the floor and headed back to his basket and his interrupted nap. Adorai paid him no attention as she extracted a thick envelope and set it squarely in her lap, where the indignant cat-lizard had been, and looked down at it for a long moment.

"Your Eminence, this is a transcript of the Grand Vicar's Address from the Throne," she said, looking up. "It's a transcript of the *actual* Address, not the . . . expurgated version that was officially circulated."

Staynair stiffened, sitting upright in his chair, and she nodded.

"I realize the official Address was severe enough in its charges and allegations against Charis, Your Eminence. It turns out the actual Address was worse. I suspect the reason it was edited before it was officially released is its explicit warning to the vicarate that the Group of Four—oh, excuse me, I *meant* the Grand Vicar, of course—has decided Holy War is inevitable."

Staynair inhaled deeply. Not in surprise so much as in confirmation.

"I was very tempted to burn her letter and simply hand the transcript to you—and to Empress Sharleyan—without telling you where it came from or exactly how it came into my hands," Adorai continued.

"To protect Nynian's identity?"

"No, Your Eminence. To prevent you from ever reading what else she's offered to do."

Staynair simply cocked his head, raising his eyebrows slightly and waiting, and she sighed.

"Your Eminence, she's offered, essentially, to become your spy in Zion. And she's offered—in fact, she sent with this letter—the contents of her own files."

"Her files?"

"Almost twenty years of meticulous notes detailing abuses of Church authority, corruption in the ranks of the vicarate, the sale of writs of attestation and of condemnation under the Proscriptions, the buying and selling of legal decisions like the one in favor of Tahdayo Mahntayl's claim to Hanth . . . all of it. They fill several trunks, Your Eminence. It's amazing what powerful men will discuss among themselves or let slip in the company of someone in her profession."

Staynair's eyes widened. For several moments, he only sat there, looking at her, before he spoke again.

"That's an . . . extraordinary offer."

"She's an extraordinary woman, Your Eminence," Adorai said simply.

"I can well believe that, from what you've already told me. Still, I must confess that I'm puzzled."

"About the reason for her offer to act as the Church of Charis' spy? Or about the reason she compiled those notes in the first place?"

"Both, actually."

"Your Eminence, Nynian has never had a great deal of reason to feel any loyalty to the great Church dynasties. To individuals from those dynasties, like me, and like my parents, perhaps, but not to the dynasties themselves. And even if she'd had any such reason, her first and strongest reaction is to sympathize with those the Church has abandoned, much as my uncle abandoned her. Worse, from the perspective of the vicarate, at least, that convent education of hers took. She believes, as I do, in what the Church is *supposed* to stand for, and that makes her opposition to what the Church actually is inevitable. And," she looked directly into Staynair's eyes once more, "I have to confess that it was Nynian who first drew me into active opposition to the internal corruption of Mother Church, not the other way around."

"But I'm still somewhat at a loss to understand why she collected all of the information you've described."

"I realize that. And, although she didn't actually authorize me to tell you this, I'm going to have to give you some additional information if I'm really going to explain. Before I do, though, please understand that what I'm about to tell you could cost scores of lives if Clyntahn should ever learn of it, Your Eminence."

"You intend to tell me this in order to clarify why you would like my advice on passing her offer along to Sharleyan?" Staynair asked, and she nodded. "In that case, Adorai, it comes under the seal of the confessional. Without your permission, I will never share it with another living soul."

"Thank you, Your Eminence."

She drew another deep breath and squared her shoulders.

"Your Eminence, there is, within the Church, at the very highest levels, a group of men who are as aware of the abuses around them as any Charisian could be. I won't reveal their names, even to you, without their permission. For that matter, I feel confident that I know only a handful of them. But Ahnzhelyk—Nynian—has been one of their primary agents for decades. They call themselves simply 'the Circle,' and their purpose is—"

. VII .

Talbor Pass, Duchy of Manchyr, League of Corisande

Sir Koryn Gahrvai watched grimly as the wounded limped towards the rear. Many of them used their weapons as improvised crutches. Here and there, one of them leaned on the shoulder of a companion—sometimes both were wounded and leaned together, supporting one another—and stretcher parties carried men too severely wounded even to hobble. There could be nothing in the world more terrible than a battle lost, he thought. It wasn't simply the defeat; it was knowing that so many men had died and been wounded under his orders for absolutely nothing.

Unlike many commanders, Gahrvai made it a point to visit the wounded as often as he could. Altogether too many of them were going to die, anyway, despite everything the Order of Pasquale could do, and he owed it to them to at least tell them how grateful he was for all they'd done and suffered. And it also kept him aware of the price of his failure.

That's not really fair, Koryn, a corner of his brain insisted. *It's not your fault the Charisians have longer-ranged artillery and those damnable rifles.*

No, another corner of his brain replied harshly, *but it is your fault you managed to get your entire army penned up in Talbor Pass like sheep in a slaughter pen.*

His jaw clenched and remembered fury guttered through his veins. The one thing he'd managed to do since that disastrous afternoon which gave him a fierce sense of personal satisfaction was to relieve Baron Barcor of his command. Yet even that sense of satisfaction was flawed, because he couldn't forgive himself for not going ahead and relieving Barcor the instant word of Cayleb's landing had reached him. The baron had taken over *four hours* to get any of his troops into motion. Even then, he'd moved with arthritic slowness, and the main body of the rear guard had still been inside the western terminus of the pass when the defeated remnants of Windshare's cavalry had come pelting back.

There'd still been time, even then, for Barcor to clear the pass and at least let some of the other troops trapped behind him get clear of Talbor's restrictive terrain. But the baron had panicked as he heard the defeated cavalry's inevitably inflated estimates of the Charisians' strength. On his own initiative, he'd suspended the advance and ordered his men to dig in where they were. By the time Gahrvai had managed to reach the rear guard to personally countermand Barcor's orders, the Charisians truly had been present in strength, and the attempt to fight his way out of the pass had ended in bloody wreckage and the loss of over three thousand in dead, wounded, and prisoners. Coupled to the losses Windshare's cavalry had taken, that had amounted to a total loss of over six thousand, and they'd actually ended up being driven the better part of a mile and a half farther east, deeper *into* the pass.

That had been two and a half five-days ago. Over the last twelve days, he'd launched five separate attempts to cut his way out, better than doubling his original casualties in the process. He'd known the effort was almost certainly futile, and so had his men, yet they'd responded to his orders with a stolid courage and a willingness to try anyway which had made him ashamed to ask it of them.

But it's not as if you had a choice, Koryn. With your supply line cut, you can't just stay here. There's no more waiting game when you've already had to start slaughtering horses and dragons. And even on short rations, supplies are going to run out in days, not five-days. It's either fight your way out, starve, or surrender.

His mind flinched away from the last word, yet it was one he had to face. Even if Corisande had possessed another field army, it couldn't have broken through the Charisian lines to relieve him. Not against Charisian weapons. And not, he admitted harshly, against Charisian *commanders*.

Food was in short supply, and the healers were running out of bandages and medicines. They were already out of almost all painkillers, and his men were suffering and dying for nothing, *accomplishing* nothing . . . except to force the Charisians to expend ammunition killing them.

His fists clenched at his side. Then he drew a deep, decisive breath.

▼ ▼ ▼

"General Gahrvai," Cayleb Ahrmahk said quietly as the Corisandian commander was shown into his tent.

"Your Majesty."

Cayleb stood with Merlin at his back and watched Gahrvai straighten from his respectful bow. The Corisandian had taken pains with his appearance, the emperor noted. He was freshly shaved, his clothing clean and pressed, but there was a tightness around his eyes, his face was gaunt, and that immaculate clothing seemed to hang loosely on his frame. Cayleb knew from Merlin's reports that Gahrvai had insisted that his officers' rations—including his own—be cut along with those of his private soldiers, and it showed.

"I thank you for agreeing to meet with me and for granting me safe conduct through your lines, Your Majesty." Gahrvai sounded stiff, almost stilted in his formality.

"General," Cayleb said, "I don't enjoy killing men. And I especially don't enjoy killing *brave* men who, through no fault of their own, can't even fight back effectively. If anything we say or do here today can keep some of those men alive, I'll count this meeting as time well spent."

Gahrvai looked into the emperor's face, and his own expression seemed to relax just a bit. Cayleb saw it, and wondered how much of Gahrvai's tension had been due to the stories which had been told—and grown in the telling—of his ultimatum to Earl Thirsk after the Battle of Crag Reach.

"Since you've said that, Your Majesty, I suppose there isn't any point in attempting to pretend my army is in anything but desperate straits. I can continue to hold out for some days longer, and the men under my command will attack yet again, if I ask it of them. But you and I both know that, in the end, any further attacks will accomplish nothing. If I believed continued resistance could serve my Prince or Corisande, then resist I would. Under the circumstances which actually obtain, I must ask for the terms upon which you would permit my men to honorably surrender."

"I can't say your request was unanticipated, Sir Koryn," Cayleb's tone was almost compassionate, "and my terms are relatively simple. I will require your men to surrender their weapons. I will require the surrender of all of your army's artillery, baggage train, and surviving draft animals. Officers will be permitted to retain their swords, and any man—officer or trooper—who can demonstrate personal ownership of his horse will be allowed to retain it.

"I regret that I can't parole your officers or any of your

men," the emperor continued. Gahrvai's eyes narrowed, his jaw muscles tightening, but Cayleb went on calmly. "Under any other circumstances, I would gladly accept your parole, Sir Koryn. While we may have found ourselves enemies, I would never question or doubt your honesty or your honor. Unfortunately, as you may perhaps have heard—" Cayleb's tight smile bared his teeth "—the Empress and I have been formally excommunicated by Grand Vicar Erek. Well, actually by the Group of Four, via their puppet on Langhorne's Throne, but it amounts to the same thing."

Gahrvai winced at the biting sarcasm of Cayleb's last sentence, and the emperor chuckled harshly.

"If I believed for a moment that Erek actually spoke for God, I'd be worried by that, General. As it is, I take it rather as a badge of honor. As my father once told me, it's true that a man can be known by his friends, but you can tell even more about him by the *enemies* he makes.

"However, it would leave *you* in a rather ticklish position if I were to ask for your parole. In the eyes of the Temple Loyalists, you'd be guilty of trafficking with heretics, at the very least. And, also in the eyes of the Temple Loyalists, any parole you granted to me would be invalid, since no one can swear any binding oath to someone who's been excommunicated. If you attempted to honor your word—which, by the way, I believe you would—then you would be twice-damned in the Temple's eyes.

"I will confess," Cayleb admitted, "that I was tempted to offer you parole, anyway. It would have been one way to help accelerate the fragmentation of Corisande's internal stability, which could only help my own cause. But after considering it more maturely, I decided that using an honorable foe in that fashion wasn't something I wanted to do. However, since this little problem about oaths and my own religious status confronts us, I'm afraid that if you and your men surrender, I'm going to have to insist on moving all of you back to the vicinity of Dairos and establishing a prisoner camp there. Towards that end, you would be allowed to retain the use of all of your army's tentage, cooking gear, and other similar supplies. We would supply whatever additional needs, medical or food, you might have. And as soon as hostilities conclude, the formal release of you and all your men would undoubtedly be covered under the terms of whatever agreement is finally reached."

Gahrvai looked at him long and hard, and Cayleb looked back levelly. He didn't know precisely what Gahrvai might be reading in his own eyes, but he waited patiently. Then, finally, the Corisandian's nostrils flared.

"I understand your concerns, and your reasons for them, Your Majesty," he said. "To be honest, they hadn't even occurred to me. I suppose that, like you, I have a few . . . reservations about the validity of your excommunication. You're undoubtedly right about what would happen if I offered you my parole, though. Under the circumstances, your terms are most generous—more generous than I would have anticipated, in fact. I won't pretend it's easy, but I have no choice but to accept them . . . and to thank you for your generosity."

. VIII .

Royal Palace,
City of Manchyr,
League of Corisande

It was remarkably quiet in the council chamber.

Prince Hektor sat at the head of the table. Earl Tartarian sat at its foot, facing him, and Earl Anvil Rock and Sir Lyndahr Raimynd, who had taken over the Earl of Coris' duties in addition to his own, sat to either side. No one else was present, and the prince's advisers' faces might have been carved from stone.

Hektor's was no better. News of the Talbor Pass surrender had arrived less than an hour ago, and the fact that everyone had known it was inevitable had made it no more welcome when it arrived. Anvil Rock, especially, looked gray-faced and ashen. It was his army which had been defeated . . . and his son who had surrendered.

"My Prince, I apologize," the earl said finally.

"There's not anything to apologize for, Rysel," Hektor told him. "Koryn did exactly what we told him to do. It's not his fault the Charisians have better weapons and control the sea."

"But he still—"

"Did you, or did you not, recommend relieving Barcor?" Hektor interrupted. Anvil Rock looked at him for a moment, then nodded, and the prince shrugged. "I should have taken your advice. However important the man might have been politically, he was an obvious disaster as an army officer. You knew that, Koryn knew that, and I knew that. But instead of letting Koryn remove him, I told him to find something 'important but harmless' for the idiot to do. Under the circumstances, and faced with those instructions from my prince, I would have done precisely the same thing he did. And it shouldn't have mattered, given the observation posts he'd set up along the coast."

"I agree, My Prince," Tartarian said. The admiral shook his head. "I still can't see how they could have broken the signal chain so completely."

"The Ahrmahks, unfortunately, have this unwelcome tendency to produce highly capable kings, Taryl," Hektor said with a wintry smile. "And it often seems to work out that when you get rid of *one* of the capable bastards, you get an even *more* capable one in trade."

"I don't care how capable Cayleb might be, My Prince," Raimynd put in. "I have to agree with Earl Tartarian. I can't see how he could have done it, either."

"It's almost enough to make you believe Clyntahn has a point about heretics and Shan-wei looking after her own, isn't it?" Hektor's chuckle contained no humor at all.

"I'm not prepared to go quite that far, My Prince," Tartarian said. "I am ready to concede that he has Shan-wei's own *luck,* though."

"I agree. At the moment, though, *how* he did it matters a

lot less than the fact that he *did* do it. And the fact that we are now well and truly screwed."

No one else spoke for several long moments. At last, Anvil Rock stirred in his chair.

"I'm afraid you're right, My Prince," he said heavily. "With Koryn's field force gone, we aren't going to be able to put another one together for at least three or four months. And anything we could cobble together would be far less well-equipped—and trained—than the army we've just lost, even if we had the time . . . which we don't.

"According to our latest reports, Cayleb already has three strong columns moving out from the Dark Hills across Manchyr. What's left of Windshare's cavalry is trying to harass him, but not very successfully. They're managing to slow him down, but I still estimate that he'll be here, outside the capital, within a five-day. The garrison we have can hold the entrenchments for a time, at least, but we'd anticipated having Koryn's forces—especially his artillery and musketeers—available as well. If Cayleb wants to pay the price in lives, he can probably storm the works. If he's willing to settle for a siege, instead, we might hold out for several months. We've stockpiled sufficient food for the city's population and the garrison for that long, but to make it last that long, we'll have to institute rationing right now. And get as many unnecessary civilian mouths as possible out of the city as quickly as possible, too."

"And his navy has Manchyr Bay completely sealed," Tartarian added grimly. "Even if the Temple were in a position to send relief, I don't see any way that it could get past the Charisian Navy."

"Neither one of you is telling me anything I didn't already know," Hektor sighed. "I think we're going to have to play for time. We might be wrong—the Temple might actually have a relief fleet on its way, strong enough to do some good. I'm not saying I believe it does; I'm only saying it's possible. And that I will be *damned* if I surrender to Cayleb Ahrmahk after this long until I absolutely have to."

The silence after his final sentence was finally said aloud was profound.

"My Prince," Raimynd said finally, "I believe we could still get you out of the capital. As long as you're free to rally the nobles, it's possible that—"

"No, Lyndahr." Hektor shook his head. "As Rysel's just pointed out, our entire stock of new weapons was captured with Koryn, for all intents and purposes. Putting troops armed with nothing but pikes and matchlocks into the field against him would be useless. And the casualties we'd take would probably be enough to turn the survivors permanently against my House, especially after people realized I'd known how bad they'd be all along. Nor do I propose to run around, like a rabbit or a hedge lizard looking for a hidey hole, while Cayleb beats the bushes for me. If I've lost, I'll take my chances on my feet, not cowering in a cupboard somewhere until they haul me out by the scruff of the neck!"

There was another moment of silence. This time, it was broken by Anvil Rock.

"I hate to say this, My Prince, but I believe you're probably right. Certainly, you're right about the uselessness of trying to fight them with old-fashioned weapons. And I'd have to say that, based on the way he's treated his prisoners, I don't think Cayleb is the sort of man to seek blind vengeance. I don't doubt he'd prefer to see you dead, especially after all of the, ah . . . animosity between your house and his and all the blood that's been shed. But if it's a choice between the pleasure of taking your head and finding the troops to control Corisande in the face of the backlash that might provoke from your subjects, I think he'll probably forego your execution."

"That's what I think, too," Hektor said. "And don't think for a moment that I don't find the fact that I'm forced to think that way . . . irritating." The last word came out covered with fish hooks. "On the other hand, I'd just as soon keep as much maneuvering room as I can. And at least we've gotten Irys and Daivyn safely out of Corisande."

His face tightened, the anxiety of a father who had sent two of his children into danger in an effort to protect them from still greater danger showing in his eyes, in the tightness of his lips. But then he shook himself.

"I'm not planning on sending him any surrender offers anytime soon," he told the other three. "As I say, there's always a chance, after all, no matter how slim. And however 'merciful' Cayleb may be feeling, I can always hope one of his own Temple Loyalists will get to him with a knife, one fine night."

. IX .

Emperor Cayleb's Tent,
Duchy of Manchyr,
League of Corisande

Should I assume, Colonel," Emperor Cayleb asked coldly, "that you have somehow failed to grasp my intentions in this matter?"

Colonel Bahrtol Rohzhyr had the appearance of a man who wished he could be anywhere else as he stood in Cayleb's command tent facing an irate emperor. The Commissary officer was effectively the chief quartermaster for Cayleb's army, and, by and large, he'd done an outstanding job so far, aided by the Charisian Navy's ability to move large quantities of supplies quickly by water. At the moment, however, he clearly didn't expect his past accomplishments to loom very large in Cayleb's thinking.

"No, Your Majesty," he said.

"In that case, perhaps you could explain to me why my instructions haven't been carried out?"

Cayleb's voice was even colder, and Rohzhyr swallowed unobtrusively. Then he stiffened his shoulders and faced the emperor squarely.

"Your Majesty, they don't *believe* us."

"*Who* doesn't believe us? Your assistant commissaries?"

"No, Your Majesty—the Corisandians. The *Corisandians* don't believe you're serious."

Cayleb's eyebrows rose, and Merlin found himself hard-pressed not to chuckle as Rohzhyr faced his emperor with an expression which was part pleading, part confusion, and part outraged virtue.

Unlike most Safeholdian Commissary officers, Rohzhyr was actually honest. By tradition, most commissaries took a ten percent "bite" off the top of all funds which passed through their hands. In most kingdoms, that was considered one of the perquisites of their position; in Charis, that wasn't the case, and Rohzhyr had never shown any temptation to emulate his more sticky-fingered counterparts in other realms.

In addition to his honesty, he possessed the virtues of intelligence and energy, but he was an outstanding example of what had once been called a "bean counter" back on Old Earth. He was organized to the point of fanaticism, and he was one of the people who'd seized upon the introduction of the abacus and Arabic numerals with both hands. Outside the regulations and requirements of the Commissary, however, he had about as much imagination as a boot. And he was possessed of a strong sense that things should be done the way they'd always *been* done, only more efficiently.

Now Cayleb settled into the camp chair beside the table at the center of his tent, looking at Rohzhyr, and the Commissary officer clasped his hands nervously behind him.

"What do you mean, they don't think I'm serious?"

"Your Majesty, I've tried to explain it to them. They just don't believe it."

Merlin wasn't really surprised to hear that.

Cayleb and his commanders were busily seizing every bag of rice, every basket of wheat, every reaper, and every horse, cow, draft dragon, chicken, and pig their foraging parties could locate. That didn't surprise the locals, however much they might have resented it. Stealing food and plundering farmers were what armies did, after all. Expecting them not to would have been about as reasonable as expecting a hurricane not to rain, although with this particular army there'd been remarkably little of the rape which often accompanied that plundering.

In this case, however, Cayleb wasn't collecting the food and other supplies for his own army's sustenance. He was collecting those items primarily to deprive Hektor of them, although he was also quite willing to use the confiscated food to feed the prisoners who'd once been Sir Koryn Gahrvai's army. That particular difference in approach had absolutely no significance for the unhappy original owners of the food, animals, and agricultural equipment involved. What *did* have a certain burning significance for them was that, contrary to the practice of virtually all other armies, the Marines were actually issuing receipts for the private property which had been seized. Receipts which would be redeemed in cold, hard cash at the end of the campaign. At which point Cayleb fully intended to tap the treasury currently in Hektor's possession in order to pay for them.

It was a novel notion, and one which had occurred to Cayleb entirely on his own. As he'd pointed out, one of the better ways to defeat the Group of Four's propaganda was to earn the trust of those people actually in contact with Charis by concrete deeds instead of printed broadsides.

"Let me get this straight," he said now. "You're telling me the Corisandian farmers are refusing to accept the receipts our foragers are handing out?"

"More or less, Your Majesty." Rohzhyr shrugged slightly. "Some of them take them, but they don't make much effort to keep track of them. And others, I'm afraid, are selling them to anyone 'foolish enough' to offer them hard cash on the spot for them."

"At what sort of exchange rate?" Cayleb asked, his eyes narrowing.

"Most of them are prepared to settle for a hundredth piece on the mark, Your Majesty," Rohzhyr sighed, and Cayleb's jaw tightened ominously.

"And are these so-generous speculators Charisians?" he inquired icily.

"Some of them," Rohzhyr admitted. "Possibly most of them. I really don't know. I only know the locals don't think our receipts are worth the paper they're written on. I wouldn't be a bit surprised if some of them are using them in their outhouses, Your Majesty."

"I see."

It was obvious to Merlin from Rohzhyr's expression and body language that he, personally, believed Cayleb's quest to actually reimburse the citizens of a land with which he was currently at war was quixotic, at best. In fact, the Commissary seemed to find the entire notion almost immoral. An unnatural act on a par with incest, perhaps. He wasn't about to come out and say it in Cayleb's presence, but it was pretty clearly his opinion that if the Corisandians chose not to accept or hang on to the receipts they'd been offered, that was their lookout, not his.

"Listen to me carefully, Colonel," Cayleb said after a moment. "The policy of the Imperial Navy and the Imperial Marines is going to be that we pay civilian owners for what we seize from them. *Civilian owners,* Colonel. I'm not going to pay a pack of greedy Charisian speculators instead of the people whose property we actually took."

"Your Majesty, I understand that, but—"

"I wasn't quite finished speaking, Colonel."

Rohzhyr's mouth closed with an almost audible click, and Cayleb favored him with a frosty smile.

"I'm afraid your clerks are going to find their workload just got a bit heavier," the emperor continued. "From this moment on, receipts for confiscated property are not transferable. They will be honored only when presented by the individual to whom they were initially issued or, in the event of his death, his legal heirs. Is that understood?"

"Yes, Your Majesty! But . . . how are we going to be able to prove the individual presenting the receipt is the one who actually received it in the first place? And what happens if someone *loses* a receipt?"

"That's why your clerks are going to be working a bit harder, Colonel. First, I want a duplicate copy of every receipt we issue, complete with date, time, and place, filed by every foraging party every day, in addition to the entries in your ledger books. And I want the recorded names of at least two witnesses to attest that the name of the individual to whom the receipt was issued is correct on the receipt. Those same two witnesses will be available to *identify* that individual before a disbursing officer, if that's necessary."

Rohzhyr's face had grown steadily longer as he visualized the additional labor involved, but one look at the emperor's expression warned him against arguing. Cayleb let him marinate for several moments, then leaned back in his camp chair and cocked his head.

"Was there anything else we needed to discuss, Colonel?" he asked pleasantly.

Rohzhyr shook his head almost convulsively, and the emperor smiled.

"In that case, Colonel, I won't keep you any longer. I'm sure you have a great many things that need doing."

. X .

Royal Palace,
City of Tellesberg,
Kingdom of Charis

Are you sure this is a good idea, Sharleyan?"

Empress Sharleyan paused, her wineglass halfway to her lips, and her eyes narrowed as she cocked her head at the Duke of Halbrook Hollow.

Her relationship with her uncle hadn't so much improved over the past few months as settled into one of mutual exhaustion. He continued to make no pretense about his disapproval of her marriage and decision to embrace Charis' cause against the Temple as her own. Nor did either of them pretend any longer that Sharleyan hadn't brought him with her to Tellesberg specifically because of that disapproval. Despite her conversation with Archbishop Maikel, their estrangement caused her more pain than she could possibly have expressed, and she made a conscientious effort to at least maintain their familial relationship, since it was obvious their *political* relationship had been largely destroyed. She knew he still loved her, and they both pretended during their twice-a-five-day suppers together that politics didn't exist.

Which made his question unexpected, and also explained why she found herself fighting to suppress an instinctive spike of automatic, resentful exasperation.

"Which idea, Uncle Byrtrym?"

She worked hard to keep that exasperation out of her tone, but it was far harder to dissemble with someone who'd always been so close to her, and his lips tightened for just a moment. Then he sat back from the table and propped his elbows on the arms of his chair.

"Actually, Sharley," he said, using her childhood nickname for the first time in far too long, "I wasn't talking about any of your, um, political decisions. Or not specifically about their political aspects, at any rate." He smiled thinly, but with an edge of affection. "I was talking about this field trip of yours."

"Oh. You mean the one to Saint Agtha's?"

"Yes." He shook his head. "I'm not happy about it, Sharley. In fact, I'm starting to regret ever having mentioned the convent to you in the first place. There's too much chance for something to go wrong if you insist on visiting it."

"I think that between them, Colonel Ropewalk, Wyllys, and Edwyrd are quite capable of dealing with anything that does go wrong, Uncle Byrtrym."

"I know you think that. And, frankly, I hope you're right and I'm wrong. But I think, perhaps, I may understand the feelings of those who don't wish to see this schism prosper a bit better than you do."

He shook his head again as her face tightened.

"I'm not trying to open that entire jar of worms, Sharley. Promise!" He managed a crooked smile, and she relaxed again . . . mostly. "I'm simply saying that emotions on either side are passionate, and what with the interdict and the excommunication, those who wish you ill are altogether too likely to feel justified in taking some sort of desperate action. Cayleb may be safe with his army, but you aren't. I don't want to see you taking unnecessary risks."

"Thank you," she said, her eyes warming at his concern for her safety, despite the differences between them. "But I'm not going to allow fear of my own subjects to turn me into a prisoner in the Palace. I especially can't afford to do that while I'm still 'that foreign woman' to altogether too many of them. This 'field trip,' as you call it, is one way of showing them I trust them enough to travel among them. And the fact that Saint Agtha was born in Chisholm but chose to spend almost all of her life here in Charis won't be lost on them, either. Besides, I've been fascinated by her biography. I really want to see the convent where she worked all those miraculous healings."

And, she did not add out loud, *because I'm exhausted. I think Rayjhis, Maikel, and I have done a good, solid job of hammering the Imperial Parliament together, and I can't believe how well Maikel's managing to integrate Archbishop Pawal's archbishopric into the new hierarchy, even with Braynair's active cooperation. But it didn't come easy for any of us. And people like your "good friend" Kairee didn't exactly help, either, Uncle Byrtrym. I need this trip.*

"All that may be true," he replied, "but it doesn't change a single thing I've said, either. I wish you'd at least take more of your personal guard from home with you."

"I can't do that, either, Uncle Byrtrym." Her tone had hardened slightly, and she grimaced, unhappy with herself at the change. "The last thing I can afford to do," she continued, trying to soften her impatience, "is to give the impression that I trust Chisholmians more than I trust Charisians. That's the entire reason for integrating my guardsmen and Cayleb's in the first place."

"But—"

"Uncle Byrtrym," she interrupted gently, "I appreciate your

concern. I truly do. Believe me, the fact that I know you still love me, despite our present political differences, is more important to me than I can say. But as you yourself helped Mahrak teach me when I was a girl, once a decision's been made, the worst thing you can do is try to second-guess yourself. And let's be honest with one another, please. My reasons for the decisions I've made can't possibly be acceptable to you. I know that, and I regret it, but it's a fact we both simply have to accept. And that means you're looking at all of those decisions from a radically different perspective. Of course we're not going to agree. If you'll forgive me, I think we both need to take it as a given that you're motivated by your love for me to worry about my safety, but that I can't allow your worries to change my mind. And on that basis, I think it would be far better if we agreed to discuss something else."

He gazed at her across the table for a second or two, then sighed.

"All right, Sharley," he said. "You're probably right. And speaking of discussing 'something else,'" he continued in a determinedly brighter tone, "what do you think of that new chestnut of mine?"

. XI .

Emperor Cayleb's Headquarters Encampment,
Duchy of Manchyr,
League of Corisande

Merlin Athrawes sat in the darkened tent, leaning back in a folding camp chair with his eyes closed. He really ought to have been lying down, with his "breathing" programmed to be slow and deep, pretending to be asleep if anyone should wander in, but that was much less likely to happen here than it had been aboard ship. Besides, he'd discovered that he actually thought better sitting or standing. Which had to be purely psychological, but made it no less true.

Unfortunately, the posture in which he chose to do his thinking did nothing to add more hours to the lengthy Safeholdian day, and as he'd told Cayleb, there was simply too much he had to keep track of. Initially, that hadn't been that much of a problem, but as the repercussions of Charis' defiance of the Group of Four reechoed around the globe, it had become a nightmare task, even with Owl's help. The fact that he'd been forced to concentrate so heavily on Corisande once Cayleb began active operations against Hektor had only made the nightmare worse, and when *he* dropped a stitch, the consequences could be dire. Not to mention frustrating as hell.

He was still . . . irritated with himself for not picking up on Hektor's plans to get his daughter and younger son out of Corisande in time, for example. The fact that the schooner *Dawn Star* had actually stopped and boarded the ship with the two of them—and Earl Coris—aboard only made his irritation worse. If there'd just been time to warn *Dawn Star* and the other cruisers that some suitably anonymous informant had told them members of Hektor's family might be attempting to flee the princedom, then her boarding officer would undoubtedly have taken a much closer look at *Wing*'s passenger list instead of concentrating on her cargo. Her completely *legitimate*-seeming cargo.

Still, he had to admit that Cayleb had been right to order him to take regular breaks each night. Two hours was probably more than he actually needed, but he could recognize a significant difference in his mental sharpness since Cayleb had handed down his *diktat*.

His lips twitched in a smile as he wondered just how Cayleb would be able to tell whether he was "awake" or "asleep" if the emperor came to check and make certain he was getting the prescribed "downtime" each night.

I suppose the point is that he doesn't have *to check. I told him I'd do it, and he took my word for it. Sneaky bastard. It's so much easier to creep around behind the back of someone who doesn't simply expect you to be as honorable and trust-worthy as he is. Besides, I might as well admit that he's got about as much "command presence" as anyone I ever served under, including Commodore Pei.*

It was peculiar how his original attitudes towards Charis and Charisians had changed, he reflected. He'd respected both Cayleb and his father from the beginning, but as he'd told King Haarahld in their very first interview, his loyalty had been to the future of Safehold, not to any specific monarch or even realm. Yet that was no longer strictly true. Since then, somehow, he'd become a Charisian himself, and he wasn't certain that was a good thing. His responsibility was to the entire human race, not to the House of Ahrmahk, however personable, likable, and charismatic the current head of that house might be. He couldn't afford to allow himself to begin identifying with the interests of Charis in a way which might distract him from his overarching duty.

But I'm not—not really, he told himself in one corner of his brain while most of his attention was concentrated on the summary of the day's take from the SNARCs which Owl was transmitting to him. *Or, rather, at this point in time, the interests of Charis are identical with those of the human race in general. There's certainly no one else prepared to take the stand Cayleb, Maikel, and Sharleyan are taking, at any rate! Even from the most cold-blooded perspective, I can't afford to lose this particular team. If I did, I'd probably never find its equal again.*

Sure, another corner of his brain replied sardonically. *You go right on convincing yourself that way.*

Oh, shut up! the first corner snapped peevishly.

He snorted. These little internal conversations of his would undoubtedly have worried any psychologist who'd been prepared to take on the challenge of analyzing an electronic pattern of memories and emotions which stubbornly persisted in thinking of itself as a human being. It wasn't as if—

His thoughts broke off abruptly and he twitched upright in his chair.

"Owl!" he subvocalized.

"Yes, Lieutenant Commander Alban?"

"Replay that last segment."

"Yes, Lieutenant Commander," the AI replied obediently, and Merlin swore silently and viciously as a dagger of ice seemed to go through his nonexistent heart.

Damn it. Damn it! I told Cayleb I had too many things to do!

Yes, he had. And as Cayleb had suggested to him, that was as inevitable as the next sunrise. He simply *had* to prioritize, which was why he'd been concentrating on matters here in Corisande and events which might directly impinge on Cayleb's operations. Besides, he knew the quality of the people Cayleb had left behind in Tellesberg, and he couldn't have personally affected anything that happened there from this far away, anyway.

Every single word of that was true, and he knew it . . . which didn't make him feel a single bit better.

He stood abruptly, still watching behind his eyelids as the SNARC routinely sweeping Sharleyan's physical location and tracking her movements detected the armed men moving steadily towards the Convent of Saint Agtha.

He didn't know who they were, but he knew they *weren't* her guardsmen or anyone else associated with her security force. That only left one real possibility for why they might be closing in on the convent. Obviously, he'd missed even more than he'd realized. Neither he nor Owl had tagged any of the men the SNARC was watching as potential threats; they weren't even in the database they'd been constructing. But they had to have contact with someone who was, or else they wouldn't have known Sharleyan's agenda well enough and sufficiently in advance to prepare as well as they obviously had.

Those thoughts flashed through his molycirc brain, and then he shook himself. However interesting all this speculation might be, it wasn't doing him any good. And it wasn't doing Sharleyan any good, either.

He stood very still, considering alternatives and consequences. It was roughly four in the morning in Corisande, which made it eighteen hundred in Charis, and he was the next best thing to seven thousand air-miles from Tellesberg. There was no way he could possibly warn Sharleyan or any of her guardsmen. But there was one possibility, only . . .

It's those kids and the krakens all over again, he thought. *Only this time, it's even worse. I can't do this. I can't risk this. It can undo every single thing we've accomplished so far, and I don't have any right to run that kind of risk,* however *much I want to.*

He knew he was right. Knew he couldn't take such an enormous chance. Knew—

"Get the recon skimmer airborne!" he snapped to Owl.

. XII .

Convent of Saint Agtha,
Earldom of Crest Hollow,
Kingdom of Charis

I think the Abbess expected me to object to the rule about servants," Sharleyan commented as Father Carlsyn, Captain Gairaht, and Sergeant Seahamper escorted her from the refectory to the Convent of Saint Agtha's guesthouse.

"If you'll pardon my saying so, Your Majesty, you *ought* to have objected," Gairaht replied, just a bit sourly. "It's not fitting."

"Oh, stop fussing, Wyllys!" Sharleyan scolded affectionately. "I knew about the convent's retreat rules before I ever asked the Abbess to allow me to come. And my imperial dignity isn't so fragile that it has to be buttressed every moment, especially on a retreat. Besides, a reputation for piety isn't a bad thing under the present circumstances, now is it?"

"And you expect me to believe you decided to accept the convent's stipulations solely on the basis of cold calculation. Is that it, Your Majesty?"

"No, but if doing what I think is the right thing works out to be the same thing I would have decided to do if I *had* calculated coldly, I'm not going to object," Sharleyan replied serenely.

"I'm relieved to hear that you have your priorities in order, Your Majesty," Father Carlsyn said dryly, and Sharleyan chuckled.

"I'm glad you're relieved, Father. On the other hand, I was scarcely likely to come up with any other answer where my confessor might overhear it, was I?"

"Except that such duplicitous thinking would never occur to someone who's had the advantage of *my* spiritual counsel for so long, Your Majesty," he replied tranquilly.

"Oh, of course not," she agreed, then looked back at Gairaht. "At any rate, Wyllys, the convent's rules are the convent's rules, and I don't intend to argue with them."

"And how many years has it been since you put yourself to bed?" the commander of her guard detail demanded.

"If you want to be technical about it, I don't suppose I *ever* have . . . except on religious retreats. Which, I suppose I could point out, if I were the sort of person who liked to repeat herself, is what this particular excursion happens to be, now isn't it?"

"And you expect me to believe Sairaih was happy to hear about this, Your Majesty?" the captain asked skeptically.

"While I realize this may be difficult to believe, Wyllys, Sairaih has learned to accept—unlike certain Imperial Guard officers I might mention, if I were the sort of person who did that—that upon occasion I may actually decide to set my royal dignity aside. And, amazingly enough, *she* doesn't argue with me about it."

Gairaht might have growled something under his breath, but if he had, he'd done it quietly enough Sharleyan could pretend she hadn't heard it. And at least he hadn't called her on her bald-faced lie. While it might technically be true that Sairaih Hahlmyn hadn't *said* anything against her imperial charge's decision to leave her behind aboard HMS *Dancer*, she'd certainly found ample opportunity to make her feelings clear. She probably could have supported herself quite comfortably as an actress, assuming she could have resisted the temptation to overact. Which, judging by this morning' performance, was unlikely.

"I at least wish Lady Mairah were here," the captain said aloud.

"And if she hadn't taken that tumble and broken her leg when she and Uncle Byrtrym went riding, she would have been," Sharleyan pointed out.

"You could have asked one of the other court ladies—" he began.

"I'm going to be just fine, Wyllys," she said firmly. "And I don't intend to spend all night arguing with you about it."

He gave her one more disapproving glance, then drew a deep breath, puffed out his mustache for a moment, and nodded.

The empress shook her head affectionately. Like most of her guardsmen—and, of course, Sairaih—Gairaht was far more sensitive to the demands of her royal dignity than she was. Perhaps that was because it *was* "her" royal dignity—well, *imperial* dignity, these days—and not theirs. She'd learned very early that she couldn't afford to allow her dignity to be undermined by the real or apparent slights of others. Whether or not she wanted to be hypersensitive in such matters was actually beside the point, given the importance of appearances in the world of political calculations. Yet a reputation for humility could also be valuable, under the appropriate circumstances, and the opportunity to step back from her persona as queen or empress, even briefly, was literally beyond price. That was one reason she'd been fond of occasional religious retreats ever since the day she'd assumed the throne of Chisholm. The opportunity to slip the day-to-day secular demands of her crown and spend some time contemplating the demands of her soul, instead, had always been welcome. And the opportunity to stop standing upon her dignity, however fleetingly, had been almost equally welcome.

Gairaht and Seahamper knew that as well as she did, and they'd had conversations very like this one many times in the past. It was an old and familiar topic, and her uncle always tended to weigh in on their side, shaking his head and wondering rhetorically why she hadn't simply gone ahead and taken vows herself.

She smiled at the memory, but the smile was brief as she remembered their estrangement. He hadn't accompanied her to Saint Agtha's, although she'd invited him, hoping the opportunity might draw them closer once more. His refusal had been polite but firm, and she wondered if it would have hurt less if she hadn't suspected that he'd sensed the same possibility . . . and wanted to avoid it.

They arrived at the guesthouse, and she reached out to lay an affectionate hand on Gairaht's arm.

"You, Wyllys Gairaht, are a fussbudget," she told him.

"As Your Majesty says." The stiffness in the guardsman's voice was belied by the twinkle in his eye, and she squeezed his mailed forearm.

"Exactly. I'm the Empress around here, after all. And, I assure you, I'll manage just fine in my lonely little convent cell. If I should suddenly discover that I'm physically incapable of getting myself into bed, I know that all I have to do is call out and my stalwart guardsmen will charge fearlessly to my rescue."

"Your Majesty, physical danger is something any guardsman is pledged to face on your behalf," Gairaht said gravely. "I'm afraid helping you prepare for bed *isn't*."

"Coward." She smiled, then took her hand from his elbow, and glanced at her confessor.

"Are you ready for bed, Father?" she asked, and he nodded.

"There, you see, Wyllys? I'll have at least one loyal soul close at hand if I should suffer some terrible nightmare!"

"And I'm very happy for you, Your Majesty," he assured her.

"Thank you," she said, and stepped through the guesthouse door. The priest stayed long enough to exchange commiserating smiles with her armsmen, then followed her inside and closed the door behind him.

Gairaht and Seahamper exchanged silent but eloquent glances of their own, then shrugged as one.

"Captain, you're not going to change her at this date," Seahamper pointed out.

"Of course I'm not, but she'd be disappointed if I stopped trying, and you know it!"

Seahamper chuckled, then looked around the convent grounds.

Saint Agtha's was located in the Styvyn Mountains above the Earldom of Crest Hollow's Trekair Bay, on the narrow isthmus dividing Howell Bay from the Cauldron. The voyage from the capital aboard Captain Paitryk Hywyt's fifty-six-gun galleon HMS *Dancer* had been a welcome diversion. The ride up the narrow, twisting track which served Saint Agtha's and the farmsteads around it had been rather more strenuous, but still enjoyable, and the convent's elevation was sufficient to actually give the gathering evening a bit of a bite.

Probably just my imagination, the sergeant thought. *I'm a northern boy, and I think I've been away from home way too long if* this *feels chilly to me!*

"Any special concerns, Sir?" he asked Gairaht after a moment.

"No, not really," the captain replied, carrying out his own survey of the convent. "In some ways, I wish she'd listened to the Duke and brought along even more men, but I think we're in pretty good shape, Edwyrd."

"Yes, Sir," Seahamper agreed.

"All right, then," Gairaht said more briskly. "I'll make one more check of the perimeter, then hand over to the Lieutenant and turn in. Call me if you need me."

"Yes, Sir," Seahamper said, exactly as if Gairaht hadn't told him exactly the same thing scores of times before. The captain smiled at him, then headed out into the gathering dusk.

Thunder rumble-grumbled from the west, and Seahamper grimaced. It rained a lot in Charis, especially by the standards of someone who'd grown up in Chisholm. From the sound of things, it intended to do some more of that raining tonight.

▼ ▼ ▼

Wyllys Gairaht heard the same sound of thunder as he stepped out through the convent's open gate, nodded to the ten men posted there with Lieutenant Hahskyn, his Charisian-born second-in-command, and turned to his right.

The ancient stone wall around the convent proper was more for privacy than any sort of genuine security. He was glad enough to see it, he supposed, but it would have been far more useful if it had been either a little shorter or else enough wider and taller that he could have put men on top of it. As it was, it was just high enough that the men on the outside were effectively separated from those on the inside, and that they'd have to use one of the three gateways to get past it in any sort of a hurry.

The main gate, in the southern wall, was wide enough for heavy freight wagons. There were smaller, merely human-sized gates in the western and northern walls, and all three of them had stood open when the Imperial Guard's advance elements had arrived. They'd promptly collected the keys to the smaller gates from the abbess, who had surrendered them readily enough. However intractable she might be about the convent's rules where servants were concerned, she clearly understood the realities of providing proper security for her empress. And, Gairaht reflected gratefully, despite the fact that she'd been the abbess of Saint Agtha's for almost twenty years, she was obviously one of the Charisians who had enthusiastically embraced the Church of Charis, as well. He'd been more than half afraid they'd been going to encounter someone with Temple Loyalist sympathies.

He reached the corner of the wall, made another right, and started through the fruit orchard outside the western wall. The abbess had been a bit dismayed by the size of Empress Sharleyan's guard detail. Convents weren't exactly accustomed to playing host to men with weapons, and her housing arrangements hadn't been up to the arrival of eighty armed and armored Imperial Guardsmen. She'd attempted to hide her dismay when they turned up, but she'd obviously had no idea where to put them, and she'd gratefully accepted Gairaht's suggestion that perhaps his men might camp in the meadow just beyond the orchard. A deep, rapidly flowing stream offered plenty of fresh water, and the location was convenient to the convent's inner grounds by way of the smallish western gate. The fact that its location also happened to give some additional security to that gate was simply a welcome side effect.

At the moment, half the detail was preparing to settle down in tents and bedrolls. In six hours, they'd be roused to relieve the duty watch, and he hoped their ability to sleep wouldn't find itself too sorely taxed if the evening's weather turned as interesting as it was threatening to do. No guardsman would ever be encouraged to sleep too deeply, but adequate rest was important if they were going to stay alert in the middle of the night, and thunderstorms were seldom exactly restful for men sleeping in canvas tents.

The eight-man watch on the western wall was satisfyingly difficult to spot. Two of its men were easy enough to find, openly sweeping back and forth along the foot of the wall with their bayoneted rifles on their shoulders. The other six, however, had found proper concealment, allowing them to maintain their overwatch without revealing their own positions to anyone who might happen by. The sergeant in charge of the detail emerged from the shrubbery to salute as Gairaht walked by, and the captain returned the courtesy.

The northern wall's duty section was equally alert, equally focused on its responsibilities, and Gairaht felt a deep pride in all of his men. Half of them were Chisholmians; the other half were native-born Charisians, and without actually hearing their accents it would have been impossible for any outsider to pick them out from one another. There'd been a certain amount of friction when the guard details were combined to form the new Imperial Guard, but these were all elite troops. They'd settled down quickly, united by their responsibilities and their pride in the fact that they'd been found worthy to guard the empress from harm.

He started his swing along the eastern wall, heading back towards the southern wall and the main gate. This was the shortest of the convent's walls, and he was just as happy that it was. The last of the sunset's bloody light, oozing ominously through the narrow chink between the storm clouds and the Styvyns' summits, was fading quickly, and the trees on this side of the convent—mature-growth forest which had never been logged off, unlike the neatly ordered fruit trees of the orchard—stood back fifty or sixty yards from the wall. The shadows underneath them were already impenetrable, and they loomed like a dark, vaguely sinister barrier, or some sort of crouching monster. The thought made Gairaht uncomfortable, and he brushed it aside impatiently as he finished checking the last post on that side and headed for the front gate.

You've got entirely too active an imagination, Wyllys, he told himself firmly. *That's probably better than being too stupid to worry about the obvious, but it's not exactly—*

The steel-headed arbalest bolt that came hissing out of the darkness under those trees struck him squarely in the throat and interrupted his thoughts forever.

. XIII .

A Farmhouse near Saint Agtha's, Earldom of Crest Hollow, Kingdom of Charis

Bishop Mylz Halcom forced himself to sit serenely at the roughly made table in the farmhouse a mile and a half from the Convent of Saint Agtha. What he really wanted to do was to pace furiously back and forth, expending physical energy in an attempt to work off the nervous tension coiling deep within him. Unfortunately, he couldn't do that.

If all was going according to plan, the attack on the convent would be beginning shortly, and he closed his eyes in a brief, silent, heartfelt prayer for the men out there in the gathering darkness who had accepted God's stern demands. The irony of the fact that such a brief time before he would have been horrified at the very thought of praying for success in a mission like this one wasn't lost upon him.

"My Lord, we have a . . . visitor."

Halcom opened his eyes and looked up quickly as the tension in Ahlvyn Shumay's voice registered. His aide stood in the farmhouse kitchen door, and his expression was anxious.

"What sort of visitor, Ahlvyn?" he made himself ask calmly.

"Me, My Lord Bishop," another voice replied, and Halcom's eyebrows shot up as the Duke of Halbrook Hollow pushed past Shumay.

"Your Grace," the bishop said after several taut, silent seconds, "this is not wise."

"With all due respect, My Lord, I'm not all that concerned with 'wise' when we're talking about my niece's life," Halbrook Hollow replied flatly.

"And how do you intend to explain your presence here, Your Grace?"

"I won't have to. Everyone knows Sharleyan and I don't see eye-to-eye politically any longer. No one's going to be surprised that I preferred not to sit around in Tellesberg when she was away. After all, it's not as if I have a lot of friends there, is it? Officially, I'm visiting Master Kairee, and the two of us are staying at his hunting lodge. I'll be back there and waiting by the time official word can reach me."

"My Lord, you've run too many risks." Halcom's voice was even flatter than Halbrook Hollow's had been. "How many people know you're here?"

"Only a handful," the duke replied impatiently. "Kairee, my personal armsmen, and the crew of the schooner that brought me."

"Excuse me, My Lord," Shumay put in, momentarily drawing both of the older men's eyes to him, "but His Grace used *Sunrise*."

Halcom's eyes narrowed for a moment. Then he tossed his head in an odd cross between a shrug and a nod as he realized Halbrook Hollow hadn't been—quite—as rash as he'd originally believed.

Traivyr Kairee's unhappiness over the sudden infusion of questionable innovations which had flooded Charis, his matching unhappiness and disgust with Cayleb's and Maikel Stayinair's decision to openly defy the Temple and the Grand Vicar's authority, and his wealth and political prominence had all combined to make him one of Halcom's first, cautious contacts when the bishop arrived in Tellesberg. He'd responded quickly and firmly, with a fierce promise of support, and he'd also accepted Halcom's direction and moderated his open, public anger and disgust. Neither of them had been foolish enough to think he could suddenly pretend he actually *supported* all of the blasphemous changes taking place around him, but he'd made it abundantly and firmly clear that he had no intention of trying to fight them. As he'd said publically on more than one occasion, the Kingdom was committed now, whether wisely or not, and to pretend otherwise would have been treasonous.

Of course, what he *hadn't* said aloud was that he was perfectly prepared to *be* treasonous, and he'd also followed through on his initial promises of support. The portions of his wealth he and Halcom had carefully diverted through "charitable donations" to the churches and monastic communities which shared his religious views, like Saint Hamlyn's in Rivermouth, had become a critically important element in the bishop's ability to successfully create, supply, and arm his Temple Loyalist organization.

Halcom hadn't been entirely happy about the fact that Kairee and Halbrook Hollow had become open friends, but he'd realized that the relationship had its advantages, as well as its drawbacks. And given the fact that the duke's unhappiness with his niece's marriage and policies was well known, it had probably been inevitable that someone as wealthy and politically prominent as Kairee, who was known to share his unhappiness, should become one of his relatively few friendly associates in Charis. Neither man was prepared to openly condemn their monarchs' policies, but there had to be a perfectly understandable "comfort zone" in their shared views. Besides, Halbrook Hollow had invested heavily in Kairee's various enterprises, and the two of them shared many of the same interests in horses and hunting, and Kairee had made his hunting lodge available to introduce his new friend to the game animals of Charis. In the end, Halcom had decided that Kairee was right; it would have looked even more suspicious if the two men *hadn't* become friends. And since everyone knew they were both avid hunters, the duke's decision to visit Kairee's lodge once again, especially while the empress was out of town anyway, was actually perfectly reasonable. Or would have been if the timing had been a bit different, at any rate.

The fact that Halbrook Hollow had used the schooner *Sunrise* for his transport from Kairee's hunting lodge in the neighboring Earldom of Styvyn to Trekair Bay was another of the very few positive elements in the duke's incredibly stupid decision to travel outside Tellesberg at this particular moment. *Sunrise* was one of Kairee's vessels, and she'd been used to make several Temple Loyalist deliveries in and around Howell Bay. Her crew had already demonstrated both its loyalty and its ability to keep its collective mouth shut.

None of which changed the fact that Halbrook Hollow had been *supposed* to be staying in Tellesberg Palace where he'd have a cast-iron alibi when news of the attack on Saint Agtha's arrived. And, of course, there was the minor fact that *Sunrise* had now sailed into Trekair Bay right by a galleon of the Imperial Charisian Navy. Which, given what was about to happen at Saint Agtha's, meant she was bound to come under intense scrutiny eventually, and that raised all sorts of unpleasant possibilities of its own.

"Your Grace," the bishop said after a moment, "I understand why you might feel anxious, but in my opinion, this was still an ill-advised decision on your part. Too many things have the potential to go wrong."

"Which is precisely why I'm here." The duke's mouth twisted in a parody of a smile. "I know how high feelings are running among our people. I want to be here to be sure they behave themselves with . . . proper restraint. Sharleyan never needs to know I was here, but *I* need to know that she's all right."

"I see."

Halcom nodded slowly, then seated himself once again at the kitchen table, facing the door. He waved one hand at the second chair, across the table from his own, and Halbrook Hollow sat down. Then the bishop glanced over his visitor's shoulder at Shumay.

"Ahlvyn, in light of His Grace's concerns, could you ask Mytrahn to step in here? Go ahead and tell him the Duke is here and—" He paused and looked at Halbrook Hollow. "I assume you brought at least one or two of your own armsmen, Your Grace?"

"Two of them." Halbrook Hollow nodded. "Don't worry. Both of them have been with me for at least twenty years."

"Good." Halcom turned back to Shumay. "Tell Mytrahn to see to any of His Grace's armsmen's needs, as well."

"Of course, My Lord," Shumay murmured, his face expressionless, and stepped out of the kitchen.

"Your Grace," Halcom continued as the young priest withdrew, "as I say, I understand the basis for your anxiety. And I suppose I can't fault you for your desire to ensure your niece's safety. Still, it would have been better if you'd been able to trust *me* to see to that while you remained in Tellesberg. All of our plans and strategy were built upon your being there, in the Palace, when news of this arrived."

"I realize that," Halbrook Hollow said just a bit shortly. "The original plan was *mine*, after all. But Traivyr is prepared to cover for me, and the fact that I'm already 'right next door' in Styvyn will get me to the scene much more rapidly. The fact that I'm already here before Gray Harbor or anyone else from Tellesberg can arrive will give me the opportunity to establish contact with Sharleyan's abductors before they do, too. It'll be much harder for them to try to ease me aside if I'm already conducting negotiations before they ever get here."

Halcom nodded slowly, although he recognized the sound of someone rationalizing a decision he'd actually made for quite different reasons. As rationalizations went, though, the bishop was forced to admit, it wasn't bad. Halbrook Hollow's plan for Sharleyan's abduction by Charisian elements hostile to the merger of Charis and Chisholm had been designed to deal Chisholm's faith in Charis a mortal blow. If the Charisians couldn't even bother themselves to adequately protect Chisholm's queen from their own lunatic fringe, the backlash in Chisholm would almost certainly be severe. Not only that, it would be most severe among Chisholm's commoners, the ones most likely to resist any machinations among the kingdom's aristocracy.

Halbrook Hollow's freely expressed reservations about the wisdom of her marriage, on the other hand, would be amply vindicated, and as the senior Chisholmian noble in Charis, not to mention his status as Sharleyan's uncle and the man who still officially commanded the Royal Army, he would inevitably be deeply involved in any negotiations with her captors. Even if someone like Gray Harbor might be tempted to exclude him, they would realize that the political consequences in Chisholm would be disastrous.

The demands of those captors would be extreme, but not impossibly so for someone determined to get his beloved niece back alive. The duke would agree in Sharleyan's name to withdraw Chisholmian support for the schism between the Temple and the Church of Charis, but only if she was returned to him alive. If his Charisian fellow negotiators objected, he would point out that Sharleyan could always countermand his own agreement later, but that for her to do that, they first had to get her back.

Once the critical point had been conceded, the "abductors" would agree to return Sharleyan to Halbrook Hollow's custody . . . but not in Charis. She would be delivered in *Chisholm*, which would naturally require Halbrook Hollow to return to Cherayth in person. And Halbrook Hollow would arrive sufficiently in advance of her return to engineer the downfall of Baron Green Mountain and Queen Mother Alahnah's regency, which would inevitably have been weakened by the proof of just how unwise the alliance with Charis had actually been in the first place. He'd have to be careful about exactly how he managed that, but given command of the army, it shouldn't prove impossibly difficult. Especially not when he accepted his old friend Green Mountain's resignation as first councilor with obvious sorrow and regret and solely because it was part of the abductors' demands.

Halbrook Hollow had no doubt that with Green Mountain out of the way, the more conservative—and ambitious—of Sharleyan's nobles would be prepared to reach a quiet, unspoken understanding with him, despite any past animosity. By the time Sharleyan herself arrived in Chisholm, he and his newfound allies would be firmly in control, at which point Sharleyan would find herself comfortably but securely—and very discreetly—under house arrest while Halbrook Hollow put "her" new policies into effect.

Unfortunately, as Halcom had pointed out to Shumay, the plan would never work—not in the long run. Which was why he had contrived his own, quite different strategy. And irritated as the bishop had been by Halbrook Hollow's unexpected arrival, more mature consideration showed him the hand of God behind the duke's foolish decision. After all, his response to what they actually intended had always been problematical, at best, whereas now . . .

"I see your reasoning, Your Grace," Halcom said in a slightly regretful tone as Mytrahn Daivys, one of the Temple Loyalists' group leaders, stepped through the kitchen door behind the seated Halbrook Hollow. "And, under the circumstances, it may not be an entirely bad thing you decided to come."

"I'm glad you can see it my way," Halbrook Hollow said.

"Now, it's important, as I say, that Sharleyan never realize I was here. So—"

His voice died in a hideous gurgle as Daivys seized his hair, yanked his head back, and slashed his throat.

Halcom pushed back from the table with a grimace of distaste as the flood of blood splashed across it. Some of the spray pattern pattered across his own tunic, and his grimace deepened. He dabbed at it instinctively, but his gaze never left Halbrook Hollow's face as the duke's eyes flared wide in horrified surprise, and then lost all expression forever.

"I'm sorry, Your Grace," Halcom said softly, reaching across the table to close the dead man's eyes. "But it truly is best this way, I think."

He drew a deep breath, suppressing an urge to gag as the coppery stink of blood and the stench of voided bowels filled the kitchen, and looked at Daivys.

"I'm sorry we had to do that, Mytrahn. He may have been a foolish man, and we all know he had personal political ambitions, as well. But he was also a son of Mother Church."

Daivys nodded, wiping his dagger clean on the duke's tunic, then cocked an eyebrow.

"What should we do with the body, My Lord?" he asked pragmatically.

"We're going to have to give that some thought," Halcom admitted. "I'm inclined to the theory that it might be best for him to simply disappear—perhaps another victim of the Charisian assassins. That will depend on how effectively Master Kairee has managed to cover himself and exactly what the Duke told people in Tellesberg he intended to do. For now, put him with his armsmen."

The Convent of Saint Agtha, Earldom of Crest Hollow, Kingdom of Charis

The marksman who'd killed Wyllys Gairaht stayed very still.

The opportunity to pick off the commander of Sharleyan's bodyguards had been an unanticipated gift from God, and he'd taken it without any order to do so. The captain would have had to die in the end, anyway, of course—there could be no survivors of this night's work—but the possibility that he might have cried out, or that one of his own men might have seen him fall, had been very real. On the other hand, the range had been less than forty yards, and the marksman hadn't missed a shot at that range since he was a boy. The odds had favored a silent kill, in his judgment, and the elimination of the bodyguards' central authority had struck him as well worth the risk.

He listened intently and heard nothing but the grumble of more thunder from the west and the sound of pre-storm wind, sighing through the trees about him.

Good, he thought, and carefully and quietly re-spanned the arbalest.

▼   ▼   ▼

Edwyrd Seahamper glanced up at the sky with a frown as full darkness settled over Saint Agtha's. The convent's grounds were dimly illuminated by the candlelight spilling out of various windows, and the convent chapel's stained-glass glowed warmly. The windows' patterns were simple, as became a convent dedicated to a saint who'd embraced a life of asceticism and vows of poverty and service, but the colors were richly vibrant.

And they won't do a thing for my nightvision, he thought grumpily.

There was just enough light to make the shadows even more impenetrable, and that was going to grow still worse, unless he missed his guess, once the rain began to fall in earnest.

Of course, I'll be able to see just fine *during the lightning flashes.*

His frown turned into a grimace at that particular thought. Contemplating the effect rain was going to have on little things like mail hauberks, cuirasses, sword blades, pistols, rifle barrels and bayonets, and anything else made of steel didn't make him feel significantly better, somehow. Still, he'd been rained on before, and he'd never shrunk yet.

He shrugged that concern aside and returned to the thought which had occasioned his frown in the first place.

Captain Gairaht should have been back half an hour ago. The captain was an energetic man who was disinclined to waste time. By now, he'd had time to hike clear round the convent twice, but there was no sign of him.

He probably found someone he thought needed a little . . . counseling, Seahamper thought. *God help anyone he thinks is slacking off on* this *detail! On the other hand, who'd be stupid enough to do that in the first place?*

His frown returned, deeper than before, and he glanced at Sergeant Tyrnyr. Tyrnyr, another Chisholmian, had been with the empress for the last eight years, which had made him the logical man to share Seahamper's watch here at the guest-house door.

"I wonder what's keeping the Captain?" Seahamper wondered out loud.

"I was just thinking the same thing," Tyrnyr replied.

"It's probably nothing, but it's not like him," Seahamper continued. "Trot over to the main gate, Bryndyn. See if he's over there."

"If he isn't?"

"Then make a circuit yourself. No, wait. If they haven't seen him, ask the Lieutenant to send one of the others around the circuit looking for him while *you* come back here."

"Got it," Tyrnyr acknowledged laconically, and went jogging off across the convent's manicured grass.

▼ ▼ ▼

The man crouched in the meadow just beyond the orchard came slowly upright once full darkness had fallen. Nailys Lahrak's face had been blackened, and his dark clothing blended seamlessly into the night about him. No one could possibly have seen him from more than a very few yards away. In fact, Lahrak himself couldn't see the other men out here under his command. Not that he was worried about them; he didn't *have* to see them to know where they were, given how often they'd rehearsed this particular task.

There'd been no way to predict with certainty where the empress' bodyguards would bivouac, but Lahrak was an experienced hunter and woodsman who'd grown up less than four miles from Saint Agtha's, and he was intimately familiar with the convent's grounds. He'd known it would be impossible for the abbess to house them inside the convent proper, and this had been by far the most logical place for them to pitch their tents *outside* its wall. There'd been two other possibilities, and they'd rehearsed attacks on those locations, as well, yet he'd been confident in his own mind that this would be the one that actually got carried out.

Now he took a small object from his pocket and raised it to his lips. A moment later, the plaintive, whistling call of a gray-horned wyvern floated through the night. The nocturnal hunter called three times, and somewhere in the windy darkness, another gray-horn replied.

▼ ▼ ▼

Captain Gairaht had posted sentries around his bivouac area, as well as around the convent itself, and those sentries hadn't been chosen for their lack of vigilance. They stood their posts alertly, yet they would have been more than human if they'd actually *expected* an attack. Especially an attack on their own encampment, rather than a direct strike at the empress. Their planning and training included the notion that the first move in an attack might be to neutralize their reserve force, but few of them had truly anticipated that level of sophistication or planning out of the sort of lunatics likely to launch a direct assault on Sharleyan or Cayleb.

Unfortunately, they weren't dealing with lunatics . . . only fanatics.

The sentries scanned the night around them attentively, yet they saw nothing. The men creeping steadily towards them through the darkness were effectively invisible, but they'd carefully located their own targets before darkness fell. They knew exactly where to find the sentries, and the guardsmen were backlit, however faintly, by their fellows' cooking fires.

For some minutes after the night-hunting wyverns had called to one another, nothing else happened. Then, abruptly, quite a lot of things happened almost simultaneously.

▼ ▼ ▼

The sudden whip-crack of a firing rifle split the night.

The sentry who'd seen his attacker at the last moment not only managed to get off his shot but hit the other man squarely in the chest. Unfortunately, the accuracy of his single shot didn't do a thing to the other two Temple Loyalists detailed to neutralize his position.

"Post Three! *Post Thr—!*" he shouted, identifying his post, but before he could complete the announcement, the other two were upon him. His rifle blocked the slash of the first man's sword, and a quick, savage riposte with the rifle butt knocked the attacker back on his heels, winning him just enough time to thrust with his bayonet at the other man. The second Temple Loyalist tried to twist aside, but he couldn't completely avoid the bayonet, and he groaned in anguish as the bitter steel slammed between his ribs.

He went down, yet even as the guardsman started to recover his bayonet, the swordsman whose first attack he'd deflected drove two feet of steel through his own throat.

None of the other sentries even saw their attackers. Two of them were turning towards the blinding muzzle flash of the first guardsman's rifle when their own assailants flowed over them; the other six were already too busy dying to even register that single shot.

Shouts of alarm came from the bivouac area, and someone began barking harsh-voiced orders as armsmen scrambled out of their tents, dropped eating utensils, sprang to their feet, and snatched for weapons. The men of the Imperial Guard responded quickly, almost instantly, with the discipline of unceasing training and hard-won experience. Yet for all the quickness with which they reacted, they were too slow. They were still scrambling for their mental balance, fighting past the stunned shock of complete surprise, when twice their own number of armed, disciplined assailants swarmed into their encampment.

Only a handful of the off-duty guardsmen were armored, and all of them were scattered about the bivouac area, where they'd been engaged in the routine, homey tasks of tending to their equipment, finishing their suppers, and preparing to get some rest before it was their turn to take over the duty watch. The Temple Loyalists were concentrated, moving in purposeful teams, and they went through the camp like a hurricane.

Men cursed, grunted, and cried out as weapons struck, and those of the guardsmen who'd managed to grab their own weapons fought back desperately. Men screamed as steel bit deep, or as the rifle butts of guardsmen who hadn't had time to load crushed flesh and bone. The night was hideous with the sounds of men slaughtering one another, and then, as abruptly as it had begun, it was over.

The meadow was littered with bodies, most of them in the livery of the Empire of Charis. Thirty-five of Sharleyan's bodyguards had been brutally eliminated at the cost of four dead and six wounded Temple Loyalists.

▼ ▼ ▼

"Langhorne!"

Sergeant Seahamper's face went white at the sudden explosion of carnage beyond the convent's wall. Despite his niggling concern over Captain Gairaht's tardiness, he'd no more expected an attack like this than anyone else. But Edwyrd Seahamper hadn't been his monarch's personal armsman for so many years for nothing.

"Rally!" he heard his own voice shouting. *"Rally!"*

Other voices shouted back . . . but not as many of them as he should have heard.

▼ ▼ ▼

The other groups of attackers had gotten as close as they could to the duty sentries, yet they'd dared not get *too* close until the bivouac had been attacked. They'd waited, straining at the leash of discipline and their orders, until the abrupt sound of that single rifle shot launched them at the guardsmen they'd been able to locate.

Half a dozen arbalest strings snapped, but this time, the darkness was the guardsmen's friend and, despite the short range, most of the bolts missed their targets. Not all of them did, but the sentries, unlike their comrades in the encampment, had anticipated that any attack on the empress would begin with an effort to neutralize them. That was why they'd chosen their positions so carefully.

Despite the intensity with which the Temple Loyalists had observed the convent since Sharleyan's arrival, they'd been unable to locate all of the guard posts outside the wall. The *moving* sentries had been relatively easy to spot as they paced back and forth, but the others were another matter. Under the circumstances, the attackers had no choice but to rely on their superior numbers and the fact that they knew approximately where any guards had to be stationed, even if they didn't know their exact locations. And unlike the sentries, they'd known the attack was coming. When the rifle shot split the night, *they* were poised and ready, and the night outside Saint Agtha's erupted in small, ugly knots of violence as they tried to rush the gates.

They failed.

Even taken by surprise, the men charged with protecting Empress Sharleyan struck back hard. Although the Imperial Guard had adopted the rifle as its primary weapon, its men knew better than to give away their positions by firing. Instead, they demonstrated to their enemies just how lethally effective a bayonet could be. The Guard was equipped with the same weapon as the Marine scout-snipers, with the same fourteen-inch bayonets, and they used the reach advantage of their weapons' length ruthlessly.

Temple Loyalists screamed as guardsmen appeared abruptly before or behind them and they suddenly found themselves transfixed by knife-edged blades of tempered steel. Unlike the surprised guardsmen in the encampment, the sentries formed coordinated teams, operating with the smoothness of long training and familiarity, and the initial assault on the main gate and on the smaller gate in the western wall failed.

The one on the northern gate was another matter. The heavy woodland had allowed the Temple Loyalists detailed for that attack to get much closer before darkness fell. They had a clearer idea of where their enemies were located, and they charged furiously, prepared to accept their own losses if they could close quickly with the guardsmen.

They succeeded . . . almost.

All eight sentries on the northern wall died, but eleven more Temple Loyalists died with them. And before the sergeant commanding the detachment went down, he turned and threw the gate key over the wall. The senior surviving attacker screamed in frustration as he realized the stout iron gate was locked, but he wasted no time trying to batter his way through it. Instead, he and his remaining men turned and ran towards the western gate.

▼　▼　▼

The ten-man reserve Captain Gairaht had posted just outside the convent chapter house reacted almost instantly to Seahamper's shout. They knew the drill for responding to a surprise attack as well as the sergeant did, and they closed in around the guesthouse in automatic reaction. It was their job to ensure the empress' safety first, rather than allowing themselves to be diverted into racing towards apparent threats which might well turn out to be diversions. Once the center was secure, they could move to reinforce the perimeter.

▼ ▼ ▼

The eight men on the western gate killed eighteen Temple Loyalists at the cost of five of their own. The sergeant commanding the detail and one of his two surviving troopers were both wounded, but they managed to retreat through the gate and lock it behind them before the surviving attackers could get themselves reorganized for another attempt. The three guardsmen fell back to join the reserve around the guesthouse, even as rifle fire began to crackle at the main gate.

▼ ▼ ▼

Lieutenant Hahskyn had been waiting for Captain Gairaht with increasing impatience. He, too, had begun wondering what could have been keeping Gairaht, even before Tyrnyr arrived at the main gate with Seahamper's message, but he'd no more suspected his commanding officer might already be dead than Seahamper had.

That didn't keep him from reacting quickly. He'd recognized the sound of the initial rifle shot even before he heard Seahamper shouting the alarm, and he and his men knew precisely what to do.

Just as the reserve's initial responsibility was to surround the empress and be certain *she* was secure, the perimeter teams' responsibility was to hold their positions at least until the situation had clarified. The ten men of Lieutenant Hahskyn's detachment didn't need him to tell them that.

They didn't need him to tell them how to do it, either, because he and Gairaht had walked the entire perimeter together immediately after their arrival. They'd discussed contingency plans for each position and briefed their men on exactly what they were supposed to do under each of those plans, and now the men on the gate put that briefing into action.

Unlike the Guard's other positions, the approach to the convent's main gate was relatively well illuminated, and Hahskyn had positioned additional lanterns farther down the approach lane, along both sides, to extend the reach of the existing lighting. Because of that, the Temple Loyalists assigned to seize the gate had found it impossible to work their way as close as their fellows had managed to do at the other gates. They had farther to go, which gave the guardsmen more time to realize what was happening, and when *they* charged, they met the accurate fire of ten rifles at point-blank range.

A third of them went down, thrashing and screaming. The others continued their charge, but the sudden carnage in their own ranks had half-stunned them and shattered their formation. This time, it was the guardsmen who met the shock of combat unshaken, and their white-hot fury and the reach of their weapons proved decisive. Only one of them was lightly wounded, and the handful of surviving Temple Loyalists fell back, leaving the approach to the gate carpeted with the bodies of their fellows.

"Sergeant Tyrnyr!" Hahskyn snapped while the gate detachment reloaded quickly. "Get back to Sergeant Seahamper and make sure the Empress is safe!"

"Yes, Sir!"

The sergeant dashed towards the guesthouse, and Hahskyn turned to his senior noncom.

"Check the other gates!" he said. "Then report back here."

"Yes, Sir!" The second sergeant saluted quickly and disappeared into the darkness, and Hahskyn looked at the remaining members of his detachment.

"All right, boys," he said grimly, "I don't know who these bastards are, but there's Shan-wei's own lot of them. Fall back behind the gate."

Faces tightened as his men realized what he was saying.

They and the other perimeter guards were supposed to be the reaction force, the ones who counterattacked once the situation had been stabilized. Closing and locking the gate behind them was an explicit admission that they were too outnumbered to consider taking the fight to the other side.

▼ ▼ ▼

"Shan-wei take it!"

Charlz Abylyn swore viciously as he surveyed the bodies sprawled outside the convent's main gate. The carefully worked out plan had visualized getting inside in the first rush, where the Temple Loyalists could get to grips with the entire strength of Sharleyan's bodyguards while the guardsmen were still stunned by the sudden surprise attack. The last thing they'd needed was to allow troops of the Imperial Guard's caliber to recover from their initial shock and confusion!

Unlike some of his fellows, Abylyn had always had his reservations about the likelihood of successfully rushing the gates, yet even at his most pessimistic, he hadn't anticipated the carnage Lieutenant Hahskyn's men had wreaked. He didn't know how well the attacks on the other gates had gone, although it was obvious they hadn't broken through, nor did he know—yet—how well the attack on the bivouac area had gone. If the other prongs of the assault had taken casualties as heavy as his, however . . .

He looked up as a runner dashed up to his position. He recognized the newcomer as one of Nailys Lahrak's men, although he didn't know his name.

"Well?" he asked sharply.

"Their camp's gone," the runner panted, his expression fierce with triumph in the dim glow spilling from the gateway's distant lanterns. "All of them—dead!"

Abylyn grunted in satisfaction. Although he didn't share the other man's obvious pleasure at the death of men who were only doing their duty, however mistaken their loyalties might have been, at least he could be confident the other half of the empress' bodyguards weren't going to come swarming up his backside while he dealt with the ones in front of him.

"Where's Nailys?"

"On his way." The runner's breathing was beginning to steady down, and he wiped sweat from his forehead. "We lost a few men of our own, and he's reorganizing. He'll be here shortly."

"That's good," Abylyn said sourly, and waved one hand at the locked gates. "As you can see, *we* lost more than 'a few men.' I haven't heard anything from the other gates yet, but it's pretty damned obvious they didn't break through, either. It looks like we're going to have to do it the hard way, after all."

The runner's face tightened as he followed Abylyn's gesture and the sprawled bodies of his fellow Temple Loyalists finally registered.

"God *damn* them!" the man hissed venomously.

"Whatever else we may think of them, they're doing their duty as they understand it, and they'll do it well," Abylyn said sharply. The runner looked at him, and Abylyn shook his head. "Don't make the mistake of thinking anything else. Not unless you really want to die out here tonight."

▼ ▼ ▼

"Edwyrd!"

Sergeant Seahamper turned towards the soprano voice. Empress Sharleyan stood in the guesthouse door, fully dressed, her expression strained, with Carlsyn Raiyz at her side, and he stepped quickly towards her.

"I don't know yet, Your Majesty," he said, answering the unspoken question in her eyes, and his voice was grim. "We don't know *anything* yet, but I'd just sent Bryndyn off to the main gate to find out if anyone had seen Captain Gairaht when all hell broke loose. From the sound of things, there have to be a lot of them. I think they hit the bivouac first . . . and I don't hear any more sounds of fighting from there."

The skin around her eyes tightened, but she didn't flinch, and he felt a surge of pride in her.

"I think we must have held at the gates, or they'd already be here," he continued, offering her the unvarnished truth, "but there's no way we have enough manpower to keep them from getting over the wall somewhere if there are enough of them. I expect to see Lieutenant Hahskyn shortly. In the meantime, please stay inside. And blow out as many of your candles as you can. I don't know for certain that there aren't marksmen already out there on the grounds somewhere, and I'd rather not give them lighted windows to silhouette targets for them."

▼   ▼   ▼

Thunder crashed louder, rapidly approaching from the west, and the first, sudden sheets of a Charisian deluge pummeled down from the heavens. Charlz Abylyn heard someone swearing in disgust, but he himself breathed a quiet prayer of thanks as he recognized the divine intervention on their behalf. The rain was bound to soak the priming of the Guard's rifles, and as far as he was concerned, that was one of the best things that could possibly happen.

"Thank Langhorne for the rain!" someone else bawled into his ear over the sudden tumult of rain and wind, as if to confirm his own thoughts. He turned his head and saw Nailys Lahrak.

"Amen," Abylyn said fervently, then leaned closer to the other man. "Your runner said you took the camp?"

"A clean sweep." Lahrak showed his teeth. "We've confirmed the body count. And as nearly as I can tell, only three or four of them managed to get inside on the other two gates."

"And how many did *we* lose?"

"I'm not sure," Lahrak replied, his voice harsher. "Not counting yours here, more than twenty, less than forty, I think. I'll know better in a few minutes; we're still coming in and getting sorted out."

Their eyes met. They'd anticipated losses of their own, and they and their men were prepared to pay whatever price was demanded of them, but losses that heavy this early were more than merely painful.

"Mytrahn will be here with his people shortly," Abylyn said.

"I don't like waiting, giving them time to get set in there," Lahrak objected.

"I don't, either, but we've already lost almost as many men as they have, and if we're going to have to go over the wall, I want enough people on our side to be damned sure we can spread *them* too thin to stop us when we do. And we're going to need all the swords we can get once we get to the other side, too."

Lahrak's expression was sour, but he grunted in unhappy agreement.

"In that case," he said, "let's get our people reorganized while we wait."

▾ ▾ ▾

Edwyrd Seahamper completed his nose count as torrents of rain lashed the convent's grounds. He'd sent a runner to the abbess, warning her to take the sisters to the chapel and keep them there, out of harm's way. He wished he could have provided them with better security than that, but he was spread far too thinly to even think about that.

"I make it thirteen, plus the two wounded," he said to Bryndyn Tyrnyr, who'd returned from the main gate.

"Plus the ten with the Lieutenant," Tyrnyr agreed.

"So, twenty-six."

"Twenty-five," Tyrnyr corrected flatly. "Zhorj isn't going to make it. He's coughing up blood."

Seahamper swore softly. Sergeant Zhorj Symyn was the Charisian-born guardsman who had commanded the picket on the west gate. He'd not only held it long enough to get his surviving men back to the guesthouse, but he'd managed to bring all of the picket's rifles, as well. Yet Seahamper couldn't afford to dwell on the knowledge that another good man was dying. He couldn't even take the time to go tell a man who'd become his friend goodbye.

"Twenty-five, then," he said harshly, and the two guardsmen looked at one another grim-faced. That was less than a third of their original strength, and they had no illusions about what had happened to any of their unaccounted for fellows.

"I think we need the Lieutenant here," Seahamper said. "Why don't you go and—"

"Why don't you stay right where you are, instead?" another voice interrupted, and Seahamper looked up to see Lieutenant Hahskyn. Rain streamed from the rim of the officer's helmet, and the other guardsmen with him were equally sodden-looking, but Seahamper had never seen a more welcome sight.

"Good to see you, Lieutenant," he said with commendable understatement, and Hahskyn smiled grimly.

"Sergeant, if you think *anything* about this situation is 'good,' you and I need to have a little talk," the Charisian said.

"I meant *relatively* good, Sir."

"Well, that's a relief." Hahskyn's smile broadened fleetingly, then vanished. "The Empress?"

"Inside." Seahamper twitched his head at the small guesthouse.

"She knows what's happening?"

"As well as any of us do, Sir."

"It isn't good, Edwyrd," Hahskyn said more quietly, his voice barely carrying to the sergeant through the sound of wind and rain. "I don't think they've given up just because we managed to bloody their nose at the gates. I think they're reorganizing, maybe rethinking, but they aren't going to just turn around and walk away. Not unless we managed to hurt them one hell of a lot worse than I think we did."

"No, Sir," Seahamper agreed harshly.

"I thought about sending a runner to Captain Hywyt," the lieutenant said even more quietly. His eyes met Seahamper's. "I didn't."

Seahamper nodded, his face bleak. The odds would have been against any runner's making it through the attackers who'd undoubtedly surrounded the convent. And even if someone could have accomplished that miracle, whatever was going to happen would undoubtedly be over and done before he could cover the eleven miles to the galleon anchored in the small port which served Saint Agtha's and bring back a relief force.

"All right, Sergeant." Hahskyn inhaled deeply. "I'll take charge of the outer perimeter. You've got the inner perimeter. And watch yourself, Edwyrd. If it all comes apart on us, you're the one she's going to be looking for, the one she's most likely to listen to."

He looked deep into Seahamper's eyes, his own eyes bleak.

"Keep her alive," he said. "Whatever you have to do, keep her alive."

▼ ▼ ▼

"It's a good thing you insisted on more men, My Lord," Mytrahn Daivys told Bishop Mylz grimly.

The bishop and Father Ahlvyn had arrived some minutes after Daivys himself, and they were as thoroughly soaked as any of the others. The bishop's teeth chattered lightly as the rain and wind chilled him, and his expression was strained as the gateway lanterns and occasional lightning flashes showed him the bodies of Abylyn's dead sprawled motionless in the rain. The sight chilled his heart far more thoroughly than the storm chilled his flesh.

Stop that, Mylz! he told himself. *You knew what it was going to be like before you ever set your hand to it. And no one promised you that doing God's will would be easy or cheap.*

"What happens next?" he asked out loud.

"Nailys and Charlz are about done sorting out their men," Daivys told him. "They're down to only about seventy between them, but my people are still intact. We'll take the lead."

Mylz Halcom nodded, but his face was tight. If Lahrak and

Abylyn had only seventy men left, then their attack teams had already lost well over half their original strength.

"All right, Mytrahn," he agreed. "God knows you're better equipped to manage this sort of thing than I am."

"You just concentrate on putting in a good word with Him for us, My Lord," Daivys said. "We'll take care of the rest."

▼ ▼ ▼

Ahndrai Hahskyn had positioned his remaining men as carefully as he could.

He couldn't disperse them too widely, especially not in the middle of a booming thunderstorm where visibility was measured in feet, not yards. Unit cohesion could vanish effortlessly under those conditions, and the one thing he was certain of was that he and his men were badly outnumbered. He couldn't afford to let this disintegrate into an uncoordinated melee. Nor could he count on their rifles and pistols to fire in the midst of such a downpour, even assuming they'd been able to see well enough to pick out targets. It was going to come down to cold steel, and that meant making his stand around the guesthouse itself.

He'd considered moving the empress into the main chapter house, but he'd quickly rejected that possibility. First, the chapter house's apparent defensibility was deceptive. Its walls were relatively thin, it had too many windows and doors, its internal architecture would have divided his guardsmen into isolated detachments, and he didn't have enough men to cover all the potential access points. Second, he was positive the empress would have refused to endanger the nuns. If not for the first set of considerations, he would have been quite prepared to haul Sharleyan bodily to the safest possible place and take his chances on her displeasure in the event of his own survival. Unfortunately, the guesthouse *was* the safest possible place . . . such as it was, and what there was of it.

On the limited plus side, the guesthouse stood well away from any of the convent's walls. Anyone who wanted to attack it would have to cross the manicured grounds, which would provide them with no concealment or cover, although the poor visibility tended to cancel that particular defensive advantage.

During the respite while the other side was obviously reorganizing, Hahskyn and Seahamper did their best to improve their positions. Saint Agtha's offered little to work with, but the sisters' three farm wagons and pair of carts had been dragged out of the stables and turned upside down to form a rude strong point covering the guesthouse's single door, and the walls of an outbuilding near the stableyard had been quickly demolished. The loose stone provided far too little building material for any sort of breastwork, but Seahamper had seen to it that the individual rocks were scattered all around their position. It wasn't as good as caltrops would have been, but in the darkness, those unexpected, all but invisible lumps of rock were guaranteed to come as unpleasant surprises to charging men.

Now the surviving guardsmen waited. All of them were veterans who could compute the odds against them just as well as Hahskyn or Seahamper. They knew what was going to happen in the end, if there were enough attackers out there to continue the assault, and their faces were grim as they thought about the life of the young woman behind them.

▼   ▼   ▼

Empress Sharleyan looked up quickly as Edwyrd Seahamper stepped into the plainly furnished, dimly lit guesthouse bedchamber. Water dripped from her personal armsman's cuirass and helmet, droplets pattering on the stone floor, and she recognized the stark desperation restrained by discipline in his eyes.

"How bad is it, Edwyrd?" she asked quietly.

"About as bad as it could be, Your Majesty." His expression was grim. "I'm pretty sure Captain Gairaht must be dead." Sharleyan winced in pain, but not in surprise, and he continued unflinchingly. "Lieutenant Hahskyn's in command now, but we're down to twenty-five men, and we don't know how many we're up against or how badly we may have hurt them. It's obvious they knew how many of *us* there were, though. If they keep coming, it'll be because they believe they've got the strength to win."

She nodded, her face tight with fear, and he reached out to take her hand in both of his.

"I don't know if we can stop them." His voice was harsh, sawtoothed with intensely personal worry, as he made himself admit the thing he feared most in all the world. "If we can't—"

He broke off, jaw clenching, and she squeezed his hand.

"If you can't," she told him, "it will only be because no mortal man could have. I know that, Edwyrd. I've never doubted it."

His mouth tightened further, and he drew a deep breath.

"We don't know what it is they want, Your Majesty—not for certain. Oh, we know they want *you,* but they may well want you alive, not dead."

"Do you really think that, Edwyrd?" she asked gently. "Or are you just trying to reassure me?"

"I think it really is possible," he told her levelly, letting her see the truth in his eyes. "Even likely. They haven't tried talking to us yet, so there's no way to *know* what they want, but I can think of a lot of ways you'd be most valuable to someone alive."

"Ways they could use me against Cayleb or Charis or Chisholm, you mean."

"Maybe, but even if they could, you'd still be *alive*, Your Majesty."

"At that high a cost?" She shook her head. "I've known since the day I took the throne that a queen—or an empress—is as mortal as anyone else, Edwyrd. I've tried to live *as* a queen, and as someone who had no need to fear when the time came to face God. And a queen—or an empress—has a final duty to her subjects. I won't let myself be used against all that I love or the people I'm responsible for."

"Your Majesty—" he began, his voice starkly appealing, but she shook her head again.

"No, Edwyrd. How long have you known me? Do you truly think I would want to live at the cost of the sort of damage someone could use me to inflict on all the people who have trusted Cayleb and me?"

He gazed deep into her eyes and saw the truth, the determination. And the fear. There was no fatalism, no eagerness to embrace death, but neither was there panic. She wanted to live as desperately as *he* wanted her to, yet she meant exactly what she'd just said, and in that moment, despite his raw anguish over what was about to happen, he felt more pride in her than he'd ever felt before.

He reached up and touched the side of her face with one hand. He hadn't touched her that way since she'd been a child, weeping with pain after a tumble from her horse had dislocated her shoulder, and she smiled in memory, despite her fear, as she pressed her cheek against his palm.

"Your Majesty—" He had to pause and clear his throat. "Sharleyan, if I don't have the chance to tell you this later, it's been the greatest honor of my life to serve as your armsman. And . . . your father would be very proud of you."

She squeezed his other hand more tightly, eyes bright with tears, and he drew a deep breath.

"It's raining too hard for anyone to fire a rifle or a pistol out there, Your Majesty," he said more briskly. "It's going to be bayonets and cold steel, but we've got nine extra rifles and an entire stack of pistols." He didn't have to explain why the rifles were "extra," and she nodded in grim understanding. "They may not fire outside," he continued, stepping over to the bedchamber's single window and using his mailed elbow to sweep every pane of expensive glass out of its frame, "but they'll fire just fine *inside.*"

He leaned out to close the shutters, drew his dagger and cut a loophole in them, then turned back to her.

"It won't stop a bullet or an arbalest bolt, Your Majesty, but it'll give you at least some concealment, and Daishyn Tayso's taken a leg wound. He's too unsteady to be much use outside, so I'm sending him in here to give you someone to reload."

"Someone to reload for *me,* instead of the other way

around?" she asked with a faint gleam of humor, despite her fear, and he snorted.

"Your Majesty, your uncle may not think it's a fitting hobby for a queen, but every man in your detachment knows you're a better shot than almost any of *them* are. And, frankly, just now, I don't really care what your uncle may think about it."

"Edwyrd is right about that, Your Majesty," Father Carlsyn said. "And I wish now that *I'd* learned to shoot one of these things. Unfortunately, I didn't, but if Daishyn shows me how, I'm sure I can at least learn how to help him load them for you."

Raiyz's expression was strained, but he managed a crooked smile when she looked at him. Seahamper smiled back at him in approval, then looked around the bedchamber one last time before he stepped back.

"I'll get Daishyn in here with the rifles and pistols, Your Majesty."

"Thank you, Edwyrd." She followed him to the door, then leaned close, rising on her toes, and kissed his bearded cheek. "I love you," she said softly.

"I know, Your Majesty." He touched her face once more. "I know."

▼   ▼   ▼

"All right," Mytrahn Daivys said to Nailys Lahrak and Charlz Abylyn. "We're all ready?"

The other two team leaders nodded. It had taken longer to get their men reorganized than they'd expected. On the other hand, the convent's isolation meant they had all night, and they might as well take the time to do it right. No doubt the guardsmen on the other side of the convent wall had been doing the same thing, and none of them were particularly happy about that thought, but there was only a limited amount Sharleyan's bodyguards *could* do.

Lahrak and Abylyn had redistributed their remaining men to give each of them slightly less than half the strength with which they'd begun the night. Daivys' so far unscathed team was still at full strength, which gave the Temple Loyalists a total of just over a hundred and fifty men.

"They've had time to recover from the surprise and get themselves organized again," Daivys continued. "They aren't going to go down easy. Be sure your men understand that."

Lahrak and Abylyn nodded again, although Abylyn's eyes flickered with a touch of what might have been resentment. He didn't need Daivys telling him what his own men had already discovered the hard way.

Daivys saw the other man's expression and started to say something else, then changed his mind. After all, if that was what Abylyn was thinking, he had a point.

"All right," he said again, instead, and smiled grimly as he pointed at the oilskin-wrapped powder charge fastened to the locked main gates. "I'm pretty sure you'll both hear the signal to attack."

▼ ▼ ▼

Ahndrai Hahskyn's head came up as a sudden thunder crack and blinding flash that owed nothing to the thunderstorm exploded in the darkness.

"*Stand to!*" he shouted, and his remaining men tightened in readiness.

▼ ▼ ▼

Daivys' men charged through the shattered gates with a snarl. They streamed through the rain towards the guesthouse, making no effort to approach stealthily. The entire reason he'd used gunpowder to open the gate instead of simply clambering over the wall had been to fix the guardsmen's attention as firmly on *his* attack as he could. He wanted Sharleyan's protectors looking his way when Lahrak and Abylyn—who *had* climbed over the wall—hit them unexpectedly from the sides.

Daivys himself was one of the first through the gate. A quarter of his eighty-five men carried arbalests, although the chance of their actually getting to use them in a fight like this one was going to be was remote. All of the Temple Loyalists carried swords, as well, but the truth was—as Daivys was well aware—that the majority of the attackers were only mediocre swordsmen, at best. Some of them, like Daivys himself, were probably as good as any Imperial Guardsman; most had only limited military experience, and he found himself wishing he'd armed the lot of them with halberds or pikes—even lizard spears!

Getting this many men into position to attack the convent without anyone noticing had been difficult enough, even using weapons which could be easily hidden in the sort of agricultural wagons that wouldn't raise too many eyebrows in such a lightly inhabited area. Trying to do the same thing with ten- or twelve-foot pikes would have been far more difficult. He'd known and accepted that from the very beginning, but he hadn't counted on how great an advantage the length of the Guard's rifles was going to give them. Whatever Lahrak and Abylyn might think, he knew they were going to take more casualties—probably heavy ones—before this night was over.

But with a numerical advantage of more than six-to-one, they could *afford* casualties.

▼ ▼ ▼

"Watch the flanks!" Hahskyn shouted as the first charging figures loomed up dimly through the stormy darkness. Then a sudden, livid flash of blue-white lightning painted the darkness purple and showed him the mass of men hurtling towards him . . . just as the oncoming Temple Loyalists hit the lumps of stone Seahamper had scattered across the approaches to the guesthouse.

The Guard lieutenant's lips skinned back from his teeth as men went down, some of them screaming with the pain of shattered ankles, and their companions' headlong charge faltered. The surprise didn't even come close to *stopping* them, but it broke them up, left holes in their ranks, and slowed their momentum significantly.

The first of them reached the Guard's position behind the

arc of wagons and agricultural equipment protecting the guesthouse's only door. They flung themselves up and over the obstacle, only to find the deadly bayonets waiting on the other side. Sharp-edged steel punched into soft flesh, opening bellies and chests, slashing throats, and men shrieked in agony as blood splashed and steamed in the pounding rain.

The bayonet drill of the Imperial Guard had been developed by Major Clareyk and Captain Athrawes. It recognized not only a rifle's reach advantage over a sword, but also the fact that a rifle was shorter and handier than a spear or pike. That it could be used to parry or block, as well as to attack . . . and that it could kill or cripple with *either* end.

The men attacking Hahskyn's guardsmen had never confronted anything like it. They'd expected the rain to neutralize the guardsmen's rifle fire, and so it had. What they *hadn't* expected was the sheer lethality of bayonet-equipped rifles in the hands of men who knew exactly what they were doing with them.

▼ ▼ ▼

Mytrahn Daivys' eyes widened as the first dozen of his men tumbled back from the improvised barricade, writhing in agony or already dead. It was impossible for him to actually see what was happening, but it was obvious that the Guard's bayonets were even more effective than he'd feared they might be.

The remnants of his front ranks drew back, and he swore as they pulled away from the piled wagons and carts. He understood their shock, but giving the defenders time to recover from the initial onslaught was the worst thing they could possibly have done.

"Hit them!" he bellowed. *"Hit them!"*

▼ ▼ ▼

Lieutenant Hahskyn felt a surge of hope as the attackers recoiled. He knew it was irrational, given the number of men out there, but it was obvious they'd been unprepared for the savagery of their reception. They drew back—not quite milling uncertainly, but clearly hesitant to engage again.

Then he heard a single raised voice.

"*Hit them!*" it shouted, harsh with command, and the mass of men snarled as it came on once more.

▼ ▼ ▼

Daivys' men surged back towards the guesthouse. Between broken ankles and bayonets, they'd lost a quarter of their strength in the first attempt, but there were still more than twice as many of them as there were of Haskyn's guardsmen, and this time they had a better idea of what they were up against. There'd never been any lack of courage or determination on their part. It was the surprise which had set them back on their heels, and this time, they weren't surprised.

They came on, shouting their hatred, hurling themselves into the Guard's teeth, and suddenly still more attackers were slamming in from either side as Lahrak and Abylyn brought their men into the assault. The guardsmen on the flanks turned to face their new enemies, but this time there were simply too many of them. Sheer weight of bodies carried them forward and over the barricade.

The guardsmen's discipline and training held them together, pairs of men fighting as teams, trying to cover one another, but the melee enveloped them, and madness reigned. Discipline and training could accomplish only so much, even with all the courage in the world behind it, and the teamwork which had spelled possible survival came apart, overwhelmed by numbers and chaos. The night disintegrated into madly swirling knots of individual combat, and there were too few guardsmen to win that kind of fight.

The Imperial Guard died hard . . . but it died.

▼ ▼ ▼

Sharleyan Ahrmahk thrust the rifle barrel through the loophole Seahamper had cut and squeezed the trigger.

The brutal recoil of the big-bore, black powder rifle hammered her slender shoulder unmercifully. She felt as if a horse had just kicked her in the collarbone, but she turned and half-threw the fired weapon to Daishyn Tayso, then snatched up the last one from the rank standing against the wall. Most of the gunsmoke had stayed outside, but the smoke from the priming pan hovered and swirled, rising towards the bedchamber's ceiling to join the cloud already hanging there.

Someone hammered at the outside of the shutter. And a cluster of arbalest bolts hissed *through* the shutter. One of them snarled past Sharleyan's head, missing her by inches before it buried itself in the bedchamber door, and she thrust the rifle's muzzle through the loophole almost blindly and squeezed the trigger again.

Agony shrieked in the night like a tortured horse, the hammering on the shutter ceased, and she dodged to one side, reaching for the first of the waiting pistols, as yet another bolt splintered its way through the disintegrating shutters and sizzled past her.

▼ ▼ ▼

Edwyrd Seahamper fell back, fighting desperately. Somehow, Bryndyn Tyrnyr managed to stay with him, covering his left flank, as they cut their way through the wild, rain- and thunder-lashed madness, trying frantically to stay between the attackers and the guesthouse door. Behind them, they heard the whip-crack sounds of gunfire, and fresh desperation slammed through Seahamper as he realized what that meant.

His mind captured fragments of memory. Lieutenant Hahskyn, bayoneting one foe, his rifle spinning in his hands as its butt crushed another man's skull, and then the sword driving in under his arm, through the opening in the side of his cuirass, and the lieutenant going down. Another guardsman fighting desperately against two opponents, somehow holding both of them at bay, until a third took him from behind and cut his throat. A sword opened a bleeding gash on Seahamper's own cheek, another hammered the breastplate of his cuirass, a third glanced off his helmet, and somehow he and Tyrnyr were still on their feet, still falling back to where the pistol shots cracked behind them.

They reached the guesthouse door, and Tyrnyr shouldered Seahamper behind him as a fresh rush surged towards them. Seahamper staggered backward, half-falling through the doorway, and his heart twisted as two swords cut Tyrnyr down before he could follow.

There was no time to feel grief. There was only the desperate need to somehow protect the empress he'd guarded since she was a little girl. The young woman he'd helped to raise, and the monarch he'd proudly sworn to serve. The Temple Loyalists could come at him only down the hallway now, and he bellowed his own hatred as he met them with his red-running bayonet. Hot blood turned the stone floor slick underfoot, and bone crunched as one of the Temple Loyalists slipped and sprawled full length and he drove the butt of his rifle savagely downward onto the fallen man's neck. His world consisted solely of that hallway, of the men storming forward along it, of the growing, terrible ache of his arms and the stink of blood.

Thunder bellowed explosively, louder than ever, shaking the entire guesthouse, but it was a distant thing, unreal and unimportant.

And because it was, he never realized that *this* thunder came not from the west, but from the *east*.

▼ ▼ ▼

The pistol roared. The shape which had loomed in the window tumbled back out of sight, and Sharleyan's slim hands and wrists felt as if she'd just hit them with a hammer as she turned to toss the fired pistol to Daishyn Tayso. But the guardsman didn't take it. He sat still and silent in his chair, hands frozen in midmotion by the arbalest quarrel buried in his left eye socket.

"I've got it, Sharleyan!" Carlsyn Raiyz shouted. He snatched the pistol from her and started reloading it as she and Tayso had taught him. His hands were clumsy with the unfamiliar task, but he jerked his head at the window. "You worry about *that*!"

▼ ▼ ▼

"Go on! *Go on!*"

Mytrahn Daivys' voice was hoarse and cracked. His throat felt raw and broken, but he continued to shout, whipping his men on with his voice. He heard Charlz Abylyn shouting in snatches even through the tumult, as well, but Lahrak's voice had gone silent.

He saw the two guardsmen fighting in the very doorway of the guesthouse, and then one of them was down, trampled under the boots of his Temple Loyalists as they stormed forward. The madness had them by the throat. Survival itself had become unreal, immaterial, beside their driving need to reach their objective.

It's a good thing we don't want her alive after all!

The thought flashed through some tiny segment of his brain, and he knew it was true. His men's bloody-fanged hatred and determination would have made it almost impossible to take Sharleyan alive now, even if they'd wanted to.

I don't—

His thought broke off as an impossible peal of thunder crashed overhead. It was scarcely unexpected—although the rain had almost stopped for the moment, the storm was far from over—but this thunder crack was so loud, so violent, that he flinched. And then, suddenly, there was one more guardsman still on his feet.

Daivys blinked, scrubbing at his eyes to clear the rainwater still running out of his soaked hair, trying to figure out where that single guardsman had come from. It was as if he'd materialized out of the air itself.

The Temple Loyalist's eyes narrowed suddenly as he realized that *this* guardsman wasn't soaked with rain. But that was impossible . . . wasn't it?

He thrust the question aside. There would be time to worry about details later; right now, he had other things to attend to, and he charged.

This one doesn't have a rifle, either, he realized as the guardsman drew two swords. One was considerably shorter than the other, and something about them joggled a scrap of memory. Something about someone who carried *two* swords. . . .

The back of his brain was still grappling with the memory when a battle steel katana, moving so fast he never actually saw it move at all, slashed his head off his shoulders.

▼ ▼ ▼

What is *it about thunderstorms and assassination attempts?*

The question darted through Merlin Athrawes' mind as Daivys' head flew just as the rain begain pounding down once more. It was a distant thought, lost below the steely focus of his desperation as he charged into the Temple Loyalists from behind.

A part of him twisted in anguish, crying out in useless protest as he saw the Imperial Guardsmen sprawled amid the tangle of their enemies' dead. He'd known every one of those men. He'd helped train them, helped select them for their duty . . . and he'd watched every one of them die through his SNARC's remotes while the recon skimmer hurtled through the Safehold sky at better than Mach five.

Just flying at that velocity had constituted a risk he knew he couldn't truly justify. Despite the skimmer's stealth systems, that kind of speed in atmosphere generated so much skin heat that an orbital scanner—like the ones which might well be incorporated into the orbiting kinetic bombardment system Langhorne had left behind—just might detect it anyway. Yet even at that speed, it had taken him an hour and a half to make the flight from Corisande.

No one on Safehold had ever heard the incredible thunder of a supersonic aircraft at low altitude. Not until tonight . . . and very few of those who had just heard it were going to survive the experience, he thought grimly. Without the courage and determination of the men who had died in Sharleyan's defense, he would have been too late, anyway. Even now, he might be, and his sapphire eyes were merciless as he sliced into the Temple Loyalists.

Most of them never had a chance to realize anyone new had joined the battle. Merlin's nervous impulses used fiber optics, not chemical transmission. When he released the governors he'd set to keep himself from betraying his more-than-human abilities too badly, his reaction speed was a hundred times that of a flesh-and-blood human, and his impossibly sharp battle steel swords were driven by "muscles" ten times as powerful as any mortal man's.

He seemed to simply stride through his enemies, moving almost slowly, yet bodies cascaded away from him. The first few men he faced died far too quickly for them to realize there was anything particularly odd about the man killing them, but as the lightning picked him out, flashed in stroboscopic spits of brilliance from his flying swords and the sprays of blood trailing in their wake, their fellows recognized, however dimly, that they faced something they'd never imagined was possible.

"Demon!" a voice wailed. *"Demon!"*

Merlin paid no attention. There were twenty men between him and the guesthouse; three of them lived long enough to try to run.

▼ ▼ ▼

Edwyrd Seahamper had no idea what was happening outside the guesthouse. All *he* knew was that the seemingly endless stream of attackers who'd been crowding in upon him had abruptly disappeared. He could still hear shouts and screams through the tumult of the thunderstorm, though, and a pistol cracked behind him yet again.

He turned and ran down the short hallway to the bedchamber door.

"It's me, Your Majesty!" he shouted as he put his shoulder to the closed door. He burst through it into a bedchamber reeking of powder smoke just as Sharleyan stepped back from the shuttered window with a raised pistol in both hands.

Gunsmoke hovered like a thick, blinding fog, but he saw the last of the broken shutters fly into fragments as a human body hurled itself against them, and a man burst half-way through the opening. The intruder froze as he found himself staring into the muzzle of Sharleyan's pistol at a range of less than three feet, and then Seahamper felt as if someone had just smashed his ears between two sledgehammers as she squeezed the trigger.

She staggered a half-pace backward with the recoil, and the back of her enemy's head disintegrated as the massive bullet exploded through his skull. He disappeared back out the window in a spray of blood, tissue, and snow-white splinters of bone, and the empress turned towards Carlsyn Raiyz for another. But the priest, too, was down, an arbalest bolt standing out of the center of his chest while blood pooled thickly on the floor beneath him.

Sharleyan's face crumpled as she saw him, but then Seahamper shoved past her just as yet another Temple Loyalist tried to force his way through the window. The new assailant looked up, then screamed, both hands clutching at his chest, as Seahamper drove a vicious bayonet thrust between his ribs. The guardsman twisted his wrists as he recovered his bayonet, and another Temple Loyalist shrieked and fell away from him as he thrust yet again.

Behind him, Sharleyan reached for the last loaded pistol with frantic haste, and Seahamper swore harshly as *another* man tried to clamber through the window. He thrust yet again, and then, abruptly, there were no more attackers.

▼   ▼   ▼

Merlin Athrawes recovered, the corpse slithered off his battle steel blade, and suddenly he was the only man standing in the convent courtyard.

He looked around slowly, literally knee-deep in bodies, and for once his eyes were as hard as the composites of which they were made. This time he could afford to leave no survivors to tell wild tales about the *"seijin."* No doubt most of those tales would have been explained away as wild exaggerations, the way all the other tales about Merlin had been. But this time, the mere fact that *"Seijin* Merlin" had been here at all would be enough to generate all the accusations of "demonic influence" which had to be avoided at any cost. He'd already dispatched half a dozen of the Temple Loyalists' wounded, and little though he liked the thought of killing men who couldn't fight back, this time he was prepared to make an exception.

It's the penalty for treason, anyway—and it's not as if I didn't "catch them in the act," he thought harshly as he waded through the tangled drifts of men who were already dead, dealing with his grim task. He closed his ears to the pleas for mercy, to the prayers, and to the curses and concentrated on dealing death as cleanly and as quickly as he could.

And then there were no living men in the entire convent courtyard. But that didn't necessarily mean none of the attackers were left, he thought. Rain and darkness were feeble obstacles to his enhanced vision, and he easily picked out the two men waiting by the main gate.

He zoomed in, and his mouth tightened as he recognized them.

▼ ▼ ▼

Bishop Mylz looked at Ahlvyn Shumay as the screams, shrieks, and sounds of combat abruptly ceased.

The bishop's eyes were shadowed and dark, sick with the reality of the bloodshed and carnage he'd unleashed in the precincts of one of God's own convents. He'd thought he was prepared for what it would be like; he'd been wrong.

Please, God, he prayed silently. *Let it be over. Let Your will be done, but I beg You to spare me more of this.*

God returned no answer, and even as he prayed, Halcom knew it would be easier next time, and even easier the time after that. He didn't want it to be, but what he wanted couldn't change what was.

At least it's finally over . . . this time, he thought, and closed his eyes as he murmured another prayer—this one for the soul of the young woman who had just died at his men's hands.

He was still praying when a deep, icy voice spoke.

"Bishop Mylz, I presume," it said, and his eyes flew open, for he'd never heard that voice before in his life.

Shock bleached the color from his cheeks as he found himself facing not Daivys, or Lahrak, or Abylyn. *This* man wore the black-and-gold of the House of Ahrmahk, and Halcom had never seen him before. But then a sudden stab of lightning blazed sapphire in the guardsman's eyes, and Halcom's heart seemed to stop beating. Only one Imperial Guardsman had eyes that color, but he was with the Emperor in—

"You can't *be* here," he heard his own voice say, almost calmly.

"No, I can't be," the man in front of him agreed coldly . . . and he smiled.

Shumay moved suddenly, his hand darting towards his belt and the dagger sheathed there. The guardsman's eyes never flickered. He didn't even *look* at Shumay. His empty left hand simply snapped out like some impossibly swift serpent, closed on the priest's neck, and twisted. Shumay jerked violently, Halcom heard a ghastly, *crunching* sound, and then the guardsman opened his hand again.

Halcom's aide slithered to the ground in a boneless heap, and the guardsman's thin smile could have frozen the heart of the sun.

"Two hours ago," he said softly, "I was in Corisande, My Lord Bishop."

Halcom shook his head slowly, disbelievingly, his eyes huge.

"*Demon*," he whispered.

"I suppose, in a way," the other man agreed. "By your lights, at any rate. But you've failed, Bishop. The Empress is alive. And I tell you this now: your 'Church' is doomed. I will personally see to it that it is erased forever from the face of the universe, like the obscenity it is."

Halcom heard someone whimpering and realized it was himself. His hand rose, trembling uncontrollably as he traced Langhorne's Scepter in the air between him and the nightmare he confronted.

That nightmare simply ignored his hand, totally unaffected by the warding sign of banishment, and Halcom's breath sobbed in his nostrils.

"Your Langhorne is a lie," the guardsman told him coldly, precisely. "He was a liar, a charlatan, a lunatic, a traitor, and a mass murderer when he was alive, and if there truly is any justice in the universe, today he's burning in Hell, with that bitch Bédard beside him. And you, *Bishop* Mylz—you make a proper priest for both of them, don't you?"

"Blasphemy! *Blasphemy!*" Somehow Halcom found the breath to gasp the word through the vise of despair tightening about his throat.

"Really?" The guardsman's laugh was carved from the ebon heart of Hell. "Then take that thought with you, My Lord Bishop. Maybe you can share it with Langhorne while you squat on the coals."

Halcom was still staring at him in horror when the katana in the guardsman's right hand sliced through his neck.

The Guesthouse,
Convent of Saint Agtha,
Earldom of Crest Hollow,
Kingdom of Charis

Sharleyan finished reloading the last of the rifles and propped it upright against the wall beside its fellows.

"What's happening, Edwyrd?" she asked softly as she started on the pistols.

"I don't know, Your Majesty." Her last surviving guardsman stood to one side of the smashed window, staying as much under cover as he could as he peered out into the rain while blood dribbled down his slashed cheek, and his voice was taut. "In fact, I don't have the least damned idea, saving your presence," he admitted. "All I can say is that if there's no more fighting and no one's trying to climb in through this window, or come through that door," he twitched his head in the direction of the bedchamber doorway, "we're a lot better off than we were. And—" he turned to give her a tight, blood-streaked smile "—if we are, I think I've just experienced my first miracle."

Sharleyan surprised herself with a laugh. There was, perhaps, a shaky edge of hysteria in it, but it truly was a laugh, and she cupped her face in her palms, pressing her fingertips against her temples.

She felt the stickiness of blood on her hands. Some of it was actually hers, oozing from the cuts on her scalp and the left side of her forehead where splinters of broken shutter had cut the skin as the arbalest bolts came screaming past her. More blood had splashed her long skirts and Charisian-style overtunic, and her face and hands were blackened and smeared with powder smoke. Her right shoulder throbbed painfully, and she didn't want to think about how badly bruised it was. If she hadn't been able to move her right arm—painful though the experience had proven—she would have believed that shoulder must be broken.

The smell of gunsmoke, blood, and death was almost overpowering despite the pelting rain's washing effect. Water blowing in through the broken window had diluted some of the blood puddled thickly on the bedchamber floor, and fresh blood still dripped from the tip of Seahamper's bayonet like thick, pearl-shaped tears. Emotional shock drew a blessed patina of unreality between her and the world about her. Her brain worked with almost unnatural clarity, yet the thoughts seemed somehow distant, and the tearing grief she knew waited for her could not yet break through.

It will, she told herself bleakly. *It will . . . when you look around and you never see all those faces again.*

She prayed desperately that at least one of her guardsmen besides Seahamper was still alive, and guilt clogged her throat as she realized how unspeakably grateful she was that if only one could have survived, it had been the sergeant. But—

"Your Majesty," a deep voice spoke from the thunderstorm, and Sharleyan's hands snapped down from her face and her head jerked up as she recognized it.

"*Langhorne!*" Seahamper hissed, as he, too, recognized that impossible voice. The guardsman stepped reflexively between his empress and the window, and his bloody bayonet rose once more, protectively.

"Your Majesty," the voice said again. "I realize this is all going to be . . . a bit difficult to explain," it continued, and despite all of the horror which had invaded this dreadful night Sharleyan heard an edge of dry humor in the words, "but you're safe now. I regret," the voice had darkened once more, "that I couldn't get here sooner."

"*C-Captain Athrawes?*" Even now, Sharleyan felt a stab of irritation at the quaver she couldn't quite keep completely out of her voice. *Don't be such a twit!* the back of her brain told her sharply. *On a night like this, even one of the Archangels would probably sound shaken!*

"Yes, Your Majesty," Merlin replied, and stepped close enough to the window for both of them to see him. Seahamper's bayonet point rose a little higher, and he seemed to settle even more solidly into place, but Sharleyan leaned around him, looking past him, and Merlin studied her expression with his enhanced vision.

She looked terrible, he thought. Her hair had slipped its elaborate coiffure and hung in random braids. Her face was smeared with blood and powder smoke, and her eyes were dark with the knowledge of how many men—men she'd known and cared about—had died to protect her. Yet even after all of that, the familiar sharp intelligence still lived in those eyes, as well. Despite shock, grief, loss, and now the fact that she was forced to confront the sheer impossibility of his own presence, she was still thinking, still attacking the problem before her rather than retreating in dazed confusion or denial.

My God, he thought. *My God, did Cayleb luck out with you, lady!*

"How—" Sharleyan paused and cleared her throat. "How can you be here, Merlin?" She shook her head. "Not even a *seijin* can be in two places at once!"

"No, Your Majesty. He can't." Merlin bowed slightly, still staying far enough back to avoid triggering any protective reaction on Seahamper's part, and drew a deep breath. "Two hours ago, I was in Corisande, in my tent," he told her.

"Two hours?" Sharleyan stared at him, then shook her head. "No, that isn't possible," she said flatly.

"Yes, it is," he said, his tone compassionate. "It's entirely possible, Your Majesty. It simply requires certain things you don't know about . . . yet."

"*Yet?*" She pounced on the adverb like a cat-lizard on a near-rat, and he nodded.

"Your Majesty, Cayleb doesn't know I'm here. There wasn't enough time for me to tell him and still get here soon enough to do any good. As it is, I was barely in time. The problem is that there are secrets not even Cayleb is free to share—even with you, as badly as he's wanted to ever since you arrived in Tellesberg. How I got here, how I knew you were in danger, are part of those secrets. But despite all the reasons he hasn't been able to tell you, I had to decide on my own authority whether to risk letting you learn about them or to stand by and do nothing while you were killed. I couldn't do that. So now I have no choice but to tell you at least a part of the truth."

"Your Majesty—" Seahamper began sharply.

"Wait, Edwyrd." She touched him gently on his armored shoulder. "Wait," she repeated, and her eyes seemed to bore into Merlin.

"No mortal man could have done what you've done, *Seijin* Merlin," she said, after a moment. "The fact that you appeared so . . . miraculously to save my life—and Edwyrd's—inclines me to feel nothing but gratitude for God's miraculous," she reused the word deliberately, "intervention. But there are other possible explanations."

"Yes, Your Majesty, there are. And that's precisely why the secrets of which I spoke are so carefully guarded. Charis' enemies—*your* enemies—would immediately proclaim that my capabilities must be demonic and use that accusation to attack everything you and Cayleb hope to accomplish."

"But you're about to tell me they'd be wrong, aren't you?"

"I am. On the other hand, I'm as aware as you are that even if I *were* a demon, I'd be telling you I'm not. I had this same conversation with Cayleb, before Darcos Sound, but he'd already known me for over a year by then. You haven't. I know that will make any explanation I can give you even harder to believe and accept, but I beg you to at least try."

"*Seijin* Merlin," she said, her lips twisting wryly, "whatever you may be, I wouldn't be alive to be having this conversation, or feeling any crisis of doubt, without your intervention. Edwyrd wouldn't be hovering here, ready to stick a bayonet clear through you if he thought you intended to harm me, either, and that's almost as important to me as all the rest of it. Under the circumstances, I suppose the least I can do is at least listen to what you have to say."

Seahamper stirred slightly, but he kept his jaw clamped tightly.

"Thank you, Your Majesty," Merlin said with the utmost sincerity. But then he shook his head with a snort. "Unfortunately, I don't really have time to give you the complete story. It's already daylight in Corisande, and no one—including Cayleb—knows where I am. I've got to get back there as quickly as possible."

"You seem to be living an even more complicated life than I'd realized," Sharleyan observed, and he chuckled.

"Your Majesty, you don't know the half of it," he told her. "I think you're going to have to, though. Know, I mean. For now, I ask you to accept—tentatively, at least—that I'm neither an angel nor a demon. That the things I can do don't violate any natural or sacred law, however the Inquisition might regard them. That I wish you and Cayleb well, and that I will do all in my power to serve and protect both of you. That there are other people, good and godly people, who know about me and my abilities. And—" he looked directly into her eyes "—that I will die before I allow men like Zhaspahr Clyntahn to go on using God Himself as an excuse to kill and torture in the name of their own ambition and perverted beliefs."

"You're asking me to accept, even if only 'tentatively,' a great deal," Sharleyan pointed out.

"I know that. If you can, though, at least until you return to Tellesberg, I'll try to prove the truthfulness of all I've just told you. I'll admit now that I can't 'prove' all of it, but if you'll see to it that the balcony outside your quarters in the Palace is clear all night on your first night back in Tellesberg, I think I'll be able to produce a friendly witness you'll feel able to trust."

"Cayleb?" she asked quickly, her face lighting, and Merlin nodded.

"Managing the arrangements so that he and I can both disappear for several hours without sending the entire army into a furor is going to be difficult, you understand. That's one reason I can't give you a specific hour for our arrival. But I feel quite confident that when I tell him about what happened here tonight, he'll insist on coming to you himself. And, now that I think about it, I have two additional requests."

"Which are?" she asked as he paused.

"First, Your Majesty, there's the rather ticklish problem of what we do about your safety and the identity of the people who orchestrated this attack."

And I still haven't decided whether or not to tell you your own uncle was one of them, he thought.

"The identity?" she repeated, and he nodded.

"There aren't any survivors of the actual attack on the convent, Your Majesty," he said grimly. His enhanced vision noticed how Sharleyan's eyes widened . . . and how Seahamper's narrowed in satisfaction. "There are a few wounded over near the bivouac area, but I'll . . . deal with them before I leave. I don't much like having to do that, but I'm afraid I don't have a choice this time. If *any* of them were to realize I'd been here, the consequences could be disastrous.

"However, there are two bodies out beyond the main gate. One of them no longer has a head, although it's close enough to the body Edwyrd should be able to find it. I think it would be a very good idea for him to do just that."

"May I ask why, *Seijin* Merlin?"

"Of course you may, Your Majesty. Up until a few minutes ago, that head belonged to one Mylz Halcom, the ex–Bishop of Margaret Bay."

Sharleyan looked at him in disbelief, but Seahamper grunted as if in sudden understanding.

"Apparently, the good bishop has been providing organization and leadership to the Temple Loyalists in Charis ever since he decamped from Hanth Town. I think it would be a good idea to take his head back to Tellesberg where his fellow bishops can positively identify it. And while they're doing that, you might mention to Baron Wave Thunder that Traivyr Kairee has been the main source of Halcom's funding. Tell him I can't prove that yet, but that I'm sure he'll find the evidence he needs if he looks under the right rocks. Tell him that, in particular, he might want to take a close look at the crew of Kairee's schooner, *Sunrise*."

And if he does, maybe I won't have to be the one to tell you about your uncle, after all. That's probably cowardly of me, but right this minute, I don't really care.

"I think we can probably manage that," Sharleyan told him, her voice equally grim. "And the second thing you wanted?"

"Edwyrd loves you, Your Majesty," Merlin said gently. "And right now, he's afraid of what I might still turn out to be. So, I'd like to ask you to do two additional things for me when you return to Tellesberg. First, speak privately to the Archbishop. Tell him every single thing I've just told you, and seek his judgment on whether or not you should listen to anything more. And, second, please arrange for Edwyrd to be there as well when Cayleb and I turn up. I think no one would be surprised if you feel the need for a little additional security after something like this, so perhaps you could insist that Colonel Ropewalk post Edwyrd on your balcony. I want him to hear everything Cayleb and I tell you *when* we tell you. I want him to be able to make up his own mind, and to know that no one and nothing is attempting to harm you."

"I can do both of those things," Sharleyan assured him, not trying to hide her relief at his mention of the archbishop.

"Thank you, Your Majesty."

He bowed deeply, then straightened and met Seahamper's eyes.

"You did well here tonight, Sergeant," he told the Chisholmian quietly. "Her Majesty is fortunate to have you."

Seahamper said nothing, and Merlin smiled crookedly.

"I know you're still trying to make up your mind about me, Edwyrd. I'm not surprised. In your place, *I'd* probably have already gone ahead and stuck that bayonet into me. If you'll allow me to, I'd like to give you a little advice, though."

His tone turned the final sentence into a question. After a moment, Seahamper nodded.

"I'm reasonably certain I've identified and dealt with—or will have dealt with, shortly, at any rate—all of the Temple Loyalists behind this particular attack. I can't be absolutely positive of that, however. And even if I could, there's no way *you* could be. So, I think the proper way for you to proceed is to assume that you and the rest of Her Majesty's detachment managed to deal with the attackers, but not to be overly confident that there aren't one or two of them left still in the woods. Under those circumstances, the logical thing for you to do would be to send one of the sisters—or their gardener, if the Abbess can dig him out of his hiding place under his bed—to *Dancer* with a message for Captain Hywyt. Tell him you want a company of his Marines, loaded for kraken, as an escort back to the ship. And while you're waiting for it to arrive, find someplace safe to park Her Majesty while you stay between her and any doors or windows."

Seahamper considered Merlin's words carefully. Under normal circumstances, he would have taken them as an order, given Merlin's rank in the Imperial Guard. As it was, he was obviously thinking about their source with a rather greater degree of suspicion than usual. After several seconds, however, he nodded again.

"Thank you," Merlin said, his smile turning even more crooked for a moment. Then he bowed once more to Sharleyan.

"And now, if you'll excuse me, Your Majesty, I really must be getting back to Corisande."

"Oh, of course, *Seijin* Merlin," she said with a faint, slightly shaky smile of her own. "Don't let me delay you."

"Thank you, Your Majesty," he repeated, and disappeared into the pounding rain.

Sharleyan looked out the window after him for several seconds, then turned to Seahamper.

"Your Majesty, is this wise?" he asked her, and she laughed a bit wildly.

"*Wise,* Edwyrd? After a night like *this* one?" She shook her head. "I have no idea. I only know that without him— whoever and whatever he truly is—you and I would both be dead at this moment. Beyond that, I don't have the faintest idea of what's truly happening here, but I do know Archbishop Maikel and Cayleb are *good* men. If they know Merlin's 'secrets' and trust him as deeply as they obviously do, then I'm prepared to at least listen to what he has to say. And

I think he has a point about you, as well. I think it is important that you hear the same things I do."

Seahamper looked at her long and intently, and then he began to nod.

"I think you're right, Your Majesty," he said slowly. "I don't know what to think about all of this, either. But you're right about one thing. That man—or whatever he really is—saved your life tonight. I owe him at least the chance to explain how he did it."

"Good, Edwyrd," she said softly, and then drew a deep breath of her own.

"Right now," she said sadly, "I think it's time we went and found the Abbess and told her I'm still alive."

. XVI .

Emperor Cayleb's Headquarters Tent, Duchy of Manchyr, League of Corisande

I don't suppose there's been any word from Merlin?"

Lieutenant Franz Ahstyn, the second-in-command of Emperor Cayleb's personal guard, looked up as the emperor poked his head out through the flaps of his command tent with one eyebrow raised.

"No, Your Majesty," the lieutenant replied. "Not yet, I'm afraid."

"Well, at least he's capable of looking after himself," the emperor said philosophically, and withdrew into his tent once more.

Ahstyn gazed at the closed tent flaps for a moment, then glanced at Payter Faircaster. The huge sergeant was the only other member of the emperor's personal guard, aside from

Captain Athrawes himself, who'd been with him when he was still crown prince. Which meant he was also the only one of them who'd served with *Seijin* Merlin ever since the mysterious foreigner had appeared in Charis.

"Don't ask me, Sir." Faircaster shrugged. "You know how much the Emperor relies on the Captain's . . . insights. If he's decided something's important enough to send the Captain off to take a personal look at it, then he must think it's *really* important. Like he says, though—the Captain can look after himself."

That last sentence, Ahstyn reflected, had to be the most mammoth case of understatement he'd ever heard in his entire life. Ahstyn hadn't personally seen the *seijin* perform any of the impossible feats legend ascribed to him. For his own part, the lieutenant was willing to assume the impossible feats in question had grown in the telling . . . which didn't mean Merlin wasn't the most dangerous man he'd ever known, anyway. All of Cayleb's personal guard had worked out against the *seijin*. No one was accepted for the detail which was already becoming known as the Emperor's Own until Merlin had personally tried him out in a no-holds-barred sparring contest, and none of them had ever managed to best him with practice blades, hand-to-hand, or on the rifle range. In fact, none of them had even managed to make him sweat. Despite that, the tales about him carving his way single-handedly through hundreds of enemies aboard *Royal Charis* at the Battle of Darcos Sound probably weren't true. *Probably.* Ahstyn wasn't quite prepared to bet money on that, but he was pretty sure he didn't *really* believe it. After all, no matter how good the *seijin* might be, he was still only a single mortal man.

Probably.

Personally, the lieutenant suspected the tales about Merlin's prodigious lethality had been quietly encouraged by the then–crown prince and his Marine bodyguards. Focusing on his deadliness as a warrior had undoubtedly been a part of the careful cover story which had been constructed to protect the truth about Merlin's greatest value to Charis. Ahstyn hadn't really believed it when he and the rest of the Emperor's Own were first briefed on the *seijin*'s "visions." It had sounded far too much like the children's tales about *Seijin* Kohdy and his magical powers.

In this case, however, the tales had happened to be true. Ahstyn had seen too many examples of the emperor using those visions to doubt that, and he understood perfectly why it was essential to keep anyone else from knowing about the *seijin*'s true capabilities. And making certain everyone knew Merlin was the most deadly bodyguard in the world—which, after all, didn't take that much exaggeration—was the perfect way to explain why he was always at the emperor's shoulder. He wasn't there as the emperor's most trusted and . . . "insightful" adviser, as Sergeant Faircaster had so aptly put it; he was there to keep the emperor alive.

Which helped to explain why the other members of the detail had been more than a little concerned when the *seijin* didn't turn up for breakfast. Merlin always ate early, before the emperor was up, so that he could be already on duty while Cayleb was served, and he was as persistently perfect in his timing as he was with a sword. So when he was a full fifteen minutes late, Ahstyn had poked his head cautiously into the small tent Merlin had been assigned for his personal use.

He'd expected to find the *seijin* sitting crosslegged in the middle of the tent's floor, concentrating on one of his "visions." That, after all, was the reason he'd been assigned a private tent in the first place. To the lieutenant's astonishment, however, the tent had been empty, and the bedroll looked as if it hadn't been used at all.

That had been totally unprecedented, and more than enough to send Ahstyn to the emperor. To the best of Ahstyn's knowledge, Captain Athrawes had never once been absent when he was supposed to be on duty. And he'd certainly never simply disappeared in the middle of the night without at least telling someone he intended to! For that matter, Ahstyn had felt more than a little miffed by the clear evidence that Merlin had somehow gotten through the protective ring around the emperor without a single one of Cayleb's guardsmen noticing him. The man might be a *seijin*, but he wasn't invisible!

Fortunately, the emperor, at least, knew where Merlin had gone. Ahstyn had waited patiently while Gahlvyn Daikyn went in and roused the sleeping emperor. Then the valet had poked his head out of the emperor's sleeping quarters and beckoned for the guardsman to enter with his message. For just a moment, Ahstyn had thought he saw surprise in Cayleb's eyes, but he'd obviously been wrong.

"I'm sorry, Franz," the emperor had said, shaking his head with a wry smile. "I told Merlin I didn't want anyone to know, but I didn't expect him to take me quite that literally. I'd assumed that he'd at least tell the rest of the detail I'd decided to send him off."

"Send him off, Your Majesty?" Ahstyn had repeated.

"Yes." Cayleb had stood and stretched, yawning hugely, before he accepted a tunic from Daikyn. "Let's just say I needed a message taken to someone who couldn't exactly be seen opening a letter from me. Not if he wanted to keep his head, at least."

Ahstyn's eyes had widened for a moment. Then he'd understood, and the fact that the *seijin* had been able to filter through his own sentries without anyone spotting him explained exactly why the emperor had chosen him to carry a critical message to one of his agents behind the Corisandian lines.

"Obviously," the emperor had continued, turning back to face Ahstyn as he belted the tunic, "I'd prefer that no one else know about this."

"Of course, Your Majesty." Ahstyn had half-bowed. "I'll brief the rest of the detail immediately."

"Thank you, Franz. And I apologize. I'd rather hoped Merlin would be back by now. I hadn't expected you to have to cover his watch, as well as your own."

"Don't worry about *that,* Your Majesty." Ahstyn had smiled. "Captain Athrawes works longer hours than any of the rest of us. I don't mind giving up a little of my own off-duty time if you need me to."

"I know." The emperor had grinned at him. "Still, it would have been polite of me to at least warn you about it ahead of time."

Ahstyn had merely smiled, touched his left shoulder in salute, and withdrawn from the emperor's sleeping tent. He rather doubted that any other king or emperor on the face of Safehold would have worried his head for a moment over the convenience or inconvenience of one of his bodyguards.

Still, it was becoming apparent that even the emperor was growing impatient. It wouldn't be fair to call Cayleb's attitude *worried,* but that might be because, like Ahstyn himself, he found it impossible to conceive of any situation Merlin wouldn't be able to handle. There had to be one, of course; Ahstyn simply couldn't imagine what it might be. On the other hand—

"Sorry I'm late, Franz."

The lieutenant twitched and snapped around in disbelief as a deep, familiar voice spoke from behind him.

"Merlin?"

"In the flesh, as it were," Merlin replied with a broad smile.

"Damn it, Sir!" Ahstyn glowered at the neatly uniformed apparition which appeared to have sprung up out of the very ground. "I know you're a *seijin,* but how in Langhorne's name did you manage *that?*"

"Manage what?" Merlin's expression was innocence itself.

"You know exactly what!" Ahstyn half-snapped. "It's bad enough you got past all of us on the way *out,* but if you can get past us on the way *in,* as well, then maybe someone else could, too!"

"Actually, Franz, I wouldn't worry about that." Merlin shook his head, and genuine contrition softened his smile. "No one else is going to be able to duplicate the technique I just used. Believe me."

"I'm beginning to think there's a lot more truth to all the old-fashioned 'magic' stories about *seijin* than I thought there was," Ahstyn said.

"It's not magic, Franz. Just training and a few enhanced abilities."

"Sure it is."

"Well, unless you're prepared to go off to the Mountains of Light and spend a couple of decades training with me, I'm afraid that's about the best explanation I can give you." Merlin reached out and patted the lieutenant on the shoulder. "I'm really not *trying* to be mysterious, Franz. Although I will admit that the opportunity to show off a bit for people who are cleared to know about my little . . . peculiarities is one of my small pleasures."

"Which is probably why there aren't more of us cleared *to* know about you," Ahstyn told him sourly. "The way we keep dropping dead from heart failure holds the numbers down!"

Merlin laughed.

"Oh, it's not quite *that* bad! Besides, you're all fit and young. I'm sure that if anyone's hearts can take it, yours can."

"That's reassuring, Sir." Ahstyn gave his superior officer a very old-fashioned look for a moment, then grimaced. "I'm sure it was entertaining to scare me out of a year's growth, but the Emperor's been poking his head out of his tent every ten minutes on the minute. I think he expected you back some time ago."

"I know." Merlin shrugged. "It took longer to find His Majesty's . . . correspondent than I'd expected. And, to be honest, not even a *seijin* can run around too energetically without someone's noticing him."

"That really is reassuring," Ahstyn said with a smile. "In the meantime, though—"

He made shooing motions towards the emperor's command tent, and Merlin nodded. Then the *seijin* squared his shoulders, crossed to the tent, and rapped his knuckles smartly against the small bell hanging outside the closed tent flaps.

"Your Majesty, I'm back," he announced over the bell's shimmering musical note.

"Oh, you *are*, are you?" The emperor sounded undeniably testy. A moment later, he poked his head back out and gave his personal armsman an equally undeniably sour look. "I *thought* you said something about dawn," he said, and glanced rather pointedly at the late-morning sun.

"I did, Your Majesty," Merlin admitted. "There were a few complications, however."

"I don't like that word, 'complications,'" Cayleb said even more testily. "I suppose you'd better come in here and tell me about them, though."

"Of course, Your Majesty," Merlin murmured, and followed the emperor into the tent.

Ahstyn and Faircaster looked at one another.

"Don't worry, Sir," the sergeant said with a broad grin. "The Emperor's very fond of the *Seijin*, really."

▼ ▼ ▼

Cayleb let the tent flaps settle back into place, then turned to Merlin, crossed his arms across his chest, and raised both eyebrows.

"Don't you think," he said, "that it might be a good idea to keep me at least *generally* informed about these little expeditions of yours?"

There was a note of genuine anger in his voice, Merlin observed, and he had a right to feel it.

"Cayleb, I'm sorry," the man who had been Nimue Alban said soberly. "If there'd been time, I certainly would have told you. Unfortunately, there wasn't. In fact, I damned nearly didn't get there in time, after all."

Cayleb's anger visibly disappeared as Merlin's serious tone registered.

"Get where?" he asked.

Merlin gazed at him for a moment, wondering how Cayleb was going to react. He'd kept watch on the encampment through one of his SNARCs the entire time he'd been gone, and he'd been relieved when Cayleb automatically covered for his absence. He'd expected the emperor to do just that, but if he'd been a flesh-and-blood human, he would have held his breath when Ahstyn went to tell Cayleb about his own absence. Fortunately, Daikyn (who also knew the "cover story" about *Seijin* Merlin's visions) had made sure the emperor was fully awake before allowing Ahstyn in to explain why he'd awakened him in the first place, and the lieutenant had obviously half-expected to be told that Cayleb knew where Merlin was.

Still. . . .

"Sit down, Cayleb," he said, waving at one of the folding camp chairs by the map table.

"Just what are you busy preparing me for, Merlin?" Cayleb's eyes narrowed, but he sat in the indicated chair.

"I'm about to tell you that. But, before I do, you need to do two things. First, you need to understand that I *did* get there in time. And, second, you need to get ready to do the best job of acting you've ever done in your entire life."

"Merlin, you're starting to really scare me," Cayleb said frankly.

"That's not my intention. But I know you, Cayleb. When I tell you where I've been, and why, you're not going to take it . . . excessively calmly, shall we say? And it's not going to be easy for you to pretend I haven't told you, but you're going to have to."

"Will you please stop trying to reassure me?" Cayleb grimaced. "If you have to, you can sit on me after you've told me to keep me from running around the camp like a lizard with its head cut off. But if you don't get busy and tell me where the *hell* you've been, you're going to see a *really* good imitation of a volcano!"

Merlin smiled briefly, then squared his shoulders.

"All right, Cayleb. I'll tell you.

"Last night, I was going through the routine take from the SNARCs in Charis with Owl. I didn't really expect to find anything too surprising, but I was wrong. In fact—"

▼ ▼ ▼

Merlin didn't—quite—need to sit on Cayleb. It was a close thing, though.

"My God." The emperor's face was ashen. "My God! You're *sure* she's all right, Merlin?!"

"Positive," Merlin said reassuringly. "I kept an eye on her all the way back to Corisande, and Seahamper's no slouch. He personally sat on her while he sent one of the nuns down to the bay, and Captain Hywyt took two full companies of Marines back up to the convent under his personal command to fetch her. She's well on her way back to *Dancer* by now, and Hywyt and Seahamper are watching her like great dragons with a single cub."

"Thank God," Cayleb murmured fervently, closing his eyes. Then he straightened, stood up, and put his hands on Merlin's shoulders.

"And thank *you*, Merlin Athrawes," he said softly, looking into Merlin's dark blue eyes. "I already owed you far more than I could ever hope to repay. Now—" He shook his head. "Would you mind very much if we named our first son Merlin? Or—" he grinned suddenly "—our first daughter Nimue?"

"Either name would probably raise a few eyebrows, but I'd be honored."

"Good!"

Cayleb gave him a little shake, then stood back and drew a deep breath.

"I can see why you said I'm going to have to be a good actor. How is anyone supposed to act like nothing happened when a pack of madmen tried to murder his wife less than five hours ago?"

"I don't know," Merlin replied honestly, "but somehow, you're going to have to. On the other hand, it could be that you've built a little bit of cover for yourself already. That business about sending me off to deliver a message was a good recovery."

"Saw that, did you?" Cayleb grinned crookedly at him, his face beginning to lose a little more of its ashen hue. "I figured you'd have one of those SNARCs of yours keeping an eye on me, wherever you were."

"Of course I did. And since you didn't tell anyone what

sort of 'message' it was, you can go right on not telling them. Let all of them assume you've got more irons in the fire than they know about. And since you're not going to tell them what the message was, or who it was to, most of them will put their own . . . creative construction, shall we say, on whatever mood you appear to be in."

"That'll work for everyone but Nahrmahn," Cayleb said a bit sourly. Merlin raised an eyebrow, and Cayleb chuckled.

"Don't misunderstand me. If anyone had ever told me I was actually going to find out that I *liked* the man, I would've told him he was a lunatic. As it happens, though, I *do* like him, and the fact that everything you've seen indicates he's genuinely decided his best hope is to be loyal to me and Sharleyan only helps. But that man is fiendishly clever."

"I believe I mentioned something to that effect quite some time ago," Merlin observed mildly.

"Indeed you did. But my point at this particular moment is that I'm quite certain he's already deduced that '*Seijin* Merlin's' abilities are even more peculiar than all of the 'wild stories' about him would suggest."

"I wouldn't be a bit surprised if you're right about that." Merlin shrugged. "One of the problems when you're using a particularly sharp knife is keeping your fingers out from under the blade."

"You're taking this suspicion of mine mighty calmly, I must say."

"It's not going to help if I *don't* take it calmly," Merlin pointed out. "And assuming the man doesn't panic if he learns a little more of the truth, then he'll be even more useful as an analyst. Not to mention the fact that we'll be able to share even more of the raw data with him."

"Should I assume from that that you're thinking in terms of introducing him to the story we've given Payter and the rest of the detail?"

"As a matter of fact, I am. In fact, I think it might not be a bad idea to ask Nahrmahn to step in here."

"Right now?" Cayleb's eyes widened, and Merlin shrugged again.

"As long as we can keep the layers of our stories straight," he said with a crooked smile. "Let's see. We tell Franz and the rest of the detail you sent me off with a message to some unknown agent on the other side. They pass that on to the rest of the army, if anyone's wondering where I disappeared to. And we give that same story to Chermyn and the rest of your officers, which will also help explain why you wanted to see Nahrmahn. After all, who could be a better adviser where skullduggery and general, all-round sneakiness is concerned? Then, we tell *Nahrmahn* that where I really spent the morning was sitting in my tent having a vision of Saint Agtha's. We tell him everything I know about the assassination attempt and who was behind it and ask him for his reactions and what he thinks would be the best way to proceed. And we tell him the 'message' story is our official cover, and that he should simply tell anyone gauche enough to ask that he's not at liberty to discuss just who you might be sending messages to, or why you might be doing it."

"I'm beginning to get a headache keeping track of who knows which part of our current set of lies," Cayleb grumbled. He thought for a moment, then nodded. "I think you're right," he said. "And I expect Nahrmahn will take it fairly well. He's smart enough to understand why we couldn't risk telling him about something like this until we'd had a chance to evaluate how wholeheartedly he'd decided to support the Empire."

"Exactly."

"All right. But in that case," Cayleb met Merlin's eyes levelly, "do we tell *him* about Halbrook Hollow?"

"Cayleb, we're talking about your wife's uncle," Merlin replied quietly, then shook his head in self-condemnation. "We all knew he had Temple Loyalist sympathies, and I should have been keeping a closer eye on him. I had the capability, but as you pointed out to me quite a while ago, I just don't have the time to watch everything. I had to prioritize, and I made a serious mistake in his case. I think I let the fact that he obviously did love her make me overconfident. And I probably counted on Bynzhamyn's natural suspicion more than I had a right to." He shook his head again. "However it happened, I didn't make watching him one of my priorities, and it almost killed Sharleyan."

"But it didn't," Cayleb told him. "And as I also pointed out to you on the occasion to which you've just referred, it was inevitable that something like this was going to happen sooner or later. There's only one of you, Merlin. No matter how wondrous you seem to be, no matter how hard you drive yourself, there's only *one* of you."

"I know, but—"

"Stop beating yourself over this," Cayleb said sternly. "It's over, and she's still alive. That's the important thing. Now, you were about to say about the Duke?"

Merlin looked at him for a moment longer, then gave a slight nod of acceptance.

"I don't know whether or not anyone will find his body," he said. "Daivys shoveled enough dirt across him and his armsmen, and enough of that whole area is still the next best thing to virgin forest, that even searchers *looking* for a grave might well miss it. But if Wave Thunder goes after Kairee, his connections to Halbrook Hollow are almost bound to come out. And explaining away his mysterious disappearance at a time like this. . . ."

He let his voice trail off then, and Cayleb snorted sourly.

"Not exactly designed to put Sharleyan's Chisholmians' minds at ease, is it?" the emperor said.

"No. And especially not in the Chamber of Commons, given his close relationship with the Army and with Green Mountain. But that's not really what you were thinking about, anyway, was it?"

"No," Cayleb admitted with a sigh.

"She's a very smart lady," Merlin pointed out sadly. "Much too smart not to figure it out eventually, whether we tell her about it or not. Especially if Bynzhamyn goes after Kairee. So I suppose the real question is whether there's any point in trying to protect her."

"And how she's likely to react when she finds out we tried to," Cayleb agreed.

"Either way, I think we definitely need to tell Nahrmahn.

First, because his advice on how we handle that entire nasty part of the problem would be extremely valuable. Second, because he's as smart as Sharleyan is. Whether we tell him or not, he's going to figure it out, so we might as well tell him the entire truth—about that, at any rate—from the beginning and save everyone a little bit of time."

"You're right, of course." Cayleb's shoulders slumped. "I only wish you weren't. She loved him like a father, Merlin. This is going to break her heart. And, to be honest, I'm a little afraid."

"Afraid she'll blame it at least indirectly on you?" Merlin asked gently. "That she'll see her decision to accept your proposal as the real cause for what he did . . . and for his death?"

"Yes," the emperor admitted.

"I can't promise she won't, Cayleb. No one could. But Sharleyan isn't the first person who's had someone close to her disapprove of her marriage. And she didn't survive that long on the throne of Chisholm without learning to understand the way people's minds—and hearts—work where politics and power are concerned. Let's face it—she brought her uncle to Charis in the first place because she was afraid she wouldn't be able to trust him back home in Chisholm. She knew that much about him before she ever married you. People can punish themselves for things that don't make any sort of rational sense at all, of course, so it's possible she'll decide her marriage did 'push him' into the actions he took, however much her intellect knows the final decision was still his and his alone. But even if she does, I think she's more likely to blame *herself* for accepting your proposal than she is to blame you for extending it."

"I'd almost rather she did blame me," Cayleb said very quietly, looking down at his hand as he toyed with a box of marker tokens on the edge of the map table.

This time, Merlin made no reply. Silence hovered for several seconds, and then Cayleb straightened once more.

"All right," he said more briskly. "I think you're right about Nahrmahn, so I suppose I'd better send word that I want to see him."

"And while we're waiting," Merlin said, "you and I need to give some thought to the minor problem of figuring out how an emperor, who's also his own field commander, can disappear from his headquarters encampment for at least—oh, four or five hours in the middle of the night, shall we say?"

"Not to mention how we get the aforesaid emperor and field commander *out* of his headquarters encampment in the first place," Cayleb agreed. He shook his head and chuckled. "I'm really looking forward to actually seeing this 'recon skimmer' of yours—scared to death, mind you, but looking forward to it. But coming up with a way to get me out of here is going to be a lot harder than simply figuring out how to accomplish something as minor as, oh, convincing Hektor of Corisande that I'm really his best friend."

. XUII .

A Recon Skimmer in Flight, Aboue Carter's Ocean

Cayleb Ahrmahk's nose was pressed firmly against the inner skin of the armorplast canopy as the recon skimmer tore through the night heavens. He was the first native Safeholdian to actually fly in well over eight centuries, and Merlin could almost physically feel the young man's delight as the emperor sat in the flight couch behind his.

Getting the two of them out of the encampment had proved far simpler than Cayleb, at least, had assumed it would. It wasn't his fault he'd overestimated the difficulties, of course; unlike Merlin, he hadn't known about things like portable holographic projectors. Like the skimmer's smart skin, the projector strapped to Merlin's belt worked best under conditions of less than optimal visibility, but they'd been fortunate in the rain clouds which had moved in during the late afternoon. The rain hadn't come down very hard, but its mistiness had reduced visibility and helped the two of them blend into their background well enough that they'd been able to get a considerably earlier start, well before full darkness had fallen.

There hadn't been much point in leaving any sooner than that, given the time difference. Nineteen hundred in Corisande was only thirteen hundred in Tellesberg, but Merlin was just as happy to have the extra time in hand. It meant he didn't have to fly at high Mach numbers this time, which was good, since there weren't any handy thunderstorms to conceal his sonic boom and he'd just as soon not fly so fast he had to worry about the skimmer's skin temperature being picked up by any orbital sensors that didn't belong to *him*. And he preferred to get there a little early if he could. He could always spend the time circling high above Tellesberg, impossible for anyone to see from the ground below, and the earlier he could set the two of them down on Sharleyan's balcony, the better.

Cayleb had reminded Merlin rather forcibly of the emperor's younger brother when he actually saw the skimmer. In fact, if Merlin wanted to be accurate, he'd seemed *younger* than Crown Prince Zhan as Owl brought the vehicle into a smooth hover and deactivated the stealth features.

"Oh, *my*!" the emperor had murmured, watching through huge eyes as the skimmer abruptly snapped into visibility and settled gently into the drift of dead leaves carpeting the woodland clearing two miles outside his camp's perimeter.

His obvious delight had caused Merlin to look at the skimmer's lean, rakish gracefulness through fresh eyes, although he could scarcely imagine how its needle-nosed sleekness and swept wings must look to someone who hadn't grown up in a high-tech universe. Cayleb's reaction underscored the vast gulf between Nimue Alban's life experience and his own in a way that Merlin's time here on Safehold really hadn't.

The emperor had watched the canopy slide back and the boarding ladder extend itself, then clambered up it just a bit gingerly under Merlin's tutelage. He'd settled into the rear flight couch, and somehow he'd managed not to jump right back up out of it as its surface moved under him, configuring itself to the contours of his body. Fortunately, Merlin had warned him what would happen, but his astonishment had been obvious, anyway.

Merlin had taken him patiently through the various displays. He hadn't bothered to warn Cayleb not to touch anything he hadn't been specifically told he *could* touch. First, because Cayleb was smart enough not to do anything of the sort, anyway. Second, because Merlin had locked all of the flight controls to the front cockpit. He'd shown the emperor how to reconfigure his visual displays so that he could direct the skimmer's after optical head wherever he wanted to, and Cayleb had spent the first thirty or forty minutes of their flight delightedly swiveling the head and zooming in on the land, ocean, and islands under them.

He'd also spent those same thirty or forty minutes chattering about everything he could see from an altitude of just over sixty-five thousand feet. But now, finally, he'd sobered.

"So this is what Langhorne and the others took away from all of us," he said softly, sitting back in his seat again at last.

"This is a *part* of what they took away from you," Merlin corrected gently. "Believe me, Cayleb. As exciting and novel as all of this is for you, it's barely scratching the surface of what Shan-wei wanted to give back to your ancestors. Oh, Langhorne and the mission planners were right about one thing—for the first three centuries or so, they had to bury any memory of the infrastructure that could have produced something like this skimmer. The stealth systems built into it, and the fact that its signature would be so tiny and hard to pick up anyway, meant they could operate at least some similar vehicles without risking anything the Gbaba could have picked up without doing a detailed in-atmosphere search. And if they'd gotten close enough to do an in-atmosphere search, it wouldn't have mattered whether Safehold had possessed advanced technology or not.

"But you could have had this back—and everything else that goes with it—four or five hundred years ago without worrying about whether or not the Gbaba would stumble across you. Or, at least, without worrying that they'd spot you because they were actively looking for you, at any rate. *That's* what they took away from you, and from your parents, and your grandparents, and your great-grandparents."

"We could have had the stars," Cayleb half-whispered.

"With the exercise of a little bit of caution, yes," Merlin agreed. "In fact, from the starting point of the knowledge Shan-wei was trying to preserve in Alexandria, by now humanity would probably have developed a high enough level of technology to go looking for the Gbaba, instead of the other way around. Not to mention the fact that the average lifespan for someone born when Nimue Alban was alive was in excess of three hundred years."

"Or the minor consideration that the lying bastards left us stuck with 'spiritual shepherds' like Clyntahn," Cayleb added harshly.

"Or that," Merlin agreed.

"You know, Merlin," Cayleb said in a rather different voice, "up until this moment, despite Saint Zherneau's journal and the other documents, I haven't really been able to wrap my mind around what you mean when you talk about 'advanced technology.' Maybe that's because I haven't really tried to. I've been too concerned, too focused, on just surviving to really try to imagine what the future—or maybe I should say the past—could have been like. I guess the fact that you're alive, and the incredible things I've seen you do, should have given me a clue, but to be honest, I've still been thinking of you like *Seijin* Kohdy. You're not 'technology,' not something one of Howsmyn's mechanics might've designed or built if they'd only had the right collection of nuts and bolts and the right wrench. You're *magic*—any ninny could tell that! But now—"

He broke off, and as Merlin glanced into the small view screen beside the pilot's right knee, the pickup in the rear cockpit showed him the emperor's shrug.

"There was a writer once, back on Old Earth," he said. "He died over three hundred years—three hundred Old Earth years; that would be about three hundred and thirty Safeholdian years—before we met the Gbaba, but he wrote something called 'science-fiction.' His name was Clarke, and he said that any sufficiently advanced technology was indistinguishable from magic.'"

"'Indistinguishable from magic,'" Cayleb repeated softly, then nodded. "That's a good way to think of it, I suppose. And it makes me feel a little better, a little less like some sort of ignorant savage."

"That's good, because there's nothing 'ignorant savage' about you, Sharleyan, Nahrmahn—not even Hektor. Within the scope of the worldview you've been permitted by the Church, you're as smart, capable, and inventive as anyone in the history of mankind, Cayleb. In fact, while I wouldn't want you to get a swelled head or anything, you and Sharleyan are pretty damned incredible, when you come right down to it. All we have to do is break down the barriers Langhorne and Bédard built to keep you all in prison, and that intelligence, capability, and inventiveness will do the rest."

"Of course, breaking down the barriers is going to take more than simply defeating the Group of Four," Cayleb said. "I know you already told me that, but now, looking at all this, I think I finally realize what you really meant. Nobody who's grown up on Safehold is going to be ready for something like *this* without an awful lot of advance preparation. And I see now exactly why you said you can't just hand this over. Why we have to learn to build it—and accept it as something which isn't 'evil'—for ourselves."

"As Maikel says, one battle at a time," Merlin agreed. "First, we break the Temple's political and economic stranglehold; after *that*, we tackle the lies in the *Writ*, itself. And that, Cayleb, is going to be an even tougher fight, in a lot of ways. The fact that eight million literate colonists left so many letters and journals and personal accounts—absolutely honest ones, as far as they knew—of how they interacted with the 'archangels,' and about their experiences on the day of Creation itself, is going to leave us with a nightmare when we try to tell everyone they're all lies. The mere fact that I have a cave stuffed with technological toys isn't going to 'magically' make nine hundred years of faith disappear overnight . . . or make the people who share that faith feel one bit happier about the possibility of falling for 'Shan-wei's snares.' That's why we need people like Howsmyn, Rhaiyan, Rahzhyr Mahklyn, and all the rest. The Safeholdian 'scientific revolution' is going to have to come from within, not be handed over by some supernatural minion of Shan-wei, and the mindset that goes with it is going to have to in-fect the entire planet. I only hope we can avoid an entire series of religious wars between the people eager to embrace the new and the people desperate to defend the old as their only hope of salvation."

"I'm not going to see Safehold building these 'recon skim-mers' in my lifetime, am I?" Cayleb asked softly.

"I don't think so," Merlin confirmed, equally softly. "I wish you were, and I suppose it could happen. But I'm afraid of what would happen if we crammed the truth at everyone that quickly. Maybe things will change, maybe I'm being too pessimistic. But I've got enough blood on my hands already, Cayleb. I don't want any more than there has to be."

"I think I'm finally beginning to understand why you're so lonely, too," Cayleb said. "You're not just the only person who remembers where we all really came from. You're the one person who's going to see people like me and Father and Sharleyan die and leave you to go on, fighting the same fight without them."

"Yes." Cayleb could hardly hear the single word, and Mer-lin closed his eyes briefly. "Yes," he repeated more loudly. "And if you want to look at it one way, I think I've got a very good chance of being personally responsible for more blood-shed than any other single person in history."

"Dragon shit!" Cayleb snapped the two words so sharply that Merlin twitched upright in his flight couch. "Don't go bor-rowing guilt, Merlin!" the emperor continued in an only mar-ginally less sharp tone. "Langhorne and Bédard and Schueler are the ones who built this mess, and Clyntahn and Maigwair and Trynair are the ones who were willing to murder an entire

kingdom to prop it up! Do you think that somehow all of that would magically stop if you'd simply decided to leave 'well enough alone'? You're not that stupid."

"But—"

"And don't give me any *'buts,'* either," the Emperor of Charis growled. "It's a mess, thousands of people are going to be killed, maybe millions of them, and you—and I, and my children, and my *grandchildren,* if that's what it takes— are going to be right in the middle of it. But in the end, Merlin Athrawes—or Nimue Alban—the truth is going to win. And part of that truth is the fact that a batch of self-serving, corrupt tyrants chose to use God Himself as a prison for all the rest of us. I remember something I read in that *History of the Terran Federation* Saint Zherneau left. Something about watering the tree of liberty with the blood of patriots. Personally, I'd just as soon water it with the blood of a few *tyrants,* but that doesn't change the truth that sometimes people have to die for the things they believe in, for the freedom they want for themselves and their children. And it doesn't make *you* responsible for it, either. Blame the people who built the prison, the ones who've spent so long trying to strangle the tree. Don't blame the person trying to tear that prison down."

Silence hovered in the recon skimmer's cockpit for several seconds, and then Merlin Athrawes smiled crookedly.

"I'll try, Your Majesty," he said. "I'll try."

Empress Sharleyan's Suite,
Royal Palace,
City of Tellesberg,
Kingdom of Charis

The Empress of Charis sat curled up in the comfortable arm-chair in her luxurious suite in Tellesberg Palace with her feet tucked under her. It was the way she'd sat when she was worried ever since she'd been a little girl, despite the best efforts of her mother, Baron Green Mountain, her uncle, and Sairaih Hahlmyn to break her of the habit. She'd never been quite certain why a queen wasn't supposed to sit that way, at least in private, and her various relatives and loyal retainers had discovered that her stubbornness extended to more than simply matters of state.

She smiled almost wistfully at the thought. It was comforting to think of such ordinary, everyday arguments and decisions, rather than the monumental upheavals of the last two days. As frightening as the world she faced had sometimes been before, at least she'd always been reasonably confident she understood it. Now, it was as if a doorway she hadn't even known existed had been opened, revealing the existence of an entirely new layer of reality, one that threatened to stand every comfortable, known fact on its head. She'd begun to feel at home here in Charis, only to find herself once again in a new and unknown land, and this time she had no map, no shelter, and no guide to explain its frightening mysteries to her.

The thought sent a stab of loneliness through her, and she looked around her suite. It was larger and airier than the one she'd enjoyed in her "own" palace in Cherayth, with the pointed arches, high ceilings, thick, heat-shedding walls, and windowed doors of Charisian architecture. She'd grown accustomed to its exoticness in the months since Cayleb's departure. What she hadn't grown accustomed to—and didn't *want* to grow accustomed to—was Cayleb's absence.

You've got more to be worried about than that, you nincompoop! she told herself sternly. *You've only been married to the man for seven months, and he's been gone for almost six of them! Don't you think it might be a little more sensible to spend your time worrying about whether or not Merlin is a demon, after all, than how much you miss a man you've hardly had time to even* start *to know?*

No doubt it would have been. And, in fairness, she had spent quite a bit of time worrying about that very point, despite Archbishop Maikel's reassurance. Her relief when the archbishop confirmed that he'd known the truth about Captain Athrawes all along had been the next best thing to unspeakable, although he'd declined to be more specific about that truth until after she'd spoken again with Merlin and Cayleb. *That* had been more than a little frustrating, but she'd had to admit that it made perfectly good sense under the circumstances. And the archbishop's serenity when he confirmed that he knew about Merlin had done more to relieve her mind than she might have believed possible, although the fact that Staynair honestly *believed* Merlin was neither a demon nor an angel didn't necessarily mean the archbishop was correct. Nonetheless, she'd told herself, if Archbishop Maikel was prepared to grant Merlin the benefit of the doubt, the least *she* could do was listen to what the *seijin* had to say. Especially since, as she'd pointed out to him herself in the smoke, blood, and bodies of the failed assassination attempt, she would most certainly have been dead along with the members of her guard detail without him.

Her eyes darkened, and she felt her lower lip trying to quiver once again as she thought about the men who had died to keep her alive. It had been their job, their duty, just as she had duties and responsibilities. She knew that. Yet knowing was a frail shield against the faces she would never see again . . . and the faces of the wives, children, fathers and mothers, sisters and brothers they'd left behind.

Stop that, she told the tears prickling at the backs of her eyes. *You can't bring them back. All you can do is to make their deaths* mean *something. You're an empress; be an empress. You know who wanted to kill you—who did kill your guardsmen. Halcom may be dead, thanks to Merlin, but there are scores of other Halcoms just like him out there. Now you've got another reason not to let them win.*

It was true, yet there were times when she felt herself being spread far too thin. When the duties and the responsibilities and the debts looming before her seemed fit to crush one of the archangels themselves. When all she wanted was to find some way to pass those duties and responsibilities to someone else. To find the time for the girlhood which had been stolen from her by a throne. Surely she was entitled to at least a little sliver of a life that was hers and hers alone, not the property of Chisholm, or of Charis. *Hers.*

And that's why you're thinking about Cayleb, she thought. *Because he is yours. You don't have all of him any more than he has all of you—the two of you are too many other people, have too many other responsibilities. But the* Writ *says that to those of whom much is asked, much is also given. It hasn't seemed that way ever since Father died . . . until now.*

Her lips stopped trying to quiver and curved in a tender smile, instead. A marriage of state, yes, but so much more. Her heart seemed to lighten magically as she remembered his smile, the taste of his lips, the magic of his touch and her own responsiveness to it. Archbishop Maikel had said a true marriage was a union of shared burdens and tasks, of two hearts, two minds, and two souls, and he'd been right. There was no challenge the two of them couldn't face together, and if it was silly of her to believe that of a man she'd actually known for barely two months, then so be it. She—

Knuckles rapped gently on a doorframe and she heard Sairaih's voice murmuring something. A moment later, Sairaih herself appeared in her bedchamber door.

"Edwyrd is here, Your Majesty," she said.

It was a mark of how shaken Sairaih had been by the assassination attempt that she didn't even frown when she saw her mistress' feet tucked up under her like some schoolroom child's. Sharleyan felt an urge to chuckle at the thought, but instead, she only nodded.

"Ask him to come in, please."

"Of course, Your Majesty."

Sairaih swept an abbreviated curtsy and withdrew. A few pulse beats later, she returned with Sergeant Seahamper.

"Edwyrd," Sharleyan said quietly. She winced slightly with the pain in her brutally bruised shoulder as she held out her hand, and the sergeant, armed and armored for duty, bent over it, kissing it, then straightened. "I see Colonel Ropewalk decided I could have you after all," the empress observed with a faint, bittersweet twinkle.

"Your Majesty, if you want me on your balcony all night, then that's where I'll be," he told her simply.

"I remember when you used to sit outside my bedroom door when I was a girl," she told him. "Right after Father died. I could always sleep knowing you were there, my very own armsman, to keep the nightmares outside, where they belonged. Maybe I'll be able to sleep tonight, too."

"I hope so, Your Majesty."

"So do I." She glanced at her maid. "Go on to bed yourself, Sairaih."

"I'm not that tired, Your Majesty. If you need—"

"If you're not that tired, you certainly ought to be. And I'm not exactly a little girl anymore, even if I do need Edwyrd to help keep the bad dreams at bay tonight. Go to bed. If it turns out I need you, I promise I'll ring and drag you back out of bed without a qualm. Now scoot!"

"Yes, Your Majesty." Sairaih smiled slightly, produced another half-curtsy, and withdrew, leaving Sharleyan alone with Seahamper.

"She's as much a worrier as you are, Edwyrd," the empress said.

"Funny how you seem to have that effect on people, Your Majesty."

"Undoubtedly because people don't trust me to have the sense to come in out of the rain."

"Undoubtedly, Your Majesty," Seahamper agreed, and she laughed a bit sadly.

"We really have been through a lot together, haven't we, Edwyrd?"

"And, if you'll pardon me for saying it, Your Majesty, I'm hoping we'll be through a lot *more* together, as well."

"I suppose that *would* beat the alternative. Still, I'd just as soon not have another couple of days as strenuous as the last two," she said, and this time, he only smiled, his eyes as sad as her own, and nodded in agreement.

"Well," she said more briskly, "I suppose we should get you out onto the balcony."

She climbed out of the armchair and tucked one arm into his armored elbow, walking barefoot across the bedchamber's cool marble floor beside him in a fluttering swirl of nightgown and steel thistle-silk night robe. He opened the latticed door onto the enormous balcony and escorted her out into the cool darkness of evening.

The sky was a cobalt-blue dome, beginning to flicker faintly with stars, and the moon was a burnished copper coin just peeking above the eastern horizon, but it wasn't quite completely dark yet. She could look out over the roofs of Tellesberg, across the waterfront to the twinkling lights of galleons moving out of the harbor on the wings of the falling tide. Other lights were beginning to glimmer across the capital, and she raised her head, savoring the cool kiss of the breeze on her face.

Yet for all the present moment's tranquility, there was a different feel to Tellesberg tonight, she thought. One at odds with the peacefulness of the scene before her. If she'd ever doubted that her new subjects had taken her to their hearts, the wave of fury which had swept across Tellesberg on the heels of the news of the assassination attempt would have put them to rest forever.

"How bad *was* it, really, Edwyrd?" she asked now, quietly, looking at the tendrils of smoke still rising down near the river. She could see them, despite the gathering evening, because they were underlit with a faint, reddish glow, pulsating gently where embers and coals still smouldered at their feet.

"Not as bad as it could have been, Your Majesty." He shrugged. "The healers are going to be busy for a while, but the City Guard got there in time to keep anyone from actually getting lynched, and the firemen held the fires to just the one block around the church."

"I wish it hadn't happened," she said softly, still gazing at the smoke, and Seahamper shrugged again. His sympathy was manifestly limited, she realized. Then again, her armsman had always been a . . . direct sort of fellow. But then he surprised her just a bit.

"They're *angry,* Your Majesty," he said. "Angry and, I think, ashamed. As far as we know, all of the bastards—begging your pardon—were Charisians, and they feel as if their entire kingdom's at fault."

"That's so foolish," she said sadly. "Three-quarters of the detachment were Charisians, too, and they died to *stop* it!"

"Of course they did. And, eventually, the rest of Charis is going to remember that, too. But not yet."

Sharleyan nodded, knowing he was right. Knowing she couldn't really have expected anything else, and grateful that, as Seahamper said, the City Guard had arrived in time to prevent any fatalities, at least. She wished the Guard could have gotten there in time to prevent the mob from torching the Church of Langhorne the Blessed, too, yet that probably would have been expecting too much.

She'd wondered, from time to time, if Cayleb and Archbishop Maikel had truly been wise to allow the Temple Loyalists who openly professed their continued allegiance to the Council of Vicars to claim one of the city's larger churches as their own. She'd been especially concerned when the people who continued to worship there began to move themselves and their families into the tenements and apartments clustered around the church, like their own little enclave in the heart of Tellesberg. What had happened today only underscored her earlier concerns, but she still hadn't been able to come up with a better solution than the one Cayleb had adopted. Whatever its drawbacks, she agreed with him and the archbishop that the last thing they could afford to do would be to confirm the Inquisition's allegations about the "bloody suppression of the true Church in heretic Charis" by actually persecuting the Loyalists.

Well, we didn't take their church away from them . . . not that the Inquisition is going to admit that for a moment!

She stood there, sharing a companionable silence with Seahamper while she felt the darkness settling fully into place, then inhaled deeply.

"I suppose I should go back inside," she told him.

"Well, if you *insist,*" another voice said. "But we just got here, you know."

She jumped, then turned with a squeak of astonishment— and joy—as she saw the two men standing behind her.

"Cayleb!"

Later on, she could never remember actually having moved. All she remembered was his arms around her, the crushing power of his embrace, and the hot, sweet taste of his mouth. She was vaguely aware of Merlin and Seahamper standing back, watching the two of them with perfectly matched smiles, despite her armsman's own astonishment at the other men's abrupt appearance, and she couldn't have cared less.

Then, finally, Cayleb's arms relaxed at least enough for her to breathe, and she heard Merlin chuckle.

"I figured they'd have to come up for air soon," he said to Seahamper. "I was beginning to think I might have been wrong about that, though."

Seahamper turned a chuckle of his own into a rather unconvincing cough, and Cayleb smiled.

"I hope you remembered to bring your cards," he told Merlin.

"And why might that be, Your Majesty?" Merlin inquired politely.

"Because you and Sergeant Seahamper are going to have to spend at least an hour or so out here amusing yourselves with something!"

"Ah, the impetuousness of young love!" Merlin replied, and Sharleyan felt her cheeks heating even as she laughed. It was odd. Not even Seahamper or Sairaih had ever displayed that sort of familiarity, and yet it felt perfectly natural— appropriate, even—coming from Captain Athrawes.

"How did the two of you *get* here?" she demanded, and Cayleb shook his head.

"That's part of what we're going to be telling you about, love," he said. "And, trust me, you're going to find it hard to believe, but it's all true. And thank God for it! If Merlin hadn't been keeping an eye on you, hadn't been able to get there in time . . ."

His voice trailed off, and Sharleyan gasped as his arms tightened almost convulsively about her once again. He realized he was crushing her and relaxed his embrace with a murmur of apology.

"Don't worry. I'm not that fragile," she assured him, reaching up to cup the side of his face in her hand. Whiskers stirred against her palm, like a brush of wiry silk, and she smiled. "And when did you grow all of *this*?" she demanded, tugging on the newly grown beard.

"I've just been a bit too busy to shave," he told her with a smile of his own.

"Of course you have." She tugged again, hard enough to make him wince, then looked past him at Merlin.

"You did say you'd bring a character witness with you, *Seijin* Merlin."

"Yes, I did, Your Grace." He bowed to her. "To be honest, I don't think I could have left him home in Corisande even if I'd wanted to. Not that it didn't take quite a bit of ingenuity to figure out how to cover our absence. Well, *his* absence, at any rate."

"How *did* you cover for it?"

"At this particular moment, love," Cayleb told her, "the 'Emperor's Own' is guarding an empty sleeping tent. They know it's empty, even if they don't have a clue just how far away from 'home' I am at this moment. As far as they're concerned, *Seijin* Merlin and I are creeping off all alone to meet a representative of a faction in Manchyr which may be prepared to turn against Hektor in return for the proper guarantees of their own positions. They weren't too happy about my going off with a single guardsman, even Merlin, but they weren't prepared to argue about it. Well, not *too* long and hard, anyway. And they—and Nahrmahn—understand that it's essential that *no one,* not even General Chermyn or Bryahn, know about these supposed negotiations. Lieutenant Ahstyn and Gahlvyn are prepared to keep anyone out of the tent until morning, but we can't guarantee that something isn't going to come up. So, much as I hate to say it, we really don't have a lot of time. And," he smiled wickedly into her eyes, "we *are* going to spend an hour or two of the time we do have together, My Lady."

"Which means," Merlin murmured with a smile of his own while Sharleyan's blush turned hotter, "that we'd better get started on those explanations I promised you, Your Grace."

▼ ▼ ▼

"No wonder you've always seemed a bit . . . unusual to me, Merlin," Sharleyan said, the better part of two hours later. She shook her head slowly, her eyes still huge with wonder, as she gazed at the guardsman who was over nine hundred years old.

Seahamper looked almost dazed. For the first time in memory, he'd obeyed her command to sit in her presence without even token argument as Cayleb began his explanation. Now it was his turn to look at Merlin, and he shook his head.

"I guess I don't feel quite so old and feeble compared to you anymore, Captain," he said. "I don't pretend to understand all of that. For that matter, I don't pretend to understand half of it! But at least now I know how you manage to do some of the . . . peculiar things I've heard stories about. You really *did* strangle three krakens with your bare hands, didn't you?"

"Not quite," Merlin replied with a crooked smile. Then he

turned back to Sharleyan. "Have we answered your questions, Your Grace?" he asked quietly.

"Oh, you've answered the ones I *knew* I had," she assured him. "Of course, you've given me at least a couple of dozen new ones!"

"It does seem to work that way, love," Cayleb agreed.

"The thing that's going to be hardest is accepting that all my life, all I was taught about God and the Archangels was a lie." Sharleyan's voice was low and bitter, and Seahamper's jaw tightened as if she spoke for him as well.

"Your Grace, you really need to discuss that with Archbishop Maikel," Merlin told her. "You already knew men like Clyntahn and Trynair could twist and abuse the faith of others. All they've really done, though, whether they knew it or not, is to follow in Langhorne's and Bédard's footsteps. The fact that corrupt and ambitious men are willing to lie even about God Himself in their pursuit of power is nothing new, I'm afraid, but it doesn't make everything you've ever believed about God untrue. In fact, as much as I hate to admit it, men like the Archbishop and the Brethren of Saint Zherneau believed the truth when they saw it in large part *because* of the values they'd been taught by the religion Langhorne and Bédard invented to enslave every Safeholdian. Things like that tend to happen when people use the goodness of God as a weapon. My own belief is that despite the best efforts of a Langhorne or a Bédard, they aren't able to keep God from creeping through the cracks when He wants to."

" 'Creeping through the cracks,' " Sharleyan repeated softly, then smiled. "I suppose that's one way to look at it, at least. And I truly do understand why the Archbishop is unwilling to challenge the Church's fundamental doctrines at this point."

"At the same time, though, we're building up a sort of inner circle of our own," Cayleb pointed out. "The four of us here, the Brethren, Dr. Mahklyn and a handful of others in the Royal College. We'll have to go on being almost insanely careful who else we tell about it, but it's a beginning."

"Yes." Sharleyan's eyes closed again, and Cayleb felt her

muscles tightening in the circle of his arm. "And I'm afraid the Archbishop's reservations about telling Earl Gray Harbor the full truth apply to Mahrak, as well. He loves me, and he trusts me, and he's fully aware of—and outraged by—the corruption in the Temple and Zion. But his fundamental faith is as strong a part of him as Uncle Byrtrym's is—*was.*"

The final word came out cracked, so quavering it seemed to have two syllables, not one, and Cayleb's arm tightened comfortingly about her.

"I'm so sorry, love," he said, bending close to press his cheek against the top of her bent head. "I know you loved him."

"I did. I *do,*" she whispered. "And I truly believed he loved *me.*"

"I think he did, Your Grace," Merlin said quietly. She opened eyes brimming with tears to look at him, and he sighed. "The original plan was his, true, but he never intended for you to be harmed. I wasn't paying enough attention to him, I admit, and it's not going to be easy to forgive myself for that. Unfortunately, I can only look at so much data from the SNARCs, and I assumed—wrongly—that Bynzhamyn and Archbishop Maikel would be keeping an eagle eye on him. Obviously, they thought that *I'd* be watching him, as well. That's how this entire plot managed to slip past all of us, and it's only underscored how important it is that none of us take anything for granted. But I've been replaying and reviewing some of the reconnaissance take I hadn't personally reviewed before, and some of it includes your uncle.

"I don't have any idea how much of his plan was driven by ambition and how much of it was driven by true horror at your defiance of the Church hierarchy. For that matter, I'm still not sure how he got into communication with Halcom in the first place. There had to be a go-between, and whoever it was is still here, I'm sure. Maybe Owl and I will be able to figure out who it was as we continue going back through the SNARCs' recordings, or maybe Bynzhamyn will find him. But I do know your uncle was adamant about seeing to it that you were captured alive. That's what took him to Saint Agtha's, and it's why Halcom murdered him, too."

"Don't make excuses for him, Merlin," Sharleyan said sadly. "I always knew he liked power. He supported me, yes, but that was partly because without his relationship to me, he wouldn't have stood at the left hand of the throne. If he'd allowed me to be set aside, the same people would have set *him* aside, because of how he and Mahrak had worked with Father, and that meant he would have lost that access to power. Yes, he loved me . . . but that love always marched in tandem with his own ambition, and it had never really been tested. Not the way it was when I decided to marry Cayleb and defy the Church. And when the test came, he chose what he chose. No one else made him, and from everything you've said, he must have been the one who went to the Temple Loyalists, not the other way around. Whatever his reasoning, whatever his motives, he was still a traitor . . . and I was still in his way."

"Believe me," Cayleb told her, "I know exactly how that feels. But at least he was insisting that you not be killed. *My* cousin set out deliberately to murder me."

"I almost wish he had, too," Sharleyan sighed. "That way I could at least be rid of this . . . ambivalence where he's concerned."

"It doesn't help," he said wistfully. "Not a lot. And it's hard learning to trust again after something like that."

"No," she replied, and he looked at her in surprise. "Not for me, Cayleb," she amplified. "But I grew up having to fight for my throne. I had to learn then that some people *can* be trusted, even if others can't. And that sometimes it's not because the ones who can't be are evil or naturally teacherous, only a matter of otherwise good people being pushed too far by competing loyalties. It doesn't make the betrayal any less a betrayal, but it does let you understand how they were driven to it."

"And that only gets worse when matters of faith get cranked into the situation," Merlin agreed.

"I know." Sharleyan gazed pensively at something only she could see for several seconds, then surprised them all with a sudden smile.

"Your Grace?" Merlin said.

"I was just thinking I'm going to need to keep written notes on who knows what," she said. "And I have to admit that I never would have thought that *Nahrmahn Baytz* should be anywhere near the innermost circle."

"I believe he's had a crisis of conscience," Merlin said dryly.

"Nonsense," Cayleb snorted. "The answer's a lot simpler than that, Merlin. Like you've always said, the man is smart. He and his princedom and his family were caught between a rock and a hard place. He had to make a decision, and now that he's made it, there's no going back. Clyntahn certainly isn't going to welcome him back with open arms, whatever he does! Which means all of his considerable intelligence is on *our* side now."

"I think you're both right," Sharleyan said thoughtfully. "I know how much *I* resented being forced to cooperate with Hektor in an attack on a kingdom which had never done me or mine any wrong. I don't think Nahrmahn liked it one bit, either. In fact, I'm inclined to think that finding himself forced to dance to Clyntahn's tune probably did push him over into an open and genuine break with the Church."

"Well, whatever happened, I think he's right about how we need to handle this situation," Cayleb said more soberly, and Sharleyan nodded.

Nahrmahn's advice, once he got over learning about *Seijin* Merlin's "visions"—which, actually, he did rather quickly—had been succinct.

"Your Majesty," he'd said, "the one thing you can't possibly afford to do, for so many reasons I can't count them all, is to try to conceal Halbrook Hollow's part in all of this. I'm sorry if that's going to cause the Empress pain, but that's all there is to it. First and foremost, you're going to have to explain what happened to him. Second, it's going to be essential for Baron Wave Thunder to 'discover' he was part of the conspiracy—and for Her Majesty to confirm it, preferably in person, and *not* by letter, in Chisholm. Even with her standing on Chisholmian soil, without a single Charisian armsman in sight, there's going to be *someone* who insists that you and your Charisians were really behind it all, and that the Empress is being constrained to lie about it. Someone besides the Church, I mean. *They* aren't going to care who testifies to his involvement. In fact, they're probably going to hold him up as some sort of martyr, murdered because of his faithfulness and then smeared with false accusations by his killers. At any rate, nothing as unimportant as the truth is going to make one bit of difference to the way their propagandists try to use this . . . affair against you.

"Since you can't do anything about the Church's version, it's particularly important that you get what really did happen across to all of your own people. And, in addition to making it clear you didn't simply do away with him because he was an irritating obstacle, it's absolutely essential to make everyone in Chisholm aware that although the assassins might have been Charisians, the two men most responsible for the entire plot—Halcom and Halbrook Hollow—were both from *outside* the Kingdom. In fact, that the man who actually put it all together not only *wasn't* a Charisian, but *was* one of the first nobles in *Chisholm*. If you do that, and if Her Majesty emphasizes the way in which her *Charisian* bodyguards fought to the last man to save her from an assassination planned by her own uncle, you can actually turn this entire thing around, at least in the view of any Chisholmian who's not already adamantly opposed to the formation of the Empire."

"I do agree," Sharleyan said now. "But I don't see any way I can personally return to Chisholm, at least until you get back from Corisande. For one thing, if I leave Charis now, won't your Charisians see that as evidence that I don't trust them? That I'm running away from them because this whole thing has made me suspicious of *all* of them?"

"I don't know, love," Cayleb said with a sigh.

"With your permission, Your Majesty?" Seahamper said diffidently.

"Which 'Majesty,' Edwyrd?" Sharleyan asked.

"In this case, both of you, Your Majesty." Her personal

armsman smiled slightly, then sobered. "I believe Prince Nahrmahn has a point. And it seems to me that if you appear before Parliament, and perhaps on Wednesday in Tellesberg Cathedral with the Archbishop, and explain frankly to all Charis that it's essential for you to return to Chisholm as quickly as possible to reassure your subjects there of your safety, and to tell them how your Charisian guardsmen died protecting you, they'll probably believe you. And, I'm certain, that if you leave Earl Gray Harbor and Archbishop Maikel to act as your regents here in Tellesberg while you're away, you can count on them to keep things running smoothly until you—or the Emperor—can return. And the fact that you trust them enough to do that should also help to reassure the rest of Charis that you really aren't running for home because you're afraid."

"I think he's right, Sharleyan," Cayleb said after a thoughtful moment. "If you hadn't been here, and if it hadn't been essential for both of us to demonstrate that we truly are equals, I would have left Rayjhis and Maikel in charge, anyway. They're certainly capable of keeping things running, as Edwyrd put it, for a few months. And, now that I think about it, having you decide 'on your own' to return to Chisholm—and demonstrate that you have both the right, the intelligence, and the will to act on your own initiative when it's impossible for the two of us to consult with one another—is only going to further strengthen our ability to share the decision-making process when we are forced to operate separately."

"I think Edwyrd and Cayleb are both right, Your Grace," Merlin said. "And it happens that this entire near-disaster has demonstrated to me that I'm not nearly as smart as I thought I was."

Sharleyan cocked her head, gazing at the tall, broad-shouldered, sapphire-eyed man she still couldn't quite think of as a woman named Nimue. She wanted to learn more about Merlin—and Nimue—and the strange, wonderful, and terrifying world from which they'd come, but she'd already realized what it was that she'd never before been able to put her finger upon where Merlin's attitudes were concerned.

She understood his comfortable familiarity with Cayleb—
and with her—now. Even Seahamper, who would have died
for her in a heartbeat, who'd helped to raise her, and who, she
knew, loved her as much as if she'd been his own daughter,
still had never managed to forget she was a queen and now an
empress. There was always that natural, inescapable edge
of deference, that inner awareness of roles and places. But
Nimue Alban had lived in a world without kings or queens or
empresses, and apparently, her father had been one of the
wealthiest and most powerful civilians in that world. Merlin
respected Cayleb deeply, there was no question in Sharleyan's
mind about that, but Nimue Alban's upbringing had immu-
nized him against that automatic, instinctual deference.

And the fact that Cayleb didn't *expect* that deference out of
him, or feel insulted when he didn't get it, said a lot of very
interesting things about Cayleb, as well, she reflected.

"*I've* always realized you weren't as smart as you thought
you were," Cayleb told him now, with a grin. "What brought
this minor fact to *your* awareness?"

"Well, Your Majesty," Merlin replied with a smile, "I could
have warned Her Grace about the assassination attempt from
Corisande if I'd only left her with a communicator. And if I
had," his smile abruptly disappeared, "all those men would
still be alive."

"Don't, Merlin." Sharleyan shook her head at him. "You
couldn't have left me any 'communicator'—whatever *that*
is—without telling me all of this before you left. And while I
can't pretend that I don't wish you *had* told me, I understand
why you didn't. For that matter, I think it was probably the
wisest decision, given what you and the Brethren actually
knew about me at that point, although obviously events have
changed that."

"I think you're being kinder to me than I deserve," Merlin
said. "You may be right, though. At any rate, *this* is a communicator."

He reached into his belt pouch and extracted a device
smaller than the palm of Sharleyan's hand and made out of
some hard, shiny, black material. He touched an almost invis-

ible stud on its surface, and a lid popped up to show a series of small buttons below a rectangular panel of what looked like opaque glass. Sharleyan's eyes rounded in wonder, and then she gasped in delight as the opaque glass suddenly glowed to life, like a magic slate board overwritten with glittering letters.

"This is called a 'security com,' Your Grace," he said. "I'm not going to try to explain everything about how it works at this point. To be honest, most of the people I knew back when I was Nimue didn't really *understand* it, anyway. All they had to know was how to *use* it, and that's all *you* need to know. Its primary function is to allow people to communicate quickly and safely over great distances by talking to each other, although it has several additional features that I've disabled, at least for now," he told her. "Among other things, this unit is capable of displaying holographic imagery—essentially, pictures, Your Grace—as well as transmitting simple voice messages. Eventually, I'm sure, you'll want to reactivate some of those features, but for now I thought it best to avoid complications. For example, it might be just a bit difficult to explain if you accidentally began playing back a holographic recording of Cayleb where someone else might see or hear it. I don't think any of us would like the interpretation most people would put on it," he finished dryly.

"Somehow, I don't think so, either," Sharleyan agreed, when he paused.

"I thought you'd probably agree, Your Grace." He smiled. "Cayleb, on the other hand, was a bit less cheerful about it when I did the same thing to *his* communicator."

"Which," Cayleb put in, "was because first he showed me how those 'holographic recordings' of his work. He can call them 'pictures' all he wants, but they're actually more like . . . like statues that move and talk. And," he gave Merlin a severe look, "he started out by showing me a 'picture' of *you*."

"In that case, it's probably just as well he's not going to show me the same thing," Sharleyan replied.

"Show you a picture of yourself?" Cayleb asked innocently, then ducked as she took a swing at him.

"As I was saying," Merlin said a bit more loudly, "it has several useful features. The most important one, for our purposes, is the ability for you and Cayleb—or for either of you and me—to speak to one another, no matter where you, or we, are. Obviously, there are still going to be limitations. For example, it's difficult enough for *me* to find anything like true privacy when I want to use something like this. It's going to be much more difficult for the two of you to do the same thing, but there are a few things we can do to simplify matters."

He touched a blinking symbol—a man's head, with an index finger vertically across his lips—on the glassy panel with a fingertip. The panel blanked, then filled with another group of letters. Sharleyan leaned closer, and read them.

"Secure relay link initiated," they said. Despite the fact that they were all words she recognized, she had no idea what they meant in this instance.

"Basically, what I've just done is to establish a link between this unit and the SNARC I have permanently parked in orbit above the Cauldron. There's one above Chisholm, too, now, for that matter. When you touch the screen icon—that glowing symbol—I touched, the com automatically seeks the nearest secure relay. The transmission is electronically steered to—"

He paused, then shook his head.

"That's starting to get into those details we don't need to get into. At any rate, when you touch the icon, the communicator links to the secure network I've set up to keep myself in touch with Owl and let me access the SNARCs. Even if the orbital array I told you about is watching for unauthorized transmissions, it won't see anything from this. But, once the link is established, Owl can connect you to me any time you need to talk to me, no matter where either of us might be."

She looked at him in amazement, as if she couldn't quite believe what she was hearing, even now, and he smiled.

"Watch," he said, and raised the "communicator" towards his mouth.

"Owl," he said.

"Yes, Lieutenant Commander?" a voice replied out of the "security communicator" after the briefest of pauses.

"Owl, I'm adding Empress Sharleyan, Emperor Cayleb, and Archbishop Maikel to the list of authorized network users. And while I'm thinking about it, let's add Sergeant Seahamper, as well, just in case. Please confirm."

"Yes, Lieutenant Commander," the voice said. "Empress Sharleyan, Emperor Cayleb, Archbishop Maikel, and Sergeant Seahamper have now been added to the authorized network users."

"Good. That's all, Owl."

"Yes, Lieutenant Commander."

"Was that *really* that 'computer' thing of yours?" Sharleyan demanded in a delighted tone.

"I'm afraid so," Merlin said, shaking his head with a crooked smile. "As computer AIs go, he's not the sharpest piece of chalk in the box, but the manufacturer's instruction manual promises me he'll get better."

"He sounds miraculous enough to *me* as it is!"

"He may right now, but just wait until you have to explain something outside his normal operating parameters to him." Merlin closed his eyes and gave a deliberate shudder. Then he opened his eyes again and handed her the device.

She took it rather gingerly, and he smiled reassuringly.

"Don't worry, Your Grace. I'll go over it all with you again, before I leave. And I'll be leaving another one of them with you, for you to hand to the Archbishop."

"Are you thinking I'm supposed to pass on your explanation to him?" Sharleyan tried to keep the trepidation out of her voice, but from Merlin's expression, it was obvious she'd failed.

"Don't worry," he repeated. "It's really a lot simpler than things you already do every day. However, there's also this."

He reached into his pouch again and extracted something else. It was hard to make out its shape as it lay in his palm, because it was made of something clearer than water.

"This goes into your ear, Your Grace," he said. "I have one of these for the Archbishop, as well."

"And what, pray tell, does it *do* in my ear, *Seijin* Merlin?" she asked a bit warily.

"Actually, you probably won't even notice it's there," he said reassuringly. "It's deliberately designed to be invisible and comfortable enough to wear permanently. As for what it does, it's an audio relay from the communicator. As long as this is in your ear, and as long as you're within a thousand feet or so of the communicator, you can hear a message from me—or from Cayleb—without anyone else overhearing it."

"I can?" Her eyes lit up again, and she looked quickly at Cayleb.

"I thought about that when Merlin explained it to me on the way here," Cayleb told her. "Unfortunately, love, while you can hear me without anyone at your end noticing it, I've still got to talk into the 'communicator' from the other end. And I'm afraid that if I sit around doing that during, oh, I don't know—a council of war, let's say—people may notice."

She laughed and shook her head at him, then turned back to Merlin.

"Will this 'relay' keep me from hearing anything else through that ear?"

"No, Your Grace," he assured her. "It's designed to pick up any sound you would hear normally and pass it on. In fact, if you wanted to, you could adjust it to a higher level of sensitivity and actually hear things you wouldn't have been able to hear, otherwise. I'd advise against playing with the settings, though, until you're used to it."

"Oh, I think I can resist *that* temptation easily enough!"

"Good."

Merlin handed her the transparent little plug, then helped her settle it into her ear. He was right. There was a moment of discomfort as the ear canal was blocked, but then the "relay" almost seemed to disappear as it conformed perfectly to the shape of her ear.

"It's also designed to let your ear breathe, and to prevent sweat from getting trapped behind it," Merlin told her. His voice sounded just a tiny bit odd. It was clearly his own, yet it had a strange, new timbre to it. It was a small thing, and she felt confident she would quickly adjust to it, but it still gave her a shivery, excited feeling to realize she was using at least a tiny part of the "technology" Langhorne and Bédard had stolen from the human race so many centuries before.

"Now, about the way you program the communicator—" Merlin began, then stopped abruptly as Cayleb raised his left hand and waggled his index finger under the *seijin*'s nose.

"You told me you'd only need a few minutes to explain all of that to her," the emperor said. "And, now that I think about it, you could walk her through it using that 'audio relay' even while we were flying back to Chisholm, couldn't you?"

"Yes," Merlin replied. "And you're mentioning this because—?"

"Because it's time for you and Edwyrd to find that deck of cards," Cayleb told him tartly. "I haven't seen my wife in the better part of six months. I intend to make up for a little bit of that lost time before you and I head back to Chisholm. Starting *now*."

"Oh."

Merlin glanced at Seahamper. The sergeant was grinning openly, and Merlin shrugged.

"Do remember we have to get back while it's still dark in Corisande, Cayleb," he said mildly.

"Oh, I will. But you're the one who told me we could have made the flight in only ninety minutes if we'd had to."

"What I said was that we could make the flight in an hour and a half in an *emergency*," Merlin corrected.

"And if my having a couple of hours to spend with my wife doesn't constitute an 'emergency,' then it damned well *ought* to."

Sharleyan was trying very hard not to giggle, and Seahamper shook his head at Merlin.

"There are some things not even a *seijin* can fight, even if he actually is an eight- or nine-hundred-year-old 'PICA,'" the guardsman said.

"So I see," Merlin said with a smile of his own.

"Come on." Seahamper twitched his head in the direction of Sharleyan's balcony. "If you didn't remember to bring any cards, Her Majesty has a couple of decks in her sitting room."

JULY,
YEAR OF GOD 893

·✦·

. I .

Prince Hektor's Palace, Manchyr, League of Corisande

I think it's time," Prince Hektor said sourly.

He and Earl Tartarian were alone in the small, private council chamber. The prince stood with his hands clasped behind him, looking out the tower window across the roofs of his capital city. Still farther out, across the broad, blue waters of the harbor, his naked eye could just make out the tiny white flaws on the horizon. Sails. The sails of Charisian schooners, hovering, watching, waiting to whistle up their larger, more powerful sisters if any ship of Tartarian's navy should be foolish enough to venture out from under the protection of the shore batteries.

At least it beats looking out in the other *direction,* he thought sourly. *Siege lines and artillery emplacements are so much more . . . intrusive.*

"My Prince, I—" the earl began.

"I know what you're going to say, Taryl," Hektor interrupted, never looking away from the harbor, "and you're right. At the rate things are going, we can hold out here in the capital for at least another three or four months. Probably longer, in fact. So, no, things aren't exactly desperate yet. But that's my point, really. If I offer to open negotiations with Cayleb now, it'll be from the closest thing to a position of strength I'm likely to find. And," he smiled thinly, "at least Irys and Daivyn are out of his reach."

Despite his best effort, Tartarian's expression betrayed him, and Hektor barked a laugh.

"Oh, I'm sure they're safely in Delferahk with Phylyp by now, Taryl! Either that, or else," his own expression tightened for a moment, "they're at the bottom of the sea, at any rate, and if Captain Harys could bring *Lance* home after Darcos Sound, he can get *Wing* to Shwei Bay. And I trust Phylyp to get them the rest of the way to Delferahk." He inhaled deeply, then shook himself, like a man brushing off his worst nightmare. "Besides, if their ship *had* been taken, Cayleb would have told me about it by now! He certainly wouldn't be keeping it a secret, given the way he'd know telling me they were in his hands would increase the pressure on me."

Tartarian nodded, and Hektor shrugged.

"As I say," the prince continued, "they're out of his reach. Unfortunately, *I'm* not, and I'm not going to be, either. Which means that from this point on, my position will only weaken."

"No doubt that's true, My Prince," the earl said, his expression troubled, "but surely Cayleb also realizes that. If I were he, I'm afraid I'd be inclined to ignore any suggestion of negotiations until the other side's position *was* closer to desperate."

"There's always that possibility," Hektor conceded. "But there are countervailing considerations, as well. Cayleb hates my guts. Well, that feeling's mutual, and he's not likely to forget that. In fact, he'll probably figure—accurately, I might add—that I'll betray him at the earliest possible moment. So you're undoubtedly right that he's going to be strongly inclined to let me stew in my own juices for at least a while longer.

"But he's also got to be looking towards what's going to happen after he wins. Let's face it," Hektor bared his teeth briefly, "one way or the other, he *is* going to win. That's not your fault, or Rysel's, or Koryn's. If it's anyone's, it's my own, but the real reason is that we just never have had time to adjust to each of those little *surprises* of his.

"On the other hand, as you yourself once pointed out to

me, Corisande isn't exactly a small territory. Especially with Irys and Daivyn out of his reach, he'll have to be worrying about how he's going to pacify the princedom afterward, and his best chance for any sort of peaceful surrender will be a negotiated settlement with me."

"But if he doesn't expect you to . . . remain conquered any longer than you must, he's not going to leave you with any more power than he can help," Tartarian pointed out.

"No. In fact, he's going to insist on everything he can think of to cut off my legs," Hektor agreed grimly. "And I'm not going to be able to resist most of the terms he chooses to impose. The best I can realistically hope for at this point is that he'll leave me technically on the throne, with 'advisers'— or possibly even an outright viceroy with a hefty garrison force—looking over my shoulder and watching every move I make like a wyvern watches a rabbit. He's no fool, Taryl, and he knows I've already killed his father and that I really don't care who takes *his* head . . . as long as someone finally gets around to it." His smile was thin and ugly. "If he leaves me on the throne at all, it'll be under conditions which make me little more than his pensioner, at best.

"But even after he conquers Corisande, even if he actually incorporates Corisande into this 'Charisian Empire' of his, he'll still have the Church to confront. At the moment, there's not a great deal the Church can do to him—not directly, not without a new model navy of its own. One of these days, though, the Church is going to *have* that kind of navy. It'll have the time to build one, anyway, because there's no way in this world Cayleb could possibly hope to conquer Howard and Haven, and once it does, there won't be any more uneven fights like Darcos Sound. So, at some point, our *dear* friend Cayleb is going to find himself fighting for his life with every man and ship he can scrape up. It may not happen tomorrow, or next five-day, but it *will* happen, Taryl. And when it does, when he's forced to reduce whatever garrison strength he thinks he can maintain in Corisande, when his attention is entirely focused on a mortal threat somewhere else, then—*then,* Taryl!—his precautions will weaken. They'll have to. And when they do, however long it takes for that to happen, I'll be ready."

Tartarian looked into his prince's hard, hating eyes, and read the savage determination simmering in their depths. If Cayleb Ahrmahk could have seen what Taryl Lektor saw in that moment, he would never have settled for anything short of Hektor Daykyn's head.

For just a moment, Tartarian found himself wishing he served Cayleb, not Hektor. It wasn't *Cayleb's* ambition which had created the enmity between Corisande and Charis, and the fashion in which Cayleb had made peace with Nahrmahn at least proved the Charisian emperor was willing to let the past bury the past under *some* circumstances. Tartarian rather doubted that any honest man could legitimately complain about the fashion in which Hektor had always governed his own people. Ruthless, yes, but also just and surprisingly fair-minded. If only he could have settled for that, forgotten his grand ambition, forsworn the "great game." . . .

But the longing lasted only for a moment. Whatever Tartarian might have wished couldn't change what *was,* and however they had arrived at their present situation, he was a Corisandian, not a Charisian. Hektor was his prince. Tartarian owed him fealty, and the way in which Hektor had ruled Corisande meant his subjects were almost as willing to stand by him as Cayleb's Charisians were willing to stand by the House of Ahrmahk.

Maybe he's right, the earl thought. *Maybe Cayleb will recognize that loyalty, realize how disastrous it would be to depose or execute him. God knows Cayleb's obviously smart enough to recognize it . . . assuming he can manage to hate Hektor at least a* little *less than Hektor hates him.*

Tartarian thought once more about the terms Cayleb had offered Nahrmahn and decided to hope for the best.

A Warehouse,
City of Manchyr,
League of Corisande

He's sent a herald to Cayleb."

"You're sure?" Father Aidryn Waimyn asked, rather more sharply than he'd intended to.

"Of course I'm sure." The other man wore the embroidered tunic of a minor court functionary or petty noble, and his voice was tart. "You don't think I'd be here, having this conversation, if I weren't, do you?" he demanded, his expression tight.

"Of course I don't." Waimyn shook his head apologetically, then looked around the dusty office of one of the many warehouses which had been idled by the Charisian blockade of Manchyr. If he was searching for something, he didn't find it, and he looked back at his companion.

"It's just . . . It's important that I be certain, that's all," he said.

"Why?" the other man asked, then shook his own head, much more quickly and harder than Waimyn had shaken his. "No. Don't tell me. I think I'd really rather not know."

"So do I," Waimyn agreed with a crooked smile. "In fact, I think it would be better for both of us if you never remembered this conversation at all."

"I'll take that as a command of Mother Church," the other man told him. He, too, looked around the dusty office, then shrugged.

"I'll be going now," he said, and eased his way out through the office door into the unused warehouse's huge, quiet emptiness.

Waimyn watched him go, then drew a deep breath and said a quiet prayer.

An intendant often found himself doing things which somehow lay outside the official parameters of his duties. Sometimes those additional tasks could provide a priest with a solid feeling of satisfaction and accomplishment. Other times, they weighed heavily upon him, like the hand of Schueler itself.

This was one of those other times. Bishop Executor Thomys knew nothing about Waimyn's private instructions from the Grand Inquisitor. Or, at least, Waimyn *thought* he didn't. It was always possible the bishop executor knew all about them and simply had no intention of admitting that he did. Not that it mattered one way or the other to Waimyn. Not really.

He drew another deep breath, then squared his shoulders, stepped out of the office, closing the door quietly behind him, and followed the other man into the warehouse's silence.

. III .

City of Manchyr, League of Corisande

Hektor Daykyn closed his eyes for a moment, savoring the feel of the breeze. Although it might technically be autumn, July had come in hot and humid, especially for the past five-day or so, which was what made today's weather so welcome. It was still undeniably on the warm side, but the morning's thunderstorms had broken the humidity, and the breeze sweeping in off the harbor was a welcome relief.

It was good to be out of the palace, he thought. It was too easy for his thoughts and his emotions, not just his body, to become trapped inside those palace walls. He *needed* this open air, the sunlight and cloud patterns, and the feel of the horse moving under him. His regular inspection trips were important to the morale of his soldiers and sailors. He knew that, yet today he was much more aware of how important getting out of the palace was to *his* morale, and he didn't feel the least bit guilty about it, either.

He glanced over his shoulder at the youngster riding along behind him. Hektor the Younger had shown rather less enthusiasm for this particular outing, once he found out it was going to require him to climb around aboard one of the navy's galleons and look interested yet again. Now he was busy practicing his "sullen obedience" look. For some reason, he seemed to find his obligatory participation in the inspection of naval units even more of a burden than his trips to tour the fortifications facing Cayleb's army on the landward side of the capital.

Hektor wondered if it was because the crown prince was remembering the brief, pointed lecture he'd delivered to him on the bloodstained deck of the galley *Lance*. If so, that was too bad, and the boy had better get over it. In fact, he'd better get over a *lot* of things.

The crown prince had been moody and depressed, especially since the surrender of Koryn Gahrvai's army. Well, that was hardly surprising. Not even a spoiled, self-absorbed, petulant prince who'd just turned sixteen could be totally blind to the peril in which he stood. Sometimes that could even be a good thing, if it made the spoiled, self-absorbed prince in question actually begin attending to his duties. Unfortunately, what young Hektor appeared to feel was mainly resentment and a sullen unhappiness if anyone asked him to exert himself in any way.

You aren't being fair to him, the disappointed father told himself, turning back in the saddle to look ahead down the broad avenue towards the navy yard once again. *Irys would tell you that . . . and she might even be right. When a sword's not tempered properly, should you blame the sword . . . or the swordsmith?*

He didn't know how to answer his own question. *Was* the fault his? Had he gone about the task of raising his son the wrong way, somehow? Or was it, indeed, something in the boy? Something lacking, that no amount of proper rearing could have magically instilled?

Sometimes he was convinced it *had* been his fault, but other times he looked at Irys and Daivyn. Whatever it was that Hektor lacked, his older sister and his younger brother both appeared to possess it in ample measure. And if Hektor had managed to raise two children, either of whom he could have seen seated on his throne after him without a qualm, then what could he have done so wrong in Hektor's case to have caused the child who actually was his heir to turn out so differently?

Is it that he knows you don't love him as much as Irys? Is that what it is? But you wanted to. You tried to. It's your disappointment in him that makes it so hard, and you didn't begin to feel that until he was—what? Ten? Eleven?

It was hard for a father to admit that he wasn't even certain he loved his own son any longer. Yet he wasn't *just* a father. He was also a ruler, and it was a ruler's responsibility to train up his successor. To feel confident his rule would be passed to someone prepared to assume that burden. And when he couldn't feel that way, when a parent's natural disappointment found itself coupled with a ruler's recognition of his heir's unfitness, the anger and the worry were all too likely to poison that same parent's natural affection.

I don't need to be worrying about this right now, Hektor told himself firmly. *There are so many* other *things I need to be dealing with. If I can't somehow convince Cayleb that it would be more dangerous to remove me than to leave me in place, it's not going to matter whether or not Hektor would have made a competent ruler after me, because he'll never have the chance.*

Of course he won't, another corner of his brain replied. *And how many times in the past have you used the excuse of "other things" to avoid dealing with this?*

The Prince of Corisande grimaced, feeling his enjoyment of the morning sunlight, breeze, and salt-freshened air slipping away from him. And mostly, he knew, that was because he knew that biting corner of his mind was right. He did have to "deal with this." It was easier to admit that than it was to figure out exactly how he was going to go about it, of course, but there were many aspects of being a ruler, or, for that matter, a parent, that were as important as they were unpleasant, and—

This time, things had been better arranged. There weren't two crossbowmen; there were twelve, and not one of Hektor's guardsmen saw them in time.

Four of the steel-headed quarrels ripped into Prince Hektor. Any one of the wounds they inflicted would have been fatal, and the brutal impacts hammered him from the saddle. It was like being hit in the chest and belly with white-hot spikes, and he felt himself falling, falling, falling. . . . It was as if he were tumbling headfirst through some impossibly deep gulf of air, and then he cried out in anguish as he hit the ground at last and time resumed its passage. Hot blood pulsed, soaking his tunic, filling his universe with pain and the awareness that death had come for him at last.

And yet, dreadful though that pain was, he barely noticed it in the face of an agony deeper than any anguish of the flesh.

Even as he fell, his eyes were whipping towards the horse behind his, and it wasn't pain that ripped that cry from him when he hit the ground. No. It was that deeper, far more dreadful anguish as he saw the three crossbow bolts sprouting from the chest of the Crown Prince of Corisande and knew too late that he did—and always had—loved his son.

. IV .

Emperor Cayleb's Headquarters Tent,
Duchy of Manchyr,
League of Corisande

My God, Merlin! You're certain they're both dead?"

"Yes, I am," Merlin replied, and Cayleb sank into the camp chair, shaking his head while he tried to come to grips with this fresh, cataclysmic upheaval. Birds sang and wyverns whistled quietly in the hot, sunny afternoon, and the subdued sounds of a military encampment seemed to enclose the headquarters tent's silence in a protective shell.

"How did it happen? Who's responsible?" the emperor asked after a moment.

"I'm not absolutely certain who's responsible," Merlin admitted. "I suspect it was Waimyn, though."

"The Intendant?" Cayleb frowned. "Why would the Church murder the man fighting against the 'apostate traitors'? I mean—oh."

The emperor grimaced and shook his head.

"It's amazing how sheer surprise can keep someone from thinking clearly, isn't it?" he said sourly. "Of course the Church—or, more probably, Clyntahn—wants him dead. He was about to ask for terms, wasn't he?"

"Exactly." Merlin nodded grimly. "In fact, he probably signed his own death warrant when he sent you that herald."

"They couldn't have him switching sides," Cayleb agreed. "And after the way Sharleyan and Nahrmahn have done just that, they couldn't be certain Hektor wouldn't do the same. Which he probably would have . . . long enough to get into range to slip a knife between my ribs, at any rate."

"Exactly," Merlin repeated. "But—"

"But that's not the only wyvern they've thrown this rock at," Cayleb interrupted him. "Oh, believe me, I see that, too, Merlin! Even if we could prove it was Waimyn, and that he did it on Clyntahn's direct orders, who's going to believe us? Especially when the Church starts trumpeting the announcement that I've murdered Hektor for his support of the true Church?"

"And the fact that Nahrmahn, who helped your cousin try to assassinate you, is now one of your inner advisers is going to play into their version of it, as well," Merlin pointed out. "For that matter, by the time the Church gets done with it, our 'ridiculous lies' about the Temple Loyalists' involvement in the attempt to murder Sharleyan are going to be seen as nothing but an additional layer of deception. Obviously the Church's true sons never tried to assassinate Sharleyan! The entire thing probably never even happened! It was all a ruse, just an act we cooked up, probably to give us an excuse to remove Halbrook Hollow—who was loyal to God and the Church—and to lend some sort of credibility to this ridiculous story about the Church's murdering Hektor and his son."

"Wonderful."

Cayleb leaned back in his chair, eyes closed as his brain came fully back on balance. He wished there were some way—any way—he could have disagreed with Merlin's analysis. Unfortunately . . .

"You do realize that the 'cover story' we put together for our visit to Tellesberg is likely to turn around and bite us on the arse now that this has happened, don't you?" he asked without opening his eyes. "Who could I have been so eager to meet privately and secretly—so privately and secretly that I only took a single trusted bodyguard with me—but the people who could deliver Hektor's death to me?"

"That thought had occurred to me," Merlin agreed sourly.

"And I'll bet you very few people in Manchyr had any idea he'd just taken the first steps towards asking for terms," Cayleb continued. "So I can't even make the logical argument that I had no reason to assassinate him when he was about to surrender his entire princedom to me!"

"Not to mention the minor fact of his popularity with his own people. I don't see any way to convince them we weren't behind this, and that's going to make maintaining order here in Corisande one hell of a lot harder," Merlin said grimly.

"You do have a way of continuing to cheer me up." Cayleb opened his eyes and showed Merlin his teeth. "Have any more . . . less than positive aspects of this situation presented themselves to you?"

"Not yet, but I'm pretty sure they will."

"So am I," Cayleb admitted unhappily. He shook his head. "You know, whatever we may think of Clyntahn, this is one move on his part that doesn't have any downside for him, as far as I can tell."

"Aside from the trivial consideration that it required him to murder a sixteen-year-old boy, as well as his father."

"Two more murders? Piffle!" Cayleb snapped his fingers, the sound like a pistol shot in the tent. "He's God's Inquisitor, Merlin—anyone he has to kill obviously deserves to die! It's God's plan for Safehold!" The emperor's voice was inexpressibly bitter, and his brown eyes might have been carved from stone. "And even if that weren't true," he continued, "what are two more murders against all the ones he's already ordered? There's enough blood on his hands to damn fifty men to Hell, already, so why not shed a little more?"

Merlin didn't reply. There was no need.

Cayleb sat glaring at a spot in the air three feet in front of him for several more seconds. Then he pushed himself to his feet.

"We'd better send for Nahrmahn," he said, and actually managed a thin smile. "How fortunate that we've admitted him to the outer arc of the inner circle, as it were. At least we can get his advice and figure out how to start putting a handle on this before the 'official word' reaches us."

. V .

Sir Koryn Gahrvai's Quarters,
Dairos,
Barony of Dairwyn,
League of Corisande

Do you believe him?" Alyk Ahrthyr asked harshly.

He sat in the comfortable sitting room of the house which had been assigned to Sir Koryn Gahrvai and his two senior subordinates in Dairos. As prisons went, this one left remarkably little to complain about. Except, of course, for the minor fact that one *was* a prisoner.

At the moment, the Earl of Windshare found himself

rather less concerned with that than with the question he'd just asked.

"I don't know," Gahrvai admitted after a moment.

He stood by the window, looking out at the two rifle-armed Charisian Marines standing sentry duty in front of the house. Beyond them, the streets of Dairos were far busier than they'd ever been before the invasion. It remained Cayleb's main supply base, which meant enormous quantities of supplies, freight, and reinforcements were constantly landing. By now, Gahrvai estimated, Cayleb's field strength really had to be up to somewhere near seventy-five thousand, which made Dairos even more important to his logistics.

It also meant Charis needed as much warehouse space as it could get its hands on, and Cayleb—to the astonishment of the Dairosian business community—was actually paying the going rate for the space he was monopolizing. He refused to allow himself to be gouged into paying more than that, but the fact that he was willing to pay *at all* was, frankly, astonishing. It also helped to explain why the city's economy was as robust as it had ever been, and the shore patrols organized by the emperor's Marines had been extraordinarily successful at preventing ugly incidents between the invaders and the city's citizens, as well. There'd been some, of course. That was inevitable. But Cayleb's military governor had quickly and publicly administered justice under the stern requirements of the Charisian Empire's articles of war. The Dairosians were still only too well aware of the fact that they were a conquered city, yet they also knew they were as safe in their persons and property under Charisian rule as they'd ever been under Corisandian rule.

Cayleb's been smart enough and careful enough to ensure that in a minor port city, Gahrvai thought. *Could the same man have been* stupid *enough to have Prince Hektor assassinated in the middle of Manchyr?*

"I don't think Cayleb was behind it," Charlz Doyal said, and reached for the cane which had become his constant companion since Haryl's Crossing.

"Why not?" Windshare growled, watching the older man

limp across to stand beside Gahrvai, looking out the window at the same scene.

"Because the one thing he *isn't* is stupid," Doyal said simply, echoing Gahrvai's own thoughts. "Look at the way he's treated *us,* the way he's insisted on maintaining public order in his own rear areas, punishing anyone who victimizes a Corisandian subject, paying fair price for the property he's seized or the warehouses he's impressed. He's taken every conceivable pain to *avoid* enraging us, our troops, or Prince Hektor's subjects. Do you really think that now that it's only a matter of time before the Prince would have been forced to surrender he's going to do something like *this*?"

"But if it wasn't him, then who *was* it?" Windshare demanded.

"That's a thornier question, Alyk." Gahrvai turned back from the window. "It's possible it was someone in Corisande—in Manchyr—who was stupid enough to think Cayleb might actually thank him for removing the Prince. Or I suppose it could've been Nahrmahn. He and the Prince were allies against Charis for a long time. I imagine it's entirely possible, maybe even likely, that Prince Hektor knew something about Nahrmahn which Nahrmahn would just as soon not have his new emperor find out about."

"You're clutching at straws, Koryn," Doyal said very quietly from behind him, and Gahrvai's expression stiffened. "You know perfectly well that if it wasn't Cayleb, it almost certainly *was* the Church."

Windshare inhaled quickly, angrily, but Gahrvai didn't even twitch for several seconds. Then his shoulders slumped, and he nodded heavily.

"You're right, Charlz." His voice was barely audible, and he closed his eyes. "You're right. And if the men fighting against God act with honor while the men who claim to be fighting *for* God do something like this, then what do you and I and Alyk do?"

AUGUST,
YEAR OF GOD 893

✦

. I .

Prince Hektor's Palace,
City of Manchyr,
League of Corisande

I hope *you* have some damned idea what we do next," the Earl of Anvil Rock said harshly.

He and Earl Tartarian sat in what had been Prince Hektor's privy council chamber, looking at one another across the table where they'd spent so many hours conferring with Hektor. The western sky, visible through the chamber's window, was an angry sheet of beaten copper, streaked with fire-edged bands of cloud.

Which, Tartarian thought, *is altogether too damned appropriate for words.*

The three days since the murders of Hektor and his son had been among the most exhausting of Tartarian's life. Probably the only man who was even more exhausted than he was was the one who currently sat across the table from him. Together, they'd managed to maintain order in Corisande's besieged capital, but how long they could continue to do that—and what was happening *outside* the city of Manchyr—was more than either of them could say.

"If you want brilliant ideas, you've come to the wrong man, Rysel," Tartarian said frankly. "All I know for sure is that right now we're riding the slash lizard . . . and you know how well *that* worked out, according to the story."

Anvil Rock's mouth twitched in a brief smile, but it never touched his eyes, and he drew a deep breath.

"We have to decide what we're going to do about the succession," he said. "And we've got to decide what to do about Cayleb's goddamned army, too."

"I'm afraid Cayleb's army is the easy part," Tartarian replied. "There's not anything we *can* do about it, which really only leaves us one option where Cayleb is concerned, doesn't it? It's not one either of us likes, but at least it has the virtue of a certain brutal simplicity."

"After the son-of-a-bitch murdered Hektor?" Anvil Rock half-snarled.

"First," Tartarian said in a deliberately calm tone, "we don't have any proof Cayleb was involved in that assassination at all. He—"

"I know he *said* he wasn't," Anvil Rock interrupted. "That's exactly what he *would* say, though, isn't it? And if it wasn't him, who else was it?"

"I don't know who it was. That's my entire point." Tartarian thought again about mentioning one unpleasant suspicion which had occurred to him and decided—again—not to. Not directly, at any rate. "It could have been Cayleb, although exactly how he could have gotten his assassins through the siege lines is an interesting question. On the other hand, it could equally well have been someone trying to curry favor with Cayleb, someone trying to force a surrender before the war did even greater damage to whatever his interests might have been. Or even someone who'd learned the Prince was planning to negotiate with Cayleb and was determined to prevent him from reaching any sort of accommodation with Charis."

That last possibility was as close as he cared to come to suggesting that the assassins might have been Temple Loyalists . . . or even direct agents of the Church. From the unhappy flicker in Anvil Rock's eyes, the army commander had caught his implication.

"The one thing that strikes me about it from Cayleb's viewpoint, though," Tartarian continued, "is how incredibly stupid it would've been. Mind you, people do stupid things, especially when there's enough hatred involved, and God knows Cayleb and the Prince hated each other. But if it was Cayleb, it was the first stupid thing he's done that *I* know of. And whether it was him or not, that doesn't change the fact that he's still got an army and a navy . . . and we don't. I hate to say it, Rysel, but we don't have a choice. In fact, with the Prince gone, we've got even less of a choice than he had."

"Even if that's true, what makes you think the rest of the Princedom would pay any attention to us?" Anvil Rock asked bitterly.

"At the moment, who else *can* they pay attention to? With Phylyp out of the Princedom with Irys and Daivyn, you're the closest thing we've got to a first councilor. Not to mention the fact that the Prince had named you as Regent if anything happened to him."

"But he named me Regent for young Hektor. With him dead right along with the Prince, I don't have anyone to be Regent *for.*"

"There's always Zhoel," Tartarian said very cautiously.

"No!" Anvil Rock's flat palm cracked explosively on the council table's surface, and his exhausted face flushed with anger. Despite the glare in his eyes, Tartarian was glad to see the emotion, for more than one reason.

"If I don't say it to you, Rysel, someone else will," he said after a moment. "If the Prince had ever contemplated, even for a moment, that he and young Hektor might both be killed, he wouldn't have sent Daivyn to Delferahk. But he did, and we're all stuck with the consequences of that."

Anvil Rock's jaw muscles ridged. For just a moment he seemed to hover on the brink of lunging to his feet and storming out of the council chamber. But then he made himself sit back and draw another of those deep, steadying breaths of which he seemed to require so many recently.

Tartarian was right, and Anvil Rock knew it, which didn't make him like it one bit better. And not simply because of the invidious position in which it threatened to place him, personally.

The previous couple of generations had not been overgenerous where the House of Daykyn's progeny was concerned.

Prince Hektor's grandfather, Prince Lewk, had produced only two children: Hektor's father, Fronz, and his uncle, Alyk. Prince Fronz had produced only two children who'd lived to their majorities: Hektor, himself, and his sister Sharyl. And Alyk Daykyn had produced only a single daughter, Fahrah, Hektor's first cousin. Both Hektor and Sharyl had been rather more prolific than their parents. Hektor had produced three children, and Sharyl had produced no fewer than five, and thereby hung Anvil Rock's problem, because Sharyl had married his own second cousin, Sir Zhasyn Gahrvai, the Baron of Wind Hook, which made her children Gahrvai's second cousins once removed.

And, of course, made them Prince Hektor's nieces and nephews.

Under Corisandian law, Prince Daivyn was his father's legal heir, following his older brother's murder. Neither he nor Tartarian doubted that Irys would have made a better ruler than her nine-year-old brother, especially under the current calamitous circumstances, but unlike Chisholm, Corisandian law had established generations ago that a daughter could not inherit the throne. And the question, unfortunately, was moot at the present moment, anyway, since neither Daivyn nor Irys was in Corisande. Their first cousins, on the other hand, were, and young Zhoel Gahrvai, the current Baron Wind Hook, stood next in the succession after Daivyn.

"I know someone's going to argue that we ought to put Zhoel in Daivyn's place," Anvil Rock said after a moment. "I can even see some pretty forceful arguments in favor of doing just that. But whatever anyone else might suggest, *I* can't be a party to deciding to do it, for a lot of reasons. Including the fact that all of my oaths were sworn to *Daivyn's* father, not to Zhasyn. And," he added more unwillingly, "even if that weren't the case, Zhoel isn't up to the job, and you know it, Taryl."

"I don't know if anyone *could* be 'up to the job' under the circumstances," Tartarian replied. "On the other hand, I do know what you mean," he admitted. "The good news is that I think Zhoel would say the same thing."

"So do I," Anvil Rock said heavily. "He's always done his best, but to be brutally honest, he makes a good baron."

Tartarian nodded. The current Baron Wind Hook was only eighteen, and he'd succeeded his father—and become his younger siblings' legal guardian—when both of his parents were killed in a coach accident, three years before. Unlike Crown Prince Hektor, he'd always tried as hard as he could to discharge the responsibilities of his birth, yet his wit was no more than average, if that. As Anvil Rock had just said, he managed to meet his obligations to his barony, if only by dint of working doggedly at them, but he would really have been happier as a simple gentleman farmer, and the thought of ascending to the Corisandian throne under any circumstances, far less the ones which currently obtained, must be terrifying to him. Assuming, of course, that the possibility had ever crossed his mind for a moment. Which, even now, it very well might not have. A probability which only underscored how utterly unsuited to the throne he would prove.

If they did place him on it anyway, he would be desperately unhappy. Tartarian could have lived with that, if he'd had to, in the best interests of Corisande. Unfortunately, the one thing it most definitely would not be was in Corisande's best interests. The amiable, hard-working, very likable young dullard would find himself the hopeless—and helpless—target of factional manipulation, with disastrous consequences for the princedom. His younger brother, Mahrak, at fourteen, would have been a far better choice. But he was the *younger* brother, and passing over Zhoel in his favor would only exacerbate what would inevitably become a ferocious succession dispute if Daivyn was set aside in *anyone's* favor in the first place.

"If it's not Zhoel, then it has to be Daivyn," Tartarian said aloud, "and that unmuzzles a slash lizard all its own."

"Tell me about it," Anvil Rock said dryly.

"There's no way Zhames is going to send him back to Corisande," Tartarian continued. "Even if he were inclined to do that, there would have to be a legitimate question in his mind about Daivyn's safety. If Cayleb did have the Prince and young Hektor assassinated, he certainly wouldn't hesitate to murder Daivyn, as well. And whether Cayleb was behind the Prince's murder or not, Zhames has to be aware of how valuable a card Daivyn's just become, especially given the fact that *he's* at war with Cayleb, too."

"And if there were any possible way Zhames might not notice it, Clyntahn and Trynair damned well will." Anvil Rock's expression was grim.

"Exactly." Tartarian nodded. "So, if we insist he's the legitimate Prince of Corisande, then we have to establish a legitimate regency in his name, and as you just pointed out, your writ of regency was for young Hektor, not Daivyn. Which means getting the Council to agree to making a nine-year-old boy, who's not even in the Princedom, and who's likely to be seen as a valuable pawn by every ambitious politician in the world, Prince of Corisande *and* to name someone as his regent."

"Wonderful." Anvil Rock leaned back, rubbing his face and eyes wearily.

"To be honest, I don't think you and I have very much choice, Rysel," Tartarian said grimly. "As you say, Zhoel would undoubtedly be a disaster on the throne, and we can't afford to fracture the succession any further than we can possibly avoid. And, unfortunately, the only two men I know whose loyalty to the Prince and to Corisande I trust—and who have the power to force a resolution of the entire question—are you and me."

"I won't be party to any coups," Anvil Rock said flatly, lowering his hands from his face and meeting Tartarian's eyes levelly across the table. "Once we open that door—once *anyone* opens *that* door—we set our feet on the road to outright civil war. A civil war with a Charisian occupation sitting right in the middle of it!"

"You're right, and I'm not suggesting any coups." Tartarian met those eyes without flinching. "I'm an admiral. You're a general. Even if we managed to seize power, how would we manage to exercise it without driving the coach straight over the edge of the cliff? Neither of us is the politician Phylyp is, but he's out of the Princedom. Without him to advise us, we need a substitute at least as good to keep us from making some sort of disastrous mistake, and I don't know another politician here in the Princedom I'd trust. The good news, such as it is and what there is of it, is that Cayleb's presence means the traditional political arrangements aren't going to apply, anyway. Or do you think Cayleb Ahrmahk is likely to leave *any* Corisandian in a position to threaten his own plans?"

Anvil Rock opened his mouth, then paused, and closed it again.

"Exactly," Tartarian said again, and produced a wintry smile. "What we're really talking about here isn't seizing power. It's going to be a matter of making the best terms we can when we *surrender* power to Cayleb. I'm sure at least some of our esteemed fellow nobles aren't going to see it that way. They're going to figure we're cutting some sort of deal with Cayleb, because that's exactly what they'd be doing in our place. Which is why I say you're the only other man in a position to act whose loyalty I trust."

"No matter what we do, we're going to find ourselves with enemies coming at us from every direction," Anvil Rock said after a moment. "The ones who think we've made some sort of arrangement with Cayleb are going to be furious that they didn't have the opportunity to do it first. And the ones who recognize that we've surrendered to Cayleb are going to blame us—and probably especially me—for the fact that Cayleb kicked our arse in the first place."

"And while you're enumerating all of the people who are going to be pissed off with us," Tartarian agreed with a grimace, "let's not forget, in order of importance, our own Temple Loyalists, the Church, and the Group of Four. Especially the Grand Inquisitor."

"Lovely."

"Trust me," Tartarian said very sincerely, "if there were any way in the world I thought we could hand the responsibility for this off to someone else, I'd take it in a heartbeat. Unfortunately, we can't."

"Well, technically, we *could*," Anvil Rock pointed out. "There's a legal quorum of the Council here in Manchyr with us, you know. We could always let them decide what to do about it."

"I can just see you doing that." Tartarian snorted.

"Actually, as you pointed out yourself a few minutes ago, we are going to have to assemble the quorum, if only so the two of us can lean on them to formally name Daivyn as Prince."

"Sure. And are you going to tell me that when we do assemble the quorum you'd trust any of them with a broken-down draft dragon? The ones who wouldn't steal it or sell it to someone else would probably starve the poor critter to death!"

"You're probably being too kind to them. And, no, I wouldn't trust them with a broken-down draft dragon."

"So we're in agreement, then?"

Silence hovered in the wake of Tartarian's question. He could see the conflicting emotions behind Anvil Rock's exhausted face, and they were easy to recognize, since he shared them fully. The desire to avoid the responsibility. The shame of admitting military defeat. The bitter anger left by the assassination, and the lingering suspicion—whatever logic might say—that Cayleb Ahrmahk had, in fact, ordered that double murder. The knowledge that whatever they decided, the two of them would be reviled by other men who hadn't had to make the same decisions . . . or whose own hopes for power had been dashed. And the awareness that it wouldn't matter to the Group of Four that they'd had no choice but to negotiate with the schismatics of Charis. There were far more reasons than Tartarian could count for the two of them to shirk the decisions which lay before them, and both of them knew it. And yet—

"Yes," Sir Rysel Gahrvai, the Earl of Anvil Rock, said heavily. "We're in agreement."

II

Prince Cayleb's Headquarters Tent, Duchy of Manchyr, League of Corisande

Cayleb Ahrmahk rose as the earls of Tartarian and Anvil Rock were escorted into his command tent.

"Earl Anvil Rock and Earl Tartarian, Your Majesty," Lieutenant Ahstyn said. The two Corisandians bowed stiffly, and Cayleb returned the courtesy with a half-bow of his own.

"My Lords." The emperor smiled very slightly and waved one hand at the other man who'd just risen from the table. "I believe you know General Gahrvai."

"Father," Sir Koryn Gahrvai said. "My Lord." He bowed to Tartarian, and his father held out his hand.

"It's good to see you again, Koryn," he said. "Although," his own smile could have frozen water, even in Manchyr, "I could wish it had been under other conditions."

The younger Gahrvai clasped his father's hand and nodded. Then Cayleb cleared his throat quietly, and all three of the Corisandians looked at him.

"My Lords," he said to them, "I'm sure all of us wish we might have met under happier circumstances. Unfortunately, we haven't. Yet whatever the circumstances, a host has certain duties. Please be seated. Allow me to offer you refreshment."

The others settled into the indicated chairs, and Cayleb nodded to the single tall, blue-eyed guardsman standing behind his own chair. Captain Athrawes came briefly to attention, then personally poured brandy into four glasses. He offered the first of them to Cayleb, but the emperor shook his head and indicated Anvil Rock, the senior of the three Corisandians. The earl accepted the glass, sipped politely, and nodded approval, and Merlin served the other two Corisandians before placing the final glass in front of Cayleb.

"I realize," the emperor said then, "that the customary rules require you to compliment me on the quality of my brandy, for me to wave off the compliments with some modest disclaimer, and for the four of us to discuss the competing virtues of our national vintages, the local hunting, and the weather before getting down to our real business. With your indulgence, and in the interests of maintaining our mutual sanity, I propose that we consider that all of those polite conversational gambits are already behind us."

Earl Anvil Rock maintained an admirably impassive expression. Tartarian's lips might have twitched slightly, and Sir Koryn raised his brandy glass again, sipping once more just a bit hastily.

"As you wish, Your Majesty," Anvil Rock replied after a moment. "In that case, however, I—"

"Pardon me," Cayleb interrupted in a courteous tone, raising one hand. "I realize that the request for this meeting came from you, but before we begin, there are a few things I would like to say. I assure you," he produced a crooked smile, "that they aren't conversational gambits."

"Of course, Your Majesty."

Anvil Rock settled back in his chair, his eyes wary, and Cayleb leaned forward, resting his forearms on the table.

"My Lords," he said quietly, "diplomacy, unspoken understandings, and polite lies no doubt have their place. In this instance, however, I think there's little point in any of us pretending that you, Earl Anvil Rock, and you, Earl Tartarian, must not at least suspect that I had a hand in the assassination of Prince Hektor and his son. In your place, *I* certainly would, and I'm quite certain much of the rest of the world is going to automatically assume Prince Hektor was murdered at my orders. And, to be perfectly frank, given the . . . history between my House and his, and the recent attack on Charis, I believe I would have been perfectly justified in having him killed."

Tartarian and Anvil Rock both tensed visibly, and Cayleb

smiled once more. This time, there was absolutely no humor in his expression, and his eyes met theirs levelly. They had no way of knowing that he had used his security com to personally view the transmissions from the SNARC which had spied upon their private meetings. Watching the holographic images had been like borrowing God's own eye. At the same time, the experience had helped him understand even better why not even Merlin could manage to keep track of everything that happened across the face of an entire planet. It had also suggested at least one possible way to ease Merlin's burden in that regard, although he hadn't brought it up yet.

More to the immediate point, however, it meant he knew exactly what Tartarian and Anvil Rock had said to one another on this very subject. More than that, he'd seen their expressions, heard the tone of their voices. It was an advantage no other negotiator in Safehold's history had ever enjoyed, and he intended to use it.

"I said I would have been *justified* in having him killed, My Lords," he reminded them, "and I believe both of you are probably sufficiently aware of all the reasons why that would have been true. I didn't say it would have been *wise* of me to do that, however. And whatever justification I might have had for having him killed, I'm not in the practice of casually killing children."

There hadn't been that many years between Cayleb's age and that of Crown Prince Hektor, but neither of the Corisandian earls saw anything ironic in the emperor's use of the word "children."

"Even setting aside all considerations of justification or justice, and ignoring the fact that the Crown Prince was killed, as well, ordering Prince Hektor's assassination would have been a particularly stupid thing for me to do under the circumstances. I fully realize that despite all of the reasons my subjects and I might have for . . . thinking unkindly of him, his own subjects saw him in quite another light. Imprisoning him, or even having him executed after giving him time to make his peace with God, would have been one thing. They might not have cared for it, but they would have understood it, given all that had passed between us. Ordering him *murdered* would have been quite another thing, however, and I can think of nothing better calculated to harden any resentment and resistance here in Corisande. Nor, for that matter," he looked directly into their eyes, "can I think of anything the Group of Four could use against me more effectively. I assure you, gentlemen, that whatever my other failings might be, I'm neither blind nor stupid enough not to understand all of the dozens of reasons why assassinating Prince Hektor would have been one of the worst things I could possibly have done."

Neither Anvil Rock nor Tartarian said anything, but he thought he saw the memory of their own conversation replaying itself somewhere behind their eyes. And he saw their faces stiffen—especially Anvil Rock's—at his mention of the Group of Four.

That's an implication he doesn't want to think about, Cayleb told himself. *From Tartarian's expression, though, it's one he's already* been *thinking about*.

"Corisande has been Charis' enemy for the better part of thirty years, My Lords," he continued. "While I realize you and I are inevitably going to have different perspectives on that enmity, I believe simple honesty would compel you to admit that up until my own current . . . visit to Corisande, virtually all of the aggression in our relationship originated in Manchyr, not in Tellesberg. I have no wish or desire to debate the causes for that, or to allocate blame. What I *do* desire, however, and what I intend to accomplish, is to put an end to the danger to Charis which Corisande represents. And, gentlemen, I intend to put an end to it *forever*."

His voice was darker, harder, with the final sentence, and he let silence linger for several heartbeats before he resumed.

"I see no need for any of us to recapitulate all that's happened since the Group of Four offered to finance and broker Prince Hektor's attack on Charis. I know, however, and I'm sure both of you recognize, that Clyntahn and Trynair never saw Hektor as anything more than a knife they might use to cut Charis' throat. I assure you, if Corisande had, indeed, been able to take Charis' place as a mercantile power, or build a true Corisandian Empire, as Hektor wished, the Group of Four would eventually have meted out the same fate to Corisande. Corrupt men don't change, and in their eyes, it would have been a simple matter of one threat to their power being replaced by another.

"What never occurred to the Group of Four was that their plan to destroy Charis might not succeed. Unfortunately for them, it didn't, and the nature of the threat we represent to their power changed drastically as a result. If we survive, we prove that someone can defy the greed and demands of venal men who abuse the authority of God, and because that's true, they have no choice but to destroy us utterly. They may cloak that fact in the rhetoric of religion and appeal passionately to the will of the God Whose laws they violate every day, but it remains true. And because it does, I cannot permit Corisande to be used as a weapon against us yet again.

"I tell you this at the outset because I refuse to attempt to deceive you. Corisande, whether willingly or not, *will* become part of the Charisian Empire. I can neither permit nor settle for anything short of that, for reasons which must be obvious to both of you. What remains to be settled are the conditions and circumstances under which that will be accomplished. Obviously, the two of you want to obtain the best possible terms for Prince Hektor's subjects. Equally obviously, I have no desire to find myself embroiled in an unending succession of local rebellions against the imperial authority here in Corisande. From the perspective of self-interest, if nothing else, then, it behooves me to impose the least punitive terms I can while providing sufficient security for Corisande's incorporation into the Empire. That, by the way, is probably the most compelling single reason why I would have avoided assassinating Prince Hektor. To be honest, I had no intention of leaving him on his throne, for several reasons, but his death, especially the circumstances under which he was killed, is inevitably going to provide a natural rallying point for the very rebellions and resistance I most want to avoid."

His reasonable tone was having an effect, he saw. Neither Anvil Rock nor Tartarian could have liked what they were hearing, but it was obvious that they'd expected a much harsher attitude out of him.

"From both of our perspectives, the perfectly understandable anger Prince Hektor's murder is going to provoke is an unfortunate thing," he continued. "The fact that I recognize the justification it provides for potential resistance to Charisian authority also means I must insist upon terms which are going to be more severe and restrictive than might otherwise have been the case. Resistance would always have been likely; now, unfortunately, I suspect that it's inevitable, and that it may well be both more severe and more widespread than it would have been otherwise. That being the case, I have no choice but to take steps which will permit me to deal with it when it arises.

"That will have consequences for you, individually, and for Corisande's nobility and commoners, alike. I regret that, but I can't change it. I also recognize the . . . precarious position in which the two of you find yourselves, the potential for factional warfare in the event of a contested succession, and all of the other intensely destabilizing consequences Prince Hektor's murder has created. Undoubtedly, the terms the two of you can accept and, even more importantly, convince or compel the other great nobles of Corisande to accept, are also going to be affected by the assassination. I recognize that, as well, and I will bear it in mind in any discussions between us. Nonetheless, any terms at which we may finally arrive will be *my* terms. I can settle for nothing less, and to be brutally frank, your military position entitles you to demand nothing more."

He paused once again, allowing his words to settle fully, then leaned back in his own chair, still regarding them across the table.

"There's a reason I'm speaking with you directly, without bevies of advisers and without screens of ambassadors. I want there to be no misunderstandings, no gray areas. And I want you to know, and to be able to tell anyone who asks, that you spoke directly to me. That whatever terms are ultimately offered to Corisande *are* my terms. That if I will accept nothing less, I also will demand nothing more after the fact."

"I appreciate your candor, Your Majesty," Anvil Rock said after a moment. "I won't pretend I've enjoyed hearing everything you had to say, because I haven't. Nor, while I can understand and appreciate your position, do I feel any great temptation to sacrifice Corisande's interests, or those of Prince Daivyn, to those of Charis. Nonetheless, I can't dispute your analysis of the current military situation, either. And whether or not you were involved in Prince Hektor and Crown Prince Hektor's murders, your analysis of the internal consequences to the Princedom closely parallels Earl Tartarian's and my own view of them. Neither of us wants a situation in which armed resistance to Charisian rule, or even conflict between our own internal factions, results in punitive Charisian measures against Prince Daivyn's subjects."

He'd watched Cayleb's expression carefully while he spoke, and now the emperor smiled slightly.

"I notice that you just referred to 'Prince Daivyn,' My Lord," he observed.

"He is Prince Hektor's legitimate heir," Anvil Rock pointed out.

"True," Cayleb agreed. "Unfortunately, he isn't in the Princedom at the moment, is he?"

Both Corisandian earls stiffened, and Cayleb shrugged.

"I realize that isn't common knowledge, even in the Palace, gentlemen. Nonetheless, my agents and I have become aware of his absence, and of the absence of Princess Irys. In fact, I rather think one of my cruisers came very close to snapping the two of them up. Tell me, am I correct in suspecting that the Harchongese galleon *Wing,* which, for some peculiar reason, was carrying a cargo of Charisian farm equipment from Charis to Shwei right through the middle of our blockade of Corisande, was actually carrying a rather more valuable cargo at the same time?"

This time, the Corisandians' alarm was obvious, and Cayleb shook his head.

"My Lords, while it pains me to admit that my Navy isn't actually infallible, this time, your efforts succeeded quite nicely, and we sent *Wing* on her way with our blessing." He grimaced, but there was a slight twinkle in his eyes, as well. "Certain of my other sources have confirmed Princess Irys' and Prince Daivyn's absence from Corisande, however, and an examination of the report from *Dawn Star*'s captain indicates the presence of three passengers aboard the mysterious *Wing*. I also note Earl Coris' absence from our meeting today, and I rather doubt the two of you would have simply absentmindedly left him behind. And, finally, if I'd been Prince Hektor and I'd decided to send my daughter and my younger son to safety, I can think of very few of my councilors to whom I would have felt comfortable entrusting them. In fact, I can think of only three or four, and two of them are sitting on your side of the table this morning. That suggests to my powerful intellect that the 'merchant factor' and his two children shown on *Wing*'s manifest were, in fact, Earl Coris, Princess Irys, and Prince Daivyn."

Tartarian and Anvil Rock looked at one another. Then Tartarian turned back to Cayleb.

"Since there's no point in pretending otherwise, in the long run, I suppose we may as well admit that you're correct, Your Majesty."

"I thought as much." Cayleb nodded. "And, in answer to the question you haven't asked, My Lord, I would assume all three of them reached their destination safely. Obviously, no one can guarantee the vagaries of wind or weather—you, as an admiral, will know that as well as I do—but your little ruse completely fooled the only one of my cruisers to actually intercept *Wing*, for which I compliment you. Although it does rather complicate both of our problems at the moment, doesn't it?"

In fact, Cayleb knew that Irys and Daivyn had reached Shwei Bay without further incident.

"I believe you could say it does represent at least a *slight* complication," Tartarian replied wryly.

"It could hardly be otherwise," Cayleb agreed. "And from your choice of words, My Lord," he looked at Anvil Rock, "it seems evident you and Earl Tartarian—and, I would assume, the Council—have agreed to acknowledge Daivyn as Prince of Corisande, despite his absence. And despite any other potential contenders for the crown."

"We have," Anvil Rock said shortly.

"I think that was probably your wisest choice, under the circumstances," Cayleb said. "On the other hand, it will undoubtedly create several difficulties. I'll be frank, My Lords—given Charis' relations with Corisande over the years, the notion of leaving any member of Prince Hektor's house on the Corisandian throne, even as a vassal of the Charisian Empire, scarcely appeals to me. The notion of having the heir to the throne outside the Princedom and—forgive me, but we all know this is true—in a position to be used as a tool against Charis by our enemies is even less attractive."

"However attractive or unattractive it may be, Your Majesty, Earl Tartarian and I have neither the right nor the desire to depose our legitimate prince."

"And I see you intend to be stubborn about that." Cayleb's brief smile deprived his words of most of their sting.

"We do, Your Majesty," Anvil Rock replied unflinchingly.

"This may surprise you, My Lord, but I not only respect your integrity, but in many ways, I agree with your decision, as well."

Despite himself, Anvil Rock's eyebrows rose slightly, and Cayleb chuckled harshly.

"Don't mistake me, My Lord. Agreeing with you isn't the same thing as liking the situation. Nonetheless, creating a succession dispute would serve neither of us at this time. Which means I'm prepared to recognize young Daivyn as Corisande's legitimate prince, and as Duke of Manchyr."

Both Corisandians' body language seemed to relax slightly, but Cayleb wasn't quite finished yet.

"Precisely what will ultimately become of Daivyn's claim to the crown remains to be seen. If he wishes to retain it—or, for that matter, his duchy—he will be required to swear fealty to me and to Empress Sharleyan, which will also hold true for every other member of the Corisandian nobility. And I will not confirm him in any of his dignities so long as he stands upon any other realm's soil. I won't *deprive* him of them, but

neither will I confirm them until I can be certain he's his own
man and not under the control of anyone else. Until such time
as I can be certain of that, his duchy will be administered for
him by someone of my own choice. I would prefer for that
someone to be a Corisandian, rather than a foreigner imposed
upon Manchyr, and I would appreciate your suggestions for
an appropriate steward."

Anvil Rock and Tartarian looked at one another again.
Neither of them spoke, however, and they turned back to
Cayleb.

"What, precisely, do you require of Corisande, Your
Majesty?" Anvil Rock asked bluntly.

"I think I've already laid out my essential points, My Lord.
Specifically, I will require that Corisande acknowledge
Charisian sovereignty, and that all members of the Corisandian nobility swear fealty, individually, to the Charisian
Crown. I will require the cooperation of your own Parliament
and your own law masters in integrating Corisandian and
Charisian law. I will require formal Corisandian recognition
of the dissolution of the League of Corisande, and recognition of Zebediah's already-accomplished permanent integra-
tion into the Empire as a separate province. I will appoint a
governor for Corisande, acting in the names of myself and
Empress Sharleyan and supported by a Charisian garrison.
All Corisandian warships will be surrendered and integrated
into the Imperial Charisian Navy, and all Corisandian army
units will be disbanded. And I will insist, for reasons I'm sure
you'll both understand, upon severely limiting the number
of armed retainers any Corisandian noble is permitted to retain."

The Corisandians' faces had tightened again while he spoke,
but he continued in that same calm, measured tone.

"In return, I will guarantee the protection of the persons
and property of Corisandian subjects. There will be no general seizure of private property, and the property of the
Crown will be respected, although it will also be integrated
into the imperial structure. All of the rights of Charisian sub-

jects will be extended to any Corisandian who swears fealty and faith to the Empire, and Corisandians will be permitted to serve in the Charisian military, if they so desire."

"And the Church, Your Majesty?" Tartarian asked softly.

"And the Church, My Lord?" Cayleb's voice was almost as soft as Tartarian's, and his smile was unpleasant. "The Church of Charis follows the Crown of Charis."

"Which means precisely what, Your Majesty?" Anvil Rock asked, his voice harsher than it had been.

"Which means the Church's bishops and serving clergy in Corisande will be required to affirm their loyalty to the Church of Charis and to acknowledge Archbishop Maikel as the primate of that church," Cayleb replied flatly. "Any bishop or priest who cannot, in good conscience, make that affirmation and acknowledgment will be deprived of his office. He will not be imprisoned for his refusal, nor will he be forced into exile or deprived of his priest's cap. As Archbishop Maikel has agreed, a priest is a priest forever, and despite the Group of Four's accusations, we have no desire to punish or victimize anyone simply because he cannot, in good conscience, agree with the position and organization of the Church of Charis. We *will* punish any treasonous acts, regardless of their justification, and regardless of who the traitors may be, but there will be no arbitrary arrests or imprisonment."

"Many of our people will reject your right to dictate terms to Mother Church, however reasonably you may dress them up, Your Majesty," Anvil Rock said warningly.

"For themselves, as individuals, they have every right to do so," Cayleb said unflinchingly. "If they step beyond matters of personal conscience into open defiance of the law which binds all men, or into organized resistance to the Crown, then they become criminals, and they will be treated as such. Although," his eyes became harder than brown agate, "I would recommend to their consideration the fact that Archbishop Maikel has specifically rejected the teachings of *The Book of Schueler* dealing with the 'appropriate punishment' for heresy. Whatever the Group of Four may choose to do, the Church of Charis will not be responsible for atrocities like those inflicted upon Archbishop Erayk. Nor will the Charisian Empire burn innocent cities or murder, rape, and terrorize their citizens as the Group of Four proposed to do to Charis."

Anvil Rock tried to meet those hard, brown eyes. After a moment, his own fell.

"For what it's worth, My Lords," Cayleb said after a few moments, his voice rather lighter than it had been, "you can console yourself with the knowledge that Empress Sharleyan and myself remain under Grand Vicar Erek's writ of excommunication. Theoretically, I suppose, that means any oath you may swear to us is nonbinding, in the eyes of Mother Church. Or, perhaps, I should say the Council of Vicars and the Group of Four. Mind you, I intend to enforce any oaths you may swear exactly as if they *were* binding, but if it helps you or any of Corisande's other nobles where your consciences are concerned . . ."

He shrugged.

"Your Majesty, we—" Anvil Rock began just a bit sharply, but Cayleb shook his head.

"Forgive me, My Lord," he interrupted. "I didn't mean to sound as if I were making light of the situation, nor would I for a moment impugn the personal honor of you or Earl Tartarian. On the other hand, whether we wish to acknowledge the point or not, all of us know *someone* in Corisande is going to take precisely that view in order to justify active resistance to the Empire. It's going to happen, My Lords, and all of us know it. When it happens, I will do all in my power to avoid overreactions, but there *will* be consequences for those responsible, and those consequences will be severe. I have no more choice in that regard than any other secular ruler, however those involved may choose to justify their actions. I won't attempt to deceive you on that point, nor would you believe me if I did."

Anvil Rock looked at him for a moment, then nodded with genuine, if perhaps grudging, respect.

"At any rate, My Lords," Cayleb said more briskly, "I believe we all understand both sides' beginning positions. As I say, my terms and requirements are essentially simple, although I'm not so naïve as to believe that giving effect to them won't be complicated, difficult, and—unfortunately—quite possibly accompanied by additional bloodshed. I would suggest at this time that you return to Manchyr to discuss them with the other members of the Council. Unless you disagree, I would recommend we meet again tomorrow, when you can give me the sense of the Council's response and we can continue these discussions, if that should be the Council's decision. In the meantime, the truce between our two armies will continue."

"I believe that sounds reasonable, Your Majesty," Anvil Rock agreed gravely, although he must have recognized as well as Cayleb that, ultimately, the Council had no option other than to accept Cayleb's terms. And, Cayleb suspected, whether Anvil Rock cared to admit it or not, he and Tartarian had to recognize that Cayleb's demands were not simply reasonable, but minimal, under the circumstances.

"Before you return to the city, however," the emperor said, "I hope you'll do me the honor of dining with me and my own senior officers. I've arranged for certain of our guests to join us at table," he added, and if his smile was small, it was also warmer than any which had yet been exchanged as he nodded sideways at Sir Koryn.

"Your Majesty," Anvil Rock said with a smile of his own, "the honor will be ours."

III

Royal Palace,
City of Cherayth,
Kingdom of Chisholm

Empress Sharleyan looked around the small, familiar council chamber.

She'd gotten a lot accomplished in this chamber, over the years, she thought. And she'd never before been away from it for so long, either. It was one year and two months, to the day, since she'd left Chisholm to marry Cayleb Ahrmahk, and there were times when she found it impossible to believe that so much had happened in so short a time.

She crossed to the open window, put her hands on the sill, and looked out it, and her eyes softened with memory. It was true absence made one see familiar things through fresh, new eyes, she thought, and savored the vista of hills, roofs, and trees. Beyond them, she could just see the living blue marble of Cherry Bay, and the air was cool, not quite crisp, as if to warn her Chisholm's autumn was on its way. No doubt it seemed even cooler to her, after her long stay in Charis, and she shivered inside as she gazed at leaves hovering on the brink of seasonal change and thought about the approaching winter. If she thought Charis had made her sensitive to *this* coolness, winter was going to be icy, indeed! Yet even as she thought that, she realized there was something about the idea of winter that seemed almost comforting, a part of the life she'd always known, and her shiver turned into a smile as she thought about the ways in which this winter was going to be different.

And how much warmer your bed's going to be, you mean, she told herself, and chuckled.

"You don't know how much I've missed hearing you do that," a voice said behind her, and she turned with a smile.

Her mother smiled back, then crossed to seat herself at the conference table. Baron Green Mountain got there before she did and pulled the chair out for her, and she looked up at him over her shoulder as he pushed it back closer to the table once she was seated.

"Thank you, Mahrak," she said.

"You're welcome, Your Majesty."

He bowed to her with a smile, and Sharleyan's eyes narrowed in sudden speculation. Green Mountain's wife of more than thirty years had died three years ago, and Queen Mother Alahnah had been a widow for almost thirteen years. They'd known each other literally since childhood, and they'd always been close, even before King Sailys' death. Since then, they'd worked with one another—and with her—as political allies who relied upon one another absolutely, and the empress suddenly wondered how she'd managed to miss the other ways in which they'd grown steadily closer.

I wonder if—?

She cut that thought off in a hurry. Mostly because it was none of her business, as long as they were discreet enough to keep their relationship from becoming a political issue, but also because she'd thought of them as Mother and Uncle Mahrak for so long that thinking of them any other way seemed obscurely wrong, somehow.

"How much you've missed me doing what, Mother?" she asked now, innocently.

"Laughing," Queen Mother Alahnah said simply. "Of course, I've missed hearing you *giggle* even more."

Sharleyan grinned and shook her head, then turned her back firmly on the window and took her own place at the table.

"I've missed you, too, Mother—and you, Mahrak," she said, her expression more serious.

"The feeling is mutual," Green Mountain told her, "and not just because we've got such a stack of documents waiting for you. Of course," it was his turn to glance somewhat pointedly at the window, "we'd rather expected you home some time ago."

"I know—I know!" she said repentantly. "It was just one thing after another, and Cayleb and I both thought—"

"Darling, we all know what you and Cayleb thought. For that matter, we agreed with you," Alahnah said, reaching out to lay a slim hand on her daughter's forearm. "I won't pretend I didn't resent the decision that kept you there so much longer . . . until I met Cayleb on his way through to Corisande, that is." She smiled warmly at her daughter and rolled her eyes. "Such a delicious young man! You managed to land quite a catch with that one, Sharley!"

If her object had been to listen to her daughter's giggle, she succeeded admirably, and Sharleyan shook her head at her.

"I can't disagree with any of that, Mother," the empress said. "On the other hand, you might want to think about the fact that he's made more visits to Cherayth over the last, oh, half-year or so than he has to Tellesberg."

"Of course he has. That's how I know your decision to stay in Tellesberg was one of state, based on cold political calculation and your sense of duty, my dear. Given how . . . tasty he is, that's the only conceivable reason you haven't been right here all that time!"

"I'm glad you appreciate the sacrifices I've been willing to make."

"We certainly do," the queen mother said rather more seriously. "And the fact that we may have agreed with your decision doesn't mean we didn't miss you."

"If only I could be in two places at one time," Sharleyan sighed.

"If you could, life would be a lot simpler," Green Mountain agreed. "Since you can't, we'll just have to do the best we can, won't we?"

"And if I haven't mentioned this before, I want you to know how thankful I am that I have the two of you to help do that," Sharleyan said with utter sincerity.

"I believe you *have* mentioned it, a time or two," he said.

"Possibly even more often than that," the queen mother added. "I'd have to check my diary to be certain, of course."

"Good." Sharleyan smiled. "My mother raised me to thank

people whenever they did me little favors like, oh, running my kingdom for a year while I go galavanting off to get married."

Green Mountain laughed, but the skin around Alahnah's eyes tightened.

"It wasn't the getting married that worried me, dear. Not, at least, after we met Cayleb." She tried to keep her voice light, but she failed, and it was Sharleyan's turn to touch her arm with a comforting hand.

"Mother, I can't begin to tell you how sorry I am," she said quietly.

"Don't be silly," Alahnah said. The briskness she put into her voice was belied by the unshed tears glistening in her eyes, and she straightened in her chair and drew a deep breath. "Byrtrym always made his own decisions—you know that, if anyone does. He made that one, just like all the others, and no one else is responsible for its consequences. I only thank God that that monster Halcom didn't succeed!"

"You can thank Edwyrd and the rest of my guards for that, Mother," Sharleyan said somberly. "Without them . . ."

She let her voice trail off, shaking her head, and Green Mountain nodded.

"I already have—thanked Edwyrd, I mean," he told her. "I offered him a more substantial token of my gratitude, as well. He turned it down."

"Politely, I hope?"

"Yes, Your Majesty." Green Mountain smiled at her. "He was *very* polite, in fact."

"Good," Sharleyan said again, then leaned back in her chair, thinking about the past few five-days.

She'd been back in Cherayth for almost a full five-day, and every one of those days had been an incredible whirl of events. She could scarcely sort them all out in her memory, and she felt relatively certain that several of those memories had gotten themselves arranged out of order, but despite her sense of exhaustion, she'd found herself feeling an enormous relief, as well. She'd had her mother's regular letters, of course, and Green Mountain's—and Cayleb's—for that matter, but that hadn't been the same thing as actually being here. After more than twelve years on the throne, it had seemed . . . unnatural to have to rely on the reports of others, no matter how much she trusted those others. And it had to have seemed even odder to them to have their monarch off living in another kingdom, entirely.

"I have to admit," she said aloud, after a few moments, "that, overall, things have worked out even better than I'd hoped they would."

"Aside from any minor plots to murder you, you mean?" Green Mountain's voice was just a little edgy, and Sharleyan realized he'd been less calm about the assassination attempt than he tried to pretend. Her eyes softened at the thought, and she smiled at him.

"Aside from that, of course," she conceded.

"I must say, dear, that however well we might have managed in the long term with you in Tellesberg, the decision to come home was a good one," her mother said. Sharleyan looked at her, and the queen mother shrugged. "When word of the attack on Saint Agtha's reached us, the public reaction was . . . unhappy."

"As always, your mother is a mistress of understatement," Green Mountain said dryly. "On the plus side, I expect that any of your nobles who may have been feeling restive again about the keenly felt injustice of finding themselves saddled with a mere queen have rethought their positions. Meeting Emperor Cayleb face-to-face would probably have produced much of that effect, anyway, of course. While he may not have struck them as a 'delicious young man,' I rather doubt that any of them would like to find him angry at *them*. And even if they were prepared to risk that, the Kingdom's reaction to the attempt on your life should have been sufficient warning for anyone but a complete idiot. Your people haven't forgotten what happened to your father, you know, Your Majesty."

"Neither have I," Sharleyan said darkly.

"No, of course you haven't," Alahnah said, and her own eyes were hard. "I'm rather looking forward to paying our debt to Hektor Daykyn. In full, with all deferred interest."

"As we all are, Mother," Sharleyan replied, reminding herself that word of Hektor's assassination hadn't yet reached Chisholm. Or, rather, it hadn't reached anyone *else* in Chisholm. That was going to change almost momentarily, of course, but she was beginning to fully appreciate the enormous advantage Merlin Athrawes' "visions" and the ability to communicate information over vast distances almost instantly truly conferred.

Not to mention the pain in the posterior Cayleb must have found it when he couldn't share that sort of information with me.

"The most important thing, aside from the fact that you're still alive, is how well you succeeded in communicating who was truly behind it to everyone here in Chisholm," Green Mountain said. She looked at him, and he smiled at her approvingly. "Your mother's right about your decision to come home. No message from you could have been as convincing as actually seeing you here, on Chisholmian soil, and it's a very good thing that you arrived so close on the heels of the news itself. Whatever anyone else may say now, for the first five-day or so there was an enormous amount of suspicion. Halcom's plan to drive a wedge between Chisholm and Charis almost worked. In fact, if he'd managed to kill you after all, it *would* have worked."

"I know. I was afraid of that from the very beginning," Sharleyan admitted. "That's why I waited long enough for Baron Wave Thunder's investigation to confirm at least some of the details. I needed to be able to tell people here who really planned the attack, and why."

"And the price your Charisian guardsmen paid to keep it from succeeding," her mother said softly. "I'll never forget what those men did for you, dear."

"Neither will I."

Sharleyan felt her eyes burn once more and made herself draw another deep breath.

"Neither will I," she repeated. "But since they did manage to keep me alive, I suppose it's time the three of us got down to work."

"Of course, Your Majesty," Green Mountain said rather more formally, and she smiled at him.

"First, Mahrak," she said, "I'd like to discuss your view of the way Uncle Byrtrym's allies on the Council are most likely to react to all of this. Then I'd like your personal impressions—and yours, Mother—on how our own Temple Loyalists are likely to respond. After that, there are a couple of treasury issues I promised Baron Ironhill I'd look into. It's past time Cayleb and I got a common imperial currency established, and now that we have the Imperial Parliament just about fully organized, we can start thinking about other things. So—"

Her mother and her first councilor sat back, their expressions intent, as Sharleyan set briskly to work.

▼ ▼ ▼

Sharleyan looked up as Edwyrd Seahamper opened the door and cleared his throat politely.

"I beg your pardon, Your Majesty, but a courier has just arrived from the Emperor."

"He has?" The empress's eyebrows arched, and Seahamper nodded gravely. Without, she reflected, so much of a flicker of expression to betray the fact that he and Sharleyan had already known the man was on his way. She smiled mentally at the thought.

At least there's one *person I can discuss things like this with without worrying,* she told herself. *Cayleb may have Merlin, but* I've *got Edwyrd, and that's almost as good.*

"He says his dispatches are urgent, Your Majesty," her personal armsman added, and she nodded crisply.

"In that case, by all means, admit him at once."

"Yes, Your Majesty."

Seahamper withdrew briefly, and Sharleyan looked around at her mother's and her first councilor's faces. She was a little surprised by how much they'd managed to accomplish since lunch. There was still far more *to* accomplish, of course. It could scarcely have been any other way, after her long absence, but they'd made a sizable dent in the backlog. It was fortunate that so much of it consisted simply of approving and confirming decisions they'd already made.

And the best of it is that, for all intents and purposes, Mother has been ruling Chisholm in my stead, and there hasn't been even a hiccup. Not on the secular side, at least. Maybe I've actually managed to convince the Kingdom that a monarch doesn't have to be male?

Of course, there was always the religious side. The good news there was that between them Archbishop Pawal, Green Mountain, Sir Ahlber Zhustyn, Chisholm's equivalent of Baron Wave Thunder, and Earl White Crag, the Kingdom's Lord Justice, had managed to keep their feet firmly on the neck of any Temple Loyalist temptation towards some sort of active resistance. The fact that it had been Temple Loyalists in Charis who had attempted to murder their queen—and the fashion in which the rest of the Kingdom had reacted to that news—had undoubtedly strengthened the inclination for Chisholm's Temple Loyalists to keep their heads down.

Unfortunately, that didn't mean they'd decided to accept Sharleyan's "heretical defiance of Mother Church." Thanks to Merlin and his SNARCs, Sharleyan was probably better aware of that even than Zhustyn or Green Mountain, neither of whom cherished any illusions in that respect. In fact, Sharleyan knew that at least three members of her own council were currently in communication with the deposed Bishop Executor Wu-shai.

At the moment, she and Merlin were both convinced they'd identified the "major players," as Merlin described them, but that, too, had its drawbacks. Knowing who to watch was a priceless advantage; fighting down the temptation to have them arrested for what she knew they were doing but would find difficult to prove in open court wasn't easy. In fact, she'd found herself sorely tempted to manufacture the evidence she needed. Fortunately, she'd decided long ago that policies like that were what got kings and queens overthrown by their own nobles. The fact that she'd always been scrupulously just in her treatment even of her enemies among the Chisholmian nobility was a major factor in the readiness with which the majority of her nobles accepted the justice she handed down when she had clear and compelling evidence of wrongdoing by one of their own number.

Well, eventually you're going to give *me that evidence, My Lords—or, at least, show me where one of my merely mortal agents can "discover" it. And when that day comes . . .*

The council chamber door opened once more as Seahamper returned with Cayleb's courier.

"Your Majesty," the courier—a Chisholmian, Sharleyan noted—said, bowing profoundly.

"Your name?" she asked.

"Commander Traivyr Gowyn, Your Majesty." Gowyn smiled, obviously pleased that she'd cared enough to ask. "I have the honor to command the armed schooner *Sentinel.*"

"Thank you," she said, smiling back at him, then sat back in her chair. "Sergeant Seahamper says your dispatches are urgent, Commander Gowyn?"

"I fear they are, Your Majesty." Gowyn's smile had disappeared into a sober expression.

"In that case, Commander, may we have them?"

"Of course, Your Majesty." Gowyn opened his dispatch case and extracted a thick envelope, sealed with Cayleb's personal seal and addressed to Sharleyan in Clyfyrd Laimhyn's clear, strong script. He laid it in her extended hand with another bow.

"Thank you," she said once more, weighing it in her palm. "Does your vessel require supplies or service, Commander?"

"I would prefer to take on fresh water before returning to sea, Your Majesty. With that proviso, *Sentinel* could sail within the hour."

"I don't believe we'll need to pack you back off quite that quickly, Commander Gowyn," Sharleyan said with a smile. "I'm pleased to hear that we could if we had to, but I expect you'll have time for at least a fresh salad and a shore-cooked meal before we send you back to Corisande."

"Thank you, Your Majesty," Gowyn replied, bowing once more as he recognized his dismissal. Seahamper escorted him back out of the council chamber, and Sharleyan turned to Green Mountain and her mother.

"And now," she said whimsically, her smile crooked as her slender fingers broke the heavy wax seals, "let's see what fresh bad news Corisande has seen fit to provide us with."

▼ ▼ ▼

". . . so I'm none too sure they believe you."

If any of Empress Sharleyan's subjects, aside from her personal armsman, had happened to glance into her bedchamber they might have had significant reservations about their monarch's stability. She sat in one of the huge, overstuffed chairs, with her feet tucked up under her, speaking to apparently empty air. It was very late, and she'd sent Sairah Hahlmyn off to bed hours ago. Mairah Lywkys was still recovering from the injury she'd suffered when Byrtrym Waistyn had "arranged" her riding fall to keep her safely out of the way at Saint Agtha's, and getting her to turn in reasonably early hadn't been difficult, either. Now Sharleyan sat in the candlelit bedchamber, watching the silver orb of Langhorne, Safehold's single moon, climbing steadily higher beyond her window, and cocked her head to one side while she listened.

"I wish I could say I was surprised to hear that," Cayleb's voice said in her right ear. "Unfortunately, if I were they, I might very well have thought I'd done it, too."

"I think they'll come around to accepting the truth eventually," Sharleyan assured her far distant husband. "Mahrak is already more than three-quarters of the way to acknowledging just how remarkably stupid it would've been for you to have Hektor killed at this particular time. At the moment, he seems to be torn between admiration for your apparently ruthless pragmatism, wondering just how you could have been dumb enough to do it, and concern over what it says about your character in long-range terms."

"And your mother?"

"Well, Mother already thought you were a 'delicious

young man,'" Sharleyan chuckled. "I think she's been both pleased and surprised by how much she likes you, and to be honest, the thought that you might have had Hektor murdered after what happened to Father only makes her like you even more. Frankly, I think she's going to be disappointed when she finally realizes you really, really didn't do it."

"I suppose that's better than having her running in horror from the cold-blooded murderer who could do such a thing," Cayleb said dryly.

"Trust me, Cayleb. The only thing that could have made Mother love you more than the notion that you'd collected Hektor's head would be the birth of her first grandchild. Which, by the way, she mentioned rather pointedly to me this afternoon. She seems to be of the opinion that having you in Corisande and me in Charis or Chisholm isn't very likely to provide for the succession. A thought which has also occurred to *me,* if not for such purely pragmatic reasons."

"You're not the only two people it's occurred to," Cayleb said with feeling. "And, as you say, not necessarily for purely pragmatic reasons."

"So just when are you going to darken my doorway so we can begin working on this little problem?" Sharleyan asked, and her own tone was rather pointed, Cayleb noticed.

"Soon, I think," he replied more seriously. "This afternoon, I met with Tartarian and Anvil Rock for the fifth time. There were a couple of points they wanted to talk about, but they obviously realize they have no choice but to sign on the dotted line in the end. They're going to, Sharleyan, and as soon as they do, I'm installing General Chermyn down here as my interim viceroy, and *Empress of Charis* and I are setting sail for Cherry Bay."

"Good!"

"The only question in my mind is how I'm going to be greeted when I arrive," Cayleb continued.

"If you mean here in the Palace, I don't think anyone could care less, either way, whether or not you had Hektor murdered," Sharleyan replied. "Oh, some people are going to be worried about it, and still more are probably going to pretend to be horrified by the very notion, but the truth is that everybody knows Hektor would've had you and your father assassinated in a moment if he'd thought he could get away with it. In fact, I'd estimate that half the nobles in Chisholm think he was involved in Tirian's assassination plot, whatever Nahrmahn—or you—might have to say about it. And the possibility that you did order it is working in our favor, in some ways. I wouldn't be a bit surprised to find out Merlin's SNARCs are reporting that the members of the nobility most likely to conspire against us with the Temple Loyalists are . . . reevaluating their positions in light of the belief that you'll simply have them killed if they turn into too much of a problem."

"Wonderful." Sharleyan's imagination could almost literally see Cayleb rolling his eyes. "Who was that Old Earth political writer you mentioned to me the other day, Merlin?"

"Machiavelli," Merlin replied. His voice was even clearer than Cayleb's, and that, Sharleyan realized, was because it was being transmitted directly from Merlin's built-in communicator.

"That was the one," Cayleb agreed. "I guess I'm going to find out whether he was right about its being better to be feared than to be loved." He sighed. "Well, Father always said it was essential that your *enemies* fear you. I'm not too sure I like the notion of being feared by my own subjects, though."

"I think you only have to worry about that where the nobility is concerned," Sharleyan said reassuringly. "The common folk are even more inclined to think you had Hektor killed. The difference between them and the nobility is that they don't have any reservations about it, if you did. In fact, they've been lighting bonfires to celebrate Hektor's death—and in salute to you for having brought it about—ever since the news broke. I have mentioned that Hektor wasn't very popular here in Chisholm, haven't I?"

"Once or twice, I suppose," Cayleb conceded.

"Well, there you have it." Sharleyan shrugged. "We can't do anything about the way the Church is going to use this for propaganda, and Nahrmahn and Merlin are both right. Even if the Church—or Clyntahn, at least—didn't actually order the murders, they're still going to use what happened as a hammer to beat both of us with. But as far as our own people are concerned, even if we did it, it's perfectly all right with them. As a matter of fact, some of them actually seem to regard it as a sort of appropriate vengeance for Halcom's attempt to murder *me*."

"What?" Sharleyan heard the confusion in his voice and giggled.

"Of course it is, silly! I know we've officially exonerated Hektor of any involvement in Halcom's plot, but there's no way my people are going to give up a perfectly good conspiracy theory!"

"Wonderful," Cayleb said again, his tone more than moderately disgusted. "If *they* all believe it, then it's going to be damned hard to convince anyone *else* of the truth."

"We'll just have to do the best we can. And in the meantime, getting you back here to Chisholm to spend a few months with *both* of us in residence—like the Empire's constitution requires, if memory serves—should pretty much finish cementing Chisholm's acceptance of the new political arrangements. Of course," she smiled wickedly out the window, "that's going to mean you get to spend the *winter* here in Chisholm. We have this thing here that you may not have seen in Charis. It's called 'snow.'"

"I *have* heard of the phenomenon," Cayleb told her with dignity. "But surely you don't mean to say it's so cold in Chisholm that it actually sticks to the ground without melting, do you?"

"It has been known to happen," she assured him solemnly.

"Well, in that case, from now on we're spending the winters in Charis."

"That would be my choice, too, all things considered together. Or maybe not. Not at the moment, at any rate."

"Why not?" He tried to keep his tone light, but she heard the sudden spike of worry in its depths, and smiled again.

"Don't worry. It's not because I mistrust our Charisians

any more than I mistrust our Chisholmians. It's just that it's just occurred to me that it *is* going to be cold here in Cherayth, isn't it?"

"And?" Cayleb asked with suspicious caution.

"Well, if it's *really* cold, then a poor, thin-blooded southern boy such as yourself is going to be looking for any source of warmth he can find."

"And?" Cayleb repeated.

"And," she said sweetly, "right off the top of my head, I can't think of anything much warmer than a nice, big bed right here in the Palace, with big, thick quilts and comforters. If we manage it right, we might not have to come out at all before spring."

SEPTEMBER,
YEAR OF GOD 893

✦

. I .

The Temple,
City of Zion,
The Temple Lands

We spend too much time in council chambers like this, Rhobair Duchairn thought. *For that matter, we spend too much time inside the Temple, and too little time out in God's world. We're too busy enjoying the luxury of the Temple to appreciate the rest of the world the Archangels built for us. And the one everyone else has no choice but to live in all year round.*

It was a thought which had occurred to him with increasing frequency over the last year or two, and he'd made an effort to do something about it. Yet however hard he tried, the responsibilities of his offices, and the deepening dangers and challenges which confronted the Church on every hand, kept drawing him back.

It's going to be even worse, once winter settles in again, he warned himself. *Once the snow gets deep enough, once it gets cold enough out there, you're going to find even more reasons to stay comfortably inside, insulated from all that . . . unpleasantness.*

There was a metaphor in that, he thought. And not one that had anything to do with weather.

He looked up as Zahmsyn Trynair came through the door. The Chancellor was running late, the last of the Group of Four to arrive, and he gave them a brief, tight smile of apology.

594 / DAVID WEBER

"Forgive me, Brothers," he said. "My office had just received a dispatch from Desnair, and I thought it best to have it deciphered before I came."

"And did it say anything interesting?" Zhaspahr Clyntahn growled from his place at the council table.

"There were some interesting observations in it," Trynair replied. "Nothing particularly earth shattering. Most of it consisted of secondhand reports on what the Charisians have been doing to completely finish off Delferahk's shipping. Apparently, their Admiral Rock Point has begun sending cutting-out expeditions even into neutral ports now—in broad daylight, as often as not—to take out or burn any Delferahk-flagged ship. I've had copies made for all of us, especially for you, Allayn."

Allayn Maigwair nodded in thanks, although the gratitude in his expression was scarcely unalloyed. He'd become painfully aware that his was the most precarious position of any of the Group of Four. Despite the fact that officially it was *he* who had realized the Church was going to require a navy of galleons, not galleys, the fact remained that no one—with the possible exception of Duchairn—could really count the number of marks which had been poured into their useless galley fleet, first. And there were persistent rumors that it was actually Clyntahn who had recognized Maigwair's initial mistake. Rumors, Maigwair strongly suspected, which had originated with the Grand Inquisitor himself . . . and which carried with them a damnation of Maigwair's own judgment which was, unfortunately, only too accurate in this instance.

"Was there anything more about Hektor's assassination?" Clyntahn asked.

"Only about the rumors and speculations swirling around in Desnair," Trynair said. He looked at Clyntahn with carefully concealed speculation. "I haven't had any new reports about the actual event. Have you?"

"No." Clyntahn shook his head. "If I had, I would certainly have brought them to everyone's attention."

"Everyone," in this case, meant the other members of the Group of Four, of course, Duchairn thought sourly.

"I wish we did have more reliable information about it," he said aloud, watching Clyntahn's expression from behind outwardly calm eyes. "That whole affair still seems . . . odd to me."

"What's 'odd' about it?" Clyntahn snorted disdainfully. "Cayleb obviously had the man killed. He had reasons enough, as far as he was concerned, even before he married Sharleyan. And the entire world knows how much *that* bitch hated Hektor!"

Something about Clyntahn's dismissive, almost casual assignment of guilt clicked down inside Rhobair Duchairn. The Treasurer General's eyes flicked sideways to Trynair's, and saw the same realization there. Both of them, Duchairn knew, had wondered from the outset. Now they knew.

"Yes, well," Trynair said, "whoever arranged it," he was very carefully not looking in Clyntahn's direction, Duchairn realized, "it leaves us with some interesting dilemmas."

"We've had enough of *those* for the last couple of years," Clyntahn observed. "I don't see how a few more are going to make all that much difference."

"I hope you'll forgive me, Zhaspahr," Trynair said with just a hint of asperity, "but quite a few of *these* dilemmas are going to fall into the political arena. That makes them of rather more than passing interest to me and to my office. And, I would have thought, they'll undoubtedly have implications for the Inquisition, as well."

Clyntahn's jowly face tightened for just an instant, but then it smoothed again, and he nodded.

"You're right," he conceded, which was about as close to an apology as he ever came.

"Thank you."

Trynair settled into his place at the head of the table and looked around at the other three faces.

"At the moment, of course, as we're all well aware, all of our information on Hektor's murder is fragmentary and secondhand, at best. I'm sure we all hope we're going to get more reliable reports—from Bishop Executor Thomys, preferably—soon. On the other hand, it's already September.

It's not going to be many more five-days before the weather begins closing down our ability to send and receive messages, even with the semaphore. I think we're going to have to go ahead and decide how to begin responding to this with the information we already have, however unsatisfactory it may be in some respects."

"Obviously, the first thing to do," Clyntahn said, "is to condemn the bloody actions of Cayleb, Sharleyan, and the rest of the apostate leadership. I realize Hektor and his son were only two more lives against all of the thousands who have already died because of their defiance of Mother Church. But if they're prepared to murder reigning princes and their heirs this casually, it indicates an entirely new level of danger."

"In what way, Zhaspahr?" Duchairn asked. He was actually a bit surprised he'd been able to keep his tone so neutral.

"The sheer brazenness of it, for one thing," Clyntahn replied. "The fact that they're willing to murder their opponents so openly only underscores their contempt for the rest of the world's judgment and condemnation. And, of course, it's going to have implications for other princes and kings, isn't it? Who can ever be certain a Charisian assassin isn't stalking *them* if they appear to be some sort of obstacle to Cayleb's and Sharleyan's obscene ambition? Besides, we're talking about an act of *murder,* Rhobair. The murder of not just anyone, but of a prince consecrated by Mother Church herself, and one who was waging God's own fight against the forces of apostasy! I realize they've already demonstrated in Ferayd that they were willing to murder even priests of God, but now they've proven they'll murder anyone, and without even the benefit of a show trial like the one in Ferayd. Hektor's a martyr, yet another martyr in the holy war against Charis and the forces of Darkness. We owe it to his memory, to God, and to Mother Church to make that clear to every member of the faithful!"

"I see."

Duchairn managed to keep his gorge down, although it wasn't easy. The fervor shining in Clyntahn's eyes frightened him. It was almost as if the Grand Inquisitor actually believed what he was saying about Charis' responsibility for Hektor's death. The fact that he could first order an act of murder so casually and then exploit it so cynically was bad enough. The possibility that he was actually able to believe his own lies was far worse, especially in one who wielded the authority of the Inquisition.

"I think we can all agree with that, Zhaspahr," Trynair said calmly. "As you say, however Hektor died—on the field of battle, in bed, or struck down by an assassin's hand—he was obviously waging war against Mother Church's enemies. While I would never wish to appear overly cynical or calculating—" Duchairn wondered if he was the only one who noticed how Trynair's eyes hardened ever so briefly as the Chancellor gazed at Clyntahn "—the simple propaganda value of making that point publicly and loudly will be invaluable."

"I thought so myself," Clyntahn agreed with the merest hint of complacency.

Maigwair looked up sharply, and Duchairn felt something almost like pity for the captain general.

Just waking up to it now, are you, Allayn? he thought sardonically. *Well, better late than never, I suppose. But you really need to work on controlling your expression.*

From the look in Maigwair's eyes, he'd finally realized what Trynair and Duchairn had suspected all along, and the fact that Clyntahn had acted unilaterally, without even consulting his colleagues, must be even more frightening to him than it was to Duchairn. After all, Maigwair was the most vulnerable of the Group of Four. The rest of the vicarate had been unhappy, to put it mildly, when the entire new galley fleet was declared obsolete before its very first battle against the forces of darkness. Even those too circumspect—or terrified—to openly criticize the Grand Inquisitor, or the Chancellor, were beginning to mutter about the Captain General's apparent incompetence. Now Clyntahn had thrown Hektor casually to the slash lizards simply because the man was more valuable as a suitably deceased martyr than he was alive. If the Grand Inquisitor could do that, then he could certainly offer up the weakest and most vulnerable of his colleagues to appease the rest of the vicarate's wrath.

And he will *do it, Allayn,* Duchairn thought. *Without a moment's hesitation or a single second thought, if he sees any advantage in it.*

An image came to him—an image of ice wyverns on an island of drift ice, pushing one of their fellows into the water to see if the krakens were still there. It wasn't very difficult to imagine one of them with Maigwair's face.

"One of the dilemmas I mentioned a moment ago," Trynair continued, "is what we do about Prince Daivyn, however."

"I'm not sure there's any reason to rush into decisions where he's concerned, Zahmsyn," Duchairn said. The Chancellor looked at him, one eyebrow raised, and he shrugged. "At the moment, he and his sister—and the Earl of Coris—are safe enough in Talkyra."

"And 'at the moment' Zhames has every reason to *keep* him there, too," Clyntahn said with a deep, amused chuckle.

However little Duchairn might care for Clyntahn's amusement over the war between Delferahk and Charis which had emerged from the Grand Inquisitor's own ship seizure policy, he had to concede that Clyntahn had a point. As long as King Zhames was at war with Cayleb and Sharleyan, he was scarcely likely to surrender his wife's distant cousin to the Charisians.

And at least Talkyra's far enough inland that the Charisians can't get to it, Duchairn thought caustically. *They seem to be able to go anywhere* else *in his kingdom they choose to!*

He upbraided himself. It wasn't King Zhames' fault that the Imperial Charisian Navy could land Marines at any point along his coast it chose. It was obvious the Charisians realized there was nothing he could do about it, though, and they were deliberately and methodically shutting down every port and harbor Delferahk had once boasted. They hadn't burned any more cities, but their blockade was virtually impenetrable, and they'd continued pouncing on every military target that offered itself. By now, the Delferahkan Navy was extinct, and although the Charisians had been scrupulously careful to avoid collateral damage to non-Delferahkan property in the course of their cutting-out expeditions to seize Delferahkan merchant ships and galleys in neutral ports, no one really wanted to risk Cayleb's ire by offering those Delferahkan vessels refuge.

Still, there was a lot of validity to Duchairn's own thought about the security of Zhames II's capital city. Talkyra truly was much too far inland to be effectively threatened by any Charisian attack. Which, in its own way, summed up the ultimate limitations upon Charisian power. Despite their successes along Delferahk's coast, or their ability to invade Corisande, or even the confusing, fragmentary reports Maigwair had so far received about their Marines' frightening new weapons and tactics, they simply lacked the land-based manpower to fight their way into the vitals of any mainland realm.

"I'm not especially concerned about Daivyn's physical security or safety," Trynair said. "I'm concerned about his political value. I'd prefer to see to it that no one else tries to exploit that value in a way which might conflict with our own policies."

"Leave the boy be for now, Zahmsyn," Clyntahn said almost impatiently. "He's not going anywhere. Where *could* he go, after all? No one who isn't already actively fighting the apostates is going to want to risk fishing in waters like these, at least until we tell them to. And when the time comes that *we* need him, we'll be able to put our hand on him whenever we choose."

"It's not quite that simple, Zhaspahr. Especially not if we intend to recognize him as the rightful Prince of Corisande."

"Actually, I think Zhaspahr is right," Duchairn said, little though he relished finding himself in agreement with the Grand Inquisitor. Trynair looked at him again, and Duchairn shrugged. "It's not as if Daivyn—or Coris, who's the one who really matters in this instance—has anyone else to champion his cause. If we proclaim that Daivyn is the legitimate Prince of Corisande, and if Mother Church undertakes to restore him to his throne when the schism has been utterly defeated, that ought to be enough. Certainly Coris is smart enough and experienced enough to realize that. Let's leave him where he is, for now, at least. We can handle anything we need to handle through correspondence. Or, for that matter, we can always summon Coris here to Zion for us to give him more specific, face-to-face instructions. I think we can let a barely nine-year-old boy who's just been orphaned try to find some stability in his life before we drag him into some sort of political frying pan."

Trynair gazed into Duchairn's eyes for several moments, then nodded slowly. Duchairn was in no doubt that Trynair would sacrifice the boy without a moment's hesitation if he decided it was the expedient thing to do. But at least the Chancellor had enough compassion to be willing to let a grieving boy be until it *became* the expedient thing to do. It was possible Clyntahn, did, too, but Duchairn personally never doubted that Clyntahn's position was the result of indifference—or even of smug satisfaction with how well his murder of the boy's father had worked out—rather than of any sort of concern for young Daivyn.

"All right," Trynair said aloud. "I'll draft a message to Coris, embodying our recognition of Daivyn and suggesting ways in which Coris and the Prince might be of assistance to us against his father's killers. I'll circulate the draft to all of you before I send it, of course," he added with a slightly pointed glance in Clyntahn's direction.

That glance bounced off of the Grand Inquisitor's armor without so much as scratching its paint.

"In the meantime," Maigwair put in, "I have to admit that I'm a bit concerned over the fact that, as Zahmsyn pointed out earlier, the weather is going to greatly impede our ability to communicate in another few five-days."

"Concerned in what way?" Duchairn asked.

"I'm not that worried about our ability to coordinate our plans elsewhere," Maigwair said. "Our existing instructions are comprehensive enough that they probably aren't going to need a lot of modifications. And I think we're all agreed that it's unlikely, to say the least, that the apostates are going to attempt any major operations against the mainland until next spring. So it's unlikely we're going to have to respond to any immediate military crises."

"Any *more* immediate military crises, you mean," Clyntahn muttered in a voice whose level was carefully calculated to be just audible. Maigwair's lips tightened for a moment, but he continued as if the Grand Inquisitor hadn't spoken.

"What *does* worry me," he said, "is what's going to happen here, in the Temple and in Zion, once winter really closes in. There's always that tendency to . . . turn inward after the first heavy snowfall."

What might almost have been unwilling—and surprised—respect flickered in Clyntahn's eyes, and Duchairn found himself sharing the Grand Inquisitor's surprise. One didn't normally expect that sort of remark out of Allayn Maigwair. Although, the Treasurer General thought a moment later, Maigwair's awareness of his own weakened position might just explain it.

As Maigwair had so aptly pointed out, once winter closed in around the city of Zion, the Temple's interests tended to switch to more purely internal matters. Communications with the outside world were slowed, less reliable, and the rhythm of Mother Church's life slowed with them. Vicars and archbishops resident in Zion tended to use that time to polish up their alliances and catch up on paperwork and routine administrative matters. And animosities and pet grievances with one another tended to loom even larger than usual within the hierarchy's rival factions.

But this winter was going to be different. *This* winter was going to be spent worrying, reflecting upon Grand Vicar Erek's Address from the Throne, and thinking about the implications for the future. Charis' apparently unbroken string of triumphs was going to be a huge factor in that thinking, and so were any potential criticisms of the Group of Four's leadership. The normally somnolent winter was going to be anything but tranquil, with potentially dire consequences for the Group of Four.

Or, at least, for its most vulnerable member.

"Oh, I think we'll find something to keep us busy," Clyntahn said, and something about his tone snatched Duchairn's attention back to him. The light in Clyntahn's eyes wasn't simply confident; it was anticipatory. The light of a man looking greedily forward to some treat he'd promised himself.

Tiny icy feet seemed to dance up and down inside Duchairn's bones. Was it possible that—?

"Do you have some particular 'something' in mind, Zhaspahr?" Trynair asked. From the Chancellor's expression, he seemed to have noticed the same thing, but he asked his question rather more calmly than Duchairn thought *he* could have asked it.

"Something always comes along, Zahmsyn," Clyntahn pointed out almost jovially. "In fact, I've noticed that it tends to come along at the most surprisingly useful times."

Duchairn's stomach muscles tightened as he recalled a seemingly innocent conversation with Vicar Samyl Wylsynn. He hadn't really thought all that deeply about it at the time, mostly because it had seemed so appropriate to the moment. Since he'd been called to the orange, Duchairn had missed altogether too many of the retreats to which he'd been routinely invited. He'd been trying to make up for some of that—as much as he could fit it into his schedule's voracious demands, at any rate—and he'd found himself sitting next to Wylsynn at one of the prayer breakfasts he'd attended. He hadn't given much thought to the coincidence which had brought them together. Not then. Not until later, when he'd had the opportunity to reflect on possibly deeper meanings in what Wylsynn had said.

He'd had two or three more conversations—brief, to be sure—with Wylsynn since. All of them, like the first one, could have been nothing more than innocent coincidences, but Duchairn didn't believe that for a moment. Wylsynn had been sounding him out about something, and given the Wylsynn family's well-earned reputation, it wouldn't have been something of which Clyntahn would have approved.

If Wylsynn's really up to something, and if Zhaspahr's gotten wind of it . . .

Duchairn hadn't worked with Clyntahn for so many years without realizing how the Grand Inquisitor's mind worked. The possible opportunity to finally crush his most hated rival would appeal strongly to him at any time. And he'd take special pleasure in waiting until he could use the chance to condemn Wylsynn for "treason against Mother Church" to divert his colleagues' attention from the Group of Four's failures at the most opportune possible time. Even better—from his perspective, at least—the discovery of "traitors" within the ranks of the vicarate itself could only help to whip up even more fervor against *all* of the Church's enemies . . . and strengthen Clyntahn's hand as the man charged with rooting out those enemies wherever they might hide.

Even if that meant among his fellow vicars . . . and especially among the ones who might have dared to criticize the Grand Inquisitor—and his allies—for mismanagement of the schism.

Trynair hadn't had the advantage of Duchairn's exchanges with Wylsynn, but he, too, obviously sensed something else under Clyntahn's surface joviality. Whatever he might suspect, however, he clearly wasn't prepared to press the point at the moment.

"At any rate," he said, brushing Clyntahn's remarks aside as if they truly were as innocuous as Clyntahn had implied, "there are several more points I'd like to discuss this afternoon. First, there's the matter of the fashion in which Siddarmark appears to be conspiring to continue trading with Charis. Siddarmark isn't the only place where it's happening, either, I'm afraid. As Rhobair warned us, men who face ruin as the economic consequences of the embargo begin to bite are prone to seek solutions to their difficulties. It occurs to me that it would be unreasonable to expect anything else, which means—"

He continued speaking, dealing with the day-to-day business of administering Mother Church in such troubled times, but Rhobair Duchairn discovered that he was listening with only half an ear.

The rest of his attention was focused someplace else, worrying about something entirely different.

. II .

Royal Palace, City of Cherayth, Kingdom of Chisholm

There. See what I mean about nice warm beds?" the Empress of Charis demanded as she snuggled close to the Emperor and laid her head on his chest.

"I'm sure it will be a nice warm bed, one of these nights," he replied in the tone of a man clearly giving such weighty matters the due consideration they deserved as he draped an arm across her back and his palm settled against damp, sweet-smelling skin. "At the moment, however, I can't really say that the air temperature is all that frigid. Even here in far northern Chisholm."

He gave an exaggerated shiver, and Sharleyan chuckled. If pressed, she would have been forced to concede that she'd been guilty, during her months in Tellesberg, of just a *little* exaggeration where the iciness of Cherayth's climate was concerned. She supposed she really shouldn't have been, but it had proved impossible for her to resist the temptation to play to her Charisian audience's apparent expectations. From the wide-eyed credulity with which they had absorbed her tales, she was sure most of them were convinced Chisholmians spent the entire winter bundled to the eyebrows in furs and parkas.

Actually, she knew, the September night really was a bit on

the cool side for Cayleb's Charisian sensibilities. It was going to get much worse than that, by the time winter closed in, and she knew that, too. Just as she knew that during Cayleb's career in the Royal Charisian Navy, his ship had sailed through waters as bitterly cold as anything he was going to face here in Cherayth.

Which doesn't make it one bit less satisfying to tease him about it, she admitted to herself. *Besides, we* are *both going to treasure the warmth of our bed before the ice melts in the spring.*

"Actually," Cayleb said, his breath soft and warm on her ear, "I'm prepared to concede—not in front of witnesses, mind you, but solely in private—that this particular bed has quite a few things to recommend it."

"Indeed?" She pushed up on one elbow to look into his eyes. "And what, pray tell, might those 'few things' be?"

"Well," he replied judiciously, reaching up with one finger to draw gentle circles around one of her nipples, "first, it's big enough. I can't begin to count the number of beds I've seen which were just plain too short. Your feet hang off at one end, or your head hangs off at the other. And it's well stuffed, too. That's always an important feature. Sometimes mattresses get stuffed with straw, or even old corn husks, and that's never very pleasant. The sheets are nice, too, now that I think about it, and the embroidery on the pillowcases is first rate. Not quite up to *Charisian* standards, perhaps, but considering the limitations available to the decorator, quite satisfactory. Then there's—"

He broke off as his wife took shameless advantage of his own currently nude state.

"Now, now!" he said hastily, as her grip tightened. "Let's not do anything we'll both regret!"

"Oh, I'm not going to do anything *I'll* regret," she assured him with a wicked smile.

"Well, in that case, I suppose I should also add that the most important feature of this entire bed is that I'm not alone in it," he said.

"That's headed in the right direction," she said. "Not quite up to *Chisholmian* standards, perhaps, but considering the limitations available to the speaker, *almost* satisfactory."

"Only *'almost'*?!" he demanded indignantly.

"I am the one in position to be pressing my legitimate demands at the moment . . . among other things," she pointed out sweetly.

"Oh, all right." He grinned hugely, gathering her into his arms and sliding her body up and across onto his own. "I suppose I might as well go ahead and admit that this is the second nicest bed I've ever been in in my entire life. I trust you'll forgive me if I always have a special warm spot for our bed back in Tellesberg."

"Oh," she kissed him slowly and thoroughly, "I suppose I can forgive you for that. After all, so do I."

▼ ▼ ▼

Some hours later, the two of them sat side-by-side in the sitting room of their suite, gazing out the windows at the polished silver disk of the moon riding across a sky of blue-black velvet. Stars twinkled, and Cayleb shook his head slowly.

"Hard to believe that every one of those stars is as big and bright as our own sun," he murmured.

"Harder to believe than to believe that Merlin is a nine-hundred-year-old *woman*?" Sharleyan demanded, resting her head on his shoulder.

"Yes, actually." Cayleb smiled. "After all, I can always just fall back on the notion that Merlin really is magic, whatever he says!"

"Idiot," she said fondly, reaching up to yank on his now fully established beard.

"Do you like it?" he asked. She looked up at him, and he shrugged. "The beard, I mean. Do you like it?"

"It tickles in some fairly inappropriate places," she said severely. "And I wouldn't want it to get out of hand. No great, shaggy clouds of whiskers, you understand. But with that proviso, I guess I can stand it."

"Now there's a ringing endorsement, if I ever heard one," he said wryly.

"Well, it's going to take some getting used to," she pointed out.

"Almost as much as getting used to the notion that Corisande is now part of the Charisian Empire?" he asked, his expression turning rather more serious.

"I suppose that depends, in the end, on just how thoroughly Corisande *is* part of the Empire," she said, her own expression matching his. "At the moment, the jury is rather still out on that, after all."

"That's true enough," he agreed. "The good news is that I think Tartarian and Anvil Rock are genuinely convinced now that I didn't order Hektor's assassination. Mind you, I don't think Anvil Rock *wanted* to be convinced, but the man's got a fairly substantial streak of integrity, and his son worked hard on bringing him around."

"So you're convinced that they intend to abide by the terms of the peace settlement?"

"Merlin's shown you the same 'imagery' from his SNARCs that he's shown me, love. That means your guess is as good as mine. At the moment, though, I'd have to say I think the answer is yes. I don't think they like it. For that matter, if I were in their boots, *I* wouldn't like it, either. But they're smart enough to recognize the inevitable when they see it."

"The fact that you guaranteed Daivyn's personal safety, whether he got to retain his throne or not, didn't hurt," Sharleyan said shrewdly.

"Maybe not. But it wouldn't have *helped*, either, if they hadn't decided they can trust me to keep my word as long as they keep theirs. And whatever *they* may think, or intend, where the peace settlement is concerned, they and the rest of the Council are on the back of a particularly irritated slash lizard at the moment. No matter what happens, they're going to be in for a rough ride, and there's a limited amount we can do to help without actually making things worse."

Sharleyan nodded soberly. One of the main reasons Cayleb had returned to Cheryath was to give Sir Koryn Gahrvai,

Tartarian, Anvil Rock, and the remainder of the Corisandian Council, which was technically acting jointly as Prince Daivyn's regent, the opportunity to restore and maintain order in Corisande without his own disturbing presence for the Temple Loyalists and their Corisandian patriot allies to rally opposition around. He'd left enough Marines under General Chermyn's command, as the official imperial viceroy of the new province of Corisande, to keep a lid on things at least in the city and Duchy of Manchyr even if worse came to worst, but that was definitely not the way he or Sharleyan wanted to establish their rule in Corisande.

"There *are* going to be some rebellions, Cayleb," Sharleyan said after a moment. "You know that, don't you?"

"Yes," he sighed. "That's inevitable, given the fact that we conquered Corisande by force of arms, rather than through a mutual accommodation like Emerald's. Or even Zebediah's, for that matter. There's going to be someone who's going to try to 'throw the foreigners out,' whether it's because of genuine patriotism or as a means to seek personal power for himself. And the religious aspect is only going to make that even worse. I'm not cherishing any rosy illusions about how docile and sweet-natured our new Corisandian subjects are going to be, Sharley. But at least Tartarian and the Gahrvais want to limit Corisandian bloodshed as much as they can, and they know that, ultimately, we've got the firepower—and the naval strength—to crush almost any rebellion which could be mounted. They know we don't want to do that, of course, but they know we *can*, if we have to. More to the point, they know we *will*."

Emperor Cayleb's face was hard, determined, and as Sharleyan gazed at it in the moonlight, she realized her own expression matched his. Neither of them wanted bloodshed that could be avoided. Neither of them wanted to see towns or cities burned, men executed for treason against their new emperor and empress. Neither of them wanted to be forced to resort to the harsh measures of suppression which the Safeholdian rules of war enshrined for conquered provinces. But given the threats which ringed them about, and the long history of Corisandian enmity for both Charis and Chisholm, neither would hesitate if it became necessary, either.

"Well, assuming any rebellions are minor enough that General Chermyn can deal with them out of his available resources, what's next?" she asked after a moment.

"That's something you and I—and Merlin—are going to spend quite a bit of this winter thinking over, love," he replied. "The truth of the matter is that what we've just finished was the *easy* part. By spring, Maigwair's going to have made more progress than I'd like to think about where his galleon fleet is concerned. Thank God he wasted all that time and money on galleys first! But from what Merlin's seen so far, *someone's* actually read Earl Thirsk's reports. And by now they've gotten enough information about the new model artillery that we're going to be facing well-armed galleons in someone else's hands. Mind you, they're not going to know what to do with them as well as we will, and I intend to keep it that way by pruning them back as brutally as possible as often as possible. As my father said, it's important for any Temple admiral to be half-defeated in his own mind before he ever puts to sea against us.

"Aside from that, though, I don't know what our best option is going to be. I'm hoping you and Baron Green Mountain can help me figure that out. At the moment, it's sort of like a battle between a doomwhale and a great dragon. In our element, we should be able to beat any fleet the Temple can throw against us, even if the numerical odds are against us, if only because we'll know what we're doing, and they won't . . . yet. But if we try to put an army ashore against mainlander armies, we'll get our arses kicked. Not at first, maybe, but in the end. We simply can't get deep enough on the mainland to force the Temple to surrender before the Temple figures out how to duplicate our weaponry advantages."

"You're saying it's going to be a standoff? A stalemate?"

"I'm saying it *may* be a standoff. Or that it may start off that way, at least. But the Temple is going to be trying to figure out ways to get at us, even while we're trying to figure out ways to get at *them*, and with all those smart and determined people on both sides trying to find a way, I'm fairly sure one will turn up. Ideally, it will be on our terms, not theirs, but I'm not foolhardy enough to try to guarantee that. So far, we've come up golden at almost every point. Eventually, we have to stub our toes, Sharley. The trick is to make sure we don't fall down and break our necks when we do."

"Well," she said, snuggling down and pressing her cheek back into his shoulder, "as you say, we've got a lot of smart people on our side, too, including you and me. And we've got Merlin, and Archbishop Maikel, and—I'm fairly sure—we've got God. Between the lot of us, we ought to be able to handle anything someone like Clyntahn can throw at us."

. III .

City of Zion,
Temple Lands

I don't like it, Samyl."

Hauwerd Wylsynn shook his head, his expression grave, as he and his older brother sat facing one another across the remnants of their supper. An autumn rainstorm beat against the huge window of the dining room, running down the transparency in sheets that turned the gathering evening's cloud-struck gloom beyond into a wavering tapestry, like some oracle's obscure vision of an uncertain future.

"There are quite a few things I don't much care for at the moment, myself, Hauwerd," Samyl replied. "Would you care to be a bit more specific?"

"Don't try to be humorous," his brother growled. "I'm not in the mood for it."

"Under the circumstances, I don't think any of us can afford to simply abandon our sense of humor," Samyl pointed out. "Not unless we want to brood on all our potential troubles until it drives all of us mad and Clyntahn can be shut of us without any effort on his part at all."

"Very funny," Hauwerd said sourly. Then he drew a deep breath and straightened in his chair. "But probably accurate," he conceded. "Mind you, I don't think I'm going to find a great many laughing matters this winter."

"We'll find them where we can," Samyl said philosophically. "For the rest, all we can do is trust God."

"I'd feel better if we had His promise that trusting in Him would bring us all through this with whole skins."

"So would I. Unfortunately, He never promised that. So go ahead and tell me what it is you've got on your mind tonight."

"It's the . . . stridency with which Clyntahn and Trynair are riding Cayleb's supposed responsibility for Hektor's assassination," Hauwerd said.

"What? You don't think he did it?" Samyl asked innocently.

"Forget you're a Schuelerite and stop playing Shan-wei's advocate," Hauwerd half-growled. "First, no, I don't think he did it. I've told you that before. He's too smart to do something this stupid. And, second, whether he was responsible or not isn't really germane to what's bothering me."

"Then what is germane?" Samyl asked . . . without, Hauwerd noticed, ever actually saying whether or not he believed Cayleb Ahrmahk had ordered Prince Hektor's murder.

"It's the way they're going about it. Stacking it on top of all of Charis' 'unprovoked aggression' against Delferahk." Hauwerd shook his head. "Couple that with the Address from the Throne, and what do you see? You see them preparing the ground to declare Holy War as soon as the ice melts in Hsing-wu's Passage, that's what you see," he said, answering his own question.

"Probably so," Samyl agreed, his own expression turning rather more serious. "On the other hand, if they weren't using those pretexts, you know they'd have found others. It's the nature of the beast."

"Krakens do tend to attack when they smell blood, don't they?" Hauwerd said bitterly.

"Yes, they do," Samyl sighed. "On the other hand, there's

612 / DAVID WEBER

not very much we can do about that, aside from seeing what the power of prayer can accomplish. Which is why I'm looking at rather more immediate concerns."

"Duchairn?"

"Exactly." Samyl nodded heavily. "I don't know exactly what's been going on inside that man, Hauwerd, but I'm strongly inclined to believe we're seeing a genuine regeneration on his part. Which, of course, puts him in a position of deadly danger, that close to Clyntahn. The last thing Clyntahn can afford is a man who takes the *Writ* seriously sitting there in the middle of the Group of Four."

"Actually," Hauwerd said seriously, "that could be Duchairn's best protection. Clyntahn's constitutionally incapable of taking the faith of anyone who doesn't agree with him seriously. Or, rather, taking anyone who doesn't agree with him as a serious threat if he's motivated by genuine faith."

"No? Then what about Duchairn's warning?"

"Zhaspahr Clyntahn's not worried about us because of our *faith,* Samyl. He's worried about us because we represent a threat to his *powerbase.* And," Hauwerd added unhappily, "because he thinks we may make a splendid diversion."

"Exactly," Samyl said again.

He'd been more than a little surprised by Duchairn's warning. The Treasurer General had taken the risk of speaking to him personally, and despite Wylsynn's own efforts to speak in diplomatic circumlocutions, Duchairn had come straight to the point with devastating frankness.

"Clyntahn has to have someone inside the Circle, Samyl," his brother said now, his voice tense.

"We've been operating for a long time," Samyl replied. "There are any number of other ways we might have given ourselves away."

"Of course there are other ways we *might* have given ourselves away," Hauwerd said impatiently. "But that's not what happened, and you know it as well as I do. If Duchairn is right, Clyntahn is only waiting until the most opportune moment from his perspective. And he wouldn't be waiting unless he was confident he knew everything we're doing, knew we weren't going to suddenly disappear before he's ready to pounce. And the only way he can know that is that he has someone on the inside telling him about our deliberations, our plans. And since we haven't added anyone new, it has to be someone who was already there."

Samyl's mouth had tightened as his brother laid out his devastating analysis. It wouldn't have bothered him as much if he hadn't come to exactly the same conclusions himself.

"Unfortunately, I don't have any idea who that 'someone' might be," he pointed out. "Do you?"

"If I did, you'd be the first to know. Or possibly," Hauwerd showed his teeth in a most unpriestly smile, "the second."

"You really need to forget the fact that you used to be a Temple Guardsman," Samyl told him. "Direct action isn't always the best option. Although, in this case, I have to admit I'd be sorely tempted, myself."

"All well and good. But since we don't know who it is, what do we do?"

"I don't know," Samyl admitted. "All I do know is that we've spent too long, committed too much of ourselves to this task, to simply cut and run. I'm not prepared to abandon God's Church to men like Clyntahn and Trynair, Hauwerd. If I have to die, there are far worse causes."

"No doubt. But there are also far better deaths," Hauwerd said grimly as he recalled Erayk Dynnys' fate.

"Yes, there are. Unfortunately, we've both just agreed Clyntahn wouldn't be giving us this much rope if he didn't have someone inside. He's watching us, and there's no way we can give all the members of the Circle warning without warning Clyntahn's spy, as well. Which means Clyntahn will know anything we do if we try to alert the others."

"Don't we still owe them that warning, whatever might happen?" Hauwerd's expression was troubled, and Samyl nodded.

"Of course we do. We just can't give it to them, anyway."

"So what *can* we do?"

"I've already started doing what I can," Samyl said. "I'm getting as many as possible of our junior members out of

Zion on one pretext or another. It's taking some ingenuity to manufacture enough 'routine missions' for me to get them sent away with winter coming on, but I've already gotten over a dozen of our bishops and upper-priests out of the city. And on missions that are going to *keep* them out of the city until after snowfall. I don't know if I can come up with something to get any of the archbishops out without arousing Clyntahn's suspicions and causing him to strike sooner. Cahnyr is about the only exception to that, since he's just about due for his winter pastoral visit to Glacierheart. But as long as you and I are still here, Clyntahn should feel fairly confident that he can put his hand on us any time he chooses."

"Somehow, that fails to inspire me with a great deal of personal reassurance," Hauwerd observed dryly.

"I know." Samyl smiled at his brother, knowing Hauwerd could see the love in his eyes. "I'm sorry I got you into this."

"Nonsense. Making ourselves a pain in the arse to people like Clyntahn and Trynair has been part of the family business for as long as I can remember. In fact, it's been a Wylsynn speciality since the Creation itself."

Hauwerd's tone had shifted very slightly, and he arched an eyebrow at his brother.

"I know," Samyl replied after a moment.

"Do you think—?"

"No." Samyl shook his head firmly.

"Samyl, if we don't use the key now, when *can* we use it?"

"The key was never meant for use against those within the Church," Samyl replied. "Not only that, but it's a weapon of last resort, and it can only be used once. Schueler made that crystal clear. And do you truly think Cayleb and Charis have crossed the threshold he set yet?"

"Of course not," Hauwerd said. "We've agreed on that from the outset. But this schism is getting deeper and deeper, Samyl. It's only too likely that it will slide over into genuine heresy sooner or later, whatever Staynair or Cayleb want, if Clyntahn keeps driving this way. And if worse comes to worst for the Circle, if there's no one left to *stop* him . . ."

He let his voice trail off, and Samyl nodded somberly.

"I know," he said. "I know. But that's one reason Paityr is in Charis, Hauwerd."

Hauwerd sat gazing at him for several seconds, then sighed heavily.

"There are times I wish we'd been born into another family," he said with a lopsided smile.

"So do I . . . sometimes," Samyl agreed. "Unfortunately, we weren't. It's why the rest of the vicarate is so damned fond of us in the first place."

Hauwerd chuckled. Then he shook his head.

"You know, I was glad from the outset that Paityr stayed in Charis, but I hadn't thought about it in terms of the key."

"That's because I never told you I'd given it to him," Samyl said. "Not that I ever really expected it to come to this when I helped Clyntahn 'arrange' his assignment there. In fact, I can't honestly say that I saw *any* of this coming when he first went to Tellesberg, but God always has worked in mysterious ways. This must have been what He had in mind . . . and at least Paityr's out of Clyntahn's reach at the moment."

"And pray God he stays there," Hauwerd said softly. He himself had never produced children, and as he considered what someone like Clyntahn might well do to the families of his enemies in the vicarate, he was profoundly grateful for that fact.

"I'm sending word to Lyzbet through Ahnzhelyk," Samyl said quietly. "I'm telling her to stay home, and keep the other children with her, instead of bringing them to Zion this winter."

"You think Clyntahn won't be watching them?"

"I know Clyntahn *will* be watching them." Samyl's voice was grim. "But I know he had to be watching Adorai Dynnys and her boys, too, and Ahnzhelyk's arrangements got them out. I think she can do the same for us. I pray so, at any rate."

"You'll send them to Charis?"

"Where else can they find anything remotely like safety?"

"No place I can think of," Hauwerd admitted.

"Obviously, I'll also be warning her to make her own arrangements," Samyl continued, "although, frankly, I'd be astonished to discover that she hasn't already given some thought to that. She's not the sort to desert a sinking ship prematurely, but she definitely *is* the sort to prepare her escape route ahead of time, God bless her!"

"Amen," Hauwerd agreed with a quirky smile.

"And," Samyl said, looking into his brother's eyes once again, "I'm going to send her another letter. This one for Paityr . . . just in case."

. IU .

Royal Palace,
City of Talkyra,
Kingdom of Delferahk

The cool breeze blowing in off Lake Erdan plucked at Irys Daykyn's hair like playful fingers. Evening was setting in across the enormous lake, and she enjoyed the familiar sight of a rippling sheet of water. Yet whatever else it might be, the lake wasn't Manchyr Bay. She missed the surf, the smell of salt, the smell of tidal marshes, the sense of the colliding life of land and sea across the hard-packed sand of the tide line and the softer, looser sand of the dunes.

And she missed her father.

She stood on the battlemented wall of King Zhames II's palace on its rocky hill above the city of Talkyra. It was both a cruder and an older palace than her father's palace in Manchyr. Despite its size, Delferahk had never been as rich a realm as Corisande, and Zhames' family had tended to rely rather more heavily upon the iron fist to maintain its authority. The occasional restiveness that technique had provoked had required a palace that was still a castle, a fortress which could be defended at need. Although both the king and Queen Hailyn assured her that those days were long past now.

But I thought that about Father, too, she thought, and brushed away a tear with one angry hand. *"Never let them see you cry." I remember you telling me that, Father. I remember* everything.

Her hands settled on the hard, weathered stone of the battlements and tightened until her knuckles stood out whitely. She wondered, looking back, if her father had somehow known this was coming. If that was the true reason he'd gotten her and Daivyn out of Corisande. She hoped not. She hoped he'd been truthful with her in the last conversation they would ever have. But whatever he'd been thinking, whatever his final motive, he *had* gotten them out, and one day Cayleb and Sharleyan of Charis would discover just how costly that was going to prove.

She stared out into the gathering evening, and the eyes of her dead mother were hard, hard, as she gazed unblinkingly into the wind.

She was fortunate to have Phylyp. She knew that, even if there were times she wanted to scream at him. He'd been a spymaster too long, she thought, forgotten how to think any way except in the cold, analytical fashion of a chess player. His insistence that they still had to keep their minds open to the possibility that someone besides Cayleb might have given the order was probably appropriate for a spy, but there was no question in Irys' mind. No question of who was responsible . . . or who would ultimately pay.

In the meantime, she would take Phylyp's tactical advice. He was right that the two of them somehow had to keep Daivyn out of the Church's clutches. No matter how fervently the Group of Four might have announced its recognition of him as Corisande's legitimate ruler, he was only a little boy. Someone like Clyntahn would twist him like a pretzel, destroy him as casually as stepping on a fly, if it served his purposes. Irys had no illusions in that regard, any more than she had any illusions about the basis for King Zhames' attentive solicitude where Daivyn was concerned.

Such a little boy, she thought, her eyes prickling once again. *Such a little boy to be caught in such deep water. They'll suck*

618 / DAVID WEBER

the marrow out of you if they have the chance, Daivyn. They'll use you, then throw you away. Unless someone stops them.

And Irys knew who that "someone" had to be.

Advise me, Phylyp, she thought. *Advise me. Help me keep him safe—keep him alive. He's not just my baby brother now; he's my Prince, and all I have left. All that butcher Cayleb has left me. No one—no one—is going to do to him what they did to Father and Hektor. As God is my witness, I'll rip out their throats with my bare teeth before I let that happen!*

No doubt it was foolish for a single eighteen-year-old girl to think such thoughts. No doubt King Zhames would pat her on the head, tell her to run along and leave the worrying to those better suited to such tasks. No doubt Zhaspahr Clyntahn would be amused at the thought that she could even consider setting her puny will and minuscule resources against his own plans for her brother. And no doubt Cayleb of Charis would laugh at the thought that someday she would see him suffer every pain he had inflicted upon her and her family twice over.

But, she told herself, promised God Himself, as she stared bleak-eyed into the face of the night wind blowing out of the north, *they'll discover their mistake.*

Oh, yes. They'll discover their mistake.

CHARACTERS

ABYLYN, CHARLZ—a senior leader of the Temple Loyalists in Charis.

AHBAHT, LYWYS—Edmynd Walkyr's brother-in-law; XO, merchant galleon *Wind*.

AHBAHT, ZHEFRY—Earl Gray Harbor's personal secretary. He fulfills many of the functions of an undersecretary of state for foreign affairs.

AHDYMSYN, BISHOP EXECUTOR ZHERALD—Erek Dynnys' bishop executor.

AHRDYN—Archbishop Maikel's cat-lizard.

AHRMAHK, CAYLEB ZHAN HAARAHLD BRYAHN—King of Charis.

AHRMAHK, CROWN PRINCE ZHAN—younger brother of King Cayleb.

AHRMAHK, KAHLVYN CAYLEB—younger brother of Duke Tirian, King Cayleb's first cousin once removed.

AHRMAHK, KING CAYLEB II—King of Charis (see Cayleb Zhan Haarahld Bryahn Ahrmahk).

AHRMAHK, PRINCESS ZHANAYT—King Cayleb's younger sister.

AHRMAHK, QUEEN ZHANAYT—King Haarahld's deceased wife; mother of Cayleb, Zhanayt, and Zhan.

AHRMAHK, RAYJHIS—Duke of Tirian, Constable of Hairatha, King Cayleb's first cousin once removed.

AHRMAHK, ZHENYFYR—Dowager Duchess of Tirian, mother of Rayjhis and Kahlvyn Cayleb Ahrmahk, daughter of Rayjhis Yowance, Earl Gray Harbor.

AHRTHYR, SIR ALYK, Earl of Windshare—the commander of Sir Koryn Gahrvai's cavalry.

AHSTYN, LIEUTENANT FRANZ, Charisian Royal Guard—the

second-in-command of King Cayleb II's personal body-guard.

AHZGOOD, PHYLYP, Earl of Coris—Prince Hektor's spy-master.

APLYN-AHRMAHK, MIDSHIPMAN HEKTOR, Royal Charisian Navy—a midshipman assigned to HMS *Destiny,* 54. An adoptive member of the House of Ahrmahk as the Duke of Darcos.

ATHRAWES, CAPTAIN MERLIN, Charisian Royal Guard—King Cayleb II's personal armsman; the cybernetic avatar of Commander Nimue Alban.

BAHNYR, HEKTOR, Earl of Mancora—one of Sir Koryn Gahrvai's senior officers; commander of the right wing at Haryl's Crossing.

BAHRMYN, ARCHBISHOP BORYS—Archbishop of Corisande.

BAHRNS, KING RAHNYLD IV—King of Dohlar.

BANAHR, PRIOR FATHER AHZWALD—head of the priory of Saint Hamlyn, city of Sarayn, Kingdom of Charis.

BAYTZ, HANBYL, Duke of Solomon—Prince Nahrmahn of Emerald's uncle and the commander of the Emeraldian Army.

BAYTZ, NAHRMAHN HANBYL GRAIM—see Prince Nahrmahn Baytz.

BAYTZ, PRINCE NAHRMAHN GAREYT—second child and elder son of Prince Nahrmahn of Emerald.

BAYTZ, PRINCE NAHRMAHN II—ruler of the Princedom of Emerald.

BAYTZ, PRINCE TRAHVYS—Prince Nahrmahn of Emerald's third child and second son.

BAYTZ, PRINCESS FELAYZ—Prince Nahrmahn of Emerald's youngest child and second daughter.

BAYTZ, PRINCESS MAHRYA—Prince Nahrmahn of Emerald's oldest child.

BAYTZ, PRINCESS OHLYVYA—wife of Prince Nahrmahn of Emerald.

BREYGART, COLONEL SIR HAUWERD, royal charisian marines—the rightful heir to the Earldom of Hanth.

BRYNDYN, MAJOR DAHRYN—the senior artillery officer attached to Brigadier Clareyk's column at Haryl's Priory.

BYRKYT, FATHER ZHON—an over-priest of the Church of God Awaiting; abbot of the Monastery of Saint Zherneau.

CAHKRAYN, SAMYL, Duke of Fern—first councilor of Dohlar.

CAHNYR, ARCHBISHOP ZHASYN—Archbishop of Glacierheart; a member of the reformists.

CHALMYRZ, FATHER KARLOS—Archbishop Borys' personal aide.

CHARLZ, MASTER YEREK, Royal Charisian Navy—Gunner, HMS *Wave,* 14.

CHERMYN, GENERAL HAUWYL, RCM—the senior officer of the Charisian Marine Corps. He will be the SO for the Marines in the invasion of Corisande.

CHERYNG, LIEUTENANT TAIWYL—a junior officer on Sir Vyk Lakyr's staff; he is in charge of Lakyr's clerks and message traffic.

CLAREYK, BRIGADIER KYNT, RCM—CO, Third Brigade, Royal Charisian Marines. One of the senior Marine officers assigned to the invasion of Corisande. He is also the originator of the training syllabus for the RCMC.

CLYNTAHN, VICAR ZHASPAHR—Grand Inquisitor of the Church of God Awaiting; one of the so-called Group of Four.

COHLMYN, SIR LEWK, Royal Charisian Navy—Earl Sharpfield, Queen Sharleyan's senior naval commander. Also the equivalent of her Navy Minister.

DAHRYUS, MASTER EDVARHD—an alias of Bishop Mylz Halcom.

DAIKYN, GAHLVYN—King Cayleb's valet.

DAIVYS, MYTRAHN—a Charisian Temple Loyalist.

DARCOS, DUKE OF—see Midshipman Hektor Aplyn-Ahrmahk.

DARYS, CAPTAIN TYMYTHY, Royal Charisian Navy ("Tym")—CO, HMS *Destroyer,* 54. Flag captain to Admiral Staynair.

DAYKYN, CROWN PRINCE HEKTOR—Prince Hektor of Corisande's second oldest child and heir apparent.

DAYKYN, PRINCE DAIVYN—Prince Hektor of Corisande's youngest child.

DAYKYN, PRINCE HEKTOR—Prince of Corisande.

DAYKYN, PRINCESS IRYS—Prince Hektor of Corisande's oldest child.

DAYKYN, PRINCESS RAICHYNDA—Prince Hektor of Corisande's deceased wife; born in the Earldom of Domair, Kingdom of Hoth.

DEKYN, SERGEANT ALLAYN—one of Kairmyn's noncoms, Delferahkan Army.

DOYAL, SIR CHARLZ—Sir Koryn Gahrvai's senior artillery commander.

DRAGONER, SIR RAYJHIS—Charisian ambassador to the Siddarmark Republic.

DRAGONMASTER, BRIGADE SERGEANT MAJOR MAHKYNTY ("Mahk"), RCM—Brigadier Clareyk's senior noncom.

DUCHAIRN, VICAR RHOBAIR—Treasurer General of the Church of God Awaiting; one of the so-called Group of Four.

DYNNYS, ADORAI—Archbishop Erayk Dynnys' wife. Her alias after her husband's arrest is Ailysa.

DYNNYS, ARCHBISHOP ERAYK—former Archbishop of Charis.

DYNNYS, STYVYN—Archbishop Erayk Dynnys' younger son, age eleven.

DYNNYS, TYMYTHY ERAYK—Archbishop Erayk Dynnys' older son, age fourteen.

EDWYRDS, KEVYN—XO, privateer galleon *Kraken*.

ERAYKSYN, LIEUTENANT STYVYN, Royal Charisian Navy—Admiral Staynair's flag lieutenant.

ERAYKSYN, WYLLYM—a Charisian textiles manufacturer.

FAHRMYN, FATHER TAIRYN—the priest assigned to Saint Chihiro's Church, a village church near the Convent of Saint Agtha.

FAIRCASTER, SERGEANT PAYTER, Charisian Royal Guard—one of King Cayleb II's armsmen. A transfer from Crown Prince Cayleb's Marine detachment.

FHAIRLY, MAJOR AHDYM—the senior battery commander on East Island, Ferayd Sound, Kingdom of Delferahk.

FHALKHAN, LIEUTENANT AHRNAHLD, Royal Charisian Marines—commanding officer, Crown Prince Zhan's bodyguard.

FORYST, VICAR ERAYK—a member of the reformists.

FRAIDMYN, SERGEANT VYK, Charisian Royal Guard—one of King Cayleb II's armsmen.

FYSHYR, HAIRYS—CO, privateer galleon *Kraken.*

GAHRMYN, LIEUTENANT RAHNYLD—XO, galley *Arrowhead,* Delferahkan Navy.

GAHRVAI, SIR KORYN—Earl Anvil Rock's eldest son and CO of Prince Hektor's field army.

GAHRVAI, SIR RYSEL, EARL OF ANVIL ROCK—Prince Hektor's senior army commander and distant cousin.

GAIRAHT, CAPTAIN WYLLYS, Chisholmian Royal Guard—CO of Queen Sharleyan's Royal Guard detachment in Charis.

GALVAHN, MAJOR SIR NAITHYN—the Earl of Windshare's senior staff officer.

GARDYNYR, ADMIRAL LYWYS, EARL OF THIRSK—King Rahnyld IV's best admiral, currently in disgrace.

GRAISYN, BISHOP EXECUTOR WYLLYS—Archbishop Lyam Tyrn's bishop executor.

GRAIVYR, FATHER STYVYN—Bishop Ernyst's intendant. A man after Clyntahn's own heart.

GRAND VICAR EREK XVII—secular and temporal head of the Church of God Awaiting.

GYRARD, CAPTAIN ANDRAI, Royal Charisian Navy—CO, HMS *Empress of Charis.*

HAHLMYN, FATHER MAHRAK—an upper-priest of the Church of God Awaiting; Bishop Executor Thomys' personal aide.

HAHLMYN, SAIRAH—Queen Sharleyan's personal maid.

HAHLYND, ADMIRAL PAWAL—CO, anti-piracy patrols, Hankey Sound. (A friend of Admiral Thirsk.)

HAHSKYN, LIEUTENANT AHNDRAI, Charisian Imperial Guard—a Charisian officer assigned to Empress Sharleyan's guard detachment. Captain Gairaht's second-in-command.

HAIMYN, BRIGADIER MAHRYS, RCM—CO, Fifth Brigade, Royal Charisian Marines.

HALCOM, BISHOP MYLZ—Bishop of Margaret Bay.

HARMYN, MAJOR BAHRKLY, Emerald Army—an Emeraldian army officer assigned to North Bay.

HARYS, CAPTAIN ZHOEL—CO, Corisandian galley *Lance*.

HOLDYN, VICAR LYWYS—a member of the reformists.

HOWSMYN, EHDWYRD—a wealthy foundry owner and ship-builder in Tellesberg.

HOWSMYN, ZHAIN—Ehdwyrd Howsmyn's wife.

HWYSTYN, SIR VYRNYN—a member of the Charisian Parliament elected from Tellesberg.

HYLLAIR, SIR FARAHK, Baron of Dairwyn—the Baron of Dairwyn.

HYNDRYK, COMMODORE SIR AHLFRYD, Royal Charisian Navy—Baron Seamount, Charisian Navy's senior gunnery expert.

HYNDYRS, DUNKYN—purser, privateer galleon *Raptor*.

HYRST, ADMIRAL ZHOZEF, Royal Chisholmian Navy—the third ranking officer of the RCN. SO in Command, Port Royal.

HYSIN, VICAR CHIYAN—a member of the reformists (from Harchong).

HYWSTYN, LORD AVRAHM—a cousin of Greyghor Stohnar, and a mid-ranking official assigned to the Siddarmarkian foreign ministry.

HYWYT, COMMANDER PAITRYK, Royal Charisian Navy—CO HMS *Wave,* 14 (schooner). Later promoted to captain as CO, HMS *Dancer*, 56.

ILLIAN, CAPTAIN AHNTAHN—one of Sir Phylyp Myllyr's company commanders.

JYNKYN, COLONEL HAUWYRD, Royal Charisian Marines—Admiral Staynair's senior Marine commander.

JYNKYNS, BISHOP ERNYST—Bishop of Ferayd. He is not an extremist and does not favor excessive use of force.

KAHNKLYN, AIDRYN—Tairys Kahnklyn's older daughter.

KAHNKLYN, AIZAK—Rahzhyr Mahklyn's son-in-law.

KAHNKLYN, ERAYK—Tairys Kahnklyn's oldest son.

KAHNKLYN, EYDYTH—Tairys Kahnklyn's younger daughter.

KAHNKLYN, HAARAHLD—Tairys Kahnklyn's middle son.

KAHNKLYN, TAIRYS—Rahzhyr Mahklyn's married daughter.

KAHNKLYN, ZHOEL—Tairys Kahnklyn's youngest son.

KAIREE, TRAIVYR—a wealthy merchant and landowner in the Earldom of Styvyn.

KAIRMYN, CAPTAIN TOMHYS—one of Sir Vyk Lakyr's officers, Delferahkan Army.

KEELHAUL—Earl Lock Island's rottweiler.

KESTAIR, MADAME AHRDYN—Archbishop Maikel's married daughter.

KESTAIR, SIR LAIRYNC—Archbishop Maikel's son-in-law.

KHAILEE, MASTER ROLF—a pseudonym used by Lord Avrahm Hywstyn.

KNOWLES, EVELYN—an Eve who escaped the destruction of the Alexandria Enclave and fled to Tellesberg.

KNOWLES, JEREMIAH—an Adam who escaped the destruction of the Alexandria Enclave and fled to Tellesberg, where he became the patron and founder of the Brethren of Saint Zherneau.

LADY MAIRAH LYWKYS—Queen Sharleyan's chief lady-in-waiting. She is Baron Green Mountain's cousin.

LAHFTYN, MAJOR BRYAHN—Brigadier Clareyk's chief of staff.

LAHRAK, NAILYS—a senior leader of the Temple Loyalists in Charis.

LAHSAHL, LIEUTENANT SHAIRMYN, Royal Charisian Navy—XO, HMS *Destroyer,* 54.

LAIMHYN, FATHER CLYFYRD—King Cayleb's confessor and personal secretary, assigned to him by Archbishop Maikel.

LAKYR, SIR VYK—SO, Ferayd garrison, Kingdom of Delferahk. About the equivalent of a brigadier general.

LATHYK, LIEUTENANT RHOBAIR—XO, HMS *Destiny,* 54.

LAYN, MAJOR ZHIM, RCM—Brigadier Kynt's subordinate for original syllabus development. Now the senior training officer, Helen Island Marine Base.

LEKTOR, ADMIRAL SIR TARYL, Earl of Tartarian—Prince Hektor's senior surviving naval commander.

LOCK ISLAND, HIGH ADMIRAL BRYAHN, Royal Charisian Navy—Earl of Lock Island, CO, Royal Charisian Navy, a cousin of King Cayleb.

MAHKELYN, LIEUTENANT RHOBAIR, Royal Charisian Navy—fourth lieutenant, HMS *Destiny,* 54.

MAHKLYN, DR. RAHZHYR—head of the Royal Charisian College.

MAHKLYN, TOHMYS—Rahzhyr Mahklyn's unmarried son.

MAHKLYN, YSBET—Rahzhyr Mahklyn's deceased wife.

MAHKNEEL, CAPTAIN HAUWYRD—CO, galley *Arrowhead,* Delferahkan Navy.

MAHLYK, STYWYRT—Captain Yairley's personal coxswain.

MAHNTAYL, TAHDAYO—usurper Earl of Hanth.

MAHNTYN, CORPORAL AILAS—a scout-sniper assigned to Sergeant Edvarhd Wystahn's platoon.

MAHRYS, ZHERYLD—Sir Rayjhis Dragoner's secretary.

MAIGEE, CAPTAIN GRAYGAIR—CO, Royal Dohlaran Navy galleon *Guardian.*

MAIGWAIR, VICAR ALLAYN—Captain General of the Church of God Awaiting; one of the so-called Group of Four.

MAIYR, CAPTAIN ZHAKSYN—one of Colonel Sir Wahlys Zhorj's troop commanders in Tahdayo Mahntayl's service.

MAKAIVYR, BRIGADIER ZHOSH, RCM—CO, First Brigade, Royal Charisian Marines.

MANTHYR, COMMODORE GWYLYM, Royal Charisian Navy—was flag captain to Crown Prince Cayleb in the Armageddon Reef campaign.

MYCHAIL, ALYX—Raiyan Mychail's oldest grandson.

MYCHAIL, MYLDRYD—one of Rhaiyan Mychail's married granddaughters-in-law.

MYCHAIL, RHAIYAN—a business partner of Ehdwyrd Howsmyn and the Kingdom of Charis' primary textile producer.

MYCHAIL, STYVYN—Myldryd Mychail's youngest son.

MYLLYR, SIR PHYLYP—one of Sir Koryn Gahrvai's regimental commanders.

NETHAUL, HAIRYM—XO, privateer schooner *Blade.*

NYLZ, ADMIRAL KOHDY, Royal Charisian Navy—one of King Cayleb's newly promoted fleet commanders.

OHLSYN, TRAHVYS—Earl of Pine Hollow, Prince Nahrmahn's of Emerald's first councilor and cousin.

OLYVYR, SIR DUSTYN—chief constructor of the Royal Charisian Navy.

PAHLZAR, COLONEL AHKYLLYS—Sir Charlz Doyal's replacement as Sir Koryn Gahrvai's senior artillery commander.

PAWALSYN, AHLVYNO—Baron Ironhill, Keeper of the Purse (treasurer) of the Kingdom of Charis, a member of King Cayleb's council.

PHONDA, MADAME AHNZHELYK—proprietor of one of the City of Zion's most discreet brothels.

QUEEN YSBELL—an earlier reigning Queen of Chisholm who was deposed (and murdered) in favor of a male ruler.

RAHLSTAHN, ADMIRAL GHARTH, Emerald Navy—Earl of Mahndyr, CO, Emerald Navy.

RAICE, BYNZHAMYN—Baron Wave Thunder, member of the Council of King Cayleb, Cayleb's spymaster.

RAIMYND, SIR LYNDAHR—Prince Hektor of Corisande's treasurer.

RAIYZ, FATHER CARLSYN—Queen Sharleyan's confessor.

RAIZYNGYR, COLONEL ARTTU—CO, ⅔rd Marines (Second Battalion, Third Brigade), Charisian Marines.

RAYNAIR, CAPTAIN EKOHLS—CO, privateer schooner *Blade*.

RAYNO, ARCHBISHOP WYLLYM—Archbishop of Chiang-wu; adjutant of the Order of Schueler.

RAYNO, KING ZHAMES II—the King of Delferahk.

RAYNO, QUEEN CONSORT HAILYN—the wife of King James II of Delferahk; a cousin of Prince Hektor of Corisande.

ROCK POINT, BARON OF—see Admiral Sir Domynyk Staynair.

ROHZHYR, COLONEL BAHRTOL, RCM—a senior commissary officer.

RYCHTAIR, NYNIAN—Ahnzhelyk Phonda's birth name.

SAHLMYN, SERGEANT MAJOR HAIN, RMMC—Colonel Zhanstyn's battalion sergeant major.

SAHNDYRS, MAHRAK—Baron Green Mountain; Queen Sharleyan's first councilor.

SARMAC, JENNIFER—an Eve who escaped the destruction of the Alexandria Enclave and fled to Tellesberg.

SARMAC, KAYLEB—an Adam who escaped the destruction of the Alexandria Enclave and fled to Tellesberg.

SAWAL, FATHER RAHSS—an under-priest of the Order of Chihiro, the skipper of one of the Temple's courier boats.

SEACATCHER, SIR RAHNYLD—Baron Mandolin, a member of King Cayleb's Council.

SEAFARMER, SIR RHYZHARD—Baron Wave Thunder's senior investigator.

SEAHAMPER, SERGEANT EDWYRD, Chisholmian Royal Guard—a member of Queen Sharleyan's normal guard detail; her personal armsman since age ten.

SELLYRS, PAITYR—Baron White Church, Keeper of the Seal of the Kingdom of Charis; a member of King Cayleb's Council.

SHAIKYR, LARYS—CO, privateer galleon *Raptor*.

SHAIN, CAPTAIN PAYTER, Royal Charisian Navy—CO, HMS *Dreadful,* 48. Admiral Nylz's flag captain.

SHANDYR, HAHL—Baron of Shandyr, Prince Nahrmahn of Emerald's spymaster.

SHUMAY, FATHER AHLVYN—Bishop Mylz Halcom's personal aide.

SHYLAIR, BISHOP EXECUTOR THOMYS—Archbishop Borys' bishop executor.

STANTYN, ARCHBISHOP NYKLAS—Archbishop of Hankey in the Desnairian Empire. A member of the reformists.

STAYNAIR, ADMIRAL SIR DOMYNYK, Baron Rock Point, Royal Charisian Navy—younger brother of Bishop Maikel Staynair. CO, Eraystor blockade squadron.

STAYNAIR, ARCHBISHOP MAIKEL—senior Charisian-born prelate of the Church of God Awaiting in Charis; named prelate of all Charis by King Cayleb.

STAYNAIR, MADAME AHRDYN—Archbishop Maikel's deceased wife.

STOHNAR, LORD PROTECTOR GREYGHOR—elected ruler of the Siddarmark Republic.

STYWYRT, SERGEANT ZOHZEF—another of Kairmyn's non-coms, Delferahkan Army.

SUMYRS, SIR ZHER, Baron Barcor—one of Sir Koryn Gahrvai's senior officers; commander of the left wing at Haryl's Crossing.

SYMMYNS, TOHMYS, Grand Duke of Zebediah—the senior nobleman of Zebediah. Raised to that rank by Prince Hektor to ride herd on the island after its conquest.

SYMYN, LIEUTENANT HAHL, Royal Charisian Navy—XO, HMS *Torrent,* 42.

SYMYN, SERGEANT ZHORJ, Charisian Imperial Guard—a Charisian noncom assigned to Empress Sharleyan's guard detachment.

SYNKLYR, LIEUTENANT AIRAH—XO, Royal Dohlaran Navy galleon *Guardian.*

TANYR, VICAR GAIRYT—a member of the reformists.

TAYSO, PRIVATE DAISHYN, Charisian Imperial Guard—a Charisian assigned to Empress Sharleyan's guard detachment.

TAYT, KING SAILYS—deceased father of Queen Sharleyan of Chisholm.

TAYT, QUEEN MOTHER ALAHNAH—Queen Sharleyan of Chisholm's mother.

TAYT, QUEEN SHARLEYAN—Queen of Chisholm.

THOMPKYN, HAUWERSTAT—Earl White Crag; Sharleyan's lord justice.

TIANG, BISHOP EXECUTOR WU-SHAI—Archbishop Zherohm's bishop executor.

TRYNAIR, VICAR ZAHMSYN—Chancellor of the Council of Vicars of the Church of God Awaiting, one of the so-called Group of Four.

TRYNTYN, CAPTAIN ZHAIRYMIAH, Royal Charisian Navy—CO, HMS *Torrent,* 42.

TYMAHN QWENTYN—the current head of the House of Qwentyn, which is one of the largest, if not *the* largest banking and investment cartel in the Republic of Siddarmark. Lord Protector Greyghor holds a seat on the House of Qwentyn's board of directors, and the cartel operates the royal mint in the city of Siddar.

TYRN, ARCHBISHOP LYAM—Archbishop of Emerald.

TYRNYR, SERGEANT BRYNDYN, Chisholmian Royal Guard—a member of Queen Sharleyan's normal guard detail.

TYRNYR, SIR SAMYL—Cayleb's special ambassador to Chisholm; was replaced / supplanted / reinforced by Gray Harbor's arrival.

URBAHN, HAHL—XO, privateer galleon *Raptor.*

URVYN, LIEUTENANT ZHAK, Royal Charisian Navy—XO, HMS *Wave,* 14.

USHYR, FATHER BRYAHN—an under-priest. Archbishop Maikel's personal secretary and most trusted aide.

VYNAIR, SERGEANT AHDYM, Charisian Royal Guard—one of King Cayleb II's armsmen.

VYNCYT, ARCHBISHOP ZHEROHM—primate of Chisholm.

WAIMYN, FATHER AIDRYN—Bishop Executor Thomys' intendant.

WAISTYN, BYRTRYM—Duke of Halbrook Hollow, Queen Sharleyan's uncle and treasurer. He does not favor an alliance with Charis but is loyal to Sharleyan.

WALKYR, EDMYND—CO, merchant galleon *Wave.*

WALKYR, GREYGHOR—Edmynd Walkyr's son.

WALKYR, LYZBET—Edmynd Walkyr's wife.

WALKYR, MYCHAIL—Edmynd Walkyr's youngest brother; XO, merchant galleon *Wind.*

WALKYR, SIR STYV—Tahdayo Mahntayl's chief adviser.

WALKYR, ZHORJ—XO, galleon *Wave.* Edmynd's younger brother.

WALLYCE, LORD FRAHNKLYN—Chancellor of the Siddarmark Republic.

WYLSYNN, FATHER PAITYR—a priest of the Order of Schueler and the Intendant of Charis. He served Erayk Dynnys in that capacity and has continued to serve Archbishop Maikel.

WYLSYNN, VICAR HAUWERD—Paityr Wylsynn's uncle; a member of the reformists and a priest of the Order of Langhorne.

WYLSYNN, VICAR SAMYL—Father Paityr Wylsynn's father; the leader of the reformists within the Council of Vicars and a priest of the Order of Schueler.

WYSTAHN, AHNAINAH—Edvarhd Wystahn's wife.

WYSTAHN, SERGEANT EDVARHD, royal charisian Marines— a scout-sniper assigned to ⅓rd Marines.

YAIRLEY, CAPTAIN ALLAYN, Royal Charisian Navy—older brother of Captain Sir Dunkyn Yairley.

YAIRLEY, CAPTAIN SIR DUNKYN, Royal Charisian Navy— CO, HMS *Destiny,* 54.

YOWANCE, RAYJHIS—Earl Gray Harbor, First Councilor of Charis.

ZAIVYAIR, AIBRAM, DUKE OF THORAST—effective Navy Minister and senior officer, Royal Dohlaran Navy, brother-in-law of Admiral-General Duke Malikai (Faidel Ahlverez).

ZHAKSYN, LIEUTENANT TOHMYS, RMMC—General Chermyn's aide.

ZHANSTYN, COLONEL ZHOEL, RMMC—CO, ⅓rd Marines (First Battalion, Third Brigade). Brigadier Clareyk's senior battalion CO.

ZHAZTRO, COMMODORE HAINZ, EMERALD NAVY—the senior Emeraldian naval officer afloat (technically) in Eraystor.

ZHEFFYR, MAJOR WYLL, Royal Charisian Marines—CO, Marine detachment, HMS *Destiny*, 54.

ZHONAIR, MAJOR GAHRMYN—a battery commander in Ferayd Harbor, Ferayd Sound, Kingdom of Delferahk.

ZHORJ, COLONEL SIR WAHLYS—Tahdayo Mahntayl's senior mercenary commander.

ZHUSTYN, SIR AHLBER—Queen Sharleyan's spymaster.

GLOSSARY

Anshinritsumei—literally "enlightenment," from the Japanese. Rendered in the Safehold Bible, however, as "the little fire," the lesser touch of God's spirit. The maximum enlightenment of which mortals are capable.

Blink-lizard—a small, bioluminescent winged lizard. Although it's about three times the size of a firefly, it fills much the same niche on Safehold.

Borer—a form of Safeholdian shellfish which attaches itself to the hulls of ships or the timbers of wharves by boring into them. There are several types of borer, the most destructive of which actually eat their way steadily deeper into a wooden structure. Borers and rot are the two most serious threats (aside, of course, from fire) to wooden hulls.

Catamount—a smaller version of the Safeholdian slash lizard. The catamount is very fast and smarter than its larger cousin, which means that it tends to avoid humans. It is, however, a lethal and dangerous hunter in its own right.

Cat lizard—a furry lizard about the size of a terrestrial cat. They are kept as pets and are very affectionate.

Chewleaf—a mildly narcotic leaf from a native Safeholdian plant. It is used much as terrestrial chewing tobacco over most of the planet's surface.

Choke tree—a low-growing species of tree native to Safehold. It comes in many varieties and is found in most of the planet's climate zones. It is dense-growing, tough, and difficult to eradicate, but it requires quite a lot of sunlight to flourish, which means it is seldom found in mature old-growth forests.

Commentaries, The—the authorized interpretations and doctrinal expansions upon the Holy Writ. They represent the officially approved and sanctioned interpretation of the original scripture.

Cotton silk—a plant native to Safehold which shares many of the properties of silk and cotton. It is very lightweight and strong, but the raw fiber comes from a plant pod which is even more filled with seeds than Old Earth cotton. Because of the amount of hand labor required to harvest and process the pods and to remove the seeds from it, cotton silk is very expensive.

Council of Vicars—the Church of God Awaiting's equivalent of the College of Cardinals.

Dagger thorn—a native Charisian shrub, growing to a height of perhaps three feet at maturity, which possesses knife-edged thorns from three to seven inches long, depending upon the variety.

Deep-mouth wyvern—Safeholdian equivalent of a pelican.

Doomwhale—the most dangerous predator of Safehold, although, fortunately, it seldom bothers with anything as small as humans. Doomwhales have been known to run to as much as one hundred feet in length, and they are pure carnivores. Each doomwhale requires a huge range, and encounters with them are rare, for which human beings are just as glad, thank you. Doomwhales will eat *anything* . . . including the largest krakens. They have been known, on *extremely* rare occasions, to attack merchant ships and war galleys.

Dragon—the largest native Safeholdian land life-forms. Dragons come in two varieties, the common dragon and the great dragon. The common dragon is about twice the size of a Terran elephant and is herbivorous. The great dragon is smaller, about half to two-thirds the size of the common dragon, but carnivorous, filling the highest feeding niche of Safehold's land-based ecology. They look very much alike, aside from their size and the fact that the common dragon has herbivore teeth and jaws, whereas the great dragon has elongated jaws with sharp, serrated teeth. They have six limbs and, unlike the slash lizard, are covered in thick, well-insulated hide rather than fur.

Five-day—a Safeholdian "week," consisting of only five days, Monday through Friday.

Fleming moss—(usually lower case) an absorbent moss native to Safehold which was genetically engineered by Shan-wei's terraforming crews to possess natural antibiotic properties. It is a staple of Safeholdian medical practice.

Grasshopper—a Safeholdian insect analogue which grows to a length of as much as nine inches and is carnivorous. Fortunately, they do not occur in the same numbers as terrestrial grasshoppers.

Gray-horned wyvern—a nocturnal flying predator of Safehold. It is roughly analogous to a terrestrial owl.

Great dragon—the largest and most dangerous land carnivore of Safehold. The great dragon isn't actually related to hill dragons or jungle dragons at all, despite some superficial physical resemblances. In fact, it's more of a scaled-up slash lizard.

Group of Four—the four vicars who dominate and effectively control the Council of Vicars of the Church of God Awaiting.

Hairatha Dragons—the Hairatha professional baseball team. The traditional rivals of the Tellesberg Krakens for the Kingdom Championship.

Hill dragon—a roughly elephant-sized draft animal commonly used on Safehold. Despite their size, they are capable of rapid, sustained movement.

Ice wyvern—a flightless aquatic wyvern rather similar to a terrestrial penguin. Species of ice wyvern are native to both the northern and southern polar regions of Safehold.

Insights, The—the recorded pronouncements and observations of the Church of God Awaiting's Grand Vicars and canonized saints. They represent deeply significant spiritual and inspirational teachings, but, as the work of fallible mortals, do not have the same standing as the *Holy Writ* itself.

Intendant—the cleric assigned to a bishopric or archbishopric as the direct representative of the Office of Inquisition. The intendant is specifically charged with assuring that the Proscriptions of Jwo-jeng are not violated.

Jungle dragon—a somewhat generic term applied to lowland dragons larger than hill dragons. The gray jungle dragon is the largest herbivore on Safehold.

Kercheef—a traditional headdress worn in the Kingdom of Tarot which consists of a specially designed bandana tied across the hair.

Knights of the Temple Lands—the corporate title of the prelates who govern the Temple Lands. Technically, the Knights of the Temple Lands are *secular* rulers who simply happen to also hold high Church office. Under the letter of the Church's law, what they may do as the Knights of the Temple Lands is completely separate from any official action of the Church. This legal fiction has been of considerable value to the Church on more than one occasion.

Kraken—generic term for an entire family of maritime predators. Krakens are rather like sharks crossed with octupi. They have powerful, fish-like bodies, strong jaws with inward-inclined, fang-like teeth, and a cluster of tentacles just behind the head which can be used to hold prey while they devour it. The smallest, coastal krakens can be as short as three or four feet; deep-water krakens up to fifty feet in length have been reported, and there are legends of those still larger.

Kyousei hi—literally "great fire" or "magnificent fire." The term used to describe the brilliant nimbus of light the Operation Ark command crew generated around their air cars and skimmers to help "prove" their divinity to the original Safeholdians.

Langhorne's Watch—the thirty-one-minute period immediately before midnight in order to compensate for the extra length of Safehold's 26.5-hour day.

Master Traynyr—a character out of the Safeholdian entertainment tradition. Master Traynyr is a stock character in Safeholdian puppet theater, by turns a bumbling conspirator whose plans always miscarry and the puppeteer who controls all of the marionette "actors" in the play.

Monastery of Saint Zherneau—the mother monastery and headquarters of the Brethren of Saint Zherneau, a relatively small and poor order in the Archbishopric of Charis.

Mountain spike-thorn—a particular subspecies of spike-thorn, found primarily in tropical mountains. The most common blossom color is a deep, rich red, but the white mountain spike-thorn is especially prized for its trumpet-shaped blossom, which has a deep, almost cobalt blue throat, fading to pure white as it approaches the outer edge of the blossom, which is, in turn, fringed in a deep golden yellow.

Narwhale—a species of Safeholdian sea life named for the Old Earth species of the same name. Safeholdian narwhales are about forty feet in length and equipped with twin hornlike tusks up to eight feet long.

Nearoak—a rough-barked Safeholdian tree similar to Old Earth oak trees, found in tropic and near-tropic zones. Although it does resemble an Old Earth oak, it is an evergreen and seeds using "pine cones."

Nynian Rychtair—the Safeholdian equivalent of Helen of Troy, a woman of legendary beauty, born in Siddarmark, who eventually married the Emperor of Harchong.

Persimmon fig—a native Safeholdian fruit which is extremely tart and relatively thick skinned.

Prong lizard—a roughly elk-sized lizard with a single horn which branches into four sharp points in the last third or so of its length. They are herbivores and not particularly ferocious.

Proscriptions of Jwo-jeng—the definition of allowable technology under the doctrine of the Church of God Awaiting. Essentially, the Proscriptions limit allowable technology to that which is powered by wind, water, or muscle. The Proscriptions are subject to interpretation, generally by the Order of Schueler, which generally errs on the side of conservatism.

Rakurai—literally "lightning bolt." The *Holy Writ*'s term for the kinetic weapons used to destroy the Alexandria Enclave.

Saint Zherneau—the patron saint of the Monastery of Saint Zherneau in Tellesberg.

Sand maggot—a loathsome carnivore, looking much like a six-legged slug, which haunts beaches just above the surf line. Sand maggots do not normally take living prey, although they have no objection to devouring the occasional small creature which strays into their reach. Their natural coloration blends with their sandy habitat well, and they normally conceal themselves by digging their bodies into the sand until they are completely covered, or only a small portion of their backs show.

Sea cow—a walrus-like Safeholdian sea mammal which grows to a body length of approximately ten feet when fully mature.

Seijin—sage, holy man. Directly from the Japanese by way of Maruyama Chihiro, the Langhorne staffer who wrote the Church of God Awaiting's Bible.

Slash lizard—a six-limbed, saurian-looking, furry oviparous mammal. One of the three top predators of Safehold. Mouth contains twin rows of fangs capable of punching through chain mail; feet have four long toes each, tipped with claws up to five or six inches long.

SNARC—Self-Navigating Autonomous Reconnaissance and Communication platform.

Spider-crab—a native species of sea life, considerably larger than any terrestrial crab. The spider-crab is not a crustacean, but rather more of a segmented, tough-hided, many-legged seagoing slug. Despite that, its legs are considered a great delicacy and are actually very tasty.

Spider rat—a native species of vermin which fills roughly the ecological niche of a terrestrial rat. Like all Safehold mammals, it is six-limbed, but it looks like a cross between a hairy gila monster and an insect, with long, multi-jointed legs which actually arch higher than its spine. It is nasty tempered but basically cowardly, and fully adult male specimens of the larger varieties of spider rat run to about two feet in body length, with another two feet of tail. The more common varieties average between 33 percent and 50 percent of that body/tail length.

Spike-thorn—a flowering shrub, various subspecies of which are found in most Safeholdian climate zones. Its blossoms come in many colors and hues, and the tropical versions tend to be taller-growing and to bear more delicate blossoms.

Steel thistle—a native Safeholdian plant which looks very much like branching bamboo. The plant bears seed pods filled with small, spiny seeds embedded in fine, straight fibers. The seeds are extremely difficult to remove by hand, but the fiber can be woven into a fabric which is even stronger than cotton silk. It can also be twisted into extremely strong, stretch-resistant rope. Moreover, the plant grows almost as rapidly as actual bamboo, and the yield of raw fiber per acre is 70 percent higher than for terrestrial cotton.

Surgoi kasai—literally "dreadful (great) conflagration." The true spirit of God, the touch of His divine fire which only an angel or archangel can endure.

Tellesberg Krakens—the Tellesberg professional baseball club.

Testimonies, The—by far the most numerous of the Church of God Awaiting's writings, these consist of the firsthand observations of the first few generations of humans on Safehold. They do not have the same status as the Christian gospels, because they do not reveal the central teachings and inspiration of God. Instead, collectively, they form an important substantiation of the *Writ*'s "historical accuracy" and conclusively attest to the fact that the events they collectively describe did, in fact, transpire.

Wire vine—a kudzu-like vine native to Safehold. Wire vine isn't as fast-growing as kudzu, but it's equally tenacious, and unlike kudzu, several of its varieties have long, sharp thorns. Unlike many native Safeholdians species of plants, it does quite well intermingled with terrestrial imports. It is often used as a sort of combination of hedgerow and barbed wire by Safehold farmers.

Wyvern—the Safeholdian ecological analogue of terrestrial birds. There are as many varieties of wyverns as there are of birds, including (but not limited to) the homing wyvern, hunting wyverns suitable for the equivalent of hawking for small prey, the crag wyvern (a small—wingspan ten feet—flying predator), various species of sea wyverns, and the king wyvern (a very large flying predator, with a wingspan of up to twenty-five feet). All wyverns have two pairs of wings, and one pair of powerful, clawed legs. The king wyvern has been known to take children as prey when desperate or when the opportunity presents, but they are quite intelligent. They know that man is a prey best left alone and generally avoid areas of human habitation.

Wyvernry—a nesting place and/or breeding hatchery for domesticated wyverns.

A NOTE ON SAFEHOLDIAN TIMEKEEPING

The Safeholdian day is 26 hours and 31 minutes long. Safe-hold's year is 301.32 local days in length, which works out to .91 Earth standard years. It has one major moon, named Langhorne, which orbits Safehold in 27.6 local days, so the lunar month is approximately 28 days long.

The Safeholdian day is divided into twenty-six 60-minute hours, and one 31-minute period, known as "Langhorne's Watch," which is used to adjust the local day into something which can be evenly divided into standard minutes and hours.

The Safeholdian calendar year is divided into ten months: February, April, March, May, June, July, August, September, October, and November. Each month is divided into six five-day weeks, each of which is referred to as a "five-day." The days of the week are: Monday, Tuesday, Wednesday, Thursday, and Friday. The extra day in each year is inserted into the middle of the month of July, but is not numbered. It is referred to as "God's Day" and is the high holy day of the Church of God Awaiting. What this means, among other things, is that the first day of every month will always be a Monday, and the last day of every month will always be a Friday. Every third year is a leap year, with the additional day—known as "Lang-horne's Memorial"—being inserted, again, without number-ing, into the middle of the month of February. It also means that each Safeholdian month is 795 standard hours long, as opposed to 720 hours for a 30-day Earth month.

The Safeholdian equinoxes occur on April 23 and September 22. The solstices fall on July 7 and February 8.